THE OTHER WAY

PASSAGE TO DAWN: BOOK TWO

DERRICK SMYTHE

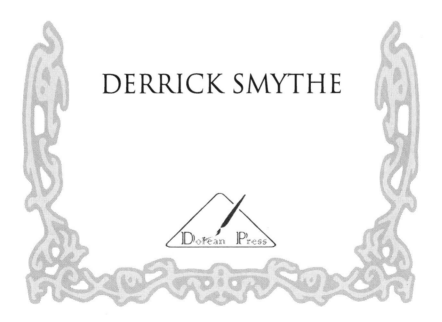

Dorean Press

Copyright
The Other Way: Passage to Dawn Book 2
© 2021 Derrick Smythe, All Rights Reserved.
Published by Dorean Press, Cicero, New York

978-1-7340953-6-4 (hardback)
978-1-7340953-4-0 (paperback)
978-1-7340953-5-7 (eBook)

www.derricksmythe.com

Editors: Carolyn Haley & Sarah Chorn
Cover Illustration: Alexandre Rito
Map Illustration: Daniel Hasenbos
Formatting: Hollow Creek Designs

Acknowledgments

ONE WEEK PRIOR TO THE publication of The Other Magic, I gave myself a belated birthday present: I told my family that I had written a book. Prior to this, knowledge of my secret decade-long project had been limited to a very small inner circle. My reasons for keeping this a secret were numerous, but no part of this decision had anything to do with a lack of perceived support. If anything, I suspected I would receive more well-meaning prodding and care than I would have wished at the time. Since learning about my not-so-little secret passion that doubles as my excuse for the occasional stints of reclusiveness, my parents, brothers, and extended family have been nothing but supportive. I am truly blessed.

To my readers, without whom this second book in the series would not have been possible, I pray that your patience and support are repaid in kind with *The Other Way* as well as the rest of the series.

To Podium Audio for transforming my stories into incredible audio content. Greg Patmore's narration breathes life into the characters and illuminates this world in ways I never thought possible.

To my local writing group, who continues to keep me on my toes, never afraid to dash the hope that I might ever write an infallible first draft.

To my alpha and beta readers, who provided critical feedback that allowed for *The Other Way* to become the best book it could be.

To my editor, Carolyn, whose remarkable attention to sequence, consistency, and all other manner of grammar has been an invaluable asset to my growth as an author; she is a master of her craft.

To my editor, Sarah, whose knowledge of the genre and eye for prose and flow brought this story to new heights.

To my biggest supporter, my wife, Kelly, whose frank critiques, and enduring patience with me, not only as a writer but as a husband, cannot be overstated, or over-thanked.

And finally, God, whose subtle nudges encouraged me to begin this journey in the first place, and who keeps me far from despair whenever things don't go according to my plan.

AUTHOR'S NOTE

I DID NOT ORIGINALLY INTEND TO include a summary of *The Other Magic* in this second book of the series. However, my most-trusted readers unanimously agreed that doing so would improve the reading experience, most notably for those who first read *The Other Magic* a year or more before picking up *The Other Way*. My goal remains to provide you, readers, with the best experience possible. I hope this story does just that. After all, reader support is a large part of what made this second book in the series possible. Thank you all so much!

The Continent of DROGEN

Summary of Events
The Other Magic

THE **O**THER **M**AGIC BEGINS WITH Kibure's inexplicable use of magic against his slave master, who instead of turning him directly over to the Kleról as is mandated, hires an unordained priestess to separate him from his powers. The rogue priestess, Sindri, quickly discovers that Kibure's magic is unaffected by her castration spell. Having been searching for a "tazamine" like Kibure since her brother was sacrificed to the God-king years earlier, Sindri works quickly to convince his master that he could fetch a pretty penny in the markets of Sire Trinkanen. She offers her services to ensure Kibure is delivered without incident, his magic held in check. She intends to take him for herself upon arrival.

However, this task proves dangerous after Sindri finds herself unable to suppress Kibure's dreams. Confused as he is by the dreams, his magic, and even the nature of the black raaven he calls Rave, Kibure is reluctant to share much with Sindri. During his visions, he radiates enough magic that seekers from the Kleról, and Magog the God-king himself, are able to sense his presence.

Magog's second-in-command is his High Priest, Fatu Mazi Grobennar. Grobennar rose to prominence alongside the God-king after recognizing the fulfillment of prophecy during one of his first posts as a young priest. Grobennar's involvement in the unusual birth provided him with instant notoriety, as well as creating a bond between himself and the God-king, a truth that would be the envy of others. At least some of his early successes within the Kleról may have been made possible because of the assistance granted by the spirit, Jaween, who exists within an amulet worn at Grobennar's neck. These spirits are relics of an older age, hidden and banned by the Kleról because of their corruptive nature and their affinity for creating chaos and mayhem. Grobennar's nemesis, Rajuban, suspected something unusual about Grobennar, and after some reconnaissance was able to discover the whereabouts of the hidden ruins where Grobennar originally found Jaween. The short story "To Earn the Sash" implies that Rajuban may have a secret of his own.

Kibure's continued use of magic convinces the God-king that this threat must be eliminated. He tasks Grobennar with capturing the source of the magic, Kibure, whom he believes is an instrument of the Dark Lord. Grobennar finds himself outmaneuvered by Rajuban and is held personally responsible for assuring Kibure's destruction. Magog also announces that another segment of prophecy is to be fulfilled: the beginnings of The Purge, which is to be a cleansing of the world through conquest and subjugation.

Kibure has another dream as his ship passes by the Lugienese capital, allowing Grobennar to pinpoint his location. During this dream, Kibure is visited by a figure whom he becomes certain is Magog himself, who attempts to kill him. He is rescued by none other than Rave, who helps pull Kibure out of the realm of dreams. Magog is incensed by this intervention and sets Grobennar to the task of destroying this Dark Lord's "agent," as well. With the help of a close friend and priestess named Paranja, Grobennar gathers a team and sets off on a ship after Kibure.

Grobennar uses the collective strength of his priests to perform a clasp on a Kraken while Kibure's ship passes through the deeper waters of Lake Lagraas. The Kraken attacks the ship, and in the confrontation performs a castration spell on Sindri, leaving her without the powers of

Klerós. Mercifully, she, Kibure, and two of the slave friends he met on board the ship are separated but manage to survive the encounter.

Kibure's raaven friend leads Sindri to Kibure and the slave, Tenk, but in their attempt to steal provisions for their trek into the mountains, Tenk is captured by Grobennar and his trackers. Without her powers, Sindri is unable to wrest Tenk from the Klerósi priests, so Kibure and Sindri are forced to leave Tenk behind. Sindri not possessing her powers provides her with even more motivation to discover the truth about Kibure's magic as they flee east. In the mountains, Sindri and Kibure are aided by a group of Palpanese smugglers who decide to help after noticing Kibure's raaven, which marks Kibure as a figure of Palpanese lore. Kibure finds himself again confused about his own significance but thankful for the help. They smuggle the two fugitives out of the Palpanese Union, onboard a trade ship, delivering the pair safely to the Isles city of Brinkwell. These trials bring about increased trust between Kibure and Sindri, and they agree to remain together in Brinkwell as they search for answers about Kibure's magic. Grobennar's failure to capture Kibure in the snowy mountains causes him to be stripped of his title. He is then sent to Brinkwell, where he is tasked with preparing the way for a Lugienese invasion.

Meanwhile, Aynward, who is fifth in line to inherit the throne of the most powerful Kingdom in all of Drogen, is shipped off to study in the faraway University of Brinkwell. The King hopes that time away from friends and home will ensure that whatever mischief Aynward cause will occur far enough away that its echoes won't reach court. Much to Aynward's displeasure, Aynward's loathsome counselor, Dolme, is sent along to accompany him. They will stay with the Queen's sister, Aunt Melanie, who left court years earlier to elope with a disreputable man who has since passed.

Once at the university, Aynward finds himself almost immediately at odds with a fellow student by the name of Theo. This older student takes pleasure in mocking high-borns like Aynward. During a hazing initiation ritual at the university, Aynward decides to fight back and is joined by a fellow Kingdomer named Kyllean who, turns out to be a

Tal-Don, blood of the Lumále riders. Their fight against the university counselors causes quite the stir, but the boys are eventually subdued. However, friendship forged by battle is strong, and Aynward has found himself his first ally in Brinkwell.

Fortunately for both boys, Counselor Dwapek, a halfling, who doesn't particularly approve of the hazing ritual, finds their heroics foolish but admirable and vouches for both in order to keep them from being expelled. In exchange, he enrolls them in a small, selective course where they'll be researching odd texts related to various magical happenings throughout the history of Drogen. Here Kyllean meets a girl name Minathi, with whom he develops a mutually romantic interest.

Concurrently, Sindri and Kibure begin searching for magic users who might be able to help them understand Kibure's mysterious powers as well as finding a way for Sindri to restore her own. Their inquiries capture the attention of a powerful wizard named Draílock, who brings the pair in for questioning but determines that they are no threat. They are instead offered an opportunity to train in the use of the *other* magic, known as ateré magic. They learn that this was the source of Kibure's magic all along. Sindri's unique perspective as a former priestess of the Kleról also intrigues Draílock's associate, who turns out to be Counselor Dwapek. He has her enrolled in his properties of magic class where she meets Aynward, Kyllean, and Minathi.

While Sindri is in class, Kibure slips into the realm of dreams and is followed by a woman before being awakened from the dream realm. Sindri senses his use of magic as she approaches their room and arrives just before Grobennar and his men. The Klerósi priests easily capture Kibure and knock Sindri out of a second-story window into the street, leaving her for dead.

After arriving home late after an embarrassing, drunken kidnapping orchestrated by Theo, Aynward is berated by Counselor Dolme and his allowance is cut. This inspires him to take up an earlier offer from Gervais, Aunt Melanie's servant, to try to steal a few rare texts from the university Special Collections. In order to do so, he'll have to infiltrate a book-thieving ring funded by an extremely dangerous merchant named

Kubal. Upon leaving a meeting with this man, Aynward sees one of the university librarians approaching Kubal's ship and realizes that he must be in on the theft. Aynward later confronts the boy and learns that Theo is at the head of the operation within the university. Aynward uses this knowledge to stage Theo's arrest; however, Theo has the university guards on payroll so Anyward's trap backfires and instead he and Kyllean are thrown into the university prison to await sentencing for providing "false" testimony.

During Aynward's interrogation by the dean, disturbing news reaches Brinkwell: the Lugienese have conquered the Palpanese Union. Knowing that the Lugienese intend to see their prophecies of conquest fulfilled and that they now possess a fleet with which to transport troops, the threat is undeniable. Once it becomes clear that Brinkwell will be indefensible against a Lugienese assault, Aynward and Kyllean are released from university custody to evacuate with the rest of the city. Aynward, Kyllean, and Minathi prepare to flee by ship, but when Minathi's name is left off the boarding list, Kyllean stays behind to help ensure her safe passage. When they don't return to the ship before it sets sail, Aynward leaps from the ship in an act of ill-conceived heroism.

Hidden within their basement lair, Grobennar becomes frustrated with Kibure's refusal to answer questions. He is also baffled by his inability to successfully delve into Kibure's mind. Even Jaween finds Kibure irritatingly elusive. But when Grobennar determines to simply kill Kibure, Jaween interferes, insisting that Grobennar's reward will be greater if the prize is delivered to the God-king alive. Grobennar acquiesces. This turns out to be a major mistake when their hideout is invaded by a group of gray-cloaked wielders, whose powers are immune to the castration spell. They steal away with Kibure, while Grobennar murders the only other remaining priest, lest his failure to maintain custody of the Dark Lord reaches Magog.

With the Lugienese fast approaching, Sindri insists on locating Kibure before it's too late. With the help of Draílock and a wizardess named Arella, Rave leads them to Kibure. They arrive at the Klerósi den just in time to find Kibure being carried away by a departing group of gray-cloaked wielders, who bar the door behind them. Sindri and company eventually break free of the lair littered with dead Klerósi priests, but by the time they do, Kibure and the gray-cloaks are sailing away in the distance.

Shortly thereafter, a fleet of Lugienese ships arrives and Aynward, Kyllean, Gervais, and an angry Counselor Dolme pass through a series of tunnels to a cove containing a small ship set aside for such an eventuality. Draílock leads Kibure, Sindri, and Arella to this location, as well. Unfortunately, a Lugienese scouting party has also discovered this cove, and the group is forced to fight their way to the ship. They manage to do so, but not before Dolme is mortally wounded. His death magnifies the rashness of Aynward's decision to leap from the ship, for had he not done so, Dolme would still be alive. Counselor Dwapek was also supposed to flee with them, but remained behind for reasons unknown to all save himself.

On the deck of the small vessel on its way to safety, Sindri stands with Aynward and professes her plans for revenge against the Lugienese, as well as a burgeoning ability to wield ateré magic. The story ends with Sindri's first entry into the realm of dreams, which reveals to her that she, like Kibure and her brother, is also a tazamine.

THE
OTHER
WAY

PROLOGUE

GROBENNAR

PLUMES OF DARK SMOKE ROSE high into the sky above the Isles city of Brinkwell; pillars of victory built from the guile and might of the Lugienese Empire. Ships burned in the harbor, homes blazed in the city, and the distant cries of those who refused to lay down their weapons rounded out the symphony of glorious conquest.

The God-king, Magog, descended the steps of the fallen palace leading down to the vast courtyard at its center. He looked every bit the picture of regality, power, of perfection incarnate. His heavy crimson cape was secured at the shoulders by two golden plates of gleaming armor, accentuating his already muscular form as he flowed down the steps like the inevitability of the sun itself. His sleeveless silken robe was heightened by thick, muscular arms, which rippled with inhuman physicality, while the crimson fabric of his cape trailed him like the blood that would flow from all those who might dare stand against him. His bronze skin glistened, but not nearly as much as the red scales that now covered much of his face, neck, and arms, a thousand souls consumed.

Magog paused at the last step and glared out at the scene before him: thirteen prisoners, a holy number to the Kleról, were strategically positioned within the open courtyard to form a perfect crescent. Behind them stood an assemblage of refugees and crewmen collected from thirteen captured vessels. Thirteen Klerósi priests stood sentinel behind the crowd, awaiting instructions from their God-king. The onlookers had followed the example of the priests, taking a knee to bow before Magog. Grobennar was no exception.

Only the thirteen prisoners remained standing. *Such a petty gesture of defiance, though their boldness is admirable.*

Magog opened his mouth and spoke the Kingdom tongue as if he'd been born to it, magnifying the sound with Klerós's power. "Citizens of Brinkwell, you know who I am. You know whom I serve. Rise now that you may bear witness to Klerós's mercy and splendor."

He waited as hesitant townsfolk stood on shaky legs. Magog gestured toward the prisoners before him with an open hand, his expression severe. "Your brethren here believe themselves above the divine law of Klerós."

He stepped down into the courtyard to approach the thirteen prisoners, ten men and three women. His voice boomed even louder. "These men and women are devout servants of their respective faiths. But will their gods protect them? Will their gods extend their hands to save their souls?"

He laughed, a chilling sound even to Grobennar's ears.

The closest prisoner, a woman, perhaps in her forties with green eyes, olive skin, dressed in a plain brown robe of the Stone Faith, cried out, "It matters not how our gods resp—"

A shot of magic burst from Magog's index finger and she spoke no further. A gasp was followed by silence, yet she appeared otherwise unharmed.

Magog's gravelly laugh cut off. "Alas, their gods will do nothing, for they are false, dead things. Ideas invented out of fear, or the greed for coin, or veneration. The one true God, Klerós, offers you the opportunity to serve him as he reshapes the world. Those who bow before him and abide by his laws shall live. You will be as servants to his chosen people, an honorable and fulfilling life free from politics, free from greed. With this comes also the gift of an everlasting life after death. But those who refuse this gift . . ."

Magog extended his arms out to either side, hands appearing to grasp some unseen essence from the air, and Grobennar felt the immense volume of Klerós's power fill the space. The prisoners in the center stiffened, then as one fell to their knees. Their bodies contorted as if invisible strings from above had taken control, which, in a sense, they had. Their chests extended forward while their arms and heads tilted back, and then came a chorus of screams.

A dog began barking angrily to the right, and Magog smiled. "Even their beloved mongrels will suffer, for loyalty to evil is a crime as heinous as the evil itself." The animal had taken up a defensive position between itself and its apparent owner, one of the thirteen.

"No, not Leo!" cried a pudgy priest. "Please, not—"

A blade of energy shot forth, and the dog released a horrifying yelp before collapsing to the ground, dead. A few gasps sounded from the onlookers, but these were quickly quieted. "There is to be no mercy where heresy is concerned. None whatsoever."

Grobennar saw thick tears streaming down the brown-robed priest whose animal had just been slain. *You will join the pup soon enough*, thought Grobennar.

Magog returned his attention to the crescent of heretics, their bodies stiffening once again. Steam began rising from their eyes, accompanied by screams of agony that bordered on inhuman.

Grobennar took this as his cue to avert his gaze. He'd seen this hundreds of times and never found it enjoyable to watch. He knew what came next, though Magog was taking it slower than usual, making sport of the public nature of the exercise. Their eyes would burn all the way through to their skulls, leaving behind charred sockets of empty space. Their skin would blister, in some places even bursting in sprays of whatever bodily fluid filled such things. No matter the nature of the crime, it took a special kind of sadism to appreciate such a sight; *Someone like Rajuban*, confirmed Grobennar.

When it was over, the crumpled forms of thirteen infidels lay as unmoving as the cobbles beneath them. Magog turned wordlessly and started back toward the stairs. "Release these witnesses and their thirteen ships."

"But . . ." The ill-advised protest of one of the Klerósi priests ended abruptly as Magog turned his head to regard him. The priest bowed until his forehead nearly touched the ground. "I—yes, of course, Your Eminence."

Magog must have been in a *very* good mood to allow such an act to go unpunished. He continued toward the stairs without further comment until he reached the space beside Grobennar. As he passed, he said calmly, "Mazi Grobennar, you will walk with me."

Grobennar shuddered, for while he believed everything had gone according to plan, the God-king had grown exceedingly unpredictable under the conniving tutelage of Fatu Mazi, Rajuban. Nevertheless, Grobennar knew he would be a fool to eschew the God-king's command. They fell into step as they ascended the stairs. "Your Grace?" said Grobennar.

Magog's air of authority remained, but there was a respect present in his tone that Grobennar had not heard in years. "You have done well here in preparing Brinkwell for the taking."

Grobennar blinked. *If only you knew*, he thought as he recalled losing the boy, and all of his priests. Grobennar's voice cracked as he responded, "Thank you." He coughed to clear his throat as much as to determine what to say next. "I am pleased to hear you say so, though it was not so difficult. These people were easy targets for ones so blessed by Klerós as us."

"Of course."

Grobennar decided to add a touch of flattery. "And with such measures as you have just taken to send messages of warning with those escaping refugees, word of both Klerós's mercy and your devastating might will quickly spread throughout the lands of Drogen. I suspect many will lay down their swords at the mere mention of your name."

Magog chuckled. "Ah, *you* understand my purpose."

Grobennar smiled, growing more comfortable as the tone of the conversation continued with such positivity. "Indeed. True genius, if you ask me."

Magog stopped walking as they reached a waist-high wall overlooking the entire fallen city of Brinkwell below. "Mazi Grobennar, I believe it was a mistake to demote you so severely, and with such haste."

Grobennar's heart skipped a beat. He was going to be restored! Perhaps Rajuban had revealed his true nature to the God-king. Oh, how he would love to see the look on Rajuban's face when he saw Grobennar wearing the golden sash of the High Priest once more.

Magog continued, "We have much to accomplish, and I believe the Empire's goals will be better served by having someone of your experience and skill back at the helm."

This is it, yes, yes, yes! Grobennar could barely contain his excitement.

"You are to be the new Fatu Ma-gazi."

Grobennar blinked. *Fatu Ma-gazi?* Grobennar's excitement buckled at those words, but only for the briefest of moments. Fatu Ma-gazi was the title for Secretary of War. With the expanded scope of the conquests to come, a Fatu Ma-gazi would wield more direct power over matters of state than even the High Priest. This promotion was still excellent news, though he couldn't help but wonder what had become of the previous Fatu Ma-gazi. Grobennar had never been fond of the man, but Grobennar was no stranger to the woes of unexpected demotion. He would need to learn what Baelgred had done, if anything, to cause Magog's scorn. This, however, was a consideration for another time. That, and the concern that Rajuban still had Magog's ear; Grobennar would still need to tread carefully.

Jaween, who had been obediently silent throughout this time, could contain himself no longer.

"*Ooooh Grobes! We're back! We're—*"

Magog interrupted the spirit's celebratory comments. "See to it that a plan for the conquest of the rest of the Isles is ready to present in two days' time. We'll work out the logistics from there. Now, go. Celebrate.

I know what this restoration means to you, Fatu Ma-gazi. I have other tasks that require my attention."

Grobennar stared out at the conquered city of Brinkwell in stunned silence as the God-king departed, his cape ominously snapping behind him. Jaween buzzed in his head, but Grobennar hardly noticed. He basked in the wonder of a purpose restored.

CHAPTER 1

KIBURE

THE SUN CAST A WARM, comforting blanket upon Kibure's shirtless back as he leaned over to place a seed within the line of freshly-tilled earth. "That's it! Finished."

Beside him, a raaven's coo answered excitedly and he smiled. He stood up, taking the damp towel from his waist and wringing some of the cool water onto his forehead. It traveled along his body, soothing the aches and pains of labor as it did.

He glanced over to his home, a modest, single-room structure sitting alone between two fields—no, one field—while the other side nestled alongside a beautiful, lush forest filled with singing birds and plenty of game for Rave to capture. The fact that this had changed before his eyes in an instant did not seem at all strange to Kibure. Nothing was amiss. He took up his bag of seeds and returned to work, content to live out his days without a bother in the world. No one to please or displease; it was just Kibure and Rave and their ability to subsist.

A nearby voice reminded him that he was not, in fact, alone. *Who is that?* he wondered.

"I said, are you expecting rain soon? Don't tell me you've gone deaf."

Kibure looked up to see his old friend, Tenkoran, more muscular than he remembered, a smile tugging at the corners of his mouth. *Ah, yes, of course Tenk lives on the adjacent farm. How could I forget?*

Kibure felt a sudden drop in temperature at the mention of rain. "Yes, I suppose it will probably rain this very evening." He looked over his shoulder at a vast field of tilled soil. "I've just enough time to finish this last row. How goes the planting of your own fields?"

Tenk, confident as ever, replied, "Oh, I finished weeks ago. Just enjoying the view from the shade beneath my favorite tree as I watch it grow. Woulda come over here to help, but I know how much you prefer the fruits of your own labor. Couldn't rob you of that."

"That's mighty kind of you," said Kibure, sincerely.

"Sure is."

Time passed, a moment, an hour. But Tenk finally said, "Say, how'd we end up here, anyhow?"

Kibure was confused by the question. "I—I don't recall." He really didn't. He didn't know that there was supposed to have been a sequence of events leading to this place, a story about how he'd arrived at this farm. He was just . . . here. That was all he knew, and that was all he wanted to know.

But Tenkoran was not satisfied with this answer. "It doesn't make sense, does it? You're just a measly slave. So am I. We don't deserve this. We deserve nothing less than the flame and an eternal gnashing of teeth."

Kibure looked up at Tenk. Something had changed. Something in the tone had shifted, and Kibure sensed the wrongness in his words. Rave did too, for his next coo was one of warning. Before Kibure's eyes, Tenk's face and body melted into something entirely different. His arms grew, as did his chest and legs. His wool trousers became silky red and extended up to his neck as sleeves grew to cover the muscular Lugienese man. The transformation continued as deep-red scales covered his face and neck. Kibure imagined these continued elsewhere but the red robe concealed the rest of his body.

Dread replaced serenity. This was no longer his friend. The God-king laughed—a throaty grinding sound like distant thunder, and the ground beneath Kibure's feet shook.

Kibure stumbled back. "What do you want?" His voice came out weak, barely audible amid the storm of Magog's presence.

The God-king continued to chuckle. "No need to fear, little one. I cannot hurt you in this place." He looked from side to side. "Our paths will bring us together in the flesh soon enough. No, I have come here to tell you a story."

Confidence dripped from every ounce of the God-king's being. It was like a heavy fog pressing down upon Kibure, forcing him to kneel as an admission of inferiority. He trembled and swallowed hard and whispered, "All right"—a pitiful note of acquiescence.

Magog nodded. "This is a story from a time before the advent of ink and page, a story twisted by time and the mouths of those who do not wish the truth to be known. I speak of the Usurper, the Dark Lord, the Snake. He goes by many names, but he was first called Olem." Magog placed both hands behind him, then cleared his throat before continuing. "Humankind was created by Klerós to rule over all of Doréa, and the spirits were to guide and teach them. For centuries, humankind and the spirits worshiped Klerós faithfully, for without him, they would not be. Gifts of great power were given to each of the seven tribes, each with attributes specific to that tribe's purpose within the world.

"But as the centuries passed, a rebellious spirit grew jealous of the veneration given only to Klerós, and this spirit plotted against the one true God. This spirit, Olem, was clever and powerful and used his cunning to seduce the tribes, turning them against their creator. In the end, only the Luguinden tribe remained loyal, and they and a number of spirits were driven out of the sacred lands of the east. But this was not enough. The Dark Lord could not bear the thought of the Luguinden people remaining alive to worship Klerós. So he sent others out of the sacred lands to seduce and corrupt. The most notable among them were the Asaaven. They built a great empire within the Hand of the Gods as a beacon of his greatness and brought war upon the Luguinden tribes of Klerós. Though the Asaaven were eventually defeated, the Dark Lord's damaging corruption remained long after the wars. Only a single Luguinden tribe, the Lugienese, remained loyal to Klerós, and they were forced to flee to Angolia to escape destruction."

Kibure held his voice as steady as he could manage, his frustration at the rambling fairy tale giving him the courage to speak. "Why are you telling me this? What has any of this to do with me?"

The God-king smiled. "Patience, little devil."

Little devil? Oh, right, he believes me some sort of agent of the Dark Lord...

Magog had been pacing as he spoke, but he stopped, boring his angry eyes right into Kibure, who couldn't help but look away.

"A vestige of the Asaaven survived the wars. This vestige of evil has lain hidden for millennia like roaches beneath the rotting remains of these fallen lands. The women who carry you from Brinkwell are among their number."

Kibure felt a tendril of fear. These women had fought priests of the Kleról back in Brinkwell and won. What if what Magog said about them was true?

Magog continued. "The time has come for Klerós to regain his rightful seat as Lord over Doréa. These Asaaven witches intend to use you toward their own designs, toward the Dark Lord's designs." Magog shrugged. "I can hardly blame them. They fear the end of days, fear the renewed strength wielded by Klerós's chosen people. The Asaaven, or what remains of them, need you in order to escape to the sacred lands of the ancient ones, the lands held by the Usurper. They believe this will protect them from Klerós's wrath. They could not be more wrong."

He turned his head and spat, an undignified action for a kinglike figure. "This remnant of the Asaaven will fall. The ancient ones will fall. Olem will fall. *You* will fall. Klerós's time to reign supreme is coming, and there is nothing anyone can do to change this."

These words sparked something unexpected in Kibure as his thoughts went back to the attack of the Kraken and the eventual loss of the first friends Kibure had ever known. All at the hands of the

Lugienese; the hands of Klerós. Kibure thought of all the slaves still toiling daily because Klerós deemed them unworthy of anything more. And this man—no, this monster—claimed to be some sort of Klerós incarnate. Kibure fought past his fear and spoke through gritted teeth.

"You killed them."

Confusion flashed across Magog's face, but it was replaced a moment later with the knife's edge of a grin. "Ah, yes, of course, your slave friends. You should be proud. Their sacrifice serves a great purpose."

Kibure shouted with a voice as frail as his own frame, "You—you— you're a butcher! Your 'god' is a butcher!"

Kibure knew the insult did him no good, that this God-king cared nothing for the denigrations of a slave, but it felt good to shout them, nonetheless.

Magog dismissed it all with a wave of his hand. "I am what I need to be, much as you are." He spread his arms wide and continued as if Kibure had said nothing. "Alas, the time comes when you will be forced to see reason. The question is whether this will be before or after you doom millions to eternal damnation." He paused, then judged Kibure's silence as an opportunity to continue. "The Lugienese people have been chosen as heirs of this world. Chosen to bring about order and salvation—"

"You mean murder and enslavement."

Magog continued as if Kibure hadn't spoken. "The ancient ones to the east would have you believe that to submit to Klerós's rule is to surrender one's 'freedom.' This is their greatest lie. They wish only to maintain their twisted version of paradise on Doréa, and the Asaaven are no different." He shook his red, scaly head. "It has been prophesied that you, the Dark Lord's agent, will be presented the opportunity to help save the lives of many, but it is known that you will make the same selfish choice as Olem and his followers. At least now you will be unable to claim ignorance when you stand before Klerós for judgment, for you have been educated on the matter. Your damnation will be justified."

Kibure was shaking. But something about all of this seemed out of place. In fact, *all* of it seemed out of place. How was Magog here with him? Where even was 'this'? He hadn't considered either until now, but now that he did...

"You—you're not really here."

He was certain he was right. He needed to be right.

Magog's mirth returned.

Kibure continued, louder, so as to not be drowned out by the God-king. "You're not here. It is you that is a lie."

The God-king tilted his head back and his laughter shook even the sky, which was being devoured by the shadows of a great storm.

Kibure was still terrified, but if this was *his* dream . . .

His hands formed fists and his body filled with heat. He lifted both arms and shouted "This is *my* dream! GET! OUT!"

Everything went still and Magog angled his powerful chin down so his deep, bottomless eyes met Kibure's own. He sneered and nodded just before he and the rest of the storm winked out of sight.

Kibure felt weak and his legs collapsed beneath him. He melted into the soil below, tears streaking his cheeks before dropping to stain the earth as he too faded from this place, from this dream, from this nightmare.

CHAPTER 2

KIBURE

KIBURE SUCKED IN A DEEP breath of air, and the musty smell belowdeck returned him to reality. He opened his eyes and yelped. Rave's beady eyes were just a handsbreadth from his own. Rave responded with a coo then leaped into the air, circling the space before returning to land upon Kibure's chest.

The hatch to the deck opened above and a beam of bright light shot down, causing Kibure to raise an arm to protect his still unadjusted eyes. A woman scurried down the companionway and rushed over to kneel beside him. "What afflicts you?" asked Vardya.

Kibure considered the question as he oriented himself with a world of wooden planks and ageless gray-robed women. His heart was still pounding and a cold film of sweat coated his skin.

"I . . ." It had been different from the "demon dreams" he had previously experienced. This one had color and sound, and Magog hadn't even attempted to kill him this time. There was certainly nothing real about Kibure being free on a farm of his own—or Tenk being anything other than—

Kibure closed his eyes tight at the thought. Tenk was dead. Kibure winced. He had abandoned his friend, left him for dead.

Vardya stared at him. "Well?" Her expression of concern quickly shifted to one of agitation, eyes narrowing, pale complexion flushing.

Kibure shook off thoughts of Tenk. "Bad dream. I'm okay."

Vardya rolled her eyes, then offered him a water skin. "Drink."

He took a long pull from the skin before standing. "Thank you. I just need some fresh air."

He followed Vardya to the main deck then found a space alone to lean against the smooth wooden railing toward the bow. The breeze whisked away his remaining sweat. The smell of salt and the taste of the sea air helped calm his nerves after both the intrusion of Magog and the reminder of Tenk's inevitable demise. *Will the guilt of that choice ever fade?*

Rave flew over and perched upon his shoulder. *At least I still have Rave.*

"Where are we headed, little buddy?" A rhetorical question. He knew Rave wouldn't, couldn't, answer. But the little black creature nestled in tighter, and Kibure relaxed as he looked out at the endless expanse of water illuminated by the rising sun along the horizon. It was a peaceful, calming sight.

"Wherever it is, it can't be worse than the Lugienese Empire, or even Brinkwell, right?"

Kibure followed the group of eight women through the knee-deep water to shore, then across a narrow beach toward the wild forest that dominated the island. Kibure detected a small release of magic as Vardya extended a hand; the thick jungle brush fell away to reveal a pathway marked by flat stones worn smooth from use. Kibure followed Vardya along the path but slowed as the light of day was replaced by gloom. He turned to see the forest close behind him, the sand and sea disappearing from sight. After weeks stuck on a small ship, he was glad to finally be moving, but there was something foreboding about the sudden disappearance of day.

Rave flew alongside the other raaven up ahead, providing Kibure the shred of confidence he needed. Rave had been a good judge of character thus far. If Kibure could trust anyone or anything, it was Rave.

They crossed several minor stone bridges spanning brooks and gullies, the gentle sound of trickling water coming and going as they did. Movement caught his eye off the right of the path. A fallen tree was slowly drifting along the ground, twisting ever so slightly as they passed—*eyes! That's not a tree.* He gasped but tried to keep his composure. The serpent's body was thicker around than his own and many times longer. He'd seen the vipers of the desert consume rats twice as thick as their own bodies. By Kibure's calculations, a human would be no difficulty at all for this colossal serpent.

One of the women who walked behind him must have noticed his change in posture. She said softly, "You need not fear Svetlana. You are no concern of hers, not so long as you're accompanied by us."

Kibure gulped. What sort of people kept a pet snake the size of a wagon?

Up ahead, the women in his retinue began disappearing one by one directly into a wall of stone. As he neared, Kibure held out a hand and watched in amazement as it disappeared from sight. Vardya guided him through the illusion into the hidden passage, the sound of the water suddenly dampened once and for all.

As they moved through the stone channel, Kibure noted the contrast to the roughly hewn corridors he recalled from Brinkwell. This passageway was marked by perfectly rounded ceilings, shaped as if by . . .

Dread returned as Kibure realized how helpless he was in the midst of such powerful wielders, friends of monster snakes and all.

That thought dissolved as the corridor opened up to a balcony overlooking a massive chamber. Kibure sucked in a quick breath and held it as he marveled at the sight before him. Concealed within the massive cavern lay an entire city, visible by the yellow light of a hundred softly glowing orbs. Kibure stared in wonder, counting dozens of stone buildings, all marked by the shadows cast by curving arcs and pillars, each etched with geometric shapes, letters, and even creatures hewn deep into their surfaces. At the city's center lay an amphitheater with seating enough for dozens upon dozens of spectators.

Vardya startled him with a hand on the shoulder. "Welcome to Purgemon."

CHAPTER 3

KIBURE

KIBURE'S ESCORTS BROUGHT HIM DOWN a sloping walkway to the floor of the cavern, then through a street lined by rows of the exquisite structures. A number of the city's occupants paused to stare before returning to their tasks. Unlike in Brinkwell, these folks did not have the perpetual urgency to their movements that he had come to expect from city dwellers; everyone here appeared to be going about their tasks with the kind of practiced grace one might gain from a lifetime of experience but without the frail, strained movements of the arthritic. These people managed gracefully youthful movements that reminded Kibure just how far from normal this was.

Kibure noted that even here, every person he saw wore a similarly fashioned cloak of gray—no, not gray—silver. Unlike the unremarkable wool cloaks worn by his escorts, these garments shimmered. They seemed to almost glow in the soft light cast by the unnatural spherical orbs that lined the streets.

Then Kibure noticed something more disconcerting. Of all the people he had seen, not one soul appeared to be male. And while he was no expert on the rules of procreation, he was pretty certain men played a role in that process. Surely a city like this could not survive generations as these women claimed, not without at least a few men. A chill captured Kibure's breath as he was directed into a building to the left. Had he been taken here for the purpose of reproduction? He shook his head. *No, this can't be like that.*

The small room was dominated by five ornate chairs set upon an elevated curved platform arranged in a semicircle. Opposite the chairs were two long stone benches arranged for small audiences. Kibure was directed to sit on the bench closest to the raised platform housing five chairs. His escorts took their seats, Vardya to his left, a woman called Emin to his right, and Andra beside her. Upon the five chairs rested four women; the chair at the center was currently unoccupied. If Kibure's "liberators" had appeared eerily ageless, which they certainly did, the women in the chairs before him were no doubt ancient. Whereas the women who had stolen away with him in Brinkwell had pale skin and jet-black hair much like his own, the women before him had hair of stark white, and their skin, while not crinkled with age, seemed stretched too thin across their bony faces. And their eyes, which he now realized bore into him like knives, appeared to hold within them the kind of depth found only from years of seeing, judgment passing with every blink of their primordial lids. These four women wore the same silver robes as all the other women in this strange city, only the fabric of their collars was a shimmering gold.

The women on the platform rose to their feet. Everyone else in the room did so as well, so Kibure mimicked the action, unsure why until he saw another woman enter from a dark passageway behind the platform. She too wore a silver robe with a golden collar, except hers was accompanied by a long golden cape. As she moved to stand before her chair on the platform, Kibure watched in awe as the cape floated behind her as if the fabric was somehow lighter than the air around it. Everything about it seemed *very* wrong. In any case, this ancient-looking woman with long white hair and a magical golden cape held the attention of every person in the room, a specter to be obeyed without the utterance of a single word. She extended both hands before her and only then did everyone in the room sit. She then took her own seat.

One look at this central woman framed by the four others made Kibure wonder if he hadn't been passed from one evil to another.

He felt the weight of their collective stare. He also felt the subtle touch of magic, closer to what he had felt from the Klerósi priest who had invaded his mind, though without the same sense of revolting violation. This was more like a pair of soft, ethereal hands reaching out to brush against him as he passed. He still found it unsettling, as if he was wearing far less than the simple white robe he had been given to wear onboard the ship. Even Rave had nestled himself around Kibure's neck, clinging tight as if someone was pulling at him in an attempt to separate the two of them.

Kibure could not hold the gaze of any of these women, so he looked at the ground until the inspection had ended. Fortunately, that came swiftly, replaced by a voice. Kibure looked up to see the ancient one seated at the centermost chair leaning forward as she said, "Welcome to Purgemon. I am Lady Atticus of the She'yar, the remnant. You are the child of the prophecies? The one with the power to wield the kosmí and cultivate the seed? The one who will return us to the lands of old?"

Magog's warning about these women from within his nightmare flashed through Kibure's mind. *The Asaaven, or what remains of them, need you in order to escape to the sacred lands of the ancient ones.* He reminded himself that it had been nothing more than a meaningless nightmare, and he knew this was true, but still . . . a strange coincidence? It didn't help that the woman speaking to him was downright terrifying.

Kibure glanced from side to side to confirm that her glare was directed right at him. He was supposed to respond in some way. The woman—Lady Atticus?—had spoken an intelligible version of Lugienese, but what she had said made such little sense. What had she asked? Something about a seed? Knowing some response was required, but that he had no answer to give, Kibure compromised with, "I—I do not know."

The woman's glare sharpened without a single change in her expression. Kibure sighed with relief when those eyes, penetrating as they were, plunged instead into Vardya.

"Vardya, you have traveled all this way with him, yet the boy is not even aware of his own purpose?"

Vardya bowed. "Lady Atticus, as I last reported, he has demonstrated the ability to touch the natural world, enter the spiritual realm of his own accord, and was being held captive by the enemy beneath the skies of the concurrent moons. More signs than this are beyond my calling to assess. I leave the telling of futures and purpose to those best qualified." She bowed her head toward the ancient beings before them.

An awkward silence passed over the room before the caped woman stood, her hands gripping the arms of the chair to help her rise. "If he is the one, his training will need to begin in earnest. The enemy will be ever zealous now that they know we have the boy."

Kibure felt exposed once again as the ancient one moved her gaze over him. "Once again, I am called Lady Atticus. What do you call yourself?"

His voice was embarrassingly shaky, but he was glad to at least know the answer to a question. "I am called Kibure."

"Well, Kibure, as you may or may not be aware"—she glanced back at Vardya for a moment before continuing—"my people, the She'yar, have been searching for you for a long time. We have been cut off from our ancestral lands for millennia. The She'yaren people believe that you are the one destined to return us home. However, we will not force you to do our bidding, for doing so would be a violation of more than one of our core tenets. Therefore, you must elect to do this of your own free will."

Lady Atticus paused to let that sink in, which was good because his mind felt like a clogged drain and any further words in that moment would have stagnated anyhow. What had already been said was enough to make him weary of regurgitation.

The fact that he was being given a choice put some of his fears about these women at ease. An evil demigod like Magog would have forced him to do his bidding, probably would have tortured him. These women were at least kind enough to ask.

He felt the eyes of everyone upon him. They were waiting for a response. "Um . . . what would I need to do?"

He cursed to himself. *They must think I'm an idiot. I can hardly use whatever powers they think I have, and I'm speaking about as well as Rave at the moment.*

The ancient one did not smile, but her voice grew softer, almost enough to suggest there was at least one fiber of compassion within. "You will need to undergo a strict regimen of training. If you are to do what you were created to do, you must learn to harness your abilities to the fullest extent."

Kibure gulped. "And what happens to me should I not agree to this?"

Ah, there's the old glare, he thought. His moment of inner humor faded as the severity of the woman's expression threatened to empty his bladder.

"Should you choose to ignore your calling, you will be cast out. Sent to a village far to the east where you will be under careful watch but free to live your remaining days in this world. You will receive rudimentary training before being allowed to leave, but only so much as what will be necessary to keep you from harming yourself or others."

Kibure felt his own scowl coming on. "So I would be free in name alone?"

Lady Atticus's voice took on an agitated edge. "You would be one of the only human visitors to have ever entered Purgemon and left with their life. We do not often allow such a thing."

Kibure felt frustration building. They hadn't rescued him; they had stolen a tool needed to perform a task, nothing more. Emboldened by this realization, he responded, "You really should have mentioned this *before* bringing me down here. That would have expanded my options."

How Lady Atticus's glare managed to sharpen further, Kibure did not know. *Any more so and she might cut her own face with it.* "Your options were set at birth," she said. "You did not choose these paths, nor did we; they were set before you. We have simply added to them. Or would you have preferred to remain in Lugienese custody?"

His confidence waned at that remark. It was a fair point. But did it mean he owed these people his life? Perhaps so. Did this mean he needed to sacrifice his freedom entirely? Oh, the irony of this "freedom" he was being offered!

He considered this and wasn't certain he wished to enslave himself to them simply because they had rescued him. After all, they had only done so because of what they had to gain if he agreed now to do their bidding.

The pressure to make a decision weighed so heavily that Kibure wondered how much longer his chair would support him. He was being offered the opportunity to finally learn how to wield his magic. The vile curse that had been at the center of all of his problems in the first place could soon become an asset. And yet in so choosing that path, he would forfeit his chance at experiencing freedom, at least in the near future. *Am I willing to give up my own freedom?* He knew the answer and finally shook his head.

"No. I will not forfeit this chance at freedom. I am grateful to have been rescued from captivity, but I do not wish to condemn myself to servitude once again, even temporary servitude."

Murmurs spread through the small chamber, though Lady Atticus seemed unfazed by his words. In fact, she appeared to have expected them. "We live in a fallen world filled with lust for self. Most would choose the same; to cherish such freedom for the brief time it exists before the Lugienese come to sweep it away for good."

Kibure had averted his eyes, looking instead to the stone floor, but he glanced up at those words. "Lugienese?"

Lady Atticus nodded. "Surely you know we are entering into the end of days here in this world, or at least this part of it. The Lugienese will not end their purge with Brinkwell or the Isles. The prophecies are clear: the evils of the west will consume the land until they have ravaged everything to the easternmost peaks."

She stopped to let the gravity of her words sink in. It did. Kibure felt a tug on his heart, though he attempted to ignore it. After an uncomfortable silence, he said, "And you believe I am the only one capable of keeping this from happening? But only if I agree to enter into your service, to be trained as a wizard?"

Lady Atticus answered matter-of-factly, "In a manner of speaking, yes, though wizard is probably not the right word for what you would become."

He considered the Lugienese. What would they do with him when they eventually found him, even if it was months or years from now? He considered his time in captivity, the man who had violated the innermost sanctity of his mind. Perhaps *this* was reason enough to enslave himself to this apparent enemy of his enemy.

He knew he was being manipulated on some level, perhaps many levels, yet the mere thought of facing Lugienese captivity again was so paralyzing that his mouth moved almost of its own accord and words flowed forth. Even if he chose to remain behind, he would face the Lugienese as a wielder of magic, not a helpless babe. "I will do it."

There was a quiet stirring among all in attendance. "I do what you need of me," he added, "and then you will release me entirely. I will be free to leave this place, with or without you."

The murmurs halted, and the ancient one smiled with her lips only. "Very well, Kibure. Once you have completed the tasks of our prophecy, we will release you to your own fate."

Feeling the fabric of his white robe sticking to his sweaty skin, he added, "And I want one of those fancy robes."

Lady Atticus replied stoically, "You will be provided a robe if, and only if, you demonstrate competence. We still don't know for certain that you are indeed the one who was foretold."

Heads nodded in agreement like leaves bobbing to the same gust of wind.

It was worth a try, he thought as he squirmed uncomfortably in the musty garment.

Lady Atticus continued, "The training will be difficult, but once it has begun, this choice of yours cannot be undone. You will need to see this through. Do you understand?"

Not really, no. But he nodded yes, cleared his dry throat, and replied, "I understand."

The ancient one nodded in return.

"Vardya, you will see to this, and then you will return to me. We have much to discuss regarding your time away."

Vardya inclined her head once again. "Yes, mistress, of course. I will see him to a room, then call upon Lady Helda to join us at the Acrogean as soon as—"

"No!" Lady Atticus's voice slammed down upon Vardya's own like a wood-splitting hammer. "We haven't the time to go about his training through traditional means. The enemy moves. The boy must be sent to the Paideia. I will send for Lady Drymus. Go now."

Everyone in the room had risen to their feet, an act of respect, Kibure figured, or perhaps because this woman rising signaled an end to the meeting. In any event, they were all standing as he was ushered back into the street. Kibure noted the nervous glances passing among the women. He had the feeling that wherever he was being sent, it would not be as pleasant as he had hoped.

They followed the main street through the beautiful underground city. As he walked, he felt occasional prickles of what he could only assume were uses of magic. These tingly flutters, however, were smooth and faint, unlike his recollections of Sindri's magic before she had lost it. This was more like walking through the forest beneath the Drisko Mountains with leaves and pine needles brushing his skin.

As Kibure followed his escorts, the magnificence of the city was increasingly muted by the tension in the body language adopted by his escort at being told to take him to . . . wherever it was they were headed.

Rave emerged from overhead and came to land on his shoulder, nestling his nose into Kibure's neck. This gave him much-needed comfort. With all the change he had experienced, Rave was the most consistent thing he knew. The furry little enigma was his rock, the little guardian who was always there for him.

They reached a tall, elaborately framed door at the other side of the city, carved into the wall that curved toward the towering stone roof above. A sweep of the woman's hand, another ripple of magic, and the door opened to allow their entry into a dark corridor.

Rave released a loud coo, then raced away, out of the space that would be his newest prison.

So much for always being there for me, thought Kibure wryly.

He sighed and followed his escort through an unlit tunnel; Vardya lifted a hand as an orb of light sprang to life, illuminating the space before them. A short while later, the path widened to expose a circular room devoid of anything but the stone that marked its walls.

"I will see you when this portion of your training has been completed."

Vardya didn't meet his eyes before turning to leave, taking her magically summoned orb of light with her. Something about this small gesture and its lack of decorum made Kibure uneasy. That, and the absolute darkness as a stone door closed behind her, a door that had not been there when they entered the room.

CHAPTER 4

RAJUBAN

HIGH PRIEST RAJUBAN WOUND HIS way down the dank steps below the ancient foundation of the palace. His desire to be closer to the Lugienese conquests in the east was deferred by the picturesque preparations he made while remaining in the capital. At least for now. *I've always preferred to play the long game. The foundations of this great construct are nearly complete. There will be ample time to decorate later.*

He smiled to himself as he recalled the years of subtle comments, favors, and humiliations he had been forced to endure before he was able to finally dislodge one of his oldest enemies, Grobennar, from his seat of favor with the God-king. There had been times when he had despaired, believing the task too great even for his masterful schemes, but at long last he had succeeded in ascending to the highest position possible, and his momentum would continue until he was marked the greatest High Priest ever to don the sash, and perhaps more.

Of course, Grobennar continued to claw at the grave. The God-king had taken one trip without Rajuban's "guidance," and suddenly Grobennar was christened Secretary of War, a position second only to Rajuban's own. Apparently the invasion of Brinkwell had occurred without flaw. Rajuban chided himself for not being more involved.

Grobennar had a particularly annoying way of defying mundane odds. Rajuban would need to continue to ensure that Grobennar's odds were anything but ordinary.

He sighed. *For every great accomplishment seen in the light, one must complete a great many more in the shadows.*

His nose twitched at the powerful scent of sulfur while the hem of his robes grew heavy with the mire from the perpetually damp stone corridor. Rajuban carried in his left hand a single torch, the illumination from which served only to confirm that the door he sought remained several paces away. *I really should talk to Magog about having this prisoner relocated to the main dungeon. How dangerous could the old man manqué truly be? Yet, the best-kept secrets are best kept secret.* He nodded to himself and increased his pace.

Reaching the door at last, Rajuban pulled out the key he had borrowed from the pair of guards stationed at the entrance to this long-neglected wing of the archaic fortress. The hinge creaked as the High Priest pushed. The mixed odors of human waste, filth, and sulfur assaulted his senses, and Rajuban shuddered as he worked through an incantation that would dull them. Even still, he could taste the stagnant, putrid air. He strode over to the sconce along the adjacent wall and lit an additional torch, then set his own on the floor beside the stone chair he had coerced the guards to transport several moons prior.

A tangle of greasy, shoulder-length curls obscured a downcast face. The former High Priest sat with his back against the wall, knees akimbo, elbows resting atop them, leaving his forearms and hands dangling limply above bare feet. He looked the part of a defeated man one thousand times over.

Rajuban did his best to greet the man in a voice of joviality, though he knew there was no way he could wash away the sound of condescension that came with his station, especially when conversing with the man who sat before him, a living obscenity. "Now, now, is this any way to greet your High Priest, old friend? I know it has been ages since you yourself wore the robes of honor, but this is not my first excursion here." He exhaled. "I only ask for the smallest semblance of deference. After all, I'm the closest thing you have to a comrade in all the world. You should be grateful I come at all. Klerós alone knows the depths of suffering that comes with all these years in isolation."

The man did not move, hadn't so much as acknowledged his arrival. Rajuban leaned in closer, listening now for breathing. *Don't tell me the bloke has perished on me.*

He took a step closer, then squatted, just beyond reach, and listened. He heard only the faintest sound of air, a wheezing of the lungs. *Alive. Good. Splendid. I need to have him fed a little better, though. He is far too close to death for my liking. How am I to extract secrets from a man so near death that he might cross over at the mere suggestion of pain?*

"Baldemar, you know why I have come."

The man remained a statue. Rajuban grunted, then stood so he could pull out the loaf of bread he had brought, along with a skin of wine. The cheese he set aside; that was the treat this man would be denied until he offered a proper greeting. Rajuban took a long pull from the skin, reinserted the plug, and dropped it between the man's feet. He then extended the loaf of bread. Baldemar still gave no reaction.

"Hey!" Rajuban smacked the living corpse across the face with the bread. "Take your gifts, heathen. Unlike you, I have a schedule. You know, with events and engagements. You remember having responsibilities now, don't you? Yes, did you know? The purge is well underway. I believe this slipped my mind during our last visit. Anyway, I've many strings to pull in order to stay ahead of my enemies, both within and without the Empire."

Bloodshot eyes slowly rolled up to meet the extended bread. Then a set of grimy, shaky hands took hold.

"That's it, marvelous. To receive a gift with gratitude is a sign of a healthy, humble spirit. All right, then. Shall we begin?"

Rajuban walked over to sit in the chair opposite the prisoner, then brought hands to his lap. "Now. Word of our conquests has brought about renewed interest in a topic that I believe you may be able to assist with. In exchange for your compliance, I am willing to offer you something grand. Are you ready to hear my offer?"

The broken soul looked up through his tangled hair and said in a hoarse voice, "I have been down here for many years. I have told you, and the High Priest before you, and the one before that everything I know. Just let me pass on to the next life of suffering that awaits me. I could use a change of scenery."

Rajuban scoffed, "I am not like the others. They were all insipid buffoons with no grasp of the larger board upon which this game is played. Now. Questions. Word has traveled here from our conquest of Brinkwell that there was a contingent of women who wielded a form of magic that resisted castration, much like the tazamines we find from time to time within the Empire. They were said to wear gray cloaks."

The prisoner attempted not to react, but he was no master of deception like Rajuban. His face may as well have gone wide-eyed in recognition.

Rajuban continued, "It is my understanding that the prisoner who seduced you all those years ago fit the description of these women, including the garb. Well, that is, before she was imprisoned. It was also said that she resisted the castrations set upon her. You spent months questioning her before she convinced you to betray your loyalties to Klerós and the Empire. And as I said, I am no patsy. I have a new theory about the extent of your relationship."

Rajuban tsked and walked over to crouch before the man. "I believe that you betrayed more than just your political oaths . . ." He awaited a response, but the man showed nothing so he continued, "You defiled your oath of purity to the Lugienese race. You allowed not only one prisoner to escape, but two."

The man paused as he chewed the bread, but only for a moment before resuming. He offered no other reaction. *Let's see how he does with this.* "We have found the child, though this abomination is now grown. However, the expected propensity for betrayal appears to be hereditary and has been revealed to the fullest extent. If you aid me, I will allow you to see the fruit of your lust. It will not be long until this anathema, this abomination, has been taken into our custody. And after this, I may even allow you to, at long last, enter into the next life. But none of it can happen if you don't first help me understand this witchcraft of theirs."

The prisoner began to struggle for breath. Was he choking? *I'm going to have to touch this disgusting bag of flesh, aren't I?*

Just before he did, he realized he had misjudged. Baldemar wasn't choking; he was laughing. Rajuban's blood boiled. *How dare he! And what could possibly be so humorous about this? I'm offering to reunite him with his only living kin before finally concluding his torment.* He drew in his magic, a dark rage threatening to overtake his need to keep the prisoner alive.

Baldemar spoke then. "Finally. I thought she had been wrong. After so many years, I'm ashamed to say that I doubted. I started to believe that I had imagined her last words." He resumed his madman's laughter, the sound echoing around the small prison of stone and mud, each hearty exhalation a slap to Rajuban's pride.

"What are you—stop laughing!"

Baldemar did not stop. The chilling sound intensified as he spoke, each word blending into infuriating guffaws. "I feel your magic, but you won't kill me. Not yet. Not yet. Not yet."

Rajuban felt his grip on restraint slipping. The man was taunting him. *He's gone completely mad. There is no use for him.*

"She was right all along," Baldemar continued, his words stilted by his boisterous laughter. "You are a fool; you'll fail to collect all of the pieces in time to stop them. You'll—"

Rajuban's ire overtook his good sense, and he sent a wave of air at Baldemar, slamming him hard against the wall. But recognition of the man's last words prevented Rajuban from finishing the job.

He can't possibly know about the stones. He must be speaking metaphorically. He's a raving lunatic. But if Baldemar did know about Magog and Rajuban's active search to reunite the ancient relics of power, what else did he know? Rajuban had attempted to delve into the man's mind on two occasions but had found nothing but dead ends. Baldemar's mind had been somehow damaged, or perhaps protected. But he was right about one thing: Rajuban could not eliminate him. Not yet. He needed to secure this man's kin. Perhaps that would be enough to turn him.

Rajuban turned and started out of the cell, then paused and stooped to retrieve the cheese he had set aside. *Indubitably, no gift today.* Rajuban's fury had become a nervous energy that he had not felt in some time. This was a wrinkle in his plans he had not expected, and the unexpected was always perilous. He clenched his jaw as he slammed the door to the cell closed behind him. *The man is trapped hundreds of feet below ground. He is no threat to anyone.*

Then the voice in his mind that had remained obediently silent spoke. *"You should just kill him. He reeks of the enemy's schemes. Every wretched breath he takes is a step toward disaster. Feed his blood to the stone beneath your feet!"*

Rajuban's hand went to the place on his chest, just beneath the skin where the red gemstone had been buried. "I will not discard valuable information. Not yet." That last word resulted in a mouthful of bile as he recalled Baldemar's maniacal words: *Not yet. Not yet. Not yet.*

"As you wish, Raj. But do but not think to blame me when the enemy's wicked scheme comes to pass. And I will not withhold the 'I told you so's.'"

Rajuban ignored the spirit, and as he passed into the refreshing air of the palace beyond the stairwell, he barked to the guards, "Ensure that the prisoner is nursed back to health. He may have an injury to his head." The guards nodded their understanding. "And double his rations. I need him healthy for questioning when next I visit."

Rajuban tossed the cheese to the guard nearest him then headed straight for Magog's chambers.

CHAPTER 5

SINDRI

SINDRI STOOD BESIDE AYNWARD, APART from the rest of the crew. He had pulled her aside while the ship was being secured to the dock in the Isles city of Tung.

"Are you sure you won't accompany me to Salmune? It's likely the safest place in all the world at this point. I could sure use your *unique* perspective in attempting to convince my father that the Lugienese threat is indeed very real."

Sindri did her best to maintain an expression of heartfelt consideration. Perhaps Prince Aynward was wholly concerned with keeping his Kingdom safe, but he was also a young male who had been stuck on a small ship for weeks with only three other women for company. One of them, Minathi, appeared fully taken by the other boy, Kyllean; and Arella, well, she was nearly as odd as the wizard, Draílock.

It was therefore no surprise to Sindri that she had caught Aynward goggling on more than one occasion during the voyage from Brinkwell to Tung. He had not yet mastered the subtleties of the sidelong glance that some of his older male counterparts possessed. While she found it flattering, Sindri had no time or patience to deflect his advances, should they come.

She smiled, then sighed for effect and hoped that her improving control of the Kingdom tongue would convey the intended balance of thankfulness and polite refusal. She was still far from confident with the language. "I thank of you for such kind words and offer; alas, I cannot go of this place with you. For now, I have need to be here in Tung." Then she added, "Maybe our path crosses in the future." That last part was pure fiction. She knew they would never see each other again. She expected her life would end sometime in the next few weeks, depending upon the ambitions of the Lugienese.

"You sure? The heart of the Kingdom is probably the safest place in the world right now."

She shook her head. "I have spoken."

He nodded his understanding, eyes downcast.

Sindri took no pleasure in the disappointment she saw in the boy's expression, but she was well adapted to all forms of disappointment. "Farewell, Prince Aynward." Raising her voice to include the others, she said, "Many thanks to all of you. I have wishes for your long life and health."

The dark, creamy-skinned woman named Minathi extended arms toward her, and Sindri had no choice but to accept. The embrace was warm and genuine. Minathi said to her, "I can't believe you're forcing me to have to travel the rest of the way alone with these two louts. But I understand your choice and I wish you well." She released the hug and stepped back. "And do please kill as many of those blasted fanatics as you can!"

Sindri looked up and gave her a devious smile. "I intend to."

Next came Kyllean, though he extended only a hand, as was proper. "If all the new magic learning stuff doesn't pan out in time, don't forget your aptitude with those blazing daggers of yours!"

Sindri smiled sadly at that remark. She had especially enjoyed sparring with the Tal-Don boy, whose unique skills with a sword had helped sharpen her own. She had sparred with both boys, and while Aynward was very skilled, Kyllean was fluid to the point of artistry.

In fact, if she wasn't mistaken, she would say he utilized some form of subtle magic, himself. She would miss it.

With nothing left to say, she nodded and turned down the gangplank, glad that Draílock and Arella had remained below for her departure.

"Sindri, just where are you going?"

Ugh. She turned to see Draílock standing at the edge of the ship.

Must I repeat myself to everyone? She continued moving and shouted back, "I have already told of you. I go to find where I can be in this city to kill Klerósi priests when they arrive."

Draílock had attempted to convince Sindri to continue east with him and Arella, as had been her initial intentions, but with her magical abilities improving over the last few weeks, and the certainty that they would not be able to find Kibure even if she wished, Sindri had decided instead upon vengeance. She figured if the Lugienese waited several more weeks before arriving, as was the best estimates at this time, she would be strong enough to kill many of her old brethren before falling herself. Granted, her improvement would likely slow once she was no longer under the tutelage of two skilled wielders; there was nothing to be done about that. She had made up her mind. No more running.

A shape materialized beside her as she neared the edge of the dock. Sindri turned to face Arella.

"Sindri, staying here accomplishes nothing."

"Staying means less Klerósi roaches to infest of the world."

Arella shook her head, keeping up with Sindri's quickening pace. "You can accomplish so much more than this if you remain with us. Don't you still wish to help find your friend, Kibure? I thought that was your plan."

Sindri ground her teeth. "Yes, it was. But we have no knowledge of his location. I rather spend time killing bad people, not running from them."

Arella took hold of Sindri's sleeve and spun her around to face her. "You will do nothing more than die if you stay here. You're not ready to face Klerósi priests. Trust me, you'll have plenty of opportunities to kill as many of them as you wish in the coming moons. Wouldn't you rather do so once you're truly equipped to do so?"

Sindri ripped her arm back and attempted to turn, but Arella held firm. She reached for Arella's wrist then, but the woman let go just as Sindri's hand moved and Sindri swatted only air.

Sindri turned and nearly walked into the straight-backed form of Draílock, who said calmly, "Will you abandon yet another soul in their time of need?"

"Wh—" These were only words, but they were an unexpected sharpened spear, and they stabbed her right in the heart. Her legs felt weak, her posture suddenly deflated. Yet Draílock knew nothing of her brother. She had not revealed that part of her past to anyone, except Kibure. He had known something of this, but Draílock hadn't had any time alone with him, had he? No, of this she was certain. "What is your meaning?"

He smiled, yet his eyes remained cold. "I speak of those left in the wake of your departure from the false god."

Sindri felt a mixture of anger and horror. *No, there's no way he knows. He's grasping at air. Even still, how dare he compare this to that!* Anger was beginning to win her inner battle.

Draílock continued, "I mean you no disrespect. I believe you were right to question an oppressive regime that crucifies wielders of ateré magic. And I speak without the knowledge of specifics, of course." He smiled coldly. "But I don't need any. No rebellion takes place without collateral damage. I merely remind you that this decision to challenge your roots has brought you here, to a place where your actions will affect not just you but others for whom you care. You have an opportunity to do something great, that is, if you have the strength. You have the opportunity to master this magic and perhaps reclaim that which you have lost. And with these tools, you might someday truly capture the revenge you seek against the people who have betrayed so many of their own."

Sindri managed to keep her anger in check. "My actions are mine. For me only. Many people have tried to manipulate my choice. You are transparent like air."

Draílock was emotionless as ever as he said, "You are not wrong. I do work to manipulate you. And yet, you should take care to consider my words in spite of this fact. I was planning to show this to you during our voyage to the Kingdom of Scritland, but we can do this now. If you feel the same after hearing this, I will bother you no further."

He reached his hand into the folds of his robes and retrieved a sheet of parchment.

Sindri placed hands upon her hips. "If I listen to this, you leave me alone?"

He nodded and handed the parchment to Arella. "Care to do the honors? You're better at translation than I."

Sindri asked, "What is this?"

Arella took the parchment, and the question. "This is a replica of an artifact retrieved by Hadrian the Mad, a famous Scritlandian explorer. It was obtained during his last voyage as captain, the one that gave him the title 'mad.' He captured several artifacts during his visit to the Hand of the Gods, as well as a madness of the mind much like others who have visited these accursed lands."

Sindri scowled. "How do you have of this now? We barely escaped Brinkwell!"

Arella gave her a patronizing look that said, *Dear child, you know so little. Let me enlighten you.* "Dwapek planned well for our escape from Brinkwell. He had several of his most valuable belongings loaded onto the ship before we arrived, including all the food we've been enjoying during this time. Back to the matter at hand, this document is just one of many to have taken on new meaning in light of what occurred in Brinkwell."

Sindri motioned with her hands for Arella to continue. She wanted to be away from all of these people as soon as she could.

Arella glanced to Draílock, who nodded. "The author of this document writes: *'This war is lost, the Empire destroyed. You must now keep the stones hidden and await the coming of the one who will guide us through the storm once and for all. Our sisters prepare a place—"*

Sindri waited for more, and when none came, responded, "Where is the rest?"

Arella shrugged. "This was all that was recovered."

"Those words have no meaning to me. I wish of you safe travels."

Draílock held up a hand. "Do not see what this letter means?"

Sindri rolled her eyes and shook her head; she had no idea and cared very little at this point.

Draílock lowered his voice and said, "This was found among the wreckage of a ship along the Strait of Spirits. It is believed to have been written by one of the last inhabitants of the Hand of the Gods at the end of what Scritlandian scholars refer to as the Great Scourge. What the Lugienese refer to as Hakbar's War."

Sindri leaned in and lowered her own voice. "This paper does not make of me to wish to kill less Klerósi priests."

Draílock's expression remained impassive as he continued calmly, "I believe the gray-cloaked women who stole away with Kibure are the descendants of this author."

Sindri narrowed her eyes. "Hakbar's War occurred over five thousand years ago. You believe that the remnant of a people from more than five thousand years ago appeared in Brinkwell to capture of Kibure? You are much a fool. As fool as the Lugienese."

The stony wizard smiled. "Perhaps. But it does seem curious that those gray-cloaks spoke so much of prophecy, then stole away with the very person that Magog himself sought for the same, if opposing, reason. I may be, as you say, a fool, but there's enough corroboration surrounding Kibure's significance, no matter our lack of understanding as to why. I believe Kibure may be more important to the coming war than you know. Of course, you'll be long dead by the time this comes to fruition, should you stay here to try to kill a few minor Klerósi priests. Still, I won't take a prisoner on this journey. The choice must be yours." He gestured to Arella with a hand. "Let's go. We must gather a few more provisions for the journey. We leave on the morrow to begin our search for the boy."

They departed, leaving Sindri to brood alone. All she wanted to do was kill Klerósi priests. But Draílock's words—*Curse him!*—hung in the air burdening her more with every passing breath. As much as she wished for vengeance in the short term, she knew that she would go with the two mages. Draílock had defeated her resolve to stay the moment he suggested she was abandoning someone in their time of need. She thought back to so many years earlier. The voice she had heard from the shadows: "Perhaps someday you will not fail to keep the ones you love from harm. Perhaps someday this name too will be laid to rest."

She had returned to that day and the voice dozens of times. Part of her believed that it had been nothing more than her grief playing tricks. Nevertheless, the accusation clung to who she had become. *I will not die, nor will I change this name until I have earned the right to call myself something new.*

Sindri let out a heavy breath, and with it went the last vestiges of her plan to remain in Tung. She admitted to herself that this had been her way of giving up the fight. While some may have thought it courageous, she recognized now that it had been nothing short of surrender. A suicide for someone who was too afraid to commit the act themself. Disgusted with herself and angry with Draílock for revealing it, she clenched her fists and started back toward the ship, a tear streaking down one cheek as she worked to control her emotions. *I owe it to Lysan to find Kibure. Let my brother not have died in vain.*

CHAPTER 6

KIBURE

KIBURE SAT IN THE DARK silence of the stone room waiting for . . . anything. Instructions? Food? Someone to tell him what in Doréa he was supposed to be doing. He continued waiting for what felt like an eternity. Maybe this was part of his training? Was he supposed to somehow escape the room? *Would be nice if they gave me some direction!*

As time stretched, Kibure finally rose to his feet. Recalling as best he could what he had seen in the room before all light was removed, he felt his way to the nearest wall. Devoid of even the slightest hint of light, he may as well have been blind. Pure nothingness.

Then he thought he heard *something*, a barely audible scratching sound. He stopped moving to listen and willed his eyes to see into the blackness, but as before, he saw nothing.

"Hello?"

Nothing.

He slumped to the floor in defeat. *I should have let them know that I'm not much for riddles.*

He shook his head in frustration. He was no more free now than he had been upon the drogal farm or even in the captivity of the Klerósi priests. *At least then I was able to see.* Time continued to pass and his mind

floated along the timeless abyss of his confinement before returning to
the present predicament. *Perhaps this is some sort of test?* He shook his
head in the dark. If this was a test, he would fail. He had no idea of the
goal. Then again, they did believe him some sort of mage, didn't they?
So if this were a test, he would be expected to use magic. That made
sense. That would also be quite difficult, considering his utter lack of
ability.

No, not ability. He had used magic before. He could no longer
deny that fact. But it had not exactly been his intention. The first time
had occurred during a moment of impulsive fury, while the others had
come from the depths of reactive, desperate fear. In spite of his current
captivity, he felt little emotion at all. Something akin to melancholy, not
the kind of extreme emotion that would serve as a catalyst for accessing
his magic. He felt only a numb sadness. It reminded him of how he
had felt during the annual harvest day celebration back at the estate.
On that day, all the slaves were treated to a special meal of charred meat
and other treats usually withheld from them. But as a young boy and
an outsider even among the slaves, he was relegated to the back of the
line. Most years, by the time he reached the table, all the meat was gone.
Then as now, his dreams of freedom had been close enough to smell,
close enough to begin salivating at the thought of tasting something so
long denied him, yet he had reached the container housing it and found
only the empty bottom of the bucket; he chewed only lies and defeat.

This was something he had been conditioned to feel, and right now
it felt like putting on an old shirt, tattered and worn. He knew it wasn't
how it was supposed to be, but it was the only thing he had, so he wore
it anyway.

He finally conceded. *May as well try something.* Kibure attempted
to relax his mind as he had done back in Brinkwell when first training
alongside Sindri under the direction of the wizard Draílock. He recalled
feeling the tingly energy within the creepy little crickets. Perhaps that
was what he was supposed to do now. Placing his hands upon the cold
stone upon which he sat, he willed himself toward the static energy
within to feel its power. He focused every shred of his attention into the

stone, then extended that will further and further into the depths of his stone container.

Then he gasped and sucked in a deep breath. He felt nothing, not unless one counted the burning sensation in his lungs from holding his breath. Yes, that was it. He had been concentrating so hard that he had forgotten to breathe. *Idiot.* He was fairly certain that this was *not* the right technique. Reasserting control over his lungs, he tried again to relax his body while extending his mind in search of the power Draílock claimed could be found in all things, living or not.

This time he did feel something. No, he didn't feel it. He saw it. It was difficult to hold within his mind's eye. It was as if he saw the room take shape. It wasn't exactly like seeing, but he did have a sense of where he was in relation to the openness of the space, the places where little to no power at all resided. It was like seeing an inverted version of his surroundings, the space where nothing existed became the solid stone, while the floor, ceiling, and walls of the cave cell became a space for his mind to move about freely. But how did he take what he felt and borrow its energy? How would he apply that energy even if he took hold of it? *This is useless.*

But he continued to probe the space. What else did he have to do? Nothing but—*wait.* He felt his mind slide over something different. Where had that been? He did the mental equivalent of backpedaling. Not only had this object felt solid, it had felt…blurry? That was the best his mind could come up with to describe it. He scanned the area again but felt nothing.

Come on, he thought.

Kibure swept the area once more, attempting to relax his mind and body even further. He felt it again and stopped. Yes, this was most certainly not stone. If the stone was a thing of static energy, unwilling to budge, then what he felt now was like finding the last piece of meat in the pail, the grease making it impossible to grip. His mind slid right off it, but he did sense that it was there, and it seemed quite large, considering he had previously felt nothing. Had it been here the entire time?

With every scrap of his attention focused on holding this sense of the object within his mind, he rose to his feet and crept toward it. As he drew closer, he felt a texture develop. He realized that whatever this was, it had layers of complexity, perhaps different materials? He walked straight toward it, then stopped suddenly when he felt it move. It could only be described as a faint ripple, but it was enough to give him pause. His heart began to pound, and his lock on the object began to fade until . . . the utter blackness observed by his bodily eyes returned, his sense of the space fleeing like a rodent escapes with its prized crumb.

Then a jolt of pain struck his eyes. He stumbled back, nearly falling as he covered his eyes. When he opened them again, he realized he was seeing light. And illuminated by this light was a woman, sitting in a simple chair within his stone dwelling.

If the five women sitting in the chairs earlier had appeared ancient, this woman was old enough to be their great-grandmother. Her wrinkly skin hung from her cheeks, seeming near liquid and ready to slide to the stone floor below. And instead of a thick head of stark white hair, this woman had merely a few wisps of the snow-white stuff, which seemed unable to rest against her otherwise bald scalp. Yet in spite of her obvious age, her eyes buzzed with energy.

This must be Lady Drymus.

She spoke with the even, dry tone of someone who would rather be somewhere else but couldn't be bothered to move. "Well, this is promising. It seems you aren't entirely without ability." Like the others, she wore a simple, silver robe; however, hers glowed like the steel of an unearthly weapon as it reflected the bluish orb of light she had summoned in her hand. It hovered a few inches above her palm, then remained in place as she lowered her extremity.

"I was beginning to fear that you were as ignorant of your powers as they claimed. Yet I see that you detected my arrival . . . eventually." She rasped, "Then again, they would not have sent you to me if you weren't in need of significant remediation. And even then, not unless they were already desperate. Sensing magic is not the same as drawing upon it. Or employing it with purpose and precision . . . as you must eventually do."

Kibure noticed a steaming beverage resting upon Lady Drymus's lap, her bony fingers holding the tip of a spoon, stirring the liquid. *Was that there when she first appeared?*

"My name is Lady Drymus. The darkness moves. We must begin at once." She extended the mug toward him. "You will drink this." She waited expectantly.

Kibure took the mug and brought the steaming beverage up to his nose to inspect. The liquid gave off a pungent smell and Kibure wriggled his nose in revulsion. He finally found his voice. "Ugh, what is it?"

"Poison."

Kibure's grip loosened at the word and the cup fell from his hand. Except, it didn't fall. He felt the slightest tingle of magic. The cup hung in the air, floating.

"None of that. Now, take the mug."

His heart pumped even harder.

"Oh, stop with the nerves, already. What sense would poisoning you make? Just take the mug and let's get on with it. Time is not our friend, nor is cowardice."

Kibure hesitated, gulped, then did as commanded. The beverage was warm, if bitter, but he was hungry and it felt good as it coated his stomach. It tasted far better than it smelled.

"Go on, drink up. Your training will begin once you have reached the other side."

Her words made little sense. But as he gulped down the last of it, the image of the woman before him flickered, and then began to fade. She looked up and said, "You may wish to lie down so you don't go banging your head as you slip into the spiritual realm." Then she cackled.

Kibure felt like he was already tumbling down a hill. By the time he made it to his back, the room had stopped spinning. But he realized that his vision was different.

"All right, on your feet."

Kibure came bolt upright. The sound had come from within his mind. That's when he realized the change in lighting; the blue light was drained of color, and he knew exactly where he was, sort of. He was in the realm of dreams like before, or whatever this place was.

He opened his mouth to ask why in all of Doréa she had sent him to this place when he was supposed to be learning magic, but when he tried to speak, his words made no sound.

"*I'm a decent reader of lips, but this will be easier if you simply learn to communicate from within this plane of reality—not that I wish to hear your whining.*" She paused. "*In fact, I do very much enjoy silence.*" She nodded, then looked up and shook her head. "*Then again, an inability to speak will prove rather problematic should you have questions, thus slowing your already stunted developmental growth. Very well.*"

She spread both arms wide. "*Let's start over, shall we?*" She stared at him expectantly. "*Ah yes, of course. You don't yet know how to speak!*" She chuckled to herself, sending faint echoes of her enjoyment into his mind.

Glad I am able to provide you with a source of amusement, Kibure thought coldly.

"*Welcome to the spiritual realm, the reflection, if you will; it is called many things by many people. You have been brought here that you might learn to impose your will upon the magic you draw from the world around you. We begin here because using magic here is safe, or safer, than practicing in the physical realm, the realm of the waking. That, and you don't need to be able to summon magic in order to manipulate the world around you in this place; we call this the other way. So your first lesson, it seems, is to will your desired speech into my mind. As you may have noticed, sound does not exist within this place. This is easiest to do when the intended recipient is also fully in the spiritual realm.*"

Kibure wondered, *Does that mean I could also speak to someone who is not in the spiritual realm?* The memory of his visit from Magog resurfaced for a fleeting moment before he cast it aside. *This is no time to worry over nightmares.*

"*Let's start with something simple, an object you can visualize easily within your mind's eye. I want you to focus all of your mental will on the existence of a single object, or as much as you can muster while still listening* to what I am saying to you." She paused to give him an opportunity to do so.

Kibure wondered, *What to choose?* What was something simple he could think about? A type of food? An article of clothing? He had no possessions to think of, so . . . what? He looked around for ideas but saw only the emptiness of the cave cell. Food then.

"*Ready?*"

He glanced over at an expectant Drymus, then shook his head. *Think. This is easy.*

"*Well?*" urged Drymus.

Not easy if you keep interrupting my thoughts.

He shook his head again, attempting to ignore her. *How about . . .*

"*I see I'm going to have to hold your hand at every step. This is going to be tedious.*"

Kibure ignored her. Then, the cup of tea from which he had drunk earlier suddenly appeared before his eyes, suspended in the air.

"*Visualize this mug.*"

Well, it's right in front of me; I don't have to visualize it.

"*Once you have it, close your eyes, but continue holding the mental image.*"

Ah. He did so.

"*Okay, now focus on the idea of the thing itself, the idea of the mug.*"

He screwed his face and did as he was asked, or tried to.

"*Okay, now keep this idea firmly within your mind and shift some of your attention to me. Visualize me and project the mug as if speaking the word to me as you would in the physical realm.*"

That entire premise felt like a knot of confusion, but he tried to follow what she had said. He imagined himself saying the word *mug*, then repeated that visualization with Drymus standing in front of him and imagined her hearing the idea of the word.

He opened his eyes and saw her standing before him, arms crossed, waiting expectantly. *It didn't work.*

He closed his eyes and tried again. He clenched his teeth and furrowed his brow in concentration, as if this was a matter of physical strength. Nothing happened. He let out a breath of frustration and opened his eyes.

Drymus glowered. "*Let's try something a bit simpler. Being able to communicate reciprocally would certainly make things easier for us, but it appears you're not ready for that so we'll just have to make do.*"

She rapped her fingers against one another in thought. "*Okay. Let's take this same premise, but apply it to this realm, not another person's mind. Take the idea of the object, the mug, and project that onto your hand.*" She demonstrated this by holding out her hand, which suddenly held a mug like the one she had been holding in the real world moments ago.

"*It is merely a matter of focusing your attention, your belief, and your will. You are forcing the energy within this place to react to your desires, much like we do in the physical realm; only, the availability of the magic there is limited to the existing energies around you and your physical ability to channel them, while here, the only limitation is that of the mind itself.*"

Seems simple enough, he thought.

He held out his hand and silently told the mug to appear. When nothing happened, he attempted to concentrate harder on the thought of the mug. He imagined the contours of the handle, and the shiny gloss of the baked clay.

There! It worked! The mug popped into existence, and to his surprise, he actually felt the cold touch of the clay mug in his hand just before it winked out.

Drymus gave him a wry look. "*Well, there's . . . something. It appears you are going to need a great deal of practice until you master this most basic technique. You must train your mind to hold on to these things which you summon into existence, much like you must eventually do so with energy summoned within the waking world. This takes time, discipline, and much more practice.*"

How do I leave? How long will I be stuck in here?

His questions, of course, did not reach Drymus's mind so she did not respond. But perhaps she noted the expression upon his face because she more or less answered. "*The tea will wear off in a few hours and your mind will travel back to the physical realm. I will have food sent.*

"Oh, and one more thing. If you wish to leave the confined space of the cave, you are permitted to move about this reflection of the city. This is merely a matter of will. Simply focus your attention on a specific place within the city and will yourself there. This would be a good exercise to practice, though it's more challenging than willing a simple object into being so you'll want to do a bit more work on the latter. But ambition plays a role in the will, so who knows, perhaps you'll find the former task less a challenge. Your mind won't, however, be able to leave the city itself, even within the spiritual realm. We have cast protections against that. This is to keep you and all of the others here hidden from those who might wish us harm. Would hate for you to frustrate yourself trying to travel to somewhere beyond. It seems you'll find frustration enough in doing what is permitted. Evening."

She disappeared.

Kibure opened his mouth to scream, but as with all things in this place, no sound could be heard. Moving from one captor to another agonized him. The fact that he had sort of agreed to this newest confinement didn't make him like it any less. *When will I be wholly free?*

He simply could not understand what these women, who were clearly more powerful than he, could possibly want from him. What could he ever accomplish that they could not? Then again, at least the women were going to teach him to use his magic, strange as their conventions might be. Perhaps if he managed to learn to wield his power well enough, he could eventually escape.

He considered for a few moments, then nodded. *I will let these women train me, but once my powers are realized, they will be mine to use as I see fit.*

Kibure swiveled his head in the darkness of the cave, then raised a hand and willed an orb of light into existence. After only a momentary delay, the cave was illuminated, but unlike the mug, this time he was able to hold the light within his mind's eye and it remained where it was, floating above his right palm.

I can see! I'm a real-life—

The orb disappeared and darkness enveloped him. He sighed the word *wizard.*

Then he mustered his will and illuminated the cave again. Now able to maintain it, he smirked in satisfaction, then decided he needed a change of scenery. *Let's see about getting out of here.* He visualized himself standing back in the center of the street where he had followed his captors before meeting the committee of elders. Seemed as good a place as any to begin. He focused his mind on that place, then closed his eyes, and—

He opened them to total darkness. Pinpricks of fear spidered throughout his body. Had he transported his consciousness into a wall? Could he even do that? Wouldn't that kill him? He recalled the warnings from the first woman who had visited him in his dreams what seemed a lifetime ago. He knew there were dangers here within the realm of dreams. But surely he would have been warned against such a danger as that. Plus, the fact he was alive and thinking about it must mean he hadn't killed himself.

Then, he realized what had happened and he felt his face go slack with embarrassment. He had lost the light he summoned to the cave in his attempt to transport himself. He summoned another light into being and sure enough, he was right where he had been in the cave. Summoning the light had been even easier this time. But he was still frustrated that he had been unable to transport himself. If he was going to be stuck in the cave for a time in the real world, he very much desired to be elsewhere while he was in the realm of dreams.

He closed his eyes and tried again to imagine himself in that same place within the city. He envisioned the buildings on either side of the street and willed himself there once more. This time when he opened his eyes, he saw the glow of magical orbs every twenty or so paces. The entire city was similarly lit, and Kibure let out a long-held breath of triumph as he smiled.

All right, I did—

Everything went black again. *—it.*

He ground his teeth and summoned an orb of light to confirm he had returned to the cave. A saying came to mind: *Two steps forward, one step back.* This was a very slow way to get to where one wished to go, and as far as he understood his situation, he needed to get to where he was going more quickly.

He flexed his hands a few times to regroup, then set his face in determination.

Kibure closed his eyes, then once again willed his consciousness into the city.

It was easier this time, and he felt more in control as he strutted down the empty streets. He was drawn to the central amphitheater he had noticed upon first seeing the city. As he moved in that direction, he noticed that all of the streets, even the side streets, seemed slightly angled toward the amphitheater like rainwater toward a puddle.

Ahead, the street widened and Kibure's destination came into view. But that was not all. Upon the amphitheater's lowest row of stone seating sat a woman clothed in a silver silk robe. She didn't look up as he approached. As he drew near, he realized that while he couldn't hear her sobs, her shoulders heaved up and down and her hands covered her face. She hadn't noticed him yet and he started to leave, but her obvious distress moved him to turn back. Before he knew it, his mind was forming the idea of words.

Not like she's going to notice if it doesn't work.

"My name is Kibure. Um . . . what is wrong?"

Did I just attempt to convey the idea of "um"? he wondered. *Good thing it didn't—*

The woman moved tear-filled hands from her face and looked up. Her eyes narrowed, and she tried to wipe them dry. To Kibure's surprise, she looked young. The ageless appearance held by most of the women he had met here, especially his captors, did not apply to this girl. She had the same inky-black hair, pale skin. There was a small dark mark on the skin of her cheek. A mark of the gods, as they called it in the Lugienese Empire.

She spoke to his mind: *"What do you care about what's wrong with me?"*

Kibure jumped. *She heard me!* He willed his thoughts to her again, concentrating much more on the act of conveying his thoughts, and much less on what thoughts he was actually sharing. "*I guess—I guess I don't. I just wondered why you were here. And then why you were crying.*" Kibure cringed after he finished.

"*At least you're honest. That's more than I can say about most of the rest.*"

Kibure was puzzled. Wasn't she one of them? "*What do you mean?*"

She gritted her teeth. "*I mean, most of the people here are liars or at best self-important hypocrites, hoarding all the important stuff like the fabled dragons and their gold. Anyone who asks questions gets a breath full of fire.*" She looked back down at her hands.

"*What questions did you ask?*"

Her eyes returned to meet his, then glanced to the side as she said, "*It doesn't matter. I'm just a girl who wants more from the world than our leaders are willing to permit.*" She stood. "*You are the one everyone has been talking about. Kibure, right?*"

No sense using his concentration up on something he could accomplish more easily. He nodded his response.

"*My name is Arabelle.*" She extended a hand.

He hesitated, staring like a fool instead.

She explained, "*I only visited your homeland for a short while before being recalled home, but I seem to remember the folks greeting one another in this way.*"

Kibure shook the hand awkwardly just as she began to retract it. He was surprised to feel warmth in a place that seemed so otherwise cold.

"*Nice to meet you, Kibure. Would you care to be shown around, or have you already had a tour?*"

Kibure was unprepared for the general change in her demeanor. "*I . . . yes. Please. I don't know how long this tea lasts, but I haven't anything else to do while stuck here, anyway.*"

"*Tea? They have Drymus teaching you, then.*" She shuddered. "*You must really be . . .*"

"*Hopeless?*" he finished for her.

"*I was going to say, struggling.*"

"*Both.*"

Arabelle nodded. "*I see. I've only worked with her a few times, but I can attest to the fact that her methods are . . . effective. She is the oldest living among us, probably the oldest living person this side of the Endless Mountains, now that I think about it. Thus, she knows a great deal.*" Arabelle started walking away from the rows of ascending stone steps. "*Let's start with the garden. It is my favorite place.*" He followed her away from the amphitheater, and for the first time since arriving, felt welcome.

As they walked, Kibure noted the occasional warping of the air. It reminded him of the hot days in the desert when the air over the sand would ripple as if boiling. As they neared an impressive stone arbor tall enough for a giant, Kibure stopped, his eyes following a moving distortion as it passed through. He was afraid he would walk right into it and didn't know if it was something that might hurt him.

Arabelle had noticed him pause beside her. "*You're wondering about the ripples of air you keep seeing?*"

Kibure nodded, glad that it wasn't his eyes playing tricks on him.

"*You're seeing the soul's reflection in this place.*"

He inclined his head. "*Ah.*"

Arabelle stared at him for a moment. "*You have no idea what that means, do you?*"

"*No.*"

She squinted in thought then said, "*To put it simply, you're seeing people, sort of.*" She paused to gather her thoughts, then continued. "*Everything that exists within the waking world is reflected here in corporeal form. However, our souls cling so tightly to our bodies in the waking world, or, as I prefer to call it, the physical realm, that we see only the slightest hint of the body's reflection here.*" She reached a hand out, and as one such translucent figure flowed by, her hand passed harmlessly through. "*You don't need to worry about any of these. You can't interact with them, nor they with you.*"

She stepped past the arbor and into the garden. As Kibure followed, he realized that this was no ordinary garden. He stared in wonder at an impossible marvel of natural splendor. Tall stalks of something akin to drogal trees grew all about, large fruit hanging low enough to pick.

Vines circled the trunks and branches, offering berries of all shapes and sizes. Kibure was hesitant to continue forward when he saw that he was stepping upon a ground made up of flowers of every kind.

"*Don't worry about those. They grow back almost instantly,*" said Arabelle as she beckoned him to follow.

They passed through an opening in the base of a massive oak, then exited the other side where Arabelle turned left and started up a set of stairs that seemed to have grown out of the tree itself. They circled the trunk until they came to a platform at the top. Much like with the stairs, Kibure saw no nails, seams, or any other evidence that they had been hewn from a tree. It was all a single, organic surface.

"*How is this possible?*" he finally asked as he met her at a wooden railing around the edge decorated with curling flowers.

Arabelle smiled. "*The magic of the world is ours to shape as we see fit. This garden is a small tribute to the one who gave us this power, this world, life itself, so they say.*"

"*Klerós?*" said Kibure without much thought.

She shook her head. "*Gods no. Klerós is . . . well, I just wouldn't say that name around here unless you wish to take up cursing, but even that might be a touch vulgar. I have my own thoughts on this matter, but around here, we call the creator Olem.*"

Kibure shrugged. He placed little weight on theology unless it explained his supposed role within the prophecies, which he was pretty sure were misguided if he were truly anywhere near their center. Most likely, they had captured the wrong tazamine. But at this point, he needed to at least learn to use his powers so he might escape before they realized their mistake.

"*We've been separated from him for thousands of years. The only proof we have of his existence is the magic embedded within this world. He doesn't answer our calls for help, nor does he offer us his power. As far as I can tell, Klerós is more real than Olem, but you didn't hear that from me.*"

"*I am no priest, but it sounds like you have need of some religious remediation.*"

She glanced at him and nodded. "*More than I care to admit to anyone but perhaps an outsider like you. You can keep my secret, can't you?*"

Kibure returned his gaze to the perfect circle of beautiful garden lodged within an underground city lit by magical luminescence. "*I— of course.*" Though he couldn't understand why she would share such sensitive information with someone she had only just met.

"*I come here often. When I doubt our purpose, I come here and look at the beauty and it reminds me that Olem must be out there, somewhere. And yet, in the same moment, I recall that it was we who built this city, and we who grew this garden. And so I doubt again.*" She paused before continuing, "*There is not a single person alive who has spoken to or even heard the voice of Olem. Even Drymus, the eldest among us, is thousands of years removed from the last living soul who walked in the supposed birthplace of our people.*"

She was quiet and Kibure had no idea what to say to any of this so he, too, continued in silence.

Arabelle's tone became determined. "*If you are who they say you are, we will know the truth of this all soon enough. You will help us finally reunite with our people, our land, and perhaps our God. Or we will fail, and the truth of our self-deception will be known. In either case, I will see the answers revealed within my lifetime, and for this I count myself blessed for I do not believe myself devout enough to spend an entire lifetime working toward something I could never be certain existed.*"

Kibure needed to say something, but what? Too late. She continued, "*I am young by our standards, yet I grow tired of waiting for the future. If you are the one to return us to our homeland, I wish to see this come to pass sooner rather than later. And if not, I will not be waiting around here for the next failed messiah.*"

The *next* failed messiah? What did that mean? He was about to ask when she started toward the center of the garden at a jog and waved a hand. "*Come on, you must see the flower sculptures.*" Her dark mood seemed to have withered away in an instant and Kibure thought it no longer appropriate to return to such a discussion.

His own unease lingered.

CHAPTER 7

GROBENNAR

THE OBSIDIAN LIQUID RIPPLED AS if alive as Grobennar pulled the quill to write. Meanwhile, the light of a single candle continued its eternal war against the gloom of the stone palace suite, even as late in the morning as it was. The Klerósi priest released a heavy breath, then smiled as he resumed the last of his missive.

"See that there is no room for confusion as to the culprit of the crime. This transition must occur without flaw. We will take advantage of the instability this creates within the Kingdom ranks. It would be better, of course, to kill them both, but two deaths will draw unwanted attention. His assumed role in the crime will serve our needs. You will find great reward when the sun sets on these plans. Send word when it is finished."

Grobennar folded the parchment into thirds, then poured the blue wax onto the seam. He fumbled in his pocket for Count Gornstein's ring. *There.* He pulled it out and pressed the face of the ring into the hot substance and felt the satisfying squish of the wax as it took on the contours of the steel emblem. This was a near-perfect replica, a gift from the pirate, Kubal, with whom Grobennar had increased dealings since his arrival in Brinkwell weeks earlier.

He didn't fully trust the man, but then, how could he? Kubal was a pirate, a heretic by birth, and a proud slave to gold. And yet, for now, their paths were aligned toward a common goal shared by Klerós himself. The man would eventually need to be declawed, or more likely killed, but for the moment, he was a useful tool.

Grobennar rolled the ring around in his hand and smiled. If the letter was intercepted, the Lugienese Empire would be in no way associated with the plot.

Grobennar grew optimistic about his plans to unseat Rajuban beside the God-king. His meeting with Magog weeks earlier in Brinkwell had gone far better than he could have hoped. Rajuban would surely have attempted to spin the ease with which Brinkwell had been conquered, but Magog had come alone and Grobennar's vital role could not be denied. As a result, Magog had restored Grobennar's honor by naming him Fatu Ma-gazi, Secretary of War. Grobennar needed to use this opportunity to its fullest before Rajuban had a chance to ensnare him in whatever traps lay ahead. One could no longer ascend peaks of permanent favor within the Klerósi faith. Instead, one ran alongside the God-king, hoping to keep up. The irony was that Grobennar had helped establish this model of rule on behalf of the God-king, thinking his role in doing so would keep him permanently ahead of the rest. Grobennar shook his head. *A painful irony, indeed.*

Grobennar walked to the small window and stared out at the cages containing the flying creatures the locals called dordron. They were birds of massive scale. Many had taken to describing them as simply overgrown eagles, but Grobennar knew they could be so much more. It had been Grobennar's idea to capture and control a contingent of them to ride into battle like the legends of old Luguindia. This would neutralize the Kingdom of Dowe's Lumáles and their famed riders. The Kingdom's elite aerial fighting force was said to have turned the tide in many a battle over the centuries, and his research thus far supported the truth of this. Surely the Empire's Klerósi battle priests would reign supreme regardless, but if another weapon might give his side further advantage, why not use it? Plus, the idea of being able to travel from city to city in days instead of weeks would prove very handy, especially when engaging in intercontinental conquest. *This would be the sort of advancement worthy of another promotion,* thought Grobennar. For in spite of his new position, he needed to unseat Rajuban. His current title was suitable during the Lugienese time of conquest, but its significance would be quickly reduced once the war was complete.

Jaween remarked, "*Imagine the chaos we'll sow with your flying friends. Too much fun!*"

"It will be much better than mere chaos if we can actually get them to do our bidding," grumbled Grobennar. "If we can control enough of these things, they'll rival the Nephilim of legend."

Jaween hissed. "*Ooh. I do hate those things.*"

Grobennar paused, taken aback. "You've met a Nephilim?"

Jaween didn't respond for a long time. Then finally he said, "*Those days are fuzzy. It hurts my head to remember too much.*"

"You don't have a head."

"*Still hurts,*" remarked Jaween.

Jaween's claim was absurd, Grobennar thought. The last time the monsters known as Nephilim were said to have roamed Doréa was thousands of years ago during Hakbar's last purge of the Hand. Grobennar had been jesting about the Nephilim. They were nothing more than a confused translation, hyperbole, or at best, an evolution from truth stretched to unrecognizable lengths on its way to becoming myth. The same appeared to be true of Jaween's recollection of the distant past.

In any case, Grobennar's claim about the dordron appeared to be just as fanciful. They had captured several dozen of the beasts, but they were wild things and Grobennar and his priests had found no efficacious means to even tame, let alone domesticate, them.

Grobennar had initiated a mental clasp with one but seeing and sensing through the eyes of the dordron while riding atop it was dangerously disorienting, not to mention the amount of magic required to maintain the clasp over a creature that never ceased to resist. The dordron's will had been stronger than any creature he had ever controlled.

Still, even if they couldn't ride the things, having a contingent of them could prove minimally beneficial should the Lugienese need to launch a defensive attack in the skies. Even clasping and controlling them from the ground could prove useful.

But as Grobennar looked out the window, he saw a priest climb up and take flight from atop one of them. Grobennar's heart soared with hope. A young, promising priest by the name of Wendrikor clung to the shiny black feathers at the base of the beast's neck, whooping as he was lifted into the air. The sun struck the black sheen and hints of purple reflected, while the multicolored head rippled in the wind.

"Beautiful," remarked Grobennar.

"*This is promising,*" commented Jaween.

Grobennar's mind drifted to visions of himself landing one of the massive creatures gracefully before Magog's throne, dismounting to accept his rightful place, that of the—

A shout rang out as Wendrikor was ripped from his seat by the sharp, golden beak of the dordron. Before Grobennar or anyone else had the chance to intervene, the poor lad crashed into the cobbled courtyard below accompanied by a distinctly fatal crunch of bone and flesh. Grobennar winced.

"*Not the best landing,*" remarked the spirit matter-of-factly.

"Indeed," admitted Grobennar through clenched teeth. He braced his arms on the stone that shaped the window, leaning heavily as he stared down at the unmoving form of the priest below.

He shook his head. Perhaps the hatchlings they captured could be reared to be friendly to humans, but that would be a legacy program, not something to improve his current plight. Grobennar needed to reap the benefits of these beasts in the immediate future, and for that, he needed a new strategy.

He turned and glided down the stairs toward the courtyard where several dozen of the dordron were held. Paranja, one of his closest friends and allies, had recently come to Brinkwell. She sat beside one of the cages, attempting to puzzle out the very same riddle.

"What was it like?" she asked.

"Sorry?"

"To fly?"

"Oh. Mostly terrifying. I had to close my eyes in order to focus solely on the bird's sight, but their minds are different from anything I have clasped before. The idea of directing it based on where my own body was, was dizzying. The advantage to riding during the clasp, of course, would be that it would require less magic than should we remain aground. But this would not do in a battle against Lumále riders, who can act independent of their flying mounts. I just wish there was a way to . . ." He trailed off as an idea struck, not a new idea per se, but a new approach to an old one. "What if there was a way to execute a partial clasp?" He looked at the dordron and considered attempting such a feat right then and there, and reconsidered.

Looking around, he found a guard by the door to the courtyard. "Hey! You there! Yes, you. Come here, now."

The man shook off his surprise then approached, bowing a few paces away. "Yes, Fatu Ma-gazi."

"Fetch me an ox. Here, take this." Grobennar handed him a folded parchment he kept on hand for such times. "Show this to anyone who gets in your way or questions the demand. And get help should you need it."

The guard took the document with Grobennar's signature and the seal of his rank and bowed. "I will do as you demand, Fatu Ma-gazi."

"Good. Now make haste!"

The man took off at a jog.

Later that day, an animal with shoulders as tall as a man's head squeezed through the southern entrance to the courtyard, and Grobennar set down the tray of cheese and fruit that he and Paranja had been picking over. They had spent the afternoon working out the details of altering the clasp as best they could from a theoretical standpoint and had arrived at something Grobennar believed might actually work. *Serendipitous timing.*

Grobennar tossed the guard and two companions a silver toman each and gave them the afternoon off. There wasn't much to do in the city, pillaged as it was; only a handful of its citizens had been kept alive, namely, those who added some value to future conquests such as farmers, cooks, or spies. The rest were useless mouths to feed and were therefore eliminated. Grobennar had thoughts about that policy as well, but those would not serve him here and now. He would ruminate on that later.

He stood on tiptoes to secure a lead rope to the harness attached to the ox's head and mouth, then directed the massive animal to the vacant center of the courtyard. This particular beast was docile and simple, unlike the dordron's stubborn and distrustful disposition. It would be the perfect trial, Grobennar thought. He placed a hand on its muscular ribs and delved into its mind. He was able to take hold of its will with ease but separating out the vision and sensations of the creature was more difficult. Even for a creature of such simplicity, he found the strands of sensory and will so interconnected that he could make little sense of the tangle. He needed to separate these, to hold only the will of the beast, not the complex carnal information that came with a full clasp. *Perhaps if I complete the clasp, then released certain aspects . . .* He did so, but as soon as he released his connection to the ox's sight, the entire clasp failed and he was left with no connection at all. He tried and failed several more times, then shouted and kicked the ox in the stomach— nope, the ribs. It grunted but seemed otherwise unfazed, while his big toe burned after striking the hard flesh. Embarrassed, Grobennar bit his lip and blew air from his mouth instead of whimpering or crying out like he wished.

The goal was simple enough in theory, but the execution was quite another thing.

Grobennar let go of the rope holding the ox and limped over to the cages housing the dordron. Gripping the bars, he ignored, Paranja who was asking him something. *How do I connect to your will without having to take on the rest?*

He extended his mind into the creature and immediately sensed its boiling fury. It was hostile, and he felt it desiring to hunt and kill. Grobennar took hold of the dordron's will, blasting through its natural desire for autonomy. These creatures were among the most challenging he had attempted in terms of their natural mental barriers, but his own current mental state left his mind sharp with anger and determination. A rush of sensation poured through the connection, and he suddenly saw himself through the eyes of the beast, closing his own eyes to complete the connection.

Then, he loosened his grip on the creature's will the way he might when allowing a clasped creature to execute tasks that the human mind could not, like flight. Grobennar could, for instance, order an eagle to fly to a certain place or attack a certain thing, but if he attempted to control the actual instinctual body mechanics that allowed the creature to do so, the general result was disastrous for both parties involved.

As Grobennar relaxed his control over the creature's will, he felt its attention shift to him, felt its desire to break free of the cage and attack the one it felt was responsible for its confinement. This will was so strong, so palpable he could almost—

He sent his will into that single strand, that connection of animal desire, and gripped it with his mind as tightly as he could, then released everything else.

The sensations he had felt coming in through the connection disappeared, and he opened his own eyes. He stared at the monstrous bird that stood twice his own height and watched as it stalked toward him. He saw as much as felt its intelligence, overpowered by rage. Still holding on to that strand of will, he pulled. The bird suddenly stopped and Grobennar sent a mental command through the connection. "*Turn around.*" This didn't translate in a phonetic sense; it never did. But the desire, if made clear by the person controlling the creature, was easy enough to convey.

To Grobennar's utter surprise, the massive bird spun and was suddenly facing the other direction. "*Sit down.*" The dordron squatted and sat.

Grobennar's eyes went wide with shock and glee. "Open the cage!"

Paranja was standing but failed to move, confused.

"Open the cage—now!"

He was afraid to move himself, afraid he might lose his grip, though as of that moment, he felt firmly in control, more so than even an ordinary clasp.

Paranja undid the latch of the cage and the door swung open. She backed up quickly and Grobennar could sense she had gathered Klerós's power in case whatever Grobennar was doing did not work.

"*Come to me.*" The dordron responded instantly. "*Sit.*" It did so. Grobennar reached up and took hold of a handful of feathers as he had done during his full clasp the day before. But unlike before, he saw only through his own eyes, feeling almost normal but for the itch in his mind where the connection to this beast's will remained.

He climbed upon its back, settled in, and commanded it to fly. Its wings extended out fifteen paces to either side, and Paranja was forced to dive out of the way as the dordron flapped its wings to take him into the air. The sound almost blocked out Paranja's voice from below. "I hope you know what you're doing!"

Grobennar's pulse was racing as the palace and city shrank beneath him. He had been afraid and nearly sick when he rode while in a full clasp on the back of the dordron the day before. It had been a difficult feat, and he considered himself lucky to have been able to return safely. But this was unlike that in almost every sense. He was able to appreciate the cool air as it tickled his skin and looked out on the vast bay and city. Grobennar saw the rise of mountains behind the city and willed the creature to fly toward them. He had seen such views from the ground through the eyes of smaller birds during a clasp, but to be in the air himself, seeing it all through his own eyes, was an experience unequaled.

"This is it! I've done it!" he shouted.

The wind blew cold and fast in his face as it rushed past, but he had no difficulty hearing Jaween. "*This is just wonderful! It seems very similar to the magic used to control these creatures before the Luguinden wars. I'm so glad you were able to puzzle it out.*"

"Wh—" Grobennar nearly lost his grip. "You . . . knew how to do this? Why didn't you tell me before?" shouted Grobennar.

Jaween did the mental equivalent of a shrug. "*My memories come and go, especially those from before my days inside this stone. I didn't remember until now.*"

"How convenient," muttered Grobennar.

"*Indeed! Imagine if I had remembered a few days ago! The timing was almost perfect! Just a few days off.*"

Grobennar turned his attention back to something less vexatious. Using the link to control the dordron, he bade it to angle them back toward the count's former palace. He would need to begin training others priests to master this method. And harnesses would need to be designed to make the riding experience safer for warfare and general travel. He grinned to himself.

At Grobennar's command, his selected priests had maintained their connections for three full days without experiencing any notable bone degradation. Grobennar eagerly awaited a time when he could share his discovery with the God-king but decided he would do so only after he had utilized this secret weapon to its fullest and could take credit for the ingenious idea and the victories that would come with it. He needed to outpace whatever schemes Rajuban continued to employ.

The spirit residing within the pendant worn at Grobennar's neck remarked with great joviality, "*You grow so devious in your old age, Grobes. The coming moons are going to be very exciting for both of us.*"

"Yes, I suspect they will."

Perhaps his proximate successes would finally earn him the favor he needed to retake his rightful position beside the God-king. However, he would still need to find a way to discredit the conniving Rajuban, or Magog would have no reason to replace him.

"*You needn't worry so much about him. You'll get yours, and he'll get his.*"

"Who?"

Jaween scoffed, "*Always so coy. You know who. Your pulse quickens and your temperature rises the moment his name brushes your mind. I'm acutely attuned to these things, you know. I can always tell.*"

Grobennar ignored the spirit, continuing to plot his next move now that the dordron were viable pieces on the board. *Not too hasty. We'll conquer the Isles city of Tung by traditional means and use that as a staging ground for the first use of the dordron. The rider-priests need more time to train before we send them out to battle. Glory can't be rushed.* He knew this all too well and needed to believe it more strongly than ever lest he lose hope in his triumphant return to Magog's side.

CHAPTER 8

AYNWARD

AYNWARD STOOD AT THE PROW of the ship as the city of Salmune, capital of the Kingdom of Dowe, came into view. He stood alone.

Count Gornstein had remained behind to secure defenses in the Isles city of Tung, while Sindri had insisted upon her own path. Kyllean had ventured home, determining that he would best serve the defense of the Kingdom by joining the elite force of Lumále riders monopolized by his family line in East End, and Minathi had likewise returned home to Quinson. Even Aunt Melanie had returned to her family estate, hoping to make amends after years of absence. And so Aynward was without allies as he gazed up at the steep cliff upon which rested the palace of Salmune, seat of the most powerful nation in Drogen, and a father who Aynward knew would be nothing short of disappointed with his son. The mound of tension in Aynward's stomach rolled over and he swallowed hard.

After such strong reservations about leaving his home more than a year earlier, Aynward thought it ironic that he now wished he could be anywhere but home. Seeing one of his closest confidants, his only sister, Dagmara, as well as his mother, would be consolations, of course, but small when compared with what he expected from his father.

Aynward's spirits lifted when he was greeted in port by a familiar, if surprising, face: Gervais. He was also extremely confused by the sight.

The servant bowed. "Greetings, young master. I pray your travels are completed without complication."

Aynward gestured with both arms. "Here in one piece, so there's that." Then Aynward tilted his head and said, "Gervais, don't take this the wrong way, but what are you doing here in Salmune?"

Gervais smiled. "Didn't you receive my letter?"

Aynward looked around confused. "Um . . ."

Gervais cursed softly. "Never mind that. The short of it is that in light of Dolme's passing—so sorry for your loss, by the way—your aunt thought you might wish for a familiar face upon your return home and leased my services to you and the crown as soon as I arrived in Quinson. I was merely pleased to have still arrived ahead of you. You must have remained at port in Tung for over a week before continuing?"

A wave of sadness washed over Aynward at the mention of Dolme, but he swallowed it, pleased by the distraction of another question. "Yes, well, we also seemed to stop at every city along the way. You probably could have walked faster. Had I known the ship you took from Tung would arrive first, I would have joined you. But I still don't understand the why of you being *here*."

"Aynward, at your aunt's request, and with the approval of the King himself"—Gervais bowed low, then rose to face Aynward—"I'm to be your new counselor."

Aynward could only gawk. He had assumed Dolme, his counselor since childhood, would not be replaced at all. All of his older siblings had been relieved of their counselors as soon as they began their specialized training. Had Aynward been allowed to attend university closer to home, he had expected Dolme to be dismissed upon Aynward's matriculation, as well. Then again, none of his siblings had been as obstinate as Aynward in their youths. But still—he was back home and had completed nearly a year of university training. Surely he was beyond the age of personalized supervision.

Gervais interrupted Aynward's ponderings. "Worry not. I've already spoken with your father about your courageous actions in Brinkwell in the midst of such horrible circumstances. I suspect you'll be regarded with some measure of respect after having survived such an extraordinary and trying endeavor. Count Gornstein's message echoed my own words, strengthening the validity of these claims. Aynward, don't go getting a big head or anything, but you're a bit of a hero."

"I—thank you?"

Not the reception I was expecting, at all. About time Kitay made an appearance in my life, thought Aynward of the goddess of luck whose absence of late had been irritatingly noticeable.

"Of course," said Gervais, bowing once more. "Now, if you would, a celebration has been arranged for tomorrow." He held up a finger. "But more on that later." Gervais wrinkled his nose. "The first order of business includes a hot bath, I think."

He gestured toward a carriage at the end of the pier. "This way, Your Grace. Your belongings from the originally scheduled departure arrived weeks ago, and the water is being drawn and heated as we speak."

Aynward had been a year away from such accommodations so when he entered his rooms, the confirmation of Gervais's words energized him. He sank into the perfectly warmed waters of the stone basin and felt the worries of his travels melt away; he closed his eyes just as a knock came at the door. "Your Grace?"

It was an unfamiliar voice. "Yes?"

"Are you proper?"

Oh, right. I don't have to break my arm reaching to scrub my back anymore! "Yes, come in," said Aynward, happy about the help, even if his help being female was a touch scandalous. Considering the filth from his skin that already clouded the water, he certainly had no reason to feel "exposed."

A thin girl, perhaps a few years older than he, appeared with a pail and sponge. He could describe her as nothing more than common: auburn hair, gray eyes, dressed in servant's clothes. She stepped forward and bowed deeply. "My name is Carlotta. I will be assisting you today, Your Grace."

"Pleased to meet you, Carlotta." He closed his eyes again and let his head rest against the smooth stone at the rim of the basin. "Ahh," he sighed. "I just need a minute to enjoy the feeling of warm water. It's been a while."

"Of course, Your Grace. Take your time."

If the afterlife is real, and half as wonderful as this, I really need to do something about my level of devotion, Aynward mused.

He finally opened his eyes and began to sit up, ready to call Carlotta over to scrub his back—but he caught the profile of another person seated in one of the chairs beside a large chest filled with his belongings. Before he had time to identify the intruder, his mouth released a decidedly *not* masculine squeak. At the same time, his hands flew out of the water to grip the sides of the tub, sending waves of water sloshing onto the stone floor. With his entire body tense, he finally inspected the trespasser. He recognized her, but he did not relax.

"Dagmara! What in Doréa are you doing here? Can't you see I'm— for the love of the gods, don't you care to knock?"

He glanced behind him and noted that the servant had a hand over her mouth; it did not cover the subtle movement of her shoulders: laughter. He was about to scold her, but Dagmara responded, "First of all, brother, hello, and welcome back. It's nice to see you, too." She smiled innocently. "That's at least a cursory greeting for a sibling long unseen. Second, you needn't blush; the water is practically brown with your filth. And lastly, I needed to know if you'd outgrown that girly squeak of yours! Couldn't have answered that last question if I had knocked, now could I?"

She turned her head to regard the servant. "Thank you, Carlotta."

She bowed. "It was nothing, Your Grace. You are finished with me?"

"Yes, you may leave."

Aynward raised an eyebrow. "Wait—then who's going to scrub my back?"

Dagmara looked skyward in thought as Carlotta exited the room. "Huh, it seems I overlooked that part. I suppose you're going to just have to make do with the places your own hands can reach."

Aynward grumbled to himself, then said, "I see you haven't changed one bit, sis." Then he allowed a genuine smile. "I think I almost missed you."

A moment passed in silence before Aynward thought to take advantage of the situation. "Say, while I have your ear, what's with this banquet feast tomorrow? Gervais tells me Father scheduled it to coincide with my arrival home but implied there was more to it than that. He wouldn't say more."

Dagmara shrugged. "Honestly, I'm not entirely sure. No one is. I know the palace has quite a few more foreign dignitaries than normal, all awaiting this banquet, but Father has been tight-lipped about the whole thing. No offense, brother, but you're right about one thing: this banquet is set for more than just a celebration of your safe return."

Aynward figured that was just as well. He did not wish to be the center of attention at some feast. He would much rather observe from the fringes so he could actually enjoy himself. He couldn't do that if all eyes were trained on him. He began to scrub his arms and chest with the block of pine-scented soap he found at the bottom of the basin. "So, what's new with the King's favorite—well, only—daughter?"

"Oh, a great deal, I suppose. Much has happened here in your absence. I've become quite the lady."

"Is that right?" Aynward laughed as he massaged the filth from his auburn mop with the soapy, if discolored, water.

"Indeed. You should see just how proper I've become without the corruptive influence of a particular younger sibling of mine. Why, I can manage an entire meal without more than a few minor glares from Mother. My table manners are nearly impeccable!"

"Important skill, that."

"Ever so!"

The levity of the conversation slowly fizzled after a few moments of silence, and neither party was able to transition onto another topic. Aynward dunked his head into the water to rinse the grime and soap alike. He ran his hands along his head, forcing much of the water out of his thick hair to return to the basin.

Dagmara stood and sighed. "Well, I have need to be off. The duties of court life call my attention. We have an exciting dinner to attend soon, after all."

Dagmara seemed to return from somewhere distant, though it had only been a few moments. Her eyes snapped back to the present and she rose to her feet. Aynward noted that while she looked much the same, she had shed the childlike appearance she'd been holding on to before he had left for Brinkwell. He couldn't pinpoint a single defining change in her features, but she really did look like—like a woman grown. He pictured her with her small sword and trousers, hair pulled up in a knot. Neither image seemed possible. That had been a different girl altogether. He saw something subtle there, a momentary expression between interactions, that forebode something darker. Then again, what did he know? He hadn't seen his sister in half a year. And she did still maintain the playful air about her that confirmed this was still his sister.

Dagmara stopped at the door and smiled. "I'll inform your servants that they may attend to you now."

She slipped out of the room without another word.

CHAPTER 9

DAGMARA

DAGMARA POKED AT HER FOOD as she surveyed the ballroom-turned-banquet hall. This hastily assembled celebration called in honor of Aynward's safe return wasn't quite the size or scope of a royal wedding ceremony, but it was close. She was certainly glad for the music; there was nothing quite like the melodic duet of harp and lute, and the singer's voice seemed an instrument of divine making unto itself. The trio of sounds flowed about the room like the tireless servants.

Dagmara sat at the long rectangular table reserved for those of the royal line and their spouses, in order of succession. Her own place at the table was permitted only by virtue of being the unmarried daughter of the King. She would be relegated to one of the side tables after her wedding to the Scritlandian prince, scheduled to coincide with his coming of age in three years' time. Glancing over, she spotted the boy, her future husband, seated at the neighboring table and wondered why such a contingent of his family and servants had bothered making the trip. It was a gesture of respect, to be sure, but they had already curried enough favor with her father to arrange the first Scritlandian-Dowe wedding in over four generations. Perhaps they were here with hopes of increasing the dowry?

Catching Aynward's eye across the table, several seats closer to the King, she couldn't help but laugh to herself as he prattled on about one thing or another while Duke Gafford, one seat further from the King, sulked and scowled. Their gray-haired uncle had always resented his own distance from the throne, which had only increased with the birth of Tito and Marco, Prince Kirous's sons, while their other brother Prince Perja's wife, Elena, sat plump with pregnancy. Doctors assured everyone this child would also be a boy. This of course would bump poor Duke Gafford to eighth in line, adding to the man's already sour disposition.

Seeing the duke's glare reminded Dagmara of the game she and Aynward invented as children to pass the time during such gatherings. Each royal had a card, and upon each card, a description, brief genealogy, imagined supernatural abilities, and weaknesses. They had done their research and spent as much time learning the secrets of as many within the court as they could. Duke Gafford had been one of the few to be awarded more than one power—access to unlimited building supplies, namely hardwood; but also his ability to immobilize enemies with his penetrating glare, which he executed to full effect as Aynward released a haughty laugh at one of his own jokes. Aynward said something else that Dagmara couldn't quite catch, and Duke Gafford began coughing uncontrollably—not coughing, but choking.

His wife, Lady Geneva, yelled out as she realized the same thing. Aynward was on his feet in an instant. He sidled up to the duke, placed one hand on his chest then slammed the other down on the duke's back.

The duke's face went from red to purple, and Dagmara thought she was about to bear witness to the first death of her life when something shot out from his mouth to splatter on his plate. Aynward apparently didn't notice, for he continued to pound the man's back like he was a percussionist deep in the passions of a performance.

The duke fell forward, face landing on his plate before he finally had the awareness to yell, "Enough! Get off of me, you bootless dew-beater!" Then he turned and knocked Aynward away with both arms, pushing him awkwardly onto the lap of Prince Kirous.

Aynward stayed there and lifted his shiny polished boot above the height of the table for all to see. "I'll have you know that I am not without boots. As you can see, mine are in fine repair! But if you would like to repay my life-saving kindness with a new pair, I'm all for it."

He hopped down from Kirous's lap. "A generous thank you would have sufficed." Then he pulled in his own chair and resumed sitting as if nothing had happened.

Duke Gafford ignored Aynward's theatrics, instead wiping the smears of food from his face and beard while Lady Geneva reminded Dagmara of her power: that of a soothing touch, her delicate fingers sliding deftly along the back of the duke's neck to calm the inferno to a mere crackle.

That recollection reminded Dagmara that it had been years since she and Aynward had played their game and several young newcomers had come to the court, either by marriage or birth; they were all currently without cards. But Dagmara knew each well enough to at least assign a label or two. None of this, of course, meant their behavior would be wholly predictable. For instance, next in line to the Dukedom of Gilliden, Duke Gafford's son, Baron Chandlen, was heir by marriage to the Bronjiornyn city of Pramjer to the north. But he had foregone his seat at the royal table to sit with his sister Jasmen, the recently elevated princess of Kael. While the two were siblings, both of their spouses were from kingdoms that traditionally held no love for each other, yet they all seemed to be getting along well enough at the moment. *Curious.* Dagmara placed a mental bookmark there for later investigation.

Then her gaze settled on a pale, dark-haired man two seats down and across the table, a guest of honor accompanying Braden of Braxton, Lord of East End, emissary to the Tal-Don riders. Dagmara had never outgrown her fascination with the magical creatures known as Lumáles, nor those who tamed and rode them. King Lupren and the heir, Prince Perja, were technically riders, as it was Kingdom tradition to be trained and bound to a Lumále, but neither one held the kind of aura about them as the few true riders she had seen visit the capital here in Salmune. King Lupren sat quietly eating his food among the din of conversation around him, answering questions upon request, but as she watched, he appeared more occupied with a continual search of the room, as if he expected someone to pull a knife at any moment and did not wish to be caught unawares. Perhaps this was just a side effect of being a true warrior, while the rest of the sword-carrying pretenders in the room sat relaxed, boastful, and oblivious.

Her eyes were drawn away from the rider as the music stopped and the room went silent. Dagmara turned her head to see that her father, the King, had risen to speak. When silence had fully consumed the room, he leaned forward to place his hands on the table.

"I would like to thank you all for being here this evening," he said. "Some of you have traveled great distances to be here, while others left important business unattended, all of this to celebrate the safe return of my youngest, Aynward, and his return from disaster at the hands of Lugienese aggression in the Isles."

He raised a hand, index finger pointing to the sky. "I have sent diplomats to treat with the Lugienese, to learn of their ambitions, and to seek peace in spite of recent violations of freedom of trade across the Glass Sea that we, the Kingdom of Dowe, work so hard to maintain."

His hand returned to the back of his chair and he shook his head. "They have rejected all reasonable requests, and I do not believe for a moment that their ambitions will suddenly come to a close. Even now, I fear their eyes are fixed upon the Isles city of Tung."

Several heads around the room nodded their agreement, accompanied by murmurs of affirmation. The King quieted the room with a hand.

"We cannot remain idle. Not with such a threat on our doorstep. With that in mind, I would like to announce an additional purpose for inviting such a contingent of friends, family, and allies from across the continent."

Dagmara stiffened and her stomach turned over. Now it all made sense. The pieces fell into place as her father spoke; the motion out of the corner of her eye merely confirmed her suspicion about what was about to be said.

"We will need strong allies now more than ever, and few things bind kingdoms better than the joining of blood."

The young Scritlandian prince proudly approached the King's outstretched hand and took it in his own. Her father continued, "I am pleased to announce the wedding of my daughter, Princess Dagmara, to Prince Aldrik of Scritland, in three weeks' time. A dowry has been renegotiated to satisfy the immediate needs of the Scritlandian people in the wake of last year's drought; their armies are to be well fed as they prepare to defend not only their own borders but ours as well. With the two most powerful kingdoms aligned to meet the Lugienese threat, I have no doubt we will be able to either dissuade them from any further consideration regarding an invasion of the mainland or, if needs be, turn them away by force. We may even be able to assemble an army in time to defend the Isles city of Tung."

The reactions of those around the room were immediately mixed, but Dagmara's ability to absorb them withered as the crushing weight of her father's words pressed down upon her. She felt her view shift and realized that her body was answering the call to come forward. It was as if she were attempting to remember a weeks'-old dream, the details obscured by the haze of her disbelief. The shock was so visceral; her body became a mindless sheep to her father's words.

The King had not spoken to her about this change in plans, and yet here she was, standing before dozens of representatives from the neighboring kingdoms; her future, a commodity exchanged alongside food and wares.

CHAPTER 10

AYNWARD

AYNWARD WAS JUST AS SURPRISED as the rest of the guests to learn of this alternate timetable for his sister's wedding. Dagmara certainly appeared dumbstruck by the news. She walked to the front of the room as if controlled by an invisible puppet master, her arms limp at her sides as her legs propelled her forward, devoid of the excitement she almost always radiated. The sudden lack of color in her face served as further proof.

Aynward was close enough to hear Prince Perja, heir to the throne, grumbling his displeasure. In fact, his voice grew loud enough for the entire room to hear.

Well, this isn't good, thought Aynward as his brother stood.

Having his wine goblet refilled a number of times during the first course of the meal was likely playing a partial role in Perja's lack of decorum.

"Some deal . . . at least for the Scritlandians, isn't it? Dowenese princess, free trade, and the large part of our stores of grain. Wonder how much of this grain the Scritlandians will be sending the 'Luggers' in exchange for their own peace? I mean, why else steal from their longtime allies like—"

"Silence!" boomed the King.

At this point Aynward recognized just how different his father looked from the man Aynward had known before leaving for Brinkwell. The King's expression of exasperation sat just below the outward anger and authority he exuded as he prepared to reprimand Perja.

Aynward also noted the unkempt beard, stubble left unshaven upon the King's powerful jaw for at least three days in spite of the occasion. He'd never seen his father's face, or anything else, left in such a state of dishevelment. Therefore, he couldn't say whether or not the dusting of gray within the beard was new. It was certainly an unexpected sight. His father had seemed almost ageless, stuck in a perpetual state of adulthood, unchanging for as long as Aynward could remember. But he had little time to digest the oddity.

The entire Scritlandian entourage had already risen to their feet at the insult. They had not drawn steel, but Aynward saw several hands twitching in anticipation, ready to defend their honor if the King did not do so on their behalf.

Turning to the nearest set of guards, King Lupren said, "Please see Perja to his quarters for the evening. It seems he has had too much to drink." He pursed his lips and added in a low growl, "He is not thinking clearly."

The guards did not hesitate to do as commanded. But Perja moved without their assistance. Goblet in hand, he made a show of slamming it down on the table, red liquid spraying those closest to him. He addressed the room, but his words were aimed at the Scritlandians. "Your words may be true, Your Majesty, were the wine not of Scritlandian make, lacking any of the promised effects, much like I suspect of this deal you've crafted behind closed doors. Please do excuse *us*; I need to relieve my stomach of this vulgar liquid and see that my family finds better company." His wife stood and moved to retrieve their two daughters from the neighboring table, her pregnancy bulge turning her swagger into more of a waddle.

It seems he is still bitter over that Scritlandian princess. His proposal to the eldest daughter of the ruling Scritlandian faction had been rejected a decade ago. The fact that this princess had, just weeks earlier, accepted a betrothal was immaterial so far as Perja had been concerned. The betrothal had been to the Prince of Kael, the Kingdom's long-standing enemy. Perja had never forgiven the slight and had rejected future negotiations with other Scritlandian factions in the following years. But rejecting marriage negotiations was far different from the direct insult to an entire nation's honor that Perja had just issued.

Poor form, brother.

The guards, all staged along the perimeter of the room, had adjusted their footing and now gripped the hilts of their weapons. Their caution was not unwarranted: the Scritlandians, the young betrothed included, appeared to be seriously considering their chances at cutting down the prince before the guards could stop them. If the rumors of their fighting prowess were true, Aynward suspected they would make quick work of it before reinforcements might arrive to overwhelm them by sheer numbers alone.

King Lupren spoke again in an attempt to further defuse the situation. "My apologies. My son, Perja, speaks for himself alone, and this behavior will be addressed, of this I promise." He glared at the back of Perja's long auburn hair as the prince stormed out of the room with his family.

Aynward decided to try his own hand at diplomacy; after all, this was originally supposed to be a celebration of his safe return home. Waiting to be certain that Perja was out of earshot, Aynward spoke to the room, but looked over at the Scritlandians, who were retaking their seats. "Don't take Prince Perja's comments too personally, or seriously. He's always been one to hold a grudge. Hell, he still hasn't forgiven me for the time I accidentally poisoned his favorite hound, and that was ages ago."

Aynward glanced over at Dagmara, who met his eyes for only a brief moment before shaking her head as her gaze returned to the King—who, Aynward noticed, was glaring in his direction. Aynward shrank back into his chair but offered a final statement as he raised his glass. "Wine's good."

Aynward looked around the room for support but found no allies. None except . . . the Tal-Don rider sitting a few seats away. *Well, there's that,* thought an otherwise deflated Aynward. The rider raised his goblet and nodded to Aynward. "As is the berry juice. Fine vintage, indeed."

This caused a few chuckles around the room, as he was likely the only person besides the children who wasn't drinking the Scritlandian wine. Aynward had never understood it, but it was known that these riders never consumed alcohol. In fact, Kyllean's affinity for the stuff really was downright curious. Perhaps being away from home and the rules therein had given him cause to experiment with stuff. Home or not, Aynward found it difficult to imagine Kyllean refusing a drink. Perhaps those rules would only apply if he actually decided to join the family business, donning the uniform and claiming a Lumále.

CHAPTER 11

KYLLEAN

KYLLEAN SWIRLED THE BUBBLY ALE in his mug, enjoying his last supper before leaving to begin his training. His mother smiled softly. "I'm glad you've decided to join, son."

She wasn't his birth mother, but she had raised him alongside her own children, and the connection between them was just as strong for him as it was for his two half-sisters.

The door to the Salty Bowl Inn swung wide, streaks of sunlight illuminating the dusty air as a lean warrior dressed in leathers entered: Kyllean's father. The man continued forward, flagging down a waitress as he walked to order a hot meal.

Kyllean rose to his feet and extended an arm in welcome.

"Greetings, son," said Kelson as they clasped forearms.

Kyllean's father took his seat beside his wife and gave her a quick peck on the cheek. "Heather."

She elbowed him. "You should have come sooner, Kelson."

He shook his head. "Our work has doubled since word of war reached the fort."

She huffed. "Always excuses. Would you have even visited had I not written you about your son?"

Kelson ignored Kyllean's mother, turning instead to inspect Kyllean, whom he had not seen since before he left for Brinkwell.

"You're looking rather somber. Rethinking your decision to join the ranks already?"

Kyllean took a sip of bubbling ale, then continued to swirl the contents about the container as he considered his initial inspiration. It had not been something he had ever envisioned himself doing, and he made no secret of this before leaving for Brinkwell. But he had returned with a different perspective, and a divided heart. There was the matter of a beautiful woman to consider, after all. And yet it had been Minathi's own words that had compelled Kyllean to join.

They had traveled together all the way from Brinkwell to the city of Quinson, where she had found her uncle resupplying one of her father's warehouses. The uncle had agreed to escort Minathi the rest of the way to the family's holdings.

Kyllean had enjoyed getting to know such a brilliant mind, with a heart the size of a glutton's belly, and a bold enough personality to keep his foolishness mostly in check. The exotic beauty draped in creamy, caramel skin didn't hurt, either. He felt a warm tingly sensation whenever he was with her, but he didn't know if this was love, or adolescent yearning. He had little difficulty imagining a life with her, but as they neared Quinson, she had crushed these thoughts when she made him promise to join the Tal-Don riders so he could avenge all that had been lost at the hands of the Lugienese. Her proclamation had laid to rest any dreams of a future with her, and he knew she would not be traveling to the town of Talmune for him to marry, should he earn the sword and mount. He thought he saw regret in her eyes as she said the words, but he knew she was right. It would be selfish to seek after love when there might not be a land within which to enjoy such a bond, should the Lugienese succeed.

Whatever his feelings, they had been strong enough that he agreed to fulfill a promise to her that he would become a rider. And he had promised himself that he would put forth a full effort toward this end.

"Well?" his father demanded.

Kyllean shook off the memory and finally replied with a partial truth. "Seeing the Lugienese attacks; the brutality; the ruthlessness of their conquest in Brinkwell. It sobered—" He took another sip. "Well . . . maybe sober isn't the right word. A figure of speech—you know what I mean."

"Oy. Well, sober is good if you're to become a rider." He chuckled.

"Huh?"

"Oh, nothing."

Kyllean's mother elbowed Kelson again. "You're not going to tell him?"

"Let the boy learn it the same way I did. Like taking off a bloody bandage. Best to just rip it off in one fluid motion rather than drag it out."

"Tell me what?" protested Kyllean.

Kyllean's mother looked at his father expectantly, then finally said, "Riders are forbidden to partake in fermented beverages."

Kyllean was quiet as he digested that. "Come again?"

She narrowed her eyes. "You heard me loud and clear."

"No ale?" He searched his memory for examples that might dispute this claim. Looking to his father, he said, "I—I was pretty sure you didn't." Then, more slowly, he continued, "*And* I suppose I can't exactly recall a specific example of another rider doing so . . ."

His father nodded.

Kyllean eyed him. "But . . . that's actually a rule?"

"It is."

"Sure, but it's not actually, like, an official rule everyone *has* to follow, though. More like celibacy and Chrologal priests, right?"

His father's expression hardened. "Have you ever seen me take a drink, even a sip?"

"Well—no. But you're never here. Doesn't mean you don't. Plus, you're . . . you're *you*. Not everyone is so adherent to rules, especially when no one is watching."

"In this they are. This particular rule is enforced by . . ." He stopped, groping for the right word. "It's difficult to explain without revealing that which should not be spoken before taking the oath, but I'll do my best to give a vague explanation." He reached down and touched the sword at his side and continued, "First, alcohol has been found to erode the link between the rider and their blade, which I recognize makes no sense to you right now, but I assure you, it's important. Furthermore, alcohol affects the link between the rider and his Lumále, that is, if you are deemed worthy of such a pairing. So, yes, if you succeed in the training, you will not touch a drink again, ever."

Kyllean couldn't believe it. *Link? What does that even mean?* "But . . ." He was thoroughly befuddled.

"But nothing. Lumáles are unable to cleanse and repair their minds the way we do, so to them alcohol is permanently debilitating. When paired with your own, the disorienting effects of the alcohol will leak through the connection and cannot be removed from the Lumále without severing the link itself, and even then, it takes an expert of the mind to try to filter out all of the damaging remnants."

His father was right about one thing. None of this made a lick of sense to him.

Kelson smiled as if having caught his son in a trap he had long ago sprung for him. "Still wish to join? This is but the smallest price to pay. There will be more."

Kyllean stared into his mug for a long while, then finally mumbled, "Oy, but this whole thing sounds rather boring now."

His father reached across the table and patted Kyllean's shoulder. "You won't be bored once the fighting begins. And let me tell you, it can be just as intoxicating and dangerous as the drinking used to be. Only now you get to do a little good. After all, we've got a Kingdom to save."

Kyllean gulped. *This had better be worth it. I'm now losing two of my favorite things in the whole world.*

An elderly-looking woman stood before a group of eighteen initiates recruited from the town of Talmune. Ten boys, eight girls.

Speaking to the entire cohort, she said, "Before I begin your first demonstration, I invite you to take a few moments to consider leaving. This is your last chance to do so unless you succeed in earning a blade. For if you stay here until the end, you will have learned things, secrets, that cannot be trusted to the rest of the world. Secrets about our people that are not to be spoken beyond the safety of these walls." She gestured with her arms to the enormous, ancient fortification that was the Tal-Don fortress.

"If you fail to earn the blade, or you decide this life is not for you, it will be too late. You will not be permitted to leave. We cannot risk you taking our secrets with you."

One of the boys shouted, "But my dah lives in Talmune and he's a rider."

"Yes, Tavis. Your father has earned the rider's sword, but not the Lumále. This is not uncommon, nor is it shameful. Any who earn the blade are considered 'riders'; however, less than half these ever earn the mount. And some small few never earn the blade, and cannot be permitted to leave the fortress, for we have no means of tracing their whereabouts the way we can with those who wield the blade. I will explain this at a later time. But what you need to understand is if you remain today, you will either settle in Talmune, or be forced to remain within this fortress. There are no other options for our kind."

The woman continued, "So. You're here. Look around and decide if you're willing to risk the possibility of never leaving these walls again, ever. There are eighteen of you. Statistically speaking, sixteen of you might never earn a blade, and another three might not do so before the war comes to us. So I ask you all one more time to consider this choice against the possibility of not succeeding."

There were some grumblings, but no one moved from their seats. No one would agree to join the Tal-Dons only to return home the following day. It was one thing to return home from university with skills and ambitions to do something besides becoming a rider; somewhere around a third of the eligible in the town of Talmune chose this course. But to pledge to join the riders only to return so soon . . . that would be far too great a disgrace. Plus, no one imagined themselves to be one of the few who might fail.

"Well, now that we have that settled, let us begin. I am your instructor. I will be teaching you the preliminary magic required to claim a blade, among other things. You may call me Master Hilde."

The eyes of those in the class went wild, though no one dared speak. *Magic? Kyllean thought. We're going to learn magic?* Did that mean his father was some sort of mage? Perhaps they were only to learn about it since they would be fighting against those who might wield it? Yes, that made far more sense.

"Kyllean. Would you be so kind as to come forward?"

Master Hilde had spoken his name and was staring right at him. What had she said?

"I . . . uh . . ." He tried to replay what he had just heard in his head. *Ah, there it is.*

He stood uncertainly and started forward.

"It's quite all right; you've nothing to fear but loss of pride." She smiled. "I have selected you to come forward. Your name was put forward as one of the best swordsmen in the group."

Master Hilde held up a hand to stave off the objections and chuckles from others.

Kyllean looked about, accusation in his eyes as he searched for the culprit. Someone had decided to nominate him because he was the newest arrival. He was sure of it. Many had been here several weeks waiting for others to arrive for the beginning of this unprecedented emergency cycle of enrollees. Sparring had been one of the few things they could do to pass the time. And having all grown up with swords in hand, it was only natural to wish to get a measure of the others as they waited for the training to begin. Kyllean had been here for just one day.

He saw mirth in the eyes of several others. A group effort, then. *Wonderful.*

Master Hilde continued, "You can see I am an old woman, well past my prime. And yet, I will demonstrate precisely what you will be learning under my tutelage, and more importantly, why.

"I selected practice swords because I knew many of you might attribute what you will see to Kyllean's fear of hurting an old woman." She smiled and patted Kyllean on the shoulder. "We needn't worry about any of that."

She placed a wooden weapon in his hand, then she stepped back and said, "First to three touches. Begin."

Kyllean took a stance in front of Master Hilde, but before his feet were even set, the old lady had slipped past his sword and held hers at Kyllean's throat.

"That's one. Please be ready next time."

Kyllean blinked. The woman had moved *very* quickly.

This time Master Hilde waited for Kyllean to advance, and, now embarrassed and a little bit angry, he attacked with vigor.

Master Hilde retreated and Kyllean smiled, increasing the intensity of his attacks, but then she brought her free hand to her mouth . . . and yawned as she continued to defend. *No way.* A moment later the woman flowed in and around Kyllean's sword with such speed and fluidity it seemed like his efforts had ended altogether.

"Two."

Kyllean shook off his surprise, and this time took a more conservative approach. It didn't matter. A few moments later, Master Hilde held Kyllean's wrist in one hand while her dull wooden blade pointed at his armpit, positioned perfectly for a lethal blow.

"Three."

She released her dominant position and bade Kyllean be seated.

"Now, I heard some grumblings from others who believed themselves the superior swordsmen. Any care to take on an old woman to complete the demonstration?"

The gathering was quiet now.

"Oh, come now. No one?" She pointed to a boy named Bastion. "Bastion, you were the one who put Kyllean's name forward. I've seen you with a blade and I suspect it was only your humility that prevented you from putting forward your own name. No need for that here. Come forward."

He scowled.

Kyllean recognized him from the sparring grounds. If Kyllean had been the one to select a challenger, he would have chosen this boy, as well. He was tall, broad, and formidable.

Master Hilde tossed the wooden weapon to Bastion and said, "Thank you for coming forward, Bastion. Same rules, understood?"

Bastion nodded and readied himself so he would not be caught off guard like Kyllean had.

It made no difference at all. The old woman made Bastion out to be nothing more than a clumsy boy with a stick.

"Thank you." She patted a deflated Bastion on the shoulder, and he glared at Kyllean as if this were somehow his doing. "You did a fine job of demonstrating precisely what I wished to convey. You may return to your seat."

Then to the rest of the class, she said, "Now, the purpose of this demonstration was not to embarrass your peers. They are both fine swordsmen. The purpose, however, was to demonstrate the elite abilities you will possess if and when you complete your training. Part of this ability involves wielding magic as I just did."

Eyes grew wide, Kyllean's as much as any other's.

I'm really going to learn magic? It was like being told he would wake up the following day with extra fingers. He would have a difficult time believing it until it happened. But at the very least, he felt a lot better about having just been beaten up by an old lady who, by appearances alone, should have a difficult time walking without a cane.

His mind returned to magic. *I'm going to learn magic! But . . . people don't just wake up and decide they wish to learn magic, do they?* He supposed priests did, so maybe this would be like that. *Wait—this means my father is . . . a mage? Does Mother know about this?*

Every kid in town had a father, mother, aunt, or uncle who was a rider or knew a rider, and not a one of them had ever spoken of magic besides the occasional fireside myth. Then again, maybe some of those stories were based in truth . . .

"I am an old woman, and both Kyllean and Bastion are by all accounts, fine swordsmen." The master puffed up for a moment as she said, "I would have still defeated both of these boys, but it would have taken longer without the magic and it's even possible that one of them might have scored a touch." That drew some laughs from the assembled.

"The magic I used is the same that will power your initial link to your rider's blade, should you earn one, and similar to that which will allow the connection between you and your Lumále should one of the few remaining decide you worthy. Both of these weapons allow our riders to face down wizards and live to tell of it. This unfortunately may be put to the test sooner than any of us might like with the coming war."

Kyllean knew that last truth all too well.

A hand shot up. "You say there are only a few Lumáles left?"

The mention of only a few Lumáles was a blow to Kyllean's vision of himself flying through the air in triumph.

"Indeed. And to be truthful, one of these few is likely not to choose at all." She looked about conspiratorially and placed a finger to her lips as she half whispered, "She's an old, stubborn creature." Hilde looked from side to side, then added, "They have remarkable hearing." Then in a normal voice: "We have been through six cohorts of initiates without her selecting a rider, so we're beginning to worry that she may simply lack the innate ability to offer the link. We're looking into that possibility.

"The good news is that you're all descended from a long line of innate wielders and therefore should almost all be capable of at least earning the blade." This caused another round of stirring throughout the assembled. "Raise your hand if you bear the bastard name Don-Votro."

Kyllean did so hesitantly, along with only two others. The rest were either full-blooded Tal-Dons or were illegitimate children whose mothers were from Talmune and therefore bore the surname Tal-Votro. The surname thing didn't make sense to Kyllean, but that's how it had all been explained to him.

Gesturing to Kyllean and the two others who had raised hands, Master Hilde said, "This is one of the few times when you can be proud—well, maybe not proud; how about thankful—for your heritage. I can't get into the details, for even I am not privy to the centuries-old arrangement but suffice it to say that the Don-Votro bloodline extends more directly into the ancient days of high sorcery than those bearing the Tal-Don or Tal-Votro names. The Don-Votros have rumored ties to the Hand of the Gods, if you wish to believe the most audacious of the theories. Regardless of the lineage, the proof is in the . . ." She looked to the heavens as if for help. "Well, I don't have a clever alliterative phrase to finish the thought so I'll just say it plainly: Don-Votros are likely to have an easier time tapping into the source and wielding it toward our purposes. They're also likely to be blessed with a much longer life than even the Tal-Dons or Tal-Votros, though you all possess longevity beyond that of outsiders who've seen enough of us to notice the slower than normal aging. Then again, with the coming war, this blessing may well be forfeit."

One prospective rider, a boy named Gerico, spoke up. "So you're a Don-Votro?"

Master Hilde smiled. "I am a woman. There is no such thing as a Don-Votro woman."

Kyllean considered this and attempted to refute it, but he was without example. He had simply never considered it.

One girl spoke up. "Why are there no female Don-Votros?"

Master Hilde responded, "A question for another time, perhaps."

Then another asked, "How old are you, then?"

The woman raised an eyebrow. "Hasn't anyone ever told you it's rude to inquire after a woman's age?" The boy shrank back but didn't wither altogether, and the eyes around the gathering were glued on Master Hilde in wait for the answer.

So, no offense taken to asking about her bastardness, but asking about age is a cardinal sin?

"I have walked Doréa for one hundred and seven years, give or take."

Mouths hung open, and no one moved. Kyllean knew they were all thinking the same thing. *Impossible.* The woman looked to be little more than fifty years old. What did that mean about Kyllean's father's age? Was he even more ancient? He was a Don-Votro, after all.

If so, how many children had he fathered? How many wives had he taken? The whole surname business now made slightly more sense. For even if a Don-Votro had a legitimate child, they would take the surname Tal-Don. Not that Kyllean had ever cared enough to puzzle it all out. These things had simply been parts of their culture in the small town of Talmune. Curiosity about such a thing would have been like asking why the sky was blue.

Master Hilde continued, "Let's keep moving. How many of you felt a slight tingling sensation develop in the back of your neck as I sparred with Kyllean or Bastion?"

More than half of the students raised their hands.

She nodded. "This indicates that your innate abilities are already beginning to manifest. How many of you have had dreams where you find yourselves in a place with no sound or color?"

This time only a small few raised hands.

"This is another indication that your magic is manifesting. This is a touch more on the dangerous side, however, so we'll want to schedule you to meet with the healer. She will guide you through the process of suppressing or departing such as soon as possible. I never experienced these dreams, myself, so I would not be a good resource as I only know what I've been told."

Kyllean felt a pang of disappointment. He had felt nothing during the sparring and had experienced no such dreams, yet he was supposed to be one of the more innately gifted by virtue of his heritage. The only thing he felt was sick to his stomach, but this was likely due to his lack of alcohol. His consumption had only increased after his escape from Brinkwell . . . and more so after Minathi told him he needed to join his father as a rider.

As if hearing these thoughts, Master Hilde said, "Not to worry if neither of these applies. Given our need for haste in this training, impending war and all, we're going to awaken your senses no matter how dormant they may be. This used to be a more difficult task, but thanks to our very own Kelson Don-Votro, we've now a tea with the means to awaken even the most dormant of abilities."

Kyllean's eyes went wide. His father had discovered a tea that could awaken . . . ? *What in the cold snow's turd was going on here?* His father was no herbalist. Then again, Kyllean had also been ignorant to the fact that his father was a wielder. It seemed Kyllean actually knew very little about his father and that which he did know was perhaps wrong. He felt betrayed. The more he learned, the more questions he had.

Master Hilde droned on, "However, before we dare risk awakening your innate senses and perhaps some of your abilities, we'll need to spend a few days learning about the power you may soon wield. It is known as elemental magic, or, as some of our more scholarly folks refer to it, atrérian. Names aside, understanding the fundamentals of how this works is crucial to your safety."

This would ordinarily be the point where Kyllean would tune out the lecturer, but in this instance, Master Hilde had his full attention. *I'm going to become a wielder! If Aynward only knew!*

CHAPTER 12

AYNWARD

AYNWARD WAS DRIED OFF AND dressed in layers of stiff formalwear in short order. As he advanced up the stairs and down the long corridor leading to his father's quarters, he was surprised to see guards posted nearly every ten paces. Aynward didn't remember ever seeing more than one guard outside the King's quarters in the years before leaving. Apparently imminent war with the Lugienese Empire had the King on high alert. Considering the infiltration of Lugienese into Brinkwell, he could hardly blame his father.

The guards each acknowledged Aynward with a bow of their heads as he passed, returning to statuesque positions of attention as soon as the show of respect was completed. Tall, arched windows lined the hallway leading to the King's quarters, stained-glass murals honoring his forefathers and the victories that forged the Kingdom in ages past. Aynward felt his unease intensify. His freshly cleaned hands were already covered by a film of sweat and there was a tightness in his muscles. No matter how many times he psyched himself up for this inevitable meeting, he realized he would be just as nervous. Aynward gripped the iron handle of the door and pulled.

The imposing oak door swung soundlessly to reveal the enormous study connected to his father's bedchamber. Like the rest of the palace architecture, the room was circular. Leather-bound books and scrolls lined the walls, while the rest of the room remained bare, with the exception of a Kingdom tapestry, and a Scritlandian runner in Kingdom blue and white leading directly to the mahogany desk in the center. The space was lit by a window with tall curtains on either side, and— something new: a dozen chairs formed a half-circle with the desk at its head. *This is interesting,* thought Aynward. *Has Father been holding meetings with his advisers right here in his personal study? He has a war room for such gatherings.* This would be yet another sign of . . . concern? Fear? Paranoia? *Something very strange is going on with him.*

To Aynward's surprise, his father rose from his seated position as the door closed behind. Then he rounded the desk and moved forward. Aynward noted that the King's stride remained regal in spite of the outward signs of age. His hair was still long, accentuated by a sharp widow's peak, and his face held its usual iron expression.

King Lupren's deep voice echoed around the study as he closed the gap between them. "Son, it is very good to see you returned and in one piece."

"Yes, well—" Aynward was without a witty retort, especially as his father's arms opened for an embrace. The King's strong arms pulled him in, though Aynward's confusion made his own movements perfunctory. Once separated, the King's stony face managed to form a slight smile. Another rarity. Everything at the dinner the evening before had been so formal. The King had hardly acknowledged Aynward. Aynward had assumed this was because he didn't wish to berate his son in front of the guests.

"If the reports are to be believed, you survived quite an ordeal, and not without some manner of heroics, if perhaps a foolhardy decision to remain behind in the first place."

What is going on here? wondered a befuddled Aynward. "I must admit, Father, I was expecting a bit more of a—stern homecoming."

"Yes, well, I can't honestly say that I expected to receive word from the Count of Brinkwell singing your praises. But your new counselor, Gervais, has corroborated these accounts. Son, I was hesitant to send you away as I did, but I was just as reluctant to keep you here in Salmune. It seems Brinkwell managed to carve a good man out of you after all, though the circumstances surrounding this experience are regrettable."

Aynward attempted to respond, but his bewilderment choked his words. "I—"

As he opened his mouth again, he felt a lump develop in his throat. "I—I believe much of the credit goes to the late Counselor Dolm—Dolmuevo."

The King placed a hand upon Aynward's shoulder and shook his head. "He was a decent man, but in the end, it was greed that caused his death, not you."

Aynward leaped back in shock. "What? What are you talking about? He was killed in the defense of my life. He didn't have to come back for me."

"Aynward, perhaps you should sit down."

The King walked back to his desk and gestured for Aynward to sit in the seat closest, facing him at an uncomfortable angle.

His father spoke again. "Aynward, it was discovered that Counselor Dolmuevo returned for you in order to deliver you to the Lugienese. He was tasked with ensuring that you remain behind, but alive. We suspect you would have been held for ransom by the Lugienese."

Aynward could not believe what he was hearing. "No. There is no way Dolme would have betrayed the Kingdom. He was one of the most loyal men I have ever known!"

The King lowered his head with a sad expression, or perhaps one of pity, as he said, "Son, we have letters confirming his involvement with the Lugienese. I'm sorry. I, too, was skeptical, but it is the truth."

Aynward scrutinized Dolme's every action through this new lens, looking for proof that the accusations were false, but everything Dolme had done seemed to fit. Everything except—

"But how could he have known I would jump from that first ship? How would he have delivered me if I were safely ferried away?"

His father just shook his head slowly. "He knew you too well, Aynward. Why do you think your friend's name wasn't on the list for your ship? Was that an honest oversight, or could it have been a calculated move to keep you in the city long enough for the Lugienese to arrive?"

No. This just can't be.

"Listen, son, none of this is your fault. In fact, whatever guilt you were carrying over his death can be cast aside. He was a traitor. The gods delivered their justice. And I fear he was not the only traitor in our midst."

Aynward could hardly comprehend what he was hearing. "I just— he seemed so . . ."

Aynward's statement trailed as movement to his right caught his attention. A dark shape emerged from behind the dark-blue curtains. It was so unexpected that Aynward hardly registered what he was seeing. The shape wore all black and carried a sword!

Aynward sprang to his feet. "Father! Behind you!"

The shadowy figure was already upon the King, slashing just as he spun to face the danger.

The King's movement saved him from a fatal blow, but the blade still cut away the King's mobility with a deep slash to the thigh, a spray of blood trailing the shimmering steel of the blade. King Lupren remained upright, one knee on the stone floor, the other leg helping him balance. Aynward was only two strides away. He let out a bellow, hoping to draw the assassin's attention away from the King.

King Lupren let out a grunt of pain as his arm deflected the swing of steel away from his body. The assassin was not dissuaded, flowing directly into his next swing. This one missed as his father hobbled into the open space between the window and his desk. "Guards!" he yelled. "Aynward, run!"

Help would not be here in time. His father was weaponless and bleeding from two serious gashes. Aynward was also without a means of defense, but he couldn't stand by and watch his father be cut to pieces.

King Lupren's movements became those of grace in spite of his injuries. He dodged several more attacks, moving with speed that seemed to defy natural law. The assassin too seemed taken aback, tilting his head to the side after a string of completely missed attacks. *How is he doing that?* Aynward had never seen his father, or anyone, move like this. Aynward had stopped where he was, mesmerized by the spectacle. His father might just last long enough for the guards to arrive.

The assassin growled and his attack lost its graceful flow, taking on a brutality, a blood lust that could no longer be predicted like the movements of a trained swordsman. This time even the unnatural speed of his father's defenses was not enough as the two bodies collided. Out of this tangle, the King was knocked to the floor, a deep gash in his other leg rendering him completely immobile.

Aynward started forward again, but the assassin must have heard his footfalls for he turned and swung.

Aynward came to a halt just in time—the metal hissing as it passed mere inches from his throat. The figure immediately closed the gap and swung again. This time Aynward had no doubt he would die. He just hoped help would arrive in time to save his father. "Guards!" he yelled. "Guards!" *Where are they?*

The blade arced down and across on its way to cleave his chest, but the assassin spun away. Aynward stood frozen in disbelief, unprepared for the assassin's foot which then took him square in the chest. Aynward's body struck the hard cold floor followed by a sound that stole his breath: a groan of pain from his father. It was a dignified sound, the sound of a great man, a proud man, but a dying man. Aynward rolled to his stomach, then crawled to his knees, ready to take his turn at death when he heard the clang of steel upon stone.

Looking up, he saw the assassin dart for the window. It swung open soundlessly. Aynward jumped to his feet to give chase but the assassin was too quick. Aynward arrived just in time to see the cutthroat land far below. Then with a flick of his wrist, the snare holding the rope to the stone fell loose. There was no chasing this man, not unless Aynward could fly.

Aynward rushed to his father, whose breathing was ragged. He lay on his back, blood oozing from his chest.

"Father . . ." Aynward whispered, pulling him close, cradling his head. He didn't know what else to do. The King tried to sit up but lacked the strength.

The King spoke, but his words were garbled by blood. "Betrayal. More betrayal. Your—"

A crimson river flowed from his open mouth, choking his speech.

Then the door to the study burst open and guards rushed in, swords at the ready. They were breathing heavily, followed by an imposing figure dressed in formal military garb, heir to the throne, the King Apparent, Perja.

Aynward's eldest brother stared down at him, then pointed. "Guards, seize the assassin."

Aynward didn't understand what was happening. Not until he spotted the sword the assassin had left behind. *His* sword. The blade was still slick with his father's crimson blood.

CHAPTER 13

DAGMARA

DAGMARA'S HEART TUMBLED YET AGAIN. Her father, the King, dead? It seemed impossible. He was so strong. She had partially believed the man would outlive all of his children if for no other reason than his refusal to give up his throne.

Dagmara sat on her mother's bed, holding her as much as her mother held her. She had been summoned there to be given the news of her father's murder. After the initial wave of grief passed, Dagmara's considerations expanded and she felt a new pang of worry.

"What of Aynward?" she asked, eyes still teary. "Wasn't he to see Father near the time of—?" *Dear gods, Aynward must have been one of the first to see Father's corpse. Or worse yet, what if he too had fallen?* It would be just like her mother to try to break the bad news into smaller, digestible portions.

The Queen hadn't answered, but her eyes went to the floor and Dagmara felt her heart twist. *No. Not Aynward, too.*

"He's okay, right? Mother? Aynward *is* okay, right?" She felt her throat tighten.

Her mother looked up and firmed her expression. "Your brother lives, though perhaps not for long."

Oh gods. He's been badly wounded. "Where is he being held? I should visit."

The Queen shook her head slowly. She looked awful. It was to be expected to some extent, but this transformation was almost inconceivable. She looked like someone who'd had the spirit sucked out of her heart. When she finally spoke, her voice was hoarse with grief. "They're saying it was *he* who killed your father, and Perja says—" Her mother returned to a fit of crying. "Says no Kingslayer can be allowed to live, no matter his bloodline." The Queen sobbed, "A dead husband, and now my children set out to kill one another . . ."

The Queen's words hit Dagmara like a hammer blow, like a boulder careening down the hill to crush those below. *Aynward, a murderer?* No, not possible. His relationship with the King had always been strained, but—murder? And yet, what did she know of his time in Brinkwell? Even his last days there? Perhaps his escape from the Lugienese attack had changed him. Yet there seemed hundreds of explanations besides the simple possibility that her brother was a cold-blooded killer. But none of them were good, and Dagmara cried. Her tears did not care why they had been summoned, nor did her mother's blouse, which absorbed them without hesitation.

Dagmara finally pulled herself away, her sorrow slowly transitioning to anger. She felt a fist form in her right hand. *Aynward must have had other options. There are always other options. He could have said something.* She needed to know what really happened before Perja had him hanged. She needed to look into Aynward's eyes and hear him tell why he felt the need to take their father's life, and, by extension, his own. She almost said as much out loud, but the timidity of her mother gave her restraint. The Queen would advise against this, perhaps even prohibit such a visit. In fact, being allowed to see the King's assassin would likely require a fair amount of persuasion beyond that of her mother. She needed to act quickly.

"I'm so sorry, Mother." She pulled the Queen in for one more hug before departing. "This is a lot to take in. I need to be alone. To think." Her tears were gone, swallowed by determination, at least for now.

"I know, honey," said her mother in a soft, sweet voice, still weak with grief. Her mother took Dagmara's hand and gave it a final squeeze. Dagmara brought her free hand to cover her mother's and said, "I love you, Mother. Thank you. I think I may take a ride to clear my head. I'll see you for supper."

The Queen nodded her understanding and Dagmara turned to leave. By the time she faced the door, Dagmara's eyes were narrow, her mouth a hard line. Yes, she was definitely going to pay her little brother a visit.

CHAPTER 14

GROBENNAR

THE CONNECTION BETWEEN GROBENNAR AND Magog solidified, followed by the touch of another mind, causing Grobennar to curse. Then he reconsidered; perhaps this was a good thing. Allow Rajuban a front-row seat to Grobennar's successes, at least those he wished Rajuban to see. Perhaps ol' Raj would slip up and reveal his true loyalty, which was only to himself.

"Welcome, Fatu Ma-gazi," came the powerful voice of the God-king, Magog.

"Thank you, Your Excellency. I am glad to feel your presence through the connection. I pray that your return to Sire Karth went without discomfort or complication." Grobennar did not bother acknowledging the *other* presence.

Magog replied, "It did. Now, on to your reason for requesting this meeting."

"Yes, yes, of course." Grobennar did not care for the annoyance he sensed in Magog. No matter, he had done a great deed on behalf of the Empire and he would gloat. He had earned that right. "I have great news about our successful conquest of Tung, as well as the upcoming conquest of the Kingdom of Dowe."

"Go on," urged Magog.

"Dowe's King is dead, or will be any day now. Confirmation of the deed should reach my ears soon. Moreover, the prince who escaped Brinkwell will no longer be a problem. Best of all, no one will suspect our hand in any of this. I have an agent with access to the soon-to-be-crowned King, Perja, albeit indirect. He will gather information about the strengths, weaknesses, and locations of their forces. We could launch a calculated, full-scale invasion in less than a full cycle of the moons."

There was a long pause, and Grobennar began to worry that the connection had failed. Then Magog said, "You have done well. But we will not be invading the Kingdom of Dowe just yet."

"I . . . I see." *Has he gone mad? They're ripe for the taking.* It took every bit of self-control he had to keep the mental tone of his next question limited to curiosity. "Might I ask why?"

Another lingering pause, then the voice of Rajuban entered his mind. "Should I explain this one?"

Magog answered, "Please."

"Many thanks, Your Excellency. Grobennar, while there is merit to your strategy, it remains blunter than may be necessary or advantageous. I have devised a plan that includes a bit more . . . finesse. This has been aided by a *direct* contact within the palace in Dowe, I believe the very same man your contact works through. I've just cut out the extra exchange. But I did allow the assassination to take place, with only a few modifications. My contact believes it would be more effective to first exacerbate existing tensions between Dowe and Scritland lest an invasion of Dowe unite these two powerful forces against us. Instead, we're going to broker a peace with Dowe, for now, while we cripple their neighbors to the south, Scritland, who will be less suspecting."

Rajuban, cursed Grobennar. *That slimy worm!* Rajuban had beaten him yet again, hijacking the fruit of his labor. In fact, Grobennar's scheme had strengthened Rajuban's own. *He must have somehow discerned my plans.*

Magog added, "Fatu Ma-gazi, you will continue your aquatic invasions. I'm aware that the sacking of the Isles city of Tung was a great success. You are now to take the Free Cities along Drogen's western coast. Our offer of peace will be negotiated from a position of strength once established there. Then we will turn our sights on Scritland. Dowe will be an easy target once this has taken place. I will have Fatu Mazi Rajuban send a courier with these newest details."

Grobennar's mind reeled. Rajuban was going to take credit for everything! Even with Grobennar's new title, he was nothing more than Rajuban's lackey; the whole glory of the successful conquest of Drogen would be Rajuban's. The thought made Grobennar nauseous.

"Thank you, Your Excellency. It will be done."

"I know. You will contact me when you have taken the last of the Free Cities."

"Of course."

The connection ended, and Grobennar pushed past the priests who had lent the necessary strength for communication over such a vast distance.

One of them, a young if ambitious priest, said, "Fatu Ma-gazi, what word from Sire Karth?"

Grobennar ignored the question as he stomped toward the suite within which he had taken up residency. He needed to think. Praise be to Klerós, Jaween must have sensed his frustration for he had remained sil—

"*Quite the damper on your plans for a glorious return to power.*"

"Not now."

"*But don't you wish to finally do something grand?*"

Grobennar shut the tall oak door to his chambers and sank into a chair beside the large, goose feather bed covered with silk blankets. Rolling his eyes, he sighed. "What do you mean? Speak plainly."

"*You recall that prisoner who directed us to the last holdouts of resistance, as well as the places of hidden riches within Brinkwell? He had been working with Kubal on the scheme that was supposed to allow us to capture the prince. Did Kubal not claim this boy to be a bastard of royal Kingdom blood?*"

"Yes. What of it?"

"*This boy's loyalties appear to favor the highest bidder and that of self-preservation, yet he has connections to Kingdom royalty. Are we not then in a position to bid very high?*"

Grobennar was close to dismissing the ramblings of the spirit, whose advice was often more changeable than not, but something about his words felt promising. A smorgasbord of connections to plans and their possible outcomes floated into Grobennar's mind, and he started to see potential paths to glory take shape. He finally said, "You might actually have something here, Jaween."

The spirit released an imitation of giddy human laughter. "*Ohhh, I always have something.*"

"Yes, the veritable quality of that *something* is the problem. Now if you wouldn't mind, I'd like a few moments of uninterrupted quiet to string together some plans."

"*Veritable like the pastries of only the best in human kitchens. So many, and all so very delicious.*"

Says the spirit with no taste receptacles, thought Grobennar. He allowed his annoyance to leak through the connection until Jaween's tedious prattling finally departed, leaving Grobennar to scheme in silence.

Grobennar had brought only the most useful of Brinkwell's prisoners with him to the sacking of the Isles city of Tung. It was easy to kill a man once he proved to have exhausted his worth, but it was impossible to make them less dead if one later realized further use.

This philosophy served Grobennar well on this day. The prisoner had been helpful back in Brinkwell, and Grobennar had rewarded him with a cell containing a bed here in Tung. Grobennar left the door open just a crack as he stepped inside. The boy looked up and glared.

"Look, I don't know anything more. I could pretend to and maybe give myself a few more days, but what's the use? Let's be done with it, already."

Grobennar attempted to give him a thoughtful look, though he wasn't certain how well his face could lie. "Theo, was it?"

The boy nodded.

"Theo, I brought a friend with me today. I believe you and he have had some dealings in the past. And I also believe you may be able to serve yet another purpose, the reward for which may go far beyond simply sparing your life."

Theo squinted and tilted his head. "Well, I've nowhere else to go, so let's hear it."

Grobennar felt his eye twitch at the disrespectful tone, but now was not the time for chastisement and pride. He turned back toward the cracked door. "Enter."

The flamboyant pirate swung open the door and strolled in as if entering his own home after a long time away. "Theo! I see you have proven resourceful, a wise choice. One that will continue to benefit you should you heed my words." He bowed a few inches to acknowledge Grobennar, then directed his words at Theo. "My apologies that our last scheme was foiled by the count, but I think this next one will be of far greater value to you."

Grobennar noticed the boy perk up at the sight of Kubal.

"Yes, my imprisonment back there was most unfortunate. What is it you wish me to steal?"

The pirate smiled and folded his hands over the multicolored belt that cinched his purple doublet at the waist. "Your birthright."

Theo blinked. "My what?"

Kubal's smile widened. "Theo, haven't you ever wondered why the Count of Brinkwell took such an interest in you during your years in the orphanage? Paid your tuition into the university, and even helped you out of imprisonment after you were caught cheating the clothes merchant a few years back?"

Theo stumbled back a step. "I . . . he just, he—"

"He fed you a line of sewage. He never cared about you or your circumstances. He was acting on behalf of Lady Melanie of Quinson, sister to the Queen of Dowe, who couldn't bring herself to mother you, yet refused to leave the city where you were to grow up."

"Even if this is true, what has it to do with me now?"

Kubal huffed as he said, "Why, everything. Bastard or not, you are still her son." Kubal paused, allowing the shock of what he was saying to sink in.

To Grobennar, the boy appeared unmoved by the news; either that or he had missed his calling to the stage. Then, Theo's eyes darkened. "How long have you known about this?"

Kubal's expression firmed in defense. "That is of no consequence. It was not my secret to tell. Not until now, when I believe it will save your life, and, more importantly, benefit my own interests." He stroked the long chain of gold he wore around his neck. "I am a man of business, after all."

Grobennar was repulsed yet again by the man's vile addiction to wealth, but he reminded himself that it served a greater good to endure the blasphemous existence of such a one, for now.

Kubal flung his hands about as he explained the plan. "Okay, so let's pretend that I'm some sort of royal bastard. What is it that you suppose I will be able to do with this?"

Kubal glanced up at Grobennar, seeking permission to reveal their plan. Grobennar nodded.

"You're going to enter the court in Quinson," Kubal stated.

Theo stared at him, incredulity painted thick upon his face. "I'm just supposed to show up in Quinson and announce, 'Hey, Mom. I know you've ignored my existence for the past twenty years, but I think it's time you formally recognized my heritage'?"

Kubal chuckled. "Well, more or less, yes."

Theo waited. Kubal elaborated, "You're going to be transported there with my help, delivering an opportunity for your aunt to save your life in exchange for formally recognizing your legitimacy, as well as delivering a message to an uncle of yours who I think will be very interested in what the Lugienese have to offer."

"And what's to stop me from betraying you once I'm safely there?"

Grobennar stood and walked over to the boy, towering over him. To his credit, Theo didn't cower. He stared back in defiance. *The boy has stones, thought Grobennar. Good. He's going to need them.*

"The assassin's guild was recently hired to kill your uncle, the King of Dowe. They have instructions to eliminate you at my word should any number of things not come to pass as I see fit, foremost among these, your aunt's need to formally recognize you. From there, you'll need to convince your uncle to accept our offer. If I catch so much as a whiff of disloyalty, of trickery, you will be marked." Grobennar leaned in close, lips brushing the boy's ear as he said, "They are professional killers who pride themselves on customer satisfaction."

Stepping back, he added, "My friend here, Kubal, speaks highly of your wit. I suspect you'll be able to find a way to make this work. After all, your life depends on it." He turned to leave. "I'll let you two work out the finer details. Kubal, you will report to me once the wheels have been set into motion."

Grobennar strode out of the room, gleaming at the prospect of seeing his plan take shape. He would have contacted the boy's uncle more directly but having a contact on the inside would provide an additional layer of separation for both parties, and invaluable insight into the inner workings of their plans.

"I haven't heard a thank you yet. Are you really going to gloat like this entire idea was your own?"

Grobennar reached up and patted the pendant about his neck as if it were a dog that had just performed a stylish trick.

Jaween added, *"Not exactly what I meant."*

Grobennar was too high of spirits to deny even this silliness from Jaween. *"Very well. Thank you, old friend."*

A beam of joy spread across the connection. *"Oh, you are most welcome. You know me, I just enjoy seeing you succeed. Are we to celebrate now?"*

"I think that would be premature. But I am feeling a bit famished."

"What a joy. What a joy! To the kitchen we go!"

CHAPTER 15

SINDRI

YOU'RE LEAVING ME HERE ALONE? Now?"

Draílock gave no outward reaction. But he answered, "Arella and I have things that we must do before we can go. You have things you must do. Would it not be better that we both do these things at the same time so we might sooner leave to find your friend?"

Sindri opened her mouth to protest, but the logic of the statement forced her lips back to their thin line of frustration at Draílock's incessant way of always being right. Arella would be no help, either. This had become a near constant for Sindri as she traveled with the pair all the way from the fallen city of Brinkwell to Tung and now to the center of the Kingdom of Scritland.

Sindri regained her composure. "So I ask of this Ruka woman for the location of the most cursed place to go by ship? I still don't see how this helps us find of Kibure."

Draílock gave her that fatherly look that said, *Dear child, I know so much more than you. Please do as I say and all will be well.* All he actually said was, "Yes. Just tell her what we're looking for and that will be enough. She is quite skilled in matters such as these."

He handed her the purse filled with coin, and whispered, "Oh, and don't mention either of our names to Ruka." And then the pair was out the door.

Sindri endured the frustration that was Draílock in part because he had agreed to help her find Kibure, and in part because he had continued training her to master her newfound abilities with ateré magic.

Sindri rose to her feet, shaking her head and cursing Draílock as she crossed the room. Then, she exited and locked the door to Dwapek's old safe house. She stood motionless on the other side for a few heartbeats to regain her sense of purpose and calm. *I have a job to do.* She started a prayer but it fizzled away before taking any real form now that she wasn't sure to whom to direct it. The corruption of the Kleról had thoroughly twisted her faith in Klerós and she wasn't confident that the other faiths of the world were any better. Sindri turned and sucked in a deep breath of dry, crisp air. The sunlight warmed her face and improved her mood if only a little. Looking out into the cloudless blue sky, she could not deny the existence of some sort of creator. *Perhaps I'll just start my own faith.*

She enjoyed the sparsely traveled streets along the outskirts of the city before entering the more heavily traveled commercial center of Scritler, capital city of Scritland. Sindri wore the robes of a warrior monk but went without the accompanying sword. Draílock had explained the warrior class here was highly respected, and so long as she didn't reveal her Lugienese identity by removing her hood, she would be given a wide berth, even if her lighter skin marked her as a foreigner. The Scritlandians valued skill above all else, so anyone, male or female, who demonstrated wielding potential could petition to receive training. According to Draílock, he, Arella, and Dwapek had all been such cases. The thought of Dwapek and his still unknown fate evoked an emotional response that Sindri could not afford to entertain, not now. She swallowed hard and tucked the thought away for a later time.

Draílock had been correct about the respect held for anyone wearing the robes. Common folk didn't dare to so much as make eye contact with her, and the few who wore similar sleeveless brown robes nodded in mutual respect as she made her way. She deduced that their numbers were large enough in the capital city that seeing an unknown member caused little suspicion. Then again, she could be from a different city altogether, which was the story she was given to use by Draílock should she be questioned. She considered her days within the Kleról and accepted that this would likely have been similar. No one would dare wear the robes unless they had earned them. That and obtaining the robes themselves as a nonmember would have required stealing from a priest who had earned them, which would be a sure way to die.

Sindri's self-consciousness persisted, but it was muted by the reinforcement of Draílock's words as things unfolded precisely as he had predicted.

She followed the main thoroughfare to the river, then turned east until the river became a lake. According to Draílock, Ruka had a very well-known, yet unadvertised, business of selling and creating artifacts and maps to merchants, captains, and smugglers.

She spotted the landmark she sought, a bridge spanning the river just before the lake, then looked for the inn that would lead her to the bakery that would lead her to the shop. *Nothing can ever be simple, can it?* Ruka's place was a business was called Volshecart, which, of course, would not be discoverable by any signage. It was supposedly located between an inn marked by a nautical wheel, and a bakery that faced the opposing street. She had been given instructions on how to enter through the bakery.

When she arrived at the bakery, she saw no indication it was anything but that. Sindri supposed that was the point.

A rotund man behind the counter glanced in her direction then returned to his work of pounding dough, flour dancing in clouds to the rhythm of his fists.

"Um, excuse of me," Sindri said in a loud voice, concerned that her foreign accent might give away her true heritage. She spoke the Kingdom tongue, which Draílock said would be understood by most within the city, especially those involved in the business of selling food and wares. *What was his name again? Garon? Gardbol? Gerold. Yes, that's it.* "Excuse of me, Gerold?"

The man paused and looked up again, this time holding her gaze, appraising her as he held the dough in both hands. He finally nodded. "Need something?"

Sindri tried to steady her breathing, and her voice. "I was told that you could help of me find Ruka of the Volshecart."

The man's eyes didn't leave hers, but he made no move to do . . . anything. Then she remembered. "I have of the fee."

Still Gerold failed to move, not until she had reached into her purse to produce the coins. She found what she was looking for and pulled out two heavy silver disks. She placed them on the counter in front of the man.

He set the dough down and wiped his hands on his apron, then reached for the coins. He turned them over a number of times, weighing each in his hands, smelling them as if he could detect fraudulent metal. Finally, he grunted and pushed through to an opening in a large cabinet alongside many others.

Sindri was beginning to think he would not return but dared not follow without express permission. Then she heard his loud steps approaching and he emerged. He left the cabinet door open behind him and said, "She awaits you. Straight ahead, knock seven times. Not eight. Not six."

"Thank you," said Sindri as she started around the counter toward the cabinet door.

Gerold returned to his work on the dough without another word.

Sindri was careful to rap on the door precisely seven times. She heard shuffling on the other side, but no one answered for nearly sixty heartbeats. *Did I not knock loud enough?*

She was contemplating whether to try again when the door began to slowly open. A dark-skinned Scritlandian woman wearing a colorful headdress and scarf turned from the door and glided to her seat behind a large desk filled with scrolls, maps, and various other parchments. There was a door behind the desk that probably led to somewhere in the inn, perhaps a small apartment hidden back there.

The woman's smooth movements did not match her aged appearance. Locks of gray hair lined with white spilled out from beneath the head covering, and her obsidian skin had the leathery look of one who had seen more summers than most. The light of two oil lamps illuminated an otherwise dark, windowless room, casting soft shadows about the clutter. There was also an array of glittering stones and jewelry in various stages of assembly, in addition to the two large green emeralds dangling from the woman's ears. Sindri took her to be a jeweler, though she saw no tools.

Ruka gestured toward an empty chair in front of her desk as she took her own seat. Narrowing her eyes, she began speaking Scritlandian, of which Sindri did not understand more than a few phrases. But Draílock had prepared her for this.

Sindri smiled as if she understood, then responded with a phrase spoken in the Kingdom tongue provided to her by Draílock. "My apologies, dear Ruka. While my training as a Scritlandian wielder goes well, my command of the language does not."

Switching seamlessly to the Kingdom tongue, Ruka replied, "Ah, a Lugienese monk of the order who speaks only the Kingdom tongue? Can't say as I've ever seen the like, nor have I ever heard of such an odd pairing. You surely did not train here in Scritler; this sort of oddity would certainly have reached my ears. Where, then?"

Sindri said as instructed, "I train at Adonis. Komkor Juden gave of me leave to travel of this place as a part of my quest." Komkor Juden was a well-known martial trainer in Adonis, one who would have enough students under his tutelage that few would question the lie. The story needed only to last long enough to obtain the information she sought.

Ruka lapped the air with her lips as if tasting the validity of Sindri's words. She smiled, and yellow teeth shone bright as she said, "You have been trained well. This is a good lie."

Sindri's heart accelerated as Ruka chuckled. "A good lie, indeed. So the question then becomes, do you lie because what you wish to know will help you do some evil? Or do you lie because it is the only way you know to do good? And finally, what is it about the truth that convinces you to conceal it?"

Sindri's leg muscles were tense, coiled and ready should this discovery mean trouble for her. Ruka appeared aged, but Sindri didn't know if there were others nearby who weren't. *I need to answer.* Draílock had not prepared her for this. *Curse that man!*

Fear took over and the words flowed out of her before she had time to consider why she chose them. "I search of my brother. He goes missing. The witches who took of him wear gray cloaks, the sigil of a scroll is worn of the left chest of each. They travel of ship and I believe they go of somewhere unknown to most. Perhaps a coastal ruin upon the Hand of the Gods, but this is only a guess. They have of magic very strong, yet no one knows of who they are."

Again the woman tasted the air, tasted Sindri's words. She was like a snake seeking prey and Sindri wondered if she hadn't just given herself over to the woman's poison. Then Ruka's expression became soft and her eyes concerned. "Tell me more about these women who have taken your brother."

Sindri did so, telling the woman everything she knew of them while leaving out the source of much of this intelligence.

"This is a most unusual, very specific thing that you ask."

"Can you help of me?"

Ruka had brought a hand to her chin and tapped her index finger upon her lips in thought. "Perhaps. There is one place in particular that could fit, though I have never personally tested the rumors. However, before we can proceed any further, there is the small matter of payment. This knowledge I've spent my life collecting at my own risk does not come free."

Draílock had at least prepared her for this portion of the transaction. "I have the coin here." Sindri jingled her purse.

"That is well. This information will be yours for . . . eight golds."

Sindri's jaw dropped. Draílock had instructed her to feign surprise at whatever the price and to negotiate from there. Her expression of shock, however, required no false embellishment. "Eight golds? Surely you joke! You do not even have certain if the information will help of me! Maybe this is worth of a single gold piece." She had the money to pay, but Draílock had made it clear that she should not take Ruka's first price. Now she knew why. This woman was a criminal, preying on desperation, and Sindri had handed that right to her with her story.

Ruka didn't waver. "I work under the principles of supply and demand. You have shared a story with me that conveys a high level of demand, and I know for certain that I am the only person perhaps in all of Doréa who might have the means to help you find your brother. Demand is high and supply is low. My price is apt."

Sindri rose to her feet. *Draílock, you'd better be right about this part.* "This is insane. You don't know where he is, and I need this money to find out who does. I'm done here." Sindri started for the door. *If you're wrong, you can come here yourself to get it,* she mumbled to the absent mage.

When she reached the door, she heard an unexpected sound. She stopped moving in order to listen. It was clapping. The woman was clapping. "Impressive."

Sindri pivoted on her heel then did her best attempt at a death stare. Ruka continued, "Yes, truly powerful theatrics." Then she sighed. "Very well. Four golds it is." The price was still criminal, but Sindri could afford it. She returned to her seat.

"Tut, tut." Ruka extended her hand and flexed her fingers. "Gold first."

"Half now, and half after you prove to have of something for me," replied Sindri.

Ruka rolled her yellowed, aged eyes. "Of course."

Sindri pulled out the four gold pieces and displayed them in her hand before placing two of them neatly on the desk for Ruka to examine.

The old woman picked them up in her wrinkly hand and turned them over a few times before sliding them into a pocket. She then rose to her feet, whistling happily as she moved to a chest to Sindri's right, nestled between two shelves filled with scrolls, tomes, and several disturbing glass containers hosting the preserved corpses of strange creatures.

She selected a small, leather-bound book, which Sindri guessed to be some sort of journal based on similar artifacts she had observed in Brinkwell. Ruka paused her tune for a moment, then nodded and moved to her right to rifle through a pile of flattened scrolls on the shelf. She pulled out a single sheet, placed it on top of the other item, then moved over to the other shelf. Ruka bent over to pull out a box then carried it along with the two items she had gathered and set them upon the mess of other documents that filled her desk. From the box, she unfolded a colored map. It was one of the most beautiful things Sindri had ever seen, an artistic marvel of ink on a cured animal hide. Sindri recognized the continent of Drogen, but the scale of the map allowed for detailed coastlines, topography, and even geographic markers like forests, deserts, lakes, rivers, and . . . islands.

Ruka sat and opened the journal. "Let's see." She thumbed through the pages, occasionally pausing to read. "Mmhm. Nope. Little later. Mmhm. Nope." Then she set the journal down in front of her, face-up, pointing her finger at a place on the page. "Here it is. A written account scribed by the one and only Captain Jasper, an unusual skill for a pirate in those days, and little known because he seems not to have sensationalized his experiences as some of the more famous pirates of legend. But this feature lends more credibility to his claims. Jasper writes . . . and please bear with me, as I will need to translate from old Scritlandian as I read. 'We followed the cursed ship south beyond the Sotaric Sea, around the blighted Land of Ghosts'—an old name for the Hand of the Gods—'toward the depths of the Blue Hells.' That's an old name for the better-known Sea of the Lost," clarified Ruka. "'Our quarry has done as no other ship I have ever known: match speed with my very own *Wind Splitter*. This be a feat impossible considering their measly dual-sailed vessel, even if its make be unknown. I do believe them be witches. 'Tis the only explanation for such unnatural speed. Blast our luck that my own wielder, Ferris, went missing before the theft occurred. I now wonder at the suspicious timing of that. But consequences be damned, no one steals from Captain Jasper and lives to tell of it.'"

Ruka skipped a few pages, then continued, "'We lost them. Sure as the sun is bright, we lost them. Never before has such prey evaded the clutches of the *Wind Splitter*, not like this. Ship simply disappeared. After rounding a small cluster of uninhabited isles south of the Land of Ghosts, the entire ship all but disappeared.'" Ruka pointed to a place on the map about as close to the edge of the world as Sindri had ever seen. "'We circled the isle a number of times, even changing direction once to be certain.'"

Ruka scanned the next page, then read, "'It has been two days since One-Eye Olsen and Scratchy Jed disembarked to search the island. I'm not fool enough to risk sending others after them, and the crew is near to mutiny over the whole ordeal. We lift anchor today and I vow never again to return to these cursed waters. I have said my prayers to the maiden of the seas in thanks that she spared the *Wind Splitter* and the remaining crew. Them witches can have their blasted rubies. No stone's worth my precious *Wind Splitter*.'"

Ruka closed the journal, then picked up the other parchment. But before she began reading, she paused and said, "Might I interest you in some tea? Coffee, perhaps?"

Sindri attempted to sound polite as she masked her annoyance at Ruka pausing at such a time. "I like of Tea, but only if you already plan to prepare water." Sindri didn't even like tea, but she figured it was the right thing to do. Women like Ruka could be turned off by the smallest perceived slight, Sindri knew, and she was still clinging to the hope that this woman actually had some information of value. She had her doubts, considering the next source was a single page.

Ruka's hands disappeared behind her desk, then returned with two clay mugs. She moved a few stacks of parchment to another already cluttered space on the desk and placed them there. Then she pulled a box from a drawer in her desk to reveal a bag of dried leaves. To Sindri's surprise, Ruka also pulled out a small decanter and poured what must have been lukewarm water into the mugs. *I'm no expert, but isn't hot tea generally steeped in . . . hot water?* But Sindri remained calm and quiet, waiting patiently for the woman to finish her business.

A tingling sensation sent chills shooting through Sindri's body. *Magic.* Positioned so close to the source, she wouldn't have needed the enchanted powers of the amulet Draílock had given her to sense Ruka's magic.

When Sindri's gaze drifted up from the now steaming cups, she noted the look of confusion in the woman's expression. She also noted that it was quickly transforming into anger. Sindri stared into two cold, dark orbs and saw murder. She then noted that Ruka was not staring back into her own eyes; her glare was slightly lower. Then it struck her: the glowing blue light of her amulet. Sindri brought her hand up to slide it back into concealment, but it was too late.

"Where did you get that amulet?" Ruka demanded.

"I—I—"

"*He* sent you, didn't he?"

"I—" *Is there any use denying it?* This woman clearly knew Draílock. Or perhaps Dwapek? Did it matter? Draílock had sent her alone with specific instructions that she *not* mention his name. *A warning about keeping the necklace hidden would have been nice.*

"Do you know who cut that stone?" asked Ruka, her tone flat, but with an undertone of danger.

Sindri shook her head. She had no idea how to navigate this situation back to safe waters.

Ruka pointed at her own chest. "I cut it myself, at the behest of a *friend.* Or someone I *thought* was a friend. I labored for days to get the size and mounting just right, free of charge! And do you know how I was repaid?"

Sindri averted her eyes, desperately fearing what was about to come. "I have much sorrow for this thing he—"

Ruka cut her off with a shout. "He betrayed me less than a fortnight later!"

She suddenly calmed, rapping fingers on the desk in thought, then her fingers went still and she growled, "The wages of sin shall be worse than death!"

Any further considerations disappeared as Ruka's right hand slipped behind the flap of her shawl. Instinct shouted the warning of steel before it came hurtling through the air. Sindri's own daggers were free from hiding just in time for the first to deflect the spinning weapon that would have slammed into her heart. But this was just a distraction as a blast of magic zipped toward her.

Sindri's former training in the priesthood saved her once again— that, and Draílock having improved her use of ateré magic during their long journey here from the Isles. She was now at least competent with her renewed magical skills, though still nowhere near as deft with these ateré-drawn powers as she had once been with the power drawn from Klerós. Sindri tapped into the energy hiding within the vast array of hardwoods and used it to deflect Ruka's next magical attack. The strike that would have obliterated Sindri instead crashed into the adjacent wall, converting Ruka's ancient scrolls into a cloud of floating shrapnel. Draílock had worked with Sindri on redirecting forces of magic as opposed to simply meeting strength with strength, a brutish strategy good for exhausting her limited abilities. She still had a nearly full reservoir of power at her disposal.

"I warned him never to return to my city!" shouted the furious Ruka. "So the coward sends his new whore on his behalf? I think not!"

The woman shot another blast of power, this one broader. Her fury affected her precision, which made her more difficult for Sindri to predict. Sindri ducked, shielded by the desk as the blast of energy struck the door behind her, eliciting a loud crack as something snapped.

Sindri rolled to the side, reaching the nearest shelf in the room. As she stood, ready to send a return attack, another assault was on the way. This time she rolled forward, avoiding the brunt of the attack but not all. Energy ripped at her left shoulder, turning her roll into an awkward tumble. She collided with another shelf of books, many of which fell atop her. Sindri lifted a behemoth tome just in time to catch the next blast head on, which slammed the book and its holder back into the shelf.

Sindri didn't know how much longer Ruka could keep this up, but without knowing what kinds of jewelry the woman held, she could not assume she was limited to a wielder's physical capacity. Sindri needed to put Ruka on the defensive. She had no intention of killing anyone today, especially not in a foreign city where she might be tried and hanged as a heretic for posing as a monk of the order, but neither could she be as careful as she liked when facing mortal danger. *Think!*

She hated losing daggers, but this was no time to worry over trivialities. She threw one of her daggers at the woman's leg. The blade might not strike flesh, given Ruka's impossible spryness, but it would at least give Sindri time to get herself out of there. She sent a bolt of energy at the base of the oil lamp, knocking it from the wall, and, more important, spilling oil and flame along the wall and the nearby clutter of dry parchment.

Ruka turned and saw why Sindri's secondary attack had not been aimed at her, and both magicians paused in wonder as the oil and flame met a great source of fuel. The flames erupted. As did Ruka's shriek. Sindri snatched a handful of parchments and shot them across the room into the flames with a touch of magic to propel them the rest of the way. Ruka shrieked once more as she turned away from Sindri to deal with the flames.

Sindri stepped toward the desk and snatched up the map, and several other items of interest to her, hoping one of them was the one Ruka had planned to share. She quickly folded the map and other papers then shoved them into her purse and started for the exit.

"No, no, no!" Ruka was pounding out the flames and cursing. Sindri smiled as she reached the door she had entered through. But it didn't open. She let out a curse of her own and stepped back to slam her shoulder into the solid wood of the door, then yelped in pain. It didn't budge. *No use.* Ruka's first attack must have collapsed the jamb, putting the weight of the entire wall upon the door. She would have to escape out the door on the other side of the room.

She turned to do so but was struck by a wave of air. It was not as powerful as the other attacks, which meant Ruka was likely nearing the safe limits of her powers, but it was enough to knock Sindri off her feet. She hit the floor hard and rolled, releasing a groan. On looking up she saw Ruka had extinguished the flames and was striding toward her, smudges of ash upon her black Scritlandian skin. The room was now dark, lit only by a single lamp just above Sindri's position, enough to highlight the menace in Ruka's eyes. "You're going to pay dearly for that, witch."

The surprise attack stole Sindri's focus and she released the power she'd been holding. *Not good.*

Ruka snatched something from a shelf as she approached. Another knife. *Not good at all!*

Sindri sank into a defensive crouching position, single dagger in hand. Normally she could outmatch a woman thrice her age at least, but nothing about Ruka seemed right and she had not fared well thus far. Sindri decided she'd rather not find out and drew power from a few specific places in the floor between them, hoping it would be enough.

Ruka's voice was lathered in contempt. "I was going to kill you all quick and nice. But I think it's going to be—"

Ruka released an undignified yelp as the wooden plank she had thought would support her next step collapsed beneath her, her leg sinking to the knee. Sindri lunged forward and kicked that same leg. Jammed as it was in the floor, it had nowhere to flex and Sindri heard as much as felt the bone snap. This time Ruka's shrill cry spoke of great pain.

Sindri was pretty sure the woman would survive the wound but thought it would be best if she didn't stick around to find out. She ran to the other exit, yelling behind her, "I'm sorry this had to happen this way." And she was. But Kibure was in danger, and Sindri would do what she must to find him. She would not let what happened to her brother happen to him.

She brushed off the ash from the brown monk's cloak as she entered the street and pulled the cowl up to hide what must have been all manner of dishevelment. No sooner had she done so than she saw a similarly dressed warrior monk running toward the building. He yelled something at her.

She screamed inside. *I can't fight another magic-user!*

She had no idea what the man had said since he'd spoken in Scritlandian, but she hoped he had not told her to stop. Thinking quickly, she decided to take a gamble. She nodded at the monk and pointed at him, then at the door to the clothing shop she had just fled, which was located on the other side of Ruka's hidden lair. She then pointed to the alley and ran toward it—praying all the while that the monk would believe the ruse that she was going to check the other side.

She chanced a look back and thanked whatever god was up there that the monk had not attacked or followed. She saw him disappear into the shop, then she turned around and ran back in the direction he had come from. She slowed and turned down another side street before collapsing into a pile of relief right on the alley floor. Rolling to her side, she reached into her purse to feel the stolen items and reflected on the ordeal she had just been through to obtain them. Her mood remained dark as she considered the blue amulet that had given her away. Draílock was *not* on her list of favorite people right now, and she was going to make that very clear to him at their rendezvous.

CHAPTER 16

SINDRI

"M Y, MY. YOU LOOK LIKE you've just returned from a journey to the underworld," remarked Draílock, a hint of mirth in his visage.

Sindri narrowed her amber eyes.

He coughed and his amusement vanished abruptly. "I take it Ruka was unable to help?"

Furious, Sindri spoke in Lugienese. "Oh, she had some information, and was in the middle of explaining it all to me when she used a bit of magic and your little trinket here," she clutched the amulet that had betrayed her and rattled it, "started glowing blue."

Draílock gave Arella a look, then his gaze returned to Sindri.

Sindri sneered, "Yeah. Would have been nice to have been warned that she might recognize such a thing."

Draílock ignored the last remark and returned the conversation to the Kingdom tongue. "Am I to assume Ruka is now dead?"

Sindri just continued to glare. "What would cause of you to believe that?"

Draílock rolled his eyes. "Ruka would not have allowed you to leave alive, not if she knew you were associated with me. Not unless—" Draílock's voice took on a tone of concern rarely heard as the cruel realization dawned on him. "Never mind, we must assume you were followed. Arella, grab our gear and take Sindri straight to the Jerico home to try to lose the tail. I'll go see what I can find from Ruka's. It's going to be ugly, but if it's the only way . . ."

Sindri said, "That may not be necessary."

Draílock responded, "It is."

Sindri pulled out the map and parchments, folded haphazardly but otherwise intact, and slammed them on the small table of the cramped dining area.

Draílock stopped. "That's not . . ." He nodded and actually smiled. "I must admit, I'm impressed. How did you manage to escape with your life *and* these treasures?"

Sindri furrowed her brow. "I took of these things from her desk as I fled for my life. No thanks to you! But this document is supposed to have of some information. Maybe it has of value for us. She also read of something else, an old pirate's journal, but I don't have of that."

Draílock sighed. "You'll tell me every detail when we're safely out of the city. We need to leave. Now."

"What did you do to make of an enemy of her? Why does she have hate for you?"

Draílock shrugged. "Let's just say we had different views on the nature of our relationship."

Arella handed him a pack, which he slung around his shoulder. "Thank you."

Looking back at Sindri, Draílock added, "That, and Arella and I may have stolen a few artifacts of hers during our last visit to Scritler."

Sindri remained seated, her expression one of incredulity. She returned her speech to Lugienese for it was a much better language to curse in. After a barrage of expletives, she asked simply, "Remind me, why should I trust any of your plans now?"

Draílock responded in Lugienese as if to remind her that he understood the tirade in full, yet cared . "This was...not my best work. But we really need to be leaving. I will draw the first tail away. You two wait five-hundred beats, then head straight to Jerico's to lose the other—yes, there's likely at least two."

Sindri was still too furious to comprehend his instructions. "Wait. The other tail? Where are we going?"

Draílock snatched up the map and parchments. "We're leaving the city to go find your friend. In addition to Ruka's wealth of information, she is also the lead on one of the largest spy networks in all of Drogen, so we're making sure that her eyes don't join us on the road."

"Great. That's just great," spat Sindri as the door closed behind the insufferable wizard.

Arella handed Sindri a pack, then rose to her feet. "Come. We will leave through the rear."

Sindri followed Arella through a narrow hallway past a few small rooms and out a back door that opened up to a quiet alley running perpendicular to one of the wider, less filthy roads skirting the poor district. This was not the nicest place for a safe house, but it was a good place to disappear, and she suspected the rent was cheap.

They continued, hoods up, for a few thousand heartbeats before being pulled down a stairwell beside another door. Arella dragged her by the arm to expedite her descent.

"Come. We must be quick."

Sindri considered the benefits of abandoning the treasonous pair to find her own way to Kibure now that she had a lead. These two had almost gotten her killed, after all. Then again, they had also saved her life more than once. And something in the tone of Arella's voice left no room for disobedience. Sindri followed.

Arella closed the door and retriggered the locks behind them, then firmly grasped Sindri's hand and guided her down a flight of stairs through inky darkness. To her right was the faint line of light from a door at the top of another staircase. They scrambled up the steps and Arella opened the door to a stuffy apartment that smelled of stale *everything*. They exited swiftly out a different door before Sindri could so much as remark upon the decor.

Once back on the street, Sindri felt her tension melting away with every step. The ability to track their movement through this last set of maneuvers would have required resources and skills beyond Sindri's imagination.

In spite of this confidence, Sindri realized she was still tensing her entire upper body. It wasn't until she spotted Draílock standing beside a line of carts at the city's edge that she felt herself fully relax.

"Ah. You made it," he remarked.

Arella nodded and replied, "How did you—" Then she held up a hand. "Never mind. I'm sure the boastful explanation will only further aggravate me."

Draílock brought hands to his chest. "You wound me. My modesty is renowned. My timely arrival at our agreed-upon checkpoint was nothing more than strict adherence to well-devised planning. I would certainly never suggest a failure on your part to do the same."

"I could have sworn I asked to be spared this explanation," mumbled Arella to Sindri.

Draílock allowed a smug smile, but it melted as his eyes drifted to something behind her and Arella.

Arella noticed the uncharacteristic concern on his face first. "What is it?" she asked, turning.

Sindri followed Draílock's gaze to more than a dozen Scritlandian monks fanning out as they approached, their target clear, their eyes fixed upon her. She had imagined herself besieged by Klerósi priests countless times. This was no less terrifying.

Sindri turned back to Draílock, ready for him to yell for them to run or fight, but he did no such thing. His face had returned to its expressionless stone, his lips a flat line. This was as good as a scowl. "This will be a bit of a setback in our departure."

A sharp command rang out from the mob of monks. "Imposter! I address you now in the Kingdom tongue that you may understand my words. You are under arrest for the crimes of unprovoked violence, theft, and heresy. You will turn yourself over to us now."

Sindri whispered a desperate plea to Draílock. "Aren't we going to do of something? They'll surely hang of me!"

Draílock responded loud enough for the monks to hear. "We don't wish to add resisting arrest to the charges. This is all just one big misunderstanding. I'm sure we'll be able to get this settled soon enough."

He then said something in Scritlandian that Sindri did not understand as one of the monks stepped forward, shackles in hand. Sindri was teetering between rage and utter horror as she extended her wrists toward her captor.

Draílock said quietly in Lugienese, "Don't worry; I'll take care of this. Don't do anything to provide them further fuel. For now, I doubt they have proof of anything worthy of the gallows."

He doubts? Does that mean he's not certain?

The monks continued to encircle them as Sindri's shackles were secured. The metal clinked into place and the man detaining her said, "You two, as well." Two others appeared from behind and presented cuffs to Draílock and Arella.

Draílock did his best not to react, but Sindri noticed something of a twitch to the left side of his lip. "Might I ask the charge?"

"Heresy! Theft! And an abundance of lies!" The familiar voice came from behind the line of monks that surrounded them. Sindri looked toward the sound and saw Ruka, limping toward them. *She must have found a healer right away.*

"That last one isn't a formal charge, but I have enough proof for the first two to put them on spikes by nightfall," shouted Ruka, eyes blazing as she pointed directly at Draílock. "Be wary; they're wielders."

Draílock lowered his head, but his eyes met Ruka's and she allowed a sinister smile. "I've been waiting a long time for your return. Thank you so much for making this so easy."

Arella whispered in Lugienese, "Draílock, what are we going to do now?"

"You are permitted to worry," was all he said.

CHAPTER 17

SINDRI

THIRTEEN PRISONERS WERE ESCORTED TO a platform at Scritler's central plaza, where a tribunal of thirteen warrior monks sat stoically awaiting the proceedings. Their ominous robes of dark silk represented the judgment they would pass on behalf of Tecuix, the almighty creator, judge over the entire Chrologal religious pantheon.

Sindri had learned about this and more from Arella the night before while crammed into a tiny sandstone cell, separated from Draílock shortly after being arrested. Men and women were not permitted to share cells. Arella must have known something of Scritlandian law because she had asked the jailor how many criminals the prison had awaiting the tribunal of heresy. Arella had cursed when the jailer answered, "Twelve." She explained to Sindri, "That means we might only have a few days. The Scritlandians only hold these tribunals upon arriving at the holy number of thirteen."

Unfortunately, some other poor soul must have been brought up on charges that very night because by morning, Sindri and Arella were marching their way toward their deaths.

They were roused early so that their sentences might be passed beneath the full light of Tecuix. Sindri's cuffs were too tight, causing her

126

hands to ache and her wrists to itch. Both hands were also covered by a woolen sack, tied tightly just above the wrist. Sindri wasn't certain how the magic was supposed to work but something about their bindings prevented the women from wielding. Nevertheless, there were still an additional thirteen monks besides the council of judgment, perhaps as a show of force to keep angry mobs from mutiny should they disagree with the sentencing.

The taste of bile was strong in Sindri's mouth as she laid eyes upon the contraption looming above the black-robed monks at the center of the smooth marble stage. It looked like a doorframe made for giants, but instead of housing an actual door, this one held a razor-sharp blade suspended high above the open space below where Sindri guessed someone's body—no, their neck—would go. Her stomach lurched and the mealy breakfast she had been fed that morning decided to make a return, splashing on the cobbled ground to wet her ankles.

She brought the sack covering her bound hands up to wipe her lips. That's when she noticed the monk holding the end of a rope that would engage the monstrosity. Unlike the other monks, this one wore a red sash across his shoulder as he stood sentinel beside the menacing weapon of judgment. He had turned his head to stare in her direction. He glared, spit, then turned his attention back to the crowd.

The line of accused was made to stand in a neat row beside the platform where they would await their individual trials. Sindri looked back to see Arella directly behind her, Draílock further back. Sindri hoped the judgments might begin with the other end of the line, but the first to be taken forward was the solitary figure in front of her. She sagged and thought perhaps it was best to go sooner. That way she wouldn't have to watch her companions die. Her legs, she realized, were not simply trembling but shaking to the point of instability.

She started to teeter when the closest monk slid her curved sword free and pointed it directly at her. She said something Sindri didn't understand, but she grasped the general threatening nature of the gesture and guessed something bad would happen should she failed to remain standing.

Sindri willed herself to overcome the shakes enough to satisfy the woman with the blade. The sword returned to its sheath. She attempted to think about something else, but her thoughts did not cooperate, the current of fear too strong for anything else to stay afloat within her mind. *How can it end like this?* All she had endured, her many brushes with death . . . could that all have been for naught? Some part of her had come to believe that Kibure really was connected to something bigger. That he was one of the forces that would restore order to this broken world, and that perhaps she might have her own role to play in events. Sindri had escaped the clutches of the Lugienese on a number of occasions, defying the odds of reason. If there was a God up there, why would He allow her to escape the magical attack through the Kraken, the chase through the mountains, and even the sack of Brinkwell, only to have her wind up dying halfway around the world without having come any closer to understanding or rescuing Kibure? Perhaps God had abandoned her after all and this was just the randomness of the world playing itself out to a meaningless end.

Or perhaps her helping Kibure escape the Lugienese Empire was as far as her role was to take her, and now whatever god had used her to aid his escape saw no further purpose in keeping her around. She let out an anxious breath of air. It would all be over soon.

The black-clad monks rose to their feet. One of them stepped forward to speak to the crowd of jeering Scritlandian citizens who had come to watch the spectacle. Suddenly everything went deathly silent and the solitary monk's voice rang out for all to hear while all in attendance bowed their heads. A prayer. Sindri understood none of what was being said, but she knew the general idea. *These people before you stand accused of heresy, a violation of the most sacred laws put forth by the almighty gods . . . blah blah blah . . . now the gods or, rather, their ambassadors here upon the world, shall judge them.*

Then all in attendance spoke the same three syllables in unison and all heads rose, eyes opening. The monk who had spoken the prayer addressed the alleged heretic before him. His intonations suggested a question. The accused shook his head, and the monk yelled something to the crowd. A woman stepped forward and pointed an accusatory finger at the man on trial, if it could be called that. Her face scrunched up the way faces do when the wearer is so enraged they care not for their appearance. Between this and the spittle flying in every direction, her meaning was clear. The lead monk nodded then spoke to the crowd again. There was silence for a moment, then a man's voice was heard from further back in the crowd, which parted so he could be seen by the tribunal. He spoke calmly but loudly enough for all to hear. The monk nodded his thanks, then yelled out to the crowd again. The response was an eruption of angry shouts and excited cheers. The monk held up a hand and the crowd was silent once again. He turned to face the other members of the tribunal and they each nodded an approval in turn. The lead monk faced the accused and spoke a two-syllable word that could have meant nothing less than condemnation. The bloodthirsty crowd entered into excited frenzy.

Meanwhile, two of the brown-robed monks guarding Sindri and the others climbed upon the stage and took the man by the arms, dragging his unwilling body to the death machine. The man squirmed, but there was no spirit in his movements. He knew he was dead. Everyone did. The red stains upon the marble floor were eerie premonitions of what was to come.

Sindri wanted nothing more than to pray, but she had no idea to whom. Instead she extended her mind to the world around her, feeling for magic in spite of what Arella had said about the bindings. She failed. Sindri's desperation pushed her to try again. Instead of pleading with a god she didn't know, she pleaded with her current reality. She pleaded with the rope that somehow neutralized the part of the mind that permitted the transfer of magic, priestly or otherwise.

Sindri turned her head away as the man's neck was fastened into the contraption. Then she closed her eyes tightly. *Please,* she prayed as she reached her mind out into the world around her. But as before, it was as though her mind was a hand that had lost all feeling. She knew the magic was there, knew it could be used, but simply couldn't touch it. Couldn't even feel it.

Then there was a shout from the monk who appeared to be in charge, followed by a sound like that of a sword drawn quickly from the sheath of a giant. A loud thud was felt as much as heard, trailed by a chorus of hoots from the crowd. Sindri knew she shouldn't look, knew she should keep her eyes closed, focused on the impossible task of wielding her magic if for no other reason than to remain distracted. But she didn't. She opened her eyes to see the two monks who had marched the accused toward his death now dragging the same body, headless and pouring blood all over the light marble platform.

Sindri's heart began to beat harder and faster while her chest became tight. The two monks tossed the headless corpse unceremoniously onto a large collection of wood that rested several paces behind the weapon of death. She had failed to notice the large pyre for the looming machine in front that had stolen her attention. Sindri realized their bodies would be burned following the executions. She also saw thirteen spikes encircling the pyre and shuddered. The heads of the heretics would stand witness to the burning of their respective corpses.

The two monks gripped her arms and dragged as much as guided her to stand where the last man had been staged. Looking out into the crowd, Sindri saw the excited whites of eyes set within the dark Scritlandian faces, all thirsting for blood. Sindri's body tingled with nervous energy.

The monk who led the proceedings approached and drew back her hood to reveal her undeniable heritage. He yelled something at the crowd, and she heard some variation of Lugienese and something that might have even been *Kleról* or *Klerós*, but her mind was hardly able to process it.

She turned to look at the monk as he switched to the Kingdom tongue. "I speak now in a language you can understand, not that you deserve as much. You stand accused of theft, unprovoked violence, and heresy for wielding in the name of darkness. How do you plead?" This was followed by what must have been the Scritlandian translation, shouted for the crowd to hear. They waited impatiently for her response.

"I—the violence was not unprovoked. I was attacked. I did take a few items on my way out, but I paid two gold coins for them, and was prepared to pay another two when I was attacked. As for the heresy. Well, I suppose it doesn't matter what I say. Probably for any of this. No one will be coming forward in my defense. The only two people I know in this city are in line to die alongside me. But that doesn't make this justice. This is barbarity. This is—"

She felt the tingle of magic a moment before her throat constricted. Then she choked on her words. The monk stared at her with death in his eyes, hand gripping the air. This hand then slowly shifted to a single vertical finger, which he moved to cover his lips. Then he released the magical hold and Sindri sucked in a large breath before beginning a fit of coughing. The monk's attention returned to the crowd as he yelled something in Scritlandian.

This must have been the part where he asked for witnesses to the crimes to step forward and speak. It was no surprise that Ruka cleared a space toward the front of the crowd. She rattled off her story in Scritlandian. Hatred oozed from the crowd at hearing her account of things. This was followed by the baker, Herald, who gave a shorter explanation, no doubt corroborating everything Ruka had said.

As expected, no one stepped forward to deny the charges. This was it. Her end was here. Sindri looked to Arella as the monks approached to guide her toward her death. Arella appeared frozen in shock, as if watching this actually come to fruition was an impossibility she was unable to comprehend.

The monks reached Sindri and took her arms and squeezed, hard. Sindri's hopelessness was overrun by her fury. She was no heretic. Well, perhaps she was by Scritlandian standards . . . and Lugienese, but at least her heresy was justified! Whatever gods these people worshipped were no more real than the idea of Klerós himself. Then again, Klerós did grant powers to his followers, as did these people's many gods, so she couldn't deny their existence altogether. So what then? Might there be an entire pantheon of gods, none of which willing to share the full truth with their followers for fear of losing even a single soul to a competitor? Were humans just the pawns of a celestial game of chess?

She would never know the answers to these questions. But was this how she wanted to spend her remaining moments alive? Wondering over the heavens and their lies? Or listening to the crowd while observing the self-satisfied looks upon the monks sitting in judgment? No. Sindri's last vestige of passive resistance died. She would not allow this to happen. Not like this. Her anger flared and it burned red-hot as she was brought before the mechanism of death.

Her mind was molten with fury as it dove deep into the world around her, but unlike the nothingness she had found before, this time she felt *something,* a tangible barrier separating her from the energy all around. Her will pushed hard against this boundary but was rebuffed. Yet the tendrils of her seething awareness held on, found purchase, and then pushed back. With an unfettered roar, Sindri's mind split the magical barrier like parchment. As a bright light might shine suddenly into existence, so too was the sudden rush of magical sensation. After having her ability to touch the power around denied her, the sudden ability to feel it was an ecstasy so satisfying she nearly forgot her own anger—but only *nearly.*

Still covered by the sack, the magical ropes around her wrists dissolved like dust, and the metal cutting into her wrists softened as she drew the static power from them. Metal was not an easy item from which to draw power, for while it was dense like gemstones, steel's base energy was deeply distorted and confused by the smelting process. Yet Sindri needed to be free of her shackles in order to fight, so she had no other choice but to draw as much stability from them as possible. She glanced at Draílock to see his head tilted to the side, an amused expression upon his face. Only he could appear to be both surprised and aware of exactly what was happening.

Her gaze shot back to the line of monks sitting in judgment. They would be the first to pay. The way they glanced around in confusion told her they sensed the use of magic, but no one moved. They must not have believed it possible to defeat the magical cuffs.

As the two monks handling her forced her head down to secure her neck into place, Sindri's shackles and the cloth covering them fell in a heap upon the marble. Sindri's hands flew forward to brace against the death machine, stopping her forward momentum. Her mind dove into the vastness of marble beneath her feet, and she felt a wave of power rush into her like a breath of crisp, clean air after holding one's breath underwater.

The monks holding her arms let go in surprise at the sight of her twisted shackles on the marble, and Sindri pivoted to face them. They would be her first victims.

Motion to her left stole her attention. The monk with the red sash yanked the rope to engage the blade. *Oh no!*

She lifted her head and slid backward as steel cut the air on its way down to decapitate her. The thud reverberated as the heavy plate slammed into the space where her neck had been just seconds ago. The crowd erupted with gasps and shouts as mere strands of her hair were left behind on the side of the death machine where they expected a lifeless head.

Sindri's will began to shape a narrow blade of energy. She would only have moments to act before the overwhelming number of practiced warrior monks had their way with her. But she would take down as many of these hypocrites as she could before that happened.

She threw out her hands to deliver her first debilitating attack upon the closest two monks, but a wave of air swept her feet out from under her and the next thing she knew the marble ground slammed into the back of her head. All of the energy she had drawn in poured out like an upturned pot of water. She tried to right herself, but her head spun with pain that throbbed with every heartbeat.

The crowd gasped again, then went silent as a voice rang out. "No further harm is to come to this woman." Sindri looked around, but in her daze she had no idea who had spoken. They had done so in the Kingdom tongue, followed quickly with Scritlandian. Only the man in charge of the ceremony, whose voice she recognized, dared reply.

He was interrupted by a word she recognized—*Królest*—which Sindri knew was Scritlandian for Kingdom. The monk switched to the Kingdom tongue.

"High Priest Malakin, the tribunal has ruled her a heretic. We have heard from the two witnesses. The gods demand justice for her sins, foremost among them, blasph—"

"And justice they shall have." The voice boomed. "Tecuix is just, and this woman's sins will be repaid. For now, she and her compatriots have entered into my protection."

"Of . . . of course, High Father," responded the monk in charge, his tone missing any sense of genuine contrition.

Sindri managed to sit up and saw the source of her rescue, an enormous man standing at the base of the marble platform, his height nearly matching that of the monks standing upon it. He wore a white robe with a shiny steel breastplate, a brown sash wrapping the shoulder, and a mammoth sword to match his proportions. His black skin seemed to sparkle like smooth, volcanic glass, and his posture spoke of power beyond his already intimidating physique. This was the leader of House Diorne, the most powerful man in all of Scritland.

But Sindri's eyes did not linger upon High Father Malakin; they were drawn to the much smaller figure standing beside him, dressed as an ordinary warrior monk. His red beard and childlike size left no doubt in Sindri's mind as to his identity. He smiled as he hopped onto the stage with the agility of a desert cat.

He approached her and immediately lent a hand, which she took. Standing, she asked, "Dwapek! How did you . . ."

"We can speak of this once you're all safe."

He glanced over his shoulder and Sindri saw Ruka slinking away. Several others quietly dissolved into the otherwise attentive crowd. *The danger has not yet passed,* she thought.

❦ ❦ ❦

The palace of House Diorne would be more aptly called a fortress. It was certainly more akin to the Lugienese Empire's seat of power in Sire Karth than it was Count Gornstein's comparatively parchment-thin palace walls back in Brinkwell. According to Draílock, it was the long-standing competition between the seven houses of Scritland that led to the construction of seven similarly fortified structures all within the confines of the greater walled city of Scritler itself.

House Diorne was named for their patron god, Diorne, the god of magic. Sindri was aware that the Kingdom of Dowe also followed the Chrologal faith, but it wasn't embedded into their political system the way it was within the Scritlandian Kingdom.

House Diorne was the current ruling family, finishing its final year in the seven-year cycle before the next election by the council of seven. The Scritlandians, she thought, seemed to have an odd obsession with the numbers seven and thirteen.

"Tea?" asked High Father Malakin.

Sindri shook her head, while Dwapek, Arella, and Draílock responded with the customary Scritlandian bow of the head, which served as simultaneous acceptance and thanks. Arella gave Sindri a look that suggested she had done something wrong in denying the offer. Sindri whispered, "What? I do not like of tea."

Arella didn't quite roll her eyes, but she sent her sight skyward to show disapproval.

Soon after, plates with biscuits accompanied steaming cups of tea. Sindri was not given either and regretted her decision to refuse the bitter beverage as her stomach growled with hunger.

Sindri looked at the sprawl of city that extended as far as she could see from the top of a circular turret set within the central courtyard of the palace. Green and purple vegetation grew wildly from large planters set between merlons, giving the turret a near lifelike appearance. She could almost imagine where the palace was built had once been home to a massive, ancient tree. This turret could be the remaining trunk and the palace built around it in tribute to what remained of the colossal edifice.

High Father Malakin waved the servants away and the conversation began.

"Dwapek, I have risked much in saving your heretical compatriots from what appears to be a well-deserved end. Were it not for our *history* and Ruka's own affinity toward dark dealings, I would not have done such a thing. This puts my house's standing in jeopardy for the upcoming election of the seven. So, it is time to explain yourself. You bring news of grave danger from the west. A warning you have already shared with me in brief."

Dwapek crossed his miniature left leg over his right in a relaxed posture and said, "The Lugienese are coming. This is known. But what was previously unknown is that yours or anyone else's magic will be rendered useless against them."

The man wastes no time getting to the point, Sindri thought.

Malakin stared at Dwapek in anticipation of further explanation. Dwapek provided none. "You're going to have to give me more than that, old friend."

Dwapek grunted. "I have said it. The Lugienese mean to conquer you, and as of right now, it is my belief that they will have little difficulty. Your magic will not be effective against theirs."

Malakin shook his head. "I did not ask for you to parrot yourself. *Explain.* How is it that you know this? What makes their magic stronger than ours? Do you blaspheme our gods?"

Dwapek growled, "I saw with my eyes. I stayed behind in Brinkwell to observe the destruction. Not only do they use a castration spell, they perform it en masse. One broad stroke and anyone within their line of sight is castrated in an instant. Cut off from whatever gods with whom they commune."

The man scoffed. "Impossible. Castration is far too complex."

Dwapek responded curtly, "And yet they manage to do it."

"We will simply reverse it," argued Malakin.

Dwapek looked up at the man, a single eyebrow raised in question. "In the middle of a battle embroiled in magic? How many priests are required to perform a single retethering? Five, six? And how much power would be required? Do I really need to explain the flaws of this strategy?"

Malakin narrowed his eyes and growled. "You observed all of this with your own eyes, yet here you stand, alive and well. This also deserves explanation. If you stayed behind, observed the destruction and were stripped of your connection to the gods, how did you manage to escape?"

"My connection was severed, yes. However, I carry with me . . . additional protection."

Sindri's mind wandered to the subject of retethering. She figured it meant reconnecting one with their ability to wield Klerós's power, though it sounded as if the process was the same no matter the god. These people could fix her! Her heart leaped at the thought, then she resumed listening to the exchange between Malakin and Dwapek.

Malakin eyed Dwapek skeptically. "Speak plainly. I grow tired of your vagaries."

Dwapek grunted. "Very well." He hopped down from his chair and began pacing as he spoke. "You remember my departure from Scritler decades ago."

Malakin nodded.

Dwapek continued without looking up, "I did not disclose the reason, and that's going to be very important in the dark days that lie before us.

"You know my story; barely escaping death within my homeland. I did so in large part because of my people's magic, calling upon the power given to the world of the Earth Mother. My people, the Renziks, are considered heretics by Scritlandian standards, calling upon powers beyond the pantheon of the Chrologal faith. I, however, do not believe this is actually in conflict with the Chrologal faith."

Dwapek took a bite of his biscuit. "Mmm, you folks sure know your pastries." He took a few more chews then continued with his mouth only partially filled with food. "You trained me to summon the powers of the Chrologal faith. For that I am grateful. I excelled quickly because I already had a foundation in channeling magic. But what I never told you, and what I must tell you now, is that my mastery of the *other* magic, that which I had used nearly since birth, never ceased."

This caused a visible stiffening of Malakin's shoulders, and Sindri thought for a moment that she would witness a duel between the two.

Dwapek stopped pacing right in front of the still-seated Malakin. "I know this story reeks of betrayal the way a drunkard reeks of booze. But there's a truth that supersedes all of this."

Malakin's lips were quivering, but he nodded begrudgingly for Dwapek to continue.

"While training here, I asked questions about the nature of the magic used by my kin to the north. I found the answers to be . . . insufficient. I continued my search for such information in secret. And in my search, I happened upon one source of particular curiosity. This, after being accepted into the monastery here in Scritler. It was this last discovery that caused me to leave for Brinkwell. And while I'm loath to admit it, I later lost interest because this source alone was insufficient."

Malakin exhaled heavily. "On with it. I have limits to how long I can suffer to hear this blasphemy."

Dwapek resumed pacing. "Ruka had just returned from the travels that granted her such local notoriety and allowed her to establish a powerful network within the city's underbelly. I encountered her through another source who said she had quite an obscure set of documents, the nature of which went beyond the censorship of the Scritlandian library."

"You mean heresies," growled Malakin.

Dwapek shrugged. "Perhaps. But one in particular caught my attention. I paid two months' salary just to have a look at it. It was said to be a direct, unadulterated copy of the writings of Theopoles the Thorn, Diorne's first apprentice."

Malakin's eyes became narrow slits.

Dwapek continued before Malakin had a chance to interrupt. "Yes, I know Theopoles was burned at the stake for betraying the faith and set up as a warning against false prophets, but his theories, all of which have been erased from the records, well . . . I believe them to be true."

Dwapek held up a hand to silence Malakin's open mouth, a comical scene considering the drastic difference in stature and position.

"He theorized there are actually three streams of magic. One from the gods of light, one from the gods of darkness, and one separate source derived from the energy from the world of Doréa itself outside of the realm of good and evil. His writings allege that even Diorne knew of this, only he worried about the logistical difficulty in monitoring such magic."

"Lies!" Malakin stood to tower over Dwapek. "How dare you come here asking for *my* help all while blaspheming my own patron god, blaspheming the faith itself!"

Sindri felt the warning of magic in the amulet that had been returned to her—it flared. The sister amulets worn by Dwapek and the others all glowed blue, and Sindri knew Malakin was preparing an attack. She glanced at Arella, who sat poised to defend, while Draílock appeared disturbingly unconcerned.

Dwapek's voice shifted to become one of authority, cutting right through Malakin's own. "You *will* hear me, friend. Do you think I am here as a favor to myself? I am here to help *you*, your people, and perhaps the entire eastern world. Now sit down and listen to what I have to say. *All* of it."

Sindri saw blood lust in Malakin's eyes. She tried to imagine someone speaking to Malakin's equivalent within the Lugienese Empire, former High Priest Grobennar or his like, in such a manner. It was too ridiculous to even consider.

But the man returned to his seat, eyes ablaze.

"As I said," Dwapek continued, "Theopoles claims that Diorne knew of this other magic but did not trust the people with this knowledge. He believed it would be too difficult to discern the difference between heresy and the benign uses of what I have come to call physical or ateré magic. It was this matter that caused the rift that resulted in Theopoles's demise, though of course this truth could not be allowed to survive."

Dwapek gestured with a hand. "I had Draílock and his apprentice, Arella, steal this work from Ruka before we fled to Brinkwell to continue developing my command of this magic, and my study of it." His tone became gentle as he pulled out a stack of parchments. "Malakin, please, review these writings for yourself. They are authentic.

"And whether you believe me or not, I can assure you, the Lugienese are coming and they will castrate and kill all who stand against them. But they, like you, appear oblivious to the power of ateré magic. If you stand against them with only those powers granted by the gods of the Chrologal faith, Scritland will fall."

"And just how do you know this with such certainty?"

Dwapek stopped pacing and stared right at Malakin. "I told you. I stayed behind to observe the Lugienese in Brinkwell. The few priests of the Chrologal faith that remained in the city were separated from their gods in an instant, then slaughtered like the rest of the commoners who remained. I risked my life to observe the severity of the threat they might pose to the rest of the world. Were it not for ateré magic, I would not be here at all."

Malakin scoffed, "Your heresy, you mean."

Dwapek eyed him. "Do you truly believe that?"

"More than I believe the words of a convicted heretic written on parchment taken from a scaff like Ruka. How much did you say you paid her just for a glimpse of these scribbles?"

Dwapek's voice lowered and his tone became even more serious. "Malakin, you know me. I am the very same person you trained with all those years ago. I came here to help you save your people. I gain nothing from being here, from telling you this."

"You kept your friends from the gallows."

"I would not have sent them here in the first place if I did not have intentions of coming myself to tell you of the imminent danger. Malakin, this is a matter of importance that cannot be ignored."

Malakin shouted, "You're right about that, old friend!"

Sindri's heart hit the floor. They were going to go right back to the city square to hang. Her nerves itched at the danger. Her momentary hope of being retethered by these priests also disappeared.

"Guards!" yelled the High Priest. Several materialized at his word.

He pointed at Dwapek. "You and your compatriots are henceforth and forever banned from the city of Scritler. The next time I see you or anyone with whom you claim association, you will beg to recant your sins, for you will all face the final punishment."

Dwapek appeared unaware of the gravity of the situation. "Oh, I think it will be much the contrary, *friend*. I'm just sorry that you are unable to hear the truth and wisdom of my warning. I pray you live long enough to—"

"Not another word. Not a single word!" The High Priest loomed over Dwapek. Sindri suspected that if Dwapek ignored this warning, there would be no trial. It would be death here and now for all of them.

The amulets worn by Draílock, Arella, and Dwapek all glowed brightly as the High Priest readied his attack. *Oh no, please no,* Sindri thought.

Malakin finally said, "Guards, escort them to the fortress gate."

Dwapek huffed but said nothing further as rough hands directed them down the spiral stairs of the turret, their gems glowing all the while.

Draílock was the first to break the silence many heartbeats later as they were making their way out of the palace grounds. "Your tact was slightly off today."

"Silence!" One of the soldiers swung a heavy hand to clap the back of Draílock's head but nearly toppled over as he hit only air.

Draílock had bent over to adjust the tie on his sandal at the very moment the man swung. It could not have been a coincidence, and yet, how Draílock knew to dodge the hand from behind him was beyond Sindri. Maybe he heard a shift of the man's feet? She shook her head as the guard dusted off the hands he had used to catch himself.

He turned, ready to launch an attack, but another guard wearing a blue sash of command held up a hand. "We lead them to the gate. Nothing more."

The angry guard growled, "They were told to remain silent or face judgment. *He* opened his mouth!"

The guard who had just saved their lives shook his head and motioned for those at the gate to open the portcullis. Then instead of looking at his own men, he looked directly at Dwapek as he said loudly,

"Should we see any of you in this city after sundown today, there will be nothing anyone can do to save you. Nothing."

Sindri felt arrows of scorn piercing her back as she and the rest began their march through the gate. Thankfully, the guards did not follow them out of the palace.

Arella was the first to speak. "Thanks for saving us. Eh, what's the plan now?"

"You three will continue to search for the boy," answered Dwapek. "He may be more important now than ever."

"And you will be doing what, exactly, while we do this?" asked Draílock.

"I have matters elsewhere to attend to, although these may not be enough to make a difference now. Scritland and the Kingdom will be overrun as soon as the Lugienese realize just how weak and divided they truly are. You do have a lead on the boy's whereabouts, do you not?"

Draílock nodded. "We will find another caravan headed west to Alder, then continue south along the tail of the Dragon Spine Mountains through Nodersos until we reach Orrin. We'll head east from there to Anakolpos to procure a seafaring vessel to get us the rest of the way."

Dwapek nodded and said, "Good," as if he expected nothing else.

Sindri found it aggravating the way both of them always acted like whatever happened was precisely what they predicted. Arella was little different, but something about her delivery generally made her words more palatable. *May I never end up like them,* thought Sindri as she followed the retinue of outlaws from yet another city to which she could never return.

CHAPTER 18

KYLLEAN

KYLLEAN'S FATHER FOUND HIM SITTING on a stone bench outside of the cramped rooms occupied by the trainees. He was dabbing his sweaty forehead with a cloth.

"How you holding up, son?"

Kyllean looked up and did his best to appear in good spirits, concealing the cloth in his hand.

"Fine. Very well. Looking forward to getting into the good stuff, like using one of those black blades and being chosen by a Lumále."

"What about the withdrawals?"

Kyllean looked from side to side as if he had just been caught with his hand in the honeycomb, then decided it wasn't worth the bother to try concealing it. He shrugged and lied, "Not that bad."

"Then you're a stronger lad than I. I remember the fevers, shaking, headaches, and nausea."

Kyllean scoffed, "I can hardly imagine you deep in the cups, though I'm sure it would be a sight."

Kelson replied, "There was once a time when I was much like yourself, perhaps worse. But that's a tale for another time."

Kyllean did his best to grin through clenched teeth. "Well, I'm doing just fine here."

"Ah, well, I'm glad to hear it. Perhaps you can share this with a friend who might be feeling the effects of withdrawal more strongly."

His father pulled out a thin package wrapped in large green leaves. He peeled back one of the leaves to reveal a collection of purple flowers. "I went to the trouble of gathering some of these. They certainly helped me through the worst of my symptoms. Just steep two or three petals in hot water, add some honey for flavor if you like, and you, or whoever is using them, will be quickly relieved of symptoms."

Kyllean accepted the package from his father's outstretched hands.

"It's called passionflower," Kelson said. "It grows further up the mountainside. It seems someone else had this problem at some point and thought others might, too. There's an entire field of the things growing a short walk from here if . . . anyone you know needs more."

Kyllean coughed to conceal his surprise. "Well, that's a—right nice of you. I'll be sure to keep an eye out for anyone who might need some."

"Glad to help," said his father, before turning to leave.

"Hey."

Kelson stopped and faced him. "Yes, Kyllean?"

"How do you go about life never telling even your own family about what you really do?"

He gave Kyllean a puzzled look. "I'm a rider. This is no secret."

"How about the fact that you're a mage and, by all accounts, healer or herbalist? I know virtually nothing about you and I'm your own son, allegedly."

Kelson attempted a smile, but it was strained. "You are. Don't you ever question that. As for the rest, I take my oaths very seriously, as do we all. I knew the cost. And I find that the higher the cost, the more worthy of making the payments. I know my secrets keep my family's future secure. You'll understand soon enough."

He left without another word.

Kyllean took several minutes to digest his father's words. Then he vomited much of his dinner and decided it might be a good idea to get something warm to drink. *Be a shame to waste the gift.* Tea didn't have to be limited to old women knitting quilts. Plenty of young, strapping lads drank the stuff . . . after being cut open by sharp metal on the battlefield and fed by a healer against their will. He shook his head. He didn't care.

An hour later, he sank into his stiff, uncomfortable bed in the common room he shared with several others and fell fast asleep wondering why people didn't drink this tea all the time. Compared to what he had been feeling earlier, he now felt . . . much less terrible.

The other initiates looked about the room, anticipation written on their faces as they sipped and waited for the effects of this *other* tea to manifest. This tea would help them sense her magic.

Master Hilde drew a blacker-than-night blade from the sheath at her side and began a series of movements. She flowed gracefully along the sword dance Kyllean knew as the jaguar, then transitioned into leaves upon the wind, followed by fire smoke. It was poetry with a sword. Then she stopped and looked out at the expectant gathering of young men and women and said, "Did any of you feel the magic?"

Kyllean had felt nothing. He felt better as he looked about the room and saw only two hesitant hands rise.

Master Hilde narrowed her eyes and glared back and forth between the two. "Now that *is* interesting, considering I wasn't using any, and the tea takes at least another dozen minutes to begin its work."

The young man and woman who had raised their hands sank deep into their seats, and Master Hilde returned her attention to the class as a whole. "Don't be so eager to impress that you make liars and fools of yourselves. It won't help you progress, not here.

"Let me begin by telling you a little more about what you're going to feel. First, I'm not going to begin using magic. Nor will you. In a few minutes you're going to feel the energy that exists all around you." Pulling out a small sphere of sapphire stone, she held it up and continued, "For instance, you'll soon be able to detect the static potential that exists within this stone, within which is a great deal." Then she walked away from the outdoor platform beside the initiates' sparring field and plucked a blade of grass. "You will similarly be able to detect the energy in something as insignificant as this living object." She bent over again and scooped up a handful of dry soil and repeated the sentiment.

"Everything in the world is made up of this energy; it cannot be increased or destroyed, only temporarily borrowed." Then she held up both hands in warning. "But before you go stumbling around blindly to play with the powers of the elements, you will need to be made aware of how to summon them, how much is safe to wield, and, of course, how it is we, the Tal-Don riders, use this magic to do what we do. Attempting anything beyond what is assigned to you under my supervision could result in the injury or death of you or those around you. Does everyone understand what I'm saying?"

Several initiates mumbled their understanding.

"Do you understand me?" she shouted.

"Yes, master," shouted the initiates in unison.

"Good." She softened her voice. "We Tal-Don riders are not wizards, sorcerers, or mages. So what are we, if not any of those things?" She raised both hands in question, palms facing the sun.

One sheepish hand went up a few seats ahead of Kyllean, who slouched in the back.

"Yes, Jenkins?"

"Riders?"

Master Hilde considered for a moment, then nodded. "A clever response. We are that, yes. But what does it mean?" Before anyone had a chance to answer, she continued, "When you get to the crux of it, we are all *warriors.*"

Master Hilde continued to elaborate, but Kyllean was drawn away from her words by a tingling sensation deep within his mind; a recognition of power around him. It was like swimming in warm water and suddenly crossing a pocket that is cooler than the rest, only this was no passing feeling; it was like descending into a new pool altogether. Judging by the sudden expression or position changes in the others in attendance, he guessed he was not the only one distracted by the sensation.

Kyllean extended his arms and combed through the invisible energy with his hands. "Whoa," he whispered.

"Well, then, I see that many of you are now beginning to feel the surrounding energies. Let's talk about what is to be done with all of this potential power, as well as what is *not* to be done with it."

CHAPTER 19

AYNWARD

AYNWARD LAY ON A BED of straw, his left wrist shackled, a length of chain running to an iron ring in the stone wall. *At least I have use of my arms this time,* he thought as he recalled his imprisonment on board the *Royal Viscera,* wrapped up like a cocoon. Or even his time in the prison at the university in Brinkwell, wrists chained painfully overhead. He sat up and nodded to himself; *A relative paradise, all things considered. I've even got a window.*

Apparently Kyllean's borderline-deranged optimism had left a lasting mark. Aynward cursed the lackadaisical swordsman. And yet he cracked a smile as he imagined himself telling Kyllean to shut up so he could think.

With the imaginary Kyllean silenced for the time being, Aynward did his best to clear his head of the deep ache of betrayal. Not just the betrayal from his own brother, but the inevitability that everyone he cared about would believe he actually murdered his own father. He could hardly blame them, but it hurt. A lot. The only way to free himself of this feeling was to discover a way to prove himself innocent. Toward that end, he needed a clear head to think.

Someone had wished to see his father dead, as well as ensuring Aynward took the fall for the crime. But why? And how could he prove his innocence before his brother, Perja, condemned him to death on the wheel or some other ghastly end? He laughed to himself, a laugh of insanity. *They found my sword with Father's blood on it, and no assassin, none besides me. I have no defense.*

Then he heard the jangle of keys. It was too soon to be his next meal. A visitor, then. Aynward felt his face redden, probably Perja. He heard the creak of iron as the door to the dungeon swung open. Then a familiar voice, but not one he expected.

"I will take it from here. Thank you."

The deeper, less nasally voice of the guard said, "I have been given orders not to allow him to be alone with anyone."

There was a long pause, some faint whispering, and then finally the guard responded, "Very well, you have five minutes."

"Thank you."

Sunlight streaked in through the small opening near the ceiling of Aynward's cell to illuminate Gervais's rodent-like face as he stepped into the doorway of the stone tomb. He wore a solemn expression. Considering everything, this was mild.

Aynward said, "Gervais, great to see you again so soon. I must apologize that your tenure as counselor will be so short-lived. On the bright side—bear in mind I can't currently confirm this, as I'm unable to travel to the library of records, but I think there's a chance that you'll find your name forever memorialized within the royal annals."

Gervais remained standing where he was but said nothing.

Aynward gave an awkward laugh. "Very well, I'll just tell you. You're to go down as the record holder for shortest royal career in Kingdom history."

Gervais's flat stare indicated that he was not amused. Aynward's attempt at finding the golden coin in the chamber pot that was their collective situation was, indeed, quite lacking. *He probably thinks I really did it and knows he'll be relieved from the palace altogether by mere association.*

"If it makes you feel any better, I didn't actually do it."

Gervais nodded and finally replied. "Of course, Your Grace." Gervais's tone suggested he was merely humoring Aynward's plea of innocence. He continued, "Yet the evidence against you is unfavorable."

"That's an understatement," mumbled Aynward.

Gervais nodded. "Indeed."

"So, why are you here?"

Gervais smiled. "To save your life."

Aynward did not expect this answer, and his face must have said as much.

"Aynward, your brother, the soon-to-be King, will torture and execute you for this crime. While he benefits from your father's untimely death, it would be imprudent to do anything less to the person responsible for the murder of a King. I have brokered an opportunity for you to escape death, and your brother has agreed to the wisdom of this compromise . . ."

Aynward could not believe what he was hearing. *Compromise. Probably will have to go without hands for the rest of my life.*

Gervais continued, "You will be allowed to live out your days with all of your needs provided for. As far as the residents of the Kingdom will be concerned, you will remain a permanent resident of the palace dungeon. However, your brother is willing to compromise with closely guarded house arrest at the edges of the Kingdom. You will not be allowed to leave the premises of course, ever."

This can't be true. What's the catch? There must be a catch.

"All you have to do is admit your guilt, publicly."

And there it is.

Aynward was silent for a time. The idea of admitting to regicide, and—worse yet— patricide, when he had done no such heinous act, galled him. How could he do so? And yet, if he was to be condemned either way, wouldn't it be better to admit guilt to save his own life?

Gervais said, "I know this decision is no easy thing, but I would urge haste. Your brother will be visiting as soon as he is crowned. The ceremony is scheduled to commence in three days' time, and he expects an answer before then. Should you refuse this offer, he will obtain your confession through *other,* less palatable means. Should it come to that, the offer of life, albeit life in isolation, will also be forfeit."

What is my honor worth? After what happened to Dolme, do I have any honor to begin with? "I will think on it."

Gervais bowed slightly. "Please do, Your Grace."

His new counselor turned to leave but Aynward stopped him. "Gervais?"

He swiveled on his heel. "Yes?"

"Thank you."

Gervais gave a sad smile then bowed. "Of course, Your Grace."

Aynward was left alone with his thoughts. He imagined the mass of stone above him and thought how much heavier his choices weighed upon him. If only there were someone standing sentinel over the heavens, for it seemed someone had committed an even worse crime than regicide, for the goddess of luck, Kitay, was clearly dead.

CHAPTER 20

DAGMARA

DAGMARA STOOD GLARING AT THE guard as she watched her purse empty into his outstretched hand.

"I will remember your face."

He swallowed hard, but his hand remained where it was until the last of her coins clinked. He opened the door without another word, and she continued her glower until her eyes were needed to guide her through the opening. *Greedy scum.*

She rounded the corridor to Aynward's cell and saw him seated upright in the corner, head resting between the two stone walls. His eyes met hers and he feigned alacrity. He couldn't possibly be anything but terrified.

"Sister, so nice of you to visit." Nodding toward the chamber pot, he said, "My apologies for the smell. The food here does not agree with me."

She stomped her way over, anger rising at his levity in the midst of his circumstances. He didn't move as she approached, and before she knew what she was doing, her open hand had crashed down upon her brother's face. She had expected him to defend himself, but he didn't. Her surprise caused her to lighten the blow at the last second, but the sound still echoed throughout the cell.

Aynward appeared unfazed. He continued smugly, "Said I was sorry. Blame the cook staff for serving red meat. I've been dieting on fish this past year."

This time she didn't hold back as she smacked him across the face. His head bounced off the wall, and for a moment, she thought she had knocked him unconscious. Then he lifted his head, temple bleeding where it had struck the rough stone. He smiled, but the mirth was gone. *Good.*

"Did you do it?" she demanded.

He chuckled to himself. "Do you seriously have to ask that question?"

She nearly struck him again but held herself in check. "Well? Did you?" Her voice cracked as anger mixed with the underlying emotions of helplessness and sorrow.

He looked up but didn't say anything. Finally, he whispered, "The assassin was there, waiting. And he had my sword." He continued speaking through clenched teeth, "He stabbed Father with *my* sword. I tried to stop him, but—"

A tear ran down his cheek. "I couldn't."

Dagmara had always been able to sniff out Aynward's lies, at least when directed toward her. She sensed only sincerity here and a wave of relief washed over her. *He's innocent. Thank the gods!* This relief, however, was short-lived, swallowed by other doubts. It made no sense.

"Why frame you?" Dagmara whispered. "Why not simply assassinate the King in the night and be done with it? The risk of being captured was surely greater with a witness to the crime. What if you had been carrying a knife and managed to injure or kill the assassin?"

Aynward shook his head. "I don't understand it myself. Perja has the most to gain as heir, but why he would include me in this, I just don't know. He has long disapproved of my antics, but to frame and execute his own brother? That seems too extreme, even for him."

Dagmara's anger toward Aynward dissolved. She . . . believed him. The loss of her father still stung but knowing that Aynward hadn't betrayed their family took the lion's share of the weight of her grief away. She had been so thrilled to hear of his safe escape from Brinkwell and his return home. To have that taken away in such a manner would have torn her heart asunder. The drive to substantiate his innocence reenergized her.

"Aynward, if it wasn't you, there has to be a way to prove it."

Aynward shook his head. But Dagmara would not be so easily cowed.

"*Someone* else had to have seen the assassin flee the palace grounds."

Aynward looked up, doubt written in his expression. "If someone did, they were likely paid very well to *un-see* it. Dagmara, if this was Perja, there is nothing to be done about it. He's going to be crowned in three days and already has access to all the resources of a king." He held up a hand to silence her response. "Dagmara, all is not lost. He offered to spare my life if I admit guilt. I'll be sent to the edges of the Kingdom to live out my days under guard, alive and well taken care of."

Her eyes bulged. "You're not going to do it, are you? Admit to killing your own father?"

She saw self-loathing in his eyes, but also a shred of determination, of stubbornness. "What choice do I have? It's that or the inquisition. I have no illusions about my ability to maintain the truth of my innocence in the face of one of those monsters' knives. I'll tell them whatever they ask of me if it will mean an end to the torture; of this I have no doubt."

Dagmara wanted to argue with him. The thought of an innocent Aynward admitting to such a heinous crime for no other reason than physical coercion was sickening. It would be wrong in every way imaginable. She wanted to demand he never give in to such wrongness. To not make Perja's obvious scheme roll out so flawlessly. But when she imagined Aynward under the knife, screaming for mercy, and finally breaking under the torturous pain, the result was much the same. Aynward had always been the pragmatic one, while Dagmara remained the idealistic voice of virtue. This time such ideals would be like vapor in the wind.

"I understand," Dagmara finally managed. "But I have to try. There may yet be a way to prove your innocence."

Aynward smiled, but his expression shifted to one of worry. "Dagmara, if this was Perja, and you get in his way, he'll go after you, too. Don't martyr yourself for my sake. You're going to be a Scritlandian Queen in just a few weeks. Don't jeopardize that."

"Perja wouldn't dare place that alliance at risk. Not with the Lugienese acting as they are. He needs Scritland."

Aynward considered this for a while then conceded, "I know I won't be able to dissuade you from your course. Just be careful. If Perja has to choose between his throne and an alliance with Scritland, he'll choose the throne, and your fate might be worse than mine."

"I'll be careful," she assured him. "But I must go if I'm to find anything useful before Perja seeks your confession. I'll try to visit once more before that time."

Ignoring the smell, she knelt down and gave Aynward a hug. "Hang in there, brother."

He attempted a laugh, but it lacked conviction as he said, "This isn't much different than my room on the ship from Tung, minus the chains, of course. I think I can handle a few more days."

Dagmara departed. She was not nearly as confident as she let on about her chances of uncovering anything of value. Perja was not one to miss details. He would have considered every angle and in a similar manner, he'd conceal them with finesse. And yet, where one finds arrogance, one also finds mistakes. Perja was certainly guilty of the former so perhaps—

"Your Grace?" said the guard she had bribed minutes earlier.

"Yes?"

"I was told to give you this message after your visit with the prisoner." Her blood went cold. She had not told anyone she was coming and was certain she had not been followed. She extended a shaky hand to take the note, then opened the small, folded parchment. A tingling sensation tightened her chest as she read; it was a summons from her brother, Perja.

He was playing with her, while also demonstrating he was already steps ahead of her, and therefore unconcerned that she might uncover anything in speaking with her brother, who would surely deny his guilt. Perja must have also known she would be powerless to help him.

Dagmara's hands trembled with the strain of keeping her fear in check, but she refused to give in to such weakness. Instead, she forced her hands into fists, crumpling the note in the process. Then she resumed her departure from the palace dungeons, thanking the god of creation for the gift of anger, for without it, she would have been unable to overcome the immobilizing effects of dread. She let her anger feed into a sense of rebellion, of confidence, even if that confidence was sorely lacking.

Perja wants to play games with me? I'll play. But he's not going to be the only one making the rules. Dagmara allowed her newfound determination to take the reins as she made her way to see the heir to the throne, the traitor, Perja.

CHAPTER 21

DAGMARA

DAGMARA GLARED AT THE SOON-TO-BE King. Perja had mastered their father's imposing, stone-faced expression of stately indifference. This was the same countenance their father had maintained while holding court, listening to the petitions of farmers and statesmen alike. Dagmara was not here on some petty business; she was his sister, and *he* had summoned *her*.

There was also something in his expression that she had never seen in her father. It was nearly imperceptible, a mere hint, but it was there, a glimmer of *something*, and it was not good. She saw it in his eyes, a sinister bearing, a conniving hidden by the rest of his face, a mask, and his true self had slid beneath the person who sat before her.

The mask finally moved, producing sound, and Dagmara returned from her musings.

"I knew you'd wish to speak of our brother, but this is not why I have summoned you. We have other, more pressing matters."

"More pressing than our brother—" She stopped herself short of pleading his innocence. If Perja was indeed responsible, it would be better that she not let on that she believed this to be the case. "—our brother's incarceration for the murder of our father?"

Perja's expression did not shift in the slightest. "Our brother's fate is sealed one way or the other. No, this meeting is informative in nature, but it pertains to you and your duty to this Kingdom."

Dagmara's brow furrowed in confusion.

Perja continued, "You will not marry Prince Aldrik. Not unless they change their stance regarding the Lugienese Empire."

Dagmara should have been relieved to hear this. She had not chosen the engagement, and certainly did not look forward to becoming the property of a foreigner four years her junior whom she had only met a handful of times. Yet her stomach twisted in a knot because she knew that Perja would now be in control of the replacement engagement. She was of an age where this would need to be done in short order, lest she outgrow desirability. He would select another suitable match soon, one of equal advantage in the changing political landscape.

Perja continued, "The Lugienese attack of the Isles has produced some *difficulty* in our relationship with Scritland. They press for war before a Lugienese invasion of the east. I wish to avoid an invasion altogether."

Dagmara felt her heart drop into her already twisted stomach. The implication did not need to be further elaborated. He planned to sue for peace, or an alliance through marriage, and he would sacrifice her toward this end. The idea of being offered up as a sacrifice to the Lugienese Empire terrified her. It suddenly made her former engagement seem a match ordained by the heavens themselves. Her ability to control her emotions withered like an early-morning fog.

She stood abruptly and yelled, "No!" She pointed an accusatory finger. "I am not chattel to be sent to the slaughter!"

Perja's expression showed no signs of anger or concern but his powerful voice echoed through the room. "Sit. Down."

His voice was so imposing that she obeyed as a reflex. And he lectured her like an insolent child. "You are not chattel, true. You are much more than that; you are a princess. And as such, you have a responsibility to serve the Kingdom. You were to be married on Father's command to strengthen our alliance with Scritland. I'm simply reassigning you to someone who will better suit our needs at this time. You only get one marriage and we need to consider how best to utilize it." His voice became uncharacteristically soft. "Mara, your sacrifice will save thousands. Are you truly so selfish that you would condemn so many to die in a war for the sake of, what, better dinner conversation?"

She stood, emotions having been stretched in several directions all at once. Shaking her head, she said with teary eyes, "This is different from what Father arranged for me and you know it. I am not for sale. I am not a commodity. You're the King. Figure out another way to deal with the Lugienese. I won't do it."

Perja tapped his fingers on the desk, still unconcerned. "We'll certainly have to do something about this spirit of rebellion; they prefer their women far more subservient. But we have some time to tame the worst of you before I'm forced to send you into service. We'll begin by finding you a more suitable counselor."

Dagmara had turned away, heading for the door, but stopped and spun to regard her brother, anger flaring at his last remarks. "My sacrifice would be in vain, *brother*. You're too much of a fool to do anything but run this Kingdom into the ground. If you truly cared about this Kingdom, you'd abdicate."

She turned to leave, concealing a smile of satisfaction at the expression she saw on her brother's face, that of rage. Considering what she was planning, this was perhaps not the best tone to have taken with him. Her small victory in finally rousing his emotions could result in greater catastrophe later, but she had already determined to forego good sense. If she were going to sacrifice herself for anyone, it would certainly not be Perja. She just had to figure out how to see to her plans before Perja locked her away like Aynward. She needed to see counselor Brenna. She would know what to do. Perhaps Brenna could even help her do it.

CHAPTER 22

KIBURE

OLD CRONE, AYE?"

Kibure swallowed hard. That part of his thought wasn't supposed to reach her. He really needed to get better at controlling his thoughts while in the realm of dreams. He had felt comfortable with the concept by the end of his last visit, but he needed more practice. "*I . . . I didn't mean—*"

"*Save it for someone who cares. Aye, it's an apt description, anyhow. And your mental slip is a good lesson to be learned. One must be precise and intentional with their thoughts if opening up for mental communication with others. And mastering this has its advantages in the physical realm, as well. The more time you spend in the spiritual realm, the more measured your words elsewhere. Thinking carefully before speaking is a skill many would do well to learn.*"

Shifting topics, she asked, "*So, did you manage to get yourself out of this cave before being returned to the physical realm or did you spend the rest of your time under the power of the tea sulking in one spot?*"

He focused his energy on not sharing his thoughts this time. *Stay calm. She is trying to agitate.* Kibure then projected, "*I spent some time walking the city.*"

"*Good. So you're not completely useless. Now conjure a weapon. You and I are going to do a little sparring.*"

Kibure stared at her as if . . . as if . . . well . . . as if she was the oldest human alive and wanted him to fight her.

"*If you're worried about hurting me, think again. You won't, not in this place. You had best just worry about yourself.*" She smiled. "*My spiritual body may resemble my physical body, but it does not hold to the same physical limitations.*" She crouched down and then jumped as high as the cave ceiling would allow, bringing her knees to her chest while in the air before landing dexterously in a fighter's stance. A sword had at some point materialized in one hand.

"*Meet me at the amphitheater.*" And then she disappeared.

It required less thought for Kibure to transport his spirit out of the cave but willing a sword into being proved a fair work of concentration. He squeezed his eyes shut and willed a blade into existence.

Drymus stood, relaxed, in front of him in the open space of the stage. She had turned her steel weapon into a wooden practice sword. He asked, "*Should I also be using wood?*"

She smiled wryly. "*That will not be necessary.*"

A question that Kibure had been wondering since the first time he was attacked by Magog in the spiritual realm returned to the forefront. "*Can one be killed while in this place?*"

She chuckled. "*You really needn't worry over that just yet, but it's a good question. The answer is yes, your spirit can be slain while here. And if that happens here, the body in the physical realm also perishes for there is no longer a spirit to return to the body. But as I said, you need not worry over this right now. No one's spirit is to be slain today.*" She angled her sword toward him and bent her knees. "*Your lesson will not be without pain, however. Are you ready?*"

Not really, he thought. He took up a stance, though in truth, he had no idea what he was doing and had no business holding a sword, imaginary or not. "*I . . . suppose so.*"

"*Good, now defend yourself.*"

She completed a half pirouette and suddenly Kibure's hand shook and his sword winked out of existence. Her wooden blade was at his throat.

He relaxed, embarrassed at how quickly he had lost his steel weapon to a wooden one, illusory or not. Then pain exploded in his chest and he flew through the air to land in a heap several paces away. He looked up to see Drymus's foot still extended after executing a spinning kick.

"*Ow! What was that for?*"

"*That,*" she resumed a relaxed posture, "*was for the old crone remark. And to remind you that in this place, a summoned object is only as strong as the strength of will used to create and sustain it. Just as in the physical realm, a spell is only as strong as the amount of summoned energy imbued within it. But worry not, the skills acquired in this place will translate to the physical realm, much like our words here do.*"

He had wondered about that. The language barrier and accents seemed not to disappear while in this place. Ideas moved flawlessly from one mind to the other.

Kibure coughed, which was strange in the way it made no sound, yet still had the satisfying effect of clearing the throat he would not actually use to speak. "*I see.*"

"*Do you? Let's try this again and see if that's true.*"

This time she summoned a thin stick that looked more the part of a whip than a sword. And yet when she struck his conjured sword with it, the effect was much the same. And this time she struck each of his arms with her weapon.

"*Yeow!*"

"*Put some effort into your weapon and maybe my little twig won't be able to cause you so much pain.*" She moved her hands in a circular motion. "*Again.*"

This was repeated more than a dozen times before he was able to put enough will into his sword to withstand the attacks. Finally she struck several times without his weapon faltering. *Hah, take that!* He didn't dare share such a thought, but he may as well have.

Drymus shifted tactics and instead of aiming for a blunt attack on his weapon, she began a fluid choreographed dance, while his own reactions were awkward and delayed. Several bursts of pain emerged amid such motions as the thin stick struck him again and again without warning. Before he realized what had happened, his sword was gone and several more shots of pain blossomed.

He had assumed a crouch after losing his weapon, opting to cover his face and neck with his arms and hands as best he could.

"You have to be able to maintain your focus, no matter the external stimuli. There is a strong connection to the training of the body in the martial arts, and the training of the mind in the magical arts."

She positioned her feet far apart and seemed to almost sit in the air. *"Now that you're alert, let's begin your training in full. I want you to mimic my position and motions. I'm going to take you through a series of movements that you are to practice daily. This will develop your footwork, as well as the body-to-mind connection which will improve your magical potential."*

Kibure did so grudgingly. To his surprise, however, by the end, he did feel much of his frustration disappear. He couldn't explain how or why that happened, but it did. He also experienced no muscle fatigue, which he had expected would happen during such difficult poses and motions. By the end, Drymus had him moving and swinging his summoned weapon, cutting at imaginary enemies, and his body performed twists and turns that were less and less unnatural the more times they were repeated.

After a complicated sequence of movements, Drymus stood up straight and announced, *"That is enough for today. Continue to practice these forms, as well as summoning objects to test the strength of your will upon them."*

Then, as if the idea had just occurred to her, she walked over to an object toward the back of the floor area of the amphitheater. He hadn't noticed it before. She placed a gentle hand upon an egg-shaped object the size of a human head that rested atop a pedestal. *"This is called the 'seed.' It is a relic of great importance to our people. It is also, very, very dense. To provide you with some incentive to improve your will, I will make a deal with you. If you are able to sink a summoned sword into this object, I will allow you to begin your training in the physical realm, with real magic.*

And once you're able to demonstrate competence with that, you'll be allowed to leave this cave for good."

Kibure's eyes widened in excitement and he nodded his understanding. She had his full attention now, and for each and every lesson moving forward until he was freed from the claustrophobic cave. *She should have led with that.*

Drymus disappeared, leaving Kibure alone with his thoughts about failure.

Before calling another sword into existence, Kibure walked over to examine the "seed." The pedestal upon which it rested was as thick as a human body, made up of multiple strands twining upward together like a tree, and that is precisely what it looked like. The base actually shared a shocking resemblance to a drogal tree. However, unlike the drogal tree, which extended several branches, each holding an array of low-hanging fruit, this stone carving of a tree presented only one piece of fruit, the "seed." Kibure reached out and touched it, feeling an irregular texture he realized, upon closer inspection, was actually symbols. If it was writing, it was no writing he had ever seen. Then again, his knowledge of such things may as well have been nonexistent. He did recognize one unmissable symbol, as it was carved into the top of the seed, larger than the others. It was a ship with three sails, and something smaller written on it that he could not read.

"*Beautiful, isn't it?*" The voice in his head startled him and he felt the chills of surprise as he turned to see Arabelle.

Recovering his wits, Kibure said, "*I suppose.*"

"*It's more beautiful in the physical realm, with sound and color. You'll see as soon as you're allowed to leave the cave.*"

Kibure sent the mental equivalent of a laugh, or tried to, anyhow. He followed it up with, "*I worry I'll be an old man by then.*"

She started to circle him. "*Oh, I don't think that's true. You're already able to travel at will within the spiritual realm, and able to summon objects of your choosing. These are both skills worthy of promotion from status of novice to apprentice.*"

She summoned an object as she turned and started circling the other way in front of him. "*One of your greatest deficits, as I see it, is your mastery of the body, which I'm sure Drymus has mentioned. This affects the mind's agility with its magic, especially under duress."*

He wondered to himself, *Is she talking about my fighting abilities? Was she—*

"Were you spying on my lesson with Drymus?"

She spun the recently summoned weapon in her hand with the dexterity of someone who could kill with one hand while eating fruit with the other. *"Spying? Me? No. Well, maybe yes. I spend a lot of time in this place. And I do wish to see you advance as quickly as possible. So when I happened upon your training, I decided to watch for a while, that is, until I tired of watching Drymus pummel you."*

Kibure scowled. *"So what's with the weapon? I was just beaten by a woman who is old enough to be . . . Well, I don't even know, but she shouldn't be able to do what she did to someone young like me."*

Arabelle smiled and stepped forward, pointing the sword at him. *"That's precisely it."* Then she flipped the blade in the air and caught the tip between two fingers. *"I figured I might teach you a thing or two about swordsmanship. That is, if you'd like to learn. Besides, checking for fault lines in the barrier becomes quite boring."* She extended the hilt toward him. *"Use this. It will be one less thing to keep your attention. You can work on improving your will later."*

She twirled, then summoned her own sword and swung it in an arc straight toward him, too fast and unpredictable for him to have done anything to stop or avoid it. He flinched as the blade stopped just short of his neck. Backing up a few steps, she said, *"Are you ready?"*

Kibure decided that it would be nice not to be beaten quite so severely by Drymus. Getting on with his real training would be preferable, and if this would help, then so be it. He nodded.

"Good." She assumed a position of preparedness, then said, *"The first thing you need is a better stance."*

CHAPTER 23

SINDRI

DUSK APPROACHED AND CAST STRETCHING shadows upon Sindri, Arella, and Draílock as they sat around a small cook fire beside the first oasis south of the city of Alder. The wood crackled, fresh flames feasting hungrily upon the dry wood they had gathered. The coals needed to cook their food were still a palm in the sun away. Sindri's stomach growled as she looked over the string of meat the caravan leader, Henrik, had haggled as they set up camp.

Draílock drew her away from thoughts of food with his imposing stare.

"What?" she blurted more angrily than intended.

Draílock shook his head as though he were shaking off a haze. "That was quite impressive what you did back there."

Sindri shrugged, unable to think of anything to say.

Arella did not let the topic conclude so easily, though she directed her question at Draílock. "How is it that she managed to break her bonds back in Scritler when neither I nor you were able?"

Sindri had been wondering the same thing but didn't wish to insult or appear a fool.

Draílock remained silent, perhaps considering the question, so Arella added, "Not to insult, Sindri, you've been progressing at a better than average rate with your training, but . . . I would not have expected *you* to be able to do *that*."

Sindri just stared into the flames, still unsure of what to say.

Arella was right, of course. Draílock and Arella were both far greater practitioners of ateré magic and yet they had remained restrained by their bonds.

Draílock finally offered a response. "Magical dexterity and magical strength are not necessarily one and the same."

Arella nodded. "This is true."

Sindri considered this for a moment, thinking back to her time within the Kleról. There had generally been a correlation between the strength of wielders and their level of skill, but as she thought further, she admitted that there were exceptions. One priestess in particular came to mind. Sindri had only known the girl, Tamar, for a few months early in her training, but Sindri recalled the jealousy she felt at how quick of a study Tamar had been in their introduction to basic healing. Yet this had suddenly come to an end when Tamar repeatedly failed to complete some of the more magically taxing spells. Tamar had progressed no further in her training and had been likely relegated to some minor town far from anywhere of significance. Everyone had different physical limits to what their mind could handle, no matter their skill.

The same principle must apply to ateré magic. But did that mean that she had more potential as a wielder than even Draílock or Arella? That seemed impossible. But there was another explanation, which she offered.

"Perhaps it was your belief that the bonds could not be broken that hindered your ability to fully commit to doing so, while my ignorance allowed me to push past the limits of the bonds."

Draílock nodded. "How very philosophical of you, Sindri. And perhaps you are correct."

She repressed the urge to roll her eyes. *Only Draílock can manage to both patronize and praise in the same breath.*

He turned his head to stare at the recently arrived wagon set up three dozen paces away. "I don't like late additions."

Sindri gave him a quizzical look.

Draílock continued, "It leads me to suspect iniquitous activity."

Arella didn't hesitate to roll her eyes. "You do realize that *we* were late additions to this caravan, right?"

Draílock smiled with his eyes but nothing else. "Exactly my point." Then he stood, winked, and disappeared into the chaos of activity beyond their camp.

"I don't think I'll ever get used to that man," said Sindri. "It's a wonder his blood circulates at all, icy as it must be."

Arella nodded slightly but didn't immediately respond. Finally, she said, "He is a good man." Then she pulled a dagger and glared into the flames as she began twirling the steel between fingers. "A good man with impeccable instincts."

Sindri glanced over to the wagon in question, where a woman, a slender man, and a girl perhaps nine years old were sitting around a cook fire in much the same way they were. The family had joined up with their small caravan as they were readying to depart the city of Alder earlier that morning.

Unlike Draílock, however, Arella smiled, and Sindri remembered that this woman had been trained by and worked alongside Draílock for nearly a decade. This suggested no small measure of lunacy in her own right.

Sindri said, "You're both crazy."

Arella's enigmatic grin did nothing to argue the statement.

Draílock returned just in time for dinner, speaking no further of his paranoia, but Sindri thought she had seen an unspoken exchange take place between him and Arella as they ate. Sindri didn't bother asking. She'd learned by now that Draílock would tell her what he wished her to know and nothing more, and Arella was not much better.

Sindri wasn't sure what caused her to wake, but upon hearing nothing, she gripped her blanket and rolled over to go back to sleep. She was beginning to fade again when she heard *something*.

Near to sleep as she was, she hardly registered the faint tearing sound. It was slow, and it came and went with the hush of an intermittent breeze. Sindri opened her eyes but remained still out of instinct. She was beginning to pass the entire thing off as nothing when she noticed the faintest line in the canvas of the wagon a few arm lengths away. She squinted, wondering if she wasn't imagining this, as well. Then she heard the sound again while the line extended further down.

Her body stiffened and her heartbeat went from a trot to a gallop. Someone was cutting their way in.

Silently, Sindri reached to the right to notify the shape in the dark that marked Arella's sleeping form. She placed a hand on Arella and pressed gently so as to not alarm her but something didn't feel right. Pressing harder, she realized that she was touching a pile of straw covered by Arella's blanket. *What*—

Before Sindri had time to puzzle out what was going on, the sensation of magic washed over her, reminding her that she should fill her own reservoir in preparation for whatever lurked outside the wagon. Still silent, she drew upon the stored power of hard wood around her, as well as the straw that lay upon it.

She stared hard at the tear in the canvas and watched it grow once again, preparing to launch an assault. Then she heard the same sound coming from the other side of the wagon and turned to see another growing rip in the canvas. Looking again to the pile of straw that should have been Arella, Sindri crawled over it to where Draílock lay and felt her hand sink into that shape, too. *Where are they? Is this some sort of absurd test?* She wouldn't put it past Draílock to orchestrate something like this in an effort to evaluate Sindri's readiness to defend herself.

The newest line in the canvas parted, and Sindri froze in place as a dark, featureless silhouette was revealed by the light of the moons. The glint of steel did not go unnoticed, nor did it remain stationary.

Sindri's years of combat training took over and her body twisted as it dropped to the wagon floor, her own dagger in one hand, magic ready in the other.

The steel weapon of the intruder careened through the air, alongside a sudden release of magic, not her own. Sindri heard the thud as much as she felt it. She turned to peer at the dagger, which had stuck in the wooden floor of the wagon, close enough that a few strands of her hair pulled as she moved.

Her eyes returned to the opening in the canvas but nothing was there. Something about the way the knife had landed was wrong, too. It had fallen as if thrown upward, a flimsy toss as opposed to having been thrown at her with any force.

Having had all of her attention on this nearest intruder, Sindri had forgotten the rip in the canvas had been started on the other side of the wagon. Just as her eyes shifted to her right to assess the other threat, another expulsion of magic washed over her, this followed by a thud and a moan.

Sindri moved toward the flap in the back of the wagon, quickly undoing the buttons that still held it in place. She slid outside, knife at the ready. Whatever was going on out here, she'd rather see it on her own terms than sit helplessly inside of the dark, covered wagon.

She readied to dart to her right to measure the danger of that most recent commotion but was stopped short by the huddled figure of a child a dozen paces away beside a neighboring wagon. She gripped the knife in her hand in spite of herself as she approached.

The child's shoulders were moving, almost convulsing, crying, she realized. Not wishing to startle, Sindri said softly as she neared, "What's wrong?"

The child looked up from beneath a hood, hair matted to the face by cheeks streaked with tears. *A little girl.*

She whimpered, "They left me back at the wagon. I don't know where they went. I heard something over here. I'm scared. My daddy said the tall man would hurt us. I think Daddy might have come here to stop the bad man."

This poor little girl. Knowing that Draílock and Arella had not been in the wagon at the time, and having felt the release of magic, Sindri suspected this girl's parents were likely now captured or dead. Then again, perhaps this had been the fate of her own companions. Either way, Sindri needed to find out right away, and this little girl should not be present to see the outcome. *What kind of parent brings a child along for a job like this?*

"Come this way. Quickly," whispered Sindri. "I'm going to take you back to your wagon then see if I can find your parents."

The girl sniffled then nodded. "Okay," and she followed close behind.

Thank the heavens, thought Sindri as she led the way.

As they neared the girl's wagon, Sindri turned ever so slightly to her left and spotted the swift movement of shadow cast by the moonlight. She whirled just in time to see a knife racing straight for her chest. Having placed her own weapon back in its hiding place within her robes, she had nothing with which to deflect the attack. Unable to get a hand up in time, she pivoted and turned her body, just barely moving beyond the worst of her attacker's strike. Heat like a burning pan struck her right shoulder and blazing pain followed. The surprise caused her to also lose her grip on the magic she had summoned.

Her assailant retracted the blade just as quickly as she had plunged it into Sindri. Just as shocking as the attack, however, was the fact that it had come from the little girl. Sindri attempted to reach into her robes to take out her own blade but found her right arm wouldn't follow her commands. The little girl wasted no time, shuffling practiced feet in order to launch another attack.

With her arm dangling loosely by her side, Sindri was forced to adjust her stance, leading now with her left foot forward. "What are you doing?" she asked.

The child ignored the question and stabbed forward while Sindri's still functional arm just barely pushed the attack aside. The little girl was far more skilled than any child should be. Spinning with the momentum Sindri had created with her block, the little girl's foot swung around to strike hard at Sindri's knee, buckling her entire leg.

By some miracle, Sindri managed to maintain her upright position, only falling to her throbbing knee. But she was still unable to reach her weapon without stretching all the way across her body to fumble around at the handle with her uninjured arm. *Why did I not leave both daggers strapped in?* Sindri instead attempted to draw upon the energy from her surroundings, but her attacker gave her no respite. Sindri's ability to draw ateré magic was not second nature like her priestly magic had once been and gripping it under duress proved beyond her ability that moment.

Yet she felt this power all around her, the dry, Scritlandian dirt beneath her feet, the wood of the wagon a few paces away, even the weeds that had managed to survive footsteps, wheels, and campfires over years of travel through this barren region. But the energy she felt slipped from her grip like greasy meat as her attacker continued her pursuit.

Sindri reached up to block a straightforward swing then ducked as the girl adjusted toward her face. With her unusable arm and awkward position on one knee, Sindri lost her balance, falling face first onto the dirt. Weaponless, yet unwilling to die, Sindri groped to find a substitute, which proved to be a brittle weed. She rolled to face the threat.

This came not a moment too soon, as the girl came crashing down upon her, blade leading the way. Sindri swung her makeshift weapon of roots and dirt, striking the young assassin squarely in the face, the weed extending half an arm further than the fist the girl had expected. The sudden explosion of organic material in the girl's eyes weakened her thrust, allowing Sindri to roll out of the way. The girl shrieked and clawed at her eyes. But Sindri knew she had only bought herself a few extra heartbeats. She needed a real weapon.

Sindri contorted to reach across her body to the right side where she had her dagger hidden away. Fingers fumbled around, trying to secure the handle well to pull it free. *Come on. Come on. Yes!* Fingertips locked around the bottom of the hilt and yanked, then she spun it to secure an effective grip just in time to deflect an incoming strike. Frustrated, her attacker rolled away, then sprang back and kicked, connecting with the side of Sindri's head. Sindri's vision went black for a heartbeat. Disoriented, she swung her good arm blindly and was surprised when she actually hit something.

"Swine!" screamed the little assassin, as she fell to her knees beside Sindri.

Unfortunately, this didn't stop her from launching another assault. Sindri's side exploded in pain and she felt the warmth of blood pouring from the wound as the girl pulled the blade free. Sindri needed to act quickly or she was finished. This girl was small, very small. Sindri realized that her tactic had been all wrong. Biting her lip and ignoring the pain of her injuries, Sindri prepared a different approach. She just hoped it would work, and that she wasn't too late.

Instead of attempting to block the knife as the girl stabbed down, Sindri dropped her own weapon so she could catch the girl's wrist. Without losing the momentum generated by the girl's motion, Sindri pulled.

Grappling had never been Sindri's strong suit, but her greater size gave her a significant advantage once on the ground, that is, if she could get rid of the girl's knife. Sindri pulled the girl's wrist as she rolled from her back to come up on top. Using her thumb, she pressed into the soft underside of the girl's wrist and the blade fell from her hands. Once on top, Sindri straddled the girl's slender frame, and for the moment kept the squirming figure from wriggling free. Sindri picked up the fallen metal, absorbing the strikes from the child as they came. Sindri knew what she needed to do. She could not detain or subdue this girl, not injured as she was. She needed to kill.

Sindri lifted the blade, prepared to plunge the knife into the neck of the fierce little assassin who couldn't have been any older than Kibure, or her brother. The thought stopped her arm where it was, suspended in the air. *I . . . I can't.*

The little girl's fist struck the gaping wound in Sindri's side and her vision swam. This weakened her position atop her opponent, and she felt a hand down by her leg. Sindri was in too much pain to imagine what the girl might be doing down there. Not until she saw the assassin's secondary blade coming straight for her throat. She had no time to react.

A voice shouted something from behind, but it may as well have been a thousand leagues away. Her vision was fading as the killing blow approached, as if her mind had told her body that this was the end and wished to save her the trouble of watching it unfold.

Then a tingle of magic and a blast of air propelled her body sideways to slam hard into the wagon several paces to her right. She struck hard and everything went blank.

CHAPTER 24

KIBURE

KIBURE SENSED DRYMUS'S ARRIVAL TO the cave. "Good morning."
She didn't return the salutation. "I see your ability to sense the
energy around you has improved."

"Nothing better to do once the tea wears off."

She lit an orb of light. "True enough." She considered for a moment
then nodded. "Perhaps it is time to change that."

Kibure nearly yelped with excitement. *She's going to let me out!*

"You're going to learn how to come and go from the spiritual realm
of your own accord. No more tea for you."

His heart sank and he said nothing.

"Your body already knows how to enter as well as how to leave.
This is merely a matter of teaching the mind how to be as smart as the
unthinking body."

That sounded like nonsense to Kibure, but he nodded. The ability
to come and go as he pleased would be nice. This didn't exactly help
with his sink-the-sword-into-the-seed problem, but it allowed more
time to practice.

Drymus interrupted his musing. "When a person tires, an ordinary
mind transitions directly into sleep, where they will experience several

dreams which they may or may not recall upon waking. These dreams take place within a realm of reality that we refer to as the dream realm— yes, we're a rather creative bunch, are we not? Anyhow, these dreams are constructed from the chaos of subconscious 'will' within which the mind becomes the host. Before you ask, yes, the dream realm is a layer of reality unto itself, entirely apart from the spiritual realm."

Just when Kibure thought the world couldn't get any larger, an entirely new one was revealed to him. He prayed there were no more.

"When the mind recedes into itself for sleep, the consciousness reaches a sort of crossroads. This crossroad has two doors that may be opened; one leads to the dream realm while the other would take you into the spiritual realm. For most people, the pathway leading to the spiritual realm is so finite one would be unable to ever locate it on their own. However, for some small few, this path is more obvious, more accessible. For those people, the spiritual realm might even be accessed by accident during the transition into sleep. Sound familiar?"

Kibure nodded, recalling several chance visits to the place.

She continued, "It is said our people's tribe was originally given this talent as a gift from God as a means of meditation and communion over distances. We were the protectors of our homeland, after all. That is, before some among us took the seed and journeyed into the forbidden."

Our people? She continued speaking for a moment, but Kibure wasn't listening anymore.

"What do you mean, *our* people?"

Drymus eyed him for a moment as if trying to decide if the question was worth her time. Kibure would insist that it was.

She chuckled. "You haven't figured it out yet?"

Kibure felt his frustration growing. "Would I be asking if I had?"

"Who's to say what you might ask or why. Children often say and do strange things." She rapped her leg with her fingers, then continued. "Our people trace unadulterated roots to one of the original seven tribes of the ancient lands. We left those lands many generations ago, but we are still the closest thing to pure blood as can be found on this side of the Endless Mountains, and therefore, our gift remains strong.

Most 'tazamines,' as the Lugienese calls them, are nothing more than anomalies whose blood contains enough of the old that some of the gifts manifest. Only without training, they don't know how to control them so they are deemed evil to those who do not understand, and more so by those who do."

"You have still not answered my question," said Kibure through gritted teeth.

"That's because it doesn't matter. Your mother was a wonderful person, a friend of mine, *or* your mother was a whore, never met her. It's of no consequence either way."

Kibure felt his anger inching toward a point of no return. Much like grabbing handfuls of sand in frustration, he had sunk his mind deep into the stone around him, drawing it into himself with each breath. He suddenly tingled with energy, poised to release it in anger. His fists were white as they clutched at his fury. But this rage had become raw energy, the cause sitting directly before him.

He looked up to meet her smug expression, only there was nothing smug about her face right then. She actually appeared—what—concerned?

"Kibure." She held up a hand, then spoke in a calm, steady voice, all mirth vanishing from her tone. "I need you to release your hold on that energy."

He stared back at her, a rush of excitement at the sensation of so much power right at his fingertips. *I could do whatever I want with this much power, couldn't I?*

But his anger was already beginning to drain away and in its place came rationality, and with it, the reminder that he had no idea how to use such energy in the first place. He might lash out at Drymus, maybe even kill her, though he doubted that she would allow such. But even if he did, he'd still be stuck here in this cave. The others would never let him out if he did something so stupid as to kill the person who was supposed to be training him. Plus, he wasn't a murderer. The rest of his frustration transitioned into mere annoyance at Drymus's cantankerous disposition. All that remained was a cold emptiness; he felt normal again.

And normal meant that he still very much disliked Drymus and the way she treated him like he was less of a person than everyone else on account of his ignorance.

He decided to address this problem in a way that she might understand—sarcasm. "Please allow me to apologize for ignoring the vast array of schooling I was provided during the majority of my life spent in servitude. Please also pardon my choice to begin life as a slave in the first place. It seemed like a promising profession, but I'm sorry that these *choices* have left me ignorant of so many of the things you believe I should know. So there it is. Now, would you mind answering my question about my heritage?"

Lacking the reproachful tone from before, she said, "Are you finished?"

"I don't know. Are you?"

Drymus blew out a breath, nodded, then said calmly, almost gently, "I don't know anything about either of your parents, not specifically. I am certain they were not from among the women here. However, there was a diaspora among our people following the collapse of the Asaaven in the Luguinden Wars. We know a few splinters have remained hidden from the rest of the fallen world. We have encountered a few such over the years while exploring the spiritual realm. What we do know about you is, it was prophesied that he who was to come at the appointed time in the appointed place would be of the Asaaven line. I can tell you no more on the subject of your parentage, for I know nothing more. But we are in a sense, kinsmen. This is why I refer to *our* people."

Kibure's already dark mood soured further. There was something familiar about that name, Asaaven, but he couldn't place it. It was probably nothing, but the story made him uneasy. Plus, the thought of learning who his parents were had given him hope, though he didn't know why. What did it actually matter?

"Would you like to get back to the gift of our people?"

Kibure nodded begrudgingly.

"Very well. The management of this gift is generally taught to our children at a young age. Likewise, the ability to harness the power of the natural world is a talent shared by all of the original seven tribes but has faded from most of the fallen world."

"You mean ateré magic?"

Drymus's eyes widened, then narrowed with suspicion. "Where did you hear that word?"

Kibure was taken aback. Then smiled to himself. "I heard it from a wonderful person, a friend of mine. Or perhaps it was a whore. It's of no consequence either way."

Drymus glared, then said stiffly, "Point taken. Now, if it please you, answer the question."

Kibure considered taking the conflict further, but Drymus was right. He had made his point. Perhaps they might both be a little more honest moving forward.

"A man named Draílock used this word to describe the borrowing of power from objects around us. Is this wrong?"

Drymus didn't react other than to ask, "This Draílock. Who was he exactly?"

Kibure shrugged. "I don't know, an old wizard, but not ancient like the wo—" He coughed and considered a different description. "He was tall, pale skin, dark hair, sunken eyes, a beard about yea long." He mimed a distance of about a hand's width from the bottom of his chin. "Icy blue eyes."

"Has to be a coincidence. There's no way . . ." she said to herself.

Kibure asked, "Do you know him or something?"

Drymus shook her head. "I doubt it. But that word, ateré, it is very old. It predates the diaspora, and that was thousands of years ago. I only know of it because of the recitation of an old story told by one of our keepers." She paused then asked, "This Draílock, you say he is a wizard?"

Kibure nodded. "He was supposed to train me and Sindri. That's how I learned to sense the power around me. He had us practice with crickets because their power is more difficult to summon but easier to sense. I learned to feel their energy, but we never made it further than this. He had only just started training me when I was kidnapped by the Lugienese." He felt a wave of chills return at the thought of the mental intrusion he had experienced by whatever entity that Grobennar man had possessed. "Then your—our—kinsmen stole me from them and carted me here."

Drymus nodded her understanding, but her eyes had grown distant, her mind was somewhere else. Then she snapped out of it. "I see. Let's return to your ability to enter the spiritual realm at will. I'd like to finish this lesson sometime before dinner."

That was strange.

"Where was I? Ah yes, the crossroads. Your mind will come upon a sort of crossroads as you near sleep. The tea I have been providing you is a combination of two leaves, with two different attributes. The first pulls your mind into itself toward sleep while the other widens the pathway to the spiritual realm. If you were not of the 'gifted,' we would have had to adjust the tea further, but this has not proven necessary. With the pathway widened, the pull in that direction becomes dominant and the mind is drawn to it without further action."

Kibure considered this and nodded, but he still did not quite understand. "But you say some people are able to enter the spiritual realm at will, without first falling asleep?"

She smiled; a disturbing image, given her aged face. "This is what I am going to teach you to do." She brought forth a cup of tea from behind her seat. "I want you to take only a small sip, not more, just a sip."

Kibure reached out and took the cup. Then another question emerged, one that had been troubling him since the voyage here and the disturbing visit from Magog. "You say there are two doors, or something like it. Is it possible to enter the door into the dream realm at will?"

She shrugged. "Sure. It's a bit of a different experience to do so from a mental state of consciousness, knowing your own will is constructing the reality that you see. But yes, it's possible."

Kibure had to know. "Would it be possible to enter someone else's dream from within the dream realm?"

Drymus nodded slowly, eyeing him carefully. "Technically, yes. But it is far more difficult, and far more dangerous. The dream realm is a place of chaos, and each dream is its own warped reflection of the physical realm as the mind chooses to see and construct it, which means each dream behaves unpredictably."

Kibure pressed her. "But it is possible? Possible to enter the dream realm and someone else's dream specifically?"

Drymus eyed him curiously. "It is . . . but one would have to either know precisely where the intended person's physical body lay in order to locate their dream, or at least have had some sort of interaction with that person's mind from within the spiritual realm to use as a marker, else you'd never be able to find that specific mind within the dream realm. Searching without a marker would be nearly impossible and at great risk to one's safety."

Last question. "Would it be possible to harm someone from within their own dream?"

She narrowed her eyes. "Is there a reason you're so interested in this? You're not thinking of trying something so foolish as to enter someone else's dream, are you?"

Kibure shook his head. And what could he say about Magog's visit to his own dream? At this point, he still wasn't certain that Magog's visit had been anything more than that, a nightmare of his own creation. "No. I wouldn't. I won't. Just . . . curious. I know that if one is killed while in the spiritual realm, the soul dies in the physical world, as well. I just wondered if the same applies to the dream realm."

She nodded her understanding and chuckled. "Having some nightmares, are we?"

A flicker of fear gripped him. She knew? No—she was mocking him again. He considered returning the sentiment but couldn't think of a worthwhile insult quickly enough, and furthermore, he didn't think this would help get him the answers he so desired. *Let's try humility.*

He lowered his eyes. "Yes. I've had a few lately."

Drymus actually sounded *almost* kind as she said, "You need not worry over your nightmares. I have never heard of someone being harmed from within their own dream. However, there was a time when our people attempted to establish a line of communication through the dream realm, and this is where the danger lies. One can be killed while visiting the dream of another. We lost several sisters before it was decided that this practice should be prohibited altogether. I was young at the time and did not ever do so myself so I cannot speak from personal experience."

Sounding a bit more agitated, Drymus said, "Suffice it to say, this is something that should not be pondered further. You should under no circumstances attempt to enter someone else's dream. Is this understood?"

He lowered his head. "Yes, Lady Drymus."

"Good. Now let us return to the task at hand."

Kibure held up the cup. "Just one sip?"

She nodded. "One sip *should* be enough to begin the process, but not enough in and of itself to push you through to the spiritual realm. If this amount is off, we'll just have to adjust for next time. I will coach you through the process as you fade."

She then explained some of the specifics. When she had finished, Kibure lifted the cup, then took his sip. "Ready."

It took longer than usual, but the effects of the tea eventually dragged his mind away, only this time he felt the strength to resist. He was able to control the speed of his descent. Once he had established control, he allowed his mind to retreat at a measured pace. Ordinarily, the transition happened so quickly it felt like he was free-falling, a short burst of vertigo before opening his eyes to the spiritual realm. This was different, and he was able to hear Drymus speaking to him from the physical realm.

"You should begin to feel two opposing forces pulling on your mind; one will lead you to the ordinary dream realm, the other to the spiritual."

It wasn't long before he reached it. He opened his eyes within this place between places, and saw nothing but dark gray, shadows all about. He tried to close his eyes but this new sight did not dissolve, for in this place he had no eyes. He felt the sensation of two forces, each reaching for him, and he began to see the shadows coalesce in a manner that resembled two faint pathways. One appeared more solid and the pull was stronger than the other. *That must be the spiritual realm.* He reached out with his hand where some part of his mind remained in the physical realm.

"You feel the pull?" she asked.

"Yes," he said, surprised to still have some control over his body in the physical realm.

"One should be noticeably stronger than the other."

"Yes, I feel that."

"Before you follow this path, I want you to extend your mind in that same direction, like you might do in order to sense the power around you in the physical realm. This will allow you to get a feel for the unique design of this place so that you might find it in the future without the tea."

Kibure did as he was instructed. At first he felt nothing besides an enticing "current" pulling his mind toward a single point in the distance of his mind. But he anchored a part of himself to where he was at this crossroads, holding tight to the sensation that pulled in the direction of the dream realm. Then he reached out and felt for the point that called to him. As he drew near, the strength intensified and he had to resist with more fervor, concentrating instead on the construction of this path. It was like being in a cave. The closer he came to the entrance, the brighter the light, but it also allowed him to observe the makeup of this path. Lines of deep contrast as opposed to the messy haze of the crossroads.

"Do you sense it?" she asked.

Kibure answered, "Yes," but his voice sounded more distant.

"Good. Now, I want you to retreat back to the crossroads. Let me know once you've returned."

This was difficult. It reminded him of his swim to the coast after being attacked by the Kraken. The shore had seemed so close, yet they had kicked their legs for hours to finally reach it.

He eventually arrived and lifted a hand with his physical body.

"Return now to the physical realm. Push against the pull you feel from the spiritual realm. You should be able to follow this line of energy. Attempt to feel the energy at your feet in the waking world and use this to guide you."

This was even more difficult. He could feel his body, which was how he was able to respond and move, but he felt numb. It was like attempting to sleep in the cold of the Drisko Mountains while on the run with Sindri. The thought of Sindri caused him to lose focus and his mind went tumbling off course. The pull toward the spiritual realm took hold of him and he was suddenly careening toward it. He lashed out and snatched the lesser pull of the dream realm and yanked. His descent slowed and finally stopped. His heart was racing. Navigating this place within his mind required a significant amount of mental discipline.

He worked his mind back toward the crossroads and then began feeling for the energy that resided within the physical realm, drawing his mind toward that. It was easier this time and within a few moments he felt himself pass the boundary. He opened his eyes and saw Drymus.

She sat with her summoned orb of light, fingers interlocked over her crossed legs as she sat in the chair facing him. She smiled. "Good. I worried you lost your way."

"I nearly did."

"All right. We haven't much time before the tea's effects fully dissipate. Now that you have a sense of what it feels like to be drawn into the spiritual realm, I want you to try to find it again. You will signal to me before entering. The remaining effects of the tea will make it easier to bring your mind to this place, but as you are currently fully awake, it will require you to do more of the work. As you do so, take note of the path you take. You *should* be able to do so without any assistance from the tea."

"Okay," said Kibure. But he wasn't entirely sure how to proceed. He didn't know *how* to find his way back.

Drymus stared at him impatiently. "Most people begin by closing their eyes."

"Ah."

This did help. With his eyes closed, he was able to sense the faint tug and follow it back down toward the crossroads. Once his awareness had slipped into his mind, he opened the mental equivalent of his eyes and confirmed he could see the slightest point of lighter gray in the direction he felt the tug. Without the added pull of the spiritual realm from the tea, he was certain he would never have been able to find his way back. But with that assistance, he could see the marker amid the shadows of darker grays and black that made up this portion of his mind.

Within a few more moments, he stood at what he now knew was the precipice of the spiritual realm, holding tight to the line he had cast toward the realm of dreams to keep himself in place. He signaled with a hand.

Drymus said, "Good. Now, I want you to imagine that you are climbing down a cliff, lowering yourself down ever so carefully, ever so slowly. Much like being able to pinpoint your access point toward the crossroads, you will want to mark your entry into the spiritual realm. This is what allows you to find your way out should you wish to leave before your body does so of its own accord. This also allows you to remain longer as you develop a better sense of what is happening when your mind begins to pull you out."

Kibure did as instructed and was amazed that he actually could slow his descent. He had previously just appeared there, or so he thought, but he now recognized that this was merely an illusion wrought by the speed with which his mind ordinarily traveled between realms.

He arrived at the spiritual realm's reflection of the cave and instinctively summoned an orb of light. Drymus was there waiting for him. She smiled and it looked to him that she wore an expression of genuine satisfaction. "*Good. Find your way back.*"

Doing so was easy enough. Moments later, he was back in the waking world.

"Excellent. Now meet me at the amphitheater for your training."

In a matter of thirty heartbeats, Kibure stood before Drymus in the spiritual realm's reflection of the amphitheater, summoned sword at the ready.

Her smile became a frown. "*Now that you are able to come and go as you please, you should begin progressing more quickly. You need to strengthen your will.*" She pointed at the seed. "*I will be back to see you in a few days. I expect to see notable improvement.*" Then she raised a finger and said,

"Be certain not to stay here for too long. While the residual magic used by the body to bring you here is minimal, it can still be dangerous to remain for too long. As you know, our bones need time to heal and restore themselves after wielding magic. If you start to feel a deep thrumming or throbbing sensation while here, that's your body telling you it's time to leave. This is one reason why I do not remain here for any longer than I do. My physical body is not what it once was, so even with the help of a few gemstones, my body reminds me very quickly if I've spent too much time in this place."

She pointed a finger at Kibure. *"Your youth will allow you more time than I, but this is not infinite, and your bones have not built up much of a tolerance. In time, they will strengthen and you'll be capable of channeling more power before causing harm. Listen to your body."*

Then she disappeared.

Kibure felt a sense of pride at having mastered a new skill, yet when his sword winked out of existence the instant it struck the seed, he realized he had a great deal further to advance. After more than a dozen failed repetitions, he stalked over to one of the trees that grew in the unnaturally lit cavern city and swung hard at that. This was not the first time he had done so. He had walked the city slashing at nearly everything he could find until finding something he could cut without seeing the sword vanish from sight. A leaf . . . on the third try. But this time he walked right over to the thick trunk of the tree and much to his surprise, the blade remained after his swing, though it bounced off as harmlessly as if he had struck stone. *Improvement.* He inspected the place where he had struck and found a tiny sliver cut into the bark, a thin nick.

A voice resounded in his head, startling him, and he lost his mental grip on the sword. It vanished. *"What did that tree ever do to you?"*

Kibure quickly summoned his tool back and turned to see Arabelle.

Embarrassed, he replied, *"Uh, nothing. I'm just . . . well . . . I don't know, seeing if I can cut something less impossible than that seed thing that Drymus seems to believe needs cutting."*

"Any progress?" She inched closer to inspect the tree. *"Is that a scratch I see there?"*

Kibure's small victory seemed foolish now. "*I . . .*" He lowered his head in resignation. "*Yeah. I have a long way to go.*"

She danced around him and swung her own blade at the thick trunk. It sank deep before she pulled it free. She repeated this and a wedge of wood fell loose. One more swing and the tree began to topple over. Kibure dove out of the way just before being completely crushed. A branch smacked his face in a shower of dark-gray leaves.

Kibure yelped, "*What in the dark was that for?*"

Arabelle smiled playfully. "*Just wanted to see if our training has improved your footwork.*" She glanced over at the fallen tree, then at Kibure who had managed to escape the worst of it, though without any semblance of grace. "*I think there's still room for improvement.*"

A whole drogal barn's worth of room for improvement, thought Kibure.

Coming to his feet, he pointed at the thick trunk of the tree and said, "*I could have been killed by this thing!*"

Arabelle brushed the dark hair away from her left shoulder, appearing unconcerned as she said, "*I was pretty sure you'd make it out of the way in time.*"

"*And if I didn't?*" Kibure bristled.

"*Well, then I suppose that would answer the question of whether or not you were meant for any great feats of savioring, eh? Not that I believe destiny is necessarily fixed, but I get the impression that these prophecies contain at least a few pillars of inevitability.*"

"*What about the tree? Isn't someone going to be upset about the large tree now lying in the middle of the street?*"

She stared at him, puzzled, then understanding dawned. She chuckled. "*This tree will return to its original state in here within a few hours and is completely unaffected within the physical realm.*"

Kibure stared at her, still confused.

"*Drymus didn't explain this to you?*"

Kibure shook his head.

"*What in the world is she teaching you?*" A rhetorical question. Extending her arms and spinning, she said, "*Everything you see here is a reflection of its true existence in the physical realm. We can add to, or alter, the things in here at will, but the reflection only goes one way. Any change you make here will revert back to its reflected state rather quickly. The smaller the change, the quicker the return. We are the only things that can be permanently altered while here, on account of us having souls, and that's only in terms of dying. I have heard of physical harm here transferring to the physical realm if the mind believes it strongly enough."*

Kibure looked down at the fallen tree. *"So this tree is completely unaltered in the physical realm?"*

"That is so."

Kibure was silent for several heartbeats before finally saying, *"Well, this has been . . . interesting. But I really need to be working to improve my 'will.' Drymus won't begin my real training until I can somehow get this stupid sword into the seed. And she expects improvement soon. I really shouldn't be wasting time playing at swords."*

He had to admit to himself that he enjoyed their time together. He hadn't felt this kind of companionship since meeting Tenk. Even Sindri had eventually proven a trusted companion, but she had kept him at a distance, treating him more like a subject than a friend. Arabelle was different. She appeared genuinely interested in *him,* which was nice even if it was for no other reason than sheer boredom.

Arabelle rolled her eyes. *"Fine. How about I help you cleave this tree in two, then we can 'play' swords. If I observed correctly, you're now able to come and go from here at your discretion?"*

Kibure nodded in response to both questions, then said, *"Again with the spying?"*

She ignored the question and walked over to sit near the base of the tree she had cut. *"Okay. Let's see what you've got."*

Kibure followed, feeling self-conscious all the while. He stood before the hewn tree, sword held high above his head and swung with all of his might, hoping that maybe this time his sword would just magically sink deep into the wood like it had for Arabelle.

The imaginary sword struck with great force, but the wood did not give way and the handle reverberated so hard that Kibure lost his grip and it disappeared from sight. *Yeow!*

Kibure turned to see Arabelle looking away, hand over her mouth to cover laughter.

"*Yes, hilarious, isn't it?*" Kibure sneered. "*I'm supposed to be a prophesied something, but I can't even complete the simplest of tasks in a fake version of the world.*"

Arabelle regained herself and faced him, smile gone. "*You know what you need?*"

"*What's that?*"

"*Confidence.*"

Kibure rolled his eyes. "*Some actual improvement would help with that.*"

Arabelle jumped to her feet. "*I couldn't agree more.*" She pointed at her temple and said, "*I have an idea.*"

Kibure stared at her expectantly.

"*Okay. I think part of your problem is that your mind holds on to the belief that the things reflected here are so real that they can't be redefined, altered, or displaced. But this is not the case at all.*" She nodded at the fallen tree beside them.

"*Here's what I want you to do. I want you to summon another tree. Just like this one. And put it right over here on the other side of us.*"

Kibure gave her a puzzled look.

"*Just do it.*"

He looked over at the fallen tree, then to the space on the other side of them and did his best to recreate it. He closed his eyes and tried to visualize the thickness of the trunk and the smooth bark, then the extending branches. This was a complicated item to will into existence, much more so than a simple sword. He agonized over the details, then finally decided what he envisioned was close enough and forced it into existence within this place.

Opening his eyes he saw a near exact replica of the fallen tree to his right. *Did I really just DO that?!* Caught between astonishment and a deeper joy than he had felt in ages, he just stood with his arms akimbo, beaming.

Arabelle nodded in approval.

Kibure followed the trunk up to the leaves and saw that his creation lost some of its craftsmanship, but that was immaterial. He had a pretty good idea of what Arabelle had in mind for him.

Returning his gaze to the trunk, he hefted his imagined sword and said, "*Shall I?*"

She smiled. "*Yes, just make sure to maintain your grip on both items as you—*"

His sword was already in motion and he swung with all of his might, but the tree simply vanished as soon as the blade reached it. Meeting no resistance meant the sword went straight into the stone of the street where they stood. Only it didn't go into the street, it struck hard and, as with striking the felled tree, the sword reverberated back, sending pain shuddering all the way up to his shoulders.

Kibure growled to himself in frustration.

Arabelle spoke confidently. "*Do it again. Only this time focus very hard on keeping the tree here.*"

This is just as pointless as striking the seed itself, he thought. But he did as she advised.

On his sixth attempt, he was able to maintain his hold on both objects and to his delight, his sword actually sank into the tree. It felt good. No pain. He pulled the sword free and swung again, this time with more confidence, and his blade sank even further. Again and again he did this until this tree, too, toppled over.

Arabelle clapped silent hands. "*Okay, okay. I think you've made your mark on the tree. Now I want you to close your eyes. Keep your sword and your tree fastened here with your will as you have been doing.*" She walked over to his side as he closed his eyes. Warm hands touched his shoulders, and he felt an odd tingling within his stomach. It was similar to sensing magic, yet not quite the same. "*I'm going to spin you a few times, and I need you to keep your eyes closed as I do so.*"

He nodded.

"*Okay, here we go.*" She spun him a number of times, then stopped and let go. A few heartbeats later, she said, "*Keep your eyes closed and swing downward just as you did before.*"

He knew what she was doing, but he went along with it. He held tight to his will, keeping the summoned sword and tree fastened to this realm, then swung hard and felt the blade slide easily into the wood just like before.

"*Good. Let's try again.*" She spun him again.

How many times will she do this before she has me try on the real one? he wondered.

The plan made sense and he applauded the theory. He just didn't have much confidence that it would work.

"*Okay, swing!*"

He did so, half expecting to feel pain shoot up his arms as he struck the impenetrable real thing. His blade slid into the wood, but not as far as the last had.

"*You hardly tried on that turn. Come on, Kibure, I want you to swing like your freedom depends on it!*"

She spun him again and this time, annoyed and wishing to prove to her that he knew exactly what she was doing but the issue did not rest with his effort. He put every ounce of strength into this swing. Something overtook him and when he swung, he felt a rush of power and the blade slid right through the summoned tree and . . . into . . . the . . . stone walkway. He let go of the sword with both hands and opened his eyes.

His sword remained upright, tip lodged deep into the cobblestones.

"*See? It's all in your head.*"

Kibure stared in disbelief. He had to turn around once just to confirm that what he was seeing was correct. The summoned tree lying down behind him had no marks. The real reflection of the tree before him had been cut clean through and had two other large slashes into it from his other swings.

"*You . . . you tricked me!*"

She smiled brightly then hopped up onto the tree, assuming a swordsman's stance. *Or would it be a swordswoman's stance? Never mind that.*

"*So are you ready to 'play' or what?*"

Kibure was speechless, but he figured that between his ability to come and go as he pleased, and now this, he had made more progress today than in all of his other training combined. He nodded and did a little twirl of the sword around his wrist just like Arabelle routinely did. He felt a confidence that he had never before known.

It didn't take long for Arabelle to humble him with the sword, but even this as unable to steal away his festive mood.

Lying on his back after being knocked from his feet with a hard spinning kick to the face, Kibure turned his head and stared over at the pedestal bearing the seed. He considered trying his luck at it right then and there, then recalled all of his victories today and thought better than to spoil the mood. He sprang back to his feet like Arabelle had taught him a few days earlier and said, *"Let's go. One more. I've got a good feeling about this one."*

Arabelle grinned expectantly. *"Good."*

Kibure flowed through the movements, feeling more natural in them than ever. Arabelle actually gave ground for a few steps before pushing one of his swings aside to create one of those angles into his defenses that she was always talking about, but he moved with her, maintaining his position against her own. *I'm really starting to get the hang of this.*

Then he saw his opening, the first of its kind, and acted just as he had been taught, turning his blade at the last second so as to not actually cut into her—

Both legs were swept out from beneath him, but the attack had come from behind him. He slammed backward headfirst into the ground. Groaning silently in the soundless space, he opened his eyes. *"You . . . cheated. I had you."*

"Did you? Hmm, I should think if this were so, it would be I, not you lying face up on the ground."

"You're forgetting the cheated part," said Kibure as he sat up, far less enthusiastic than the last time.

"Cheated? I suppose we'll have to look into the rules of combat." To that end, she summoned a large tome and began thumbing through the

pages before stopping midway. She then pointed. "*Ah, here it is. 'The winner is the person who . . . wins. No other criterion is to be considered.'*"

Kibure walked over to stare at the page, but having no knowledge of letters, could not verify the truth of what she read. "*Is that even what it says?*"

She slammed the book closed and it winked out of existence.

"*Maybe. Maybe not. In any case, what I did is the next step in your training. Adds a whole new element. Granted, it's a skill limited to fighting within the spiritual realm. I do not recommend trying it while on the other side, since to my knowledge it's not possible. But I sure do look forward to the first time you do this to Drymus. You'll need to do some practicing before you attempt it with her. It will only work once.*"

CHAPTER 25

AYNWARD

THE CREAK OF METAL NOTIFIED Aynward that someone approached. *Too early for another meal, and too soon for the confession. Who then might this be?*

Gervais appeared once again, a tray of food in his hands. He smiled as he advanced. "Aynward, I managed to obtain some additional comfort on your behalf, as well as good tidings for the future." He set the tray down and Aynward's mouth immediately moistened, his ravenous stomach yearning for real food.

"Gervais, I don't think you understand just how much I love you right now."

Gervais smiled, then bowed. "Then perhaps you should wait to confess this love until I reveal to you yet another token of my generosity." He reached into one of the many folds in his loose-fitting robes and pulled out a bottle. "I'm told that this particular vintage was exceptional. You will need to finish this before the guard changes. I have only bribed the one, and he has been instructed to take the bottle with him when he leaves. But I pray you have a very important speech to give on the morrow, so I thought that perhaps this may calm your nerves. I know your previous counselor would have objections regarding the use of intoxicants, but I know you have been through a lot, and you find yourself in a difficult position." He handed the bottle over to Aynward.

Aynward reached out and took the gift. "You spoke with Dagmara, then?"

Gervais offered a quizzical look. "I fear not. Should I have done so?"

"Well—no. It's just—you now appear to doubt my guilt. Yet, you admitted the evidence against me is irrefutable."

Gervais frowned. "Yes, that. The evidence is indeed without blemish. You will surely be found guilty. I know that you could not have committed this crime, at least not alone."

To Aynward's own surprise, he took offense to the comment. "You don't think me capable?"

Gervais shook his head. "Nothing like that, though . . ." He brought a finger to his chin, then nodded. "You are not the murdering type, Your Grace. Plus, there is the matter of the sword. You did not have the murder weapon in your possession upon entering your father's chambers. It was I who arranged for the transport of your belongings from the ship to your chambers. They should have still been in transit from the ship when the murder took place. I attempted to explain this to your brother, but his ears are closed to reason. He prefers to remain limited to the ignorance provided by isolating the evidence from the scene, not the circumstances beyond. To believe otherwise would imply a more complex scheme within the palace."

"A scheme he himself orchestrated," muttered Aynward.

"Perhaps."

"So you know I'm innocent, yet you assume I will confess my guilt?"

Gervais allowed his gaze to sink to the stone floor of the prison, then strained to return to meet Aynward's own. "Unfortunately, the Kingdom is not a place of true criminal proceedings, or," he scoffed, "a place of trial by jury as seen in the Free Cities. No, the King has passed judgment on your guilt, and it is his will alone that stands. Your 'trial' is merely a show for the sake of public appearances. He'll not allow you to present your side of events unless he can be assured that it aligns with his own. Therefore, agreeing to confess is the *only* sensible course. The alternative is torture, which you and I both know will end in a signed confession. In either case, your presumed guilt remains. I don't take you to be the sort to endure pointless suffering, not when a comfortable life awaits you elsewhere. That is part of the good news I have to share. I managed to squeeze more information out of the powers that be." He grinned. "This place you'll be staying, this *prison*, is quite lavish."

Aynward doubted very much that Dagmara would manage to prove his innocence. He had therefore been teetering between his two remaining courses. *May as well make an informed choice.* He finally said, "You have my attention."

Gervais nodded. "Good. The crown has secured a beautiful home right on the river in the city of East End. You'll be guarded closely, of course, but I'm told you'll be allowed to swim in the river. And the home itself sits upon a small rise, boasting an elevated turret with an enclosed reading nook beside an outdoor balcony. It won't be quite the view you have here atop the south wall of the palace, but the description speaks of a certain beauty all the same."

"That does sound rather pleasant. Boring, but pleasant." This was not an uncommon *punishment* for nobles. Political connections made execution more of a hassle than they were worth. Such an outcome for him came with many benefits. He would have none of the responsibility he had feared all of his life, and he would be able to read all of the books he had wished to read but never had time. He might even be given a woman, one proven to be infertile, of course, but a woman all the same. That is, if he wished to subject someone to the very same fate as he. He wasn't certain how he felt about such a thing. But he would have a great deal of time to ponder all of the moral questions of the world if he chose the way of confession.

Finally, he said, "My brother seems to be stacking the chips very heavily on the side of confession. And while I realize I am being bribed, he makes it very difficult to refuse."

Gervais smiled slightly. "Well, as your counselor, I would advise for you to remain alive. His offer is quite generous. Yet, I understand the hesitation in confessing to such a heinous crime as patricide, especially given your innocence. This will be no easy course, though once done, I think you will feel relieved."

Aynward lifted the bottle, not certain what it contained. Besides his return banquet, it had been weeks since he had consumed any wine, spirit, or ale. He did not care what it was, so long as it numbed his aching spirit. He tipped the bottle and drank deeply. Several gulps later, he pulled the bottle away, spilling the red liquid down his neck in his haste.

"Good wine." He paused and released a loud belch. "Thank you, Gervais, you have given me much to consider, but the liquid courage will help." He set the bottle down and shook his head hard, as the wine was bitter when swallowed by the gulp.

"Yes, of course. Though I might advise sipping."

Aynward ignored the suggestion, taking another large swig of the dark liquid. "Considering the task before me, I think sipping will be inadequate. A few more bottles would be greatly appreciated."

Gervais bowed. "I will see what I can find, Your Grace."

Aynward set the bottle down and leaned against the stone wall of his cell.

CHAPTER 26

DAGMARA

AGMARA'S COUNSELOR, BRENNA, SAT ACROSS from her, sipping tea at the small table set upon a balcony overlooking Lake Salmune and the city that surrounded it. Her ebony skin glistened with an oily sheen after her morning exercises. Dagmara had missed today's lesson with the sword, but that would not have stopped Brenna from completing her own.

The Scritlandian woman-turned-counselor had been recruited to teach Dagmara the ways of the Scritlandian courts and their womanly customs, but Dagmara had also convinced her to continue teaching her with the sword where Aynward had left off. In this case, if caught, she would argue that this fit within the scope of Scritlandian court training since women in Scritland were just as much warriors as men. Knowing that she would no longer have to hide her training was at least some consolation.

But right now she had more important matters to discuss.

"We have a very big problem, Brenna. The betrothal is to be ended between Aldrik and me as soon as Perja has the crown. And Aynward is going to confess to a crime he did not commit!"

Brenna lifted the dainty teacup to her lips, a smooth, elegant movement that belied her callused hands and firm muscles. "That seems more like two problems, though unrelated."

Dagmara nodded. "Yes, two very big problems. Only, I have been thinking that perhaps there might be a single solution to the both of them. But I can't do it alone, can't even plan it on my own. Too many moving pieces, and we don't have much time."

Brenna narrowed her eyes. "I am listening, but I already dislike the type of talk of which you speak."

Dagmara knew this would be the case, but she had no one else she could trust. And Brenna would tell her if her idea were truly insane rather than say so out of simple fear like most others would be likened to do.

Dagmara explained her intentions as best she could, possibilities coming to mind even as she spoke.

When she finished, Brenna said, "All of these things would make a traitor of you. Should I participate, I too would become an enemy of your Kingdom, perhaps at the expense of my life."

Dagmara winced. Brenna was right. The voice in the back of her mind screamed recklessness. But she needed to hear someone else say it, lest she remain ridden with guilt as Aynward lived out his life in exile. And while in this particular case, Aynward was truly without guilt, he would not have been such a prime candidate to be framed had it not been for the many sins of his past. Therefore, he wasn't wholly innocent. She would have to remind herself of this many times before she would be rid of the guilt she would feel at having done nothing to help.

Brenna coughed to regain Dagmara's attention. *Blast, Brenna has been speaking.*

"I believe that to do nothing would be just as irresponsible. This is a fight worth fighting." Brenna rose to her feet. "Excuse me, Your Grace. I think we will need to continue planning over dinner. I will have our meal brought here and a message sent to your mother outlining your wishes to dine in while grieving the loss of your father. Your mother will be able to communicate this to any who ask after your absence from the Great Hall this evening."

Dagmara was left speechless. She had hardly expected Brenna to do anything besides explain how terrible her idea was. All she could manage to say before Brenna exited the room was, "Thank you."

After Brenna left, Dagmara melted into her chair, ideas swirling, a surreal sense of lightness about her. None of this felt real; her father's death, Aynward's incarceration, and most of all, the thought of defying the Kingdom itself. And yet the only thing that frightened her at the moment was her lack of fear. *Quite the paradox, that.* "Tecuix help us," she whispered to the god of creation.

CHAPTER 27

AYNWARD

THE AFTERNOON SUNLIGHT WRIGGLED ITS way into Aynward's cell in the same persistent way the cold of winter might creep into the walls of the palace no matter how many fires one lit to ward against it. The same could be said of Aynward's next visitor, whose arrival was equally beyond the scope of Aynward's ability to defend.

"Greetings, brother," said Perja.

Aynward eyed his brother. "You're looking rather regal, almost kingly. Only, what's that all over your hands?"

Perja lifted his hands in question as Aynward continued, "Is that . . . yes—it seems Father's blood remains. I don't think you've cleaned them well enough. Better fire your wash servant."

Perja's eyes narrowed as he glanced down at the clean white skin of his hands, but his arrogant smile returned. "Always the forked tongue, even from the depths of hopeless despair." He shook his head. "I'll make sure the inquisitors earn their pay to obtain your confession. I'll instruct them to begin with the toes. I suspect it won't take long before you're telling a grand tale of treachery."

Aynward smiled in return. "A tale that will be, isn't that right, *Kingslayer.*" Aynward lifted his own hands, chains and all, to cover his mouth. "Ohhh—my mistake. *You* didn't kill our father. Never you. *You* wouldn't dare get your own hands dirty. You're far too much a coward to do the deed yourself. The stain on your hands must have come from soaking our Kingdom banners crimson."

Perja reacted as Aynward hoped, bristling as he said, "You never knew when to shut your mouth. I would have you killed right here, right now, were it not for the need for a public trial. It appears you're going to go the way of pain first. And before you get any bright ideas, know that a written confession alone will not preclude death by execution. I will not spare your life unless this confession is spoken aloud during the public hearing. However, unlike Father's coddling, you'll only have one chance to get this right. And you're too stupid and prideful for that."

Without thought for how foolish it was for him to continue provoking his brother, Aynward spat back, "While we're on the topic of stupid, I was thinking you'll make a fine vassal King to the Lugienese. That's what this is really all about, isn't it? It suits you so well, no thinking involved. Just following orders and with the illusion of importance. No real change for you there, that is, until they stab you in the back with an all-out invasion."

Perja shook his head. "You can't possibly believe the nonsense you're spewing. Or are you deranged to the point of believing your own lies? That would explain why you're so good at weaving them."

Aynward responded, "Hold on, are we still talking about me? I thought derangement and lies were more your thing."

Perja shook his head. "It's a wonder I feel any guilt at all in handing you over to the inquisitors. Thank you for making it at least a little easier on my conscience."

"Conscience? You have one of those?"

Perja turned and strode out of the cell. "See you at the trial, *brother.*"

"There's a reason the fat beggar earns less coin," shouted Aynward after his brother but this earned him no response. Aynward chuckled. *I'm turning into Dwapek, aren't I?* He considered Dwapek's fate in Brinkwell, then winced. *In more ways than one.*

Later that day, Aynward lay strapped to a table in a room down the hall from his cell. He was still deep below the palace; no one would hear him scream. Two associate inquisitors stood by quietly. They had assisted the Senior Inquisitor with securing their prisoner, as well as carrying the various tools of torture.

The Senior Inquisitor wore the typical white robes to indicate his purity in qualifying for a position dedicated to finding the truth, no matter the cost. Aynward believed the white was more to serve as a reminder to others when they swaggered around the palace after their sessions, blood-staining their white clothes for all to see.

The man in white addressed Aynward with a low, nasally voice. "You have been accused of murder, and the evidence surrounding the incident is damning. Do you contest that which the evidence claims?"

Aynward considered what he knew he was supposed to do versus what he, in that moment, wished to do. He allowed himself to release a few deep breaths before replying, "I did not murder my father."

"Of course," said the man. "Let us verify the truth of what you say." One of his henchmen opened up a kit lined with small metal tools. "With pleas of innocence, I find very few remain as innocent as they first claim, though some small few have managed to take their 'innocence' to the grave. I pray you will be wiser than this. I take no pleasure in what I must do next."

Aynward felt his breath thicken, as if the air in the room had suddenly become an invisible jelly.

The man took hold of Aynward's foot, squeezing the knuckle at the base of the big toe. Aynward nearly confessed just then. *I have to be strong or Perja won't believe it. It's just pain. Be strong, be—*

The metal forceps dug in painfully beneath his toenail and Aynward gasped. Then the man let go of the knuckle, taking the other side of the forceps to clamp down on the nail. Aynward felt the tension, the dull pain where the bottom tooth dug into the sensitive tissue beneath the nail.

The man whispered, "This can be over before it begins. All you need do is confess."

Aynward opened his mouth to speak. "I—I—" He had to endure. This was his only chance. "I'm in no—"

Pain exploded from the place where Aynward's toenail had once been and he screamed. His voice reached pitches both high and low at the same time, a guttural shriek of horror. The rush of anguish was worse by far than the warm sting he recalled from the sword wound several weeks earlier. He strained against the straps, but they held firm to the table.

The wave of initial suffering did eventually level out to become a barely tolerable throbbing and he could hear himself continue to moan. He was vaguely aware as the forceps dug into the toenail beside the one he had just lost. The inquisitor offered another chance to escape. "Confess. All you need do is confess."

Aynward ignored the pain, and the voice of the inquisitor in front of him.

He shouted once more as the second nail was removed, then a wave of nausea washed over him. *One more. One more should be enough. You can do this.*

The room swam before his eyes as he waited for the inquisitor to remove yet another piece of his flesh. He felt as if he was floating outside his body, observing the torture from beyond himself.

"Confess!" shouted the inquisitor before ripping the third nail. Aynward moaned, but it morphed into an unhinged gurgled laugh. The nausea was like an intoxicant and Aynward felt his sanity drifting away. *Get ahold of yourself.*

As the metal forced its way beneath yet another nail, Aynward exhaled, "I confess." He hardly recognized his own voice. The inquisitor held the forceps in place, and Aynward felt himself panic. *He's going to continue!*

"I confess!"

The forceps held firm, the man had taken the tool in both hands and pulled on the nail. "To what do you confess?"

The haze in Aynward's head fell away, replaced again by urgency and fear.

"Everything! I killed my father. I slew the King with my own blade." He felt tears flowing from his face now. "Please, I'm guilty."

The man in the white robe smiled, holding fast to his grip on the nail. He gave a final tug, but not enough to remove the nail. Then he released and handed the instrument of torture to one of his minions.

"See? That wasn't so bad. Does it not feel better to simply relieve yourself of the guilt?"

Aynward ignored the sadistic inquisitor and said, "Provide me the requisite materials and I'll scribe the formal confession I am to read to the court tomorrow."

The man didn't initially respond to Aynward, but finally gave a nod to his henchmen and they began loosening the straps holding him in place.

Aynward was surprised at his body's ability to adjust to the throbbing discomfort of his injuries, accepting this as a new normal. That new normal did not apply to walking, however. He was acutely aware of the damage done to his foot as his toes pressed against the stone floor with each step, leaving a trail of blood behind. They would wait to clean him up until they were satisfied with his confession. Should he fail to hold up his end of the bargain, he knew they would eagerly return to torture. He had no desire to resume such activities.

He was escorted into a torchlit room down the hall. It had been prepared with the items necessary for written confession. This was not the first time they had gone through this routine, Aynward knew.

Aynward collapsed into his chair and dipped the quill into the ink. His fingers shook, but this became less noticeable once he started writing. His penmanship would show signs of distress, but that was to be expected. This was not the first written confession to have been extracted under duress. He wrote exactly what his brother would wish to see, detailing a full confession of guilt in the crime of regicide, patricide, and treason against the crown.

Hours later, he heard the familiar creak of metal, the sound of a guest. Dinner had already arrived, so he prayed this was—Gervais's decisive steps brought him into view, and with him, a small pack bearing gifts.

Gervais gave him a sympathetic smile. "It would have been a difficult thing to watch your execution, Your Grace. I am glad that you decided to end the suffering. The public would know of your alleged betrayal no matter your confession. At least this way you are able to live out your days with a semblance of comfort."

Aynward glanced down at his bandaged foot. "A semblance. Speaking of, do you have in your pack what I think and hope you have?"

Gervais gave him a crooked smile. "Oh, I think you will be pleased indeed." He pulled out two bottles. "Aged Scritlandian, two very good years, I'm told." He knelt down and loosened the cork to the first.

Aynward nodded to the second. "May as well open the both of them. I haven't much of a tolerance right now, but I'm going to try very hard to forget the pain in my foot and the lie I'm to repeat before tomorrow's proceedings."

"Very well, Your Grace. Just be sure you're able to speak with some clarity by noon of the morrow. I suspect that your brother would not take kindly to an incomprehensible confession. This will, after all, be his first public appearance after the coronation. Be mindful of the fact that your level of comfort in the coming years remains contingent upon your compliance here. I know you're innocent, but I also know you've no other choice. You may as well make the most of what you're being given."

Aynward popped the cork from the first bottle and drank. He swallowed a gulp, then said, "Oh, I intend on making the very most of tomorrow's events. Worry you not; I know exactly what I must do." He took another swig, a small one this time.

Gervais rose to his feet.

"Gervais?"

"Yes, Your Grace?"

"Thank you. I wish we would have had more time together."

Gervais bowed. "As do I, Your Grace."

He left the cell, and Aynward set down the bottle and waited. It was going to be a very long night, and an even longer tomorrow.

CHAPTER 28

KYLLEAN

LUMÁLE HEIGHTS WAS AN EERIE place, even for someone who knew the danger was minimal. Kyllean's father had brought him there as a child, and he recalled how frightened he had been even with his father beside him. The fact that it was after dark and they were only able to see by the grace of the two moons gave the experience an even more sinister feel. Sure, the bright moons provided ample illumination on their path, but the depths of shadow found elsewhere in the night attempted to dampen even the merriest of moods.

Still, Kyllean eagerly ascended the slope alongside two initiates he had taken a liking to. Evra had progressed so quickly she was planning to test for her blade the following day. It had been her idea to visit the Heights before she left Kyllean and Levi behind to continue their training. She was confident that she would pass.

"Hurry up. Must you two be slower at everything?"

Kyllean focused on the surrounding stone and drew in a bit of power, then took two steps and leaped higher than any ordinary human could to land upon the switchback above. He called down, "I was thinking the exact same thing." Then continued up the slope as if he'd been in front of them the entire time.

"Show-off," grumbled Levi from below.

They reached the lowest level of nests on the next switchback, but these were vacant, and had been for who knew how long. *My father probably knows*, thought Kyllean.

The nests were small depressions carved into the stone of the steep rock face of the mountain, and the Tal-Don fortress had been built at the base of this mountain. Kyllean didn't know which had been introduced first, the switchback path or the nests themselves. They seemed to both exist as if they'd been there as one since the beginning of time. He, Evra, and Levi continued to climb, passing empty nest after empty nest, dozens upon dozens of them, all devoid of life. This reinforced the truth about the dwindling majestic creatures. Master Hilde said that at one time every nest had been occupied and new nests had to be built above the others.

Being creatures that adhered to a hierarchy, the highest roosts were now occupied by the oldest Lumáles, which were said to move themselves periodically as better spots became available. However, the Lumáles they sought had not yet claimed riders. The first would be fourth from the bottom. Without riders, none of these had been given a name.

They walked on quietly until Levi mused, "Wonder when the new heir will be sent here for training."

Evra responded, "Hopefully soon. Maybe having a child earn the blade before either of you might inspire you to speed things along."

"Erm, did I miss something?" asked Kyllean.

Levi nodded. "Uh, if you're not sure what we're talking about then yes, you did. Speaking of, I meant to ask you about this. Wasn't it that youngest prince who was at Brinkwell with you? What was his name?"

Kyllean nodded. "Aynward, but he's not the heir."

Levi laughed. "Well, I know that." He shook his head. "You really don't know, do you?"

"Know what?" said a frustrated Kyllean.

Levi stopped, and Evra followed suit before exchanging a look. Levi said, "Okay. I just assumed you knew. Everyone was talking about it yesterday at the evening meal."

"I skipped last night to practice. Now get on with it!"

Levi put a hand on Kyllean's shoulder. "Prince Aynward murdered his father, the King, in cold blood. Slew him in his own chambers. Rumor says the guards found him alone with the dead King, murder weapon in hand. He's set to stand trial in a few days but it's just a formality."

Kyllean felt like he had been punched in the chest with a hammer.

"That—that can't be right." Kyllean turned away and closed his eyes, trying to wrap his mind around the image of Aynward, a cold-blooded murderer. *No way.* "His father and he weren't close, Aynward made that pretty clear, but still, he's no murderer."

Levi shrugged. "You said yourself that you both killed several Lugienese during your escape, and didn't he lose his counselor in the fight? They say that kind of thing can change a man. He experienced both in the same day. Perhaps he's not the same person you knew back in Brinkwell."

Kyllean shook his head in disbelief. "I—I just don't see it. We traveled together from Brinkwell. Nothing about his demeanor suggested murder. Not even close." But even if it were true, the idea that his friend was to be executed for . . . anything, still hurt. Aynward had risked his own life coming back just to see that Kyllean and Minathi made it to safety. They then fought alongside each other in battle to narrowly escape death. That was a difficult bond to break.

The trio resumed walking and Evra patted Kyllean on the shoulder. "I'm sorry. Maybe seeing the Lumáles will be a welcome distraction."

When they turned up the next switchback, Levi exclaimed, "Finally!"

All three of them slowed as they approached the first nest occupied by a living, breathing, Lumále. Unlike a bird's nest, this was no crude thing of sticks. Three paces from the path, covered by a roof of stone, grew a spiraling set of vines that stretched toward the center, forming a perfectly circular opening just large enough for one of their vast heads to peer out should they choose. The vines were decorated with flowers of every color. Kyllean knew that the vines could separate at the behest of the Lumáles but had no idea how any of that worked.

Levi said, "My mother and father have both taken me to see their Lumáles a dozen times each. I'm still no less awed by them."

Kyllean's own father had only taken him the once, but watching Evra, he kept that complaint silent. She had never been allowed to come here. Her father was a sword bearer but had never been chosen by a Lumále and had therefore never been permitted to bring Evra to the Heights. Only initiates, blade bearers, and Lumále-tethered riders were permitted. And only the riders were allowed to bring guests.

"Amazing . . ." she said, trailing off as she stood staring.

"Yeah," agreed Kyllean, feeling a little relieved by the diversion from darker thoughts.

After few moments had passed, Levi spoke up. "Come on; let's do what we came here to do."

They continued to climb, passing mostly empty nests along the next switchback. A man passed them on his way down, grumbling, "The old spinster's never going to choose." Kyllean presumed this man was as of yet a blade bearer untethered.

Kyllean had known to an extent, but had never reconciled the fact that the initiates were not only competing with the other initiates, but also with every untethered blade bearer in the fortress. For as many centuries as the Tal-Don riders had been here, they'd never been able to decipher the secret of the Lumále pairing process. Lumáles chose who they chose, when they chose, sometimes ignoring the same blade bearer a dozen times before suddenly offering the link. There were only five remaining untethered Lumáles. Four of them were still relatively young, and the fifth actually did have a name, sort of. She was referred to as the old spinster, for she was well beyond the age of choosing. Nearly all Lumáles chose a rider before they reached the age of twenty. But Master Hilde remained optimistic even about the old spinster, stating that there had once been a Lumále that had held out fifty years before finally choosing their rider.

"Can hardly blame them for being so selective," said Levi. "In fact, I'd say it's a wonder any of them ever choose a rider."

"And why's that?" replied an incredulous Evra.

"Well, think about it. What do they get in return?"

A fair question, agreed Kyllean.

Levi elaborated, "They become slaves to whomever they choose. Compelled by magic to obey the will of the rider they select until one of the two of them passes, and even then the sudden severing of the link often renders them magically impotent. Why offer such a thing to us?"

They had reached the dwelling of the first untethered Lumále and the question died there.

They stared at the opening in the center of the spiraling vines, trying to catch a glimpse of the creature inside. Levi approached the nest. "Hello?"

Kyllean and Evra remained where they were, less comfortable in spite of the fact that Lumáles weren't known to harm visitors. Then again, few visitors frequented Lumále Heights so the probability was low.

Levi edged closer, his face only a hand's breadth away from the opening. Kyllean joined him, trying to see into the darkness behind the vines.

Then Kyllean felt warmth in the air in front of his face and the vines moved ever so slightly, swaying. The smell was . . . unsettling. A rank mixture of death and the flowers of the vine, which slowly parted to reveal the monstrous head of a Lumále peering out at him. He stumbled back, bumping into Evra, who caught him and Levi alike.

"Watch out!" she yelped, pushing both boys off of her.

Neither paid her any mind as the Lumále's head flowed out of the opening in the parted vines. Its large, gray head inched closer, the mouth large enough to easily clamp down around a human torso. Attached to the head was a long, narrow neck, longer than a full-grown man was tall. The rest of the creature was hidden behind the vines, but Kyllean knew what lay beyond. The serpentlike neck connected to a body three times the size of a large ox, all covered in thick, shiny gray fur. Holding the body upright were two thick legs ending with dangerous black talons the length of curved swords. There was also the barbed tail, ten paces long, that could be used like a whip to open wounds in flesh as easily as any blade. The size and scope of the wings simply made everything else seem all the larger. With wings fully extended, one of these creatures could measure fifteen paces from end to end.

The Lumále's snout sniffed the air with keen interest before producing a grunting noise. It then disappeared back behind the vines and everything went still.

"Well, that was . . ."

"Awesome!" finished Levi. "A little bit terrifying, but still . . . awesome!"

They continued up the slope and repeated the process for the next three occupied, untethered Lumáles, though only one actually opened its vines to meet them and they were wise enough not to attempt entering uninvited to the others.

"Still have one more," said Evra, unaffected by their failure thus far.

Kyllean grumbled, "The spinster? Aren't you tired yet? That one is still a ways up, and everyone knows she's not going to choose a rider."

Evra puffed out her chest and steeled her jaw. "She hasn't met me yet."

Kyllean recognized the determination for what it was and nodded. "Okay, let's go."

The moons continued to move across the night sky as they climbed yet further and Kyllean ventured a look out over the edge of the steep slope to the fortress below. They illuminated the rectangular shapes of vast stone used to build the structures that made up walls as well as the buildings within. A few lamps glowed further, but most of the light clung to the source itself, swallowed by the darkness of night.

He saw the faint glow of the Talmune, a few leagues away, though from here it appeared quite close.

"Come on!" said Evra from up ahead and Kyllean returned to the climb.

They finally arrived and understood what the rider had been grumbling about on his way down.

"She's not even here!" groaned Levi as he peered into the nest through the vines.

Disappointment at having climbed all the way there for nothing attempted to surface, but it never made it past Kyllean's sense of relief, for he would not have to face the pressure of failing to be chosen yet again.

Levi continued, "All this way for nothing!"

Kyllean saw Evra's expression and his relief died. *I'm so selfish.* She appeared ready to cry. Then her eyes widened and her mouth opened. She stumbled back, eyes fixed on something above, but Kyllean didn't have the chance to follow her line of sight because he saw where she was headed: over the edge.

He took a quick step and leaped.

CHAPTER 29

KYLLEAN

A S HE SOARED THROUGH THE air, Kyllean caught Evra's wrist just as her right foot skidded off the edge of the walkway. A tumble down the steep slope would surely be fatal. He yanked her wrist right as his body struck painfully flat upon the stone path. Unfortunately, he didn't have enough leverage to stop her momentum altogether and the rest of Evra's body continued over the edge. Kyllean held fast and slid to the edge as Evra slammed against the cliff that would be her doom. And then, thankfully, all movement stopped.

Kyllean held Evra by the wrist, his body flattened against the path up to the shoulder while the rest of his arm extended down, keeping Evra from certain death as her body brushed against the side of the upright stone face of the mountain.

He tried to pull, but with his arm extended as it was, her body didn't move. He drew in magic and attempted again, but he still lacked the necessary leverage. *I can't do it.* "You're going to have to pull yourself up. Draw upon your magic!"

"I—I'll try," she whimpered.

He felt her other hand clasp his arm higher up, while he remained perfectly still for fear he might be pulled over with her. This worry was minimized when Levi took hold of his foot to stabilize his position. "Thank you!" he yelled back.

Evra's next grip caught Kyllean's tunic and she pulled herself up from there. Just as she climbed to safety, a shadow descended and all three initiates looked up to see their field of vision taken up by the massive form of a Lumále, wings outstretched to the fullest extent as it prepared to land . . . right where they lay.

Kyllean and the others scooted on their hind ends as fast as possible to make way. They stopped when their backs pressed against the wall of the opening to the creature's nest. Vast as the creature was, it landed almost soundlessly. And while Lumáles were not known to be dangerous to visitors, the humans' primal sense of self-preservation triggered a quickened pulse as the imposing bird-thing stared down at them.

Kyllean swallowed his fear and decided to try to break the ice. He pressed his hands to the wall behind to help guide him to his feet while remaining flat against the stone. He inclined his head. "Greetings, O majestic Lumále. You look quite . . . erm . . . lovely today."

No response.

Keep talking. That will fix it. "So, uh—we have come to visit you with the hope that you might find one of us worthy of—you know—choosing to send the magical link thingy."

No response. But it did blink. *Blinking seems like a good start.* "We're a little bit eager. There's a whole bunch of Lugienese gearing up to come this way to kill us all, so we were thinking it might be better to take and kill them instead."

The Lumále tilted its head so just one of its eyes faced him.

He gulped but continued to pretend that he wasn't ready to soil himself. "Where are my manners? My name is Kyllean," he gulped again, "if it please you." Gesturing slowly with each hand, he added, "This here is Levi, and this is Evra. Any one of us would be a fine choice, though I must admit, I am best suited."

This convinced Levi to chime in as he too came to his feet. "Both of my parents are tethered to other Lumáles. Their Lumáles are called Salgor and Prayden; you probably know them. Fantastic creatures."

The massive head moved again, this time directly in front of Kyllean and Levi. Even their forced bravados were unable to rally, and no further words followed. The nostrils flared, then seemed to breathe in deeply, Kyllean's tunic rippling as the creature took measure of him. It made a sort of snorting noise, then moved on to Levi. This noise was repeated before moving on to Evra, who Kyllean saw was shaking beside him.

He reached out a hand and took hers in his own. "It's okay," he whispered. "Just stay calm."

The Lumále continued to sniff her, and Kyllean heard her say, "Please." Kyllean wasn't sure if she was pleading for her life or to be chosen.

The creature backed its head away and turned its other eye to face her. A moment later it extended its head toward the heavens and released a vast shriek, then turned and leaped from the edge, outstretched wings lifting it into the air.

All three trainees released their own form of sighs while Levi went so far as to sink back to the ground.

"Whoa," was the most intelligent sound Kyllean could muster.

A short while later, the trio descended from the roost. Joviality having withered on the way up, the trip down was mostly quiet. As they approached the bottom, Levi stopped and pointed to their left and said, "Hey . . . guys . . ."

Kyllean looked up to see the silhouette of a bird, color removed by the blinding backdrop that was the sun, but he quickly realized why Levi seemed so concerned. The shape was growing quickly, very quickly, and this was no bird.

The Lumále soared toward them at an alarming speed and soon all three of them darted for cover in the nearby vacant nest. The gray Lumále pulled up at the last moment to land more heavily than before, talons scraping the stone as it skidded to a halt. It then stalked forward, claws clicking the stone. This time there was no sense of curiosity, though Kyllean couldn't explain why he felt that was the case. Once closer, the creature brought its nose right up to him and pushed.

He fell over, then scrambled to his feet. "Hey, what—" It did the same thing to Levi, who bumped into Kyllean's recently recovered form and they both fell in a jumbled heap. Untangling themselves, they returned to standing, and this time the Lumále was gentler as it guided them out from within the empty nest, leaving Evra alone as the Lumále turned back to face her vulnerable, shaking form.

"Oh no you don't," said Kyllean, taking a step toward the animal as he drew his . . . he didn't have a weapon with him, not that it would have done him any good. The creature's head turned back and it opened its huge maw filled with sharp teeth and released a shriek that pierced his bones, sapping any desire to do anything but curl up into a tiny ball and hope he was forgotten.

It repeated the noise and he started backward. "Evra, get out of here while she's distracted!"

But Evra didn't move.

Then the Lumále opened its wings as much as it could in the confined space and Evra disappeared behind them. That's when Kyllean felt the tingle of magic, which elicited confirmation that something very bad was about to happen to Evra. Lumáles were creatures with innate magic, but class discussions of Lumáles had yet to reveal precisely what these abilities entailed.

There was of course another possibility.

"Evra, are you okay in there?" he called.

"I—I—" Then she yelped as a bubble of magical sensations was released. Whatever was going on, Lumále magic was involved.

"That's it." Kyllean moved not knowing exactly what he could or should do to rescue her but felt compelled to do *something*.

Levi shouted, "Kyllean! No!"

Kyllean used his own magic to speed his approach and lined up to kick the big bird in the ribs, or kidney, or whatever existed in the side he saw covered in gray fur above the supporting legs.

"Evra's being tethered!"

Kyllean's misguided rescue attempt died at those words, but his momentum did not. Instead of the kick he had been planning, his entire body pivoted off the foot he had planted, and he fell awkwardly into the side of the creature between the wing and shoulder area. *Nothing like a face full of fur,* he thought.

He pushed off and stumbled back just as the Lumále whirled, its wing knocking him to the ground. *I deserved that.* He just prayed the retaliation ended there.

Kyllean wasn't certain what a glare looked like coming from a Lumále, but he thought he might be experiencing it as the creature peered down at him. "Very sorry about that." He made no sudden movements, hoping this would help his chances of being seen as nonthreatening, in spite of his most recent action.

The creature bent its head toward him and slowly opened its mouth. Sharp teeth the size of fingers gleamed back at him. Kyllean went completely rigid. "Please. Please. No." He'd never heard of anyone in the fortress being attacked by a Lumále, but that didn't mean he couldn't be the first, or that they simply kept such things quiet.

It was too late to run, or even scoot out of the way. The open mouth closed over his torso and flinched, eyes closed as the pressure of its jaw increased. Then he was lifted into the air. The teeth did not seem to be quite as razor sharp as they appeared at first glance; in fact, he was pretty sure nothing pierced his skin. His next concern was not that of being crushed or impaled, but when he opened his eyes, he saw that it had swung its head out over the edge of the cliff. There was nothing beneath him but open air for another hundred feet.

That would probably be a better way to go than being chewed to death, he supposed. He had always wanted to fly, though he had imagined it going slightly different than this.

Then he heard Evra say, "Put him down . . . on the walkway."

Kyllean saw her standing tall beside the creature.

Nothing happened for a time, and Kyllean played out his fall down the cliffside a dozen times before he was finally deposited beside a speechless Levi. He collapsed unceremoniously to the stone path, then stood and brushed off the saliva, which meant smearing it along his tunic.

"Thank you, Evra."

"You're welcome. Thanks for, well, trying to help."

The Lumále beside him continued to glare, then finally snorted and turned away as it lowered itself to the ground and extended its wing as much as the space beside Evra permitted.

Levi found his voice. "I think it wishes you to ride."

She turned, then glanced back at Levi and Kyllean. "I—should I? Don't I need a saddle?"

Levi shook his head. "My parents have flown without one. You just hold on to the fur. Saddles are more for long flights and warfare."

Turning back to the Lumále, she slowly climbed up and came to a sitting position, legs dangling just below the shoulder of the wings. She looked over at Kyllean. "Like this?"

Kyllean shrugged and looked to Levi. "Looks right to me," Levi said. "She's not going to fly unless she thinks you're . . ." The statement died as the Lumále extended its wings and flapped, causing its body to lift from the ground even as Levi and Kyllean ducked to avoid being hit.

Minutes later, Kyllean sat with his legs dangling over the edge of the stone path, watching as Evra flew away upon the majestic animal.

"It seems we're just not destined to ride," said Levi, longing in his voice.

"There are still a few more left," replied Kyllean.

Levi shook his head. "As I said . . ."

Kyllean took on a more serious tone. "We can still earn our blades. I've every intention of killing at least a dozen more Lugienese before my end. I was hoping to do it from the back of a Lumále, of course, but I'll take it however I can get it."

"Suppose that's the best attitude to have with so few Lumáles left to claim a rider. I've just dreamed of riding since I was a kid."

"Yeah," agreed Kyllean, though he didn't think his experience of longing matched that of Levi's. His own desire to ride had been one of curiosity, not true longing. It hadn't been until very recently that he finally felt compelled to embrace his heritage as a rider. Too late, it seemed. He felt more guilt over his previous attitude of indifference than disappointment over having missed the opportunity to become a full rider. Not that he really believed this would have changed the outcome, but he did believe that he didn't deserve to be chosen, not when there were others, like Levi, like Evra, who had wanted nothing more for their entire lives.

Staring out toward the east, Kyllean watched the shrinking form of Evra and her Lumále, along with three others flying about, practicing aerial acrobatics in preparation for the coming war. Kyllean was glad that at least someone had been claimed. They were going to need every advantage they could get.

"Let's go. I need to give my mind a rest. Let's practice killing bad people," said Kyllean.

Levi followed him down the slope toward the practice yard without another word.

CHAPTER 30

DAGMARA

THE DOMED GREAT HALL WHERE Dagmara's father, the late King, held court was now home to the fallacious trial of her brother, Aynward, who was escorted into the room by two guards. He walked on unsteady feet, one of them mutilated, she knew, bandaged inside of the boot he now wore. He stumbled and nearly fell, the guard to his right the only reason he remained upright.

Her older brother, Sylmis, fourth youngest of the Dowe children, leaned over and said, "It appears our brother came upon some drink while in the dungeons."

"So it would seem," whispered Dagmara as she nervously adjusted her tiara. She hated wearing the thing, but it was a required piece of her princessly ensemble. No matter how she had it arranged within her hair, it always found a way of poking at her scalp.

The entire royal family, their spouses, and any children present in the city sat in the front row of the Great Hall to bear witness to the public trial. Nobles were positioned in the second, third, and fourth rows, followed by a row of guards, and behind them, a section for the general populace. The room was filled to capacity; not an unheard-of occurrence, but a rare one. The death of a king by his own son's hand was cause enough to intrigue even the most dispassionate. The doors had been closed; the room filled long before the trial was set to begin that afternoon.

Dagmara's new seat was a change. She was accustomed to sitting on the platform as a child of the King. The entire arrangement was new, in fact, though she had sat here during the coronation ceremony the day before. Dagmara glanced over at Brenna, who stood along the side of the room with the other counselors, mostly counselors to Dagmara's siblings' children.

Perja sat primly on his new throne, the throne that should still have been home to her father, to his father. His wife, the new Queen, was seated beside him, his own two daughters beside her, and Dagmara's mother had retained a place of honor to his other side.

Aynward reached the seat near the lectern where stood a priest of the Chrologal faith, the faith loosely followed by the Kingdom of Dowe, adopted by the line of Dowe after the fashion of the Scritlandians who had assisted in the overthrow of the Lothlem hundreds of years ago.

The lectern was positioned at an angle to face both the gathered crowd and the King. The priest quieted the room with a lifting of his hand. "We are gathered here today to bear witness to a matter of the gravest of nature, a dark stain upon the very fabric of our great Kingdom. In accordance with Kingdom law, the accused must stand trial before his peers, but is to be judged by the creator, Tecuix, and his lieutenant here on Doréa, the King.

"Only a unanimous decision by the High Council itself may reverse such a judgment." The room was silent as the man spoke. This was still routine, and yet the man's voice commanded their attention. "As is custom, I will read the accused a statement of law under which he is being tried, followed by the description of evidence against him. This will be followed by the testimony of witnesses. After these have been heard, the accused will be allowed an opportunity to speak in defense or to accept guilt of the crime, offering any pertinent evidence and one witness should he deny the claims. Once all has been heard, his

Holiness, King Perja Dowe, will cast judgment and the matter will be settled beyond dispute."

The crowd applauded, though it was laced with tension. Having their own monarch murdered by his son put the people on edge. Such things simply did not happen in the civilized nation that was the Kingdom of Dowe. It was an act more akin to the heathens to the north or the mysterious evil that lurked in the Trolich Forests to the east.

The priest droned on about the evidence stacked against Aynward, though it wasn't a lengthy description of events. The evidence was quite simple, just irrefutably sound. There were no witnesses to dispute what had been found in the room: their King lying dead in a pool of his own blood, with the "impetuous" Prince Aynward and his bloody sword the only logical causes.

The priest returned to the lectern after the witness spoke his piece. They brought forth the guard from the hallway leading to the King's chambers. He had seen no one else enter or leave the room. He also corroborated the evidence found at the scene. The priest then gestured to Aynward, who sat sloppily in his chair waiting to be called upon to defend himself.

"The accused is known by the name Aynward Dowe, the victim's son, and a prince of the crown. He will now speak on behalf of his guilt in the matter. May the gods grant him wisdom and truth as he does so."

Dagmara felt her own nerves through the tingling in her stomach and the sweat in her palms. *I don't know if I can do this,* she thought. She glanced up to the balcony overlooking the room and found Fronklin, Aynward's childhood friend, now a member of the guard. He stood poised in his chain mail and breastplate alongside the rest of the archers. He met her gaze, winked, and then smiled.

Aynward moved to stand, bringing Dagmara's attention back to the lectern. He leaned forward and put his hands on his knees for support, then stood on wobbly legs nearly falling on his face, catching himself at the last moment. The crowd murmured at his obvious intoxication.

Dagmara spared a look at Perja and saw his fury barely in check. Aynward was making a mockery of this trial already, Perja's first real appearance as King. Dagmara noticed his wife's hand reach over to touch Perja's thigh, an attempt to keep him from standing.

Aynward reached the lectern and fumbled through his jacket to find a piece of parchment. As he did so, he made eye contact with Dagmara; she gave him the nod of confirmation. With slurred speech, Aynward spoke to the crowd. "Greetings, my fellow friends, citizens." Then, turning to regard Perja: "And others. My apologies for the delay here, these cuffs make difficult work of even the most mundane tasks."

He finally managed to grasp the parchment and pulled it out. But then fumbled it in his hands as he tried to flatten it out on the lectern to read. He reached down to pick it up then cleared his throat and the murmuring stopped once again.

"My name is Aynward Dowe, son of Lupren Dowe. I am a prince, though my chances to inherit are about as likely as a butcher opening a smithy." This caused awkward laughter to spread through the room, though the mood remained tense.

"I have here a written confession of guilt regarding the crime described by the priest minutes ago. They only had to take three toenails to convince me that I should just admit to the crime of which I was accused." He blew out a hard breath, his nervousness apparent in spite of his drunken state.

"Okay, so without further delay," he made a show of staring directly at the written confession, "I, Aynward Dowe, do hereby declare my guilt. I have committed the crime of—" His fingers slipped from the parchment and it rolled up once again. Aynward scrabbled about in his chains, knocking the written confession to the ground for a second time.

King Perja stood up from his throne, indignation in his voice as he said, "Oh for the love of the gods! Unlock the cuffs so the man can get on with his confession!"

One of the two guards who had escorted Aynward into the room moved quickly to do as commanded.

"You are too kind, Your Majesty."

Perja sat without acknowledging Aynward's remark, but his hands clutched the arms of his throne hard enough to turn the knuckles white.

Aynward started speaking as the guard worked his keys. His speech was no longer slurred as he said, "I have committed the crime of . . . being the best candidate to frame for the murder of a king. I am guilty of being in the room while an assassin used my own sword to slay the King. But I did not commit this heinous act, and no amount of torture will cause me to say otherwise!"

Gasps rang out from the crowd, and the guard working Aynward's shackles looked up in surprise. But it was too late; he had turned the key and the cuffs fell to the ground just as Aynward pulled the man's wrist forward so he could reach his weapon. Aynward pulled it free, the sound of drawn metal ringing throughout the room. Aynward then stepped to the side and kicked the side of the man's knee, toppling him to the floor. Aynward was no longer the drunken fool, his movements fluid and precise.

Perja stood up and shouted, "Stop him! Now!"

The room erupted into chaos, and Dagmara played her own part. "Guards! To me!" Four of the closest formed up at her command. She saw Brenna moving toward Aynward. There were only three guards set about the lectern where he stood, and Brenna surprised the first by coming from behind to slip both hands around the wrist that held his sword. She twisted and the man spun through the air before collapsing to the ground, wrist surely broken, and no sword. Brenna took on the next closest guard while Aynward engaged the third.

They would have to move quickly before the other guards in the room made their way through the mob of people fleeing in the other direction. Dagmara needed to get over there herself, though she had the advantage of sitting in the first row. Of the four guards protecting her, one turned and said to the others, "You two stay here to protect the princess. Jeffries, with me." With that, two of her guards departed to engage Aynward and Brenna, who had just dispatched their foes. This was Dagmara's opportunity. She prayed her secret martial training would be enough. She kicked the first guard in the back of the knee then reached in from behind and pulled his sword, which he had yet to take up. "Tecuix, forgive me." She sliced his hamstring before he had time to understand what was happening.

The other guard pulled his own sword but Dagmara swept out his foot as he pivoted to face her, throwing him off-balance. Her blade met the flesh of his other ankle. She had no desire to kill Kingdom guards on this day, or any day for that matter. But Aynward would die if she couldn't at least hurt a few.

Her brother, Sylmis, called from behind her, "Dagmara, what are you doing?"

She turned to see him just a step away, knowing he would try to stop her.

Without another thought, she pivoted and swung. Sylmis brought his weaponless hands up in defense, but she had no intention of striking down her own brother, at least not *this* brother. She just needed him not to see her other attack coming. With his feet firmly planted, he left himself open to a less permanent, yet still debilitating, blow. She kicked up with her foot, taking him square in the groin. He fell as if struck from behind by a volley of arrows.

"I'm sorry, Sylmis. Aynward is innocent. I have to help him."

She turned and ran before he could respond.

Perja's voice boomed, echoing above the bedlam, his rage unchecked. "Archers, fire at will!"

Dagmara prayed that Fronklin's role went according to plan or this escape would end much sooner and deadlier than she would like. She glanced up to the balcony above as she ran toward the exit in the back. Twenty archers fit arrows at the King's command.

A shaft fell harmlessly below as the first guard's string snapped. Shouts from the others rang out over the pandemonium, their strings all snapping when pulled. Dagmara caught up to Aynward as he struck the guard, Jeffries, unconscious.

"Let's go!" he said.

Dagmara shot a look up to the balcony and her eyes met Aynward's old friend. She mouthed the words, "Thank you." Fronk just winked again, then resumed acting surprised at his own broken bowstring.

Aynward led the way to the hidden exit behind the dais where sat the royal family, though those seats were now all empty. Then two members of the King's own guard moved to block the back exit. They had been positioned behind Perja during the trial. These two would not be dispatched so easily, and yet Aynward, Dagmara, and Brenna had only a short window of time before the rest of the guards broke through the sea of fleeing people to surround them.

Dagmara had no illusions about her own abilities with a sword. She prayed Aynward's alleged skills were no exaggeration and that Brenna's own lived up to the Scritlandian prestige.

Aynward lifted his sword but stopped and yelled, "We wish only to leave in peace, you need not—"

Aynward's words ended midsentence as he noticed the knife protruding from the closest man's shoulder, just beyond the breastplate. He would not be lifting his sword anytime soon. Brenna's leg shot out, followed by a spinning kick with the other that took the surprised guard square in the face.

Dagmara glanced over to the other guard, still wobbling on unsteady feet, a knife in his thigh. *When did that happen?* Dagmara wondered. Brenna continued to flow forward like a rolling fog. She was ready for the guard's off-balance attack, blocking before she slammed the pommel of her sword into the side of his head. He fell silently to the floor. Dagmara shot Brenna a questioning look, and she responded curtly, "No time for chatter."

They rushed past the guards and Aynward found the stone to open the hidden door, which swung inward to reveal a narrow passage designed as an escape for the royal family in the event of a palace breach. Brenna ushered Aynward and Dagmara into the opening, following close behind, then she grunted in pain. Dagmara turned to see Perja's form looming in the doorway. Brenna shrugged off the attack and turned to face the new King. She thrust her sword toward him, but he brushed it aside with ease. Brenna pressed the attack with a series of maneuvers, all of which appeared to do nothing more than amuse the King. Dagmara stared in awe as Perja fended off Brenna's attacks with disinterest, his eyes trained on Dagmara.

Two guards stepped forward to attack Brenna on either side, but Perja held up a hand, "She's mine."

They obeyed and Perja spoke again, his voice deep and measured. "This was a big mistake." Then his eyes zeroed in on Brenna, and Dagmara had a sinking feeling that the tide of battle was about to turn against the Scritlandian woman. Perja's movements seemed to exist within a different reality of space and time, and Brenna was suddenly being driven back toward the tunnel, sword flashing faster than Dagmara's eyes could follow, just to stay alive. What Dagmara was able to see was the emergence of crimson upon Perja's blade as he continued his assault.

She's going to die. We're not going to make it.

Aynward said, "Close the door!"

Dagmara was taken aback. "Without Brenna?"

"She will not win, but *we* can still make it."

Aynward attempted to wrest Dagmara from the doorway to close it himself. Dagmara held firm.

"We *need* to go!" urged Aynward.

"Then go!" said Dagmara as she stepped back out of the opening. Thinking only of Brenna's life, Dagmara stepped forward and swung her own sword at her brother, but he easily deflected it then resumed his assault on Brenna, who was somehow still on her feet in spite of Perja's impossible speed.

Dagmara looked down and spotted her tiara on the ground in front of her. It must have fallen in the midst of her attempt to strike out at Perja. She squatted to retrieve it, then shot it at Perja. With the tiara being so small, and with most of his attention on Brenna, he did not see it coming. He cried out as it struck him on the side of the face. This was quickly followed by a howl of pain and he dropped his weapon, blood running down the side of his sword arm.

Before Dagmara knew what was happening, she was pulled back into the tunnel by Brenna. Aynward slammed the door shut behind them. The guards who had been hanging back suddenly slammed into the door in force, but they may as well have tried to cut steel with water. The sound of the lock bar thudding into place further ensured their safety, at least for the moment.

Perja's voice boomed through the door. "You're a dead woman, Brenna. You all are."

Brenna responded, "And you are a coward, sending assassins to do the work of our enemy. See how long you last on your own."

Dagmara exhaled in relief. Neither Perja nor his men would break through that door; this was precisely how it had been designed, after all.

Brenna lit the torch. Then said, "Come on, we have a head start, but they'll know exactly where we are headed. This tunnel has only three exits. We need to get there before they do!"

CHAPTER 31

AYNWARD

EAVY BREATHING AND FOOTFALLS ECHOED down the empty
corridor so loud it seemed to Aynward that everyone in the entire
palace should be able to hear them. It wouldn't matter, their potential
destinations were limited. The three fugitives reached the first split in
the tunnel; the passage to the right would produce a dizzying set of
stairs set deep into the cliff upon which rested the palace. These would
lead to an alcove where a small schooner was stowed, always well-
maintained in the event of an unexpected attack. This tradition had
lasted many centuries, a protocol no one had been willing to end in spite
of its antiquated status during such an era of peace. The boat was large
enough for the King, a few guards, and a dozen or so of his closest kin.

The fugitives continued straight toward the two remaining exits up
ahead. The schooner would have been too obvious, and too difficult to
operate by just the three of them. And they weren't improvising; they
had at least some semblance of a plan.

Minutes later they reached the second split in the tunnel. Aynward
held the torch high to make sure he took the intended path, then turned
right. "This way will put us just beyond the palace walls by the west
bridge. You have everything prepared at the exit?"

Dagmara nodded, much of her hair sticking to her head, which was slick with sweat.

Brenna placed a hand on Dagmara's shoulder and inclined her head toward the left, the other tunnel. "I must go this way, Your Grace."

Dagmara's eyes went wide in astonishment, especially as she took in the blood leaking through a number of places along Brenna's torso and legs. "You're injured! Plus, we discussed this, you are coming with us. You'll be tortured and hanged if they catch you."

Brenna shook her head. "In spite of whatever sorcery the King possesses, he did not land any blows of substance. I have no intention of being caught. Secondly, you voiced your plan and I agreed to help, but that doesn't mean I will do as you decide. Punish me all you wish when we next meet, but I am acting in accordance with your best interest, not your fervent demands."

Brenna made to step in the direction of the alternate route but Dagmara said, "Oh no you don't!" and grabbed the taller woman by the arm.

Brenna spun with shocking speed and completed a maneuver that disengaged Dagmara's grip from her arm. Instead, Brenna held both of Dagmara's arms and turned her away. Dagmara's resistance may as well have been water trying to penetrate a solid stone wall. Passing the struggling Dagmara to Aynward, Brenna said, "Please ensure that your sister follows you. You have only a brief time to escape without notice. I hope to buy you a bit more time with a merry little chase through the countryside before I, too, disappear."

Aynward felt his sister's fury, his one arm clamping her to his side while the other continued to hold the torch. Brenna had taken her own torch from the sconce at the juncture and lit it using his.

Dagmara shouted in pure frustration as Aynward held her. He said in a strained voice, "Thank you, Brenna. I know how much you've risked." Brenna had visited Aynward to explain the plan, along with her intention to draw attention away from their pursuit, an aspect she had known Dagmara would reject if she knew.

"Don't waste it," said Brenna. Then she hurried in the other direction, the long tunnel leading to the east gate, far away from where Aynward and Dagmara were headed.

Dagmara finally shouted after Brenna, "You'd better survive! Or I'll—I'll—" She was crying. "I'll petition the gods to hold you captive until I enter the afterlife so I can punish you myself!"

Brenna was already growing distant, but her single parting word was clear enough. "Hurry!"

Aynward released his sister. "Come on."

For a brief moment, Aynward thought Dagmara would stand her ground, or even turn to follow Brenna, but she finally met Aynward's torchlit eyes. Then she turned and ran, Aynward following on her heels until they reached the solid stone door a short while later.

Aynward paused before undoing the locking mechanism. In theory, they would open the door to find nothing more than the hedge spanning the juncture between the outer palace walls and the east bridge, a break wall connecting the two. Brenna had been sent earlier to stow their change of clothes behind that hedge. This part of the plan would only succeed, however, if they had reached this place before the guards. The escape passages were unknown to all but the royal family, and the King's guard, but Aynward had no doubt that Perja would risk exposing the location of the tunnels for the sake of capturing his fugitive brother and sister.

Aynward passed the torch to Dagmara, undid the lock, then pushed on the thick stone door, which groaned as it swiveled on resistant hinges. He poked his head out, then hopped down. "Coast is clear, for now."

Dagmara followed him out, torch in hand, then tossed it over the adjacent wall to be extinguished in the water. She located the hidden pack and rummaged through the contents to find their traveling cloaks while Aynward closed the tunnel door. This was nothing new for Aynward, who had often used the tunnels to sneak into the city from the palace unnoticed. The real trick had always been slipping back in, since the tunnels could not be opened from the outside. Bribery had been the most effective method, though he had been caught enough to know the limitations of coin when it came to loyal guards.

The outline of the door disappeared, the seams becoming nearly invisible unless one knew where to look.

Dagmara threw a brown cloak at Aynward. "Here."

Aynward caught the jumble of dyed wool, then looked up just in time to avoid being struck in the head by two large, dark objects: boots. Good idea. He had been dressed in his formalwear for the confession, and the traveling cloak would have been little disguise with shiny noble's boots jutting out from beneath. He scrambled to take off his filthy doublet, then ripped off his boots.

"Ohh," he moaned.

In the midst of the fighting and the running immediately to follow, he had nearly forgotten the removal of three of his toenails, a sacrifice he had made in order to not draw suspicion to their plans. Now, he wondered at the wisdom in that choice. His toes were bandaged, but the blood had soaked through. His socks were crusting over with the stuff. And yet, removing his shiny footwear was nowhere near as painful as squeezing into the new pair. But he had no time to whine; he would deal with the pain later.

Dagmara stood over him as he pulled on the second boot, a weathered and worn-looking thing, precisely what he needed. Dagmara held the dress she had been wearing in her hands, a simple, form-fitting garment selected with the forethought of mobility, as well as ease of removal. She reached out a hand. "Give them here."

Aynward added the boots, sword, and doublet to Dagmara's pile, then she tossed it all over the wall. Aynward stood and threw on the cloak. Then Dagmara handed him a belt and a long, sheathed dagger, which Aynward instantly secured to his person. "Good thinking, though hopefully I won't have to defend us with this any time soon."

"Worry not, brother. I have my own protection."

He looked up and noted a high belt and a few other straps she appeared to have been wearing beneath her dress. What she had not been wearing was the short, curved sword sheathed in leather that she slid into place at an angle across her front side from shoulder to hip. She then donned her cloak to complete the transformation.

Aynward stared at her, dumbfounded.

"What? It was a parting gift from Brenna. She's been training me to fight with the Scritlandian scimitar, and it just so happens that they have also mastered the art of concealing their weapons."

Aynward shook his head in astonishment. "Are you able to sit while wearing that thing?"

"Not comfortably, but if needed, yes."

"Amazing." He shook his head as if awakening from a dream. "We need to move."

Dagmara peered over the thick hedge. "Our ship should be ready to travel as soon as we arrive."

"South Wharfs?"

Dagmara nodded.

Aynward led the way to the place in the hedge he had cut away years ago in order to sneak into the city to meet with friends. The hole was overgrown from disuse, but they managed.

Dagmara followed Aynward through, then stood and brushed herself off. "Well, I supposed there's at least one positive to the foolishness of your youth. I can't imagine fitting through that bramble otherwise."

The pair earned an odd look from a passerby, but he was the only person in sight. The middle-aged man appeared uninterested, continuing toward wherever he was headed. They were one street away from the main thoroughfare, a wide street dividing South Shandon, the old city district leading to the west bridge, which would lead to the South Wharfs before the street turned toward the newer portion of the city, the walled keeps of the nobility.

The two fugitives approached this street through an alley between two small buildings. They gave each other a look, then put up their hoods. Aynward peeked out from behind the building to his left. The street bustled. A great deal of this traffic included the gentry fleeing the confession. Most were in carriages, but others had simply fled on foot, likely too flustered to wait for their carriages; they now walked quickly.

The nobility would be the ones most likely to recognize Aynward and Dagmara.

"How are we going to get to the ship without being recognized?" asked Dagmara, concern swirling around each word like a spring gnat.

Aynward tried to sound more confident than he felt. "Just act like we belong. Trust me, we'll melt into the crowd like hot butter to a biscuit."

"Hot butter?"

Aynward shrugged. "Water to a stream?" He sighed. "People don't see what they don't expect, and they certainly don't expect us to pop up here dressed in traveling clothes."

Dagmara appeared unconvinced but gave him a slight nod.

"Come on, we need to go." He stepped into the midafternoon traffic. He tried to appear purposeful as he did so, matching the determined pace of many of the others in the street.

As they crested the east bridge, he turned to see a small contingent of guards in the distance moving to intercept them should they emerge from the tunnel. He sighed in relief and prayed they had left no obvious evidence of their passing.

Brenna, he knew, would leave the tunnel by the east gate open, making it appear as though the three of them had fled in that direction. Perja's men would fan out to search the East King's Road instead of the King's River where Aynward and Dagmara were headed. If Perja's men actually managed to capture Brenna soon enough they might discover the ruse, but by then Aynward and Dagmara should be leagues away.

After the initial hopelessness of his imprisonment, his closeness to freedom felt almost surreal. Yet he was now a fugitive within his own Kingdom. And with Perja on the throne and the assassination of his father staining his name, he would never truly be free, would he? He shrugged those dark thoughts aside for the moment. *I need to be further away from Salmune than the east bridge before I fall into despair and self-pity.*

CHAPTER 32

SINDRI

SINDRI OPENED HER EYES TO a gray, dim version of the world. Even the shadows lost the crisp blackness they might otherwise maintain. Considering how dark the wagon had been even during the day, sight alone was not the distinctive indicator that she was not fully awake. It was the eerie silence of the place. Not a single sound could be heard. Sindri remained wary. Kibure had spoken of being attacked by Magog himself while in his dream world. Yet she had to admit that waking here was better than not waking at all. *Must not be dead yet. That's good.* Then again . . . the afterlife she had been promised by the Klerósi faith now appeared to be completely defunct, so . . . *Perhaps I am dead and this is where people like me go when they die, at least for a time.* Walking the world in utter silence seemed like a mild punishment after the lifetime of sin she had led.

This was only her second visit to the dream realm, the first having taken place during the first night of her voyage from Brinkwell.

Arella had felt the magic but Sindri had ultimately asked her not to say anything until Sindri had time to puzzle out what it was she had just experienced. So far as Sindri knew, Arella had kept this promise.

Sindri sat up, recalling her last waking memory. She reached over to touch her shoulder where she had been stabbed. The fight with the child assassin seemed like it had just taken place, yet there was none of the pain she would have expected. *Perhaps Draílock or Arella healed me already.* Then again, she could be walking the world as the soul of a dead person. *No, this is the same dream realm as before.* But she did not know how long she had been "sleeping" or the severity of her injuries. She had been too consumed with her struggle to survive to take note of her injuries.

Sindri glanced over to where Arella and Draílock should have been within the wagon but knew she would see no one there. One could see inanimate objects, though absent of color, but one could not see people, or at least not the way one might ordinarily see them. There were small, subtle suggestions of what she thought might be people in the waking world but it was impossible to determine who was who without context.

Sindri crawled over to the tent flap and undid the buttons holding it shut. She was greeted by a brighter light than she expected. Surveying the area, she saw the muted, gray sun edging its way toward the horizon, framed by two immobile wagons. The rest of a caravan remained intact within the surrounding area. Their travels must have ended for the evening and while the area initially appeared devoid of others, as she relaxed her focus she realized that the camp was actually quite active. Light ripples in her vision represented what she believed to be the movement of men and women throughout. She saw a pile of wood beset by gray tongues of flame, a cook fire set beside her wagon. She saw two small distortions, trailed by much larger ones, all moving toward a small creek to her left. Horses?

Sindri approached an empty place beside two suggestions of people who had to be Draílock and Arella. She could hear nothing, of course, but she did notice something strange. A pot of something, probably stew, suddenly winked out of sight. It had been resting above the fire on the grate they had purchased early in their journey. The pot suddenly reappeared between her companions. Upon a stump between the two disturbances of air.

Sindri pondered this. *Ah,* she thought. *You can't see clothing worn by people here, either. Perhaps, like clothing, anything touching a person in the real world becomes muted within this dream place. But why does the ground not do this beneath our feet? Or even the seats where we sit?* She sat puzzled for several heartbeats, then decided to find something else to occupy her thoughts. She had no idea how to enter or leave this place but moving around would surely take her mind off of the many questions to which she had no answers. The only thing she knew for certain was that her previous visit had been brief and had ended inexplicably.

Sindri started walking along the line of a dozen wagons until she reached the one in the front. She reached up and opened the flap. The wagon was filled to capacity with large barrels. Judging by the number of tents set up, and the fact that these were all merchants hoping to transport one product or another, she concluded that most wagons would be filled with freight like this one.

She decided to look for something more interesting, a tent. She had learned that the merchant who had organized the caravan owned the first four wagons. He was the one who had taken care of hiring the small team of mercenaries paid collectively by each of the caravan goers. This man had the largest of the tents in their camp. Unlike most, which were low to the ground with only enough room for those who would sleep in them, his was tall enough to stand upright inside. Sindri looked both ways out of habit, felt foolish for having done so, then entered the tent.

The space did not seem to match the plain canvas that she saw from the outside. Once she crossed the threshold of the tent flap, she felt like she had entered a small palace. Her gaze was immediately drawn to the animal fur, soft pillows, and silky sheets spread along the floor. Whoever this man was, his taste was extravagant. He was probably skimming some of the collected mercenary fees right into his own pockets. There was a table set up in the back of the tent and Sindri walked over to inspect its contents. She noted a few small leather books, but most of what lay on the desk appeared to be ledgers. What caught her interest was the map, half covered by another piece of parchment. This map was not as detailed as the one Ruka had *provided,* but Sindri picked it up, anyhow.

That was when she noted another aspect of this dream place. The portion of the map that had been openly visible to the eyes remained unchanged; however, the portion that had been covered by another item remained completely blank. *It must be that only items readily visible can be seen in this place.* She had wondered about spies, and the threat posed should they know how to utilize this dream realm. Magog clearly knew how to navigate it. But there seemed to still be limitations to what one could uncover. Just to confirm her theory, she reached picked up one of the books and opened it. The title was written in Scritlandian, which she did not know how to read. She opened it anyway and found it to be just as devoid of writing as the blank half of the map.

She inspected a few more items, grew bored, set them back haphazardly, and then departed. As she stepped into the brighter gray light of the fading sun, her attention was caught by movement ahead, or at least she thought as much. Whatever it had been was no longer there by the time her eyes focused on the place in her peripheral vision where the movement had occurred. *Another person?* The thought terrified her. Anyone visiting this place would likely know more about its rules than her and was likely no friend.

Dread seeped into her. Was there such a thing as an assassin who worked from within the dream world? She was only aware of two beings with the ability to walk this realm. Then again, her brother, Lyson, had also likely been entering this place before his capture all those years ago. Any tazamine could likely come here, but that was not the possibility that frightened her. Did any of Magog's priests also know how to enter the world of dreams? She had no idea, but it seemed plausible.

Her curiosity overpowered her fear, driving her to investigate. She ran, taking no care since her footfalls would make no sound. The shape had disappeared behind a wagon more than three dozen paces away. Sindri raced for the other side to catch whoever or whatever this was. Behind the wagon lay only the barren vegetation of the Scritlandian desert. There would be nowhere else to hide.

She reached the wagon with surprising speed. In fact, it almost felt as though her steps extended further and faster than should be possible. On a whim of precaution, she attempted to draw magic from her surroundings, but there was nothing there from which to draw. Not in this place.

She wished that she had asked Kibure more about his dreams, or, rather, that he had been willing to share when she had asked. He probably understood little more than she did about the rules governing it, but perhaps she could have made some sense of this had she had time to ponder. Kibure had claimed that Magog himself had attempted to kill him, but she didn't know how that might have been accomplished. Could he use his powers in this place while others could not? Or had he attempted a more mundane method? Or perhaps Kibure was mistaken altogether about whom he had seen. She shook her head angrily. None of these questions could be answered right now.

She swallowed hard then slowly peered around the wagon.

There was no one there.

Whoever, or whatever, must be hiding along the other remaining side, the very back of the wagon. She knew this person or thing would see her just as much as she would see them, but she needed to know. She crept along to the corner and once again peered slowly to find—nothing.

Had this being disappeared completely? Or had they had jumped into the wagon itself? She did notice the flap was not secured. Stealth abandoned, she parted the canvas and hopped inside to find a great many crates filled with fruit. But nothing more.

Did I imagine that movement? It was possible.

She felt the vagueness of the dream world begin to fade as she climbed down from the back of the wagon. She would find no answers this day.

⊰⊰⊰

Sindri's vision came into focus, and so too the pain radiating from her shoulder and side. Her injuries did not feel as severe as they should have been, all things considered. In fact, they itched more than they throbbed.

The wagon did not jostle with the movement of travel, for which she was thankful, and light leaked into the place where she lay in the back of the wagon. She brought her good arm up to rub her face. Satisfied, she decided to attempt the other. She was relieved to find that it responded as intended.

"Ah. Welcome back to the world of the waking," sounded Draílock's voice, both condescending and indifferent as always.

Sindri grunted and sat up, feeling dizzy as she did.

Draílock said, "You're going to wish to drink some water. We've done our best to keep you fed and hydrated, but one can only do so much for the unconscious." He handed her a waterskin.

Taking it in her hands, she asked, "How long have I been asleep?"

Draílock glanced at Arella as if she were more qualified to respond. "A fortnight."

Sindri had just taken a large gulp of water but her quick intake of air mid-swallow caused her to choke, spittle flying every which way as she started a fit of coughing. Finally clearing her lungs of water, she exclaimed, "A fortnight? How is that—?"

Arella answered, "The wound to your side was quite serious, and we could only use so much magic to heal you. The rest needed to be handled by your body from within. You were very near to death."

Sindri had no words.

Draílock added, "I must apologize for what happened to you, Sindri. I feel at least partially responsible."

Sindri tilted her head. "You saved of my life."

"Well, yes, that is true. However, I should have warned you about the danger. That they use children."

"Who is *they*? Did Ruka hire these people to kill of us?"

Draílock looked over at Arella, then back at Sindri. "Yes, we assume that Ruka was behind this, but the real problem is more the matter of the *who* she hired." He paused, and pulled something from a pocket, then extended his hand to her before dropping a small object into her palm.

She rolled the thing around in her hand, then held it between her thumb and forefinger to look more closely. There was a stone on the top and bottom with a hole at the top. She imagined this was worn as part of a necklace. The center was glass. Still puzzled, she asked, "What is this?"

"*This* is poison," said Draílock disgustedly. "These aren't your average thugs paid to knock skulls for coin. It appears Ruka hired the Somiternum. They are fanatical, and as you have now learned, they start them very young."

Sindri didn't understand. "Why do the Somi—whatever—not poison of us in the first place?"

Draílock shook his head. "That is not their way. The poison is to ensure they aren't captured for questioning. She got to it before I got to her."

Arella added, "The other problem is that Ruka knows where we're headed."

"So you think more will be sent?" asked Sindri, concerned.

"Certainly. However, it will take some time for them to realize that this first group failed. We may yet reach our destination before they are able to find us. And they will wish to catch us before we depart the Banch-Lihn city of Novaya. Even the Somiternum will not follow us into the cursed waters around the Hand of the Gods."

Arella added, "Either way, we should be safe at least until we reach Orrin to the south. It is possible, however, that the Somiternum sent word ahead as a precaution against our survival."

Draílock nodded then said in a lower tone, "For now, I'm more curious about the fact that you were radiating magic while you slept. We felt it from where we ate by the fire, more than a dozen paces away." Looking over at Arella, he said accusingly, "I'm told, though belatedly, that this is not the first time this has taken place?"

Draílock's glare flitted between Sindri and Arella. Sindri would need to explain why she had not disclosed this to him sooner.

"I . . . had a dream."

Draílock's stare was going to puncture something if he didn't soften it soon.

"Not a normal dream. I believe I entered a different place altogether, if such a thing is possible."

Sindri thought she caught a look of concern crossing Draílock's expression, but with him any flash of emotion lasted so briefly one usually wound up believing they had imagined it. He merely said, "Go on."

Maybe he knows something about this place. I'm a fool for keeping it from him. She said, "It's like here, only there is no color or sound, and I can't seem to affect anything so far as I can tell." She ended her statement with the inflection of a question. Perhaps turning this into an investigation of the dream realm itself, as opposed to her keeping it from him, would reduce Draílock's anger that it had been kept from him in the first place.

"You should have spoken of this sooner."

"Why, what do you know about this place? What does this mean?"

Draílock hesitated for just long enough to tell Sindri that he was going to employ a deception. "I am aware of its existence, though I have had few direct dealings with it. As for what it means, well, I am not entirely certain. It does mean that your mother was likely not of Lugienese blood."

Sindri's eyes snapped up to meet Draílock's gaze. Her father's last words, *Your mother. She was no slave—* She never understood his meaning. Sindri had resigned herself to accepting his last words as the meaningless drivel of a dying mean, nothing more. She had seen countless people die and knew that the last moments before death often lacked lucidity. But his words now took on new meaning. Why would he specify that her mother was not a slave? Of course she wasn't. But if she was not Lugienese, then this clarification could, in fact, be *very* telling. She could be of a different race entirely, yet because her father was Lugienese, the physical attributes passed on would cause her to appear to be Lugienese. That was why it was so difficult to detect the bastard children of Lugienese men, while the bastards of Lugienese women met instant condemnation. Even so, this revelation revealed more questions than it answered.

One concern surfaced above the rest. "Is it dangerous? This place? Can someone die while in there?" This would answer the question of Magog seeking Kibure in that way.

Draílock did not hesitate to answer. "Yes."

Yes what? Yes to both?

He elaborated, "My understanding is that one can affect everything within this place at will, including other people. And while most things return to their original state after some time, if someone's spirit is affected to the point of mortality while there, and their mind believes it, the spirit's reflection here in our reality also passes. That person then ceases to be."

This surprised even Arella, who said, "You've never spoken of this before."

He gave his cold smile, then his expression turned thoughtful. "I knew someone, a very long time ago, who visited the spiritual realm. As for why I never mentioned it, well, I've never had a reason. However, had you mentioned this dream to me when you first learned of it, I would have surely told you then."

Sindri then told Draílock everything she knew about Kibure's dreams, as well as her own, including the possibility that she had seen someone or something while within the last one.

Draílock appeared none too pleased. "Well, whoever it was, they know where we are right now. We're just going to have to pray that they are friend not foe."

Sindri needed more. "What else can you tell of me about this place? I think I cannot have magic while there. How is one killed? Is it like here, knives and swords?"

Draílock shook his head. "Truly, I know very little. My understanding is that magic does not exist there, at least not in the way we know it, that the rules governing this plane of existence are different. I have heard of travelers' minds traversing vast distances in an instant. They call this the other way. How it functions, I could not say. Let us pray that you are able to keep from returning there until we are able to find someone who can answer these questions further."

"You know of someone?"

Draílock's reply was like an icy hand to bare skin. "I have my suspicions that when we find Kibure, a great many of our questions will be answered."

CHAPTER 33

KIBURE

L ET'S SEE WHAT YOU'VE BEEN *up to,*" said an unenthusiastic Drymus.

Kibure stood before the seed, sword poised to strike. "*To confirm, you're going to allow me to learn real magic in the waking world if I can sink my sword into this thing?*"

Drymus nodded. "*That is so. But why don't you worry about simply holding on to your weapon before we get too excited about reward.*"

Kibure was careful not to let his insults for Drymus leave the safety of his mind. Then he prepared his mind. *Believe in yourself. It's just like the tree. None of this is truly real.* Kibure readjusted his grip and gritted his teeth. He punctuated every word as he prepared to swing. *I. CAN. DO. THIS!* He imagined his sword sliding clean through the center of the seed, splitting it clear in half like he had done with the tree and several other objects since then.

He visualized the cleaved seed right up until the moment his summoned weapon made contact. Then pain shot up his arms and he dropped the blade, cursing.

Kibure shook out his hands, picked up his weapon, and swung again to similar effect. Then again.

"*Perhaps next time,*" remarked Drymus, amusement in her mental tone. "*At least you were able to keep the sword from leaving this realm.*"

Kibure took several angry steps away from the pedestal, then threw his sword as hard as he could in frustration. It spun end over end, sinking hilt deep into the pedestal upon which the seed was fixed.

Drymus's eyebrows rose. "*Improvement. Definite improvement.*"

Kibure didn't respond.

"*Let's work a little more on your forms.*"

Drymus took him through the warm-up routine, not that his body needed to be warmed up while here, but this had been explained as a calming strategy to prepare the mind. If that were the case, however, it was ineffective this time. His mind raced as he wrestled with the question of why he was unable to cut the seed. The day before, he had cut through every other object he could find throughout the city. What was so different about the seed? Was this some trick designed specifically to keep him from succeeding? He didn't understand why that would be the case, but he didn't understand much about this place or his role within it.

"*You appear much more comfortable in your forms. You have been practicing.*"

Not much else to do, he thought to himself.

A few bouts into their sparring reminded Kibure just how much more he had to learn. He could prolong his demise, slowing a few of her attacks with defensive measures taught to him by either Drymus or Arabelle, but nothing more. Kibure decided to change tactics by executing a counterattack whereby he stepped in instead of away from her offensive. He was rewarded with—an elbow to the face, followed by a knee to the stomach, topped with a kick that took his feet out from beneath his disoriented body.

She loomed over him and said, "*I see you have been practicing more than just your forms.*" There was a hint of accusation. She seemed to ponder something, then said, "*Be advised, if your extra training is coming from whom I suspect, there is likely something more at play, and you are just a knife being sharpened toward one of her schemes.*"

Kibure thought to himself, *She's teaching me more than you are. Wait until I master transporting myself from place to place the way Arabelle does. Then you'll really see.*

Drymus turned and started walking away. With her back to him she said to his mind, "*Continue to focus on your forms and your will. Your progress is hopeful, though slower than we would like.*" She turned back to eye him. "*And you have been warned about the girl.*"

Then she winked out of sight.

CHAPTER 34

KIBURE

KIBURE'S WEAPON SLICED ONLY AIR. He ducked, pivoted, and swung, correctly guessing that his opponent would reappear directly behind him. Air again. Understanding the ruse, he rolled to the side and saw out of the corner of his eye that he had just narrowly escaped defeat.

He came out of his roll springing to his feet, but before landing, he transported himself to the other side of his enemy, thrusting forward as he appeared. Arabelle spun out of the way, then she, too, disappeared. This time Kibure leaped inhumanly high into the air, a feat he would have been unable to accomplish in the waking world, but one that in the spiritual realm required little more than a dash of will.

Arabelle reappeared just in time for his descent, but she popped out of sight just as his sword neared her unguarded scalp. A solid kick to the back took him before he landed, and then a fist to the face as she reappeared before him.

And just like that, it was over. He lay on his back once again, reeling.

"*Much better. So much better!*" applauded Arabelle. "*I dare say that was almost fun!*"

Kibure worked his mouth opened and closed a few times, then felt at the throbbing pain in his jaw with his hand. "*Yes. So very fun.*" He sat up and then stood.

Arabelle said, "*I think I was right to transition us to wooden swords for sparring. One of these times you're actually going to hit me and I'll be glad for the change.*"

Kibure spun his weapon absently around his wrist as he said, "*You have a special way of complimenting and insulting all at once. Is that a trait of your people? I find that Drymus also possesses this talent.*"

She merely smiled. "*How goes the quest to sink your sword into the seed?*"

Kibure's mood darkened. "*I can cut clean through anything I wish here in the city. Anything but that blasted seed!*"

She shook her head. "*You've made progress everywhere else. I don't see why Drymus thinks you need to be able to do that before she'll train you to use magic in the waking world. I doubt anyone can pierce the seed. So far as I can tell, you're more than ready to train with physical magic. I would come train you myself if I were allowed.*"

Kibure considered for a moment. "*You've tried to cut into the seed?*"

Arabelle nodded. "*Everyone has. I honestly don't think it's possible.*"

Kibure bristled. He was spending all of this time on a task that could not even be completed. He felt betrayed. *Liars.* He was sick of all of the lies. *I'm going to learn to wield physical magic and get out of this cave, get out of this city, whatever it takes.*

"*Let's go again.*"

Kibure maintained perfect balance as he moved about in an ever-shifting stance, ready to intercept, deflect, and reattack. His body glistened with sweat as he worked on his forms within the darkness of the cave. He had decided it would be good for his physical body to mirror as close as possible what his body's reflection had been doing in the spiritual realm. Plus, he couldn't spend all of his time there, anyhow. He had overdone it a few times and paid a heavy price. He spent nearly an entire day feeling the deep, throbbing ache of his bones as they worked to restore their natural density. He was growing more in tune with his body's limitations and being careful not to exceed them.

As he worked through the motions, he felt the presence of Drymus approaching from the corridor. He was able to align himself closer to the residual energies of the world around him as he emptied his mind during his forms. He had also begun to feel as though he could grasp chunks of this energy. Where before he had felt like the power he sensed around him was covered in oil, he now felt his mind brushing up against textured objects that could be easily lifted and used should he simply will it.

"Welcome back, teacher," he said coolly.

"Many thanks for the warm welcome. Good to see that your sense of the world around you continues to improve. I suspect you'll be out of here in short order."

Kibure doused his anger at her mockery. "Yes. Yes, I think I will."

"Shall we go then to see where your progress stands?"

Kibure sat upon the ground, legs crossed, as Drymus took her seat in the chair. "Of course."

Seconds later, they faced the spiritual reflections of each other in the amphitheater, the seed looming over them in spite of its stout height a dozen paces away.

"*Well? Let's see if you're ready to learn your physical magic.*"

Kibure grinned. "*I have an alternative proposal for you.*"

Drymus was not impressed. "*I was not aware that this was a negotiation.*"

"*It's more than fair.*"

Drymus rolled her eyes. "*I'm listening.*"

"*If I can defeat you in a sparring bout, you begin training me in the physical realm, wooden swords, of course. First to gain a potentially lethal position or strike.*"

Drymus stared at him, expression devoid of emotion. "*My, my, that's quite the offer. Let me just make sure that I understand this correctly. You have given up attempting to do as you were asked with the seed and have instead begun working to improve your sparring so you can challenge me to a bout, assuming your chances are greater in achieving the latter. Is that it?"*

Doubt started to creep into Kibure's previously optimistic spirit.

"I . . ." He became angry. *"I know that the seed can't be pierced. Arabelle can't do it, and she's far stronger than I. So, yes, I think my chances of success with my offer are greater."*

Drymus's expression didn't change, but her voice took on a hint of disgust. *"Arabelle."* She did the mental equivalent of a scoff. *"That girl doesn't know a great many things, first among them is that what I am asking you to do is something that only you can do. If you are who we believe you to be, you will be able to do as you have been asked."*

"And what if I'm not?"

Drymus stared at the ground, then slowly looked up to meet his eyes. *"Then our time here is coming to an end, and in case you're wondering, we don't have another one of you sitting in reserve."*

Kibure wasn't about to let her manipulate him like this. He was done with that. *"If I am who you think I am, you should be doing everything you can to train me. Don't you need me to be able to perform actual magic, not stick swords in stuff in the pretend realm? What does my offer hurt? I'll probably lose, anyway. If I do, I'll go back to working on your pointless task with the seed."*

Drymus stared him down for a dozen heartbeats before responding, *"One chance. After this, you return to what you're supposed to be doing. Is that clear?"*

Kibure's spirit rejoiced for just long enough for him to recognize that he now had to actually defeat her, or all of this would have been for nothing. There did not appear to be sweat in this place, but that just meant that all the nervous energy pooled in his mind without an outlet. He nodded.

"Say it," she demanded.

Kibure summoned his weapon, the wooden weapon he had been using to practice with Arabelle. *"If I lose, I will return all of my efforts upon the seed."*

"*Very well. Let's be done with this foolishness.*" A wooden sword materialized in her hand.

She stood in place, looking bored as she waited for Kibure to attack. He did so with caution, and she easily deflected each cut and thrust. "*I thought you wanted to learn real magic. You're going to have to hit me if you wish to see that happen.*"

Kibure had been intentionally playing it safe, knowing he had no chance of breaking past her defenses with his elementary skills alone. A few weeks of training would not change that.

But he did need to get her to attack more strongly in order for his plan to work, and Arabelle had given him one more weapon with which to use.

"*I'm not the first supposed savior of your people, am I?*" he said as he swung low for her legs, then swept up toward her body.

Drymus brushed his attack aside like it was a pesky fly, but still did not press the attack.

Since she didn't answer, he continued, "*Other students of yours have failed, haven't they? What happens to someone who is told that they are a prophesied savior, but later realizes they're nothing more than an ordinary nothing?*"

This got her attention and he saw a change in her demeanor. He launched a weak attack and was rewarded by a series of return parries that nearly ended his scheme then and there. He spun and backpedaled out of the way enough to gain a temporary respite.

He would need to spring his trap now, or she would defeat him before he had the chance. "*I don't wish to end up like your last student.*"

Kibure stepped back in anticipation, and not a moment too soon. The flurry of movement that came his way made him realize just how far beneath her skill he really was. There was no way he could defeat her. At least not by traditional means.

Drymus's sword continued to gain speed, blurring the air, and Kibure wondered just how his own sword was keeping up. He had no time for strategy, no time to counterattack. His body took over protecting him by reflexes developed in his training, reflexes that were not prepared to defend against his opponent's speed and skill. Drymus knocked the sword from Kibure's hand, then prepared to place the blade upon his neck, but as she did, her sword met only air.

Kibure smiled as he vanished from sight. He reappeared directly behind her, a momentary sense of ecstasy that he had timed it so perfectly. He didn't have to be better, he just had to plan better. And with Arabelle's help, he had just done the impossible. He quickly extended his newly summoned sword toward Drymus's neck to claim his victory.

Then the ground pulled his face toward it, and pain exploded along the side of his head. He wasn't sure which had happened first, until he registered the glimpse of an elbow that had appeared just after Drymus had disappeared from sight in front of him.

He felt the wooden sword pressing down hard against the back of his neck. It hurt, but not as much as the realization that he had failed.

"Fool boy. Did you really think your little trick would work? I've been around for centuries. I've seen every scheme imaginable. Then again, this wasn't as much your plan as it was hers, was it?"

Kibure had no response. Only anger. Anger at himself for thinking he would succeed, and anger at Arabelle for convincing him that he could.

"Nothing? Fine. While I have your attention, let me address your question and why you had better pray that you are who we think you are. I don't know which details Arabelle chose to share and which to withhold, but you're right, you are not the first. The difference last time, however, was that we discovered him before the threat from the west had truly manifested. We believed the Lugienese would begin their conquest much later in the savior's development. This time, the west is already here. So if you aren't the one, we're all doomed for there is no one else."

She finally lifted the pressure from the back of Kibure's neck. *"Now get up."*

Kibure did so, slowly, ashamed that he thought to exploit Drymus's personal life, and without a full understanding.

Drymus's voice took on a softer tone. *"I don't know exactly how to accomplish what the prophecies say regarding the seed. But I know that if you can't find a way to do it, we will be destroyed before we have any chance of survival, let alone victory."*

Kibure was unable to meet Drymus's eye. Instead, he walked toward the seed, but as he did, he felt a mountain of weight tugging down upon his shoulders. It was like carrying a long pole with the buckets of water on either side, only he attempted to carry dozens of buckets. He sank to his knees with the weight.

Drymus said from behind him, "*I know this isn't easy. But you must find a way. I offer you this last piece of advice on the matter and then I will leave you to your task. The more your mind is able to ignore, to block out, the more focused your will becomes within this realm.*"

Kibure didn't respond, didn't move.

Drymus walked past him, then continued past the pedestal upon which rested the seed. "*I think it's time I had a conversation with our mutual friend.*"

CHAPTER 35

SINDRI

THE SILENCE OF THE DREAM was not so different from hearing a sudden cacophony of sounds. Both were jarring, disturbing, and rendered the sense of hearing useless.

Sindri cursed the moment she recognized the eerie silence for what it was. The last week of travel toward the Scritlandian city of Orrin had been mostly sleepless, as Sindri determined that the best way to stay free of the dream realm was to keep from sleep altogether. She had found, however, that after two days without any sleep at all, her body began to fail and she would suddenly wake from bouts of sleep that she hadn't realized she had begun. This current flight from consciousness was no different.

They were less than a league from the city of Orrin. Camp had been set beyond sight of the city walls, which from this direction was all that could be seen of the city. Orrin had been built upon a tall rise in the foothills just south of the Dragon Spine Mountains. After being one of the first cities conquered by the Lothlem invaders of old, rebuilding had been the first order of business upon gaining their freedom. They would never be conquered again. At least that's the story Draílock told right before Sindri awoke to the silent nightmare that was the dream world.

She inspected the camp nervously, expecting—she wasn't sure what—something bad. But she found herself to be completely alone.

Still, sitting out in the open seemed a risk not worth taking, so she started walking toward their wagon where she could just wait until she was returned to the world of the waking. Just as she reached the wagon, she wondered, *Is it wise to corner myself in a place with nowhere to run if someone or something does come looking for me?*

Yet sitting out in the open to be easily spotted seemed just as foolish. She surveyed the camp and settled on a place along the outer edge where she could see the entirety of the gathering, sequestered between two wagons with a tent blocking most of her body from sight. She smiled nervously. *This is as safe a place as can be found to wait.*

Sindri stood motionless for a long while, tracking the occasional ripple in her vision representing the camp-goers as they moved about in the waking world. *I should be joining them there any moment.* But a small part of her felt rising tension. A foreboding. She was ready to run, but she didn't dare move until she at least saw the threat. That sense of being watched was so powerful that she turned to see if someone was behind her in the open area beyond the camp. She turned quickly but saw no one. Just a small grove of pines on the other side of the road at the base of a steep rise.

She wondered, *If everything that happens here is a mere function of the mind, then perhaps that is how people travel vast distances while here? Could it be as simple as closing my eyes and imagining myself in another place?*

Sindri glanced around, still seeing no one, but with a growing sense of impending doom as if an enemy were closing in. *It's worth trying.* She closed her eyes and forced her mind to visualize a place . . . *hmm, where would I go?* Her mind was quick to jump to places within the Lugienese Empire merely out of familiarity, but that idea dissipated as quickly as it appeared; returning there in any capacity seemed foolhardy, even in this realm; perhaps especially in this realm.

She opened her eyes again to ensure she was still alone. *This is absurd. Just choose a place.* She decided on the square in Scritler where she had nearly been executed. She would have no difficulty visualizing it, of that she was certain. She closed her eyes and focused on the imagery of that place. The marble platform, the monstrous contraption that would have separated her head from her shoulders had Dwapek arrived only a few moments later. She saw the rough, sand-colored bricks, and adobe construction that surrounded the open area. She saw the array of palm trees that lined the main thoroughfare leading up to this place from the main gate at the northern end of the city. *I'm here,* she whispered to herself, though the words made no sound.

She saw the glint of marble just before her vision flickered and blurred and then she was . . . exactly where she had started. She cursed and noticed something far worse than having not moved; there before her stood the unmistakable image of a man no more than ten paces away. He stared at her with what might have been surprise, as if he had not expected her to open her eyes, or perhaps at seeing her at all. Then he winked out of existence.

Wh—

She looked around in all directions but saw no one. The man was gone. *There's no way I imagined that.*

As startling as seeing someone had been, and seeing that same person disappear right before her eyes, there was something else that disturbed her even further. There was something vaguely familiar about the man she had seen. Yet from where, she could not recall. Skin tone was difficult to decipher in this colorless place, and she had only seen the man for an instant, but she was fairly certain he had been of the Lugienese slave race.

Then her grip on the dream realm slipped and she opened her physical eyes to the waking world. The first sensation she felt was the need to cover her mouth, which she did. She crawled to the back of the wagon where she had been resting, pulled back the canvas flap, and an explosion of vomit spewed from her mouth.

Wiping her mouth with her sleeve, she turned back to see the forms of Draílock and Arella, both sitting with legs crossed as if they had been drinking tea at a show. Knowing that she had been the performer and recalling the experience itself caused her no shortage of further frustration. "Enjoy the show, did you?"

She couldn't see Draílock's expression, shadowed as it was, but she could imagine his flat stony lips curling up at the edges just enough that only an observer familiar with his idiosyncratic might recognize that he was enjoying himself, but otherwise so subtle that any accusation might be turned around to make the plaintiff seem anything but sane.

As expected, Draílock ignored the question. "I attempted to follow the strands of energy into this dream place, hoping that I could follow you there. However, it seems this gift is not so easily shared."

"*Gift*," she scoffed. "A curse."

"It is certainly not an ideal time to have these episodes." Draílock's cool, even tone annoyed Sindri more than normal.

"No, it is not." She considered not telling him, but knew she needed to. "I . . . I saw someone."

This piece of information at least managed to cause a shift in Draílock's tone. It wasn't concern, but it was certainly closer to excitement than normal. "Well? You appear to have escaped with your life. Did this person *do* anything?"

She shook her head. "No." She paused before continuing, "The person seemed more surprised to see me than anything else. He disappeared moments after I spotted him."

"Well? Did you recognize this . . . man?"

Sindri opened her mouth to respond but paused. "I . . . I'm not sure. I only saw a glimpse before he disappeared. But I did get the sense that I had seen him before. Perhaps it will come to me later."

"Of course." Draílock's response was distant. Sindri understood that he was archiving this new information somewhere deep inside of that long skull alongside thousands of other puzzle pieces collected like a roving tinker.

Arella seemed to understand that Draílock was no longer fully with them and decided on her own question. "Anything else?"

Sindri thought back to her failed attempt to transport herself to another location within the spiritual realm. She recalled the flickering of her vision as she opened her eyes, but she didn't know just what it was and finally understood Kibure's hesitation to be forthcoming about his own experiences within this place. She simply answered, "No."

Draílock returned his awareness to them. "Be ready to leave at dawn. I will go now and finalize the details for our entry into Orrin. We're returning this wagon to Gentry, who will transport it to the market to resupply the caravan. This will afford us the necessary stealth. He's going to need a few extra silvers to keep the guards at the gate from checking the contents of the wagon. They don't look favorably upon human cargo, no matter the cause."

Draílock returned just as the camp was picked up, and the caravan prepared to travel the last distance to the gate less than a league away. He climbed inside their wagon and said, "You can come out. I have some unfortunate news to share before you enter the city."

Sindri and Arella climbed out from their hiding places within the cargo of the wagon. Draílock looked them both in the eyes, Arella then Sindri. "I am leaving you two to complete this task. Other matters have progressed more quickly than I would have liked, and I must see to them at once."

Sindri looked at Arella, expecting an argument, but Arella simply nodded as if she expected this development.

How can she just let him go like this? We need him. "How are we to find of information about Kibure? How are we to get out of Orrin? And what will we do even if we find of him? We'll need of your help then most of all!"

Draílock showed no sign of emotion, only certainty, as he replied, "I've spoken with Henrik, he's as trustworthy a merchant as we could hope to find, and he has agreed to help find you transport, for a fee." He handed Arella a purse filled with coins. "Once you're in the city, he will assist in securing you safe transport to Anakolpos. You'll give him the rest of his payment only after he has successfully arranged your transport. There is enough here to pay him his fee, your transport to Anakolpos, and still more than enough to convince a seafaring ship headed to the south to take a detour."

Sindri wasn't ready to give up yet. "How long will you be gone? How will you find us when you have finished?"

He chuckled. "I know where you're headed. And you two aren't exactly the most inconspicuous pair." Draílock paused for effect. "I'll have no difficulty locating you once my other business has concluded." He looked at Arella. "You'll do your best to keep her safe." It was not a question.

Arella nodded. "Of course."

"It is likely that the two of you will encounter Klerósi priests before this is through, and those gray-cloaked sorceresses are not likely to greet you with hospitality. You'll need to be nimble of hand and mind at every turn from here on out."

Arella said, "We will continue with caution and will flee the fights we cannot win."

Draílock smiled. "See? Arella will take very good care of you in my absence. Some days I believe she is more competent than I with such a charge."

He bowed and said, "I take my leave. Good luck to you."

Sindri rose to her feet to try to stop him, but Arella's voice caught her. "Sindri. Let him go. We need to get into hiding. We must be close to the gate by now."

Draílock slipped out of the moving wagon without another word.

CHAPTER 36

SINDRI

ARELLA SAT BESIDE SINDRI AT the dockside inn, both nursing their sour ales more for appearance than enjoyment. The pair had made friends with one of the members of the caravan, a wool merchant named Galdred and his son, during their—praise the gods—uneventful easterly float down the river. Galdred was destined for Novaya, not Anakolpos, but Sindri agreed with Arella that Ruka's spies would most likely be looking for them in Anakolpos, anyhow. They were now just a few days north of the coastal city of Novaya.

Turned out, Novaya was a more suitable place than Anakolpos for more than just reasons of safety. According to Galdred, Banch-Lihn cities like Novaya tended to have more dealings with the merchants to the south, which was where the pair ultimately needed to go. This southern influence became apparent as Sindri and Arella walked the crowded streets of the market browsing the wares. If the fashion of the townsfolk was any indicator, Galdred was telling the truth. There was certainly far more color worn here than in Scritland, where most clothing consisted of drab browns, tans, and the occasional shades of green. Jewelry studded with polished bone and jade was further proof that the merchants of Novaya spent time exchanging in Luguinden ports. Even the populace showed ethnic ties to the Luguinden, with several folks appearing more akin to the bronze of Sindri's skin than the onyx of their Scritlandian guide, Galdred.

But just because ships traveled south did not mean convincing one to take a detour to the Cursed Isles would be easy. Sindri and Arella were hoping Galdred and his son, Keldred, would increase their chances. The pair occupied the two chairs opposite the women at their table. The wool merchants looked right at home with their dark Scritlandian skin and dusty-brown tunics. Alone, they'd have drawn the attention of no one. Seated as they were with two hooded women, they appeared only slightly conspicuous. Even still, if Ruka's spy network extended into Novaya, word may still have reached them to be on the lookout for a Lugienese and an Isles woman. With this in mind, Arella had provided Galdred with an additional stipend to help them locate and negotiate transport to their final destination. The added finder's fee would be worth avoiding the notice caused by two foreign women skulking around the city asking about the Cursed Isles.

Sindri whined from beneath her hood, "Must we drink of this ale? It tastes of urine, or how I think urine to taste."

Galdred chuckled. "Around these parts, the water is not so clean so they drink this. You get used to it, and if not, it's still better than turning your bowels to porridge. That's killed more than one visitor who didn't know better."

Sindri swallowed another mouthful and grimaced. *I pray I never get used to this.* Looking around at the perpetual scowls of the patrons, Sindri added, "Shouldn't an entire city of drunkards have more . . . joy?"

Galdred shook his head. "Hah! You'd have to drink a few pitchers just to get tipsy on the sour ale. Folks around here hoping to forget their sorrows have to order the harder stuff, and that gets pricey."

The inn hosted a peppering of folks from all over. Merchants, ship-hands, and a smattering of locals from what Sindri saw. Galdred had led them here for just this reason. They needed to find a merchant vessel willing to carry them into waters believed by most to be cursed. No easy thing, especially while attempting to remain unnoticed. This simply wasn't the kind of inquiry that went "unnoticed."

The reality of the difficulty was reinforced a short while later as Galdred sat a few tables away speaking with a ship captain. The potbellied man wore a shirt with torn edges at the bottom so extreme that Sindri guessed it had to be a thing of fashion. The man leaned in and nodded and Sindri grew hopeful. She saw him look up to the ceiling in thought, perhaps calculating cost. A few more words were exchanged and then without warning, liquid sprayed from the man's mouth and he leaned back in his chair howling. "The Cursed Isles?" His voice was loud enough for everyone in the place to hear. "Why in the splitt'n silver would any captain take a ship out that way?"

Galdred's finger went immediately to his mouth to shush the man, but Sindri knew the damage had been done. Arella knew this, too, and motioned for Sindri to follow her out. Cowls drawn to conceal them, they attempted to tactfully slip out the back to escape association with the outburst. It was too late.

A thin man had risen to his feet and blocked the exit. His disheveled black hair was peppered with gray and his haggard sunburned skin suggested many days spent baking in the sun. He smiled as he said, "Now where's you folk head'n all of a sudden? Ain't you with them two men there? Seen you come in together, didn't I?"

Sindri's mouth went dry, but Arella answered, "We were just heading home. Had a long day and thought we'd put in for the evening. Excuse us."

The man frowned and crossed his arms, showing off stains on the elbows of both sleeves of his otherwise off-white shirt. "I thought you was hope'n to hitch a ride to the Cursed Isles."

Arella's eyes darted from side to side. "Yes, well, it doesn't appear that's going to happen today. We really must be going." She attempted to continue toward the door, but the man held out an arm and she stopped just shy of bumping into it with her chest. Sindri saw the measured restraint on Arella's face and wondered how much more she would endure before she made a real scene in here.

"Easy does it, lass." He spoke calmly, quietly, so just the three of them could hear. "See, a friend of mine just informed me that there was a pair o' women might be head'n our way look'n to find a ride to some place out in the Cursed Isles. A Lugienese-look'n one, and a pretty Isleslander. There's somethin' of a reward for capturing such folk, dead or alive. You musta done somethin' real bad to make this kinda list, as most of our jobs come local. This one come from on high."

Sindri was already fingering one of her daggers and looked about the room to see if there might be others. There were. A woman at a table to the right had been absently nursing a dark liquid, but had repositioned her feet, ready to spring into action. Another man who had been lurking along the back wall now had his hand in his coat, likely ready to draw steel. She had to assume she was missing others. This was not good.

The thin man blocking the exit must have sensed that Arella was preparing to strike because he said, "Now listen here, I'm offerin' to bring you in alive, but if you—oh no you don't."

The arm he had extended returned to him while the other suddenly held a blade and shot forward with deadly speed and precision. Arella, however, was no ordinary human. She slid back as her own dagger swatted the attack away, then she kicked out and the man screamed and fell to the side, clutching his knee.

Sindri knew they should avoid drawing the attention of others in town by using magic, but they might have no other choice. For now she drew her steel and went to work on the nearest threat, the woman she'd seen with the dark drink. Now standing, she was nearly a head taller than Sindri, a behemoth in every sense. She barreled forward with a long, curved dagger. Arella had already found another foe so Sindri was on her own. Her back was literally against the wall. Ordinarily she would have attempted to circle the woman toward the wall to free up her own space to maneuver, but that would expose her flank. She was forced to face this mammoth head on.

In a matter of seconds, her body reacted for her by ducking the neck-level swing of her attacker. While she was down there, she plunged each of her knives into the woman's thighs or tried to. One sank deep into the meat of the woman's leg, but the other slid off the leather breeches and out of her hand. Then, the woman's forward momentum knocked Sindri onto her butt, and the next thing she knew something hard collided with the side of her skull, a knee, she presumed. This put her on her side and she immediately rolled to her back to defend. Her ribs absorbed one painful kick as she pulled another dagger, then she captured the next boot between her body and arm and squeezed while she drove steel into the woman's calf.

Crying out, the woman tried to bring her knee down on Sindri's chest. Sindri slid forward and managed to kick her leg up high enough to strike the base of the woman's spine. Sindri scooched forward and came to her feet, then pounced on the far larger woman who had fallen to her face and dropped her weapon. Sindri landed with her own knee to the woman's back, resulting in a loud groan. The woman went still when she felt the cold steel of Sindri's blade at the side of her neck.

In this moment of control, Sindri looked up to see how Arella was faring. She spotted the thin man who had begun the assault heaped beside the exit. Arella stood still with dagger drawn. Sindri's relief disappeared when she followed Arella's line of sight to see Galdred held from behind at knifepoint.

"Move another muscle and I paint the floor with your pal's blood."

Sindri looked back to Arella, who continued to glare at the brawny fellow who held Galdred's life in his hands. Galdred's son stood frozen, two paces away, a dagger held in a slack hand, eyes wide with fear.

Sindri's own weapon remained firmly pressing the skin of her opponent's neck. *Is my life worth more than Galdred's?* That was what it boiled down to. Him or her. Then she felt Arella drawing in power and knew there was a third option. Drawing magic would only be discernible to any users in the room, but should Arella actually use her magic, their whereabouts would become apparent to *anyone* with the talent on this side of town. Sindri supposed they needed to be leaving anyhow, so perhaps this was the best option after all. There was more than simply her own life at stake. She needed to rescue Kibure.

"Put your weapons down and we can discuss how to proceed from there," growled the man holding Galdred.

Sindri likewise drew in power and prepared to end the attack once and for all. This drew the attention of Arella, who glanced her way and nodded slightly.

Before either could act, Galdred shouted, "No!" and tried to wriggle free. The man holding him lost control of Galdred's waist. Seeing his advantage slipping away, he stabbed the knife into Galdred's neck. Sindri shouted and drew her other knife with her free hand. Keldred cried out and started toward his father's murderer. He held a knife in his hand, but Sindri knew he had no chance of winning. He was a merchant, not a fighter. Sindri threw her knife.

Keldred collided with the man a moment after the knife plunged into his chest, ending the man's defense against Keldred. They went down together in a heap and Sindri knew she needed to intervene. Choosing to limit her death count for the day, she simply cracked the butt of her knife into her captive's temple, knocking her out.

By the time Sindri arrived to help Keldred, it was clear he was not the one in need of assistance. She stopped short at the sight of the young man driving his knife repeatedly into the other man's neck. He lost his grip after a few times, the handle slick with blood. Unwilling to sacrifice time to retake the weapon, he simply continued to pummel the man's face with just his fists until Arella pulled him off.

"We need to leave," hissed Arella.

The truth of this was confirmed by the voice of the barkeep. "You stay right there. City watch is on the way to sort this all out. Don't you think about leave'n this mess for me to explain by myself!"

Arella responded, "Apologies. That will not be possible. We've urgent business elsewhere."

She had the courtesy of dropping a few silvers as she pulled a shaky Keldred along. The clink of the silver ended prematurely as it splashed into the pool of blood beside Galdred's murderer.

"Somebody stop them!" shouted the barkeep.

Sindri guarded their retreat out the back, noting that the few remaining patrons seemed uninterested in doing anything besides steering clear of wherever the three chose to go.

As soon as the door closed behind them, they took off at a run, Arella pulling Keldred along until he followed of his own accord.

The street was still ablaze with activity, which would have played to their advantage but for the fact that Keldred's face was splattered with blood.

A voice rang out from behind just as Sindri stepped into the street. "I can help you!"

They melted into the throng, at least insomuch as foreigners could do so. Their situation worsened as Sindri spotted the street parting for uniformed men up ahead. A man who had been sent to retrieve the watch spotted them and pointed. Sindri didn't hear what he said, but it was clear that the watch had them in their sights.

Sindri and her companions turned and sprinted in the other direction. *Not good. Not good.*

A man fell in, running alongside Sindri. She pulled one of her daggers, prepared to cripple him, when he shouted, "I can take you there."

His ethnicity was that of the Banch-Lihn, creamy tan skin, a black beard, and head of dark auburn hair. He wore a tan cloak accented by a purple headdress common among the people here, but she recognized him from the inn they had just left.

Sindri continued running and said, "You're a little bit late."

He continued alongside. "Yes, things got out of hand before I had time to offer."

Arella said, "We need to get out of the city right now."

They shifted to single file to pass the wagon they had been trailing, but the man kept up and was scuttling beside Sindri again once past. "They're going to catch you, and it will be very bad for your chances to reach the Cursed Isles. My ship is up ahead, but you must follow me now or your chance is gone."

Arella said, "Why should I trust you?"

He dropped behind and started toward the other side, toward Arella. He yelled over his shoulder. "Because you need to escape this city. Follow me and we can discuss terms after you're safe."

Arella said between labored breaths, "We'll take our chances."

Sindri, however, had other plans. This was exactly what they needed. She would hear him out. Arella had been sent by Draílock to protect her, but that didn't give Arella authority over her. Sindri snarled, "I'm going with you."

The man nodded and yelled, "Turn right up ahead. We passed by the ship, but it's not far."

Arella said something, but Sindri wasn't listening. She was not going to get caught here, and she wasn't passing up the chance to find Kibure. She was too far in.

Sindri heard Arella's voice behind, "Sindri, this is a mistake." Then slightly quieter, "Come on, Keldred."

The din of the chaos was dampened for a few breaths as they cut down the smaller street to a meet up with docks that lined the bay and fed into the Sea of Giants. They took another right to follow the man. After thirty paces, Sindri risked a look back and spotted Arella and Keldred close behind, but also noted men from the watch emerging onto the wide, if cluttered, avenue. She returned her attention to see where she was running and nearly collided with the Banch-Lihn man in front of her.

He stopped and turned to face them. He pointed to a stack of crates piled two high, four wide, one of which was being lifted by two men. He yelled to them, "Put that back down!" They obeyed and he said to Sindri and the others, "This way now," as he waved them behind the crates. "Stay here."

He spun and stepped back toward the busy street.

Sindri's heart was beating hard and the burning in her lungs leaked all the way into her throat. The trio was huddled behind the crates, and Sindri shifted so she could see the street through a narrow vertical space between two crates.

This was it. If the watch had seen where they went, or if the Banch-Lihn man betrayed them, they would have no choice but to use their magic and hope to escape the city alive, but without a ship. She had been forced to release her hold on the magic from back at the inn; that was too far away. Unlike priestly magic, which could be held indefinitely once drawn, ateré magic was proximal to the object from which it was drawn. Therefore, she needed to draw in a new swath of potential energy, and Arella did the same. "You had better be right about this," said Arella, sounding none too pleased.

Sindri held her breath as the watch approached. They had slowed, but whether because they had seen where Sindri and the rest had gone or because they had lost sight of their quarry was unclear.

The man who promised to help stepped forward to greet the watch. *Oh no.*

But then he pointed to a street leading back to where they had begun and yelled, "If you're seeking the bloodied man and two foreign women, they went that way!"

Sindri counted six watchmen in total, but there may have been another she couldn't see. They were led by a pedestrian from the inn, who appeared to be the reason the watch had not been moving more quickly. He was potbellied and looked near to collapsing from the exertion. "That's got to be them," he said, panting.

"Thanks," said one of the gray-uniformed men. They disappeared in that direction.

That's a good sign, I think.

The Banch-Lihn man returned as soon as the watch was out of sight. "Come, come. We need to get on board the ship before the ruse is discovered."

Keldred appeared to be stuck in a state of shock, while Arella was still holding fast to her magic, ready to put an end to the Banch-Lihn man should this prove to be some sort of farce. Sindri stood. "We need to leave."

The Banch-Lihn man agreed. "Yes, hurry, hurry."

They followed him up the gangplank onto a vessel about twice the size of the one they had taken from Brinkwell to Tung, though still smaller than many others in the bay.

"Come now, below deck."

Arella stopped where she stood. "I'm not going a step further until I know who you are and why you're helping us."

The man released a sound that would have been amusing had the circumstances been anything but life and death. He gave an impatient bow, then said, "My name is Taldar. I am a merchant of spices . . . and other things. My vessel is bound for Nineveh. I observed you closely at the inn, so I am aware that you have the coin to pay me for this detour of yours, and that you have few alternatives available to you that do not result in imprisonment or death."

Arella nodded. "This is all true. What is your fee?"

He smiled hesitantly. "Of course."

His initial price was surprisingly lower than expected and Sindri joined in on the conversation to haggle him down from there. If there was one thing she had learned from Draílock thus far, it was that just because you had the coin, didn't mean you should pay full price. Since they had no idea if or when they would see the wizard again to refill their purse, it seemed wise to use their remaining coin sparingly.

Taldar continued glancing back toward the city. "Are you satisfied? May we find safety below? I do not like the idea of implicating my entire crew."

Arella growled, "Last thing. You will tell me why you've volunteered to help us."

Taldar rolled his eyes. "Yes. Yes, of course. Well, first of all, this is not *my* ship, but I do foot the bill. I am new to merchanting so I have hired this ship and its crew to carry my wares for the duration of this year, but they are not forever mine. I am hoping to be able to net enough profit this year to purchase my very own ship."

Taldar looked from side to side and spoke low so only they could hear. "Toward that end, I have traced rumors of a great treasure in the Cursed Isles, but I did not have the coin to finance such a journey. Your timing could not have been more perfect."

Sindri actually sympathized with the man. She much doubted they would find treasure, but if his belief would get her, Arella, and Keldred to the Cursed Isles, she would not argue. She worried about escaping the Isles after rescuing Kibure, especially now if this "treasure" wasn't discovered, but that was one of many concerns she didn't have the luxury of worrying over.

There was also Keldred. They couldn't very well abandon him, and yet they would not be able to take him with them to help capture Kibure. *Never mind all that,* she thought. For now, she needed to simply thank whatever god was out there that they'd found a way to the Cursed Isles and go from there.

Sindri turned to Arella. "Satisfied?"

Arella harrumphed, then gave a slight nod of approval.

"Wonderful!" exclaimed Taldar. "Let's get you out of sight so we can discuss the rest of the particulars from a position of relative safety."

They climbed down to the deck below and Taldar relaxed a great deal.

"Before we go any further, I'll be needing that payment—to satisfy the captain that the financing is covered. We'll need to stop for more supplies along the way since we'll be departing this place earlier than anticipated." He winked.

Sindri trusted the man only as far as her desperation required, but she was no fool. "Half now, half upon our safe return."

He narrowed his eyes for the briefest moment, then bowed. "Of course, of course."

Sindri noted the captain and much of the crew were lighter skinned than most of the inhabitants of Banch-Lihn. It reminded Sindri of her time in Brinkwell, where many of the merchants and peddlers bore the lighter tones of the northwestern coast of Drogen.

In any case, she and Arella were greeted without too many glares, though Sindri wouldn't have called the stares warm. No doubt the crew would see none of the fee she had paid Taldar, yet they'd all take on the inherent risks of the Cursed Isles. The captain must have been a good one, for Sindri heard not a single complaint, even if such feelings existed beneath the surface.

After introductions were made, Taldar escorted them to their cabin. "My sincerest apologies, but this was the best we could do on such short notice." They descended another ladder past the crew's quarters and found themselves in a cramped space amid crates of cargo.

"I managed to round up some blankets, though you'll want them mostly to lie upon, as it gets stuffy down here during this time a year. The trip back may be a little tighter if we find the treasure, but we'll be heading directly to Nineveh then, a shorter journey."

Sindri replied, "Thank you, Taldar, this will do just fine."

"Excellent. I'll come down to notify you when it is safe to return to the main deck."

Taldar disappeared up the ladder and Sindri turned to regard Keldred. "How are you doing?"

He was quiet for a while, but the question forced him to acknowledge what had happened. The single lamp was enough to illuminate tears that formed once again in his eyes before they began the journey down his cheeks.

"I'm so sorry about your father," whispered Sindri. "And so sorry that you've been forced to flee here with us. I would never have taken his help if I had known what would happen. Once our business has concluded here, I would like to help you."

His lips formed a flat line, then he spoke in a voice filled with more certainty than Sindri expected. "He offered his help to you. Fool he may be for doing so, but that was *his* choice. I am glad I was there to take vengeance upon his killer. There is nothing more to be done."

He turned away and Sindri pressed the issue no further. Arella gave Sindri a look that said, *Leave him alone,* and so she did. She was grateful when the awkward silence was extinguished by Taldar's return a short while later.

"We are safely out of the harbor. You may return to the deck."

CHAPTER 37

DAGMARA

DAGMARA'S FOOT MET THE SOLID, unmoving planking of the pier in Quinson with trepidation, half expecting guards to spring from behind buildings at any time. None did.

The two-day journey south along the King's Sea to the city of Quinson had given the pair plenty of time to worry over what might await them upon arriving at their mother's ancestral home. They hoped to meet up with Aunt Melanie, who would have arrived weeks earlier, a refugee of Brinkwell like so many others. Aynward was adamant that she could be trusted to help hide them or get them out of the country even if pigeons had brought word ahead that they were enemies of the state.

Enemies of the state! That thought was beyond Dagmara's comprehension; a concept so alien to her existence that reconciling it with her former status as beloved Princess of Dowe seemed nearly impossible. She had never been an enemy of . . . well, anything. She had ignored a rule here or there, but she'd never been caught with her hand in the sugar bin, so to speak. Helping an alleged assassin escape justice, along with fleeing her duty to marry whomever the new King planned to sell her off to, seemed about as extreme a shift as one could make short of killing the King herself. In the current climate, that seemed like a contender for the best option available to her and Aynward if they ever hoped to resume any semblance of normality.

"Hey, Dag—oh—Dagnabbit!" Aynward glanced behind him to see who might have heard his near slip. He then decided on, "Woman, get over here." When he was closer, he whispered, "Would you stop walking like you're in a funeral procession!"

"I'm not! And guise or not, you'll regret calling me over like a serving maid should you do so again!"

He stopped and tilted his head at her, his face barely visible beneath the cowl of his upraised hood. "Well, you look like your feet and head wish to take you in opposite directions, it's suspicious, the very opposite of what we wish to appear. That, and we won't find an audience with Aunt Melanie before sundown if you shuffle along like you're doing the 'I just wet myself' shame walk."

Dagmara harrumphed, but increased the speed of her feet, outpacing that of her brother to prove to him as much as to herself that he was wrong. She slowed just a few paces beyond the dock to let Aynward take the lead, as she realized she had no idea where they were going. Neither of them had ever been to Quinson, but Aynward was without a doubt more experienced in the navigation of cities. He had spent a full hour ostensibly memorizing a map of Quinson that he convinced the captain to allow him to borrow the day before.

As they walked, Aynward pulled out a long strip of what could only be described as leather-gone-wrong. He bit into it with obvious effort, then yanked what remained free, a mouth-sized piece missing. He extended the shriveled, dark-red stuff her way. "Jerked meat?"

They had not had anything to eat that morning and her stomach had already been rumbling, but something about the look of this alleged *meat* reminded her of the value of intermittent fasting.

She shook her head. "I'm sure we'll pass a place that sells *real* food soon enough. That stuff looks like it was trampled by an entire squadron of soldiers, then left out in the sun to rot."

Aynward just shrugged and grinned. "More for me."

Dagmara had been reluctant as it was to eat the dried fish Aynward had scrounged while onboard the cargo vessel they had taken from Salmune. This trampled meat was something entirely beneath a princess of, well, anywhere.

Aynward directed them out of the bustling docks region, where crates and people moved about like ants after the removal of a rock they had used for a roof. He said, "The manse is situated along the southwest corner of the city. Judging by the map, Quinson is less than half the size of Salmune, perhaps smaller. We should be there in short order so long as we don't get lost along the way."

Just then they rounded a corner and the scent of freshly baked bread sent Dagmara's mouth into a state of salivation far beyond what should be permitted of anyone of royal station. Her eyes immediately searched for the source of this heavenly aroma, finding the oven in front of which stood the rack filled to capacity with various breads.

Dagmara tugged on Aynward's sleeve. "We're going to need to take a quick detour here."

He bowed slightly. "Yes, of course. Your Highness mustn't go without her bread, though this appears to be tailored more to the common folk. Are you sure your delicate palate can survive yet another low-born meal? I assumed you would requisition the kitchen at the manse before seeking Aunt Melanie's assistance."

Dagmara's lips tightened and her brow furrowed, but only slightly. "This will do just fine, thank you."

Her body relaxed minutes later as she ripped into the loaf of still-warm bread, all attempts at etiquette abandoned to instincts more akin to a street dog. The bread was certainly common fare, far more granular than what she was accustomed to, but she was not about to voice a complaint that might feed into Aynward's claims that she was too prim to survive without a palace staff on retainer. And texture aside, in the context of her ravenous state, the bread may as well have been baked in the heavens. She made a loud "Mmm" as she bit into the much-too-large-to-chew-comfortably hunk. That should keep Aynward quiet on the subject, at least for a while.

⤛⤛⤛

The midday sun broke through the clouds, bringing the full force of its strength upon the fugitives. Dagmara was already breathing heavily as they neared the crest of a seemingly endless ascent.

Aynward panted, "The map should have had warning signs about the topography of this accursed city."

Dagmara simply replied, "Are we at least close? Seems like we've trekked a dozen leagues."

"Yeah. I think we're close."

Not only was Dagmara tired, but she was also growing increasingly doubtful about the wisdom in coming to Quinson in search of help. Yet Aynward insisted that Aunt Melanie was their best hope. *She won't be much help if we're recognized and captured. Or if we pass out along the way from exhaustion.*

Aynward turned right down a wide avenue. The pervasive traffic of the docks was all but gone by the time they entered the residential area of homes built upon the hillside overlooking the dregs of the city and the King's River below. Fortunately, most of the locals on the streets took little notice of the pair.

Dagmara followed Aynward as he turned down another smaller street, where he suddenly stopped.

"That was it."

"That was what?" replied Dagmara.

"The Elden Villa."

"Where?"

Without turning, Aynward said, "Back there. We just passed the south wall."

"But . . ." Dagmara hadn't seen anything resembling her image of what the place would look like.

"The yellow wall."

The wall to which he referred was hardly the fortifying barrier she had expected from a long-standing family of influence.

"If the villa is back there, why are we standing here in this alley?"

Aynward sighed. "We only get one chance at the gate. I wanted to take a moment to regroup and go over our story before we go to the gate and sound more suspicious than we already are."

Dagmara met Aynward's eye and pretended that she was not afraid herself. "Is the great master of schemes nervous about a little role-playing?"

Aynward scoffed, "Just want to make sure *you* don't go and mess this up." He rolled up his sleeves and rubbed the cuts from his shackles, which had scabbed over. "I would very much like to avoid being held prisoner again. Not to mention, I doubt Perja's offer of life under house arrest still stands. It'll be the headsman for me. So . . ."

"Point taken." Dagmara drolled, "We're friends of Aunt—the Lady Melanie. We escaped the Lugienese assault on Brinkwell. Our names are Min-ath-i and Kyllean. We wish to continue discussions over a business proposition that was cut short due to the invasion."

Aynward gave her a satisfied nod. "Minathi."

"Minathi," repeated Dagmara, this time with more confidence.

"Good. Okay. We're going back down the street the way we came then circle the block until we run into the gate."

Dagmara gestured with a hand. "After you, Kyllean."

Aynward strode onto the street, a confident swagger now part of his adopted persona.

Now that Dagmara knew that the yellow-painted wall was part of the villa, she studied it, noting the intricate scrollwork etched into the upper portions. It was only about eight feet tall, very climbable. Behind it she could see portions of the clay roof, and a few of the multi-level buildings and towers within. As unimpressive as the protective barrier, the area enclosed within the walls appeared much the opposite. They passed three streets on their left before finally turning the corner to continue along the other outer wall of the estate. Looking down the line, Dagmara could see two men leaning against the wall. She noted the matching yellow tabards and the curved scabbard attached to the nearest man's hip and supposed that these two were guards. They had found their gate. Her heart thumped more franticly than she would have liked.

CHAPTER 38

AYNWARD

THE GUARDS TURNED IN UNISON to greet the approaching Aynward and Dagmara. It did not go unnoticed that the two guards had exchanged quiet words after spotting the oncoming fugitives, or that they had both reached down to loosen their swords in their sheaths. The men attempted discretion, playing it like they were merely adjusting their trousers, but Aynward watched everyone and everything with scrutiny these days.

Whispering from the side of his mouth, Aynward said to Dagmara, "I think word of our escape has reached Quinson. Either that or those are the most suspicious guards I have ever seen."

"Should we turn back?"

"Too late. If they think it's us and we turn away now . . ."

He needed to say something to these men without hesitation. Attempting his best imitation of a Brinkwell native's accent, Aynward spoke. "Greetings, Quinsonians. How fare you on this bright—uh—what day is it again?"

The nearest guard, a short, pudgy fellow with red cheeks and wispy brown strands of hair caked to a sweaty, otherwise bald scalp narrowed his eyes and replied, "Secondsday."

The man opened his mouth to continue but Aynward gave him no such opportunity. "Of course! Of course. My apologies." Glancing at Dagmara Aynward continued, "Rats and fleas! My ignorance has cost us precious moments once again, my dear Minathi. Precious moments, indeed. With such an arduous journey from the west, I just haven't been able to keep track. No track at all."

Aynward hoped this guard would not have the worldly experience to know just how poor Aynward's accent really was.

"Kyllean, quit your yammering. Time is for us to ask these kind men to see if they might fetch the attention of Lady Melanie at our behest."

God's above! Dagmara's Scritlandian accent is superb! Aynward realized his jaw hung open in surprise. He quickly returned to his best mask of affability, and the conversation. "Right you are. Right you are. Words of wisdom." Aynward implored the two guards with a wide, sweeping gesture of his hand. This resulted in both bringing hands to their respective hilts.

Aynward jumped back, not having to fake his concern, though keeping up the pretense of character remained a challenge. *Okay, no more sudden movements.* "Dear me. You needn't draw steel. We are but travelers seeking the audience of Lady Melanie. We're acquaintances of hers from Brinkwell. She told us to call upon her if ever we made it to Quinson. We were in discussions over a business proposition before . . ."

Dagmara stepped forward, slowly, and placed interlocking fingers upon Aynward's shoulder. Speaking in the most innocent voice Aynward had ever heard from her, she said, "Well here we are." She tilted her head and added, "We only ask that you send word to Lady Melanie that her dear friends Kyllean and Minathi seek her pleasure at the gate. I assure you she will require you to escort us inside. We are more than pleased to wait here. We would never presume to ask entry into such a place without one of the residents' say-so. Dear me, no. Never would we think such thoughts."

This provided the guards with their first clear opportunity to return words since the fugitives had begun their frivolous greeting. The two exchanged confused looks before the pudgy one finally narrowed his eyes. "Wait here one moment. I need to discuss—uh—matters of security."

Dagmara leaned in close while the two guards stepped inside the gate for their own private conversation. All of her false confidence was gone as she said, "We should leave while we still have the chance. We can find our own way south to Scritland. This was such a bad—"

She was interrupted by the pudgy guard. "Tad will remain here with you while I send word to Lady Melanie. Please do step inside as you wait."

Dagmara pleaded with her eyes, looking from Aynward to the freedom that remained beyond the gate. Aynward had his own reservations, but this was still their best option. "Wonderful. Just wonderful." Aynward inclined his head toward the departing guard. "Much obliged. Much obliged."

"This is a mistake," hissed Dagmara, loud enough for only Aynward's ears.

Aynward maintained his feigned smile as he whispered, "You're just being paranoid."

The pudgy guard disappeared through the tall double doors of the villa. Aynward didn't like the awkward silence that settled over the entrance to the gate so he decided to strike up a conversation with the other guard. "So, Tad, tell me, how do you like it here in Quinson?"

The young guard who couldn't have been much older than Aynward himself seemed taken aback. "I—I like it just fine, I suppose. Don't know nothing else. Lived here my whole life."

"A true Quinsonian through and through. And guarding the Elden Villa gate? Seems a dangerous job. I would be far too frightened. Too frightened, indeed. Too many brigands in the world these days." Aynward brought a hand to his mouth. "Oh my, here I am bringing my troubles with me. Surely Quinson is safer than Brinkwell."

Tad shrugged. "Can't speak for Brinkwell but serving the Elden family here seems safe enough. I mostly only draw steel in the practice yard. And it pays well enough to raise a family. What about you? What did you do in Brinkwell?"

Dagmara's continuous glare in Aynward's direction only encouraged him further. He decided to go off-script.

"Oh, nothing near as glamorous as guarding a villa. I raised chickens. Yes, I did. One of the reasons I'm here, actually. Hoping Lady Melanie can introduce me to a few of the important farm folk in these parts so I can return to doing what I know. Say, you've a wife, Tad?"

Tad had relaxed his posture at some point in the conversation and now leaned against the gate comfortably. "Yessir. Wife, two little ones, and a third on the way."

Gods above! He can't have seen more than eighteen summers! "My oh my. I was going to suggest—"

The door to the villa opened and a different guard stepped through. "Lady Melanie will now see you, please follow me."

Aynward smiled at Dagmara and the two walked toward the open door.

Meanwhile, a second guard stepped past the first and approached the gate. Tad asked confusedly, "Hold on. I don't recognize either of you. What happened to Bradford? We were only halfway through our shift."

Aynward paused, his excited steps slowing.

The guard who held the door responded without hesitation, "The earl requested additional guards sent here from the city watch on account of the royal fugitives. Bradford has been reassigned to the stables until the danger has passed."

Aynward sucked in a breath of cold air at the mention of royal fugitives—at least the air now seemed cold. *It's a good thing we got inside when we did.*

Aynward was unable to resist the opportunity to learn more. He maintained his not-at-all-Kyllean facade. "What's this business about royal fugitives? I'm a glutton for good gossip. Yes, indeed. Kyllean loves a healthy dash with every meal."

The door to the villa closed behind them.

Dagmara replied before the man could answer, "Kyllean, don't bother the guard with your frivolities. Surely Lady Melanie will have more than enough gossip for the both of us."

The guard led them through the foyer, speaking without turning while he waved a dismissive hand. "No worries. Word will carry to the streets soon enough. A pigeon brought news last night that the Kingslayer escaped sentencing with the help of his sister and perhaps a servant. We're told to be on the lookout for them in case they're fool enough to seek refuge at their mother's ancestral holdings here in Quinson."

Aynward gulped hard, then did his best to deliver a hearty laugh. "Ha ha. That would be right bold. Yes. Right bold and foolish, indeed. I would head straight north. Wouldn't stop until I was deep in the Renzik frosts. That is, if I were a Kingslayer on the run."

Dagmara was bulging her eyes at him and gesturing for him to stop talking. She was probably right.

Their escort turned his head and smiled. "The royal family has no lack for boldness or foolishness."

While Aynward did not disagree with the man's statement, he was surprised by the candid nature of the remark. Guards were not usually so loose with their tongues, especially when their words could be considered treason, and certainly not while within the walls of a place so directly connected to the royal family about which he spoke.

Aynward's circumspection was snuffed out as the man opened a door at the end of a long hallway. "Lady Melanie awaits you in the gardens."

Aynward held out his hand for Dagmara to lead the way through the opening. They stepped into a world of purple and green, cropped only by the outer courtyard walls of yellow stucco. At first glance, it appeared as though the entire courtyard consisted of nothing more than wild growths of tree, flower, and vine; greens and purples, punctuated by a cobbled walkway extending both left and right.

When the guard did not move to follow or lead, Aynward asked, "Uh, which way?"

"I don't believe it matters. It all leads to the same place."

With that, the man departed, closing the door behind him.

Dagmara shrugged and started to the left. This path traveled nearly to the edge of the courtyard before revealing another path to the right, which she took. This became another right-hand turn before showing another long, narrow walkway through the dense foliage built up by waist-high beds held in place by stone half-walls. The path zigzagged in this fashion another five times before spitting them out into an open area furnished with four tables, twelve chairs, four small flowering trees at each corner, and one taller tree towering over the rest at the center of the patio. From within this central sitting area, Aynward observed that the design of walkways, hidden as they were from the eye, gave the appearance that one was entirely alone, surrounded only by the garden itself.

Aunt Melanie sat cross-legged at a table to the far right of the clearing, stirring a steaming cup with a spoon. She looked up and shook her head sadly.

"You should not have come here." She sighed and stood. "But it is too late to change that." She smiled as Dagmara approached, then embraced her niece. As Melanie released Dagmara, her eyes turned to Aynward and her smile became a scowl, yet she opened her arms for a hug and Aynward did not dare deny her. As he stepped in, she closed her arms and instead reached up and took hold of the bottom of his head and pulled, hard.

"Ow!"

"What were you thinking getting your sister mixed up with this nonsense!"

"I—*ow*—didn't—*ow*—exactly—*ow*—plan this!"

"Oh?" She twisted.

"Yeow! No! She insisted!"

"Then *you* should have insisted more! She's your sister and you've done and got her—"

Aynward finally wriggled free of Aunt Melanie's grip and stumbled away from within her reach as she trailed off. He rubbed his ear and gave her his own glare.

"He speaks true, Aunt Melanie. I gave him little choice in the matter. I wasn't going to let my brother confess to a crime he did not commit, or, worse yet, refuse and be executed."

"Couldn't have been a little quicker with that?" complained Aynward, the sting from Aunt Melanie's work on his ear finally beginning to fade.

"You still deserved it."

Aynward harrumphed.

Dagmara ignored Aynward. "Aunt Mel, you don't seem particularly surprised to see us, or concerned at seeing an accused Kingslayer."

Aunt Melanie rolled her steel-gray eyes and scoffed, "Aynward is many things, but Kingslayer is not one of them. As for seeing you here, well . . ." She sighed sadly. "You wouldn't have the resources or connections to get much further than here unnoticed, and I'm one of the few people alive in the Kingdom he thinks he can trust." She picked up a leather pouch the size of a grapefruit and set it on the table. It jingled and Aynward knew he was looking at a bag filled with coin.

Melanie continued, eyes darting from side to side, "Which is also the reason why this meeting should not be. As happy as I would otherwise be to see the both of you, I am not the only one to have guessed that you might come here."

In spite of the ear pull and comment about being a fool, Aynward looked at the bag of coin and felt a bit of satisfaction in having guessed that Aunt Melanie would be willing to help, especially with all of Dagmara's doubts. "See, Mara, I told you Aunt Melanie could be trusted."

They were hoping she might be able to help hide them for a few weeks until things with the search cooled off.

Dagmara seemed to hardly notice the comment. She was scanning their surroundings intently.

"What is it?" he asked.

Continuing to search, she said, "Thought I saw something."

Aynward did his own visual inspection but saw nothing besides the green and purple foliage.

Returning his gaze to Aunt Melanie, he said, "I see the coin, but where would you suggest we go from here, O Wise One?"

She slouched in her seat. "Honestly, you don't have many options, but if I were you," She chuckled at that before continuing, "If you manage to make it out of the city alive, I would make my way east. You could probably make fine lives for yourselves in the cities of Anshan without much to worry over, especially with some coin to get you started." She jingled the purse. "Sad to say, but so long as Perja sits the throne, the two of you will not be safe anywhere in the Kingdom, perhaps the world. And if you're thinking of heading south to Scritler with hopes of convincing them to make good on Dagmara's betrothal without Perja's blessing . . . I would advise against this. That betrothal is gone. The Scritlandians do not wish to join lines with someone who cannot be 'controlled.'"

Aynward noted Dagmara's gaze dropping to the cobbles. She was likely relieved at the broken betrothal, but they had discussed seeking refuge in Scritland, and it was one of the better options they had come up with.

Melanie continued, "But even getting east at this point will be no easy thing. From what I hear, he is not only setting up checkpoints on all of the major roads, but he has set a hefty bounty on your head, Aynward."

"Is that right? How much am I worth?"

Melanie narrowed her eyes. "More than you should be."

Aynward shuffled in his seat.

Melanie continued, "You understand what that means, don't you?"

Aynward nodded sadly. "We have to worry about mercenaries and cutthroats as well as Kingdom authorities."

Melanie nodded. Glancing at Dagmara, she frowned. "There is a bounty on you, too. The only difference is Perja wants you returned alive. However, I wouldn't expect much grace with regards to that. Not if you're traveling with Aynward."

Dagmara sighed. "Can't choose your family . . ."

Aunt Melanie frowned. "Indeed. However, you've been forced to do just that. Aynward here, while drawn to acts of utter stupidity, at least seems to have a good heart in there somewhere. It is unfortunate that Perja is the one sitting the throne with the resources of an entire Kingdom at his fingertips."

Aynward leaned in. "Aunt Melanie, that is quite possibly the nicest underhanded compliment I've ever received. Thank you!"

Her tone became stern and her eyes hard. "Consider it a parting gift and try to avoid the main roads as much as possible. You two need to be going. But before you go, you should know that I—I have a son. I've just sent word formally recognizing him as an heir, though he stands to inherit little from me."

Aynward was taken aback. "A son? Since when?"

"Since before you were born. He's a few years your senior, Aynward. I believe you met in Brinkwell."

Dagmara gave Aynward a look that said, *How could you have not known?*

His expression was pure shock. "Who?"

His aunt looked at the ground, ashamed. "It's part of why I can't help you any further. I don't trust him, yet I couldn't see him killed. I had no choice. But I do know he is planning something with Duke Gafford. Come, you need to leave."

Aynward and Dagmara did so, and Dagmara rushed over to give Aunt Melanie a hug. To Aynward's surprise, Aunt Melanie was crying. Tears streamed down her cheeks freely. *Something is off here.*

She held Dagmara tight, clutching her as if this were a funeral. In a sense, it was. *We can't ever return.* The thought struck Aynward hard. He had known this, of course, but the act of actually saying good-bye to someone forever brought the reality of it to the surface in a way that he had not yet fully digested.

Then it was Aynward's turn. But before he could get his arms around his aunt for an embrace, she reached up and took hold of his face in her hands. "Aynward, I'm so sorry. It was either you or him."

Aynward had no idea what she meant, but the fact that she seemed so upset about it gave him reason to worry. He responded nervously. "Me or who? What are you talking about?"

Aunt Melanie sniffled. "My son."

Aynward stood there in a state of bewilderment, arms still out stupidly waiting to hug her and be gone. "Aunt Mel, could you do me a favor and make a little more sense. As you said, we kind of need to be going. Who is he?"

She just shook her head. "Theo."

Then she pulled him in tight. Aynward returned the hug, but his arms grew weak. The sadistic lunatic who had strung Aynward to a tree in his small clothes after a beat-down was her son, Aynward's own cousin . . . it stole the warmth from his embrace.

"You two need to be going. It's not safe anywhere in this city." Then Melanie gasped and Aynward felt something bite his shoulder. He sprang back and reached up to feel where she had stabbed him. How had she managed that? Did she have a spike somehow hidden in the cloth of her dress?

Then he saw the arrow sticking a few fingertips out of her chest. It had entered her back and angled across to stab out at him. He quickly took her in his arms and lowered her to the ground, then yelled, "Dagmara, get down!"

Something buzzed past his head.

He cringed as the sheathed sword he had wrapped to his chest jabbed into his flesh. It wouldn't draw blood, but it certainly didn't feel good. He would also be unable to draw it while crouching in this position. He grabbed the wooden chair he'd been sitting in and hoped he had correctly guessed the direction of the archer. He also prayed that there weren't more.

He held his aunt, warm blood pouring all around the hand on her back. The arrow had taken her in the heart. Fatal.

In spite of this, the spinster still managed her classic glare before saying, "Leave me, you fool!" When he didn't move, she pushed on his chest with weak arms, and her voice came out more of a soft gurgle. "Go!"

With the threat of death to propel him, he reluctantly obeyed his aunt. "Dagmara, stay to my left, and run!"

Holding up the chair as a shield, he sprinted toward the nearest opening, one of four paths leading out of the garden. The chair slowed Aynward down, but he felt the thunk of another arrow and said a prayer of thanks. He was about to drop it as he reached the cover of the garden path, but a guard stepped out to block their path, sword drawn.

Without time to hesitate, and without slowing to give the man time to adjust, Aynward twisted the chair in his grip so it was held in front of him like a battering ram. He used it accordingly.

The guard lifted the sword to swing but Aynward lowered his head and drove the legs of the chair forward. The steel of the sword bit into the wood just as Aynward and his chair slammed into the man. The momentum carried both the guard and Aynward into the flowery brush of the waist-high bed. Aynward pulled himself free of the tangled mess first and hopped down, working frantically to undo the straps that kept his short sword sheathed. The guard rummaged through the brush, cursing. He suddenly turned, sword in hand, before Aynward was able to free his own weapon.

Aynward froze.

"Don't you dare," came Dagmara's hard voice to Aynward's left. She stood with a scimitar extending toward the guard's throat.

The guard didn't move. Aynward breathed a momentary sigh of relief before the man glanced at Dagmara and smiled. *That doesn't seem like the correct response to having a sword at one's throat. Does he think she won't do it?* Aynward prayed she would.

Then a different voice said, "Drop the weapon. Now."

This voice came from behind Dagmara. Aynward turned his head slowly to see a second guard, swordpoint resting at the corner of Dagmara's neck and shoulder. Aynward recognized defeat. He also recognized the face of the man holding the sword. Aynward had last seen him running from the scene of his father's murder.

CHAPTER 39

DAGMARA

AGMARA STIFFENED AT THE FEEL of cold steel on her neck, but she didn't immediately lower her blade. She just stood there in a stalemate, similarly prepared to kill the guard before her. She had never taken a life, but in this moment she believed she could. However, that would mean losing her own. Would Aynward be able to escape if she sacrificed herself here?

Still refusing to move, she attempted to meet Aynward's eyes but he was staring behind her at the man holding the sword to her neck. He had gone pale, but as she looked more closely, she saw that his expression was changing to one of anger—no, not anger. Hate. His eyes took on an icy, callous quality that did not fit his ordinary visage.

"Put down the sword, Mara. We're finished, but you're still valuable alive." Even his voice was different. It frightened her. Not because of the sound itself, but because of how it sounded coming from Aynward's mouth. Then she realized what he was planning to do.

"Aynward, don't do it. There may still be a way to work something out with Perja."

He didn't blink. "No. I don't think so."

The man behind her said, "Aynward is right. He will die today. I have my instructions. You, girl, do not need to do so." The man's tone contained no hint of satisfaction, no smug air; it was just matter of fact. He may as well have been explaining the inevitability of the sun setting this evening.

Dagmara glared at Aynward, frustrated that he might be right. Worse, if she died with him, there would be no one to speak of his innocence. One can't seek justice from the grave. Her shoulder burned with the weight of the weapon, outstretched as it was, but the thought of Aynward being struck down as soon as she lowered her blade prevented her from moving. She imagined his death moments from now, and the wave of sorrow caused her to waver.

She blinked away tears in order to see, then slowly did as she was asked.

Then the man behind her grunted and the steel of his blade slid from its perch between Dagmara's shoulder and neck. This was followed by an unmistakable thud and she looked down to see his face strike the ground beside her right foot. The man whom she had been holding in check with her blade thought to take advantage of the distraction and his sword shot out toward Aynward. Dagmara reacted without thinking, sending her own weapon forward; it plunged into the side of the man's abdomen. The sharp metal slid through his flesh more easily than she would have thought possible.

His gaze met hers, and there was a moment of surprise before his expression turned to anger. She brought her other hand to the hilt and drove the metal deeper, as far as it could go. The cross guard finally prevented it from going any further. The man's eyes started to glaze over with death, but Dagmara continued to push and the man shuffled back until his heels were stopped by the raised stone flower bed behind. He opened his mouth to speak but only blood spilled forth. Dagmara felt the warm liquid as it flowed over her hands and her anger was only further aroused. She continued to push but the dying man simply refused to fall.

Then she felt a hand touch hers and she screamed, a feral sound that hardly sounded like her. It was Aynward's hand. He was standing beside her.

"Shh. It's okay. He's gone. You can let go of the sword now."

He peeled her fingers from the grip and took it with his own, then pushed the man away from the blade, allowing his body to collapse into the garden behind him.

CHAPTER 40

AYNWARD

DAGMARA WAS SHAKING AND AYNWARD wrapped an arm around her as he wiped the blood from her blade on his dark traveling cloak. He understood the shock of killing another human all too well. But they didn't have time to reflect at the moment. He turned her around and noted the body of the other guard, an imposter, lying unconscious on the ground. Behind him stood Tad, the guard from the gate.

Aynward said, "Thank you, Tad."

Tad knelt down and picked up the fallen guard's sword and tossed it into the garden. "Don't thank me yet." His tone of voice held no hint of the friendliness from earlier. Then Tad pointed his sword at the unconscious man on the ground. "These men bear the tattoos of Quinson's thieves' guild, and they killed several of our guards in order to get to you. This is not typical criminal behavior, even for them, which leads me to suspect that you are not who you said you were at the gate, *Your Grace.*" There was no reverence in the lad's use of the honorific.

Extending the point of the blade in Aynward's direction, he continued, "Put down the weapon, Kingslayer."

Oh rats, thought Aynward, his emotions already worn down to powder. *Confidence. Be confident.*

"As much as I would love to get into the details of how I am very much *not* a Kingslayer, and how the man whose sword you currently hold is the actual person guilty of said crime, I currently have no means of proving such, nor do I believe the new King would be willing to hear evidence even if I had any. So . . . I was thinking it might be better if instead of us squaring off right now with steel and you getting all cut up and dead-like, how's about you just sort of, don't do all of that, and my sister and I leave quietly. Although, before we go our separate ways, my sword here does have business with the fellow lying on the ground, just in case he's not quite all the way dead."

Tad stared at him incredulous. "You're serious?"

Aynward gave his best attempt at producing a crazed smile before responding, "Yuuup." *No one wants to mess with crazy, especially when crazy is brandishing a sword.*

"You know I can't let you go. That would be treason."

"Well, you know I can't let you *not* let me go; that would also be treason—of a sort. Treason against my own sense of self-preservation, and I value my own life far above that of *my brother,* the pretender King."

Aynward did his best to continue on with his forced smile, meanwhile drawing his own blade as he returned Dagmara's. It looked like there was more blood to be spilled.

Pain suddenly shot through Aynward's left side and he stumbled, almost toppling over his sister. After a split second of confusion, Aynward understood. *The archer! Idiot!* He must have moved from his concealed position on the other side of the dining area where he had struck and killed Aunt Melanie. *How could I have been so stupid?*

Fortunately, this arrow had only grazed Aynward's ribs. *Unfortunately,* the archer would no doubt nock another arrow before they had time to run back in that direction to find a different exit. And the same fate would await them if they remained where they were. Yet Tad was barring their only other means of escape.

Aynward decided that he liked his odds with Tad much more than giving the archer another shot.

Just as Aynward moved to attack, the unmoving assassin on the ground sprang to life, kicking out at Tad's ankle, causing him to fall to his knee. The assassin's other foot then kicked the hand holding Tad's sword and the metal spun upward into the air. With agility beyond even what Aynward recalled from his father's assassination, the man swung both feet like an acrobat and stood upright ready for battle. He caught the airborne sword in this same motion.

"Oh come on," blurted Aynward. Then his eyes widened further. Dagmara had slipped away from him during the chaos and was darting toward the upright assassin. "Dagmara, no!"

It was too late. She was upon him even as the warning left Aynward's mouth.

Much to *everyone's* surprise, Dagmara's scimitar was used as nothing more than a distraction. Her real attack came from a foot that landed square between the recently risen man's legs. The assassin dropped his weapon and groaned as his position wavered. Dagmara then landed a punch square in the man's face as he fell, speeding his descent to the ground.

Whatever state of shock had befallen Dagmara as a result of killing the guard, she had recovered, at least for now. Or perhaps her shock had simply manifested as a fearlessness bordering on insanity, Aynward thought. Regardless, he now had an opportunity to seek vengeance on the man responsible for their father's death and his status as a fugitive.

Aynward stepped toward the roiling assassin, hand squeezing the grip on his weapon. This was going to be *very* satisfying.

But then movement to Aynward's left forced him to alter course. He ducked below the cover of the raised bed of flowers, vines, and greenery; this saved his life. An arrow sliced the air where his head had just been. The zip of the shaft overhead was more than enough to propel him onward.

Aynward crawled back, abandoning the assassin, then sprang to his feet, hoping he was beyond the archer's sight, though he had to assume that the man was on the move.

"Come on!" he yelled to Dagmara, who was still a few paces back standing over the fallen assassin.

She had sheathed her own blade and held up Tad's weapon, which the assassin had dropped as he fell. Then she turned and led Aynward around the first bend in the garden maze.

"Hey, that's my sword!"

The two fugitives paid Tad's cries no mind but he followed close behind.

They reached the door leading out of the enclosed villa gardens only to discover that it was locked. Aynward shook the handle in frustration, then kicked the bottom. Pain exploded from his still tender toenail-less foot and he cursed.

Turning, Aynward tried his best to sound respectful as he addressed Tad. "Tell me you have a key."

Tad glared. "I do, but as I said, I can't just let you two escape."

Aynward pointed his blade at the fool, though he was several paces away. "Then all three of us are going to die in here, but you'll surely be the first!"

Tad crossed his arms across his chest. "So be it."

Dagmara surprised them both as she twirled and spun, slashing out toward Tad with his own blade. She had become a great deal more skilled under the tutelage of her Scritlandian teacher than Aynward realized. Her swing did not hit Tad; it wasn't intended to, but it allowed him to see that she could have killed him then and there with no difficulty. She bowed slightly. "We are not the enemy, Tad. And Prince Aynward is no Kingslayer." Then she spun the blade so the hilt faced the guard and extended it for him to receive. Her other hand pointed back to the garden. "*That* is the enemy."

Tad appeared just as confused and conflicted as Aynward felt about Dagmara returning the man's weapon. Aynward knew they didn't have time for such folly. "Mara! Have you lost your mind?" But Tad nodded, snatched his sword, then took out a key.

The guard shook his head as he worked the lock. "I can't believe I'm helping—"

"Get down!" yelled Aynward as he pushed Tad out of the way. A knife clanged against the stucco where Aynward had just been standing.

That knife was aimed at me, not Tad, Aynward realized. He turned to face the assassin. The man pulled another knife and smiled, brandishing one in each hand, but he was still far enough away that Aynward didn't feel nearly as threatened by him as he did by the man who then emerged from the maze carrying a bow as he nocked an arrow.

Aynward shuffled a few steps away from the door. "It's me they're after. Tad, get Dagmara out of here."

Without warning, the assassin threw the knife. Aynward dodged to the side as he flicked the object away with his blade. His move to avoid the first was exactly what the attacker had been hoping to achieve and Aynward felt the sting as the second blade bit into his left leg. Aynward howled.

Then he looked up and saw that the other imposter guard, the one with the bow, was aiming right for him. Aynward would have no answer for that. His only consolation was hearing the door to his left squeak as it opened.

Aynward glanced over at his sister. "I love you Dagmara! Now go!"

Aynward returned his sights to the man who would end his life and he steeled himself against the expected pain. Perhaps the archer would miss his first shot. Aynward assumed he would die, but he didn't have to die quickly. The longer it took the two to end him, the more time Dagmara had to escape. He reached down and yanked the small knife from his thigh and threw it blindly in the archer's direction, then dashed away from the door. But with a throbbing foot and a deep knife wound in his thigh, his run manifested as more of a pathetic hobble.

Seconds later he looked up, wondering why the archer hadn't attempted his shot yet, and saw the man drop to his knees, both hands holding his throat as red liquid flowed between the fingers. The hilt of a knife rested at the center of his hands. Aynward knew this could not be the knife he had thrown.

Aynward followed the surprised gaze of the other assassin and it led him to the visage of Dagmara standing casually in the open doorway, her expression a mask of anger. She took a step to the side and bent over to retrieve the other knife that had missed Aynward earlier. With her sword in one hand and the knife in the other, she yelled to Aynward, "You're going the wrong way, brother."

Unbelievable. Aynward shook his head and tottered back toward the door, each step bringing excruciating pain. His sights focused on the assassin, who had drawn two more of his knives from beneath the folds on his stolen guardsman uniform. He appeared unconcerned with Dagmara, his attention remaining fully upon his primary target, Aynward, now only a few steps away from the relative safety that lay beyond the door.

He let both knives fly, and like before, one of the two met flesh. Aynward screamed as the metal cut deep into the tissue of his upraised arm, which managed to save his neck, and his life.

Aynward was only a pace away from the door, but the jolt from being struck again along with his other injuries sent him tumbling. A pair of strong arms caught and dragged him the rest of the way and he heard the jingle of keys as the door was locked behind them.

Dagmara spoke with the authority of a true princess as she said to Tad, "We need to get out of this city. I know about the bounty and the rumors, but *please*, Tad. On my word as Princess of Dowe and a devout follower of the gods of the Chrologal faith, Aynward is innocent. I assure you, I would not have helped my brother escape if I did not know for certain that he had been framed in the first place. They're going to hang him if he's caught, and gods only know what the King will have in store for me for helping him escape. Tad, please."

"I—I—I'll lose my job, or worse yet, join Aynward on the gallows."

Dagmara shook her head. "Neither one is necessary. No one has to even know about us, or at least who we are. As far as anyone else is concerned, these cutthroats came here to kill my aunt, Lady Melanie. That much is true, anyhow. And you've got bodies to support that. Heck, you get to take the credit for slaying two of them in your attempt to help capture the rats who did this. Your bravery will likely be rewarded."

"This is insane," growled Tad. "Totally insane!" He ground his teeth. "Come on."

He brought them to a nearby storage closet, Aynward held upright by Tad as they hurried along. When they were safely inside, Tad said, "All right, I need to find the rest of the guard to take down that imposter in the garden. He's trapped in there for now. But if someone finds you two before I get back, I'm denying any involvement. Understood?"

They nodded and Dagmara said, "If it helps, there is a purse full of coin beside Lady Melanie. Take that and use it to get us out of the city; keep the rest for yourself. For your trouble."

Then Aynward added, "And Tad, if you get a minute after killing the assassin, could you do something about getting me some bandages? I think I might be bleeding."

Tad rolled his eyes and shut the door. Aynward's vision went black as the door closed.

CHAPTER 41

DAGMARA

AFTER A FEW WORRISOME HOURS of unconsciousness, Aynward was now fully astir. His restful state during the bandaging had probably been for the best and being awake in time for them to leave was also to their advantage. Unfortunately, he had full faculty of his mouth.

"Escaped?" exclaimed Aynward. Tad nodded.

"But I thought you said he was trapped within the garden, all the exterior doors locked. You said he was trapped!"

Tad shook his head. "He was." Shrugging, he added, "And now he's not." Tad opened the door to the storage room the rest of the way and ushered the pair out into the dimly lit hallway.

"How could you just let the guy escape?"

Tad shushed Aynward, then whispered, "Do you want my help or not?"

Aynward grunted but said nothing further. He reluctantly allowed Tad to assist him as he hobbled on his bandaged leg. Dagmara was no healer, but she was glad to have been able to provide a pair of steady hands to at least apply a rudimentary poultice to Aynward's most severe wounds, especially the one on his upper right arm, a difficult place for him to reach with his opposite hand. Tad had also brought them a pack that contained new clothes, but his plan for sneaking them out of the estate made changing into these clothes seem like it might be a better idea for after they were beyond the walls.

Dagmara did her best to breathe through her mouth, which helped, a little.

Aynward whispered, "I could be wrong, but I'm confident that Tad totally stopped thinking about ways to get us out of here the second he came across this idea."

Dagmara muffled a cough. "Stop whining. He's risking everything to help us."

"I know, I know. But seriously. There had to be another, less fecal means to escape than—"

Aynward's words were cut short as the flap to the cart was pulled open. Dagmara ducked her head and remained motionless as a servant began shoveling the morning collection of . . . she covered her mouth to prevent herself from vomiting. The smell of human excrement threatened to overwhelm her. The blanket covering the two did nothing to prevent the stench from reaching their noses.

Tad had sent the servant in charge of collecting the contents of the evening and morning chamber pots on some errand when he reached the area closest to the closet where they had been hiding for most of the evening. Dagmara hadn't heard exactly what Tad said to the servant, but whatever the task, it had given Tad time to shovel out a place for them within the already collected waste, cover them in a blanket, then shovel it around to disguise their presence within the wagon. It was a clever, sensible, plan. But Dagmara would be glad to be done with this portion of it.

She peered out from beneath the blanket to confirm that the servant was no longer shoveling filth into the wagon but instead was now emptying it. *Thank the heavens.* This was their cue to leave. Dagmara swallowed her pride, and her revulsion at the smell, then hopped up from hiding and exclaimed, "That's it! There is simply no place for privacy in this city, is there, Thebolt?"

The servant shoveling the human waste stumbled back in surprise at the emergence of two humans from the thick of the filth inside the wagon.

"Wh—"

Dagmara did her best harrumph, then added, "No privacy at all. Please excuse us."

"But how did you . . ." The servant trailed off.

Looking to Aynward, Dagmara said, "Perhaps we'll have more luck in a stable, and less of the stench." She threw her arms up in frustration and said to the servant, "There's just no good place for forbidden love to bloom, is there?"

He opened and closed his mouth, but no words emerged.

Dagmara heaved the heavy pack that carried their weapons and a change of clothes, then hugged Aynward as she helped him walk. "You really need to ease up on the brandy, my love. You can hardly stay upright."

Dagmara glanced back, saw the servant was out of sight and shoved Aynward away. "Disgusting! I'm not ever doing this again!"

"Which part?"

Dagmara rolled her eyes. "Either!"

Knowing the filth of much of the city was dumped in this place in the narrow tributary, they traveled upstream to where the water would be less "muddy." They continued until Dagmara's legs could go no further without rest. Aynward's injured leg was not faring much better, even without the weight of the pack. They both collapsed in a heap, breathing heavily for a few hundred heartbeats before wading into the stream to strip and wash.

They didn't have time to relax within the soothing cool water, but Dagmara felt mildly refreshed as she emerged to change into a second set of clothes provided by Tad.

They now had nothing more than this fresh set of commoner's clothes, traveling cloaks, and one weapon each. Aynward clutched the purse tied to his waist and mumbled something Dagmara assumed was displeasure about how little coin Tad had left to them. Dagmara figured they should be grateful that Tad had been willing to hand any of it over. She and Aynward had been completely at Tad's mercy, after all.

They would have several long days ahead of them if they hoped to avoid being discovered, and less if the servant mentioned what he had seen to someone wise enough to puzzle out their scheme. They would not rest again until nightfall and would need to stay off any well-traveled roads on their way east, which they had decided was their best option. Aynward claimed Minathi had family holdings east of Quinson nestled at the base of the Dragon Spine Mountains. If they could get in touch with her, they might be able to make it east beyond the Kingdom.

CHAPTER 42

GROBENNAR

THE WORDS OF THE MISSIVE gave Grobennar a renewed sense of hope and vigor for his plans in Drogen. Theo had been formally recognized by the aunt and approved by the Lord of the Estate. He was now a member of the royal court, if an unrespected bastard to an unrespected member of the family. Nonetheless, Grobennar now had his own man on the inside, and better still, the boy's uncle, Duke Gafford, had agreed to meet, which meant Grobennar's plans could be set into motion sooner rather than later.

It wasn't all good news, however. Rajuban must have hired the assassin's guild to hunt down and eliminate the prince, who had somehow escaped the trial with the help of his sister. The fools had killed the aunt and yet two fugitives escaped. Theo was none too pleased that his mother had been killed and seemed to believe Grobennar was behind the hit.

The priest ran his hands through his translucent hair as he pondered how to proceed. He considered writing back to explain the truth: that he had nothing to do with the violence that had taken place, that there were political schisms within the ranks of the Klerósi hierarchy and this had been the work of someone else. But as he attempted to organize these thoughts, he considered how such an admission might later be used against him. Best to maintain the facade of total control. Grobennar came to this conclusion just as he heard the sound of laughter within his mind: Jaween.

"*Oh, this is just wonderful! The boy is going to be afraid to relieve himself without your permission for fear of your power.*"

Grobennar considered this. "I suppose assumptions that leave him fearful could be used to my advantage." But a tickling somewhere in the back of Grobennar's mind caused him to continue mulling over nuance. He thought back to what he knew about Theo. The boy had mentioned dealings with the prince while in Brinkwell. This brought about another idea.

"What if Theo was made to believe Prince Aynward was directly responsible for Lady Melanie's death?"

"*Oh? More scheming? I loooove scheming. Go on.*"

"We play to the existing hatred between them. We remind Theo that it was Aynward who fled to Aunt Melanie's estate, knowingly putting her life at risk and therefore the one responsible for her death. We promise Theo that once Duke Gafford ascends the throne, he can be personally tasked with finding and killing the prince as a reward. We can even provide 'help.' He should be more than satisfied with a chance to earn retribution, and it gets him out of the way so he cannot be turned against us later by one of Rajuban's pawns. Once Duke Gafford agrees to our 'arrangement,' the royal court will be staffed with Lugienese wielders of my choosing to enforce the agreement. Theo's role within the court will then have been served, and if he is able to find and kill the prince, all the better for everyone."

"*Yes, yes, yesss! A brilliant plan. Klerós's light has finally come out from behind the clouds.*"

The more Grobennar considered this notion, the more he believed Klerós was indeed interceding on his behalf. As the saying went, "Coincidences that occur in the favor of his followers are evidence of Klerós's hand rewarding their service."

Warm tingles washed over Grobennar's body and he smiled to himself. The paving stones on the path to redemption were being set before each step. He simply needed to keep his feet moving. Next on the list: the Free Cities.

As far as the Lugienese fleet was concerned, Grobennar was onboard his ship and not to be disturbed as they approached the landing site just north of the Free City of Drebrose. However, Grobennar wished to utilize his newfound weapon, the dordron, so he and Paranja had visited the secluded training grounds for the fledgling force of riders who now trained outside of the city of Tung.

He and Paranja had taken flight upon their respective dordron to meet the invasion in Drebrose by air.

Grobennar had taken a liking to one dordron in particular and had gone so far as to give her a name, Frida, meaning redemption and he had little doubt that she would live up to it. He felt the warm Isles air become cool and crisp as they rose above the sleeping city of Tung. No longer afraid of falling to his death, he found the experience of flight exhilarating. It was exhilarating. The wind buffeting his face and neck, and the raw speed these creatures reached during flight, was nothing short of glorious. He looked down to see a thousand yellow and orange dots sprawled out below, the contours of the coast evident by the black nighttime water. Tung was not a beautiful city, not compared with the Lugienese capital that had been Grobennar's home for much of his adult life. However, at this moment, Grobennar could hardly deny the beauty he saw here in the Isles city.

They departed in the night so as to go unseen, which was not unusual for any of those training atop the beasts. Grobennar was adamant that none of their training activities be seen; he had no idea how many spies Rajuban might have secreted around the city.

Grobennar established a mental link between himself and Paranja as they traveled. This was no difficulty to maintain, since the partial clasp with their winged mounts used so little energy now. Grobennar reveled at the wonder of flying atop a creature of such simultaneous beauty and wrath.

Paranja remarked as if reading his thoughts, "*This is almost as euphoric as drawing in Klerós's power. I hope I'm not asked to part with this newfound ability any time soon. I suspect that to do so would be nearly as devastating as a magical castration.*"

"*I don't see any reason why we should be parted from them,*" agreed Grobennar. "*They are the spoils of our own labor, after all. Only Magog himself can take this from us, and I can imagine no reason for him to do so.*"

This was not entirely true, of course. Should their plans in the Free Cities, and especially the Kingdom, go afoul, Grobennar suspected that more than just his dordron would be taken from him. But it was a risk he needed to take; the reward could place him on equal footing with Rajuban, one step away from total redemption.

Grobennar agreed with Paranja's sentiment regarding the experience. He too would come to miss the ability to fly should it be removed. In the weeks since discovering the ability to control the dordron, he had found that Frida grew less and less resistant to his control, and he wondered if perhaps someday this creature might come to even appreciate the link they shared, becoming an ally, not a slave. How much more power would he have at his disposal if he didn't have to continue to enforce the link?

Jaween interrupted Grobennar's thoughts. "*Grobes, I have a tickling in my memory regarding these creatures. I don't recall just what it is, but I have a certain inkling that something isn't quite right . . .*"

Grobennar disliked the sound of this, but it was by no means the first time Jaween had voiced concerns based on fragmented memories that later proved benign or never manifested at all.

Then Paranja's mind spoke to him from up ahead. "*Fatu Ma-gazi, something's wrong.*"

He saw her dordron up ahead, faintly visible through the light of a moon partially hidden behind a cloud. She was turning back away from the mainland of Drogen, the outline of which was apparent below. "*Care to elaborate?*"

"*My dordron is defying my command to continue east. I can't seem to stop it from turning back.*"

It didn't take Grobennar long to understand, for his own mount suddenly turned of its own accord. Grobennar did the mental equivalent of squeezing the connection but to no avail. Its will was suddenly a thick, immobile wall of resistance.

"Jaween, a little help here?"

"*Gladly.*"

Grobennar waited patiently, his own mind still attempting to break down the barrier. It was as if he held the reins to a horse built from steel. Then he felt a release on the will and was able to turn the dordron once again.

"That seemed to work."

"*Hmm I'm not certain it was anything I did,*" said Jaween, confused.

"Whatever the cause, I am fully in control once more."

To Paranja, he said, "*I've been able to wrangle control back from my dordron. How goes it with you?*"

"*Mine too appears to have relented. I'll follow you.*"

Grobennar was now in the lead and had turned his dordron back east toward the mainland and the continent of Drogen. A few moments later, he felt the same sudden resistance as his giant bird changed course, turning from Grobennar's intended destination.

"Demon dragons!" cursed Grobennar. "What is going on?"

Paranja shouted into the connection, "*Mine too has turned away.*"

Jaween commented to Grobennar, "*Hmm . . . this tickles a memory.*"

"Well, it would be great if you would dig that memory out of the archives for a few minutes so we can figure out what in the demon is going on here. My squadron of dordron won't do me any good if they go rogue the moment we get close to Drogen!"

Jaween did his impression of a sigh through the connection. "*I'll try.*"

Grobennar rode on in silence as he waited upon Jaween. He and Paranja had turned their dordron back toward the Isle of Tethro, outside of the city of Tung, where the fledgling force of dordron and their riders had been relocated from Brinkwell.

Just as they prepared to land, Jaween exclaimed, "*I remember! Er, I think I remember. Well, sort of.*"

Several heartbeats passed in silence before Grobennar finally said, "What? Are you waiting for permission? Out with it, already!"

"*Oh yes. I remembered something, I think. Some sort of war, don't ask me when or why, probably something to do with human procreation. That seems to be the cause of a great many spats. It's—*"

"Focus, Jaween!" Grobennar was losing his patience quickly.

"*Right. Erm . . . war—spat—humans—yummy pastries—ah yes, here we are. There appears to have been some sort of spell cast to keep these creatures from entering the lands of Drogen. Yes, that seems right.*"

"A spell to keep the dordron from entering the continent of Drogen?" Grobennar punctuated each word, his anger building as he did. "Well, isn't that just perfect? I'm going to have to have Frida here drop me in the sea for a swim if I'm to even take part in the conquest of Drebrose. All that work to subdue the beasts, and for nothing! You wouldn't happen to have any specific memory of this somewhere in your . . . little, tiny brain, if we can even call it that."

"*Unfortunately, no. Nothing specific. Just a vague sense that this is what took place.*"

Grobennar gripped the amulet and squeezed. "I should toss you into the sea for all the good you do me."

"*Hey-hey-hey, no-no-no. Let's not do anything . . . rash. There may still be a way around this.*" Jaween's mental bearing was one of grave concern, and rightfully so, for Grobennar was seriously considering the notion. "*If a spell can be made, it can be unmade. Perhaps I-I-I can still be of some help.*"

Grobennar clutched the amulet until he felt the edges cutting into his skin. Finally, he responded, "We had better be able to undo this."

"*You should turn the creature around.*"

"This is part of your plan to help?"

"*Why, of course. Since neither of us felt the spell before, we should assume it's buried, perhaps even disguised within its mind. But . . . it is somehow activated by proximity to Drogen, so I might be able to feel my way into the spell and have a look as it is activated.*"

Grobennar considered the logic and figured it made some sense. He spoke into Paranja's mind: "*Continue back to the training grounds. I am going to see if I can locate the source of whatever is keeping these things from entering Drogen.*"

"*As you wish, Fatu Ma-gazi. Please, just be careful.*"

Grobennar turned back once again toward Drogen. Minutes later, he approached the location where the creature had prevailed over Grobennar's control. As he did, Grobennar pried into the connection to feel for the source of whatever it was that was overriding his own hold over the dordron during the transition away from his otherwise iron grip upon this beast's will. He sent his mind deep into the creature's will as he sped toward the Drogen coast. But as it turned away, he still felt nothing. It was like holding a heavy object with the help of several others only to have them all suddenly let go.

"I pray you had better success than I in sensing the source of this irregularity."

Jaween was silent within his mind for a long while, then said, "*Turn the beast back toward Drogen.*" Grobennar repeated the process more than six times before Jaween finally said, "*I think I may have located the spell.*"

"Okay, so now what?"

"*You're going to need the help of at least one more priest to help break down the spell, but I am confident that it can be done. You will have to break down the spell individually for each creature.*"

"That can be done." Grobennar sensed there was more. "What else?"

Jaween did not immediately respond. "*You are not going to like this.*"

"Don't be coy. Out with it."

"I'm going to have to guide both you and the other priest to the place within the dordron where the spell resides."

"I don't understand the problem."

Another pause. "*You will both have to give your wills over to me during this time.*"

Grobennar flinched. He had done this only once before, early in their relationship, and the result had been a catastrophe that nearly ended his time in the Kleról. The spirit's appetite for chaos was insatiable and once in control of another's will in corporeal form, Jaween had nearly lost control. The idea of giving his will over to Jaween again alongside the power of another: it was more than reckless. Not to mention, he would have to explain the spirit to whomever he chose. His first thought was Paranja, for he trusted her, but would she go on trusting him if he revealed that he had been hiding a weapon strictly forbidden by the Kleról?

That was a secret he wasn't sure he could trust with even Paranja. But what other choice did he have? He had selected a team of priests in whom he had the utmost confidence, but this was a secret that would not only ruin him politically, it could mean death.

Solving this problem would require two very great risks. *How far am I willing to go to achieve my goals?*

Some time later, Grobennar sat with Paranja and another loyal priest beside a cage housing a particularly prickly dordron.

"I don't know why you're so hesitant about this plan," said Jaween. *"What happened back in Sire Karth all those years ago was an . . . aberration. I ordinarily have great self-control."*

Forgive me if I don't share your confidence, thought Grobennar. With others in the vicinity, Grobennar answered only with a displeasured grunt. In spite of his past quarrel with Paetar, there remained a pang of guilt at what would transpire.

"You are prepared to do what must be done?" asked Grobennar of Paetar, the male priest between himself and Paranja. Paetar had been invited to assist in the task just hours earlier, which was when the truth about Jaween had been revealed to him. Grobennar had taken him aside to explain everything, including Jaween and his role in this feat. Grobennar was careful to keep Paranja apart from the full truth of what was to take place.

Paetar had blanched at the revelation that one of The Forbidden was among them, but Grobennar had implored him to consider the greater good that might be done in spite of the means by which it would be achieved. After all, the sentient gemstones were not considered to be evil unto themselves; the Kleról simply considered their powerful potential to persuade too dangerous to risk falling into the hands of a wayward, ambitious priest. They had been blamed for the Chaos Wars after all. This was shortly after Lesante's founding of the Empire. However, many of Jaween's comments indicated that he predated even this time. Any records of where or how The Forbidden had originally come into being had been destroyed, but there were many theories.

Paetar looked hesitantly at the pair, swallowed hard, then nodded. "I am prepared to serve, Fatu Ma-gazi."

"This is well. You do yourself, your family, and the Empire a great honor. Your strength and sacrifice today will ensure victory over our enemies."

Grobennar patted him on the shoulder. Paetar would need to allow the spirit to take hold of his will in order to accomplish their goal. Grobennar himself doubted the intelligence of this plan so he could only imagine how Paetar must feel. And yet, he was here. It was commendable.

"Paranja, your role is to ensure our safety and add your strength, if needed, as Paetar and I explore the mind of the dordron in search of the spell that keeps it from the east." Grobennar turned to Paetar. "Are you ready to begin?"

Paetar gulped and nodded, beaded sweat running down his face. "I am."

Grobennar felt his own nerves coalesce in his chest and knees, which began to tremble.

"Let us begin." *Lord God, please protect and forgive me,* he prayed to Klerós.

Grobennar immediately felt the probing touch of Jaween, like an ice-cold hand on the bare skin of his back, only this touch wrapped around the most intimate place of his mind, his will. Grobennar knew this was to happen, yet he still recoiled out of instinct, like the tingling sensation one feels while standing at the precipice of a great height. His initial reaction was to step back to safety, maintaining control over his will, his sense of self. But he stepped back to the edge, leaning forward, relinquishing his will, transferring ownership to Jaween. He just prayed the spirit would do the same once the job was finished.

Jaween exclaimed, "*This . . . this . . . I have not felt something so wonderful in a very, very long time.*"

The excitement in Jaween's mental connection was chilling.

"*Do you have Paetar's mind, as well?*" asked Grobennar. As the question was asked, Grobennar felt Paetar's presence. In fact, he felt Paetar so strongly that Grobennar wondered if Jaween hadn't sent Grobennar's mind into the other man's. It felt much like a clasp of another creature, only Grobennar wasn't in control, or at least, not fully. He could feel the priest's utter fear, his mental whimpering.

Then he heard him speak to Jaween through the connection. "*I am ready.*"

Grobennar had to credit the man. He may have been afraid, but he was loyal to the task.

"*Oh, what a joyous day to destroy a spell!*" cackled Jaween.

Grobennar's mind was suddenly plunged into that of the dordron. He recognized the creature's powerful will and the malice that pooled within a being caged and controlled by another against its volition.

Jaween's ability to navigate the creature's mind was nothing short of astounding. The giant bird had begun to thrash about the cage at the intrusion into its mind, but Jaween put a swift end to that with a precise mental touch to the exact place where the modality was controlled. All priests trained to clasp were capable of doing so, but it was the speed and effortlessness that astonished Grobennar, whose skill with a clasp was unmatched by any he knew. His paled in comparison. And it had to have been hundreds of years since Jaween had had the opportunity to do this. It brought confidence to Grobennar that they might accomplish the task at hand, yet it also gave him cause to fear what might happen should the spirit not keep to their agreement. The destruction that this being could bring about was almost unfathomable, and he understood why the prophetess, Lesante, had banned the use of such things within the Empire.

Jaween moved throughout the mind of the dordron so quickly Grobennar could barely understand where the spirit was leading his and Paetar's minds. Grobennar was certain Paetar would have no idea what was happening. Where Grobennar would break through a creature's will and then detour around the swirls of instinct that drove a beast to behave the way it did, Jaween brought them straight through this portion of the creature, speeding up and slowing down at odd intervals that Grobennar did not understand. All the while, Jaween transmitted an emotional glee like that of a hound set free after prey, only in this case it was like the prey had been scattered about a field and the hound could not decide which one to attack so he bounced around from one to the other, howling with joy all the while.

Then everything stopped and Jaween said into their minds, "*I have located the area of affliction.*"

Grobennar had no ability to feel around on his own, not until Jaween returned his will to him, but he could speak through the connection. "*I don't see anything here.*"

"*Why, of course you don't. It was hidden quite well. They hid the spell within the part of the mind that drives instinct, but also in a place you might never see activated unless triggered, like the part of an animal's mind that tells it to flee from fire. That portion of its mind would otherwise remain dormant.*

"*In this case, there is a very complicated spell prompted only by proximity to a location in the center of the Isles, allowing free rein across most of the region, but keeping the dordron from entering the continent of Drogen. You might never see it unless you were doing this exact thing while flying atop the creature as it attempted to fly past the geographic barrier that activates it. And because it's embedded in the instinctual portion of the mind, it has become a part of those things passed down through reproduction. Whoever created this was a true master of magic.*"

Grobennar considered this with a sense of wonder. Jaween was right about the genius behind whoever crafted the spell. He now saw it, not only the placement of it, but the complexity. Hundreds of strands somehow connected to the portion of the dordron's mind that understood geographic location but also connected to its will. And unlike most animal instincts, Grobennar could tell it was a one-way connection only. That's why someone controlling the dordron would be able to do nothing to override it where they might ordinarily seize total control over even the basest instincts an animal might possess. This spell could not be manipulated from control over the will itself, because there was no connection from the will to it. *Such an ingenious design.* Grobennar reveled at the beauty of such a creation and could only be thankful for Jaween's help in identifying it.

He commented to the giddy spirit, *"Let's finish what we came to do."*

Jaween took hold of Grobennar's power, as well as Paetar's, and began dismantling the spell like he was unlacing a boot. Yet the weaves involved were so intricate Grobennar could only guess at their composition.

He would have liked to have studied them, but time was limited. Jaween made quick work of the spell with the shared power of two priests, then took hold of Grobennar's body and spoke through him. "The spell has been removed. Paranja, have the other dordron brought here at once so we might do the same to them." Grobennar felt Jaween manipulating his face into an expression he could only guess was . . . lust? *No, no, no. What is he doing?*

"I really appreciate all of your help, my darling."

"Jaween, what are you doing?"

"Whatever do you mean? I'm merely showing kindness to someone who is aiding our cause."

Grobennar bristled. *"My darling? And what is that look you—I gave her?"*

Paranja stared at him blinking in surprise at the informality. She then returned a warm smile. "Of course, my Fatu Ma-gazi. I would do *anything* . . . for you . . . and the Empire."

Grobennar's hand moved against his will, reached out, and patted her bottom. "I know. Now make haste."

She let out a high-pitched "Whoop!" in surprise, and her expression became a glare, which Grobennar was certain would be accompanied by a slap, a well-deserved one in his opinion. But then she smiled and laughed. "You're in odd spirits this evening. Very, very odd."

More than you could possibly know, thought the currently helpless Grobennar.

Grobennar's eye winked at her, just before she turned to complete the request.

She shook her head and disappeared over a ridge to where the other dordron were being held.

Grobennar was almost more taken aback by Jaween's provocative behavior toward Paranja than the dordron and spell itself. He would *never* behave in such a manner. Priests weren't necessarily sworn to celibacy, but most of those who rose to high ranks did indeed remain so. Families were too weighty, and relationships clouded one's judgment. Grobennar could only ever dream of discovering a relationship between Rajuban and a woman that he could exploit. Grobennar had always prided himself on his ability to ignore and overcome the bestial lusts of the flesh. Where many priests feigned celibacy, and if nothing else frequented brothels to satisfy their needs, Grobennar had simply tamed his yearnings, limited them to the occasional perusal with his eyes before reminding himself of the ever-steepening slope that would lead him to sin. And he would end there. Jaween had just set the stage for . . .

"*I think if you play your hand right, you might finally have the chance to—*"

"*No.*"

"*Hmm, perhaps I could maintain control of your will for just a bit longer than previously discussed. You would thank me after, of this I'm sure.*"

Grobennar felt a sudden surge of panic. "*No. Please, no.*" He was utterly helpless. There was nothing he would be able to do to stop Jaween from such a course if he saw fit. "*Please,*" he begged.

"*Ughh, so boring.*"

⊰⊰⊰

Removing the spell from the remaining dordron went surprisingly quickly. Grobennar was beginning to yearn for his next meal as the last of the spells were removed. His feelings grew increasingly mixed as he neared the conclusion of their work. The next phase of their plan required the obedience of Jaween in holding up his end of the bargain, which, after his suggestive behaviors toward Paranja, strained Grobennar's confidence. He very much disliked operating at the mercy of a sociopathic, amoral being such as Jaween.

Grobennar said into the connection, *"It is time to conclude the day's business."*

Paetar replied, *"Oh thanks be to Klerós. This has been . . . exhausting."*

Grobennar felt Jaween's excitement elevating. He recognized this being's elation; it reached a height to rival the clasp they had performed on the Kraken, which had resulted in the destruction of the entire ship and crew of the Dark Lord's agent. Grobennar waited with great anticipation, genuinely concerned that Jaween would abandon their plan in lieu of exploiting the potential chaos to be had in the midst of having been given control.

Grobennar knew Jaween's awareness was teetering on the precipice of this choice. He could feel the pull from Jaween's consciousness to catapult them all into the darkness of mayhem. There was joy waiting there, or at least Jaween's perception that it would be joy. Thick tension filled the moment, and more than that, fear, Grobennar's fear. He knew that Jaween could not help himself. Jaween was a jackal lured by the cries of a wounded fawn, and Grobennar was that fawn. His cries only further fueled Jaween's craving.

"Jaween! The plan! Stick to the plan!"

Jaween's mind cackled. *"But there's so much . . . wildness. We could have so much fun right now!"*

Grobennar punched back with his mind. *"To what end? This would ruin me and you would be cast away for another thousand years, or worse, destroyed altogether. Release me now and you'll have more fun, but if you gorge yourself, it could be your last meal, ever."*

Jaween's mind shouted at Grobennar's mind. *"Humans! Weakness! Bah!"*

To Grobennar's great relief and surprise, Jaween released his hold on Grobennar's will. Jaween's mental touch engulfed him in a rush, and

Grobennar suddenly understood the strange reactions he saw in freed animals over which he had held sway through the clasp.

He had been standing at the time of this release and stumbled back, right into Paranja, who caught him gently. "Are you unwell? Fatu Ma-gazi?" She held him in her arms, hands wrapping around his chest from behind, showing no interest in letting go.

"I—I'm fine." He stiffened and shrugged her off. "Sorry. And thank you, of course."

He tried to smile, careful not to suggest any hint of flirtation. "I believe my body was simply in temporary shock after so much time working within the minds of these beasts. But the job is done." Grobennar then turned his attention to Paetar. The last portion of their plan still needed completing. He placed a hand on the amulet, then spoke to the priest. "Thank you, Paetar, for your assistance today."

Paetar glared back at him and spoke, though Grobennar knew the words were not his own. Jaween still held sway over the man. "Do you recall that time back in the priesthood, during the seeker competition?"

Grobennar looked back at him, feigning confusion. "I—yes, I suppose." He paused, then added, "That was quite some years ago."

"I helped Rajuban, your greatest rival."

Grobennar nodded. "Yes? Is this story going somewhere? I would very much like to rest."

Paetar continued as if Grobennar hadn't spoken. "Had we won outright, I would have risen alongside him to a position within the Assembly inside of two years. I wouldn't be here doing menial tasks with the likes of you."

"Excuse me?"

Paetar pressed on. "I know you cheated your way to victory, setting the stage for your own rise, stepping on the shoulders of those more deserving than yourself."

Grobennar stood taller and stepped forward. "You forget yourself, Mazi Paetar. Whatever lingering feelings of jealousy you may feel, they are unbecoming. It has been a long day so I'm willing to forgive such loose speech. But my patience wears thin."

Paranja looked back and forth, and Grobennar felt her gathering Klerós's power. Or was that Paetar? Both? He gathered his own and stood poised and ready to do what must be done.

Paetar growled, "You're not going to take credit for my work here tonight. The glory will be mine." He lashed out with his summoned power, and Grobennar barely reacted in time, ducking the brunt of the blow, deflecting the rest as he assumed a crouch. He returned a magical attack of his own while unsheathing a dagger from its place of hiding on each of his legs.

Paranja also attacked, but her attempts were flicked away and returned with a blast of heat that, fortunately, she managed to defend.

Grobennar bellowed, "That is enough! Stand down, Mazi Paetar!"

"Oh, I think not. This is far too much fun," snickered the possessed Paetar.

Grobennar closed the gap between them, sending several quick slivers of molten heat to keep Paetar occupied. They dissolved before making contact. *"How in the—"*

He was close enough to attack through mundane means, and Paetar held no weapons. Grobennar pressed the advantage, stabbing and slashing with precision, but Paetar somersaulted through the air like an acrobat, a movement entirely alien to any fighting technique Grobennar had ever seen, let alone faced.

Paetar's hand became a knife unto itself, stabbing into Grobennar's flesh between the shoulder and neck, causing his entire left arm to fall slack. Paranja stepped in to assist, but her martial advance was dismantled in seconds, and she was soon careening through the air after a kick that included a boost of magic. Grobennar was certain he heard a crunch that could mean nothing less than broken ribs, perhaps more.

Upon feeling the sudden flux in magic, several other priests had emerged from the training grounds and were standing by, unsure what to do as the two priests fought each other.

"Stop him, you fools!" yelled Grobennar, who had meanwhile decided on a more practical response to Paetar's abruptly improved combat skills. Using his good arm, he gripped the amulet in his hand and removed the chain from around his neck. If he could throw it far enough away, Jaween would lose control over the man's mind and perhaps Grobennar could then finish the job.

A blast of air swept Grobennar from his feet before he could complete the throw. Then Paetar leaped atop him. Grobennar had only one arm with which to defend himself, so he was useless against the priest, who batted the knife and amulet out of his hand then clasped fingers around Grobennar's throat.

"This needs to stop. You go too—" Grobennar's shout became garbled syllables. Paetar squeezed and the light of day shrank away.

Then the light returned and Grobennar realized that Paetar had been thrown from him by a blast of power from one of the bystanders. Before anything else could be done, Grobennar scrabbled to take hold of the amulet. Then he threw it as far as he could over a cluster of bushes a dozen paces away, the opposite direction of Paetar.

Grobennar coughed, his throat aching as he came to his feet to face his foe. Paetar had also risen, but his expression was one of worry, not malice. "I—what—that wasn't me!"

Grobennar moved on shaky legs. He said nothing as he stalked forward. And Paetar's eyes darted from side to side, wide with fear. "It wasn't me. It was the—"

A dart of magic struck Paetar's throat, collapsing his windpipe. The priest choked on whatever mess Grobennar had just made of his wind passage, and Grobennar took pity on him, knowing this had been the only way. The priest was innocent, this time. But Grobennar was not one to forget a betrayal. Paetar had nearly cost him everything. The sins of the past had simply taken a long time to catch up with him. However, even Paetar did not deserve to suffer.

Grobennar knelt beside the priest, who had fallen to the ground. He whispered to Paetar, "You have done Klerós a great service today. Your sins are now forgiven." Paetar stared wide-eyed in panic and Grobennar had mercy on him, ending his life.

He rose to his feet and proclaimed loud enough for all to hear. "You have borne witness to an unprovoked attack upon a superior. Fatu Almaj Paranja will attest to this when she recovers from her wounds.

Mazi Tormonald, see to her at once. Mazi Thaetar, see to the body. As a priest who served Klerós well, the proper rights shall still be observed. It is my belief that unraveling the spell was injurious to an otherwise loyal man's mind. We shall not remember him as he was in his last moments; we will remember the sacrifice he made in his years serving the Empire."

Nods of agreement flowed throughout the onlookers, all loyal priests of the Empire—and, more important, servants of the Fatu Ma-gazi.

"Let us depart from these hallowed grounds."

The priests and priestesses returned to the training grounds while Grobennar started for the location of Jaween. He pulled up short when he saw Paranja walking toward him, a golden chain dangling from her closed fist.

She stopped in front of him and raised an eyebrow. "You appear to have dropped this during your struggle against Mazi Paetar." Her tone didn't exactly contain accusation, but there was a hint of suspicion.

Grobennar chuckled awkwardly. "Aye. It seems I did. Strange, the things people do under duress."

"Indeed," replied Paranja.

Grobennar knew she was suspicious, but he also had known her a long time. She would not force him to lie to her directly. She would not ask him outright. She expected him to take some time to decide how to tell her the full truth. And if he didn't, she would respect that decision.

Grobennar felt the weight of the amulet as it slid into his hand and considered telling her everything just to get it off his shoulders, to have someone with whom to share the cumbersome truth of his sins. But he could not burden Paranja with such knowledge. Not because he didn't trust her, but because he did not want the knowledge of the things he had done on her conscience. This was his burden, and his alone, to bear.

Grobennar slid the chain over his head and felt the familiar tug on his neck and shoulders, the ever-present pull toward the underworld that accompanied the gemstone as it dangled about his neck.

Jaween had remained silent during the exchange between Grobennar and Paranja, but the satisfaction Grobennar sensed through the connection grated on his nerves. Jaween was a glutton who had just gorged himself on human fear and destruction. There was, however, also a touch of . . . remorse? No, Jaween was incapable of true remorse, but he seemed *almost* capable of emulating a sense of being apologetic. He would cower away for a time like a pup that knows he just destroyed something important.

Grobennar would certainly need to deal with the spirit, but for now he needed to rest. Anything he said or did with regard to Jaween would be lacking. His bones were frail and his mind felt like it had been trampled by a horde of mounted warriors.

Paranja walked alongside Grobennar on his way to the tent he had ordered set up as a residence during his visits to the training grounds. This served as a reminder that he did have one issue that needed to be resolved before laying his head down to rest.

He stopped just a few paces away from the opening. "Paranja, I wish to apologize for my behavior this evening. I was . . . not quite myself."

Several expressions crossed her face before she responded, one such appeared to be disappointment. *Disappointment that I behaved as I did, or that I am now rescinding full ownership over such conduct?*

She settled on a light smile. "You were under a great deal of stress this evening. People say and do all manner of strange things under such circumstances. I accept your apology, Fatu Ma-gazi." She rested a gentle hand upon his arm, just below the shoulder. "By now, I think you know my feelings toward you, and if you don't, then you're more of a fool than I give you credit."

She turned and glided away without another word, leaving Grobennar standing outside his tent, mouth agape. He didn't need Jaween to say, "*I told you so.*" Her admittance of such feelings only caused him further embarrassment at what he had said and done. How could she harbor such feelings, especially after his buffoonery?

The idea of having a romantic relationship was out of the question, no matter their feelings. He had been careful to quash any such thoughts the moment they surfaced. A man in Grobennar's position could not afford the liability that came with romance. And while he *could* perhaps engage in some of the activities often associated with romantic entanglements, it was all part of a greater web of connectedness that he knew was best to avoid altogether, not to mention a violation of self-control and lust that made up one of the tenets of the faith. He shook all thoughts of Paranja and romance out of his mind as he entered his tent. He needed rest, nothing more.

CHAPTER 43

DAGMARA

As evening approached, Aynward took Dagmara's arm and pulled her off the narrow road they traveled along the river. "Wagons."

They found cover several paces off the road and waited for the travelers to pass them by. There was still plenty of light by which to see, so as the three wagons bumped along, Aynward tilted his head and pointed at the uncovered cargo in the second wagon. He whispered, "Wine."

Then he started to stand. Dagmara pulled at his sleeve. "What are you doing? We don't have enough coin for your—"

He yanked his sleeve free and stepped into view. "Hey," he yelled. "Hey, over here."

Dagmara's heart sank. *What have I done, trusting a drunk with my life?*

The wagons came to a halt and Aynward beckoned Dagmara to come forward with him. She forced exhausted legs to stand and followed him over.

Two dark-skinned Scritlandian men bearing the typical short, curved blades of their homeland stood beside a shorter Scritlandian. He spoke with a light accent, lighter even than Brenna's. "You've captured my attention, stopped my wagon." He looked the two of them up and down, then peered into the woods searching for others before he continued, "You don't appear equipped to rob us so I'll assume your intentions lack malice, but I am no charity. State your business."

Aynward said, "I noticed your cargo. That's Van Odla vineyard vintage, is it not?"

The guards gripped their weapons tighter at the mention of the cargo.

The man nodded. "It is." Skepticism leaked from every word.

How did Aynward know that? wondered Dagmara.

"My companion here, Ada," Aynward waved a hand toward Dagmara, "and I are friends of Lady Minathi Van Odla. We were planning a visit but were attacked by bandits and lost our way. We were wondering if you might point us in the right direction."

The man stepped toward them to examine closer. "Friends of Lady Minathi, you say?"

Aynward replied with the truth, sort of. "We took a course together in Brinkwell. She's quite the spirited girl. Enamored with a friend of mine, actually, but he's a Don-Votro, so you know, not a realistic pairing."

The man frowned. "I didn't catch your name."

"Lars. Samdred Lars, of Fremolden originally." Aynward even did a gentle bow, though Dagmara noticed him wince at the movement.

The Scritlandian in charge stepped back and nodded. "It's funny, for a moment there I thought perhaps the two of you might be those fugitives we heard about just before we our departure. Something about a brother and sister, one of whom stands accused of slaying his own father, the King."

Aynward's eyes met Dagmara's and she could see him judging the guards' positions, the man in front of him, as well as any others who might be a threat. He didn't pause long in his response. "Fugitives and Kingslayers? By the gods, that sounds like a bit too much excitement for the two of us. Truth be told, them bandits brought enough violence to satisfy us for the rest of our days, that is if the gods have mercy."

"Is that right?" The man turned away and started walking back toward the wagon. "That's too bad. I'm Lady Minathi's uncle, and she was quite distraught when news of such events reached us. Adamant that her good friend, Prince Aynward, would never commit such a crime. And I'm inclined to believe her. Probably would have offered assistance to someone like that were I to find him and his brave sister on the road in need of such aid."

Dagmara waited a few heartbeats but when Aynward said nothing she blurted, "It's us. I am Princess Dagmara, and this is my brother, he who stands accused of treason and Kingslaying."

The dark-skinned Scritlandian spun on his heel, and said to his guards, "Seize them." The men responded instantly, as did Dagmara and Aynward, but just as Dagmara drew her curved blade from hiding, the sound of laughter gave her pause.

The Scritlandian who claimed to be Minathi's uncle was heaving with merriment, a high-pitched, throaty sound. "Stand down, all of you, stand down," he said before returning to his guffawing.

Aynward looked at Dagmara, then back to the man. "Er, did I miss something? I feel like I missed something."

The Scritlandian finally relented and said, "We're taking you back to the Van Odla Estate. We'll set camp now and leave at first light. We're only three days' travel from the estate, and while the delay on making it to market with our cargo will be most unfortunate, keeping those who stand wrongly accused safe is of a higher priority." He stepped forward and held out a hand before Aynward. "My name is Grinnald. My older brother, Lord Van Odla, runs production at the family vineyard; I run the mercantile side of things. I believe he will feel similarly about assisting you. We are both of Scritland, a kingdom of law and order. It was the only climate ripe for quality grape cultivation and a beautiful kingdom woman, Lady Francesca, that brought us north of our homeland."

Aynward tilted his head. "Not to discourage the help or anything, but wouldn't helping two fugitives escape custody be a slight betrayal of law and order?"

Grinnald lifted an eyebrow and smiled, his white teeth shining bright. Then he pointed to the heavens, where the first of the moons was cresting the horizon, and said, "We follow a higher law and order than that of men, my dear friend of Lady Minathi. You will stand before my brother, and he will consult the gods over your fate. Until that time, you will be our welcome guests, though we will need to act with some measure of discretion." Gesturing to his three wagons, he said, "These men are mine, and they will not breathe a word of any of this. But as we approach the estate, you and your sister will hide within the cargo."

Aynward flattened his lips and tilted his head as he said, "I'm going to sound like a bit of a negative Nathan, here, but how do I know you won't simply turn us over to some authority to collect the bounty before entering the grounds of the estate? You know, once we're securely hidden?"

Grinnald brought a hand to his chin in thought. "A bounty? Well, I could use a few new wagons. My brother, frugal man that he is, has been reluctant to replace these rickety things in spite of my insistence that they're hardly worthy of travel."

The man's tone was jovial, but Aynward appeared ready to launch an attack at any sudden movement. Then Grinnald laughed again, haughty and boisterous. "If you're concerned, I'll send word ahead of our arrival so Lady Minathi can personally acknowledge your arrival before we pass the gates. This will assure you that I speak truth, for who would dare cross her?"

Dagmara let out a breath as Aynward's posture deflated. He replied, "That would be much appreciated, Lord Grinnald."

"Very well. But please, no lord talk around me. I've no lands to inherit. Contrary to kingdom norms, Lady Minathi has been named heiress. I live well enough as a necessary function of the family business, as will my children, should they choose it. Call me Ser if you must include an honorific."

With the tension finally broken, their camp was set and Dagmara found her growling stomach finally satisfied so they recounted their escape from the palace of Salmune and the death of their aunt in Quinson. Grinnald offered condolences, and then a cup of wine to the both of them, which Dagmara declined.

"Are you certain, Lady Dagmara? We will be dumping whatever we don't drink this evening."

Aynward piped in, "I'll take hers."

Dagmara glared at him. "Is that wise?" she asked, annoyed at his return to flippancy.

He sighed. "Surely not, though my toenail-less toes would greatly appreciate the numbing properties of overindulgence." Groaning he continued, "I could swear there's a little gremlin in my boot right now gnawing on them!" But to her surprise, he waved the cup away.

"Might I ask why you intend to dump portions of your cargo?" asked Dagmara.

Ser Grinnald replied, "Two reasons," and he gestured with his own cup toward the two fugitives.

"I . . . I don't follow."

"It's simple. If what you say about the events in Quinson is true, they'll be sending patrols in every direction from there. It won't be long before one passes through here. Perhaps we'll arrive at the Van Odla Estate before this comes to pass, but if not, I would like to be able to hide the two of you. Explaining your companionship might otherwise prove difficult."

The following day passed without incident. However, just before breaking for dinner on the second day, one of the guards fell back, and urged Aynward and Dagmara into hiding.

"Four riders. Quickly now. Quickly."

As had been discussed, the lids of two of the now empty barrels were quickly lifted, and the fugitives hopped inside. The guard remarked, "You should have enough air to last until they're gone." Then he struck each lid home with a mallet. Shortly thereafter the wagons came to a halt.

How comforting, thought Dagmara.

The barrel was stuffy and the stench of fermentation was powerful. Dagmara had to focus to steady her breathing.

Having been positioned in the lead wagon nearest Grinnald, Dagmara was able to hear the conversation well enough, and they were right to have hidden.

"Identify yourself, your business, and your destination," sounded a high-pitched voice.

Grinnald answered with an affable tone, "Well met, good sir. Might I ask under what authority you demand this information?"

"We come in the name of the King with orders to search all cargo on the road," rang the same voice.

"Ah, the King. And what is it you're looking for, exactly?"

A deeper-sounding man replied, "We will be asking the questions, *merchant.*"

Loathing was evident in the man's voice. Scritlandian merchants were viewed with a particular disfavor in southern Dowe. As they became more active in the market, they disrupted some of the older, noble monopolies on certain luxury trade items, fine wines included, making them cheaper by direct shipments instead of through trade at the border.

"Very well. I want no trouble, of course. I am Grinnald of the Van Odla Estate, taking this here wine to the estate."

"If you are of the Van Odla Estate, shouldn't you be bringing the wine *from* the estate, not to it?"

Grinnald remained good-humored. "Ah, you are a perceptive one, I see. Well, ordinarily you would be right. But as you may recall, we had a very bad spell of locusts last year, hatched just west of the Spine. Nasty pestilence on our vineyard." He leaned in to speak more quietly. "We've resorted to buying up batches from other vineyards to mix with our own in order to keep up with demand. And please, good Ser, if you could keep this secret, it would be a great favor to us of the Van Odla. In fact, take a barrel if it please you. One on us for your discretion on the matter."

"Just like a Scritlandian to pass another's work off as his own."

Grinnald laughed off the insult. "Pah, just a temporary measure until our new vines produce fruit. But you say it true, and it pains me to admit it."

The higher-pitched voice said, "Best make sure they have what they say they have, aye?"

"Aye. Good idea," said another voice Dagmara had not yet heard.

Then a loud crash, and a yelp from Grinnald were followed by the sound of rushing liquid. "Please, we paid good money for these. I don't know what you're looking for, but this is Van Odla property. Please."

Another loud crack, this one was closer to Dagmara. She couldn't tell for sure, but she thought there was only one more barrel before her own.

"Gentlemen, what is it that you want? Is it gold? I have some coin left from our dealings."

Dagmara wished right now to push the lid from the top of the barrel and drive a sword through these men, but the lid would not come off unless pried. Another loud sound thundered. This one was without a doubt the barrel directly beside her, as she felt the vibration acutely.

"Let's see this gold of yours."

Dagmara let out a breath and whispered, "*Tecuix, praise be your name, please let this work.*"

"This it?" scoffed a deep-voiced man. "Keep searching!"

Dagmara braced herself for the impact, praying that whatever they were using to bust open the barrels wouldn't also bust open her skull, or any part of her for that matter. She closed her eyes and made herself as small as she could against the back of the barrel, not that this would do any good in such a tight space.

Time seemed to stop as she waited, and waited, and finally, she heard the deep-voiced man say, "Now that's more like it. I'd almost consider letting you take the fugitives, even if you had them, for this. Yes, this will do just fine."

"I'm glad we could come to an agreement and pleased to support the King's servants of law and order," grumbled Grinnald.

Dagmara waited patiently for the patrol to depart, no longer tense with concern over being captured, but found the air within the capsule less and less satisfying to breathe. Finally, she heard a gentle knock on the barrel from the outside. "You okay?"

"Uh-huh. Just a little stuffy."

"Okay, let's get you out of there." And she heard as much as felt the metal pry bar fight its way beneath the lid, followed by a high-pitched groan as it slid free.

A rush of cooler, fresh air sank into the barrel and Dagmara breathed deeply, then released a loud sigh of satisfaction.

Aynward let out an exasperated sound of relief. "I love the smell of wine as much as the next fool, but that was a little much even for me. Hooey!"

Back on her feet and out of the barrel entirely, Dagmara said to Grinnald, "We are in your debt. Thank you. I know it's not much, but please, we have some coin. You have to take what we have. You've already lost too much."

Grinnald waved the words away with a hand. "That's part of our ordinary travel security. The guards are here in case it's a fight worth fighting, and the coin is there for when it's not." Gesturing toward the two guards, he said, "Turp and Tallad are sturdy fighters, and I'm a little past my prime, but being Scritlandian, I suspect I'm still better with a weapon than a Kingdom-born patrolman. Even still, sending those men on their way without reason to believe you two came this way is more valuable. If they didn't return, the Kingdom would know exactly where to pool their resources and the next time a patrol came through, it would be an entire squadron."

Aynward nodded. "Well, you're due a great reward. I'll probably not ever have the means to repay you, but if I do and you're not dead from old age, you'll be paid well for your trouble."

"Well, you know, that's what it's all about, after all," chuckled Grinnald. "I cast a wide net of good deeds in hopes that someone one day will repay one of them tenfold. A more reliable investment than putting money in any Kingdom bank."

Aynward laughed at that. "Especially now. My brother is going to empty the treasury in search of us alone."

Dagmara wasn't sure this was actually funny but didn't want to ruin the mood so she let out a light laugh with the others.

The remainder of their travel to the Van Odla vineyard went without incident, and soon enough they were greeted by a landscape of rolling hills lined with vines, set before the backdrop of the Dragon Spine

Mountains. The Van Odlas were not the only ones to have realized the favorable soil of this region. In fact, Aynward's questions had revealed that the Van Odla Estate had been home to a failed vineyard from decades earlier that had gone into disrepair. It hadn't been the grapes or the soil that had ruined them, it had been the storage units. Apparently they had constructed the vats wrong, thereby spoiling the wine just enough to ruin the flavor, but not enough to make it evident that this was the cause of the subpar quality. The Van Odla family had rectified this and revived the estate over the past two decades.

Grinnald yelled back, "We'll be approaching the gate so I'm going to need you two to go back into hiding. I don't want any more eyes on you than is absolutely necessary."

Fortunately, he had not insisted on having the barrels sealed shut, simply that they hide within them until they were safely inside of the estate.

When the wagon finally stopped and Grinnald knocked on Dagmara's barrel, her legs had cramped and she needed assistance to stand. She could only imagine what Aynward must have felt like confined to a proportionally smaller space. He removed the need to imagine. "By the gods, I'd rather be captured than do that again."

He climbed out of the barrel and nearly fell from the wagon on unsteady legs. Grinnald caught his arm. "Careful, Lord Aynward the former."

Aynward recovered his footing and remarked, "Thank you. Hmm, Lord Aynward the former . . . it has a certain ring to it, don't you think, Mara?"

Dagmara shrugged. "You're demented."

"Ah hah, I'll take that as a yes, then, on account of the obvious jealousy it produced."

A few moments later, one of Grinnald's men returned with two cloaks that matched those worn by his drivers and guards. "Put these on."

They complied, then followed Grinnald out of the storage warehouse where the wagon had been stopped. Dagmara looked out to see shelves upon shelves of barrels, filled with various vintages. "This is amazing," whispered Aynward.

Dagmara pulled his sleeve as they exited. "Keep your head down."

"Yes, Mother."

Dagmara released her grip and followed Grinnald, the cowl of her cloak drawn as far possible. A pair of Kingdom-born newcomers would likely attract the kind of attention that they wished to avoid. It was best to be unnoticed altogether. The two Scritlandian guards followed close behind, though they remained casual.

They were hurried from the warehouse and up a narrow path bordering a field lined with row after row of grape-laden vines. Dagmara tried to keep her head angled down but couldn't help but look up as the scale and beauty of the place became apparent. They were brought to a door designed for servants, not guests, and from there, an antechamber that led to a lavish room—no doubt, Grinnald's own quarters.

"You will wait here. Please, have a seat, and don't—touch—anything." Grinnald nodded toward the guards who remained standing at attention, expressions impassive.

Aynward sank into a cushioned chair just before Dagmara, and they both released sounds of satisfaction. Dagmara said, "This chair is heavenly. I would gladly turn you over to the authorities in exchange for such comfort."

Aynward exhaled—another loud sound of satisfaction—then replied, "I wouldn't blame you one bit, sis. I'm considering turning *myself* over under the condition I get a good night's sleep with a goose feather pillow, a day to lounge in this chair with a bottle of Van Odla's finest."

The door opened and Grinnald stepped into the room trailed by someone who could have been his twin if not for the extra fifty pounds sitting at his waist. *Minathi's father.* The man wore a purple robe embroidered in fancy furls and golden stitching, cinched at the hips with a thick, golden chain. His head was shaved and glistened as he offered a bow that landed somewhere between reverent and indifferent. He returned to an upright position and opened his arms wide. "Welcome to the Van Odla Estate. I am Herold Van Odla, owner of this property."

Dagmara and Aynward both rose to their feet and inclined their heads respectfully. Dagmara responded, "Pleased to meet you. Your vineyard is beautiful."

Aynward added, "Indeed. This is quite the enterprise you've built here. Under different circumstances, I would love to peruse."

Herold's smile faded. "Indeed. The circumstances are *not* favorable. Please, sit." Then he looked to Grinnald. "Fetch a servant and have them return with some refreshment, if you would."

"Of course."

Grinnald did not seem offended by being ordered around by his brother, nor did his brother give any sense of condescension. The exchange was mutually matter of fact, a mere understanding of hierarchy, of respect.

"Aynward. I received a detailed report from my brother. I have also conversed with my daughter, Minathi, with whom you are well acquainted, but I would like to hear the tale from your lips before making any final judgments about what next to do with you and your sister."

Two hours later, the tale had been mostly completed from start to finish and Dagmara felt like her stomach might explode from the plates of cheese, fruit, and salted meats she had nervously nibbled throughout the retelling of events. Herold rubbed his face, deep in thought, but managed only to conclude, "There's more at play here than the politics at the surface; that much is clear. But I have no guesses as to the motives or players involved. Knowing the conniving that exists in my homeland between the various factions, I find that ninety-nine percent of the time when something seems extraordinary, it's because it is. The question is: What is your role in all of this? Are you mere pawns placed on the board as part of a strategy completely unknown to you? Have you already played your part, or do you continue to affect the play? Or perhaps you were involved as active players from the start but now flee because your own plans failed?"

Dagmara did not like Herold's uncertainty about their motives. It seemed logical to conclude that he would not assist them if he believed there was a chance he might be played the fool. Minathi seemed to be the key to their safety, yet she had not been included in the process. In fact, Dagmara wondered if she had even been told of their arrival.

Aynward leaned forward and spoke with a passion and authority she had rarely heard from him. "Listen, if Lady Minathi has told you anything about me, I'm sure she described a pattern of foolhardy decisions based on youthful, self-serving, petty goals. None of that is wrong. And while I suppose I would be capable of coveting power, I'd surely not do so with an act of patricidal mania as my brother, the King, believes. I do agree that something about this entire scenario reeks of coordinated sabotage; but my and my sister's roles since the slaying of my father have been contrary to whatever forces lay behind it. I was a pawn sent out to draw blood as a sacrifice to clear the board for an attack from elsewhere. My only play since then has been to move from where I was supposed to be before the sequence could be completed. And I've now drawn another to my cause. Lord Herold, we're just trying to survive."

Aynward had been surprisingly sparing with his wine consumption throughout the retelling of events, and his sobriety was made all the more apparent with that speech. He could have eventually made a good baron or duke, Dagmara mused. Now he would be lucky to live to see another year, another few weeks, even.

Lord Herold looked the two of them over, stone-faced all the while, then said, "I will return shortly. Excuse me."

He gestured for Grinnald to follow him out of the room and left without another word.

Dagmara looked to Aynward. "What do you think? Does he believe us? You?"

Aynward shrugged, returning to his casual, relaxed persona, though she could tell his insouciance was faked. "No idea." He rubbed his stomach. "But if not, at least we managed a fantastic meal before the world comes crashing down around us."

Dagmara rolled her eyes. "Well, aren't you just seeing the fleck of gold within the mound of dung?"

That resulted in genuine laughter from Aynward, the likes of which she had not heard since before he left for Brinkwell. "That's beautiful. One of my instructors at Brinkwell would be particularly keen to steal that phrase for himself." Then Aynward's expression clouded and he returned to the more somber version of himself. While he did a fair job of masking it, Dagmara could tell he still had unresolved feelings regarding his departure from Brinkwell, or the memory of what he left behind. She knew he had seen things about which he would likely never speak. She understood firsthand now the trauma of violence. She recalled the feeling as she'd slid her blade free from the flesh of an attacker, the cold shock of taking a life, even one intent on taking her own. Aynward had seen much more of this. She was glad when the door opened to pull her from the darkness of those thoughts.

Through the opening strode a beautiful woman with jet-black hair and creamy light-brown skin that looked to have been polished for its smooth sheen. She wore a jade dress of fine fabric, though it was not an ornate gown like those worn by the women at court. This was more of a casual dress worn for tea. Dagmara knew this had to be Minathi, though Aynward's description had not done justice to her stunning beauty. She was trailed by her father and uncle.

She glared at Aynward. "Got yourself into yet another mess, did you?"

Aynward sat up straighter than Dagmara had ever seen at Minathi's arrival. Then he frowned. "This one was not by choice, but I suppose I've played my part in prolonging it."

The girl smiled and curtsied. "Of course you have."

She took another step closer to him and waited expectantly for him to stand in greeting, which Dagmara had already done. He rose with reluctance, and she forgot all formality as she wrapped arms around his neck and squeezed. "It's great to see you, Aynward. I'm so glad you're okay!"

Aynward returned the hug, though he appeared to Dagmara very much aware that he was standing in the presence of Minathi's father and uncle; his return embrace was stiff and formal.

She finally relinquished her hold on him and stepped toward Dagmara. "And you must be the Princess Dagmara, a swordswoman of legend if the rumors are to be believed."

Dagmara felt her face warm, but then thought, *These people are Scritlandians, after all. They don't hold women to such a restricted status as the Kingdom.* "Well, I'll admit to knowing which way to point a blade.

My newest tutor was Scritlandian, and she taught me a few tricks. Turns out you Scritlandians really know your steel."

Minathi giggled, then said to Aynward, "I already like her better than you." She opened her arms for an embrace and pulled Dagmara in. Then she whispered in Dagmara's ear, "Thank you for believing Aynward. I know he wouldn't be here were it not for you."

Then she stepped back, and Dagmara smiled as warmly as she could. "It is an honor to meet you. Aynward has spoken highly of you and your family."

Minathi waved the comment away. "I'm sure that's not entirely true, but I appreciate a compliment as much as any woman." Turning to her father she said, "Well, would you like to share the good news or shall I?"

Lord Herold lifted an open hand toward Minathi. "Please, they're your friends. You may have the honors."

Minathi smiled. "We're going to help you."

CHAPTER 44

GROBENNAR

GROBENNAR AND PARANJA HAD ARRIVED upon the backs of their dordron just in time to oversee the invasion of the Free City of Drebrose. They left their winged mounts in a forest glade with instructions to remain hidden where they were unless attacked. They would have to maintain their links with the creatures in order to enforce these instructions, but such simple orders would be easy to manage and the energy required to sustain the link was negligible.

They had taken care to observe the location of Lugienese troops before landing. This minimized the distance they would have to travel on foot before Grobennar arrived to assume control of a horse, as well as the assault.

The Lugienese had surrounded Drebrose's meager fleet in port, but no notable exchanges of violence had taken place as of yet. The Lugienese fleet had been instructed to wait for their ground troops to march on the city before engaging, much like they had done in Brinkwell. The land invasion had not met any resistance, and the city walls were now within eyeshot.

Grobennar dismounted from his horse just beyond bowshot, an indication that the rest of the advance should do the same. Word had reached him that the Free Cities had called on the Kingdom of Dowe for

340

aid, but Grobennar knew very well that the Kingdom was still licking its wounds after its naval defeat outside of the Isles city of Tung.

All four of the Free Cities would fall to the Lugienese almost concurrently, and the easy victories here would serve as a bargaining chip for Theo's upcoming meeting with his uncle, Duke Gafford of the Duchy of Gilliden. Grobennar's victories over the Free Cities would mark an important new methodology in terms of conquest, which he hoped would sweeten the deal with the duke.

Grobennar had ordered the Lugienese to show mercy to any of the conquered willing to proclaim fealty to Magog and Klerós. All of the converted were to be left alive and allowed to continue with their lives as vassals to the Lugienese Empire.

Grobennar had not yet disclosed this shift to Magog, reasoning that his authority as Fatu Ma-gazi, and the task of conquest, left him room for a few minor changes in strategy. He would ask for forgiveness after his plans had come full to fruition.

Paranja took a step to stand beside Grobennar, her translucent hair blowing behind her in the coastal breeze. A courier approached on horseback, pulled up beside the place where Grobennar and Paranja stood, then dismounted and knelt, head bowed.

"Rise and report," said Grobennar.

"Thank you, Fatu-Ma-Gazi. I bear a response from Drebrose." He produced a wax-sealed parchment. Grobennar snatched it up, broke the seal, and began reading. He then held out his opened hand and the message erupted in flame.

Jaween must have been able to discern enough of the message through their connection, for he giggled in the background of Grobennar's mind. The spirit preferred the chaos of utter destruction over diplomacy.

Grobennar crumbled the ashes of the response in his hand, and let them fall to the ground, swirling in the wind. "The fool wishes for death."

Grobennar gave Paranja a look and said, "Gather a squadron of wielders. We will take the city today. The poor dunce still believes that the Kingdom will come to his aid. He is sorely mistaken. But," he held up one finger for emphasis, "we will not give him the death he deserves, not exactly. We must set an example that allows for the peaceful transfer of power. This King is to be taken alive."

Grobennar stood amid a half-circle of Klerósi priests, all proficient wielders, their wills linked with his own. An army of five thousand was positioned just behind him, poised to attack at his behest. Victory was all but assured. The difficulty would be in minimizing the damage once the city had been taken. His men were not accustomed to showing any form of mercy to their enemies. However, Grobennar needed to show that the Lugienese were capable of more than simple brutality to those who bowed. This would strengthen the negotiation with Duke Gafford. Grobennar would be offering the duke an opportunity to rescue the Kingdom of Dowe from utter ruin. The duke could be a hero, protecting his people from a war they could not hope to win.

Grobennar opened the mental link he had set up between himself and a dozen other priests, scattered throughout the legions of soldiers. "Remind the troops of their duty to follow my commands of conversion. We will have plenty of opportunity for looting and pillaging, but it must be orderly. As soon as the walls go down, you are to begin the assault. This is to be a swift, but clean, takeover."

He ignored the responses of confirmation, his mind turning to the real task: the walls. His army was position just beyond bowshot. The bowmen standing upon the battlements of this beautiful coastal city were prepared to rain death upon them, but they would falter and flee.

He raised his hands, closed his eyes, and sank his mind into the cauldron of power left open for his use through the mental connection with the others. He lifted his right hand, opened his eyes, and looked out to scan his target, the eastern gate, but also a place his military architects had suggested would be best suited for the true breach, a less-defended space between the eastern gate and the largest of the defensive towers.

His gaze returned to the gate, and he readied himself to send a blast of energy. He was interrupted by a voice inside of his head. "*The anticipation is killing me. Well, okay, not killing me, but it is very bothersome how long you're taking to unleash the beauty of armed chaos!"*

Grobennar mumbled low enough that those around him would not discern his words. "Shut up. I'm trying to concentrate. And this attack will not be like the others."

"Yes, yes. Schemes of mercy. But I will still have my chance to play today, yes?"

"It is likely, yes."

"Ooh yes. Don't let me get in your way. Please do begin."

The spirit's giddy laughter faded into the background and Grobennar returned his focus to the city gate. He released a mountain of power, sending it hurtling toward the eastern gate. It exploded inward, and planks of wood and metal sprayed upward into the area that had once been shadowed by the gate. The thick wall on either side of the gate also shattered, stone and mortar tumbling down to crush its defenders.

Grobennar's men knew what to do, and without a moment's hesitation, one of the three legions on the field raced toward the gate. Once they were within bowshot, a volley of arrows filled the sky, but the legion was trailed by their commander, a talented and powerful wielder who was able to turn aside most of the arrows.

Grobennar waited patiently for his men to reach the gate, engaged by what he knew would be the bulk of the enemy forces. The Fatu Ma-gazi watched from the rise upon which he stood as the red of the Lugienese army moved across the field striking the wall like a waterfall of blood, initially contained but eventually leaking through the cracks. As streaks of red slowly melted past the gate, Grobennar reached into his well of power and sent the second wave of energy, this one three times as vast. The energy crashed into the stone wall between the breached gate and the largest of the defensive towers with a deafening boom, followed by a tall plume of smoke. Grobennar stumbled back a few steps after handling so much power, then watched as the commanders of the other two legions waited for confirmation that the wall was indeed down. One of them had the wherewithal to send a strong burst of air to clear the smoke, revealing the crumbled stone and a blank space where a section of wall had previously stood. His next motion waved the legion forward, racing toward the breach.

This flow of soldiers was slowed only by the limited size of the entrance. The city would be fully theirs by the time Grobennar reached the king's palace.

"My horse," he yelled to a squire. "Paranja, with me." The priestess nodded obediently and Grobennar asked, "Shall we claim another trophy for the God-king?"

Paranja grinned. "For the glory of Klerós, and your own." The addition to this statement bordered on blasphemy, but Grobennar enjoyed the sentiment and did not correct her.

Jaween whispered to his mind, "*I wish you would have ridden in upon the back of a dordron. What better way to intimidate?*"

Grobennar turned away from Paranja to avoid being heard. "You know why. They are to appear playthings to all but a select few. Rajuban cannot know what I have done with them, not yet."

"*Boring,*" taunted the spirit.

Grobennar turned back to Paranja, climbing into the saddle.

Jaween's desire to utilize the dordron mirrored his own. No one else knew their true purpose. He had ordered vows of silence to those priests he had trained to ride and had appointed only those he was certain he could trust. More riders would join this elite force once his plans were made public, but for now the secret must remain.

Grobennar and Paranja rode at a trot into Drebrose, which by this time was abuzz with inhabitants in the process of being subdued. Most of the defenders appeared to have either surrendered their weapons or died fighting. Civilians could be heard crying out as their hiding places were discovered, or their running was brought to a close. Many would die this day, but many more, he guessed, would choose conversion and a life of monitored obedience to Klerós and Lugienese law. It was a wonder Magog had not considered this form of conquest sooner. Obliterating the entire population left vacant, useless cities behind. Brinkwell had been a shell before moving on, and the same could be said of Tung. The mercy shown in the Free Cities would serve as an example to the rest of the continent that the Lugienese were merciful to those who chose Klerós over their pagan falsities.

And this would go more smoothly if Grobennar could convince Drebrose's King himself. By the time he and Paranja reached the king's palace, the doors had been blown down; he felt the remnants of magic as he crossed the threshold of the breach. He rode his horse through the doors and into a courtyard, then through a tall door that opened up to a throne room. The timing of his arrival was impeccable. Two soldiers emerged from an adjacent hall dragging the King by the arms. He must have been hiding in his quarters. The leader of the second legion, Fatu Gazi Lorimar, followed close behind. His teeth shone wide in a grin when he noticed Grobennar and Paranja's arrival. He opened his arms and bowed. "Your timing is perfection, Fatu Ma-gazi . . . and Fatu Almaj," he added, referring to Paranja's status as a member of the Assembly. Speaking in heavily accented kingdom tongue, he said, "King Daeman here was just getting ready to express his eagerness to convert."

The man thrashed about upon hearing this, spitting, "I will do no such thing! I'm no Lugger pawn." He then wrenched his neck around to bite the hand of one of his captors, resulting in a shout from the soldier and a retaliatory boot to the king's stomach. This put a temporary end to the fight. Grobennar extended a hand and immobilized the king, then reached into his saddle bag and tossed a rope to the soldiers, who tied the king's hands behind his back without a word.

Grobennar dismounted and approached.

With the king's hands bound, Grobennar took him by the sleeve and directed him to a window of the palace where much of the city below could be viewed. The window had no glass; it was one of many openings in the wall set to overlook a garden, courtyard, the city, and even the bay, which was filled with ships from both sides, all prepared for battle.

Grobennar let go of the king's sleeve, opting for the fabric at the back of his neck, and forced the man out the window so that if Grobennar were to release his hold, the man would plummet to his death below.

Grobennar did not believe the man would survive such a fall, and the whining squeals of the King suggested that he believed the same.

"Your city is mine. Do you see?" He extended the man further out the window, using a trickle of magic to strengthen his arm. "Do you see?"

The King whimpered, "Yes."

"Say it."

"I—I—"

"Say it!" shouted Grobennar.

Grobennar noted a dribble of liquid pooling at the man's feet. *Good, he should be frightened.*

"The city is yours," he cried.

"Good." Grobennar yanked the man's upper body back inside, then led him to his throne and gestured for him to sit. King Daeman stepped hesitantly toward the tall, purple velvet seat, its legs and arms coated in gold. Grobennar was sure he was trying to decide if this was some sort of trick and said, "Go on."

King Daeman sat awkwardly, unable to lean back with his hands tied behind him as they were. Grobennar said to him, "As far as conquered kings go, you, sir, are a fortunate man. You are the first among many to be offered a conquest of mercy from the Lugienese Empire."

The King gave no reaction. He just stared back at Grobennar, confused, so Grobennar elaborated. "You're to be given the opportunity to continue to govern yourselves within our expanding Empire. We offer you your life and even your title, in exchange for fealty to the Lugienese Empire and your conversion to the Klerósi faith. You, King Daeman, are to be our first vassal king."

The man's eyes widened, and Grobennar saw relief wash over his face, but as expected, as soon as his life was returned to him, greed and pride clouded his eyes, and they narrowed. Grobennar answered the question before it could be voiced. "You will, of course, be left with Lugienese officials to ensure your 'sincerity.' Trust is earned, not freely given. Therefore, your sovereignty will be curtailed greatly. You will be provided advisers and intermediaries to ensure that the God-king's will is never compromised, and this will be strictly enforced by a contingent of soldiers and priests left to maintain order. Your fealty will be to Klerós and Emperor Magog first and foremost."

The King shook his head. "I cannot submit to this. My line has refused fealty to both the Kingdom of Dowe and Scritland for generations. I cannot allow such a stain upon my line for submitting to a *foreign* people and their *god*."

Grobennar shook his head slowly. "Leave us. King Daeman and I will speak privately about the benefits of this offer."

Paranja nodded and reached over to secure the reins of Grobennar's horse, then led everyone else through a set of wide doors to an adjacent room. The Lugienese soldiers closed the doors behind them.

Grobennar felt Jaween's anticipation leaking through their connection. He was like a hound and the king's mind a greasy piece of meat held before his face; the drool of his desire amalgamated through their connection.

"Before we begin, I want to be clear about one thing: the voice you're about to hear is real. You're not crazy. Not yet, anyhow. Should you refuse for too long, however, there is a point from which your mind may never recover."

The King stared at him in confusion, but he would understand very soon. Grobennar grinned. "You may begin."

Jaween howled in pleasure.

King Daeman howled in pain.

CHAPTER 45

KYLLEAN

KYLLEAN SENSED THE STATIC ENERGY all around him and drew it into himself. Focusing his mental energy, he created a choke point in his mind to limit the flow of power into his body. He felt his reservoir fill, but instead of projecting it outward like a mage might do to cast spells, he projected it inward, a small, sustainable trickle of magic that would enhance his speed and strength for a substantial period without running the risk of bone degradation.

Looking up, he grinned and prepared to meet his opponent's attack. Neither he nor his practice partner, Levi, had earned blades, but Kyllean was close. Once he could project his power into an external object, he would test for a weapon of his own.

Levi charged forward with enhanced speed, sword held before him in both hands poised to strike down or across depending on the opening. Kyllean readied himself to defend, but he had reacted too slow to sidestep so he did the only thing he could. He leaped into the air, twisting as he flipped so as to remain defensible even as he completed the aerial maneuver. Levi's blunt practice sword still grazed his leg, but Kyllean avoided the brunt of the assault.

Positions now reversed, Kyllean gave Levi no time to begin anew. He launched a flurry of lightning-fast attacks, which Levi managed to dance around until gaining the advantage on Kyllean once again.

Levi was a good swordsman, but he had proven the lesser to Kyllean's own skills, at least until introducing the enhanced speed and agility of magic. These new elements disproportionately rewarded riskier, offensive tactics. Master Hilde had said defensive measures would catch up in time as the warrior became more acquainted with their newfound speed, and reacting to the same from others, but Kyllean found it frustrating to see his previous superiority temporarily diminished.

"Dead," said Levi in triumph.

"Dead, indeed," huffed the defeated Kyllean.

His father's voice interrupted. "You overextended during your riposte, exposing your right side. Your feet and hips were not in agreement about what your sword was attempting to do. I know the speed granted to you makes you feel like you're able to take more risks, but the practical reality is that the same rules apply to swordsmanship no matter the rapidity. Your newfound speed and strength cause you to overreach because you believe you can get away with more before the enemy responds." He shrugged, then continued, "This might be the case against most foes, but if you hope to stay as alive as nature would prefer, you must not sacrifice form on the altar of speed. To truly master the sword and our magic is to return oneself to fighting in much the same way you did before. Use your speed to enhance your skills, not to change them altogether."

Kyllean considered this. It made sense but would be easier said than done. "Thank you, Father."

Levi smiled. "I'm rather hoping you're wrong, Master Kelson."

"Aye, though this doesn't mean you can't still become the better swordsman, magic aside."

Levi nodded. "In that case, are you ready for another bout?"

Kyllean shook off the embarrassment at having been defeated in front of his father and agreed. Taking his stance he growled, "Very well, let's go."

Kyllean's father cleared his throat and both boys looked back to him. "My apologies, gentlemen. I did actually come here with a purpose beyond that of weapons instruction." Nodding to Levi, Kyllean's father said, "May I have a moment?"

Levi bowed. "Of course, Master Kelson."

"Thank you."

Kyllean shouted after his friend, "Don't go far. I'm still planning to leave you a few welts before class today."

Turning back to his father, Kyllean sensed the serious atmosphere and allowed his smile to fade.

Without further preamble, Kelson said, "I'm leaving today."

Kyllean looked back at his father as if to say, *Yeah, what's new?* This was the nature of being a rider, especially one tethered to a Lumále. They were frequently gone for long periods for one reason or another. Kyllean finally broke the silence with, "All right?"

"The Kingdom is under attack."

"Oh," replied a surprised and inwardly concerned, Kyllean. He knew the Lugienese were coming, but so soon? Everyone believed they wouldn't launch a full invasion until they had established a strong foothold elsewhere on the continent. The best guesses had put this at least one year away, if not more.

"I've always entrusted Master Hilde with this task, but now that you're here, I think it's appropriate that this be passed on to you." He handed Kyllean a sealed message. "If I don't return, I want you to give this to your mother. She deserves this and so much more."

"Of course you'll return. They won't send the Kingdom's greatest assets into harm's way so early in the war. You'll likely be used only for reconnaissance." But Kyllean understood his father's grim mood. He and the others could be going up against powerful mages, something that had not occurred in centuries. This, in addition to the speed and brutality of the Lugienese conquests elsewhere, was enough to convince even an experienced rider like his father to have thoughts about his mortality.

"You're probably right. But nothing is certain, son. And the Lugienese are not some rebellion of farmers. They are a force of—"

"I know what they are. I saw what they did in Brinkwell."

"Yes, of course you did. Then you understand why I'm giving this to you now."

Kyllean nodded.

"I can't get into the details of our mission, but the Kingdom is in greater peril than we thought and far more quickly than we anticipated. I pray you take your training seriously, for I believe we'll soon need every sword we can muster."

CHAPTER 46

GROBENNAR

GROBENNAR SOARED OVER THE LANDS between Drebrose and the Duchy of Gilliden. He knew the date of Theo's meeting and hoped to add an additional layer of persuasion. The ability to travel so swiftly across such a vast space opened up so many new possibilities. He could leave and return to Drebrose in a matter of days without anyone the wiser.

This also gave him further opportunity to improve his control over the dordron and the spell used to control it. Paranja flew beside him, rider and bird silhouetted the moon; it was the sort of beauty Grobennar would have rarely noticed or acknowledged, but there was something invigorating about the cool, crisp air that took his mind far away from the pressures of his station that ordinarily weighed heavy upon him.

They had departed the night prior, had slept the following day, and departed again by night. They arrived the following morning with plenty of time to spare before the meeting that afternoon.

Grobennar watched as Theo's retinue entered the palace. He and Paranja had to guess how long it might take for Theo to finish with introductions, then broach the subject with the duke. The timing of their arrival would be critical. When enough time had passed, Grobennar exhaled heavily and nodded to Paranja. "Klerós guide us."

Grobennar's giant bird rose to its full height with him safely secured in the saddle, and a beat of its massive wings took to him into the air. Grobennar and Paranja circled the fortress twice from above before spotting the balcony upon which Theo and the duke dined.

"*This is going to be marvelous,*" purred Jaween.

Grobennar wasn't certain of that, but he was certain that the duke would have to at least consider the offer. The ability to reach him directly like this all but assured such. Furthermore, he would be able to enforce such an alliance through the pirate's transport of troops once the deal was struck. Grobennar had already sent a small contingent of soldiers to the city by sea. They would arrive shortly to accompany the duke in his march on Salmune.

Grobennar gleamed as the dordron dug sharp talons into the stone of the parapet bordering the large balcony while Paranja landed upon the other side of the balcony. Grobennar slid off the side and instructed the bird to remain where it was. A swarm of men with nocked bows had run from their posts about the wall toward the intrusion and had now taken aim, though they appeared unsure which intruder to focus their attention on. Grobennar and Paranja raised their arms slowly to the sky in as nonthreatening a manner as possible.

A broad-shouldered man dressed in finery sat across from Theo at a small table with steaming mugs, two glasses, and two nearly empty plates of food. He had risen to his feet and drawn a sword. "Hold your fire, for now," he said to the bowmen. Then, looking directly at Grobennar, he bellowed, "You must be . . . Fatu-something Grobennar. My apologies, I don't know the honorifics well."

You will learn them soon enough, chuckled Grobennar.

He bowed ever so slightly in the direction of the duke, a revolting gesture of respect to an inferior, but one Grobennar felt might ease the tension with six arrows pointed his way. He did not wish to have to launch a magical attack while here, at least not *that* sort.

"I am Fatu Ma-gazi, Grobennar, Secretary of War to the Lugienese Empire." Gesturing to Paranja beside him, he said, "And this is Amaj Paranja, a powerful wielder and member of the Klerósi Assembly. As I'm sure Lord Theo has already explained to you, we are here to discuss an alliance of sorts."

The man held his sword where it was, pointing at Grobennar. "Yes, I was in the process of rejecting the offer when you arrived. I have no interest in betraying my people, no matter the reward."

Grobennar did not appreciate the aggression he sensed in the tone, or the waggling of the sword as the man spoke. He seemed on the edge of volatility, and it would only take one stray arrow placed just right to injure Grobennar even beyond Jaween's ability to heal before he passed into the next life.

"The offer we bring is generous," said Grobennar, arms still in the air. "And it would not be a betrayal to your people, but a—"

"Silence!" shouted the duke. "I am in no mood to be patronized in my own home. It has been bad enough listening to the silken bastard. But to have an all-but-declared enemy land on my walls on the backs of the underworld's winged mounts, it's beyond tolerable. I am a man of principle. I cannot be bought."

The boy, Theo, sat as stiff as a statue, knuckles white as he gripped the arms of his seat. Grobennar suspected that the boy wished he was anywhere else in the world but here, caught between two spatting men who could have him killed with a mere word.

Jaween said, "*This is not going well for you. This man seems to need a mental massage.*"

"Quiet," whispered Grobennar under his breath. More guards arrived. Grobennar was beginning to worry that violence might erupt after all. Grobennar imagined that if the man suddenly shouted out in pain at Jaween's touch, Grobennar and Paranja would find themselves deflecting arrows for a few minutes while they wiped out all of the guards.

Paranja surprised Grobennar by speaking out. "Duke Gafford. I believe you have mischaracterized our arrival here today. We are not here to discuss bribery. We are here to ensure that you understand precisely what it is we expect from you, and why. To believe this is an offer, suggests that you have the option to refuse. This is not so." She looked about at the guards and Grobennar felt magic flow from her, subtly, calculatingly. The eyes of several widened as they saw the tips of their arrows turn upward, rendering them useless.

The duke opened his mouth to speak, but Paranja silenced him with Klerós's power, resulting in nothing more than a few pathetic grunts. "You do not have a choice. But you should know that you were selected specifically for your loyalty. We believe you are the best choice to lead your people beneath the shadow of Lugienese oversight because we know you are a man of great integrity. Your own citizens will be made to see this as an act of salvation, a deliverance from utter ruin, rather than a reach for power. And this will be no lie. Word has likely not reached you of the fall of Free Cities, but rest assured, they have *all* fallen. However, the God-king, in his great benevolence, has decided to permit self-rule so long as their leadership pledges fealty to the Lugienese Empire and Klerós, a small price for their lives and positions, and a change from the precedent set in other conquered lands where all of the conquered become slaves regardless of previous rank."

Duke Gafford coughed as Paranja released her magical grip on his throat. Then he said in a hoarse voice, "The Kingdom will not fall so easily to Lugienese barbarism."

Paranja shook her head slowly. "Quite so. The Kingdom of Dowe will fall to Lugienese diplomacy and our generous offer, that which allows you to become vassals instead of meat for worms. For if you believe for a moment that the Kingdom of Dowe has a fighting chance against Lugienese on the battlefield, you could not be more wrong. Your greatest asset, the Lumáles, will be neutralized by our dordron riders." She glanced over at the towering creature beside her. "Our numbers are superior, our wielders unmatched, and our offer of life, generous." She turned and walked over to the dordron, which lowered itself so she could mount.

Grobennar shook off his surprise at Paranja's initiative. None of that had been rehearsed or expected. But he followed her lead, striding over to climb atop his own dordron.

Paranja made a final statement. "We will give you time to finalize your plans for taking the city of Salmune over dessert with Lord Theo. We will return tomorrow to hear the details."

The duke's jaw hung open, but he was wise enough to hold his tongue this time.

"Oh, and one more thing. Call Lord Theo a bastard one more time, and I'll remove a hand of his choosing as a reminder that as a Lugienese ambassador, he is to be treated with the utmost respect." She winked at Theo, and he nodded and smiled back, adjusting himself to sit more upright, more confident.

Then her dordron flapped its wings and took to the sky, Grobennar following suit. Jaween said, "*I like the way she does diplomacy, though I still vote for more killing.*" Grobennar remained silent, still in awe of what he had just witnessed.

Paranja looked back and even at this distance he could see that she was concerned. She opened a connection to his mind and said, "*Sorry to have interrupted. I take full responsibility if he does not agree and we have to resort to other measures.*"

Grobennar gathered his wits and responded with confidence, "*He will agree. And I don't have an arrow sticking out of my back, which may have been a distinct possibility had you not chimed in.*"

She didn't respond for a time. Then she said, "*Thank you,*" and they flew silently to their rendezvous beyond the city.

CHAPTER 47

GROBENNAR

GROBENNAR SAT UPON THE BACK of his dordron, Frida, surrounded by his squadron of twenty-five dordron riders. Today would be their maiden mission as they launched the assault on the capital city of the Kingdom of Dowe, the prize of the continent. Success today would give Grobennar the opportunity to show his worth as his dordron riders proved themselves lethal against the Kingdom's Lumáles. He had received no contact or rebuke over his decision to leave subjects who converted alive in the Free Cities, a major gamble for the success of his strategy in conquering Dowe. He would have had no choice but to rescind the offer and flee the Kingdom with his soldiers had such a thing occurred.

But instead, victory was at hand. The duke's army was the largest of the duchies and was responsible for the security of the northern border where an invasion from the sea was most likely. The duke also had ties through his children to the kingdom of Kael to the south, and Bronjiornyn to the north. Grobennar planned to exploit both in due time.

King Perja had left a sizable contingent in the capital city, but the rest had been sent west where an attack along the western border was far more likely, especially after the fall of the Free Cities on their border. By the time King Perja learned of Duke Gafford's approach, a known inevitability, Perja would be unable to recall enough troops to defend his city, even if he guessed the duke's intentions. Word that they were accompanied by the host of Lugienese soldiers would support any suspicions, so Grobennar didn't bother with vain efforts at disguise. Kubal had transported these troops onboard his own ships in order to avoid questions about Lugienese naval activity that might notify Rajuban and Magog of Grobennar's intentions. Grobennar had been careful to siphon his troops in small batches so as to draw as little attention as possible.

Grobennar magnified his voice so he could be heard over the din of mounted riders, whose dordron paced around the open field, just a few leagues from Salmune. "We are here to claim this city for Magog, for Klerós, for the Empire, and for ourselves. Legends claim we are not the first to tame these winged beasts but let us be the greatest! And if we are met with force by the Tal-Don riders of the Lumále horde, let us show them that our might is unrivaled, our God more powerful, and our resolve more solid than the bedrock that secures our very world."

A cheer rang out from among a group of ordinarily stoic priests, and the dordron took to the sky to begin their assault upon Salmune. The duke's army awaited the arrival of the dordron as their signal to move on the palace.

The King had sent messages demanding that the duke return home with his troops, but these had, of course, been ignored. This was no surprise. What did surprise Grobennar was the lack of archers as he approached. He had summoned Klerós power and expected to use it. Instead, he flew past the walls unmolested and noted only a few men. The palace grounds themselves appeared all but empty.

He swooped past the palace and circled back, then bade his mount to land upon the parapet. Grobennar slid down to the wall walkway and approached the nearest guard. "Where hides your King? Where is his army?"

The guard was old, much too old to be an active soldier. He stood proudly as he said, "We have all been instructed to respond with the following message: 'The duke's treachery will be repaid with blood.'"

Grobennar walked up to him and lifted him into the air with his power. While the man hovered in place, Jaween rambled in giddy excitement. "You may enter," Grobennar said to the spirit.

The man looked down at Grobennar, his fright at being hoisted into the air with magic shifting to confusion at Grobennar's odd command. Then the man shrieked as Jaween began his work.

Minutes later, the guard whimpered, "King Perja and his troops vacated the premises days ago. You will find nothing here but old men such as I."

It was then that Grobennar smelled smoke. Sniffing the air, he said, "Why do I smell smoke? What is burning?"

He was fairly certain he knew the answer already. The old guard grinned. "As I said, you foreign pile of reeking excrement, you will find nothing here but the old and sick."

Cowards, thought Grobennar.

Then he sent a blast of air at the man's feet, who somersaulted onto his face. He groaned and crawled to his knees as Grobennar approached. Grobennar crouched down and took the man by the hand, thumb biting into the palm, then lifted and twisted, forcing the guard to turn onto his back lest his wrist snap.

Grobennar stood and placed a boot upon the man's neck. He needed to confirm his words. "Your lack of respect has earned you another reward. But first . . ."

Paranja, Grobennar's old friend Penden, and three others were within earshot, all awaiting instructions since there appeared to be no foes to attack. "Penden, open the gate to allow the duke and his men entry. Paranja, Ransend, and Kindra, with me, they've set flame to the stores of grain. Salvage as much as you can."

Grobennar then sent a mental message to the rest of the contingent of riders. "*The city has been set aflame, do your best to put out as much as possible.*"

After they departed, Grobennar returned his attention to the old guard. "When I have learned what I can from you, I'm going to let my friend spend some time enjoying himself within your ungrateful little mind. We'll make plans for the rest of your pathetic life based on what remains of your faculties after this."

Grobennar delved into the man's mind to rummage through his memories. A short time later, Jaween was given a few minutes to torment, then Grobennar tossed the delinquent guard over the edge of the wall, a courtesy he probably did not deserve. The man had remained loyal to his own people, an admirable if foolish trait.

⊰⊰⊰

As the sun neared the horizon to embrace the coming of night, Grobennar dismounted from his dordron to pay a visit to Duke Gafford. Grobennar found the man standing atop the walls of the palace overlooking Lake Salmune and the city that wrapped around the small harbor.

Grobennar approached. "The city is yours and the Kingdom to follow."

He didn't look up. "Not mine, truly. And not the way I would have imagined myself ascending the throne in any case."

"If my understanding of succession is in any way accurate, you would never have ascended the throne. But you are right. You will rule as a mere vassal, but a vassal who has saved the lives of his people. Every person who lays down their sword and submits is a life that would otherwise have been taken. It was inevitable. Klerós claims these lands and so it is."

The duke sighed. "Yes, well, forgive me for not feeling more enthused about the matter. Being a vassal to my brother's Kingdom was not so bad. Being a puppet to a foreign god in whom I do not believe leaves me little to be excited over."

Grobennar hardly expected true conversion from this man, but this kind of blasphemy could not be permitted. *One final warning should do.* Grobennar brought his power to bear and brushed it against the puppet-king. This would give him a burning sensation throughout his entire body without doing any real harm.

Duke Gafford's eyes went wide and he opened his mouth to speak, but Grobennar closed it for him with his magic. "You would do well to consider that you are now under Lugienese law, under which blasphemy against Klerós, the Kleról, or the God-king is punishable by death. We care not for titles where this law is concerned. Consider the time for candid speech to have ended. From now on, assume that every conversation you have is heard by a priest, no matter how alone you think you may be. Am I clear?"

Grobennar released his hold on the man's jaw and the duke's eyes smoldered as he responded, "Yes, Fatu Ma-gazi." There was no reverence in his tone, but Grobennar believed he would do what was needed in order to remain living.

Their nearly concluded conversation was interrupted by a Lugienese soldier. "My most sincere apologies, Fatu Ma-gazi." He bowed deeply as Grobennar turned his head to inspect the intruders. One of the soldier's hands clung to the arm of a shaggy-looking Kingdom boy, who, Grobennar noted, did not bow. He couldn't have been more than ten years of age. When the soldier's head regained its upright position, he smacked the boy hard in the back of the head. Then glared and mimed a slight bow, tilting his head toward Grobennar.

The boy wrinkled his nose, rubbed the back of his head with his free arm, then performed a quick, unpracticed bow.

Definitely not noble.

This done, the guard spoke. "This boy claims to have a message for you. He was provided a single Lugienese phrase to recite in which he asks for you and you alone. I was given charge of him because I have some familiarity with the Kingdom tongue. Even still, I would have simply confiscated the message to save you the trouble, but of course he does not have it on his person. Says it's for your eyes and ears alone."

Grobennar had turned to face the pair fully, his glare at the interruption fully ablaze. Speaking in the Kingdom tongue now, Grobennar said, "Well? What is this message, boy?"

The boy appeared unafraid in spite of his surroundings. He looked up and shrugged. "I was told that I would be paid . . . two gold pieces for relaying this 'advice.'"

Always coin with these people. Grobennar ground his teeth at the boldness of the boy to come here to bargain for anything more than simply his life. Grobennar had no way of knowing the truth about the sum the boy had been promised, but the use of the code word "advice" confirmed that this was indeed a message from Grobennar's spy. Grobennar would pay any sum for this information.

Jaween spoke to his mind: "*I could very quickly learn all that you need to know from the boy.*"

Grobennar didn't hate this idea, but the boy might be needed again and Jaween didn't always leave the minds of those he touched intact. Grobennar responded, "Klerós rewards good deeds in this life and beyond. Provide the message, and you will be paid." Grobennar reached into his purse as a reflex, then frowned as his hand came up empty. Of course it was empty; he had no need of coin these days. Ignoring the misstep, Grobennar said, "Guard, you will see that the boy is compensated to the fullest. Find Mazi Ferenar; he's been assigned to oversee the goings-on at the palace bridge. Tell him I sent you and he will ensure that payment is made. Half now, half upon the boy's return here with the message."

I will have the boy repaid for his greed after the message is delivered, thought Grobennar.

"Very well, Fatu Ma-gazi."

Grobennar resumed his conversation with the duke as the pair disappeared from view.

"Your nephew will surely rally as many of his banner men as he can as he marches to . . . wherever he is headed. You will begin drafting messages at once in order to gather support from the other lords of this Kingdom, and they had best be *very* convincing. Our decision to allow you to sit the throne will remain for only as long as it benefits the Empire. Kingdom-wide resistance will severely injure your position with us. You understand?"

The duke nodded, then asked hesitantly, "May I take my leave to begin?"

Grobennar waved his hand and focused his gaze on the city below, marveling at their accomplishment. The conquest had begun and he would have the glory.

Duke Gafford finally bowed and departed.

The boy and the guard returned more quickly than Grobennar expected and the boy handed over a wax-sealed parchment. Grobennar opened it eagerly and began to read. According to his source, King Perja had not been swayed by the advice given to him to hold the palace, which would have been the preferred outcome, bloodshed aside. However, the letter did provide the false King's destination: the city of Quinson. He had sent pigeons and runners to all of his banner men within marching distance. He was preparing to dig in at Quinson to the south, which had a less impenetrable palace, but a more defensible city as a whole. The big question remained: Would the Scritlandians be able to make it to Quinson in time?

Grobennar fell into deep thought after finishing the letter. It was the boy who finally interrupted this. "So, my gold?"

Grobennar glared up at the boy and prepared to issue the order he be killed, his usefulness having expired. A sudden tug on his conscience silenced these words. He couldn't explain it in any way besides an inexplicable change of heart. He said in Lugienese to the guard, "See that he is paid for his service. Then have him sent to the nearest established Kleról for conversion. Only upon his refusal to convert may he be eliminated. See that this is understood."

The guard's expression showed disbelief. This was mirrored by the sensation that came flooding across the connection from the spirit, Jaween.

Grobennar explained to both of them, "These people need to see the generosity our God is capable of bestowing upon those who follow him. They speak a language of currency. Word of our generosity to those who convert must spread as our Empire stretches further and further from our seat of power. If this plan is to work, we can't be constantly looking over our shoulders. There will be plenty enough violence to demonstrate Klerós's wrath."

The guard nodded his limited understanding and led the boy away.

"You're getting soft in your old age, Grobes."

Grobennar rolled his eyes. "I need to find and capture this false King before he arrives in Quinson, and before he can rally his other banner men."

Grobennar ended the clasp with the hawk and smiled. Speaking with Paranja, Duke Gafford, and a dozen others on his war council, he said, "The former King and his troops continue on the march toward Quinson. Before ending the connection with the hawk, I surveyed the surrounding areas and spotted no small number of men moving in the direction of the city, led by their liege lords."

Paranja responded, confused, "Yet you appear pleased?"

"Indeed. We have an opportunity to capture the false King before he arrives."

Perja's decision to remain with his troops was honorable but foolish. Grobennar had been able to easily determine the location of his tent, and, more specifically, knew that he was inside. He ended the clasp with his hawk and said to his contingent of fifteen dordron riders, "We need only capture the King and return. All I need from you is to keep his guards at bay. We'll need to be swift, and you'll likely come under heavy bow fire. But they have few wielders and no Lumáles with them, so we should have little difficulty absconding with the young King."

Everyone nodded their understanding. He had brought fifteen of his twenty-five riders with him for this task. Capturing the King before he could hide behind the walls in Quinson with reinforcements from the region was an opportunity Grobennar could not afford to pass up. It would put an end to whatever rebellion Perja planned to wage.

With the capital taken, and the King soon to be captured, whatever resistance remained throughout the Kingdom would fizzle and

Grobennar would be responsible for a major conquest with barely a dent in Lugienese numbers.

Grobennar took to the sky upon Frida's back and his riders followed suit. King Perja had marched his entire army through the northern pass in the Dragon Spine Mountains and was now camped on a plain beside a gorge carved by the southernmost river feeding the King's Sea. The rolling hills of the area surrounding the plain provided the perfect cover for Grobennar and his dordron to hide.

They flew low to the ground as they approached the camp, which had just recently been set with the coming of dusk. Grobennar could taste glory as he flew past, shouts of alarm trailing him with such a delay they may as well have not come at all.

He spotted the ornate tent and bade Frida to land beside it. Eight others in his party landed their mounts around the tent to create a circle of defense as they sent blasts of power at the guards who had been posted to protect it. The remaining riders hovered above, their dordron flapping their great wings to hold positions in the air. Grobennar felt his party of priests and priestesses continue to utilize Klerós's magic to repel attacks from the defenders below while Grobennar was given the honor of capturing the King himself.

Grobennar hopped off and prepared himself to dispatch the two guards he had seen slip into the tent upon his arrival.

"Ooh yes. It's happening! Can you taste their fear?" said Jaween.

Grobennar cut his own way into the back of the tent, slashing the canvas with his dagger, and the guards rushed to meet him with steel. The Fatu Ma-gazi prepared a magical defense, but the men fell to their knees clutching their ears before this was required of him. He had given Jaween permission to satisfy his hunger for the minds of those they encountered, save the King, and he appeared to be taking full advantage.

King Perja rose to his feet. He was a broad-shouldered man dressed in pristine armor, featuring a white belted tunic with the Kingdom crest upon the chest that clung to the shimmering plate. His deep-blue cape rippled as he turned to face the Fatu Ma-gazi. Even Grobennar couldn't help but admit that the man looked regal. He was older than Grobennar had expected, not a boy at all. But looking the part of a king would not keep him from capture. Grobennar held his magic at the ready as the King drew his sword. To his credit, the man paid no mind to his suffering guards; he was prepared to fight, outwardly unafraid. This was yet another trait of useless value.

"Your tent has been surrounded by my dordron riders. Put down your steel or I will do so for you."

The King looked from side to side, considering, and Grobennar readied himself to attack with Klerós's power. The King slowly lowered his weapon to the ground. And yet Grobennar sensed a tension in him that suggested resistance. There was also a faint flavor of magic in the air, though he could not be certain of its origin.

"You will kneel. I will bind you, and then we will be off."

Unmoving as he maintained eye contact, King Perja said, "Where will you take me?"

"You will return with me to Salmune. Now, kneel."

The King glared at him with icy eyes. Then, just as Grobennar prepared to send a spear of pain in this direction, he lowered himself to one knee. Grobennar glared back at him, peeved that the King was taking so long to comply. He needed to be gone from here. Jaween addressed him: *"Do you sense that?"*

"Hmm?" replied Grobennar.

"The King is drawing in some sort of faint magic."

Grobennar's expertise as a former seeker made him more sensitive to magic than most, but even he had a difficult time detecting this. He extended his mind directly toward the King to confirm, and . . . yes, there it was. But the King was not supposed to be a magic user, and this did not feel like priestly magic. This was . . . the tainted scent of tazamine magic.

Grobennar extended a hand to preempt any sort of magical attack with one of his own, but the King darted to his feet, rolling to the side with inhuman speed, snatching up his sword in the process. Grobennar reacted just in time as the blade arched toward his throat, followed by a burning sensation—the man had drawn blood, a shallow gash across his neck.

By the time he recovered his wits, the King had escaped the tent. Just then, shrieks of horror escaped the mouths of his priests outside.

CHAPTER 48

GROBENNAR

GROBENNAR RACED OUT OF THE tent just as explosions of magical energy shot forth from the hands of several of his priests. His eyes widened not only at the sight of the nearest dordron having been decapitated by Perja, but also at the fast-approaching forms of more than a dozen mammoth, winged creatures—nightmares. Worse yet, his priests' magical attacks seemed to wash over the approaching forms of the famed Lumále riders. The magic dissipated as if it had never been used. The creatures were upon them in seconds, flesh meeting flesh on the ground and in the sky.

It looked little different than a traditional cavalry charge, and the results were similarly devastating for the attacked who had remained either on the ground or flapping in place to defend the tent. None had any forward momentum and they were shocked by their failed attempts at magic.

Grobennar spotted Frida waiting obediently, her instinct to flee held in check only by the powerful link of control. He watched in horror as King Perja dodged past the fallen dordron's rider and his blast of power. Perja struck the priest in the face with a fist before he could attack again, then leaped an impossible distance to swing at the next closest bird. The dordron attempted to move, resulting in a lost wing instead of a blade to the neck—a death blow, in any case.

Grobennar set his jaw and lashed out once again with his power. This time, a bolt of molten heat struck the King in the leg and he faltered.

Grobennar then rushed to recover Frida. He bade her to retrieve him even as he raced to meet her halfway. He clambered up, and the connection between him and his mount intensified; her strong animalistic bloodlust became his own. Frida no longer wished to flee, she wished to do battle. She sensed the danger but her instinct was to charge headlong into it. Grobennar spotted the King lying on the ground writhing in pain, the metal of his shin guard having been warped painfully by Grobennar's blast of energy. Grobennar fought to resist Frida's instincts and sent her to snatch Perja up in her mighty talons before taking to the air.

As soon as he had the King, Grobennar sent out a mental message to his party, "*Retreat!*"

No longer tasked with protecting Grobennar on the ground, the other dordron took to the sky, attempting to disengage. Just then a shape out of the corner of Grobennar's eye told him just enough about the coming danger for his body to react. He ducked, pressing his entire body as close to his dordron as possible. A scalding sensation grew along his back, but there was nowhere else for him to go. He looked up to see a Lumále and rider righting themselves after having turned completely upside down for the attack.

Jaween worked to heal Grobennar, who urged Frida forward, away from the rout.

Then another shadow descended and Grobennar didn't have to tell Frida; she darted to the side, avoiding the attack from—

A Lumále's long, corrugated tail snapped past and blood sprayed from Frida's side, splattering Grobennar's face as they plummeted to the ground. "Noooo!"

This Lumále had no rider. Grobennar understood, then: this creature wanted its master back.

Grobennar cleared the blood from his eyes with his wrist, then tapped deeper into the link to determine the damage to Frida. He sensed only rage. He went deeper still to locate the pain buried beneath the fury and followed it into the innermost portions of the wound. Thankfully, it was a shallow cut and Grobennar did a quick mending.

No sooner had he finished than Jaween warned, "*The King's Lumále seems intent on retrieving him.*"

The Lumále was upon them again. Frida twisted in the air of her own accord, limiting the impact of the collision but it was still jarring and Grobennar was glad for the strong stirrups and handles that allowed him to hold on. As the Lumále disengaged, Grobennar felt Frida's pain through the connection and knew she had been cut once again, this time in the chest just above the leg that held the king.

Those blasted tails!

He channeled Klerós's power through the gemstone at his index finger's knuckle and did another healing, as best he could manage under the circumstances. Suddenly he saw the riderless Lumále tumble through the air past him, a trail of blood in its wake. Grobennar flew through the spray of red mist, closing his eyes as he did.

"Ughhh."

He looked up and spotted a dordron spiraling downward ahead of him and barely recognized the streak of white across its underbelly that identified this as Paranja's dordron. The King had been quiet so far as Grobennar could tell, but he bellowed a guttural shout of pain and grief upon seeing his Lumále fall from the sky. Grobennar smiled, knowing that there would be no Lumále coming in search of him now.

Grobennar had Frida fly higher so he could join Paranja, but just as he matched altitudes with her, another Lumále and rider swooped down from higher still. The attack was aimed at her.

This slowed Paranja, and Frida hardly needed to be told what to do. He felt her rage after being cut twice by the creatures. She wanted blood, and this time Grobennar allowed it.

Even with just one free talon, the agility Frida commanded in the air was greater than he had expected, much more than she had demonstrated while he trained upon her back. This was an agility fueled by instinct and a total lack of restraint. The Lumále in their sights noticed their approach at the last moment and abandoned its pursuit of Paranja. Yet Frida's prey was unable to escape. She twisted in the air to avoid the sharp tail, nearly unseating Grobennar. Then, even with one set of talons occupied by the King, the other ripped into the underbelly of the vulnerable Lumále.

A moment later they changed course, and Frida swooped around to continue after the creature. Grobennar saw blood falling to the ground far below. Frida overtook the injured Lumále once again and this time caught the end of its wing in her strong beak and tore.

The Lumále's rider leaped inhumanly high from the back of his mount, hefting a sword high above his head, and Grobennar was nearly cleaved in two. He shot a blast of power at his assailant, whose blade twisted from a position of attack to one of defense. To Grobennar's horror, the blade absorbed the magic of his attack.

Grobennar unhooked his feet from their stirrups and turned to face his enemy. Sliding a dagger free, he still hoped to utilize Klerós's power if possible. He fired another blade of magic at the rider, a spell of immobilization, but again the man spun the blade and the spell seemed to disintegrate.

"A little help here?"

Jaween had been uncharacteristically quiet during all of this.

"*Of course. Only—I—I—this one's mind. The fortifications within are commendable, nearly impenetrable.*"

"Keep trying!"

Jaween screeched his frustration at his inability to enter this man's mind.

The rider struck out with attacks of his own, but Grobennar busied him with blast of power, forcing his foe to remain defensive.

The rider's movements were so swift and fluid, he seemed powered by magic himself, and Grobennar thought he sensed more than just the power of the blade as it somehow neutralized his attacks. Then the rider swung low and Grobennar saw his opportunity. He leaped to avoid the blade, meanwhile lashing out with his own power. This time the blast struck the flesh of the man's shoulder and he jerked to the side, lost his balance, and disappeared from sight.

Grobennar felt a flash of heat in his foot but paid it no mind. Leaping from a fast-moving object came with perils of its own. Grobennar was no longer situated at the base of the mighty bird's neck; he was—

"Arggggh!"

He let go of the dagger and stretched out both of his hands to catch what he could. Both hands grasped giant feathers at the base of the bird's tail, but those in his left hand pulled free at the force of the sudden tug. He fell to the right, slamming into the side of the dordron, and gasped. He dangled in the air by one arm, still over a hundred paces above the fast-moving ground below—a lethal fall. Twisting his body, he managed to get a second hand into the thick feathers of the bird and started pulling himself up. His relief vanished when he looked down and saw that the cursed rider had somehow managed to catch the other foot of the dordron and was readying to cut the King free.

Darkness below!

The rider's injured shoulder was clearly causing him difficulty, and Grobennar wondered how he had even managed to wind up where he was.

"*I have him!*" cackled Jaween.

The rider glanced up at Grobennar in surprise, allowing a moment of relief. Apparently Jaween was right. But then the man narrowed his eyes and smiled.

Jaween released an unintelligible shriek of frustration, followed by, "*So strong!*" Then his mood shifted. "*But ooh, what a wonder it will be to finally feast on this mind. We need to capture him!*"

"No time!"

Letting go with one hand, Grobennar sent forward a sharp blast of air, hoping it might be hard enough to knock the man from the foot without injuring Frida. The wedge of air slammed into the bird's foot just as the rider swung his sword to release the King.

The rider was knocked into the open air, but not before his blade had cut into Frida's other foot. Her talon opened just long enough to release the King. Frida reached out and snatched the air, but the King's body had moved beyond her grasp. Her talon instead caught the rider's extended arm, piercing the wrist as the King plummeted to the ground below.

"Nooo!" shouted Grobennar as his prize tumbled through the air to his death.

The rider now dangled by his wrist, and without his sword. Grobennar prepared to incinerate him then and there with a blast of searing energy but gathered his composure in time to paralyze him instead. To Grobennar's delight, the rider was unable to defend against this magic now that he was without his sword.

Grobennar urged Frida away as he climbed up her back to the relative safety of the saddle.

She sped along, leaving the pursuing Lumáles behind.

When Grobennar finally looked back, he saw few other dordron. Of the fifteen he had brought with him, he counted only six, and they were still being pursued by a host of Lumáles and their riders.

To Grobennar's relief, the Lumáles appeared to be slower and less agile than the dordron in the open air, and the distance between his riders and their adversaries grew until the Lumáles finally ended the chase.

"*That did not go as well as we should have liked.*"

"No. No, it did not."

The King had somehow suspected their intentions and set the trap. And while killing the King had not been the goal, it was better than leaving behind a leader to rally behind. Though at a cost of more than a third of his dordron fleet!

"Even these dordron are little match for those—those—monsters!"

"*Once you stopped trying to, you know, magic your way to victory, you fared far better. It seems you have to simply let the dordron do the fighting.*"

Perturbed, Grobennar shot back, "How is it that both those creatures and their riders' swords absorb Klerós's power? And you couldn't even break that warrior's mind? What good are you?"

"*I was getting close! I recall something like this from . . . before.*" There was a long pause, and then he continued, "*I just can't quite locate the memories. Perhaps it will come to me later. Yes, those riders do seem quite the foes in their own right.*"

"We'll learn their secrets, one way or another," growled Grobennar.

"*Oooh, I do like the sounds of that. So you're going to let me play with this one?*"

"Indeed," mused Grobennar.

There was a letter waiting for him upon arrival back in Salmune. It read simply, "Proceed with caution. They are prepared for an attack."

Grobennar crumbled the message in his hand, then lit it on fire as he slammed it onto the stone floor in disgust. "When did this message arrive?"

The priest who had notified him quickly responded, "A few hours after you departed, Fatu Ma-gazi."

Grobennar ground his teeth. At least his spy had *attempted* to warn him. *Much good it did.* He sighed. *No good comes from dwelling on what could have been. Plus, I have a prisoner to interrogate.* Jaween's anticipatory excitement was almost intolerable. "Yes, yes, we'll pay him a visit as soon as I've had a chance to wash up."

"*Oh goody!*" tittered the voice in his head.

CHAPTER 49

KYLLEAN

ACCORDING TO WHAT KYLLEAN AND the other initiates had been taught, nearly anyone could learn the form of magic used by the riders, but those further from the original Don-Votro line generally found it far more difficult. Master Hilde used the line of Dowe as an example. Neither the deceased King nor his heir had any known blood ties to the Don-Votros, and yet they always managed to be paired with sword and, furthermore, with Lumáles. It had been the trial of earning the blade that had proven most difficult for both of them. Master Hilde chuckled as she recounted how long it had taken the now King, Perja, to earn his blade. Six years, and his father eight. And yet, they had managed it after all.

The fact that the line of Dowe had never been without a Lumále pairing remained an unsolved mystery. The Lumále selection of riders was invariably fickle, *except* when it came to the royal line of Dowe. Master Hilde theorized that there was some sort of centuries-old magic that drew the Lumáles to the line of Dowe. It seemed the only sensible explanation, though she couldn't imagine how it might have been accomplished.

Imagining someone like Aynward learning to wield the magic of the blade had given Kyllean all the more reason to push through his own training. These thoughts also reminded Kyllean of how difficult it had been to learn the news about Aynward's slaying of his own father and the execution that had surely been carried out by now.

I could really use a tall drink right, he thought. But recalling the nausea he'd felt when stopping, he thought this a very poor choice. Not that he could find booze anywhere in the fortress, anyhow.

He pushed those thoughts aside. They were best left to a time when he no longer had a substantial obstacle looming in his path, like learning to master an unfamiliar power.

Drawing in magic for his own internal enhancement had proven little difficulty but projecting this power outward had eluded him for weeks, causing him no small amount of embarrassment as one of the few in his cohort to allegedly have the blood of the ancients on both sides of his heritage. Of all the initiates, he should have struggled the least. This time, as Kyllean filled his mental reservoir, he paused before attempting to project it. He was able to direct power into himself but had yet to send it elsewhere. He could sense the emptiness of the blade, the vacuum of potential, but it was a locked door. Every time he tried, the power flowed out into the void, wasted.

Closing his eyes, he felt the practice blade in his hands. The hunger for power within it was palpable yet it refused to accept his offering. He let his mind absorb the essence of the sword, looking closer into its construction as if it were a source of power itself. As he did so, he felt something *different.*

What was that?

His sense of the blade's shape felt different from before. Kyllean sent his mind deeper into the hilt of the sword where he had felt the ethereal protuberance and was able to locate it once again. He inspected this with his mind and sensed what could only be described as another void altogether. The closer he looked, the larger it became within his mind's eye. It was as if this space within the hilt of the blade had been condensed a dozen times over.

What would happen if I—

Power suddenly streamed out of him and into the tiny space so small he'd never before even noticed it. As if the gates of a massive dam had been opened, his power flowed into the sword. He stood in awe, holding a blade that was now filled to the brim with potential energy, much more than he had ever projected into himself. Master Hilde clapped her hands. "Well done! Well done! There may be hope for you after all."

Kyllean marveled at the sudden feeling of lightness in his hands. Even with his enhanced strength and speed, the obsidian weapon used for practicing felt heavy, clunky even. But with the magic now within it, he felt he was holding a switch, not a club.

Better late than never, laughed Kyllean to himself.

"What now?" he asked Master Hilde.

"Now we get you your own sword and some armor so you can join your classmates with Master Lauren to begin training with your new weapon and learning more of the Lumáles. Though, with so few remaining to claim a rider, you may never get the chance."

Thanks for the reminder.

She continued, "Be that as it may, should one outlive its rider, they do sometimes choose another."

"And what happens to those of us not destined to ride?"

"You'll still have your swords, and if the fight comes to us, you'll defend this fortress and, of course, the remaining eggs. We hide the eggs well, but should the enemy discover their whereabouts, the line of Lumáles and riders could be forever undone. This place is all that remains of these creatures anywhere in the world."

Nothing like living in the end of days.

Kyllean was taken to the armory shed to be introduced to Master Baradon, who crossed his arms upon their approach.

Master Hilde said, "Greetings, Master Baradon. This is initiate Kyllean Don-Votro. He has earned the blade, so if you would, we would like to arm him."

The elderly man looked as though he could still break a person in half with his bare hands. He glowered, then turned and led them down a set of stone stairs and into a vast underground bunker directly below the initiate training grounds. It appeared to also stretch beneath the practice yard of the riders, which was on the other side of a tall stone wall. They could hear the clang of swords as they listened to Master Hilde's lectures on magic, technique, and strategy before they began their own sparring each day.

"A lot of new blood these days," grumbled Master Baradon. "Not quite the same level of scrutiny as when we went through, is there?"

Master Hilde replied, "My standards haven't shifted in the slightest. But with war on the horizon, we took in a larger class of recruits. We need every man and woman with the talent."

Master Baradon grunted, "More like every boy and girl."

Kyllean ignored the jab. He knew it wasn't personal.

"Come over here, don't be shy. I need your measurements so I can shape your breastplate, mail, and the rest," said Baradon.

Kyllean was quiet as he did so, mesmerized by the array of weapons spaced along an entire stone wall, their black blades glittering in the red glow of several spherical lights.

"So many . . ." he muttered.

"Our numbers were once much greater, both riders and Lumáles," responded Master Hilde as Baradon wrapped a piece of thin rope around Kyllean's chest.

There had to be at least two hundred weapons scattered along the wall, each with its own unique design.

Once he had finished, Master Baradon, said, "Choose whichever suits you. Just know that once you do, no one else may use that blade, for the magic imbued within each creates a link to that specific user, severed only by death."

"Well, then, I'll have to choose wisely, aye?"

The number and variety overwhelmed Kyllean. Most were some variety of scimitar, the weapon most congruent with the style of fight taught at the school, but he did see a fair number of broadswords, axes, and even . . .

"A trident? Who fights with a trident?"

Master Baradon shrugged. "Some of these are *very* old."

Master Hilde said, "It is believed the riders of old were both warriors and mages. We theorize that it was not until our descendants settled here that they founded a new order with a focus exclusively on developing warriors, not mages. The scope of an all-encompassing study of magic was perhaps too great, and the development of riders fully equipped to defend suffered. That's my personal hypothesis, anyhow. There is no official record of a decision to change this, only that it's what has been done since our founding in this place. There is also the notion that every single weapon here was forged before the founding of our line in Talmune. These were all brought here by those same people."

"Huh," was all Kyllean could manage. He walked over to the wall and picked up a thin, curved weapon, the blade an inky black. He took a few practice swings. "Suppose I could take the heads off of a few Lugienese with this one." He set it back on the wall mount and continued down the line. He selected a slightly longer blade that was similarly built, though this one had a larger cross guard. He swung that one a few times and decided it felt a touch too clunky for his liking.

He repeated this a dozen more times as he moved along the wall.

"Remember, the blade will become lighter once imbued with your magic," said Master Hilde.

Master Baradon made a sound of dissatisfaction as Kyllean returned yet another weapon to the wall. "You know, choose wisely was not an invitation to spend an entire week down here playing with each and every one."

Kyllean looked over to the broad-shouldered man and said, "Hey now, apparently I have to live with this steel for the rest of my likely short life. This could mean the difference between the deaths of fifty or fifty-one of them Luggers. I don't know about you, but I like the sounds of fifty-one much better."

Baradon scoffed. "He's confident, I'll give him that . . ."

Master Hilde nodded, and added, "This one just came from Brinkwell. If one believes his account, he's already sent quite a few Lugienese to the underworld."

"Is that right?"

Kyllean completed a spin, ducking an imaginary attack, then thrust upward with his new blade. "Indeed. And that was without this super-duper speed stuff, or the craftsmanship of one of these things. Truth be told, I'm hoping to take many more than just fifty-one from the world of the living, but I try to keep my goals attainable."

"Well, then, take your time."

Kyllean stared up at a silver blade. Well, not exactly silver. It was marbled, with lines of white, black, and gray. He had never seen anything like it. He picked it up and handled it. The balance was . . . impeccable. The second he twirled it around his wrist, he felt like it had been the only sword he'd ever known.

"Don't bother with that one," said Baradon.

"And why's that?"

"Doesn't work."

Kyllean continued to thrust and parry his imaginary foes. "What do you mean? Seems fine to me. Better than fine. It's magnificent."

Master Hilde answered this question for Baradon. "The magical attributes that function within the other blades do not do so in that one. We don't know if this was a failed attempt or if the intent is different, but since no one has managed to make it work, this blade remains where it is, unused."

"Huh. Such a fine blade . . ."

He set it back on the wall and continued perusing for another dozen minutes until finally selecting a suitable obsidian weapon. "This will do."

"About time," grumbled Master Baradon.

Kyllean paused as he neared the stairs leading up to the training ground and looked back, eyes settling on the marbled blade upon the wall. "Say, would I be allowed to take that other blade as well?"

Master Baradon said, "No. One weapon per rider."

"Well, sure, but how long since anyone has taken that one? Couple hundred years?"

Baradon countered, "I take your point, but the rule is the rule. One rider, one weapon."

Master Hilde appeared intrigued by the notion. "Master Baradon, I know the rules as well as you, but we've no lack for weapons and you and I both know that not a single rider in our lives has used the thing. I don't see the harm in it."

Baradon made a growling sound, then harrumphed. "Fine. But don't complain to me when he fails to progress because he's wasting his time with this fool's blade instead of continuing to progress with the real one."

Master Hilde nodded. "A fair point. Kyllean, you will not spend any of your official training with this blade. What you choose to do with it beyond that is up to you. Understood?"

Kyllean smiled. "Oh, absolutely! Many thanks!" Then he jogged back to retrieve the second blade and snatched it from the wall. He slapped Baradon on the back as he passed him. "Thank you, too."

Baradon caught his arm and squeezed and Kyllean thought the man was going to strike him. "Hand over the blade," he growled.

"But—" squealed Kyllean.

"But nothing. The blade, now."

Master Hilde raised a finger to end the charade when Baradon explained, "This blade has no sheath. I'll need to fashion one."

Kyllean handed it over and exhaled loudly as Baradon released him. He immediately went to rolling out the flesh of his upper arm. "You've the grip of an ape!"

"Aye, working with your hands will do that to a man."

Kyllean was eager to be out of there before the man thought of another reason to take hold. "Thank you, Master Baradon."

"Come back in one week to collect your armor, sheath, and the *other* sword," he said mumbling the end of the statement.

Kyllean and Master Hilde returned to the training ground and his teacher said, "Well, let's get you over to Master Laurel to begin instruction with your new blade."

Just then, a shadow crossed overhead and Kyllean looked up to see one of the massive creatures gliding past. It landed a dozen paces away with deceptive grace. And an armored rider dismounted.

Master Hilde approached and greeted her comrade, but the rider's eyes were hard. "My apologies, but I must go directly to Headmaster Forestone. I bear grave news from the west."

Kyllean noted the dried blood upon the woman's armor, then looked back to see that the Lumále too was sprinkled with crimson stains. Kyllean could not tell for certain if the blood were its own or that of an enemy, but his excitement over earning the sword was suddenly stifled by the ominous seeds of dread he felt about whatever news this woman carried from the west.

CHAPTER 50

KIBURE

K IBURE SAT WITH HIS BACK leaning up against the pedestal of his nemesis: the seed. He had long since exhausted his mental faculties for the day. Attempting to complete the impossible had a way of doing that to a person, he mused. And so he sat alone doubting his purpose, and everything else.

If he wasn't the supposed savior, he would never be able to do as needed and they would all be eradicated by the Lugienese. That possibility frightened him. Worse was the possibility that he *was* the savior but was failing to fulfill the requirements of this role. Could his body be meant for the task, but his mind too weak? The thought of not only failing himself but the entire world was so weighty that he lost the ability to do much else but dwell upon this failure as if it had already occurred.

A voice in his head triggered a release from some of the weight, if only temporarily. *"Don't tell me you've already given up for the day."*

Kibure looked up to see Arabelle striding toward him, silver robe floating about her as if a gentle breeze had been sent just for this purpose.

"Drymus has given me a very strict quota on failures, and I exceeded that limit a while ago."

"Ah yes, of course."

With no further reaction from Arabelle and nothing to add that wouldn't sound downright pitiful, Kibure changed the topic. *"I didn't expect to see you here again."*

"And why is that? Did Drymus say something to you about this?"

Kibure shrugged. *"I don't think she appreciated you telling me about her last student."*

Arabelle appeared to release a heavy breath. *"Yes. Well, it was worth a try. It did have the desired effect. I had hoped that bringing up the death of her own nephew would not simply anger her, but perhaps weaken her focus for a time. You were so very close. I really thought you had her."*

Her words registered late, but they did register. Kibure felt a renewed pang of guilt. *"Her last student was also her nephew?"*

Arabelle nodded as if this were of no consequence.

"I used the death of her own nephew to incite her." This was not a question but a statement of incredulity. He continued in the same tone. *"She lost her own nephew and I antagonized her with this memory. I'm lucky she didn't kill me!"*

Arabelle waved the idea aside. *"If you haven't noticed, we don't keep our male kinsmen in this place. We don't experience the same level of familial attachment as cultures on the outside. Plus, this was over one hundred years ago and she had only just met the boy before the training began."*

Kibure shook his head. *"Still."* He came to his feet, the distraction lifting the weight of responsibility for now, though guilt and anger were beginning to fill its place. Arabelle must have seen his expression.

"Don't tell me you're upset about using this against Drymus."

Kibure glared up at her. *"I don't enjoy the feeling of being used. If I do something, I prefer to know what I'm doing and why."*

She rolled her eyes. *"We're always being used in one way or another. You probably more than anyone else alive right now."* She gave him a thoughtful expression. *"But I will do my best to be more transparent with you moving forward."*

"Thank you," Kibure grumbled. The exchange reminded him of another question that had been tugging at the corner of his mind since his arrival. *"So what does happen to males that are born here? And how*

do . . . you know . . . how do the women here even have children? Don't they need . . ."

Arabelle allowed a chuckle to pass on to him, then said, *"Another male?"*

Kibure looked at his feet. *"Well, isn't that how it works?"*

"Such curiosity." She nodded her head. *"We have an 'agreement' with a line of our people who have chosen to remain more connected to the fallen world after the collapse of our empire. When it comes time for some of our women to bear a child, we pay our kinsmen a visit. Our women then return here until the children are born. After one year, males born are returned to their fathers to be raised on the outside, females remain here."*

Kibure considered this. Had he been one of these males, born here but returned to wherever his father resided? How then would he have become a slave? The story he had been told was that his mother had been the one to bring him to the estate while he was still in her womb. Drymus seemed to believe he was closely related but had been slim on details.

Arabelle interrupted Kibure's musing. *"I have an idea that may help you strengthen your will without frustrating you to the point of pathetic sulking. No offense."*

Kibure glared at her.

"How would you like to break free of the defensive barrier to this place?"

Kibure tilted his head, waiting for further explanation.

"You know, travel beyond the cavern walls?"

"Why?"

She sighed, or at least that's what it looked like to Kibure. *"You've seen this place, right? My people have been stuck hiding out in a giant cavern for generations upon generations waiting for their savior. Perhaps you, perhaps not. We wait and wait, watching for the signs to align with the prophecies. We have sisters who study the stars every single day, and as soon as they knew the sign was approaching, everyone who was not already on an assignment was not permitted to leave. I had just been sent on mine but was recalled once you were located. Now I'm trapped here, and if you fail to do what you're supposed to do with the seed, we will die here waiting for the Lugienese to finally kill us. I spend as much time as my body allows in this realm searching for a way to break through the barrier so I can see a little more of the world beyond. It will be the only chance I ever get if you fail."*

"*I'm glad you're so confident in me,*" grumbled Kibure through the connection, though he could hardly fault her for doubting.

"*Yes, well . . . maybe . . . Maybe focusing on this other task will help you improve your strength of will and therefore help your chances.*"

"*Okay, but to break through the barrier? Wasn't that built for our—your protection? I know I'm just a dimwitted, illiterate, former slave, but I was under the impression that barriers and walls work not only to keep people in, but also to keep unwanted guests out.*"

She rolled her eyes. "*Yes, yes, but this was built thousands of years ago. Few on the outside nowadays even know how to navigate the spiritual realm, and fewer still would have the knowledge of its principles like any one of us do. We are more of a danger to the followers of the Dark One than they are to us, at least here in this realm. So yes, I am certain.*"

Kibure considered her logic. "*Okay, so let's say I agree to help you try to break through this barrier. What makes you think I can even help you do it? You're a stronger wielder than I.*"

She held up a finger. "*That may not be so. I am no doubt more skilled, but more powerful? No. At least not if you are what they think you are. One of the things that should set you apart is your capacity to wield. To do the things you'll need to be able to do, your potential to wield in terms of sheer volume has to be immense. So in theory, your reservoir should be vastly greater than any of ours. Therefore, it stands to reason that your magical reflection here, your potential in will, should also be vastly greater, once developed. You know that's why Drymus is keeping you in here, right? She's teaching you to strengthen and control your will without the risk of you using your abilities in the physical realm where you might cause harm to yourself or others. But even now, I suspect you could summon more energy than most, perhaps all, of us. You just have to be trained in how to use it, which, honestly, I still don't understand why they aren't already doing, risks aside.*"

Kibure wasn't certain that he wished to help her, but he was definitely curious. *"So how exactly would I go about breaking the barrier? Wasn't it constructed by a lot of powerful wielders?"*

Arabelle shook her head. *"We're not going to break down the entire barrier. We just need to make a little doorway. And I've already found the best place to do it."*

"So let's say I help you with this. What do I get out of it?"

She looked him over as if trying to decide whether he was serious. *"As I've said, you get more practice strengthening your will. This brings you closer to your real training and freedom from the cave."*

He eyed her expectantly.

She threw up her hands. *"Fine. If you agree to help me, I'll teach you as best I can from here, how to use your magic there, in the waking world. Keep in mind, I won't be able to help nearly as well as someone who is right there with you to feel what you're doing and to answer questions as you experiment. But I can probably teach you a few things."*

Kibure smiled. *"Well, then. What are we waiting for?"*

She hesitated. *"All right. Couple of things first. You know about the limitations our bodies have on how much we can wield, right?"*

He shrugged. *"I know that if I stay here for too long, my body hurts and I am supposed to wait awhile before I return."*

She nodded. *"Yes, and that's because when we wield, we're actually drawing upon the contents of our own bones to channel magic. And when we enter this place, we're still borrowing small bits of magic directly from our bones and channeling it. Novices tend to burn more while doing this than those who have been trained to be more efficient in their use. You're probably using up to twice the amount of power necessary to be here right now. I tell you this so you might understand that if you practice here to your bones' limits, then return to the waking world and use more, you could seriously harm yourself, perhaps even kill yourself."*

Now he understood why Draílock had been so hesitant to let him and Sindri practice wielding beyond the safety of that secure room. It hadn't only been because of the risk of detection. It was because there were real dangers associated with wielding too much power. *"So the more*

I use in the physical realm, the less time I will have to spend in the spiritual." Kibure kept his next statement to himself. *Another reason she hasn't been training me to wield in the physical realm. I wouldn't be able to spend as much time working on the pointless task of sinking my weapon into that seed.*

Arabelle frowned. *"Additionally, Drymus and anyone else nearby will almost certainly detect an increase in your use of magic. When you're in the spiritual realm, you use a small, steady amount. If you go and start doing other things, they'll know."*

Good, thought Kibure. *Maybe if Drymus knows I'm able to wield in the physical realm, she'll decide to start training me out there.* He responded with, *"Okay. Let's start."*

She looked up to the distant cavern roof, then back at Kibure. *"I'm going to begin with the basics. I know you received some minor training before and I don't wish to waste time with redundancy, yet some of this information is important enough to repeat."*

The growling in Kibure's stomach told him that Arabelle's lesson had gone longer than he had wished. Yet how could he stop her? This is what he had wanted since he had arrived here: actual instruction on how to use his magic.

Perhaps sensing his distraction, or perhaps having finished the lesson, Arabelle said, *"That's enough for now. Go back and do as discussed. The next time you're here, we'll do what I want us to do: make a door out of here."*

Back in the darkness of the cave, Kibure focused his attention on Arabelle's instruction. Feeling the power around him was not difficult and even gripping it with his mind was a small matter for him now. What he had been afraid to do was to draw upon it. Today would be different.

He sank his mind into the stone around him, careful to spread out the tentacles of his consciousness so as to not draw too much power from any one place enough to weaken it, though he considered this strategy would perhaps be the secret to escaping the cave should he wish to do it on his own.

His heart thumped. This was the part he had been so afraid to do, and after the warnings, he was all the more hesitant. He needed to draw in this power, but not too much of it. Arabelle had told him he would be safer to draw in a limited amount of power so that he wouldn't have to worry as much about controlling the release of it, which could be a less stable event. Kibure felt a tingling sensation and recalled this feeling, although unlike before, he wasn't filled with rage or a fight for his life. He could now just drink in the feeling, and in spite of his fear, he found that it felt . . . wonderful. Energy filled him, and he suddenly believed that he could take hold of whatever door currently contained him, and simply blow it out of the way if he willed it.

But instead, he decided on a more practical use: he was going to make light.

Holding out his hand much like he had seen Drymus do, he directed the energy into the space just above his palm. He understood now why Drymus had decided to work on developing his will within the spiritual realm first. According to Arabelle, it was a very similar concept, and he was glad for having honed his will because he found it easier than he would have thought possible. With the concept in his mind, he funneled his power into the small space, willing it to become light.

A plume of something like fire shot out from him, then circled back as he focused on the small area above his palm. Breathing heavily, he furrowed his brow in concentration. It was one thing to release his energy, and quite another to hold on to a steady stream of it, releasing it slowly to maintain the volatile ball of luminescence that danced above his open palm.

The light flickered as his concentration slipped, but he restored it and continued to work out the flow of energy that supported the conjured light. Growing a little more confident, he narrowed the stream of energy, then attempted to push more through it. The result was a tighter, brighter ball of light. It was nowhere near as clean in appearance as those lining the streets of the underground city, or the neat orb of light summoned by Drymus when she visited, but Kibure was pleased with his work.

He nodded in satisfaction, smiling wide as he did so. *I'm a wielder! A real-life wizard!* His eyes flitted around the barren stone room: circular high ceiling, a single chair positioned in the center of the space.

Kibure considered the chair only to quickly refocus on his light. The orb remained unchanged. *I am a wizard,* he repeated confidently. Holding his will tight to the ball of light in much the same way he would have done in the spiritual realm, he directed another portion of his mind toward the chair. *Telekinesis. Now, that's the mark of a true wizard!* He willed the chair to move.

Nothing happened. *Arrrgh.* Looking closer, he saw that the chair was shaking. He must not have used quite enough energy to actually move it. Reaching into his well of power, he poured more into the task, pushed again, harder, and this time—

"Whoa!" His feet slid several paces back as a wave of energy escaped; the chair was ripped from its place in the center of the cave and sped toward the wall, at the same time an opening appeared in the stone right where the chair was headed. Drymus stepped through, illuminated by an orb of her own.

Oh no. Oh no! But it was too late to do anything about it, not that he would have known how to stop her wave of power once set in motion. He cringed and his hands went to his face.

Kibure felt a slight tinge of magic and the hurtling chair changed directions just before colliding with Drymus, though her robes still billowed as if standing in the middle of a great storm. The chair slammed into the hard stone of the cave wall a pace away. Wooden splinters flew as the chair exploded into pieces.

Drymus's voice was hard and firm as she yelled, "Release your magic at once!"

Her tone left no room for question and Kibure was too spooked to disobey. He released his hold on the ball of light that he had somehow managed to hold on to throughout, leaving only the orb of light employed by Drymus.

She glared at him and his legs felt weak. He wasn't sure how much of this feeling stemmed from his fear of what she was going to do to him, and how much was a physical response to the release of a great force of magic.

Drymus stepped closer and her hand extended, index finger pointing accusingly in his direction. "What were you thinking, boy? Are you trying to get yourself killed?"

Kibure opened his mouth but no sound came out. His throat was dry.

"Magic is not a toy to be flung around for funzies. There are dangers to consid—"

She stopped speaking as Kibure's legs gave out beneath him. She cursed and a tingle of magic told him she had done something.

He landed upon a pad of air, and then floated gently to the ground.

"Fool boy. How long were you in the spiritual realm before returning here to try out your new trick?"

Kibure's weakness turned into a deep ache, and he knew this was his bones. Staring up at the ceiling of the cave, he dared not move. He tried to answer and his hoarse voice said, "Too long?"

Drymus stood over him. "Yes, much too long if you decide to do something utterly reckless like coming back to the physical realm to use a massive swath of magic immediately upon return. How did you manage to do this, anyhow? I was under the impression that you knew little more than how to sense the energy around you. Or was that a lie?"

Kibure was too dazed to carry on a conversation like this for long, but his initial shock at what he had done was giving way to other, deeper feelings, those of his frustration and impatience at not being allowed to leave the cave or be properly trained to use his real powers. "I—you refuse to teach me, so I decided to try to learn it myself."

Drymus was quiet for a time, then grumbled to herself. "*She* had something to with this. I just know she did."

Another set of footfalls drew near and he saw another woman appear beside Drymus. She was one of the women who had brought food to Kibure. She handed Drymus a mug. "Thank you, Ilith."

The woman bowed. "Of course." Then departed.

Drymus squatted down and helped Kibure sit up and held out the mug to him. "You will drink this."

"What is it?"

"More poison."

Kibure rolled his eyes and felt dizzy.

Drymus spoke again. "This will keep you from using magic of any sort until I permit such. I don't trust that you'll keep from doing so on my advice alone."

"But won't that prevent me from entering the spiritual realm as well?"

Drymus shook her head. "That is different. Entering the spiritual realm utilizes only the energy that coalesces within your bones. This is different from drawing upon the magic from your surroundings."

Kibure reached for the mug, then stopped. "You should be training me, both here and in the spiritual realm. If I'm supposed to be able to perform magic, and the Lugienese threat is as real as everyone believes, then why do we waste time pretending in the spiritual realm?"

Drymus smiled. "We do so because young wizards are rash and because I wish to be certain that you are *the* one before I trust you to wield power in the physical realm."

Kibure was not satisfied and he surprised even himself. "No."

"No?" asked Drymus, her tone somewhere between amusement and anger.

"I will not drink your tea. I am not doing anything else for you until you agree to train me in both realms. If I'm not who you hope, we're doomed anyway so what does it matter?"

Kibure swatted at the steaming mug attempting to knock it to the floor, but before so much as a drop of liquid spilled, he felt the immobilizing power of Drymus. He sat, frozen in place as Drymus pulled the mug to her chest. She then plugged his nose, tipped back his head, and poured the drink down his throat. She released his throat from her spell so he could swallow and he had no choice but to do so. None of his efforts to resist did any good.

"I am too old to tolerate insolence. I do what is best for my people, and if you are indeed to count yourself one of them, then you will do as you are told." She stood up and turned away from him and started for the exit. She released him from her power and said without turning around, "You will need to rest for some time before you can return to the spiritual realm. I will visit you then."

Days later, Kibure mustered his strength and his will, and once again swung his summoned weapon down toward the seed with all his might. The blade slid harmlessly from the surface, off to the side, and continued into the ground to the hilt. Kibure's momentum brought him down to the ground in an awkward tumble.

Incensed by his continued failure, he pulled the weapon free and took a backhand swing at the pedestal, cleaving clean through it at an angle. The top half crashed to the ground, seed and all. Feeling more satisfied with this than anything he had done thus far, Kibure stood and hacked away at more of the pedestal. Frustration fueled each swing and soon there was no pedestal with which to cut so he turned to the half that had fallen and began cutting that into small pieces as well. He sang angrily to himself as he did so. *Just like old times,* he thought.

> *Toil, toil, in the dream,*
> *New slavery we have found,*
> *Swing—FAIL—*
> *Swing—FAIL—*
> *Can't cut the seedling,*
> *But you're the savior we need you,*
> *Pick up the pace,*

Swing—FAIL—

Swing—FAIL—

Can't cut the seedling—

Arabelle's voice in his mind stilted the rhythm in his head. "*I see you're in good spirits.*"

Kibure attempted to ignore her. This was the first time she had visited since he had been forced into his regimen of tea.

"*You caused quite the excitement around the city with your not-so-subtle use of magic. Haven't felt anything since, so I'm assuming Drymus forbade you from practicing again, perhaps even has you on a diet of the inhibitor tea?*"

Kibure still didn't respond. He just continued to hack away at the remnants of stone that had once been the pedestal.

"*I did warn you that this might happen. And of course, you didn't exactly keep it subtle, did you? What did you try to do, blow the ceiling off your cave?*"

Kibure turned and faced her. "*I'm really not in the mood. As you can see, I have an impossible task to complete, so if you don't mind, I'd prefer to be left alone.*"

Arabelle smiled. "*Of cour—*" She raised a hand to point.

Kibure looked to where she pointed and dropped his blade. He had cut away at everything that had contained the seed, the bottom of which now glowed faintly. In his fit of rage, he had failed to notice. The glow was yellow. He was actually seeing color here in the spiritual realm! A faint pinkish glow!

Arabelle walked over to where the seed remained on the ground and kicked the rubble out of the way. Then she crouched down and touched the bottom glowing section of the seed with her summoned blade. She yanked back her hand and dropped the weapon as if she'd just touched a hot coal. Massaging her hand, she stood and said, "*I think that perhaps you should try.*"

Kibure snorted. "*Me? Looks like you didn't enjoy your own experience. I think I'll pass.*"

She shook her head. "*Yes, but you're supposed to be different now, aren't you?*"

He considered this logic, swallowed hard, then placed his foot upon the seed to hold it in place. He slowly moved his sword to tap the glowing portion at the bottom with the tip. His nerves tingled with the anticipation of pain. There was none. He hadn't even angled his weapon to go in. He had simply touched the glowing portion with the side of his blade. It stuck there as if this portion of the seed was made from tar.

Kibure stared in disbelief before squatting down to angle the blade in. *There's no way.* But his summoned blade slid inside as easily as if the underside were hollow, and he felt no pain whatsoever. Then his sword began to glow, as did the rest of the seed itself. He felt warmth radiating from the seed through the blade, and into his skin. He looked over at Arabelle, who bore an expression that seemed part surprise and part satisfied.

"*What's happening?*" asked Kibure in a panic.

"*How should I know?*

"*Well, what should I do?*"

Arabelle shrugged her shoulders. "*I don't believe that this has ever happened, but I suspect someone will be paying you a visit in the physical realm very soon.*"

CHAPTER 51

KIBURE

KIBURE OPENED HIS EYES TO an already illuminated cave; Drymus sat cross-legged in front of him.

"You are more capable than I believed."

"Thanks for the praise," grumbled Kibure.

She shrugged. "As you have so kindly pointed out, you are not the first we believed might be *the* one."

Kibure felt himself shrink back. "I'm sorry about what I said about you and your last student. I . . . didn't know he was your nephew."

Drymus looked up, emotionless as ever. "It is nothing. Arabelle told you what you needed to know in order to suit her goals for you. Nothing more."

Standing, Drymus said, "Come. You have been summoned. You will stand before the council once again."

Kibure made no move to rise. "Can I ask you a question first?"

Drymus rolled her eyes. "Quickly."

He hesitated, fearing his question would offend. But his concern for what might be in store for him if he failed to prove his worth weighed more heavily. "What really happened? To your nephew, I mean."

Drymus's expression clouded, and for a moment Kibure thought she would not answer, but she sighed and said, "I tried to train him, as I did you, only I trained him in the spiritual realm and the waking world simultaneously. Once we determined that he was not in fact the one slated to return us home, he changed. He became volatile, obsessing over the kosmí. He was caught attempting to remove its reflection in the spiritual realm from Purgemon."

"So what happened to him?"

Drymus shook her head.

Kibure felt revulsion welling up inside of him. He gulped. "What became of him?"

Arabelle had told him that some disaster had befallen Drymus's last training experience and that mentioning such would likely result in a reaction that could be exploited. He now had the sense that he should have asked more and, had he done so, he would not have used this information even if it would mean that she would begin training him in the physical realm.

"I was forced to put him down." Drymus's expression was stone.

"You . . . they made you do it yourself?"

She shook her head. "No, not directly, but he was my nephew, my trainee, and my responsibility. If it had to be done, it needed to be me."

Drymus turned away, walking toward the door that materialized in the cave wall. "Unless you have any more prying questions, the council awaits your presence."

Kibure felt sick as he considered a woman slaying her own nephew. Would he meet the same fate? These thoughts spun around his mind as he was escorted out of the cave.

Kibure was glad to be free of the suffocating stone enclosure, but Drymus's mood had been markedly less cheery than Kibure thought it should be, even before he asked his question about her nephew. He had just completed a monumental task, something no one else in the entire city could do. But her mood was downright scornful.

They entered the same chambers as before and the same five women sat stonelike in their seats upon the raised platform that consumed half of the small room. The only indication that the women were even alive and not well-crafted stonework was the swiveling of their heads as he and Drymus entered the room.

The apparent leader of the council, the aged woman who had spoken to him during his first visit, was the first to speak again.

"Thank you, Lady Drymus, for bringing the boy here for inspection. It has been confirmed that the 'seed' has been returned to the physical realm. However, as discussed, further confirmation is needed before we can allow you to proceed. He must be able to draw upon the stone itself."

Drymus nodded and said, "I have issued my warning. The blame will be upon your hands when this does not go as you would wish."

The council leader's eyes narrowed yet the rest of her expression remained unchanged. "Yes, you have, and we do not appreciate the repetition. It carries with it tones of disrespect that are not permissible. You will remain henceforth silent, or you will wish you had."

Kibure was taken aback to hear someone speak to Drymus with such contempt.

The leader stood, then swiveled on a heel and glided to the back of the platform to retrieve an item tightly wrapped in a golden satin cloth. He knew what lay inside before she unfolded it, but what he did not expect was to see was the scaly, onyx seed fall open as soon as the cloth that held it together was removed.

Inside the seed lay a fist-sized golden sphere, which was not cut. It was shiny to the point of appearing wet, and partially translucent. And whether it was a trick of the light or not, the sphere was glowing.

The leader pointed at Kibure. "Come forward."

Kibure had been glad just to be out of the cave, but after Drymus's ominous warning, and the disagreeable disposition of the council members, he wondered if it might be better to simply return to the safety of that place.

He paused before her and she extended her hand, the sphere resting upon her open palm.

"This is the kosmí. It is an artifact of great power, but that is only true for those with the capacity to wield it. It is otherwise nothing more than a pretty stone. We have not begotten one of our line capable of wielding its power since our departure from the old world many generations ago. Your ability to do so will be the confirmation we need in order to move forward with your training and the rest of our preparations."

Kibure looked from side to side, then turned to Drymus for support, but she sat on a chair behind him, legs and arms crossed, refusing to meet his gaze.

"Eyes here. Lady Drymus is of no concern to you right now."

"What is it you want me to do with this kosmí?"

"You simply need to draw upon its energy. This will be the final proof we need. We are aware that you have at least some ability to wield, as evidenced by your 'actions' a few days ago. If you are able to draw upon the power held within the stone, you will likely find there to be much more than you might expect. DO NOT attempt to wield this power; you need only draw upon it. Just a trickle, nothing more. We will be watching very closely. This is all."

That doesn't seem too bad.

Yet, Drymus's concern suggested otherwise. Then again, she seemed not to believe him capable of much. He dismissed her worry. *She's just overly cautious because of her experience training her nephew.* He understood to an extent, but he didn't have to share in her fear.

"All right."

He closed his eyes and extended his mind into his surroundings. He felt the smooth, orderly energy held within the hard stone floor beneath his feet, then followed that to the feet of the woman before him, whose energy could be felt but not drawn, for it clung to her like ice to the cold. He continued his mental probing along the length of her body until he reached her hand where he sensed . . . *nothing.*

That couldn't be right. If this object was supposed to be so powerful, the energy housed within should be nearly pulsating, begging to be set free, or at least that's what he imagined it should feel like. He didn't exactly have a wealth of experience on the matter.

He tried to force his consciousness to take hold of the sphere, but still he felt nothing. More than nothing. The more he tried, the more he realized that it felt more like empty air than a solid object at all. He could sense the spherical shape of the object by virtue of the absolute absence of any energy, but that was the complete opposite of what he should be feeling, wasn't it? It felt to him like someone had taken the stone and somehow sucked it clean of all matter.

He opened his eyes and said, "I—er—I don't feel . . . anything."

The woman met his eyes and narrowed her own. "You had best try harder."

Kibure did so again, quickly finding the object within his mind's eye and attempting to draw upon it. But with no energy to take hold of, it was a dead end.

He continued to work his mind in and around the stone, but still felt a nothingness so absolute he was certain that this was the truth of it. But that did nothing to help his predicament. He tried to probe into the stone but some force stopped him. If there was energy within, it was like water hiding beneath a thick blanket of sand.

He opened his eyes again and felt the glares of all five women boring down on him.

One such woman to his left spoke in a voice like the screeching of a crow. "Well, it seems Drymus's warnings were without merit. He is not *the* one."

To his right another voice, a deeper shrill whispered, "Olem help us if he's not. Perhaps he just needs further training, training from someone who can produce better results."

Kibure didn't like Drymus in the least, but the thought of beginning anew with someone worse was a prospect he did not wish to investigate.

Comments and whispers continued around him, but he pushed past them, focusing solely on the kosmí. He brought his mind to the void that was the stone. He gritted his teeth. *I know nothing of prophecy or saving, but I'm going to use this stone.* He brought the mental equivalent of a hand to the stone, feeling desperately for any sign of energy with which to grasp, but it was as if the stone was . . . *What if the stone doesn't radiate power, but it draws power into itself? How would I access it?* It would be like trying to reach a hand into a bucket filled to the brim with ice. *So if the ice represents the energy, how might I extricate it with just a hand?*

Voices were still speaking around him, but he ignored them. The women didn't exist. The world was just him and the kosmí. Someone grabbed his arm, but he hardly felt it. *I'm doing this. I'm doing this.*

It might be his last chance. *No way to find out but to put my hand into the nothingness to see if that's all this is.* He took his mind's eye and imagined it was a sharpened spear. Then with all of his might, he drove it into the stone.

He went from feeling absolutely nothing to feeling a sudden surge of power so great he thought it would swallow him whole. He recalled the winds ripping through the ravine in his escape through the Drisko Mountains; this was a hundred—no, a thousand—times more powerful. His mind was knocked around like a grain of sand amid a great dust storm, his ability to direct his course was no more existent than a stone in descent from atop a cliff.

The volume of raw power threatened to fray his mind at the seams. Pain shot through his consciousness, yet he embraced it, for it was the only sensation he recognized in all of the chaos. His ability to sense direction in relation to where his physical body existed was voided the second he entered. He had crossed the threshold of the fist-sized stone into a vast mountain of nightmarish swirling darkness. Only, it wasn't darkness, not really. It was every color, and colors he didn't even know existed. All of this flashed back and forth before his eyes until his small mind was unable to process any of it.

One thing became clear in the midst of it all: he was going to be torn asunder if he didn't get himself out of there. The pain increased and he felt like he was being swallowed. Again his thoughts went to the Drisko Mountains, this time to the drifts of snow. He had needed to be pulled from one after sinking up to his neck when he wandered off the trail to relieve himself. Only here he didn't stop sinking at his neck. His entire mind was being consumed and he had no idea which way to go in order to escape.

I'm going to die. This thought stabilized within his mind while everything else continued to tumble about. *I'm going to die within a stone the size of a fist. This is . . . just . . .* He struggled to capture the word amid the mayhem around him. *Stupid.*

That thought was the only thing that made any sense as his mind was ripped apart. *This is so stupid.* He was scared to death, and would soon join death, but he was also angry. *How can a mere stone do all of this?* And in that moment he felt a fragment of clarity. A flake of snow within an avalanche.

As his mind drifted into oblivion, he clung tight to this minuscule anchor he'd found that connected him to the world beyond. The chaos slowed around him and he realized that this was exactly what he needed to do. This was little different than the spiritual realm. It was a matter of will. With his remaining mental strength, Kibure reached out and took hold of the raw energy that threatened to consume him and threw the might of his will against its power.

Everything suddenly slammed to a halt and his mind returned to his physical body.

He opened his eyes and saw his hand extended toward the woman who held the stone, only—she no longer held it. The stone was in his outstretched hand, which he realized was painfully warm. His entire body coursed with power. He thought back to the cave when he had drunk in the energy of the stone around him. That had been a drop in the bucket compared to the sea of power he now held within his hand, within his entire body. And he was terrified.

He looked around and saw expressions of surprise, fear, and anger.

The woman who had held the stone spoke. "What do you think you're doing? You will return the kosmí at once."

Kibure held so much power in him at that moment, he feared to move at all. He tried to speak, but even that simple act seemed a task too dangerous. "I . . ." He stopped himself, certain he would lose control if he did . . . anything.

Drymus's voice sounded from behind him, calm, but he heard a slight tremble as well. "Kibure, you need to release your hold on the kosmí. Carefully."

He did not disagree, but he was too afraid.

The woman in front of him started toward him.

Drymus shouted a warning, but this was ignored. "The kosmí—now," she commanded.

She reached for it and without thinking, Kibure pulled his hand back. Some part of him refused to relinquish the power or was fearful of what might happen when he did.

He tested his voice again, still afraid that he would lose control at any moment. "I . . . can't."

His body felt like a pot of boiling water, the energy begging to be set free. He had consumed more than his body could ever hope to wield. If what Drymus had said about channeling power was true, his bones would turn to dust the moment he released even a sliver of what he now held.

"How dare you!" The woman reached for him again and Kibure attempted to turn away, too slow.

Her hand gripped the kosmí, attempting to wrench it free.

"Lady Attica, no!" screamed Drymus.

Kibure's hand was glued to the sphere of power, his fingers had become stone. A sharp pain began to blossom as Lady Attica pulled at the stone in his hand.

He heard himself saying something, but his attention had moved to keeping the lid on the mountain of power fighting to be set free.

He squeezed his hand on the kosmí and a voice that was his but was amplified many times over yelled in defiance, "Go!"

Power exploded outward in a spray of blinding light and everything went black.

CHAPTER 52

GROBENNAR

GROBENNAR TREMBLED AS THE MENTAL connection between himself and Magog solidified. Rajuban, he suspected, was present as well—*the swine*. This was it. His gambit was discovered and while not a total failure, it would not be enough to satisfy. It could have worked if only he had more time. But *if* was just another word for failure, and one did not ignore a summons of any kind from the God-king. The worst part was the fact that this communication would likely also include Rajuban.

Magog spoke calmly, which was either a good thing or a *very* bad thing. "*Fatu Ma-gazi Grobennar, you have been very, very busy.*"

Grobennar did not know how much Magog knew, a definite problem. He had no desire to incriminate himself, yet to leave something out or lie could be even more disastrous for him. He had a valid defense: he had acted within his authority as Secretary of War, and while his actions were not necessarily sanctioned by precedent, they were within his power. That was the line he needed to take if he was to survive this exchange.

"*Indeed, I have. I had been hoping to bestow upon you the blessing of conquest, the conquest of the Kingdom of Dowe as well as the establishment of a new elite fighting force of airborne Klerósi priests. The latter has come to fruition, but the former is still under way, though I suspect you've learned that we have taken the capital city, Salmune."*

Grobennar was surprised he'd been able to get so many words in without being interrupted but wasn't certain whether or not this was a good sign. He had personally utilized silence as a tool in both instances.

Rajuban, curse his soul, was the one to respond. *"Your most recent methods depart from our established policy of converting all of the conquered into a single slave class. Do you not find this curious, Your Eminence?"*

Magog replied. *"Indeed. You will explain this now, Fatu Ma-gazi, Grobennar."*

"Tread lightly, he sounds angry," said Jaween.

Would have never guessed that for myself, thought Grobennar.

"I recognize that my methods have been rather unorthodox, Your Excellency. I would like to begin by saying that my goals of conquest are in no way compromised. I am simply exploring alternative methods in order to do so with less Lugienese casualties. By giving the appearance of allying with some, we are able to step back and allow these infidels to kill one another. It is for this reason that I have begun setting up puppet leaders while allowing citizens to maintain their own sense of false sovereignty. It was my intention to consult with you after the Kingdom had been fully subdued, at which point it would be easy enough to renege on such generous terms without consequence, for the Kingdom would be significantly weakened."

Grobennar decided to take advantage of the fact that Magog had not yet interrupted.

"I might also add that while there remains no Lugienese precedent, my methods are in fact supported by the writings of the founding prophet, Lesante herself. As you know, she foretold the 'conversion of the entire world to the Klerósi faith.' Her writings are clear in stating that there must be 'death to all of the pagans of the fallen world,' but there is nothing written about hierarchy or enslavement of those peoples who convert. Conversion is the only clear requisite, though her other writings make it quite obvious that Klerós's people stand above the rest."

Magog finally responded and sounded none too pleased. *"You play games with words, but your intent remains in league with the glory of*

Klerós." He paused, then continued, "*However, these new developments will shift our timetable concerning Scritland.*"

Grobennar let out a heavy sigh of relief. He could hardly believe it. Barely a rebuke at all! He was nearly certain Rajuban would exploit the opportunity to wrest Grobennar's newfound position of favor from him once again. But Rajuban remained silent.

Magog spoke again. "*I am traveling to the city of Tung to coordinate our final plans for the Kingdom and Scritland. I'm also eager to see these dordron riders in the flesh. You will travel there immediately. If the reports are correct, you have several more dordron to tame in order to replenish the force. The next time our dordron riders face Lumále riders, I expect things to go much differently.*"

Grobennar responded, "*Yes. Of course, Your Excellency. When do you expect to arrive?*"

As if simply wishing to make it known that he was *always* with the God-king, even when it seemed like he wasn't, Rajuban spoke into the connection to answer. "*We shall arrive in Tung this very evening.*"

This evening? Grobennar could visualize Rajuban's crooked smile even through the connection. "*We look forward to your own arrival as soon as possible, old friend. This should be a good test of dordron speed and endurance, don't you think?*"

Grobennar responded to Magog, not Rajuban. "*I will leave as soon as possible, Your Excellency. I'll need to make a few arrangements to maintain order while I am away.*"

Again, it was Rajuban who responded. "*No need. It's all been taken care of. We will take Quinson before they have time to rally support from Scritland. You're free to leave as soon as this conversation ends. Although perhaps compelled is a better word.*"

"*I don't like this, Grobes.*"

Nor did Grobennar. Magog had been too . . . amenable. Then again, perhaps Grobennar had simply become too accustomed to the God-king's wrath to assume that his efforts might actually be rewarded. Or perhaps this was his own insecurity rearing its ugly head. And Jaween's outlook didn't help. Perhaps he had nothing to fear. He had been elevated after his victory in Brinkwell, after all, reassigned to a position outranked only by the Fatu Mazi and the God-king himself. And he had just subdued the heart of the Kingdom of Dowe with almost no casualties, not to mention the development of the dordron fleet. He *should* be rewarded. Magog wished to plan the rest of the conquest in person with him. Perhaps Magog was growing tired of Rajuban's whispers in his ear. *This is my opportunity to regain my rightful seat once and for all.*

"*Grobennar? Is this understood?*" boomed the God-king through the connection. He had missed something.

Umm . . . "*Of course, Your Excellency. It will be done. I will depart straight away.*"

The connection ended and Grobennar released a breath that could have supported an army underwater for hours.

"*Magog is going to kill you. You know that, right?*"

"What? No. That's ridiculous."

"*He's definitely going to kill you. Have I ever steered you wrong?*"

"Yes. Many times, as a matter of fact."

"*Even still, I'll be sure to send a message to your languishing soul about how right I was about this as I seek a new master from within your charred remains.*"

Grobennar rolled his eyes. "I need to leave."

He grabbed his travel pack and enough provisions for a couple of overnight stays since he did not wish to attempt suicide by driving his dordron to fly for two or more days without rest. As he was walking toward the palace wall where he had commanded Frida to wait for him, he heard Paranja.

"Looks like you're dressed for travel. Where might you be going that requires an overnight pack?"

"I have business with the God-king."

"Oh? What business is that?"

Grobennar was annoyed with her prying. "Nothing that concerns you. I've been summoned to coordinate plans for the completion of our efforts across the continent."

"Was this Rajuban's idea or Emperor Magog's?"

"What does that matter? I've been summoned, so I will go."

Her hands went to her hips as she said, "Aren't you the least bit concerned that you're being lured into a trap by your long-standing rival?"

"*Hmm?*" sounded Jaween innocently.

Grobennar ground his teeth. *Does no one think I could simply be commended for a job well done?*

"Even if I were, I can't very well refuse a summons from the God-king. My course has been set, I must now take it."

Paranja sighed. "You're right, of course. I only wish there was a way to separate this current Fatu Mazi from the God-king. It should be you, and I fear this whisperer of secrets has injected his venom into the mind of Klerós's own chosen lieutenant here upon Doréa."

Grobennar knew this to be true but had no intention of stirring up thoughts of rebellion. "Perhaps, but Klerós will smite the liar. If not now, then later. We have to do our best, and trust that Klerós will take care of the rest. Our own roles may be more or less significant than our own designs for ourselves." Climbing upon Frida, he concluded, "I trust that you'll watch over the work we've started here. Apparently our Fatu Mazi has sent instructions. I do not know to whom, but please do your best to safeguard our progress."

"And you do your best to avoid whatever trap has been set before you in Tung."

Grobennar made no further comment. Frida took to the air and Grobennar had nothing to do but think and pray. And occasionally endure Jaween's musings about the danger that lay ahead.

CHAPTER 53

AYNWARD

THANK YOU FOR TRANSPORTING US all this way," said Dagmara.

"Yes, thank you, indeed," Aynward followed with as he crawled out from the secret compartment in the back of the cargo wagon filled with casks of Van Odla wine.

The journey to East End had been uneventful besides a few nerve-racking searches of the cargo within which the pair had been hidden.

Placing a hand on the single largest vat of fermented *anything* he had ever seen, Aynward remarked, "Say, I've been meaning to ask, who's the thirsty fellow that put in an order of such a . . . *buttload* of wine?"

The Scritlandian merchant's reaction was flatter than the marble surface of the ballroom back at the palace, and Dagmara looked at Aynward as if he had just broken wind. "Your entire life has been leading you to this exact moment in time, hasn't it? When you could utter the word 'buttload' in the appropriate context."

Aynward just grinned back at her. She wasn't wrong.

Shaking her head, she asked, "Whatever will you do now that your life's work has been achieved?"

The drivers looked back and forth between themselves, then the louder of the two interrupted, "Apologies, but we really must be going,

409

and you had best not linger either. As you know, it is recommended that you continue east, but we can go no further than here."

"Annnnd my moment of triumph is shattered by the haste of merchants." Aynward gave the men a nod. "Alas, you're quite right. Thank you, and be well, gentlemen."

"And you."

They hopped back into their respective positions then urged the horses to pull the wagons forward, eager to be as far away from the fugitives as possible before they were recognized and captured.

Dagmara looked at Aynward. "What now?"

"I for one could go for a hot meal cooked over something other than a hastily built campfire."

"Is that wise?"

Aynward shrugged. "Long as we keep our heads down and don't do anything stupid, we should be okay, but I suppose I'm no more an expert at this than you."

"Then I say we get one hot meal and a room for the night, then work on finding our way further east. After the way our wagon was searched on the way in here, it's clear every city guard is on the lookout. I would guess we'll have to be just as careful getting out of here as we were getting in."

Aynward scooped a spoonful of barely warm stew into his mouth and tried to chew. There was no need, it was more like old porridge. "I long for that Scritlandian cook fire."

Dagmara took another reluctant spoonful of her own and remarked, "This is more fit for the trough of pigs."

Taking a sip from his glass, Aynward added, "This water isn't much better. Tastes like someone trapped a fart inside the cask before rolling it here from the river."

Dagmara spat out a mouthful of her own. "That's disgusting." She coughed. "I think I'm finished eating or drinking for the evening."

Aynward shook his head and continued working on his meal. "I'm too hungry to stop, but I'm still going to complain about it as I force it down."

The inn was located in the merchant quarter not far from the Kingdom road coming into the easternmost city, aptly named East End. The pair had agreed that while there was some risk in remaining within the vicinity of more crowded areas, they might stand out more if hiding out in less populated areas. At least at a place like this, filled as it was, they were just another pair of wayward travelers among many.

"How are the toes, by the way?" asked Dagmara.

The mention of this caused him to move them around in his boot. "Much better since the Van Oldas rebandaged them. I hardly notice them, to be honest." Prior to this, he had been growing worried about infection.

"Say, Dagmara, do you suppose we'll change the name of this city if we ever expand our borders further east?"

"I—yes? No. I don't know. Do you think we'll be expanding our borders any time soon?"

"Fair point," conceded Aynward. "But it's something to keep in mind. Were I king, I'd have my eye on that."

"Meanwhile, the Lugienese ravage the west coast . . ." mumbled Dagmara.

Aynward replied, "A king's eye should be ever focused on the present and the future, working to join the two as one."

"Your kingly wisdom is inspiring," mocked Dagmara.

The mention of kings brought an image of the gruesome death of his father, and Aynward regretted his own lighthearted comment. His mood soured and his hunger disappeared as he finished the last of his stew-flavored porridge. He stood. "Let's get some shut-eye."

They started toward their room through the crowd of patrons, but as they did, one spoke to another loud enough for anyone within ten paces to hear in spite of the background noise. "Told you them Lugienese would test the new King sooner rather than later! Pay up!"

Aynward slowed in an attempt to hear more.

An elderly man sitting across the table scoffed, "You said they'd attack the coast, not slay the king!"

"Bah, still an attack, and he still failed just like I done said," responded the portly man whose words had initially caught Aynward's attention.

The thin elderly fellow shot back, "No one could have known they'd make dragons!"

"I still called it, and you still owe me!"

Dagmara interrupted their disagreement. "I'm terribly sorry to interject. We've been on the road. What news of the new king?"

The portly man regarded her. Dagmara was dressed in a dust-covered knee-length traveling cloak, worn-out field boots from the Van Odla Estate, and a pair of worker's trousers. She hadn't sounded *too* princessy.

Aynward still attempted to obscure his face just to be safe. The price on their heads was too high for anyone with a hunch to ignore.

The man finally answered, "Well, word is them Lugienese made some sort o' dragons and attacked the King on his retreat from Salmune. Rumor is he's as dead as his father."

Aynward heard the tremble in Dagmara's voice in spite of her efforts to hide it. "Why was the King on retreat?"

The man tilted his head. "You been on the road that long? Word reached us last week about the traitor, Duke Gafford. Yeah, marched his troops into the capital alongside a force of Lugienese—"

"And dragons! Don't forget the dragons," added the man beside him.

He rolled his eyes. "And dragons. The King ran before they even arrived, coward."

The old man interrupted from across the table. "Don't speak ill of the dead."

"What? I ain't speakin' anything that ain't true. The boy ran scared and wound up gettin' caught with his back turned."

The thin man shook his head. "I heard the King still lives, just been hurt real bad."

Dagmara then asked, "What about the rest of the Kingdom army? Were they also defeated?"

The portly fellow shook his head. "They've taken up position in Quinson and are rallying as many banner men as can be found. Duke Gafford is doing the same on behalf of the Lugienese. Apparently if you swear allegiance to the Empire and their god, they'll allow you to live life as normal. The duke has already convinced two other duchies to follow him in allying with the Lugienese, though I hear not all of their banner men are following the order to lay down arms."

Dagmara nodded and thanked the men for the information, then bade them farewell. Aynward took the long way around and they met up by the hallway to the rooms in the back.

They said nothing to each other until they reached their room.

Then Dagmara said, "We've got to do something."

Aynward stared at her, incredulous. "By doing something, you mean continue east and get out of this Kingdom like we previously planned, right?"

"Aynward! The Kingdom is crumbling, and Perja might well be dead."

"Yeah, all the more reason to leave as soon as possible. Whether he's dead or not, everyone still thinks I killed our father, and you helped me escape, which implicates you as well."

She took him by the shoulders and said firmly, "This is different. We're still part of the royal line. We have a responsibility to help."

"Um, you seem to be forgetting *at least* one important fact, my dear sister." He waited just long enough to make his point, but not long enough for her to fill the silence with words. "We. Are. Fugitives. If we show up—anywhere—we'll be arrested. On top of that, they'll allocate extra guards to keep me from escaping again, meaning less guards that could be fighting the bad guys. I don't see how that could possibly help the Kingdom."

"Well, what about your friend . . . the Tal-Don rider guy?"

"You mean . . . Kyllean?"

"Sure. I don't know. The only Tal-Don rider you met in Brinkwell. Didn't you say he returned home to join the Lumále riders?"

Aynward nodded slowly to emphasize his confusion. "Yes . . ."

Dagmara stared at him as if he should be able to read her mind, then let out an exasperated "Ugh. What if we can find him and—"

"And what?" interrupted Aynward. "Find him and ask him if he believes that I didn't kill my father? Maybe he would, maybe not, but we're still enemies of the Kingdom, still outlaws. Even if Kyllean believed our story, he'd be a brand-new recruit. He's not going to be able to exonerate us of our supposed crimes, especially mine. And he'll likely not even have his own Lumále. You know how long Father said it takes to earn one, and that's if any are even left to take on new riders."

She turned away from him. "Why do you have to be so negative all the time?"

"I'm not negative, I'm *realistic*. It just happens that our current situation is quite dire. Though if you consider where we were a few weeks ago, I'd say we've made great headway to improving our situation. I just don't want to throw that all away."

But he saw her shoulders moving up and down and knew she was crying. *Great. Just great.*

He stepped forward and put an arm around her. She turned and pushed him away. "I don't want your sympathy hugs!"

Well, I tried.

"I'm going to go double up on my evening meal."

"Do whatever you wish," she grumbled.

He turned and left without another word, knowing that whatever he said would just make it worse until she had cooled off. *She'll come to her senses.*

Aynward found an empty table toward the back and seated himself, then ordered an ale. *Hope the ale is better than the food.* As the server returned with a tall wooden cup frothing with his liquid dessert, he noticed four uniformed men enter the inn. Something about their arrival didn't sit right with him. "Say, Gertrude, was it?"

The server turned. "Yes?"

He lowered his voice. "Are those city watchmen?"

She turned back to have a look. "Why yes, they are. How odd."

"Sooo, I take it them being here is not normal?"

She shook her head confusedly. "No. Not particularly."

The watchmen had approached the bar and were signaling to be served. Then Aynward noticed the thin man who had spoken with Dagmara earlier was with them.

Aynward pulled the cowl of his hood and dug into his purse for the largest coin he had and shoved it into Gertrude's hand. "Think you could go distract the innkeeper with a question or two to keep him away from those watchmen for a few more moments?"

She considered, then said, "He's a mighty grumpy man. I'm gonna need a little—"

Aynward didn't have time to haggle. He shoved two more coins into her hand. "How's that?"

Her eyes widened and she smiled. "Come to think of it, I have *several* questions for the innkeeper."

She moved swiftly to intercept him just as he was being waved over by the barmaid who was speaking with the watchmen.

Aynward disappeared back into the hallway and opened the door to their room.

"We need to leave. Now."

"What?"

"Watchmen. Here. Grab your stuff and let's go."

Dagmara snatched up her pack and Aynward did the same. "Come on!"

They rushed to the back hallway and thanked the gods that there was a back door. It was locked with two bolts from the inside. That wasn't the issue, as they were easy enough to slide open; they just wouldn't be able to lock them from the outside. "They'll know we've gone this way, but we've no other choice. We're going to have to get out of the city before they alert the rest of the city watch."

They heard shouts from the inside just as they closed the door. They must have just reached their room and found it empty.

"Come on!"

They ran.

CHAPTER 54

DAGMARA

T HE NORTH GATE WAS, AS they had feared, well-guarded. That and the sun was setting so anyone leaving the city would already appear more suspicious.

Aynward whispered, "At the very least, they all seem to have their eyes trained outward on those attempting to enter, not those trying to leave." And the gate had not been closed for the evening, another mark of good fortune. It meant they didn't have to convince any of the guardsmen to open it for them.

The pair finished catching their breath after running the entire way from the inn, then calmly strode out the gate unopposed. "This is so much easier than I would have guessed," Dagmara whispered to Aynward.

"Hey!"

Sinner's below!

"Hey, you two. Stop right there!" shouted a man from atop the wall-walk.

They froze, then turned and removed their hoods. Dagmara had allowed her hair to remain unkempt so as to look less the part of a royal. It hadn't taken long on the road for the ordinary sheen to lose its glint.

"Identify yourselves, and your business beyond the city."

Aynward opened his arms wide in greeting and responded without hesitation. His voice sounded different, as did his diction.

"Gladly, my good sir. Name's Connor. Connor Don-Votro, and this is my cousin Sophie. We're headed back to Talmune for the evening, seeing as we live there and all."

"It's a bit late for travel. What was your business in the city?" He held a bow but had not trained it on either of them . . . yet. Three other guards had become interested in the conversation and now stood beside him, bows in hand.

Aynward maintained a tone of joviality as he said, "We were there to sample the new shipment of Van Odla wine, of course. Just arrived today. Splendid vintage, you should really give it a try. Can't get any at my usual watering hole, the Salty Bowl, so I may have spent a little longer sampling this evening, hence the late hour."

The guard glanced over at his compatriot who shrugged. "What do we care about rider folk returning home?"

The guard that had stopped them to begin said, "Very well. Be on your way. Safe travels."

The pair walked as calmly as they could until they reached the first bend in the road and the forest between the city of East End and the neighboring township of Talmune.

"We need to run. Those guards are going to puzzle out who we were once the city watch notifies them of an alleged sighting of the most wanted pair of fugitives in the Kingdom. And they're going to have horses."

Fortunately, Talmune was closer to East End than either of them had believed and they arrived before the sound of hooves.

Township seemed an exaggeration for the place, more like a village. This meant that it had no gates, which was good except for the fact that this also meant there would be fewer places to hide. There was just enough sunlight remaining to illuminate the fortress looming above the village built into the side of the rocky mountain. The silhouettes of flying creatures could be seen, but in the fading light Dagmara could not be certain if these were distant Lumáles or closer birds.

"Where to now?" she asked.

Aynward looked nervously from side to side. "No idea. Haven't managed to think that far ahead. My brain doesn't work quite as well when I can barely breathe."

The town was almost devoid of activity, but the smoke from chimneys and the glow of lamp lights indicated there were at least some people here.

Aynward said, "We can't very well barge into someone's home. And this place is small enough that the watchmen could realistically go from house to house until they find us."

Dagmara said, "Kyllean's parents' home?"

Aynward shrugged. "No idea which one it is."

Dagmara nodded. "We could always just ask someone."

"No way! What happens when the watchmen get here and start asking around to see—"

She stopped listening when she saw a woman crossing the street a few paces from where they were standing in the shadow of a barn. Dagmara shoved Aynward around the corner and whispered, "Shh. Stay here."

Dagmara turned and stepped into the dim light cast by the emerging moons and the streetlamps lining the single main route through the village.

"Excuse me, ma'am."

The woman appeared more curious than frightened by the sudden appearance of a person in a place where Dagmara guessed visitors were few. "Yes? What can I do for you, traveler?"

This is a promising start. "I'm looking for the residence of Kyllean Don-Votro, but I seem to have forgotten where it is. It was much lighter the last time I visited, and that was years ago."

The woman looked her up and down, then made a strange sound with her lips before saying, "If you're hoping to find Kyllean, I believe he's joined the riders." She pointed to the massive stone structure etched into the side of the mountainside half a day's ride away. "But as you may know, the Tal-Don fortress does not accept uninvited guests. Heather Tal-Don, his mother, lives right over there." She pointed to a small home wedged between two others. "You might leave a message and . . ." She looked about. "You alone?"

Dagmara shook her head. "My cousin has come with me. We've been mistaken for fugitives by the watch in East End so we're hoping to remain inconspicuous."

The woman tsked. "Watchmen. Useless. Well, if Heather doesn't offer hospitality, I have a room for you and your cousin. In fact, it might be best if you stayed with me for the evening and paid Heather a visit on the morn."

Dagmara considered this for only a moment before agreeing. "That would be wonderful. Thank you so much. We haven't much coin," she lied, "but we're happy to share what we do." Revealing how much they did have would make them appear far more suspicious.

The woman waved a hand. "Nonsense, I won't abide any of that. I'm not running an inn, I'm offering hospitality to weary travelers. Now go gather your cousin and come along. We'll make introductions and get you something to eat."

A heavy pounding on the door shook the home just as Dagmara was finally falling asleep. The knocking was relentless and the woman, Estelle, barked, "Gods above… save the skin on your knuckles, I'm coming!"

The home was modest, one large room that served as a kitchen and living space, then two small bedrooms, one of which was currently occupied by Dagmara and Aynward. They had both pulled out their weapons, as there was nowhere to hide if the watchmen were to search the home and no window in the room from which to escape if necessary.

Dagmara peered out from behind the bead curtain that served as the door to their room. Estelle opened the front door to two watchmen, though this didn't mean there weren't more outside.

"We're sorry to bother you, ma'am, but two fugitives were seen heading this way. They are believed to be the Kingslayer and his traitor sister, the Princess. We're conducting a search of every home to ensure that they aren't hiding out in one of them."

"Dear gods. Truly? Those fugitives? There's quite the reward set on their heads, is there not?"

She's going to turn us in. We're done for.

The guards looked at each other. "Yes. There is."

"Tell me now, if I happen to spot them, then provide this information to you, who would earn the reward?"

The men exchanged a confused expression. "I, well, suitable compensation would of course be provided to anyone who assisted in the capture."

Estelle brought a hand to her chin. "So I would be relying upon the word and honor of city watchmen from East End to divide up the reward should I know anything about these fugitives?"

"Uh, that is correct. Our honor is impeccable."

"Mmmhmm. That's why there is a no-search-and-seizure clause in place between the residents of Talmune and East End, a clause enforced by the Tal-Don fortress?"

The man stammered, then said, "There is a royal proclamation ordering the capture and return of these fugitives! We will be searching this home under the authority of the King himself."

"Listen here, East Enders. I am harboring no fugitives here. And you have no authority to do anything but take my word on this. But just in case you're feeling a little fresh, you should know that my husband is the captain of the Tal-Don riders, third division. His Lumále is a lovely creature, but quite protective when it comes to my husband's safety as well as my own. And I've had a *very* good look at the both of you. You have no authority to enter my home and it *will* require an assault on my body for you to do so. I can't imagine how my husband and his Lumále would react should they learn of an assault upon my body as a precursor to rummaging through my empty home in the middle of the night on a rumor about some renegade teenagers that *you* lost track of within your own city."

Neither one said anything, then one of the men took a step further into the doorway.

Here they come. Tecuix protect us.

Then the other guard put a hand on the man's shoulder. "This is all you, Gunthry. I'm not getting involved with a Tal-Don over this, a captain at that."

The man ended his approach and glared at Estelle, who stood defiantly mere inches away, arms crossed just waiting for him to knock her aside.

They stood frozen in a contest of wills for several heartbeats before the man finally turned and stormed out of the doorway. "Come on, let's keep checking. This hag isn't worth the time."

"I'll be sure to keep an eye out for them," she yelled after the watchmen as she shut the door and applied the lock.

Dagmara stood in disbelief, heart still beating as if she had been running for hours. Then she finally relaxed and laid her weapon down alongside Aynward's.

He whispered, "I can't believe she just did that."

They heard the floorboards creak as Estelle walked toward them. She stopped at the opening to the bedroom and whispered, "They're gone. We'll worry about getting you over to the home of Kyllean's mother tomorrow. Now get some sleep."

"Thank you," whispered Dagmara, but the woman said nothing further as she continued toward her own room next to theirs.

Estelle went out for a few hours the next morning after serving the pair an unremarkable morning meal of barley bread and gruel. She did have fresh butter, which was certainly an unexpected treat to accompany the otherwise bland bread.

She had closed the shutters and locked the door, but still insisted that the pair remain hidden in the room just to be safe.

When the door opened, Estelle carried a fresh wheel of cheese. "As I suspected, those mongrels from East End were driven out of town last evening not long after they attempted the same nonsense with Jared across the way. We don't take kindly to those Kingdom folk imposing on us here."

Dagmara gave a confused look.

Aynward explained, "Talmune has a distinctive arrangement within the Kingdom that grants them legal sovereignty, making its residents sort of apart from the jurisdiction of Kingdom patrols, or in this case city watchmen."

"Meaning?"

Estelle answered. "Meaning, if I go down to East End and steal something, the city watch can lawfully remove my hand in accordance with Kingdom and local law. And the same goes for one of them coming here and doing the same. But they can't come here lookin' to impose their laws on folks that are here, and vice versa."

Dagmara shook her head, confused. "So criminals can just come here to escape the laws of East End?"

Estelle shook her head. "We're a tight-knit group, mostly all related in some fashion or another. We're quite strict on residency and we have plenty enough folks here for our liking. Not that we necessarily dislike visitors or anything. But when city watchmen come barging in here demanding this or that, we're not obliged to help. Of course, if them folks had come here asking nicely for help in locating an escaped criminal, most of us would be happy to help out. But the way them men came here bangin' on doors at that hour was just plain impolite."

Dagmara understood that portion of the woman's rationale for not helping. She chuckled. "Thank the gods they didn't ask nicely."

Estelle smiled and shook her head. "If you're a friend of Kyllean's, I just as soon leave it to him to decide whether or not you're worth helping. He's a good lad and I trust he'll make the right choice regarding the two of you, much like he finally did when he decided to join the riders.

"Speaking of, I'm going to send you over to see his mother today before dusk; she'll be able to get in touch with him. In the meantime, I don't think it would be such a great idea to have you roaming about the village the very night after those thugs came about disturbing the peace in their effort to find you. It would only take one partisan. Plus, I suspect East End will have sent at least one spy of their own into town to keep an eye out. You will remain here until dusk. Understood?"

Dagmara and Aynward nodded enthusiastically. Aynward must have been just as shocked by Estelle's words as Dagmara because his mouth hung agape but no words flowed forth.

Dagmara finally said, "Thank you, Estelle. Truly."

The woman waved the thanks away and said, "I've got me some errands to run today. Stay out of sight while I'm out. If someone's sneaking about looking in windows, I'd rather them not see two strangers fitting the description of the fugitives that East End and the Kingdom are after."

❦❦❦

Aynward and Dagmara crept along the darkened street. They didn't have far to go. The home they sought was a mere fifty paces from where they had been staying. They had crossed the street and walked with hoods drawn. The street was empty so they walked along within the shadows, optimistic about reaching their destination without any complications.

They froze in place when a figure emerged from a side street, pretty certain they would not be seen unless this person were to walk right into them. Okay, no problem, *We'll just wait for—*

The man, she could now see that it was a man, walked right up to the very home they were supposed to visit. *Now what?*

"That's him," said Aynward excitedly.

"That's who?"

"Kyllean!"

The man had just passed into the home.

"Come on," said Aynward.

They remained cautious as they approached, taking it slow to ensure they weren't seen by anyone else. A woman and child emerged from cover and Aynward and Dagmara crouched down and waited until they had passed out of sight before continuing. A few more steps and Dagmara was able to peer into the window.

As she did, she grabbed Aynward's cloak. "Wait," she whispered.

"What?"

"It looks like . . . they're crying."

Aynward turned around and positioned himself so one eye could see in the window.

"What the . . . I think you're right. But why?"

Dagmara said, "Think we should wait?"

Aynward nodded. "Kyllean is not the crying sort so whatever this is about, it's bad."

CHAPTER 55

KYLLEAN

KYLLEAN HELD THE NOTE IN his hand, the one his father had given him before he had departed. He said he wrote such a note before every mission, but now that Kyllean was there, he would entrust him with the task of delivery should circumstances permit such. Kyllean did not feel honored, he felt burdened.

He knocked on the door to the home he had known his entire life, and Heather, the only woman he had ever known as a mother, opened the door and let him in. Her expression was grim. "What're you doing here?"

"Say, whatever happened to 'Hi, Kyllean, so nice to see you!'?" he said, unable to keep himself from joking in spite of the news he carried.

She glared at him as he closed the door behind him. "There's only two explanations for your being allowed to come here and you having already earned your first leave of absence is not the one I believe most likely. That means . . ."

He heard the faint crack in her voice even as she tried to be strong, tried to keep it from showing.

Kyllean sagged his head in defeat. No sense keeping the truth from her any longer than was necessary. "Can we at least have a seat first?"

She nodded and led him to the small kitchen table where she sank into a chair. He sat in the chair beside her, the one his father usually sat in. He didn't do it on purpose, but he realized the unspoken implication yet again and knew he needed to get on with the news.

"Father asked me to give this to you in the event that . . . he . . . didn't come back." His own voice betrayed him as he finished the statement and handed her the letter.

She took it but did not immediately open it. "So? What happened?" Her tone was such that he worried she believed he had something to do with the news.

Kyllean swallowed and managed to regain control of his voice. "The capital has been taken, betrayed by Duke Gafford, who marched his troops against Salmune alongside a contingent of Lugienese. King Perja fled the capital intending to rally his banner men in Quinson. However, the Lugienese sought to capture the King before he arrived in Quinson. King Perja called upon the riders to send aid the moment he fled Salmune. This is why Father left.

"The Lugienese created a magical bond to an Isles bird called a dordron and their battle between riders. They experienced heavy losses, but we too suffered. The King fell from a great height and his condition is currently not known to us, though rumor is that he lives."

Kyllean felt his voice choke as he prepared to deliver the news his mother had been waiting to hear, even though he knew she suspected it. "Father was among the fallen."

Heather appeared unmoved by the news, merely nodding her understanding. Kyllean knew she was putting up a front and respected her strength. He was having a difficult time holding himself together and knew that the moment she broke, so too would he.

She then cut the seal to the letter and unfolded the parchment.

Her eyes watered, and then she burst into a fit of angry sobs. "Damn him! Damn that man! To rip my heart out from beyond the grave!"

She crumbled the letter and flung it across the room then continued to sob. Kyllean moved to embrace her and she accepted his arms around her as he pulled her in tight. "I'm sorry, Mom. I'm so sorry." He too sobbed.

They cried together for a long time before she finally pushed to her feet. She wiped her puffy, red eyes, and somehow regained her composure, returning to her ordinary poised self.

"Well, Kyllean. You have your training to attend to. You've done what your father asked you to do. You now have a kingdom to defend, and a father to avenge."

He nodded. "I would like nothing more than to take the heads off a few hundred Lugienese, but if doing so means they've come here, I pray this never comes to pass."

She sniffled, clearing the last of her grief away and brushed the wet wrinkles from the apron she wore over her dress.

"Be careful, Kyllean."

Then she pulled him in for another hug and squeezed so tight he thought she might crack one of his ribs.

"I will."

"I love you, Kyllean. Love you as my own. You know that, right?"

"I love you too, Mom."

He turned without another word, wondering just what that letter had said to have upset her so. Father apologized for dying, of course. He probably gave her some recommendation on who to marry next. That was something his father would do. Then again, the more he had learned about his father in recent weeks, the less he knew about the man.

The sound of shouting rang out from the street as he approached the door. *What in the gods is going on out there at this hour?*

He threw open the door to see a dozen people standing in the dimly lit street. Kyllean worked to process the scene before him. Ten men stood with blades drawn squaring off against two others, a woman and . . .

"Aynward?"

The prince glanced over, which all but confirmed his identity as he said, "Say, you wouldn't happen to be hiding a dozen or so others in there willing to defend us against the city watch of East End would you?

I'd like to at least get the chance to explain to you that I didn't do what they say I did."

Kyllean knew he didn't have much time to act but drawing metal against men of the Kingdom in an attempt to assist a known fugitive wanted for killing the King was probably not a wise course so far as his career, or even freedom, was concerned. This should not be a decision made in haste . . .

CHAPTER 56

AYNWARD

AYNWARD WAS RELIEVED TO SEE his friend but had no idea how Kyllean would respond. He was asking for more than just an extra hand to lift a too-heavy object. He was asking Kyllean to commit treason.

Kyllean grimaced, then shook his head, but remained where he stood five paces away. Kyllean looked over at the watchmen and said, "Gentlemen, my name is Kyllean Don-Votro. I am a blade bearer and sworn protector of the realm." He reached into his scabbard and pulled free a shiny black blade as proof. To Aynward's further shock, he then pulled another sword, this one marbled white and black. They were both remarkable weapons. "Allow me to escort these two to the Tal-Don fortress to be turned over to justice."

A tall thin man, the one who had first shouted for them to come out from cover, took a step closer and spit. He growled, "To the bellows of Doréa with that. They're coming with us. And so's my reward."

Kyllean bore a glare that Aynward had never seen and his voice lacked its ordinary mirth. "You break the covenant between our people by coming here with weapons drawn. Stand down and I'll forgive the offense. Otherwise, you're going to learn just what a rider's blade can do

429

to a man who decides to test its edge. Mind you, I'm having a rough day so my patience is not quite as thick as normal. I would recommend choosing wisely and quickly before I start poking holes in people."

The man flinched at the mention of the rider's blade but did not show any signs of backing down. "We checked with legal before coming back today. Turns out that seeing as these two are wanted for treason against the crown, we're within our rights to collect. The warrant for treason supersedes all other codes and agreements."

Kyllean twirled both blades simultaneously then continued to simply glare.

The watchman swallowed hard. "Look, we've no quarrel with you. No desire to clash steel, but if you stand in our way, you will be dealt with in the same manner as the Kingslayer and his traitor sister."

Dagmara said, "Before we start painting the road with blood, perhaps we could come to a compromise?"

Everyone stopped what they were doing to stare at her.

The tall man tilted his head. "You're not in much of a position to negotiate anything besides an unconditional surrender."

She nodded. "Perhaps not, but if it means you not getting your throat slit by a trained blade bearer, perhaps you ought to consider my offer." The man continued to stare expectantly. "The bounty on me is twice the value if I'm brought in alive, you know that. So, I offer to come with you, willingly, if you allow my brother to go free."

No freaking way. "She's lying," said Aynward, hoping to end the madness before it was even considered.

"No, I'm not!" said Dagmara firmly. "I'm done running. They can't do much more than punish me with words at this point. I still need to be married off sometime, though I'm sure my value has decreased significantly. It's not worth you or anyone getting killed over. I'm done. This is the most responsible course." She tossed her sword to the ground and it skittered over to land at the feet of the leader of the watchmen.

Aynward gritted his teeth.

The watchmen all seemed on edge, ready to launch an attack, but curious about what their leader might say to the proposal.

"I agree to these terms."

Aynward's heart sank. *This is madness.* "Dagmara, no."

She stepped forward and Aynward reached and caught her wrist. "No. You're not turning yourself—"

She twisted her arm away and slipped out from his grip. A moment later she was standing within the group of armed men.

The leader smiled. "Cuff her."

Aynward took one step forward and eleven blades were raised in unison.

"Aynward, it's okay. Please. Just let me do this."

He held his sword, knuckles white, lacking the opportunity to vent his frustration.

As soon as Dagmara was cuffed, the leader grabbed the fabric of her cloak and pulled her to him. With one arm around her chest, he placed his sword against her throat. "Thank you, Your Grace. You've earned me a healthy retirement."

Aynward knew what this maggot was going to do next before he opened his mouth to continue. The weight of Aynward's steel grew unbearably heavy in an instant.

The man pulled her behind the others in the group who still held their weapons at the ready. "Drop the blades, both of you, or the princess dies."

Aynward's blood boiled, but what could he do? He had no choice but to comply. It was his life or Dagmara's.

He and Kyllean slowly bent to set their weapons on the ground. "That's good. Now, kick them over to us."

Just as Aynward brought his leg back to do so, he noted motion coming from behind where his sister and her captor stood. This was followed by a loud thud. The man toppled. In his place stood . . .

"Estelle? What're you doing?"

"Giving you a fighting chance. Now pick up your weapons."

Before Aynward had even processed what had happened, Kyllean dove forward, catching the hilts of both of his weapons in either hand as he rolled toward the watchmen. He sprang forward with inhuman speed and suddenly there was one less man on his feet.

Aynward reached down to retrieve his weapon, and by then another of the watchmen was down. To Aynward's further shock, Estelle had taken down another of the watchmen with her fireplace iron!

Dagmara had picked up the unconscious watchman's blade and hefted it before her in spite of her hands being cuffed together.

Aynward had no desire to kill anyone, but it was his life or theirs, and their honor had just been severely blemished. He engaged two watchmen and found them to be competent with their weapons. *How did Kyllean take down two of them already?* Glancing over, he changed that number to three. *I really need to learn what they're teaching him up there.*

He ducked an attack from the nearest watchman, then blocked one from the other as he took a step back. He circled away from the first in order to isolate his fight with just one of them at a time. This gave him the chance to launch an attack of his own, and his desperation fueled a riskier style than was normal for him. He was rewarded with his opponent's scream as his blade slid across the man's upper arm, causing him to drop his weapon. Aynward kicked him in the knee, then cut into his other leg. The man fell over. Aynward pivoted just as the other guardsman renewed his pursuit.

Aynward down blocked, then leaped forward. Risky, unorthodox, but effective. The man barely managed to block, but Aynward was close enough to create other problems for him. He released the grip on his blade with one hand and slammed his fist into the watchman's jaw.

Pain exploded from Aynward's knuckles, but his adversary was no longer on his feet. Scanning the scene before him, he found that only four of the original twelve watchmen remained upright, and another woman had joined the fight. Kyllean's mother bore a scimitar shaped much like Kyllean's own.

She dispatched her opponent, while Dagmara remained alive, but giving ground.

"Kyllean! Help my sister!"

Before Kyllean had a chance, Kyllean's mother was by her side and Aynward was drawn back into a fight of his own. Aynward's right hand stung with every swing, but this would have to be a problem for tomorrow. His advance put the next watchman on his heels, and Aynward felt the confidence of a swordsman fully in control. Every swing of the man's sword became predictable and Aynward backed him away from the others until the man could retreat no further for the building at his back. He tried to shuffle to the side, but Aynward sidestepped; there would be no escape.

To Aynward's shock, the man reversed his weapon and dropped to one knee. "I yield. Please, don't kill me."

Aynward stopped his next attack mid-swing. "That is an excellent choice. Now if only the rest of your—" Aynward stopped talking as he noted the man's grin, and the fact that he was looking behind Aynward. He didn't need to see what was coming.

Out of instinct, Aynward ducked and spun to meet the attack. He was too late. His movement prevented his head from being separated from the rest of his body, but the metal still bit deep into his shoulder, cutting toward the neck. An acute, fire-like sensation shot down his arm and he gasped. The shocking intensity of pain sapped the strength from Aynward's legs and he collapsed to the ground in a heap.

His weapon fell from his hand and he stared up at the night sky as the man he had punched in the jaw earlier brought his weapon to bear in what would be a killing blow. His weapon came down awkwardly, as the man's grip on it slipped. *That's strange,* Aynward thought as his hold on consciousness began to slip. The man fell to the side, and a woman holding an iron fire poker stepped past. Aynward heard a few yelps from the man who had yielded his weapon. Estelle was as formidable with the heavy iron tool as any of the warriors with a sword. But Aynward was unable to even thank her as the dizzying pain from his grievous wound consumed him.

CHAPTER 57

DAGMARA

"AYNWARD!" SHOUTED DAGMARA, ABANDONING HER own safety to run over to her brother.

Kyllean intercepted the last remaining watchman who in spite of the shifted odds had decided to try to bar her way. The watchman was on the ground moaning before Dagmara had even considered changing her mind.

Dagmara reached Aynward and felt a wave of despair roll across her entire body. His eyes were closed and blood was already soaking his clothes and pooling onto the cobbled street upon which he now lay.

She overheard Kyllean in the background yelling at the watchmen, most of whom were alive, but injured or unconscious: "Go on. Get out of here before I change my mind about letting you live. And don't you bother trying to come claim your *prize* at the fortress or I swear to you I'll finish what *you* started tonight!"

Estelle crouched alongside Dagmara. "We need to stop the bleeding and get him to a healer." She looked over to where Kyllean stood shoving along the injured watchmen, insults abounding as he did. Then she looked at his mother, and the plume of smoke coming from her home.

434

"Heather, get that blade of yours into the coals of your fire. We need to cauterize this wound now!"

She nodded and immediately set to work.

Estelle opened Aynward's cloak and pulled out a small knife to cut away at the fabric at his neck. "My Lady, fetch some cooking wine or spirits from Heather's home. We need to sanitize this wound." She cut a wide strip from the hem of her dress, folded it up, and pressed it against the wound.

Dagmara returned momentarily with a bottle of something. Estelle removed a blood-soaked bandage and shook her head in disgust. Then she poured the liquid over the wound. Aynward gave no reaction. Estelle handed another strip of folded fabric to Dagmara. "Press the wound as hard as you can until I return with Heather's blade."

Dagmara did as she was told and prayed to Tecuix. *Please God, you made him. Keep your creation from death's gates. This is not his time. I know it's not. Keep him from death's gate. This is not his time . . .*

Then Estelle stood before her with a sword, the top of which glowed red-hot. Dagmara was forced to look away as the woman pressed the metal against Aynward's wound. The sizzle of burning flesh was more than enough and the smell caused her to cover her mouth with the sleeve of her cloak.

"There is nothing more that I can do. You need to get him to a healer within the fortress. However, once inside, even if they are able to heal him, they may decide to turn you over to the Kingdom."

Dagmara nodded. "Saving his life now is more important. We'll have to risk it."

Heather said, "I have horses stabled nearby. Kyllean, go fetch Penny and Theopold, I'll explain the necessity to Gendry tomorrow."

Kyllean took one last long look at the remaining watchmen lying motionless upon the ground. "Think you can handle it if any of them wakes up while I'm gone?"

Estelle picked up the poker she had used earlier. "They will pose no problem for us once you are gone. Now go! Hurry!"

CHAPTER 58

GROBENNAR

GROBENNAR WAS WELCOMED INTO THE Great Hall of the God-king's temporary headquarters within the Count of Tung's former palace. This modest residence rested neatly along the Glass Sea skirting the southwest edge of the city, protected from aquatic invasion by a steep cliff.

Upon the long table rested a vast map of the continent of Drogen, which Grobennar had commandeered during his time in the city. This map was now decorated with small wooden carvings, colored to represent various troop locations, and even the variety of troops, be they cavalry, trained foot soldiers, Scritlandian orders of monks, or civilian militias. The airborne Lumáles even had wooden representatives upon the map.

The level of detail was astounding when compared with what Grobennar had been working with, and he said as much as he took in the sight.

Rajuban responded absentmindedly, "Yes, well, I have expanded my network of whisperers in recent months. Little of what goes on escapes the attention of myself or the God-king."

Magog waved a hand. "Enough gloating. Whatever your differences, we're on the precipice of eliminating the greatest threat to Klerós's plans. The destiny of our people rests in our hands. Let us see it fulfilled."

Grobennar didn't have to try to whisper an *I told you so* to Jaween about the lack of threat from Rajuban and the God-king. Jaween's silence throughout was enough to tell him the spirit understood.

The training ground for the dordron was no longer a secret in Tung, and Grobennar, Rajuban, and the God-king watched as the few dordron Grobennar had left behind practiced aerial maneuvers with their riders.

"Remarkable creatures, especially harnessed as they are by our priests," remarked Magog.

"They are," agreed Grobennar. "Gliding through the sky upon one's back is a wondrous treat. We should prepare one for you, Your Excellency. This would reduce travel time for you as the Lugienese borders bulge."

"I was thinking the very same thing," replied Magog. He smiled in a way that Grobennar had not seen in a long time, especially not toward him.

Rajuban did his best to sound unimpressed as he added, "Yes, though the clash with the Kingdom's Lumáles proves that the number of dordron and riders likewise trained and fitted to our cause remains grossly inadequate. We will need greater numbers by thrice at least if we are to neutralize the Tal-Don riders."

He was right on that point, Grobennar admitted. Then said, "Indeed. After all, the report purports that the Tal-Don weapons absorbed all of our magical attacks, as did the Lumáles themselves. Understanding how this works would help our cause greatly. Had I been given more time before departure, I would have had more to report on the matter, for I managed to take prisoner one such Tal-Don rider. I had plans to begin interrogating him the very day I was summoned. In the meantime, I should assist in converting more of the captured dordron, yes? Is there any way we could petition Klerós to add a few extra hours in the day?"

Magog chuckled but shook his head. "Your talents will be needed for things of greater importance. The inventor of the shovel does not spend his days laboring with it, he employs others to buy and sell his genius, then begins work developing something new so he might eventually retire to a large estate."

Grobennar understood then. "You want me to teach others how to alter and tame the dordron."

Magog nodded. "There is a very important mission to the east that will require a large force of dordron riders. Rajuban was able to reverse engineer the details of the magic collar used to control the beasts, and I have brought with me more than enough magical muscle to train as many riders as we have dordron. In fact, we've already begun this process. However, I'm told there is also a geographic restriction spell that prevents the dordron from entering Drogen?"

Even Rajuban was vexed by this problem. He interjected with a tone of confidence, "Given more time, I'm certain I would have puzzled it out."

Grobennar nodded. "Perhaps. Though taming the beasts was child's play in comparison to removing the barrier. It is no surprise that this skill escaped one whose talents are geared more toward in the art of deception and—"

The God-king waved a hand. "Enough chest-puffing, both of you."

Both priests ceased speaking.

Magog continued, "We have more than enough skilled priests. You, Grobennar, will show them how to do this thing. We cannot risk such an important secret being lost should some unforeseen evil befall you, especially during a time of war."

"He means to betray you. He's going to kill you!" warned Jaween.

Grobennar ignored Jaween, though he had the same concern. He replied simply, "Of course." Attempting to mask his fear, he added a dash of lighthearted humor. "So where, exactly, is this large retirement estate for the inventor located?"

Magog grinned. "In heaven."

Grobennar nodded. "Indeed . . ." and they both laughed just like old times, or at least Grobennar tried to. Unfortunately, his "old times" still included a very unwanted guest.

Grobennar had no desire to relinquish this secret about the dordron, a secret that gave him far greater value alive. Not that he had any proof of foul play. Still . . . he wasn't fool enough to believe that the winds of Rajuban's schemes and Magog's temper could not suddenly change. Then again, Magog could just as easily delve his mind for the secret. Even if Grobennar fought against such, he had no illusions about his ability to hold tight to something if he knew in the end his fate was death. He would sing like a good choirboy in order to earn the quick death. *My thoughts wander toward dark places,* he thought.

"*Your betrayal awaits,*" hissed Jaween.

Grobennar ignored Jaween. He had no other choice, anyway. "I will do this as soon as the priests are ready. It will likely require more than twenty of them, since most will be unable to successfully remove the barrier even with training."

Magog's eyebrows rose, causing the red scales lining his forehead to sparkle.

"They await you now."

That was fast, thought Grobennar. Too fast. "Very well, let us begin."

CHAPTER 59

SINDRI

ARELLA STOOD BESIDE SINDRI ALONG the starboard side of the ship, occasionally spotting land to the west as their transport hugged the coast through the Strait of Spirits. On the port side to the east lay the Hand of the Gods. Everyone knew the rumors. Ships that traveled too close often ran aground or simply disappeared. Whether this was because of dangerous hidden reefs, or something more of a popular debate for the inns where sailors frequented, the common belief was that ships were best to steer well clear.

What bothered Sindri at the moment, however, was the fact that the very same ship that had trailed them from Novaya was still following close behind. They had stopped to resupply in the city of Rey, a bay town whose existence solely depended on the limited trade between Novaya and the Luguinden cities to the south.

The sun crested the horizon the following morning to illuminate the white sails of this other ship like a beacon. Arella stole Sindri's thought. "That is the exact same ship that followed us from Novaya," she said. "To resupply and set sail on the same timeline seems more of a coincidence than I care to tolerate."

Sindri wholeheartedly agreed. "Let's speak with Taldar."

The merchant was nowhere to be found, likely sleeping off the effects of the bottle he had been carrying around since departing Rey the day before. Arella volunteered to rouse him.

Not long after, Arella "guided" a sleepy-eyed Taldar from the direction of his private quarters near the captain.

"What is this all about?" he protested, his free hand rubbing the sleep out of his eyes.

Arella let go of his sleeve once he was standing beside Sindri, then she pointed. "See that?"

He squinted, rubbing his eyes once again. "See what?"

"That ship?" said Arella, her voice indicating a loss of patience.

He looked out, then nodded. "Well, sure. What of it?"

Arella's eyes widened. "It's been following us since Novaya. Don't you think we should be doing something about that?"

Taldar's brow furrowed in confusion. "What would we do? That is my other hired ship. Did I not mention that already?"

Arella and Sindri looked at each other, then back at Taldar. Sindri beat Arella to it. "Your *other* hired ship? No, you did *not* mention that."

He chuckled innocently. "Hmm. Well, yes. I've hired two of them. They're both coming with us to the Cursed Isles . . . just in case the treasure we find is too great for one ship to haul alone. There's also the added security in case something untoward happens upon this ship. Can't be too careful these days."

Both women stared speechless until Taldar spoke again. "Was that the entirety of your emergency? If so, I would like to return to my rest. Any other concerns or paranoia you'd like me to put to rest?"

Arella finally grumbled, "Enjoy the rest of your nap."

He stretched his arms and yawned. "Yes, yes. Very good, then."

When he was beyond earshot, Arella said, "I told you there was something off about this whole thing, and this proves it."

Sindri agreed it was strange, but that didn't necessarily prove ill intent. "Yes, he has strangeness. But now we know this ship that follows us is not of a bad intention. Mystery is solved. I must get back to my training."

The closer they drew to the Cursed Isles, the more apprehensive Sindri became. Her control of ateré magic had not reached the level of control she had known as a Klerósi priestess, and she knew very well that the women who had stolen away with Kibure were masters. As much as she wished to find Kibure, she wasn't confident that finding him and rescuing him would go hand in hand, especially now that Draílock had all but abandoned them. The closer she drew to Kibure, the further away she felt. Yet something in her gut told her that this would be her last chance. Should she fail here, all would be lost. And so she continued to train.

One benefit of them being onboard a ship far away from any known civilization was that she no longer needed to worry about exposing herself to any who might wish her harm. No one would notice her use of magic, and the crew had been made afraid of them once it was discovered that she and Arella were sorceresses. This kept the crew's inevitable desires of the flesh at bay.

Sindri had been given permission by Taldar to use the leftover straw from the crates of consumed spirits and food. He had merely given her a puzzled expression before nodding yes and walking off mumbling obscenities about the dark arts.

Sindri stepped onto the empty quarterdeck, supplies in hand, and lined up the makeshift targets of straw across the port side of the deck. She stood at the stern and withdrew six coins. She stared out at the ripples of disturbed water in the ship's wake and her mind went to her own trail of destruction. Her quest for understanding and vengeance after the murder of her brother by Emperor Magog was littered with collateral damage. Galdred was merely the most recent addition. Tears formed as she looked back at all she had done in the name of vengeance and redemption. Then she squeezed the coins in her hands and shook her head. "Let none of them have died in vain," she whispered to herself. The wrongness of the statement raked at her nerves, but she swallowed her shame and resumed focus on the task at hand.

Sindri closed her eyes and emptied her lungs completely. She waited until her lungs burned, then tossed the coins behind her. She opened her mind to the innate power around her, searching for the metal of the coins as they moved through the air. Reaching her mind's eye into the essence of this power, she breathed in and pulled. Before the first clang of metal struck the wood, she was prepared to turn the energy of these coins upon her foe. She spun and opened her eyes, then sent a bolt of energy zipping toward the first bundle of straw. It exploded in a spray of yellow fragments so small the area became a cloud of yellow floating particles quickly dispersed by the breeze.

She repeated this process a dozen times, increasing the number of coins with each attempt. "Okay, let's try for twenty-one," she said out loud to herself. But this time as she tossed the coins and spun, she sensed magic to her right and used the power to create an angled wall of air, which deflected the attack as she rolled out of the way. She came up with a dagger in hand, but managed another magical defense, which deflected the second attack. She sent a magical retort of her own, then spun out of the way of the returned fire. This time, instead of deflecting, she sent a thin blast of air. This seemed to catch her opponent off guard, forcing them to pivot out of the way.

A succession of four modest hand claps followed. "You're improving," mused Arella.

Sindri nodded and said grimly, "I have of the hope that Kibure's captors will agree."

CHAPTER 60

SINDRI

"WHY THE ODD EXPRESSION?" ASKED Arella.

"I . . . what do you mean?"

Arella smiled. "You wear a pensive, almost nostalgic, expression. I just wonder what causes this."

Sindri considered for a moment, then said, "We have followed of small hope to find of Kibure for much time. I don't think I was of the belief that we would actually find of him. Now it is happening. We have found of him and I feel more nerves for failing."

Arella smiled. "Do you know why it is so difficult to defeat a great champion in a fight?"

Sindri rolled her eyes. "Because they are better."

Arella shrugged. "Perhaps sometimes. But they often continue to defeat foes long past their prime, foes who are in fact better fighters. This is because when the opportunity is finally presented to the challenger, when the opening is finally there, most hesitate in that instant because of their disbelief, or because they had not prepared their minds for the reality that it could happen. The sudden fear of failing becomes so powerful that by the time they move to capitalize on the opportunity, the moment has passed and the weight of having missed it only serves to

444

further confirm their original doubts. This missed opportunity almost deifies the opponent. The challenger later says, 'I was right there, but I still failed. The gods must have ordained it to happen in this way.'"

Sindri stared at Arella, wondering what her past held that she could understand such a phenomenon so perfectly. Sindri identified immediately with what Arella said, for she could recall her days of training, losing to opponents not because they were better, but because she had believed them to be better. It had taken many unnecessary beatings before she had learned to trust in her own abilities as a wielder, and fighter. Had Arella experienced something similar in her own training with Draílock or Dwapek? And did this same concept apply here and now? She did not think they were the same. "You say of these words as if you know this thing, but you do not."

The warm, salty breeze swept across the deck and blew Arella's blond hair into her eyes, but she brushed it back with a hand and smiled. "I trained in Scritler under Dwapek for a time, and then further with Draílock once we followed Dwapek to the Isles. They are both formidable, but not invincible, and it took me a long time to learn this thing about them, but more so, about myself. You would do well to learn the same. It may save your life someday."

Arella hopped out of the tiny fishing boat they had used to paddle from the anchored ship to the shore and pulled it up onto the white sandy beach.

Sindri stepped out and felt the warm, fine sand pool around the toes in her sandals. By all appearances, this island was nothing but jungle. They had circled the entire thing twice while Arella confirmed that it was the one they wanted. There were other islands, just as the pirate's diary had suggested when they lost the women they had been chasing, but Arella insisted that this one was it. Sindri attempted to feel for the use of magic but felt only the residual magic of her local surroundings.

Arella stood on the beach facing the thick vegetation of the forest before them and said, "Do you sense it?"

Sindri extended a hand and closed her eyes. Nothing seemed amiss so she opened her eyes and looked over to Arella who said, "The magic used here is quite clever. These weaves are so smooth, they radiate almost no magic whatsoever."

"I still sense nothing," said Sindri, shrugging her shoulders. *Not that it matters.*

Arella nodded. "That is precisely the point. It's even more obvious now that we're closer."

Go on, thought Sindri.

"They have concealed their magic so well that sensing the magic itself is not possible. It's not unlike what Draílock did to protect the room where he first taught you and Kibure back in Brinkwell. Only, this is an entire forest, on an entire island. The scale of such a project seems impossible. I can't sense the magic, but I can detect the absence of residual energy, which is an indication that it's being hidden. The collective strength needed to create such a net is . . . almost unthinkable. We are going to need to tread carefully."

Sindri's heart thumped hard in her chest at Arella's words. They had come so far. To have this opportunity slip through her fingers now would be a cruelty from which she didn't believe she would recover.

Sindri followed the sorceress to the edge of the forest, at which point she led the way along the threshold.

"If it were me, I would make whatever entrance exists difficult to find. And filled with traps," said Arella. "There is a reason why these Isles are referred to as the 'cursed,' and it's more than just the fact that any ship to sail much further east of them seldom returns."

They spent the entire day walking the shoreline looking for a way into the forest besides blunt force, but the vegetation was seamlessly dense throughout. They stopped at a piece of thick driftwood close to where they had begun, and Sindri slumped beside it in the sand. "We don't have enough of food to walk the beach for days."

Arella looked at Sindri. "You are right, but I would rather not have gone all this way only to stick my foot in a bear trap and die within reach of the prize."

Sindri rolled her eyes. "Yes, but you heard of the captain. He waits only three days. And what happens of us if he decides to leave early? I do not wish to die slowly of the starvation. Better a quick death."

Arella smiled sadly. "A fair point, Sindri. This place is heavily enchanted, we know that much. So as they say," she changed her voice to mock the stoic wizard, Draílock, "a job worth doing, is a job worth doing well," then continued in her own voice: "I suppose we do need to begin the 'doing' part."

Sindri stood and brushed the white sand from her Scritlandian robes and followed Arella to the edge of the forest. Arella paused, then gestured with a hand. "Well? Would you like the honors?"

As pleased as Sindri was to be finally *doing* something, her fear of failure returned in full, her legs becoming laden with nervous energy as she stepped into the unnaturally thick vegetation.

CHAPTER 61

KIBURE

KIBURE OPENED HIS EYES TO a cream-colored ceiling, lit in the soft-white luminescence common to this strange underground world. He turned his head and saw Drymus, seated in a chair, knitting something with needle and yarn beside his own plush bed.

"Ah," she said, "the prophesied redeemer stirs."

That statement brought back Kibure's memory of what had happened with the kosmí. Except, he didn't know what had happened, other than he had passed out and awakened here.

"Wh—what happened?"

Without looking up from her work, Drymus said, "You drew upon the kosmí, then released a surge of power that destroyed the entire council chambers, the surrounding structures, and would have killed every single person in attendance had I not constructed a shield around you to redirect the worst of it upward instead of out."

She spoke as if recounting a childhood memory of no significance whatsoever.

"No one was killed?" He held his breath as he awaited the answer.

"No. Several are still recovering from their injuries."

"There was just so much . . ."

"Power?" she finished for him.

He nodded. "I felt like I could have moved the entire world, though I might just as likely have blown it to bits. Attempting to fit so much into my mind at once was impossible. It would have destroyed me, I'm sure of it."

She nodded and her voice showed signs of disapproval. "I warned them against testing this before I had time to train you further, but they insisted, as if you returning the seed to the physical realm weren't proof enough. The good news is I think they may actually listen to me next time they suggest something as foolish as giving an untrained wizard access to an object of such vast power. But at least now we know with the utmost certainty that you are the one we sought."

That confirmation should have been comforting, and in some ways it felt good to be told that he was important. But it also carried with it the responsibility to live up to the expectation set by prophecy, and that terrified him.

"What now?" he asked, concerned that he might be asked to wield the stone again.

Drymus finally met his gaze. "Now you need to learn how to truly wield magic. And you need to learn quickly. We lost several days to this little nap of yours."

"Days?"

She nodded. "After what you just did, I'm surprised it wasn't longer. And had you not been touching the kosmí when you wielded its power, you would have surely died."

He sat up and felt surprisingly well. "Why would touching it matter?"

She reached up and took hold of the gemstone necklace she wore. "Whenever you channel power, your body defaults to the hardest object directly connected to it. This is ordinarily your bones. That's what makes it easy to injure oneself if too much power is wielded at a given time. To diminish these effects, you can carry something with you that is harder than your bones, like, say, a gemstone ring. Not only can you wield its power if it's touching you directly, but also your body will default to the remaining power within said object before moving to draw upon your bones. Bear in mind, this has a limited effect. If you wield more power in a short period than can be handled by the given object, the rest is still pushed onto your bones.

"Your issue was not so much the bone density as it was a shock to the portion of your brain that channels magic. Attempting to wield so much power was like attempting to lift a tree with a rope of twine. It doesn't matter how strong the person pulling the rope is, the rope itself was not strong enough. Your mind, your will, these are not strong enough. Not yet."

She set her knitting on a small table beside his bed and stood. "The good news about this brush with death is that I suspect it stretched your reservoir greatly. As they say, whatever doesn't kill you, makes you stronger. However, like a tree grows, it would be better to strengthen you in a more gradual manner." She waved a hand. "Come along. We're going to do some magic!"

Something about her demeanor had changed. He couldn't quite place it, but she certainly seemed a little bit less . . . terrible. He stood on legs that felt fresh, even strong, and followed. His cheerful mood darkened as she escorted him back toward the darkness of his former residence within the cave.

"Not to worry, I won't force you to remain here any longer. But for now, this is a safe place within which to train you on the finer manipulations of your power. Strength of will and the ability to draw power from the kosmí will not be the only requirements for completing the task your future requires of you."

She turned to face him once standing in the center of the cave, the orb of light she had used to guide the way floating from one hand to the other. "I seem to recall you creating your own version of light, right before you sent that blast of air straight for me."

Kibure shrugged. "I didn't know you were coming."

She rolled her eyes. "Create the orb of light again. This time we're going to make sure it doesn't look so pathetic, and you're going to only draw a measured amount of power from the rocks around you, not the heap you did last time."

"Less power!" shouted Drymus. "Less power!" She was shielding her eyes. "I don't fancy the idea of losing what's left of my vision!"

"Sorry." Kibure managed to dampen his orb of light to a brightness that matched Drymus's own.

"Well, it's safe to say that you're able to focus your energy. Which means you're ready to begin learning the skills that mark your ultimate purpose for our people."

Kibure was both proud of his mastery, and trepidatious about moving on to more serious tasks.

Drymus held out a hand and waited for Kibure to take what she held within. He did so and she dropped a small pebble into his hand. *No, not a pebble,* he realized. *A seed.*

"Today, you are a farmer."

Kibure froze, the word returning images of a recent dream, one he did not wish to recall. The way Magog's horrible eyes had bored into him with such malevolence, and the terrible, powerful laughter of the storm, both remained vivid in his mind. He shook off the images as best he could and returned his attention to Drymus. "So, what do I do with this seed?"

"Send some of your power directly into it."

He reached his mind into the reservoir he had drawn from the cave around him and did as he was asked, sending a fragment of power into the seed. Nothing appeared to happen.

"More," she said calmly.

He sent an additional wave at the seed, but still nothing changed.

Am I doing it wrong? He added more energy to the flow and pushed that into the seed. He was rewarded with the slightest movement in his hand and saw that the very top of the seed had split open to reveal a tiny green tendril of life sprouting from within, and then it stopped.

"Whoa," whispered Kibure. He pushed more energy into the seed, much more than what he streamed into the orb of light that hovered above him.

Green life extended from the seed, then it split fully open as roots shot out from the bottom, wrapping around his hand up his fingers, and then his entire arm, strangling every one of his limbs like a vine. Then the plant extended itself toward his face as it sprouted leaves, and those leaves panned out and soon Drymus was gone from sight, blocked by dozens of fist-sized green growths.

"Stop."

Kibure ceased the flow of magic.

The no longer visible Drymus said, "You've managed the easy part, but do you notice any problems?"

Kibure nodded, then realized she wouldn't be able to see this. He took his free hand and pushed the growth out of his face so he could resume eye contact with Drymus. "This tree, or whatever it is, appears to not be growing up like it's supposed to."

Drymus nodded. "And this is why we must now get into the intricacies of growing plant life, with magic."

She extended her own hand and Kibure sensed the tingle of her magic as she poured it into the seed in her own hand. The plant acted similarly to his, only it grew up from her hand like one might expect in nature. She continued until it was half her height, nearly touching the ceiling.

"Plants are not sentient, but they have a natural drive to seek sustenance in order to survive. Toward that end, their roots know to dig into the ground in search of water and nutrients, while leaves attempt to find the sun. But when a person feeds a seed magic, but doesn't direct its growth, the plant doesn't know any better than to treat the user like it would soil and sun."

She crouched and the roots of the small tree released their grip on her hand, extending instead toward the ground. She slid her hand out from beneath and the roots flattened out until the trunk of the small tree touched the cave floor.

Standing, she said, "When growing a seed, you need not only feed it energy, you must also guide the seed's use of this energy. Growing a plant is like giving someone a sword; no matter your intentions, without the proper training, that person is more apt to harm themselves with the blade than do any real good."

She gestured with a hand. "As you can see, your plant believes you to be its source of sustenance and its growth reflects such. Reach your mind into the energy of this seedling and tell it what you want it to do."

Kibure extended his mind into the line of energy held within his plant and began sending in more, only now he followed this energy to its end and willed its growth forward. A few moments later, he stood, gaping at his creation.

Drymus chuckled. "That might be the ugliest tree I've ever seen anyone grow."

Kibure shrugged, not disagreeing with her assessment in the least. He understood the principle, and had fed and directed, but his deftness was still lacking so the result was roots that curled up at their ends at odd angles as Kibure had begun focusing on the top of the tree. The trunk too had suffered, growing uneven and tilted, topped with several jagged branches, leaves budding in sporadic patches everywhere except the ends of the branches.

"It's a start," Drymus reluctantly concluded. "Come along, you're going to watch a few of our more skilled artificers of this magic as they work in the communal garden. You will spend the remainder of the day there. I want you to send your mind into their creations to feel the way they inject their targets with power. You will join them tomorrow in growing something of your own."

CHAPTER 62

KYLLEAN

KYLLEAN POUNDED ON THE GATE. "Open up! Now! It's urgent!"

A loud voice boomed from the top of the ramparts, "Identify yourself and your business."

Kyllean backed up his horse so the two guards could see who he was.

"Kyllean Don-Votro." He waved his rider sword as further confirmation. This would allow him to bring guests into the fortress. "I bring two friends, one of whom is gravely injured so open this door now! He needs a healer!"

The door opened more slowly than he had ever recalled. *Come on.* When the horses were finally able to squeeze beneath the portcullis, Kyllean said, "I'm still new here. How do I get him to the healer?" He had heard mentions of a healer within the walls but had not yet been injured enough to need them.

The guard, Kyllean thought his name might be Briggs, or Brags, something like that, pointed to the left. "The healer has a room in the west wing of the citadel, but I can't guarantee she'll heal someone without the Tal-Don blood. You might be better off taking your friend to the general infirmary located beside the adjoining passage between the initiate and rider training arenas."

454

"Thanks," he said, then yelled to Dagmara, "Come on. Follow me." He urged his mount through the inner gate and straight toward the citadel. The situation was too dire to care at all for decorum. He brought his horse right up the steps and into the citadel. He dismounted only when he reached the first hallway too short to accommodate their animals.

Kyllean waited for Dagmara to dismount so she could help him get Aynward's limp form to the ground. The fugitive prince's breathing was shallow, deathly. "Stay with Aynward, I'm going to get the healer. I'll be back as soon as I can. Aynward told me you're quite religious. I suggest you begin praying in earnest."

She snapped, "Stop talking and go!"

Kyllean took off at a run down the hall. He had yet to see a single person, which was not unusual, but Aynward could not afford to wait while Kyllean searched every room of the citadel. "Help! Healer, I need a healer, help!" he yelled down the hall.

He had only been into the citadel twice and had no sense of its layout or design, he knew only that it was vast. The hallway took unexpected turns at slight angles as he progressed. The first two doors he found were locked. The third opened to an empty room with just a table, chairs, and a window looking out on the training grounds. Under different circumstances he might have admired the view, but with the situation as it was, he turned and darted back into the hallway, shouting once again.

At long last, a woman down the hall opened a door and peered out, looking both ways in search of the source of the disturbance. They locked eyes and Kyllean yelled to her, "Healer! Where's the healer?"

The pale, middle-aged woman dressed in a plain wool robe stepped out into the hallway and said in a soft, accented voice, "I am the healer. How may I assist you?"

Kyllean stopped running, still a dozen paces away. "Well . . . by . . . you know . . . healing!" he stammered exasperated. "This way. He's in the . . ." He didn't know if the room had a name. "The big room back this way!" He waved his hands, but the woman did not move. She turned and disappeared back into the room, though she left the door open.

Kyllean sprinted to retrieve her. "Hey! What are you doing? My friend is dying!"

He turned into the doorway and was forced to go sideways to avoid slamming full force into the woman, who was reemerging from the room carrying a bag. Probably medical supplies, he supposed stupidly. Kyllean attempted to recover some sense of not being a total crazy person and said, "I . . . can I . . . I'll carry your bag. We need to hurry."

The woman continued walking without a reaction besides holding out the bag for him to take. He did so, and then ran. He stopped when he looked back to see that the woman continued at a walk. "A little urgency would be great!"

The woman's pace remained steady. "I do not run unless chased," she said without any show of emotion. She just stated the fact, leaving no room for discussion. But Kyllean was desperate.

"Well, then by all means, lead the way and I'll chase you. I can brandish a sword if that'll help."

She stopped walking and turned to look him in the eyes. "Do you wish me to heal your friend?"

Kyllean was ready to scream at the fact that she was no longer moving toward Aynward. He responded frantically. "Yes!"

"Then speak only of your friend's condition and how he or she came to such a state. When we arrive, I will be better able to assist."

Kyllean did so, teeth grinding between words at his lack of control over what was happening. Aynward's life was completely at this woman's mercy.

They found Dagmara kneeling beside Aynward in prayer. She didn't move until the woman knelt alongside her and placed a hand upon Aynward's chest.

The woman looked back up, an accusatory expression upon her face. "He is not a rider."

Kyllean shrugged. "So? Is that a problem?"

She didn't respond immediately; her attention had returned to Aynward, which Kyllean figured was a good sign. Then he felt the tingle of magic. He figured that might be an even better sign. Then she tilted her head to the side and let out a soft gasp.

"What is it?" Kyllean asked, afraid something terrible had been discovered about his wound.

"He is of the line of Dowe."

Then she looked up and her eyes moved over Dagmara. "Ah, I see."

No one spoke for a time as she continued to run her hand along Aynward's wound, but Kyllean met Dagmara's gaze. They both knew the woman knew exactly who they were. Kyllean supposed the same was sure to happen the second officials from East End arrived, demanding that the fugitives be handed over. They might even demand his own head for his part in injuring so many of their own.

"Hand me the bag."

Kyllean handed it over and she rummaged through it until she found a small bottle. She uncorked it and poured droplets of liquid onto the wound. Then she corked the bottle and brought her hand to touch the deep gash. The tingle of magic increased and Kyllean watched in wonder as the wound slowly closed, until all that remained was a faint red line where moments ago had been a gaping chasm in Aynward's flesh.

She removed her hand, then sat breathing heavily as if she had just finished a race and needed to catch her breath.

"You will need to help me return to my room."

"I'm sorry, what?"

"Your friend's wound was grievous. It required more energy than I am used to wielding in such a short span. I would ordinarily have healed him to a lesser degree, leaving his body to finish the rest, but I suspect these two will be leaving very soon no matter anyone's advice to do otherwise. I have overtaxed myself."

"So you're not going to tell anyone who they are?"

The woman shrugged. "Not my place, though anyone with a head between their shoulders will know who they are in short order. I would suggest getting them far away from here as quickly as possible, though the boy is going to be weak for some time."

Dagmara rushed over and hugged the healer, who was struggling just to stand and tried her best to push the hug away.

"Thank you so much for saving my brother. I . . . I didn't even get your name."

"I am Lillith."

Dagmara helped the healer the rest of the way to her feet. "Thank you, Lillith. Truly, thank you."

Kyllean echoed his own thanks as he placed an arm around Lillith's waist while draping her arm over his shoulder as he prepared to return her to her room. Just then, Aynward stirred and opened his eyes slowly. Kyllean turned around with the healer.

Kyllean saw the confusion in his eyes at being somewhere completely at odds with the last thing he recalled. Aynward looked around, absorbing his surroundings until his eyes landed on the woman beside Kyllean.

He spoke in a raspy voice. "You . . . you're one of *them* aren't you?"

Kyllean turned to regard the woman, confused by Aynward's statement. Lillith smiled back at him. "You've just woken up from being healed of a deadly wound. I suspect you'll be confused for some time."

Aynward was having none of her deflection. "The insignia on your chest. Your complexion, your accent."

Kyllean noticed, then, the silver robe beneath the woolen shawl. The sigil was now visible though he couldn't place it. He also couldn't think of a reason why it could possibly matter. Lillith had just healed Aynward. What did he care for her affiliation?

"Your sisters. They stole away with a boy back in Brinkwell, some sort of wielder. And those strange performances . . . who are you and what business have you here with the riders?"

Kyllean recalled the performance he had seen in Brinkwell, which, thinking back to the mention of the wolf and the warning, now appeared to have been a warning to the city. He also recalled Sindri, Draílock, and Arella stating their intentions to track down the missing boy. He didn't see what Lillith could have to do with that, even if she was somehow related to those women.

The healer smiled and said, "You'll need to be leaving soon if you're to climb to safety." She closed her eyes for a moment, then opened them and turned to look at Dagmara and nodded, as if understanding something more. "Embrace what is to come and you may yet survive." She squeezed Kyllean's waist with her arm. "I need to rest. Return me to my room." Then to the others, she added, "I wish you safe travels, line of Dowe."

She started trying to walk and Kyllean had little choice but to follow along as her crutch.

"Wait, climb to safety? What does that even mean? Who are you?"

The brittle woman laughed. "Just a healer cursed with eyes to see what is before me."

Kyllean looked back to his friends. "I'll just be a minute. Don't go anywhere or do anything until I get back."

When they arrived at Lillith's room, Kyllean said, "Where to?"

"The bed will be fine. I just need to lie down for a while."

He helped her over, noting the large, messy room filled with vials, books, and scrolls. It was something like what he guessed Counselor Dwapek's rooms might have looked like back in Brinkwell. The thought returned him to the present danger facing Aynward and Dagmara. He needed to leave. As he stepped out into the hallway, the healer's soft voice drifted out behind him, "Do not despair, a part of your father lives on through you."

Kyllean whirled, angry and confused. He strode back toward the bed. "What is that supposed to mean?"

She smiled and her voice was a mere whisper as she answered, "Cling to this knowledge in the dark days to come." Her eyes closed and did not reopen, though she continued to breathe.

Kyllean stormed into the hallway, his feelings of gratitude at Aynward's survival dampened by the reminder of his father's death and the ominous words of Lillith the healer.

CHAPTER 63

KIBURE

YOU ARE A DIFFICULT PERSON to pin down these days, Mr. Savior."
The voice snaked its way into Kibure's room where he rested after another long day of seed growing. "Working you hard, are they?"

Kibure had not 'heard' this voice before, not in the physical realm. Yet he recognized it, he knew this woman even before she stepped through the door.

Arabelle.

She had already mastered the smooth gliding gate of the other women and used this to great effect as she drifted into the room. Arabelle was one of the few women in Purgemon still clinging to any visual signs of youth before ascending to the agelessness of most of the city's occupants. Small dimples in her cheeks when she smirked, a sliver less definition in the muscles of her exposed arms, and the gentleness around her crystal blue eyes all did their part to distinguish her from the others. Her black hair flowed to the rhythm of her soft steps., while her milk-white skin glowed in the unnatural yellow light, adding a sense of warmth that hadn't been visible from within the spiritual realm. There was simply something more genuine about seeing her in color, hearing her soft footsteps, her voice with a slight rasp to it. Kibure felt his pulse quicken, which was difficult to reconcile. *What's happening to me?*

Kibure scooched himself up to a seated position upon his bed, eyes glued to the approaching form, and then it struck him. *This woman is...beautiful.*

"Well?" She asked.

Oh right, working me hard, yes. "Yeah, sorry. Very busy. Drymus has been teaching me to—"

She looked from side to side. "You need to come with me."

Confused, Kibure asked, "Why? Where are we going?"

Arabelle's face was stone. "I'm here to collect on your promise to me before it's too late. Meet me in the spiritual realm by the entrance to the garden. I'll be there in a few moments. There's one thing I must do first."

She disappeared out the door and Kibure exhaled loudly. He took a moment to collect himself, then closed his eyes. I have a promise to keep. He focused his attention on the space within his mind, the crossroads, then dove inside.

He stared out at the flowing walkways that wound through the beds of fruits and flowers. Without much effort, he floated into the air to gain a better vantage. His control was continuing to grow both here and in the physical world. His abilities in the spiritual realm had increased dramatically once he understood that the rules of the physical world only applied here insomuch as the mind's understanding of belief in these rules might limit that person. If he could perceive himself floating through the air, then that is what he did. There had been an exception to this rule regarding the seed, and of course, the barrier constructed around the cavern, but these were not the norm. In general, people walked on the ground within this place merely because it was what the mind expected them to do. But he now saw that whatever force of nature kept people planted upon Doréa in the physical world was no more real in this place than his thought that an orb of light should suddenly burst into being upon his hand, or that he could disappear and reappear with a thought.

"Are you finished pretending to be a bird?" Arabelle spoke into his mind from below.

Kibure looked down, then lowered himself gently. *"What else was I supposed to do while I waited? What were you doing, anyhow?"*

"Nothing important. C'mon, we haven't much time."

Why the rush? Kibure kept this last question to himself.

She led him to the edge of the underground city beside an orchard of fruit trees, though unlike with drogal, they grew a fruit that could simply be plucked and eaten. But they were not here for fruit. Kibure followed Arabelle toward a space between two trees, each the width of a small dwelling, then she touched the stone wall with a hand. *"Here. This is where we make our doorway out."*

"How do you know? And just how, exactly, are we to accomplish this?"

"This is a seldom-used exit from the city, guarded only in the physical realm."

She pointed at a ripple in the air that Kibure presumed was one of the women walking by.

"I have discovered this weak point in the protective barrier inside the dream realm. It seems that the physical reflections of stone and earth help to reinforce the will-cast barrier created by my forebears. Aware of this, they appear to have reinforced the two main entrances with an additional barrier. However, they did not do the same here, which I believe is because this exit was created after the barrier was constructed. In any case, here is where we will create our doorway, if indeed it can be done."

"So what do I need to do?" asked Kibure hesitantly.

"You will begin by helping me reinforce the barrier around the door."

Kibure's face contorted in confusion. *"Aren't we supposed to be creating an exit, not a stronger cage?"*

"Yes, well, we need to reinforce this section of barrier, so when we make our door within it, the rest of the barrier doesn't collapse in around it and kill both of us. As you know, your physical body doesn't do well without a spirit."

Kibure eyed her skeptically. *"When you put it like that, this seems like a very bad idea, Arabelle."*

She tightened the area around her lips. *"You promised you would help."*

"Yes, but you didn't tell me it could get me killed."

She shook her head. *"That will only happen if you don't do exactly as I say."*

Kibure swallowed hard, an unnecessary but instinctual reaction to his discomfort. He nodded. *"This had better not get me killed."*

She took his left hand and placed it directly upon the surface of the stone wall, pressing her palm into the back of Kibure's hand to hold it in place. *"There is a corridor on the other side of the stone, right here in the physical realm's reflection of this place. If this barrier was not here, we would be able to walk right through this and out into the world beyond."* She let go of his hand and said, *"I want you to try to do so now."*

Kibure looked at her but did his best not to show his doubt. He pushed, not just physically, but with his will. As soon as he added his will to the action, he felt resistance. It was as if the wall was not only preventing him from pushing forward, it was pushing back. He felt a density to it, a weight that he knew he could not budge. It was like trying to dig out a large stone from the ground. One knew instantly whether or not the stone was going to budge, or if they had in some way loosened it. This barrier was as immobile as the cave stone itself.

Arabelle then said, *"Now that you've felt the barrier, I want you to plunge your mind into it, just like you would if you were attempting to sense the energy around you in the physical world."*

Keeping his hand on the barrier, he pressed his will into it once again. He extended his awareness into the thing that pushed upon his will and felt the power behind it. But unlike an object in the waking world, this object was not static. He felt a pulsating strength. The deeper he delved, the more power he sensed. He could feel the lines of resistance reaching into the cave wall itself, set with anchors of some sort. And as Arabelle had guessed, there was no such anchor right where he pushed because the cave wall was only as thick as the stone door. But they needed to be able to stop the energy from flowing toward a particular area of pressure like it did when he pushed against it, otherwise it didn't matter that this section was less reinforced.

"*I feel it. But I have no idea how to do what you say about making it stronger.*"

Arabelle smiled at him. "*That's why I'm here.*"

Touching the wall with her hands, she said, "*Just focus on sensing the barrier. I'm going to make a few changes. Tell me when you feel them.*"

For a few moments, he felt nothing and his concentration began to slip as he focused on the fact that he felt nothing. But as he reestablished his connection with the barrier, he felt the change. Arabelle was somehow connecting the anchors of energy that reached into the stone behind them. She was crafting a circular line of power as she connected each anchor to the next. When she finished, Kibure noted that the push against his will was actually stronger: all of the anchors around this area were working in tandem.

"*I think you made it worse.*"

"*For now. But I want you to go over there and push.*"

He released his touch on the barrier, then moved a few paces over and did as she instructed. He felt the barrier shift again to repel his will upon it.

Arabelle said, "*Push harder.*"

He did so, and felt the barrier redouble against his will.

"*Harder,*" she said, strain evident even through the mental speech.

Kibure repositioned his feet and put his entire will into the effort.

"*Everything you have!*" she encouraged.

"*I am.*"

"*More!*"

He shook his head and continued to press his will against the powerful lines of resistance. It was difficult to do when he felt no movement whatsoever, no give. There was no way to know if his effort was doing anything. But he focused on the task and tried, willing his body against the barrier.

Arabelle suddenly disappeared.

Kibure released his push against the barrier and was thrown back through the air.

CHAPTER 64

DAGMARA

KYLLEAN THREW THE NEW, NOT bloody, traveling cloaks on the bed. "Put these on and follow me. We're heading down into the tunnels."

"Tunnels?" asked Aynward. "Why does it always have to be a tunnel?"

"There are twenty watchmen from East End at the gate right now asking where the Kingslayer and his fugitive sister are hiding. I don't know what the headmaster's reaction to this will be, but I think it's probably best that we not attempt the front gate."

"Fair point," agreed Aynward.

The door burst open and Kyllean turned to face the intruder. "Levi," he said in a high-pitched, surprised voice. "Levi—these are my—uh—friends. We were just leaving."

The tall rider named Levi looked on in confusion, then recognition. "Well, you had best do so now. They're all looking for you, or, rather, your *friends.*"

Kyllean cursed, then added, "Thanks for the warning, Levi."

Levi simply nodded.

"Come on," urged Kyllean.

He led them out of the small, unused sitting room beside the empty barracks and down another hall. "We've got to get to . . ." He trailed off as he reached an intersection and peered around the corner. Then he waved them back.

Dagmara was behind Aynward so she was the first one to try the nearest door. The handle turned and the three ducked inside. They waited thirty heartbeats before Kyllean left to check the hallway. He waved them back out and they continued along the same path. They reached the door to the tunnel, narrowly avoiding two more sets of riders.

Dagmara sighed in relief as Kyllean lit the torch and they closed the door behind them. They descended a short, narrow flight of stairs, then followed the corridor in a mostly straight line. Supposedly this tunnel led beneath the mountain and out the other side.

A few minutes into their travels, Kyllean suddenly stopped. "Oh no."

"What is it?" whispered Aynward.

By this time, they could all see why Kyllean had stopped. There was a light up ahead, and it wasn't the light at the end of the tunnel, it was torchlight. And the orange glow was growing brighter. Kyllean shuffled past Dagmara and Aynward, then tried to extinguish his torch. He smacked it against the wall several times, but it was no use. The bucket of water left for such purposes was near the entrance.

"Run!"

They did. But it was too late. A shout echoed from behind. They reached the entrance and Kyllean tossed the torch into the bucket of water then they burst through the door. "This way," he shouted.

He led them down several hallways without seeing anyone, then they were blinded by the bright light of the sun as he opened a door that led outside. "Come on."

They ran behind the massive three-story building used for food storage then emerged onto a wide, well-traveled trail that led upward. It didn't take long for both Dagmara and Aynward to become winded. while Kyllean jogged with ease, repeatedly waiting for them to catch up. Short spruce lined the trail, but Dagmara looked up and noticed the exposed switchback above.

Concerned, she said to Kyllean, "Where are we going? What are we going to do on the side of a mountain exposed for all to see?"

He glanced back, expression nervous. "We're going to try to hide, wait for dark, and then take this trail the rest of the way up to the Lumále nests. It continues down the other side of the mountain to an old, rarely used gate, same place the tunnel would have brought us, I think."

Dagmara spoke up. "You think? You mean you're not sure?"

"My apologies, *Your Grace*. I've never been concerned with escaping my place of employment, so the details of its layout were not a top priority for me. So come on, we've got to get off the trail."

Dagmara and Aynward followed as Kyllean led them to the first major bend in the trail then continued straight into the foliage. "Careful to only step on rocks if you can."

The terrain was sparse compared to what Dagmara had been used to, even in the small forest around the palace at Salmune. This made it easy enough to keep from leaving tracks.

They moved along for thirty or forty paces before Kyllean whispered, "Here, quickly!"

Dagmara and Aynward followed Kyllean into the sharp needles of a thick pine as he said, "Pray they didn't already see us."

"Who?"

Then the air rippled and the branches danced as a shadow passed above. "Lumále," whispered Dagmara, mesmerized by its size and beauty in spite of her limited view. The creature glided by, just above the treetop, gray fur glistening as it flexed to maintain outstretched wings.

"We're going to have to wait here until nightfall," said Kyllean, whose body Dagmara realized was pressed tightly against her own, her own chest rising and falling distinctly upon his own due to her labored breathing.

Aynward was there, too, but he may as well have been absent, and he was soon crawling along the ground to rest against the trunk of the tree.

Kyllean reached up as if to put an arm around her neck and she panicked, but then she felt the branch that was pinning her to him release its pressure. "Your Grace." He took a small step back, as much as the area allowed. "If you would like to sit, I will cut away a few branches with my knife."

Dagmara recovered and said, "Yes. Please. That would be nice." Though she had to admit she hadn't minded their closeness, not in the least. *This is no time for pretty romance,* she scolded herself.

As they sat silently waiting for nightfall within the thick cover of the tree, a question surfaced. "Kyllean, what's going to happen to you? Aren't you going to get into some trouble?"

He chuckled as he said, "Suppose I may. Haven't really had time to worry over such things." He sounded jovial, yet there was an underlying falseness to his laughter. He had probably just begun thinking through the ramifications of helping fugitives accused of treason now that he had time to sit and wait. There was no way to deny his involvement and no way to plead ignorance.

Kyllean added, "I'll probably just get a few lashes and some extra cleaning duties for a few weeks."

"I see," was all Dagmara said. She had a difficult time believing that a place like this would be so lenient, but she wasn't about to argue with him over his own people's customs.

Aynward butted in. "At the very least, he can't be charged and tried in Kingdom court unless he takes part in a crime outside of Talmune."

Kyllean nodded. "That's true. So how about we stop all this worry talk. I'll be just fine. If I were you, I'd be far more concerned about what might happen to a prince who fled his own trial and whose head could fetch enough gold to make any man rich enough to purchase his own estate." Then eyeing Dagmara, he said, "And I'm thinking bounty hunters aren't going to be too careful with his sister, no matter her looks, if she gets in the way. The difference for you alive versus dead at this point becomes negligible."

Aynward huffed loudly. "Yeah . . . well . . . okay, you're not wrong about any of that. But since when were you so . . . pragmatic?"

He laughed. "Since always. I think this might just be the first time your ears were open wide enough to hear it."

Aynward responded, "Yeah, okay. Not to change the subject or anything, but when are you getting your own Lumále?"

Dagmara's thoughts had just been drifting away toward an imagined scene of capture, but this brought her back to the present in an instant.

Kyllean shrugged. "I'm not really permitted to speak much on this topic, trade secrets and all, but I can tell you this much: there's only one unclaimed Lumále left, and she's been so for long enough to assume that she's not interested in choosing anyone any time soon."

Dagmara heard the sound of loss in his voice, but there was also an acceptance. He had come to terms with this reality. He would probably never become a full rider. His loss was the loss of a dream.

He laughed lightly, then said, "The last eligible Lumále chose a rider just days ago. A classmate of mine. She deserved it, of course, but yeah, that's that." His mood lightened a bit as he added, "I did get these sweet blades, though." He worked them free from within the tight space and handed one to Dagmara, then stretched out to get the other to Aynward.

Dagmara turned the marbled blade over in her hands a few times, mesmerized. She hadn't noticed it in the midst of the fighting the other night. "This is beautiful. What is it made from? I've never seen anything like it."

"No idea," said Kyllean. "No one wanted it so I asked if I could have it as a second. Apparently it doesn't have any magical attributes, at least that anyone has been able to figure out."

Aynward's head shot up. "Does that mean the stories are true about these other blades being magical? I always thought that was kind of . . . you know . . . made up." Aynward appeared completely taken in by the inky-black blade in his hands, oohing and ahhing as he ran his fingers along the flat of the black metal.

Kyllean shrank back a little. "Erm, I . . . I think I was not supposed to talk about that. Then again, you're going to likely hang anyway, so I guess I shouldn't be too concerned."

Dagmara shot him a glare. "Hey!"

Kyllean smiled. "Not you, of course. Surely no one would dare touch a hair on that beautiful head of yours."

Dagmara glowered. "That would be a nice compliment if you hadn't just stated the opposite moments ago."

"Whoops."

Aynward said, "Hey sis, mind if I have a look at that one?"

"Sure." They switched weapons and Aynward continued to marvel out loud with sounds of astonishment. "So if the black blades have magical properties, does that mean you're now some sort of wielder?"

Kyllean looked from side to side. "I know you're going to probably die soon and all, but I really can't say anything more about this."

Aynward nodded to himself. "Okay, so that's a yes. Wow, I never would have imagined, my dear friend Kyllean a wielder. It's nearly unfathomable. Then again, I didn't see you do anything particularly magicky when we were fighting earlier."

Dagmara considered this as well and concluded, "He didn't have to. Or perhaps he did, but the magic of the blade isn't something you can see."

"Fair point."

Kyllean interrupted, "So how about you two tell me about your travels from Salmune. Surely there's a tale or two there."

Dagmara and Aynward took turns recapping the sequence of events from the assassination all the way to arriving in Talmune. Aynward concluded, "I mean, what luck that you happened to be visiting your mum. Kitay has been pretty reluctant in her help as of late, but surely this was her doing, eh Kyllean?"

Dagmara rolled her eyes and Kyllean's mood seemed to darken. Aynward didn't notice. "Say, what were you doing there? Looked like a pretty serious conversation going on before everything with the watch happened."

Kyllean looked down at the ground. "I was delivering a message from my father to my mother."

No one said anything for a long pause, and Aynward finally said, "So . . . am I missing something? Why is it that you got stuck delivering the message? Doesn't the fortress have a courier, or was this top-secret rider stuff?"

Kyllean shook his head, and Dagmara had a feeling that Aynward was prying into something personal. "My father gave me a letter to give to my mother in the event that he didn't return from a mission."

Dagmara looked over to Aynward as understanding washed over her. He was already there. "Oh. Kyl, I'm so sorry, man."

Kyllean shook his head. "It's all right. He was a good example, I suppose, but I hardly knew the man. I was more concerned about my mum, but she's as tough a lass as any, as you saw. Think she was angrier with him for dying than she was sad."

Dagmara reached out a hand and touched Kyllean's. He didn't pull it away; he didn't react at all. Then, as if finally recognizing what had happened, he shied away, retracting his hand in the process. "It's fine, really."

Neither Aynward nor Dagmara pressed further. They both knew full well the pain of losing a father, and that everyone dealt with grief differently. The sun was beginning to set so they would be leaving their place of hiding to brave the trail up the mountain by night. Dagmara contemplated the challenge of escaping. They would not fight these people if confronted. Run, yes, but fight, no. The riders were not the enemy. Come to think of it, neither was the city watch they had fought earlier. Those men had been following Kingdom law, though they were more likely just after the reward. Nevertheless, it was difficult to justify even what injury they had caused those men. In light of the coming war, Dagmara wondered if their running wasn't making the accusation of treason truer than ever before. And yet, to turn themselves over to judgment based on faulty evidence and speculation was also wrong. It was a downright lie, and the teachings of the faith were clear on matters of truth. *The truth is not to be adulterated.*

They sat in silence for a long time, each lost in their own web of hopes, dreams, and fears.

Some time later, a palpable darkness pressed down upon them and Dagmara looked up to see the first of the night's moons gone from the night sky. She could hardly see Kyllean but she heard him repositioning to rise. "We should take advantage of this cloud cover while we have it."

Aynward stepped past Dagmara; she hadn't even heard him rise. "I was thinking the same thing." He held out a hand for Dagmara, which she took.

Before long Dagmara and Aynward were standing behind a bit of brush at the edge of the trail. Kyllean went out to confirm that they were alone, then waved a hand for them to come out. He said, "Be careful along the edge as we get higher." He pointed up. "A fall from up there will likely not be survivable."

They moved at a brisk pace, and Dagmara quickly felt the effects of the steady climb. With Aynward still recovering from his wounds, she worried he might fall behind. He didn't, but his breathing was louder than their footfalls on the packed-dirt trail.

"You doing okay, brother?" she asked.

"I'm . . ." two breaths later, ". . . fine."

Exhausted, but too stubborn to admit it. No surprise there. Meanwhile, Kyllean might as well have been strolling through a market, browsing the merchandise. He continued a pattern of jogging up ahead, then darting back, and never once did his words fight with his breathing.

Kyllean returned from up ahead and said, "We're approaching the nests of the Lumáles, just so you know. They're harmless to us, but just so you know."

They had been passing the empty nests for some time, but they had been just that, empty. Dagmara had only been up close to a Lumáles in the palace on one occasion and that had been many years earlier. She was disappointed that this might be the only good look she would get of them, and it was dangerously dark at that. If everything went as planned and they managed to escape to the east, she might never see one again.

Her eyes had adjusted to the low light, and yet as they passed the next nest, only the barest outline of mass could be seen. She had ventured a better glance at the Lumáles on their approach to the fortress as she watched them soar through the sky.

This was for the best, of course. If she couldn't see the Lumáles, any riders still awake and searching for her and her companions would be unlikely to notice them, as well.

Then, as if her thoughts had some impact on the sky above, the clouds parted and the entire party was illuminated by the larger of the two moons.

"Quick, into the nest," said Kyllean in a hushed but firm voice.

They rushed from the exposed path into the deep impression carved from the side of the mountain. They huddled together with their backs to the stone, out of sight. Dagmara was suddenly aware that she stood only a few paces from an immense shape further within. She stared as the shadowed creature's mass moved ever so slightly up and then down as it breathed. She trembled, then released a squeak as a large white sphere popped into being on one side of the hulk that was the Lumále. The head rose up to stare at the three visitors, and all of the assurances Dagmara had been given about Lumáles being friendly disappeared behind a certainty that the massive jaws might easily close around her entire skull.

The creature sniffed the air, then rose as much as it could within the limited space of the overhang. Its wings opened partway and it shifted its body to face them directly. Pinned as they were against the wall, Dagmara knew if this thing chose to attack, at least one of them would be redistributed throughout this land as part of the Lumále's excrement.

"You're certain these things are friendly?" asked Aynward, concern evident in his voice.

"I've never heard of an attack . . . on a rider, at least."

"Well, this one seems none too pleased at our intrusion," responded Aynward.

Kyllean drew his blades. "Perhaps a pair of nonriders has never woken one up in the middle of the night."

"Wouldn't that be three?" asked Aynward.

"Well, technically, I'm still considered a rider now that I've earned the blade," countered Kyllean.

"Well, that's just downright mislead—"

"Is that *really* what we want to debate right now?" interrupted Dagmara, her heart pounding like a caged monkey in her chest.

Kyllean nodded. "Fair enough." He stepped forward, slowly, and lowered his weapons in front of him. "We're not here to cause trouble.

We're just . . . hiding here for a moment . . . if that's all right with you, great giant of the sky."

The Lumále seemed to give him the deepest possible glare, its eyes narrowing to slits as it continued sniffing the air. Then, to all their great relief, it lay back down. Its eyes remained open, never leaving the trio as they themselves sank back into the stone on trembling legs.

"See?" said Kyllean. "Just like I said." He moved slowly to retrieve his weapons.

A cloud passed overhead to swallow the moonlight, cloaking everything in darkness once again, so the three eagerly resumed their trek up the mountain. They passed several more nests on their way up. About half of them appeared to be occupied. Then spears of light pierced the darkness once more as the clouds parted. They ducked into another nest, this one unoccupied, and Kyllean said, "Well, we've made it this far without causing an alarm. We might be high enough up that we can't be seen from below. I suggest that we keep going, regardless of the light of the moons." Looking up it became apparent that their hope of cloud cover masking their travel was dwindling. A few gray specks remained, but the thick cloud cover from earlier had passed them by, leaving both moons visible.

"Let us pray you're right," said Aynward, sounding none too enthusiastic. *Tecuix guide and protect us.*

They stalked back onto the pathway and had taken only a few steps when they heard a shout. It sounded like it had come from below but with the echo, so it could have come from anywhere.

They ran.

Dagmara followed Kyllean, quickly overtaking Aynward, and they turned up the next switchback. Another shout rang out, and this one seemed to come from above. *Was that the same voice or another?* They neared the next nest when a sudden shadow turned the path into darkness.

Dagmara stopped to stare at the dark form of a Lumále flapping powerful wings as it hovered above them. It turned slightly in the air, and the silhouette of a man with a shaved head could be seen. "This ends here!" shouted the man.

The three backed their way deeper into the depression within the mountain, another nest. The Lumále before them landed and the man dismounted gracefully, drawing his sword. Dagmara spotted two more shapes growing in size within the night sky.

This is it. End of the road. Dagmara's mind ran through her return to the King, imagining what she might say to him. Then she remembered that Perja was believed to be dead. Who was ruling in his place? His son was too young, and his wife, Elena, had been too short a time as Queen to be named Regent. It must be her brother Kirous, the Duke of Vesvalen. He was a fair man, but at this point, clemency seemed improbable.

The rider stalked toward them. "Lay down your arms."

Dagmara drew her weapon and looked over to Aynward and Kyllean as she knelt to relinquish hers in surrender.

"I'm afraid I can't do that," said Aynward. "I am innocent of the charges leveled against me."

The man stopped moving forward at the sound of two other Lumáles landing on either side of the indentation cut into the mountain that they were all occupying. Two riders were quickly at the bald man's side, one man and one woman.

Kyllean said to Aynward, "Listen, friend, I believe you. These nice folks here are not going to hurt you. They're just going to return you to the Kingdom authorities. And look, with your brother Perja out of the mix—sorry for your loss—perhaps you'll get a fair trial."

Dagmara realized that Kyllean was speaking to his brethren as much as he was to Aynward. He wanted to be certain that Aynward wasn't killed here.

"I'm not turning myself over to anyone. I've run too far to just give up now. I didn't kill my father. And if these men want to kill an innocent man, that crime will rest with them. But I'd rather go to my funeral with a weapon in hand than be escorted to the end of the rope for an audience."

The male rider with the shaved head spoke again. "This is your last warning. Lay down your weapons. *All* of you."

It was not lost on Dagmara, or this rider, that Kyllean had also not yet relinquished his swords, and Dagmara suddenly felt herself reaching to retrieve her own. She could not stand idly by as her brother was executed. Then again, was getting herself killed on account of her brother's stubborn stupidity any wiser? Who did that help? Dagmara scooped up her blade in spite of the logical part of her brain shouting in alarm.

Kyllean said, "Listen, Gerald. You don't know me, but you do know—did know—my father, Kelson. I'm not looking to fight one of my own. But my friend here is innocent. I know this to my core. But if we hand him over to the Kingdom, he's going to hang for a crime he did not commit. I won't be able to live with myself if I allow that to happen. Please. Just let him and his sister go."

Gerald appeared to consider the request. He nodded. *He's going to do it. He's going to let us go. Kyllean, that beautiful geni—*

"I did know your father. He was an honorable man. And I am certain he is looking down right now in dismay at the sight of his son meddling with murderers of the worst kind. It's no wonder you've not been chosen by a Lumále. They are very discerning creatures, after all."

The man raised his blade and the other riders did the same. "Last chance," he warned.

No one spoke for what seemed an eternity. Then Gerald stepped forward. "I take no pleasure in this, but it must be done."

Kyllean stepped forward, both blades at the ready, but Gerald pulled back at the last moment, staring past Kyllean, behind all of them.

Dagmara risked turning to see what could have drawn his attention. She sucked in a breath as she turned to see the vastness of a Lumále towering above them all. It lowered its head between the two opposing groups and the riders each took a step back, though their weapons remained firm in hand.

The creature seemed to inspect the air. Gerald spoke loudly and calmly. "Lumále, we have need of these people. Please return to your nest."

The creature gave no indication that it heard. Instead it lowered its head and turned it toward Aynward. It seemed to breathe him in, then it snorted.

"Can hardly blame her there," said Kyllean.

"Really? A joke? Right now?" asked Aynward, incredulous.

Kyllean shrugged. "You really do smell something awful." Then the Lumále repeated this same exercise on Kyllean, snorting once again, the sound so much like human disgust it would have been amusing had Dagmara not been so frightened.

"Well, that's just poor taste," grumbled Kyllean.

Aynward shook his head and the Lumále brought its snout up to Dagmara. Its eyes were half the size of her head and they peered into her as fist-sized nostrils breathed her in. Dagmara saw a diagonal scar across its nose, making it all the more frightening, reaffirming a Lumále's potential for violence and war. But instead of retreating as it had with her brother and Kyllean, it continued to sniff her. It brought its head closer and closer until its wet nose touched her trembling hand. She flinched as they made contact. Then a tingling sensation ran from her fingertips all the way up her arm, then expanded throughout her body. It was cold at first but by the time it reached her toes, her entire body felt warm, very warm.

Then, as quickly as it came, it was gone, and the Lumále rose up and pushed its way past the trio of riders, who quickly stepped aside. The other Lumáles parted at the edge of the path to give way.

CHAPTER 65

KYLLEAN

KYLLEAN WAS OUT OF TIME; he needed to make a choice. Gerald, Claris, and Tumont all resumed their approach, weapons at the ready.

Gerald said, "This is your last chance to stand down peacefully. Especially you, Kyllean. Considering what you've done already, I shouldn't even offer you this chance. I do so only out of respect for your late father. He would be so disappointed."

Slight change of plans. Kyllean drew in power from beneath his feet and growled, "What's new?"

Kyllean relaxed his position, and Gerald nodded his approval, then Kyllean struck. There was no honor in the way he did so, but this man had no right to bring his father into this. Kyllean's initial attack was blocked, but Kyllean didn't want to cut the man. He slammed his other fist into Gerald's chest and heard the satisfying whoosh of air as he was knocked backward, his feet sliding helplessly against the smooth, dusty stone upon which they fought.

Then Kyllean slipped back into line with his friends. He needed to finish this now. He whispered, "I'm sorry," then he turned his weapon on Aynward, who was certainly not expecting the attack to come from beside him. Nevertheless, he managed to turn and meet the attack, shuffling back in surprise. *Not good. Your back is turned to Dagmara. Finish this now.*

There wasn't much room for Aynward to retreat, not in the direction he had maneuvered, but Aynward had made sure not to put his back to the three riders who were stalking forward once again.

"I'm," Kyllean increased his speed, burning the power he had absorbed, "sorry." He blocked one of Aynward's counter strikes then brought his elbow up as he stepped inside of Aynward's extended blade. Pivoting on his outside foot to gain the angle he needed, he slid his blade free from where they had been pressed together and swung. Without Kyllean's enhanced speed, Aynward would have been able to turn to face him in time, but instead the blunt end of Kyllean's blade hit home, striking the back of Aynward's neck.

Kyllean heard Dagmara shriek from somewhere behind him, closer than she should have been, but Kyllean needed to finish this. He used the moment of stunned surprise to sweep Aynward's closest leg out from under him, bringing Aynward's sword grip within reach. Kyllean had pulled back his weapon to swing and once again used the blunt side of the blade to strike the off-balance fighter, this time in the wrists. He knew it would hurt, possibly even break bone, but it was better than watching his friend be cut open by Gerald. Aynward cried out and his weapon toppled to the side alongside his fallen body.

Kyllean saw motion out of the corner of his eye and instinctively dove to the right, but not before a surge of pain blossomed from the back of his left leg. He bellowed and his sideways roll became more of a flop. He finished on his back, losing the grip on one of his weapons in the process. He just hoped Aynward didn't have enough time to recover before—

Steel flashed and Kyllean went rigid. "Enough!" It was Dagmara's voice, and it was her blade at his throat, blood from the back of Kyllean's leg dripping from the steel at his neck. But before Kyllean had time to be thankful that she hadn't simply continued the swing to remove his head from his shoulders, he spotted the attack from behind her as the riders closed in.

Without consideration for the metal brushing his throat, Kyllean scissored his legs, between which Dagmara had planted one of her feet. He twisted his body away from her sword as she fell, the sword of Gerald missing her head by a few hairs. Kyllean rolled into Dagmara's fallen body and wrapped his arms around her own to prevent her from struggling, hoping this would be enough to end the attack from the riders.

She had let out a shout, and her body wriggled and writhed beneath his own, but he held firm. His body lay chest to chest on her, the pain in the back of his leg muted by the bloodlust of battle and the fear for his life and that of the others. He brought his mouth to her ear and whispered, "It's over. The fight is over."

Then he lifted his head and yelled, "Yield. We yield."

Kyllean turned his head to the other side where Aynward had been knocked from his feet and thanked the gods that Aynward had been unable to recover his weapon before Claris leveled her own at his chest. Only then did the intimacy of his position upon Dagmara register. She must have also felt the sudden awkwardness of their bodies, for she began struggling anew. "Get off me. Get off of me this instant! I am a princess! How dare you!"

He held tight. "Are you done fighting? I like you better alive."

"Get off of me!" she shouted.

He reached his hand out and pushed her weapon out of reach, then rolled off of her. She slapped him across the face as he did. He took it in stride, smiling as he brought his hand to his cheek. "Well, that was nice. Though in all honesty, I was hoping for more of a thank you for saving your life, if not for the hug."

Dagmara sat up and stared death at Kyllean before turning her blazing glare upon Gerald and Tumont, who towered over them, blades extended as a warning not to move.

Gerald said, "You three will come with us. The headmaster will decide what is to be done with you."

⊰⊰⊰

Their wrists and ankles had been bound. Furthermore, they had been locked in separate rooms for the rest of the evening. But morning finally came and it felt good to have his ankles and wrists untied. Kyllean shook out tight muscles as he was escorted to the headmaster alongside the others, who filed in behind with their respective escorts. Kyllean gave Aynward a nod, but Aynward only glared back at him.

"Listen," said Kyllean as they walked. "I'm sorry about that up there. It was either that or watch you and Dagmara get cut to pieces by Gerald and the others."

Aynward responded angrily, "I was prepared to die. Die with a sword in my hand. And with your help, we may yet have escaped."

"And if not, what of your sister's fate?"

Aynward didn't say anything for several steps, and then Dagmara answered, "I'm a grown woman. I can make my own choices. Don't need yet another man making them for me."

"You're serious? I mean, Aynward I can understand, he can be a real dolt, but I thought you were supposed to be the smart one. You don't truly wish to die simply because your brother doesn't know when to quit, do you?"

The guard beside him squeezed his arm. "That's enough. All of you. You're giving me a headache."

They weren't far from the riders' arena where the headmaster awaited their arrival. They passed beneath tall marble arches and into the sandy pit encircled by three levels of marble arches, all of which were tall and wide enough for a Lumále to safely perch. The arena had appeared vast from where Kyllean had been able to see it during his training. But to stand inside was to feel like a true ant among giants. The massive pillars that supported the arches glinted in the early-morning sun, and several Lumáles rested upon the arches at various levels. It had been said that in centuries past, entire assemblies of riders and their mounts had filled the perimeter before being sent into battle. Kyllean could only imagine, and only barely.

Headmaster Forestone stood tall with arms crossed, scowling at Kyllean and the others as they were escorted toward him. His Lumále lay beside him, unconcerned as they approached, but its eyes opened as Kyllean neared and the contempt held within suggested a dangerous fate to anyone who crossed this rider. There were a dozen others in attendance, including Master Hilde, who met Kyllean's eyes with a sad expression. That look hurt more than the anger he felt palpitating from the headmaster.

Kyllean was told by the headmaster to recount his side of what had transpired. He had an audience of Gerald, Tumont, and Claris, along with their own Lumáles. The strange healer was also there, her expression as indifferent as, well, someone who was truly indifferent.

Headmaster Forestone's scowl deepened as Kyllean continued his narrative. The headmaster was a large man with broad shoulders and a stiff posture that had remained unaltered in spite of the reality that he was well beyond his fighting years. He maintained the sort of persona that would frighten grown men until his last breath no matter his true physical condition.

"Kyllean, you have brought treason to our doorstep and smuggled it into our halls. Not only did you take part, but you raised weapons against your own in order to see it done."

"To be fair. I later *unraised* those weapons and used them to disarm the alleged criminals. But I'll admit that prior to—"

"Silence!" boomed the headmaster. "We will deal with the fullness of your punishment after we have determined our course with the fugitives. For now, be it known that your status as a rider is forfeit until further notice."

The weight of those words slammed down on Kyllean like a hammer and he swayed at the sudden weakness in his legs. He had expected punishment; maybe chamber pot duty, scrubbing the floors, some sort of manual labor, but his status revoked? That was the one thing he had left over from his father, the one remaining tie. And now it had been stripped. To make matters worse, his decision to help his friend had produced no fruit, only pain. This had been all for naught. Their outcome was the same and his own outcome all the worse for it.

He opened his mouth to respond, to plead, but nothing came out. No smart remark, no clever misdirection. Only choking silence, which was struck down by Headmaster Forestone's voice.

"Prince Aynward, you are accused of high treason, patricide, and regicide. And while you may claim innocence in all of this, it is not within my authority to rule one way or the other. The covenant between the riders and the Kingdom dates back many centuries, and while we may have local autonomy, we are not exempt from a duty to uphold justice as seen by the crown. To protect you from capture would be as much an act of treason as your sister's own decision to assist in your escape, a decision that has placed her under Kingdom judgment, as well."

Kyllean's attention waned. The headmaster continued to speak, asking questions, determining the logistics of delivery, but Kyllean's mind absorbed none of it. The words were like rainwater to a freshly oiled sword. He stared out blankly, thoughts scattered in so many directions that no single idea could win his attention. His eyes were open, but his mind closed.

For this reason, the growing shape in the sky didn't register until the wind generated by powerful wings blew dark curls of his own dark hair into his eyes. Snapping back to attention, Kyllean shuffled aside as a riderless Lumále landed gently beside him.

One of the riders must have summoned it. Are they transporting Aynward and Dagmara back to the Kingdom already? The Lumále turned to face him and stared back. He recognized the deep scar across her nose, but this only increased his confusion. She gave him a curt sniff, then as before snorted and turned her attention to Dagmara.

"What is this? Would someone shoo the spinster back to her perch?" snapped the headmaster. Several riders who stood at attention looked at one another, then stepped forward.

"Yah, scram."

The Lumále ignored them, but one rider was wise enough to hop onto the back of his own Lumále and moved it forward to encourage the unwanted guest to find another place to spend its time.

His Lumále stalked toward the spinster and was greeted with a movement so quick that even his Lumále skidded back. The spinster released a low growl, and its tail coiled up behind it like a serpent.

"I've been convinced that this one was broken for years," said the headmaster angrily. "Go on, get!"

The rider on the back of his Lumále turned his creature slightly, its own tail now poised to retaliate should an attack come. "Standing by. Just give the order."

There was a long silence where no one moved as the two creatures squared up in preparation for battle. Then the spinster snorted and turned. It opened its wings and leaped into the air.

And everyone relaxed for a breath before it turned back a moment later, this time landing directly behind Kyllean, Dagmara, and Aynward.

"Oh for the love of the sleeping gods above," moaned Headmaster Forestone.

Kyllean and the others had all turned to face the erratic Lumále, but Kyllean heard the strange accent of the healer saying quietly, "Are you all so blind? Let the creature do what it came here to do."

"This thing is mad. What does an old healer like you know of such things?"

Kyllean turned to see the woman roll her eyes and shrug. "Hmm."

And then he felt it, the faintest tingling of magic. He whipped around to see . . .

What in the . . .

Dagmara's hand was reaching out to touch the snout of the Lumále, which had come dangerously close to her. There was no aggression in its posture; if anything, it showed supplication. Kyllean recognized the similarity to what had happened with . . . Evra? He stared in disbelief as the magic moved between the fugitive princess and the winged beast.

Dagmara's eyes were wide with surprise. "Wh . . . what's happening?"

CHAPTER 66

DAGMARA

WARMTH WASHED OVER DAGMARA, THAT and a sudden sense of . . . a presence? She felt thoughts within her mind that were not her own, but they weren't exactly thoughts, more like impressions. There was no monologue, only a sense of . . . irritation?

I think I'm supposed to do something here, but what? She felt a mounting pressure within her mind. It was like playing tag in the palace as kids, her brother attempting to push his way through a door she struggled to hold shut. *What would it mean to let go?* she wondered.

Then again, what have I to lose? She gave in to the feeling, let go of her hold upon the door to her mind. It swung wide open and everything she had just felt between her and the presence abruptly heightened and a part of her own mind shot out into that of the . . .

She stumbled forward. The Lumále that loomed above her moved its tail with lightning speed and caught her falling form as gently as a mother might her child. It set her upright with surprising dexterity.

Then it bumped its head into hers and lowered its entire body before her.

She felt drawn to it, but . . . *I can't ride this thing.*

And yet, the feeling was so powerful within her mind. Everything else around her seemed to fade, to blur. Only the Lumále before her existed and she *needed* to climb up onto its back. Her legs moved her uncertain body and within moments she sat atop the creature between its shoulders, hands nestling into the thick gray fur at the base of its neck.

She heard the sound of others around her, some talking, some perhaps even yelling, but they may as well have been leagues away.

Dagmara nearly fell backward as the Lumále flapped its massive wings for the first time. Her grip on the fur held firm. She looked down over the side, and in just three flaps of the creature's wings the people gathered below shrank away as if the land itself was withdrawing. The Lumále's wings seemed to move soundlessly as they propelled both of them into the sky.

Dagmara marveled at the sight below. The fortress had its own sort of beauty, nestled as it was into the side of the mountain. She peered out at the road leading to the town of Talmune, and East End beyond that. It was a narrow strip within a vast forest of green. There were squares of farmland sprinkled throughout, but there was so much forest she wondered why they hadn't just escaped into this vastness of dark green when running from East End.

Soon she was able to see the head of the Dragon Spine Mountains to the west, which, considering how many leagues away they were, seemed nearly impossible.

Dagmara had always loved riding horses; loved the feeling of her hair whipping behind her as she raced across an empty field at full gallop. She had never imagined she might travel at such a speed as this. And now, to do so with the view as if from the peak of a mountain, with the ground moving ever so slightly beneath . . .

She enjoyed the freedom, yet she also felt anticipation coming from the Lumále as it continued to take them higher.

CHAPTER 67

KYLLEAN

KYLLEAN STARED IN DISBELIEF AT the distant dot in the sky.

Not a single word had been uttered since Dagmara had flown into the air upon the back of a Lumále.

Kyllean couldn't take it any longer. "So . . . am I crazy or did that Lumále just choose an untrained, wanted fugitive to be its rider?"

Kyllean looked around at the others. All of them were frozen in the same pose.

Aynward continued staring up, but answered, "Both of those statements appear to be true."

Aynward broke the curse of silence, and several others sounded at once. Foremost among these, and most clear to Kyllean, was the headmaster. "Gerald, Tumont, follow the princess. Make sure she doesn't venture too far. We'll still need to return the girl to Kingdom custody."

"Of course," replied Gerald curtly. He jogged over to his Lumále and Tumont mirrored this. "Do you wish us to retrieve her with force?"

The headmaster shook his head. "Only if necessary. And give her a few hours first. We'll have to sever the link before returning her to the Kingdom. Let the girl enjoy the connection for now. Being chosen by a

Lumále is a great honor. Much as she may be a fugitive, she's earned the right to a good ride."

Kyllean's excitement for Dagmara was replaced with revulsion. He had learned about severing in class. Severing a link prematurely was extremely rare, and often did irreparable damage to both the rider and the Lumále.

How could they even consider such a thing? *There has to be a way out of this. I just have to think.* Multiple scenarios played out within his mind, but none of them ended well for anyone.

Except . . .

It wasn't good, but it might be the best they could hope for.

He smiled to himself, and then heard the gasps. Everyone was looking toward the sky, toward Dagmara and the riders . . . he followed their line of sight and his heart sank and his breath caught.

CHAPTER 68

DAGMARA

THE LUMÁLE STRAIGHTENED ITS WINGS, and they floated through in the air. There was something both intoxicating and terrifying about sitting so high up above the world below. Her capture and return to the Kingdom were now distant problems. She knew that she would still have to return to the headmaster and answer for the crime of helping Aynward escape. She would probably be separated from this Lumále indefinitely and returned for trial. But not now. Right now, in this moment, she was fulfilling a dream she'd fostered since childhood and nothing could stand before that. She was a rider!

Dagmara leaned over and nestled into the neck of her Lumále with the side of her face. "I don't know if you can understand me, but I want to thank you for doing this."

She was rewarded with a sudden sensation of inner warmth, not physical, but emotional. There was no other way to describe it. "I'll take that as a yes. You *can* understand me. Do you have a name? Are you able to speak back to me?"

She received no response to her question, but a wave of strong emotions flooded into her mind and she felt like she understood this creature better than most people she had met. There was a perpetual loneliness, yet she desired to be away from others. A longing for open air, which was currently being satisfied, which explained the joy she felt pouring in. There was also underlying anger, but Dagmara felt it would take a lot to stir that to the top.

"So what should I call you?" She said this out loud for the creature's benefit, even if she wouldn't receive a verbal response. "How about . . ." She searched for the right word as the Lumále soared, propped up by a steady breeze. The act of merely extending her wings seemed enough to keep them afloat, indefinitely hovering leagues above the world and all of its many problems below.

"Anila. It means air in Scritlandian. You know, because you fly."

She felt immediate displeasure pour into her.

"Okay, how about Sutanu? It means beauty. You are certainly beautiful."

The next response was not as strong, but she didn't take it as acceptance, either.

"This is more difficult than I thought. I really wish you could just speak to me."

She tried a few more to no avail. "Perhaps you just don't want a name?"

Annoyance flared. "Okay. Umm. How about Ekanta? It means lonely one."

The emotional equivalent of rejection flowed into her mind, following by annoyance.

"Well, I'm out of ideas and I probably should go back down. My brother is in a great deal of trouble and I can't very well leave him to that fate. Not that there's anything I can do now that we've been caught."

Her Lumále didn't react for a while, but finally shifted its wings and they began a meandering descent. She tingled with excitement at the movement, and her Lumále seemed to sense this because she picked up speed. Dagmara let out a laugh of raw joy. This was the most exhilarating experience she had yet to know. The Lumále increased the angle further and they picked up even more speed. The wind stung her face but she didn't care. She cherished the rush, knowing she traveled faster than she ever had and likely ever would.

"This. Is. Amazing!" Her last word became a shrill cry as her Lumále tilted further; they were speeding toward the ground at a full dive. Her excitement turned to fear as her grip on the fur began to slip. *This is too fast. I'm going to fall off.*

Her Lumále adjusted the angle of descent, but the sudden change in her weight caused what remained of Dagmara's grip to slip. Dagmara slid from her seat and into the open air with cry.

CHAPTER 69

KYLLEAN

KYLLEAN STARED IN HORROR AT the tumbling dot in the sky—Dagmara's body spun uncontrolled on its way toward the ground. His body filled with power as a reflex, but this only made the feeling worse for he knew there was nothing he could actually do. Though he did have magically enhanced strength and speed. Perhaps that would be enough . . .

He sprang forward, running as quick as his magically enhanced legs would take him. He had no idea if it would but no one else had moved.

Kyllean propelled himself forward, but Dagmara was falling—fast. Too fast. He wasn't going to get there in time. *Come on!*

He drew in even more power and felt his speed increase further. She was going to land just outside the walls of the arena and he was going to be very close. He did a quick calculation and knew what he needed to do. *Please be enough.*

He leaped higher than any normal human had a right to jump, his left foot hitting the top of the arch that made up the first level of Lumále perches surrounding the arena. He used the top of the arch to launch himself higher and further into the sky, his eyes losing sight of Dagmara's free-falling form for only an instant. He extended his arms to catch her and braced himself for a great deal of pain. This was going to hurt. They were both going to be injured greatly.

Something caught his eye to the right, but he didn't dare look away from Dagmara. Something big indeed—Dagmara was snatched from the air and Kyllean soared past empty-handed. Then something large slammed into him from the other side and his excitement that Dagmara had been snatched from the sky disappeared within a confused tumble toward the ground from a height that was sure to result in—a dizzying swirl of chaos danced across his eyes along with lots of pain, and he struck the ground, back of his head first.

Light flashed, and inextricable pain danced throughout his entire body. Kyllean heard a moan reverberate throughout himself, like a giant drum was beating within his head.

"Ow! What is—" He stopped talking. It was his own voice. It hurt to talk. It hurt to think. He had no idea where he was or what was going on. *Why do I hurt?*

His sight was blurry, but the blackness of his sight began to recede, replaced by hazy, blue sky. A fuzzy form crept into view. A long, reptilian head and a massive body. A Lumále? A smaller form moved toward him alongside the beast. Both shapes remained blurry, his eyes unable to focus.

"That was a very stupid thing you just did."

The voice was deep and less muffled. *My hearing appears to be returning to normal.* The man slowly came into focus. Gerald.

"Very stupid."

A rush of memories returned, though not everything was clear. "Is Dagmara . . . ?"

"She's fine. Rattled, but fine. Her Lumále caught her just before both of you could be killed by her fall."

That was a relief. "What happened to me?"

"You weren't the only one attempting to save the princess. My Lumále turned at the last moment as her own Lumále caught her with its talons. That's when the form of an idiot flying through the sky appeared right in our path and struck the chest of my Lumále." He reached over and patted the chest of the gray creature, which stared expressionless eyes down upon Kyllean. "She's fine enough, but I suspect you're going to need the healer."

Kyllean figured now was as good a time as any to try to stand. The throbbing in his head he had felt while lying down increased to unbearable levels and his vision narrowed. His head felt as if someone was knocking it with a hammer every time his heart beat. This receded as soon as he lay back down. He also felt a considerable level of sharp pain shoot from his neck down his left arm. Once he was fully flat upon his back again, he did an inventory of each limb. At the very least, nothing else appeared to have more than a few scrapes and bruises.

"I'll send the healer to you as soon as she's done with the princess," said Gerald, his voice lacking a single note of sympathy.

"You said the princess is all right, though?"

"Yes." There was a pause, and then Gerald turned away as he said, "Wait here." And then to his Lumále, "Let's go."

Kyllean lay on his back staring up at the cloudless afternoon sky, thankful that his help hadn't indirectly resulted in either Aynward or Dagmara's death. He considered Aynward's fate once he returned home and still felt a pang of guilt at having failed to get them through to safety. He spent the next several minutes running through scenarios in which he might have been successful; there weren't many.

The trio was brought before the headmaster again the following day. However, the audience in the arena was far larger than it had been the day before. Kyllean asked Tumont why there were so many people gathered as they entered but received no response.

He stared in awe at the Lumáles encircling the assemblage. Their riders stood armored beside them.

Kyllean spoke loud enough for everyone in attendance to hear. "Will someone please explain why it looks like the remaining riders are dressed for battle?"

Beside the headmaster stood the healer, Master Hilde, and a female rider he did not know but had seen around the fortress on a few occasions. She appeared old by rider standards, but not the frail kind of old. This was the sort of old that said to others, *Mess with me and you'll be embarrassed and hurt before it's over.* Kyllean had learned his lesson about underestimating some of the "old" riders in the practice yard since earning his blade. This woman appeared formidable, glaring directly at him as he drew close.

No one had answered Kyllean's question, and the woman's stare prevented him from voicing it again.

Headmaster Forestone silenced the gathered assembly and spoke. "We are here today to act on a number of issues concerning a matter of our responsibility to honor the covenant of the Kingdom, as well as the punishment of one of our own."

A scattering of clouds had rolled in, and one just happened to have passed over just as Headmaster Forestone spoke the word "punishment." *As if this meeting needs to feel more ominous,* thought Kyllean sarcastically. He glanced over to Aynward who looked his way, then up to the sky, and finally rolled his eyes and shrugged. He was likely cursing the goddess of luck at such an omen.

The headmaster continued, "We must return the fugitive, Prince Aynward, to the Kingdom authorities so he might be tried for his alleged crimes. This same response has been ruled necessary for Princess Dagmara. The events of yesterday, while unusual, do not supersede our responsibilities to uphold the law. I don't believe anyone relishes the idea of having to cut the connection between rider and Lumále, especially in the case of a Lumále who has been reluctant to offer a link to a rider for such a span as this."

Kyllean looked at Dagmara, who stood a few paces to his left alongside Aynward. She stared at the ground, appearing to have accepted her fate. Both siblings had defeat written plainly on their faces and their posture.

Kyllean felt powerless in his own right. How could he convince Headmaster Forestone to change his mind? Was it even possible? Kyllean didn't even have an alternative to sugg—not unless . . .

He blurted out the idea as it formed, without any thought for logistics or decorum. "Allow her to join the riders."

Gerald scoffed, "She's wanted by the Kingdom. For treason."

Ignoring Gerald, Kyllean looked directly at Headmaster Forestone. "Well . . . we make it into a sort of penance. Requesting a full pardon for the princess in return for her service to the Tal-Dons, and therefore, the Kingdom. You know as well as I that we need *every* rider we can get."

The idea seemed to have revived Aynward's spirit. "If I agree to turn myself over in exchange for Dagmara's pardon, I think with Kirous as acting King for the time being, may agree."

Kyllean hated himself for even suggesting that Aynward's freedom be sacrificed, but there was no way Aynward was going to escape now, anyway.

The headmaster peered out at the three miscreants before him, his arms folded in stern contemplation. Then he said, "Princess Dagmara. Assuming the King were to agree to such terms, what would you say to joining the Tal-Dons?"

Kyllean's heart beat faster. Forestone was actually considering this!

She was silent, staring at hard-packed dirt in front of her feet as if waiting for an answer to rise up from the ground. She finally looked up and shook her head. "I . . . I can't abandon my brother. If anything, I am more guilty than he. He at least knows for certain the truth of his innocence. I have willingly broken Kingdom law based upon the word of a fugitive wanted for regicide. A word, I believe—yes, but as far as the law is concerned, I have defied the Kingdom and raised my sword against my own people. I can't accept a pardon, not while my brother is sent to judgment."

Aynward shook his head. "No way. No way, sis. This—" He swallowed, his voice beginning to crack. "This is your chance to get out of the mess I've made and you need to take it. You've risked far more than you should have on my behalf. This opportunity is a reward from on high for your piety over the years and the valor displayed in helping an innocent man find a bit more adventure before meeting his end. You know what's going to happen if you're returned home. Worse case, they hang you, too. But even if they don't, you'll be locked away in a tower until you're married off, forced to bear an heir, and then locked away once more. Knowing you, that would be a worse fate still. You're here. You've been chosen by a Lumále. You need to do this. Tecuix has spoken."

Kyllean knew Aynward cared little for the gods, but Dagmara perked up at the mention of Tecuix. She turned and glared, wrath parsing the air. "How dare you bring the gods into this!"

Aynward shrugged. "I didn't bring them into this, they were already here. Whether I revere them is irrelevant. You who see the gods at work in the shedding of a single leaf from a tree cannot possibly ignore their hand in providing you with the very thing you've always dreamed of at a time when your life is at stake. Sister, if you can't see this, then you're more a fool than I."

Dagmara dropped her gaze and Kyllean spotted the smallest puff of dust upon the ground before her; a tear striking the dirt.

Dagmara shook her head and her voice cracked as she asked, "How could I fulfill my own dream while leaving you to such a fate?"

Aynward smiled. "This is my dream for you, too. This is the *only* thing you can do to help me."

Kyllean extended his left arm to Aynward and they clasped forearms for what Kyllean suspected would be the very last time. Even if Kyllean managed to survive the coming war with the Lugienese, and Aynward's life was somehow spared by the new King, Aynward would surely be kept under lock and key and the rider who had helped him escape capture once before would not likely be allowed to visit. Kyllean pulled his friend in for a full frontal, shameless embrace.

"I'm going to miss you," said Kyllean.

"You too, old friend." Aynward patted his back and they separated.

Kyllean smiled and shook his head. "I can't believe you managed to escape the capital, a team of assassins, and fight your way into the Tal-Don fortress, granted you had a little help on that last stretch and nearly died in the process. Still a feat worthy of song."

Aynward returned a weak smile but shook his head slowly. "I'm sorry I dragged you into my mess."

"Nonsense! I'm glad we had this last chance to cause mischief. This was the most excitement I've had since Brinkwell! I'd do it again without a thought."

Aynward's mood remained muted, but he allowed a slight grin. "Without a thought is certainly accurate."

Kyllean chuckled and was about to respond when a harsh voice from behind stole the conversation's remaining momentum. "C'mon, finish up. We need to be leaving." Aynward's rider escort stood tapping his foot beside his Lumále as they said their final goodbyes.

Kyllean sighed and nodded. "Goodbye, old friend."

Aynward reached out and gripped Kyllean's collar and pulled him in close with surprising ferocity, and whispered so only he could hear, "You take care of my sister. Promise me that no matter what, you'll take care of her." His eyes blazed with an intensity that had not been present in the fugitive prince since before they had been captured, but where his sister was concerned, nothing could be more serious.

Kyllean coughed at the pressure on his throat as he said, "I give you my word."

Aynward gave him a slight shove. "That means you need to take care of yourself, as well."

Kyllean winked. "Always do."

Aynward pulled his gaze away and focused on his sister, and the two embraced.

Kyllean turned and departed, leaving the siblings to say their goodbyes in private. He would miss Aynward—a lot.

He started toward the practice grounds so he could blow off some steam. Plus, he needed to continue to improve his skills. He was supposed to somehow protect a woman who was every bit as stubborn as her brother, but with the added danger of being a linked rider on the eve of a great war, that is, as long as King Kirous agreed to allow her to train. In any case, if and when war came, she was just as likely to try saving him, which he supposed brought him back to the need to keep up his own training. He let out an exhausted breath. *Convincing the headmaster to let her train as a rider was my idea, wasn't it?*

CHAPTER 70

DAGMARA

A KNOCK CAME AT THE DOOR. Dagmara threw back her covers and sat up. "Yes?"

"Are you proper?"

Dagmara recognized Kyllean's voice.

She rubbed her face and felt her hair full of wild tangles. "Just a minute." She attempted to brush her hair while throwing on the laundered traveling clothes that had just been returned to her.

"I really don't care how many sleeping lines your pillow left on your face."

Dagmara picked up the small mirror from the stand and noted that no such lines existed. *I sleep on my back, as is proper.*

She strode over to the door, annoyed at his early-morning arrival, and the comment. She swung open the door and Kyllean stumbled through with a surprised, "Whoa!" landing soundly on his behind.

Speaking in her most pretentious princess voice, Dagmara remarked, "You know, Headmaster Forestone provided me with a couple of chairs if you'd prefer to sit. Us 'royal' folk don't commune upon the floor if we can help it. It simply isn't proper."

500

Kyllean stood and brushed off his trousers. His expression grew serious. "Well, I hope you are enjoying your chairs, because you're not going to have them for much longer."

Dagmara looked at him confusedly. "What do you mean? Wait, has word arrived back from Quinson already?"

Kyllean nodded. "I may or may not have accidentally on purpose bumped into Tumont as he carried the message to Headmaster Forestone. Upon bumping into Tumont, the message *somehow* wound up in my possession. I'll admit, my curiosity got the better of me and I was unable to resist the temptation to break the seal and read the message."

Dagmara raised her eyebrows at the audacity. "So? Where's the letter?"

She grew hopeful, excited, yet still nervous. Her heart was thumping and her fingers tingled.

"Well, I had to go deliver it to the headmaster before Tumont realized the 'mishap.' And then I came here." His expression grew grim. "I wanted you to hear it from me first."

Her heart sank. The news was bad. Her brother Kirous had rejected the pardon, she was to be returned, and the connection between herself and her Lumále severed. She looked him in the eyes, her vision already blurred by tears.

He spoke solemnly, perhaps more seriously than she had ever heard him speak. "You're to be returned . . . to . . . your . . . training."

She stared at Kyllean, waiting for him to elaborate. He didn't. Her voice became embarrassingly whiny. "Wh—what does that mean?"

Kyllean's expression broke like an egg, a wide smile flowing forth. "You're to continue training as a rider!"

Dagmara's entire body filled with relief, excitement, and then caged annoyance at Kyllean's psychotic method of delivery. She didn't care, and yet she had to repay him in a language that he would understand. He was reclining in the other chair beside her own, feet upon the small table before the both of them. She stood and kicked the back leg of the chair upon which Kyllean's entire weight balanced. He toppled backward with the yelp.

"Yeow! What was that for?"

She just stared at him with her best motherly look that said, *You know what you did.*

He stood and brushed off imaginary dirt from the recently mopped floor. "See if I bring you the good news the next time your trial is postponed until after a war."

"Postponed? I thought I was to be pardoned."

Kyllean shrugged. "One and the same."

"Um . . . no, those are not one and the same. You do understand the difference, right?"

"Sure, sure. Minor detail."

She rolled her eyes and spoke slowly, as if to a child. "In one case, I am absolved of any accused crimes and free to join the riders indefinitely. In the other case, I train to be a rider *only* until we push back the Lugienese and then I am required to return to stand trial where I might still be convicted. Those are two *very* different outcomes."

Kyllean responded with nonchalance. "I prefer to see the silver lining in life. Do as you wish." He turned and stepped through the door. "See you on the practice field."

The door closed and she heard the guard locking the door. Kyllean said to him, "You'll be off guard duty here in just a few hours, Henrik." His voice was muffled only slightly by the thick wood between them.

"Praise the gods!" said the guard. "Standing here with nothing else to do is torture. I'd rather finish my penance cleaning chamber pots. At least then I'd get to move about!"

She heard Kyllean's footsteps fade as he departed.

Dagmara was a bag of mixed emotions as she sank back into her bed. She knew she wouldn't be able to fall back asleep. She lay staring up at the planks of wood that made up her ceiling. Her thoughts turned to her brother. She hadn't even asked about his fate, if it had yet been decided, and this made her feel even guiltier, though she knew the reason she hadn't; she feared the answer. Part of her still wished to be handed over to justice if only to have this guilt of Aynward's fate removed from her chest. If nothing else, she *should* be there. How had she let him convince her to remain behind?

CHAPTER 71

GROBENNAR

GROBENNAR SPENT DAYS TEACHING OTHER priests the nuances of preparing the dordron. The most difficult part had been teaching them to remove the magical geographic restriction. None of them had a powerful spirit like Jaween to assist, and since this was something he himself would never have been able to accomplish on his own, teaching someone else to do so was mostly impossible.

Of the twenty-eight priests given over to his care to teach, only two had managed to successfully remove the spell. The rest would be relegated to taming or offering strength to others in order to do so.

Grobennar sank onto a bench along the edge of the training field, mentally exhausted after so much monotony. *How do those kazi priests teach children, or even tadi priests? I have not the patience for such a calling.*

He watched as some of the newly tamed dordron flew about, while other riders practiced with the sword, something Grobennar had urged after his run-in with the Tal-Don riders. One particular dordron captured his attention as it approached carrying something in its talons, a large sack.

As it drew near, Grobennar realized that the sack contained a person, and he recognized the dordron carrying it. This was Paranja's dordron; she brought the Tal-Don prisoner!

That beautiful woman! If they could understand how the Tal-Don magic negated their own, the next confrontation between riders would surely go much differently.

"Ah, here comes the prize. The secret to the Tal-Don magic," came the nasally voice of Fatu Mazi Rajuban from behind.

Grobennar did not turn, but replied simply, "Yes. The secrets he holds should indeed provide great insight into the Kingdom's greatest weapon." *How did he know?*

Rajuban slid into place beside Grobennar, giving him the urge to relocate. "Is there something I can do for you?" he asked, annoyed.

"Perhaps. I want a great many things."

"As do we all," mumbled Grobennar. "Let me rephrase. Is there something that you want that causes you to be standing beside me now?"

Rajuban brought his left palm to his heart and said in feigned exasperation, "You wound me yet again. I am merely a servant of the Empire come to sit beside his biggest rival to discuss a coordinated plan of conquest."

Grobennar continued watching the approaching form of Paranja, her dordron, and the captured rider. "Someone once told me that if an enemy appears to offer poisoned wine, it is best not to drink."

"Sound advice," remarked Rajuban. "Only what is to be done when this wine is offered by a God? Such a refusal would be death no matter the choice. Surely the poison would be the better way to go."

Grobennar finally turned to regard the man. "I really do hate you."

Rajuban offered a sinister smile. "You will join me as we meet this Tal-Don rider."

"*This is it. Time to kill him. It's either him or you,*" Jaween declared into Grobennar's mind.

For once Grobennar thought Jaween might be onto something. But so too was Rajuban. He could not refuse. Plus, everything had been going so well these past few days. They had no reason to eliminate him.

Still, his gut told him he was headed for death, while his mind could not reconcile this. Besides Jaween's suspicion and Rajuban's uncharacteristic friendliness, Grobennar had no reason to believe that his life was in danger. *Perhaps that's the point,* he thought wryly.

Nevertheless, Grobennar followed Rajuban to the far side of the training ground, away from prying eyes. There were two stone tables that had not been there when Grobennar had first set up the training facility for the dordron and their riders. The tables included straps and chains meant to restrain prisoners for interrogation. Grobennar noticed a procession of cloaked figures following behind and felt his heart begin to beat harder. All of their faces were obscured, and their robes were not red, but black.

"What's this about?" asked Grobennar, stopping where he was a dozen paces from the tables.

Rajuban turned and smiled. "We're meeting the rider here. We have some questions for him."

Grobennar didn't move, just glared at Rajuban.

"Oh, you mean the ominous black-clad folks who have accompanied us here?" He raised both hands in acknowledgment of their presence and they began to fan out around the tables.

"Kill him! Kill him now. It might already be too late!"

Rajuban continued, "They are here to assist us. They are the fruit of a special pet project of mine. I've been experimenting with a few ideas of my own over the years. I've had to keep this a secret because it flirts with the edges of Klerósi law, but after seeing them in action, Magog has officially sanctioned this particular venture."

Grobennar felt doom's presence ensnaring him. He knew Rajuban was lying. But what could he do? He couldn't fight this many—whatever these people were. And what would he do if he somehow survived? He would be an exile. He swallowed hard and nodded. Then continued following Rajuban to stand beside the table.

Paranja was escorted by another group of dark hooded figures, twelve of them. They fanned out to form a ring around Grobennar, Rajuban, and the two tables. Paranja stepped inside.

"Greetings, Fatu Mazi." She bowed, then greeted Grobennar with his respective title.

She held one of the black blades in one hand, and a set of chains to lead the prisoner, who appeared to have been beaten recently, his lip bleeding on one side and a fresh bruise on his face. *Fool must have attempted something during an overnight on the journey here*, thought Grobennar.

"I present to you the Tal-Don rider."

Rajuban smiled. "You have done well, and your reward shall be great, for this and for what is to come." Nodding to the robed figures, he said, "Please secure the prisoner. We have another matter that must be settled before we continue with him."

Rajuban stared at Grobennar and the satisfaction on his face gave Grobennar all the confirmation that he needed. This was it.

Jaween shrieked in his mind, but Grobennar merely winced and continued facing his executioner. "How many I serve, Fatu Mazi?"

Rajuban smiled. "You look a little pale. Is everything all right?"

"Just do what you came here to do."

Grobennar sensed no magic. But his nerves brought a tremble to his hands, and he decided he should at least try to get in a shot before Rajuban did. He remained on high alert, prepared to launch an attack the moment he sensed a threat from Rajuban.

Rajuban sighed and his posture relaxed as he spoke. "I observed something many years ago, a most curious gemstone built into the amulet that a certain young, ambitious priest wore about his neck."

"*He knows. Kill him!*"

Grobennar felt the sweat in his hands grow cold. *No. He couldn't know. It's a rare and likely valuable gem for shielding bone degradation.*

"Yes," Rajuban droned. "I see the concern written on your face. You're wondering whether or not I know about your little spirit friend?"

Grobennar drew in power, prepared to strike.

Rajuban put up a hand but had not yet drawn any himself. "Not so fast, old friend. I'm not here to kill you. I'm here to bargain on behalf of the God-king."

"*Slit his lying throat!*" cried Jaween.

Rajuban pulled out a small leather pouch, loosened the drawstring, and produced several gemstones the same red as his own. "These shards were once a part of a larger, far more powerful spherical stone last wielded by our Luguinden predecessor, Hakbar the Uniter, who, as you know, vanquished the once powerful inhabitants of the Hand of the Gods. Lesante's seers say he was touched by Klerós, wielding not only this stone but another much like it. They say this is how he summoned the Nephilim to this plane during the last battle, if you believe such fanciful tales. I for one never did. But the more I learn of these stones, the more I wonder if perhaps the tales aren't at least in part true.

"One such stone was stolen from him years after the conquest by a remnant of those he had conquered. We are in the process of securing that lost artifact as we speak. But there are others, one of which is closer at hand even than this."

Jaween hissed in Grobennar's mind as Rajuban continued.

"The remaining stone was passed down to Hakbar's successor, who worried over its safety and the unity of the tribes so he had it splintered into five shards: one for each of the five tribes. Centuries later, the prophetess, Lesante, assumed control of a Lugien tribe on the brink of annihilation. She used her shard in a way her enemies never expected: she broke it into nine smaller shards and summoned powerful spirits from the beyond to reside within each. These shards were given to her eight lieutenants, while she wielded the last. With the strength lent by such, she and the Lugien tribe's survivors were able to defend against their adversaries and escape to Angolia, the birthplace of the Lugienese Empire."

Grobennar felt Jaween's consciousness squirming at the words, or perhaps grasping at his own impartial memories from such times. Could what Rajuban said be true?

Grobennar was genuinely curious, but worried about where Rajuban might be leading the conversation. Grobennar had not yet relinquished the hold on his magic as he said, "There is no mention of any of this in the records. Not a single page in her writings, I have read them all. Nor is there mention of this stone of power. Even still, I fail to see what any of this has to do with me."

Rajuban nodded. "Patience, old friend. You never were one for prologues, but please, this one forms the foundation for the annals of history we will be writing in the coming days. But you're quite right. The histories sanctioned by the Kleról are . . . incomplete. However, as you know, there are those dwelling among us now who were there during such times, though their memories may have gaps after the trauma of being transferred from one host to another."

Grobennar's eyes widened in shock, but he waited for Rajuban to continue.

"As you know, several centuries after the prophetess's death, the Kleról fell into a state of chaos and revolt. It was only then that the Fatu Mazi Herbikor found fault in what he believed to be the corruptive spirits hidden within these relics. So he banned their use and hid them away, ordering those who had hidden them to be slain so no records of their whereabouts might remain. He also destroyed all records of the stone and the truth about the shards from our writings. His efforts were largely successful, that is until centuries later when a small boy, playing in a stream with two friends, happened upon an abandoned tunnel. There he found a single gemstone necklace." Holding one of the red shards up between his thumb and forefinger, Rajuban continued, "But there was so much more to be found inside that tunnel had that boy continued to explore, including a single volume containing the true history of the stones, our shards included."

Grobennar could not believe what he was hearing. How could Rajuban know all of this? The other boys had disappeared years ago, presumably murdered by ruffians. Grobennar's eyes widened at the realization. *It was Rajuban.* But to keep such a secret for so long? For Rajuban to have known what Grobennar possessed, a forbidden relic, this entire time . . . he could have had Grobennar arrested and tried for treason long before he rose to the height of Fatu Mazi. Why wait?

Grobennar glanced away in confusion, unable to comprehend all the implications of this story. He spotted Paranja, but she appeared unfazed, unsurprised. Did she know, as well? Was she in on this whole scheme? That betrayal felt just as terrible as the rest. And Grobennar still didn't even know what the scheme was.

Rajuban continued, "Yes. I know. It's a lot to take in. The good news is that the God-king is willing to overlook this transgression just as he has my own. In fact—" Rajuban reached up and pulled at the neckline of his robes to reveal a thumb-sized lump beneath the skin at the center of his collarbone. "The God-king has aided me in transferring the inhabitant of my own shard into this ruby so that my shard could be added to the reunification of the stone of power that Magog will be reclaiming as his own. All the while, I remain a beneficiary of the wisdom and powerful attributes associated with my spirit friend. This same offer is now given unto you."

"They're going to banish me and kill you! Don't trust them!"

Grobennar glanced around at the twelve hooded figures, and finally at Paranja, who gave him a nervous look. "So this bargain of which you speak requires I relinquish my gemstone, my shard, and in exchange, I will be given the spirit back, transferred into a new gem, and we will continue our conquest of Drogen?"

Rajuban nodded. "This is so."

Grobennar sensed Rajuban's excitement at his acceptance of these facts. *Too easy,* he thought. "With such a generous offer, why bother with all the hoods?"

Rajuban chuckled. "Neither one of us got to where we are today by leaving anything entirely to chance."

"True enough," agreed Grobennar.

"You're going to do it? You fool. You can't!"

Grobennar reached a decision. A decision he hated, but a decision he believed was unavoidable. Rajuban had outplayed him once again and he was at the mercy of the man's word. Anything besides this was assured death. So he reached up and took hold of the golden chain connected to the amulet and lifted it over his head, reducing the strength of Jaween's mental screams.

Paranja spoke up. "Would you mind if I did the honors?"

Rajuban rolled his eyes. "Very well. I suppose you have been *pretending* to be his friend for all this time. You deserve this much."

That struck a nerve, a painful cord. Grobennar had known Paranja from his days back in the Tethiriean, the academy of seekers, and he had always counted her a friend, and he thought she wished to be more than that. Was that all a lie? There was something about the creases around her eyes that gave him pause. She stared at him as if attempting to communicate something. An apology? A warning? Or was he just so overwhelmed with nerves that he was imagining things?

As she took hold of the chain, she thanked him out loud, then leaned in and whispered, "Get ready."

Grobennar did his best not to react. *Ready for what?*

As she approached the smug Fatu Mazi, Grobennar felt the tingle of priestly magic mix with that of the faint taint of dark magic. Then everything became a complete blur of action.

Paranja's hand shot out along with the glint of steel. The knife cut into the collar of the Fatu Mazi, who shrieked as he stumbled back. Paranja followed with a blast of energy, also directed at Rajuban. He dodged to the side, but not before Paranja had snatched the pouch of shards he had been holding out in front of him. Without looking, her wrist snapped from behind her back and Grobennar's amulet zipped through the air to strike him hard in the chest. It stung, but he caught it before it struck the ground.

Grobennar looked up to see that the chains binding the prisoner had fallen to the stone while Paranja tossed the black blade to the rider. Without missing a beat, she shot a spray of fiery energy from her hands in both directions, forcing the hooded guards to block, duck, or, for a few of them, accept the painful blow with shrieks of pain that sent them writhing on the ground.

Knowing his bed had been made, Grobennar joined the melee. He shot bolts of energy at the two closest priests, landing both as they were too distracted by Paranja to see his attack coming. The black-dyed wool of their cloaks smoked, as did their skin. But there were far too many of these men for Grobennar's liking.

Paranja yelled to the rider, "Kelson, to me." She rolled backward and came to her feet beside Grobennar while the rider performed a far more impressive backflip to land in front of both of them, sword out slashing the air to absorb the blasts of retaliatory energy coming their way.

The former prisoner's blade flashed to and fro as if he were attacking a swarm of bees, dashing the oncoming attacks as the trio backed away from Rajuban and his remaining minions. One of them had lost his hood and his face revealed a crown of colorful gemstones embedded within the skin of his forehead.

What kind of twisted monsters has Rajuban created?

"Summon your dordron," said Paranja, her words rushed as she returned magic with magic.

Holding his hand over his bleeding neck, Rajuban roared, "You're a dead woman, Paranja!" Rajuban punctuated the next two words for emphasis. "Dead. Woman!" Then he growled, "And I'm going to make sure it's slow." His final words dripped with hatred, the likes of which Grobennar had never heard. "Take them alive!"

"Come on!" she yelled to Grobennar. "Kelson can hold them off for a time."

Grobennar ran, but as he glanced back, he saw that the remaining hooded figures were growing wise, fanning out. Then Grobennar spotted two freakishly large flying creatures racing up the slope, close to the ground. They pulled up a moment later and Grobennar and Paranja clambered up in a hurry.

"Let's go!" yelled Paranja.

Their mounts took to the air, though Grobennar noticed Paranja heading toward the violence while Grobennar had directed his mount to fly away. Then he saw the rope dangling from the foot of the dordron and understood what she was doing.

She yelled to Kelson, and he leaped to catch the loop at the bottom of the rope as it flew by. He continued to bat away bolts of energy from the monsters attacking below as the dordron propelled them away.

Grobennar did his best to hold on as he turned to defend himself and Frida from the continued attacks, hoping to escape onslaught from the . . . priests? Abominations, more like. How had Rajuban convinced the God-king to sanction such *wrongness*?

Then an invisible blast of air slammed into Frida's body, sending both her and Grobennar spinning toward the ground. He clung on for dear life as they careened toward a copse of trees between the training ground and the place where Rajuban had attempted to obtain Grobennar's piece of the shard.

"Noooo!"

He lost his grip and finally leaped from her back. This split-second choice ended the spinning movement so he was able to face the fast-approaching ground head on as he overshot the trees. He dug into himself and the strength lent by Jaween and threw it at the ground in a blast of powerful air. Nevertheless, he struck the ground with a painful crunch.

To his surprise, his body registered a great deal of pain but he did not lose consciousness. He tried to move and groaned from the sharp pain he felt in several areas of his body. Jaween was quick to work his power on the worst of it and Grobennar was able to crawl to his knees. "So much for escaping."

"*At least we managed to take a few down with us. With more to come, I hope!*"

But Grobennar sensed Frida's mind fast approaching and looked up to see her wings opening to land beside him. She must have somehow righted herself before striking the ground. Whatever the case, he now had another chance at escape.

He scrambled up. Once back in the air, he saw Paranja up ahead. She was not as far as he would have expected. Then, he noticed that the rider was no longer dangling from the rope but had climbed up to ride behind her. He would not trust the man once free of these lands. But he bade Frida to follow with as much haste as she could manage. Looking back toward the training ground, he knew it would not be long before they were pursued. But he also knew there were not many trained dordron riders here, and those who were had just recently learned. He, Paranja, and the rider might just escape with their lives.

But then what? He was now a man without a banner. What had he done? Why had he joined Paranja against Rajuban? Rajuban might have kept his word. But Grobennar suspected this was not so. Paranja knew the plan for him. That's why she'd acted as she did, wasn't it?

What could I have done differently? Anything? He feared for his soul. He had just stolen away with the pieces of a powerful relic that would help Klerós's lieutenants in the world reign supreme against his enemies. Would this defiance against his god's avatar mean his soul was forfeit?

He glanced behind him and saw four dordron beginning their pursuit. It looked like he would be drawing yet more Lugienese blood today.

CHAPTER 72

GROBENNAR

BLOOD SPRAYED FROM THE NECK of the Tal-Don rider, the sand at their feet rushing to soak up the red droplets as they struck.

"*Ooh. Splendid!*" responded Jaween.

Grobennar stumbled back in surprise. "What—what are you doing?" Grobennar didn't trust the man, either, and was certainly not opposed to slaying those he knew to be his enemies, but this one had just helped them escape. Grobennar had planned to convince Paranja to simply leave the rider here. They could then fly far enough away to be safe and set up camp for the night.

"Eliminating a threat," she said without hesitation. "His purpose has been served and we saved him the pain of interrogation. Giving him the opportunity to save us in exchange for a quick death was as much mercy as he deserved."

"Was he aware that this was the exchange?"

She didn't answer right away, but finally said, "He is an enemy to my people and yours."

Grobennar considered her response. "What you say indicates that there is a great deal more I do not know about you."

515

Paranja smiled. "You will understand everything soon enough. However, for now, I can tell you only this: we are on our way to meet friends."

"That's not a lot to go on," remarked Grobennar, his eyes trained on the blade Paranja wiped upon the cloak of the corpse that lay beside her.

"Yes, but right now it's the *only* thing you have to go on."

"*She makes a fair point. But I don't trust her. But ooh I like the way she thinks!*"

"At least tell me where we're headed."

"South."

One of the tribes, then. It had not escaped his attention that Paranja had included stealing the shards as a part of her plan. If she had merely wished to escape with Grobennar, she could have done so before his return to Rajuban and the extremely risky escape therein. But what did *she* want with the shards? He had to assume that she intended . . .

"You intend to take my shard. Are you waiting for me to close my eyes? Will you slit my throat, as well?"

Paranja looked sincerely hurt by the words, but he decided she was as good a performer as any he had seen to have been accepted into Rajuban's inner circle.

She said, "If I wished to steal your shard and kill you, I would have done so long ago and my plans for obtaining the others from Rajuban would have looked much different. Yes, I've kept things from you, but please believe that I have no plans to betray you. As for further answers, unfortunately, you're just going to have to trust me. I hope my loyalty to you thus far is enough to convince you to do so."

"*So very cunning. Too cunning, if you ask me, which you never do. But I know you will not kill her like you should. Let's hope I can rouse you in time to stop her from cutting you open as you sleep.*"

"Seems you've left me with few other options."

She gave him a warm smile. "Trust me, you will appreciate the options I've left open to you."

CHAPTER 73

DAGMARA

KYLLEAN STRODE OVER TO DAGMARA carrying a practice sword. "How fares my favorite princess rider on her journey to riderhood?"

Dagmara shrugged. "Well, I've got the Lumále so I'd say I'm further along than say, a Lumáleless rider without a rider's blade."

Kyllean made a gasping sound, then dropped his practice weapon to clutch his throat before falling to the ground with a choking sound. A moment later, he performed an acrobatic motion that sprang him from his back to his feet in a single motion.

"I see your tongue remains as sharp as ever. But I suppose you're right." He held up one of the two weapons he carried with him. "However, I was given my blades back this morning, though I'm still to continue spending much of my days cleaning chamber pots. Nevertheless, the headmaster decided that with the Lugienese behaving as they are, I need to continue to progress."

"Congratulations on that. You must be excited."

He nodded and twirled the single weapon in his hand. "I am." He continued a show of extraordinary movements with the blade, and she almost mocked him for showing off, only he wasn't. He was just genuinely enjoying his weapon. "It's funny. I've only had this blade a

517

short while, yet it seems like it's been with me my entire life. Being without it was . . . difficult."

"I'm very happy for you."

He chuckled. "Thanks. I'm sure it's nothing like having my own Lumále. You are the envy of many folks who have been here for years."

Dagmara nodded, and her playful smile faded. His secondary statement was truer than she would have liked. The envy to which he referred was palpable. The chasm she felt between herself and those within the fortress was wide. In spite of the fact that they were all preparing for a Lugienese invasion of the Kingdom, she did not feel the kinship with others that she had expected. Dagmara was in the precarious position of having been claimed by a Lumále but being herself unable to wield a rider's sword or perform even the slightest amount of magic to enhance her speed or strength. She was in every sense unworthy.

Because the others in Kyllean's cohort had by now all earned their swords, she had been moved over to the riders' practice yard. Even still, few would spar with her outside of the mandatory training sessions organized by Master Hilde. Anyone with the ability to use their enhanced speed and strength did not wish to waste time sparring with someone who could not. Additionally, her fighting style was far different from the Tal-Don style taught to these children from the time they were big enough to hold a stick. Her Scritlandian-influenced movements caused frustration to those who expected certain reactions that never came. This meant either easy victories for them, or awkward, accidental bruises and supposed lucky hits for Dagmara. This coupled with the jealousy that she was also learning to ride her Lumále meant that she was treated like the outsider that she was.

"So, do you wish to spar or what?"

It felt like pity, but Dagmara nodded. "Sure."

He was far better than she. That much was apparent, but he didn't gloat. After a few bouts, he even complimented her. "You know, you're actually quite a bit better than I expected. Your training with that Scritlandian gives you an interesting . . . accent, so to speak. Could prove useful, though you expose yourself too much on the right side when you thrust. As soon as someone notices, they'll feint to draw it and capitalize."

"Better than expected. Quite the compliment," she said with a sliver of sarcasm in her voice. Then she looked to the sky behind him and widened her eyes to show surprise and fear. He took the bait and turned.

Dagmara ducked and pivoted on her left foot as her other leg snapped out to sweep his feet out from under him. He landed more gracefully than anyone had any right to, but she still managed to extend her practice sword to his neck while he was down, causing him to go still.

"You know, you actually fall with far more grace than I expected."

A few jeers rang out from others in the practice yard, and Kyllean's ordinarily pale expression reddened. "I really need to stop letting you do things like that."

"Oh? I wasn't aware you *let* yourself be flopped to the ground yet again."

It was a petty move, but it felt good to "win" at something, scrupulous or not.

"Yes, yes. I take your point, though I was not attempting to patronize you. My compliment was genuine. As was my critique."

Dagmara smiled. "I know. I just really needed to knock someone down."

Kyllean stood up and brushed off the dust from his backside as best he could. "Don't count on *that* happening again."

Dagmara raised an eyebrow. "Oh?"

He ignored her attempt to continue the banter. "Care to fix your attack? I think a minor adjustment to your lead foot, and a slight change to the angle of your sword, will do wonders."

She accepted his help and they continued to spar, cementing the adjustments to her swordplay. Dagmara finally held up a hand, her lungs ready to burst with fatigue. "I . . . think . . . I . . . need . . . a . . . break."

Kyllean was either masking his own weariness, or he really was *that* good. "Very well. This was a productive session. You're a quick learner."

"Not of magic," she grumbled as she took a seat upon the ground, leaning back on straightened arms.

Kyllean waved a hand. "You're not an innate user. It will take time. Gods, it took me longer than many in my cohort and my blood is pure Don-Votro. It's really nothing to worry yourself over."

She shook her head. "Master Hilde says the same."

"Further confirming the validity," said Kyllean, smiling warmly.

"I can't even sense magic being used, let alone the latent energy around me."

"Give it time."

"We might not have time."

Kyllean looked up and nodded. He knew she was right. He responded, "Worry over the things within your control, leave the rest to the gods. Right now, the only thing you have control over is your training. If you're doing everything you're supposed to do there, the rest will take care of itself. And if not, there's nothing to be gained from worry."

Dagmara nodded. She knew this was true. Everyone said essentially the same thing. But it was difficult to believe when every other student had earned their blade. She was the only one who seemed completely inept.

He added, "Plus, everyone else has been here longer than you."

That was true, too, but it didn't make her feel any better. It didn't give her hope that something would suddenly happen.

"She gave you the tea, right?"

Dagmara nodded. "Yes, I was able to feel her magic during this time, but nothing since."

He nodded and they sat in silence for a while. And then she saw his expression change. He reached his hand toward hers, slowly, but stopped before making contact. He looked up and met her eyes. "May I?"

She looked down at her own hand, then back up at him. "W—what are you doing?"

He gave her a wry smile that felt very much in line with the Kyllean that Aynward had described. "I want to try something."

She hesitated. "Is it going to hurt?"

He looked up in thought. "I don't *think* so."

"Uh—all right?"

He waited for her to say more, but she didn't and he slowly brought his hand to touch her own. His hand was warm, and a little bit rough from the calluses of swordplay. But it felt . . . nice. Very nice. She looked up to meet his eyes, but he continued to gaze down at their hands. He was fully focused on somethi—

She stiffened as a rush of tingling butterflies ran up her arm and into her chest, then spread out from there. Her fatigue was forgotten. She felt suddenly strong. It was a similar sensation to when she was close to her Lumále, though not the same. She didn't feel the connectedness to Kyllean's feelings, but there was something.

Finally he said, "So you feel that?"

She exhaled loudly, excitedly, and nodded. "Yes."

"Hmm. I wonder . . ."

He released his touch on her hand. "Do you . . . still feel it?"

Dagmara considered. She felt no change. "No—I mean, yes. Yes, I still feel it." She was giddy with excitement at the sensation. Definitely different from the connection between her and her Lumále.

He rose to his feet. "Pick up your weapon."

She mirrored him and stood, bringing her weapon to bear.

"Let's spar."

She took her stance, then opened up with an attack. As she did, she noted the lightness of her weapon and the unnatural speed with which she moved.

She felt her eyes widen.

"It's working!" he exclaimed.

"How did you—?"

"I am pushing some of my own energy into you, much like I do with my rider blade." He laughed like a kid who had just discovered the magic of skipping a rock on the water by accident.

Dagmara reengaged; her newfound speed and strength making her feel as though she was wielding a switch, not a heavy metal practice sword. They sparred for a considerable time and it was joyous!

Kyllean paused and spoke more to himself than her. "What if I . . ." He walked over to the wall of the practice yard and retrieved his rider's blade. "Here, try this."

He did a fancy twirl with his hand and the blade spun, hilt suddenly facing her and within reach. She took it hesitantly. "This is a real rider's blade."

He nodded. "It is."

The obsidian metal glinted and lines of light danced along its edge as she moved it.

"Let me know if you feel anything change."

His face became one of stern concentration.

Dagmara waited expectantly, basking in the power she felt with the magic flowing through her veins. *Is this how the riders feel every time they use their power?* It was a wonder they didn't lose themselves in it and burn themselves out. She had been taught about the dangers of overtaxing oneself in this way, especially for novices who were less efficient in their use of drawing power from their surroundings. *I never want this feeling to go away.*

A voice cut through the practice yard and everything stopped, including Kyllean's magic.

"What do you think you're doing?" It was Master Hilde, and she sounded *very* angry.

Kyllean turned to face her. He spoke excitedly, oblivious to the fury in her tone. "I pushed some of my magic into her, and it actually worked! She was—"

Master Hilde cut him off. "Fool boy!"

Kyllean bowed his head in respect, then continued to speak. "No, Master Hilde, I don't think you understand. I was just—"

She cut him off again. "I know what you're doing and you will end it right this moment!"

Dagmara gasped as the sensation of power suddenly drained away. It was like being dropped into a pool of water, her every movement felt taxed by comparison, the color around her muted.

Master Hilde continued to berate Kyllean. "And you will *not* do it again. Pushing your magic into someone else is a sure-fire way to get yourself killed!" Glaring at Dagmara she said, "The princess is going to need to learn to wield her own magic." She shook her head and looked back at Kyllean, her tone softening. "Pushing your own magic into another like that takes a far greater toll on one's bones than pushing it through oneself. As it is, you will be taking today and tomorrow off from training in order to allow your bones time to replenish their strength. You're *very* lucky you didn't break something today."

Dagmara saw Kyllean's embarrassment, but also frustration. "You'd think someone would have mentioned this before now," he grumbled as Master Hilde stalked away.

She whirled. "We've not warned about it because we've never had a student stupid enough to try something like this without at least first asking! Which brings me to another important rule. Don't try anything else that involves magic without running it by me first."

She looked to Dagmara. "Do you understand?"

Dagmara nodded. "Yes, Master."

"Good."

Kyllean shrugged once Master Hilde was fully beyond earshot. "Was worth a try."

Dagmara gave him a confused look.

Kyllean sighed and shook his head. "Really seemed like a great idea at the time, but I think maybe Master Hilde was right about the risks." He wobbled where he stood and Dagmara saw that he was struggling to remain standing. She took a quick step toward him as he wavered. She slid just beneath his shoulder and her left arm wrapped around his waist. She let his arm drape across her own shoulders, then she reached up and took hold of his hand. "Let's get you back to your room to rest."

He grunted. "This went downhill rather quickly didn't it?"

She didn't respond.

"Well, at least you were able to experience the feeling. What did you think?"

Dagmara smiled. "It was . . . intoxicating."

"Then perhaps it was worth it after all."

She shook her head. "Not if I'm never able to wield it on my own. Now I know what I'm missing."

"All the more incentive to work harder to learn."

She stopped walking and looked up at him. "You think I haven't been trying?"

"I—uh—no. That's not what I meant. I was just—oh, uh, we can't leave my sword here." They had just reached the exit to the practice yard. Dagmara released the glare she had glued on him and they hobbled over to retrieve his weapon. He sheathed it.

She helped him back to his room without much more conversation, and then into his bed in the barracks and was glad his was the bottom bunk. She started to leave, then turned and said, "Thank you for today. It meant a lot that you tried to help. And you're right. I'm glad I was able to experience the feeling at least once. Rest up so we can spar again when you're all healed up. I don't want any excuses when I beat you."

He laughed and the rest of the tension between them disappeared like the magic she had felt earlier. She decided now would be a good time for a ride.

Once outside, she extended her thoughts the way she had been taught by the riding masters and quickly found the connection between herself and her Lumále. This was different magic, or the same magic, but not her magic. Or she wasn't the one doing the magic. Something like that. She didn't understand it all just yet. All she knew was that she could sense the general direction of her Lumále and extend her mind along the connection between them. It was just like any one of the five senses, only she was new to it so her control was weak. She found the consciousness of her Lumále and attempted to push the idea of her riding. This was the last thing she had learned and had been successful in her last two attempts.

Dagmara thought she sensed the impression of a response but wasn't certain. She walked toward Lumále Heights so as to draw less attention if and when her Lumále came. She hadn't gotten more than fifty paces along the sloping trail when she felt the sudden strengthening of their connection. She looked up to see her Lumále quickly growing in size.

At least I'm able to do one thing right, she thought as she climbed onto the back of her Lumále.

CHAPTER 74

KYLLEAN

KYLLEAN HELD HIS BREATH AS he shoveled this last load of human waste from the cesspit beneath the garderobe. The wheelbarrow was overflowing, and heavier than he liked, but this would be his last haul of the evening if he could manage it. *The things we do for friendship,* he thought as he strained to lift the arms of the cart. *I really need to make better choices in friends.*

A voice captured his attention just as he managed to get the cart moving forward up the hill. It was a deep, hollow voice, and it was familiar, though he couldn't initially place it. "You must have committed quite the crime to have been assigned to such a task."

Kyllean turned his head to the right to regard the speaker but saw only shadow. Still unable to place the voice, he asked, "Who's there?"

It was dusk, the sun having just dropped behind Lumále Heights. This left several hours of illuminated sky, but direct sunlight would not be seen again until morning. The back side of the citadel was not a well-lit place to begin with, and the space between the row of spruce and citadel was especially gloomy. There was nothing threatening in the voice, but Kyllean still felt uneasy as he resumed pushing the heavy tool up the slope on his way to dump this last load of filth.

"If it's any consolation, I believe this will be your last time performing such a task."

The voice seemed to come from the opposite side as last time and Kyllean whipped his head around to meet the mysterious visitor. This sudden movement caused him to lose control of the heavy load. The right handle took on a will of its own as the barrow began tipping to its side. "No, no, no!"

He felt the tingle of magic, the slightest sliver. The wheelbarrow righted itself. Kyllean looked up to see the silhouette of a tall thin man in a dark billowing robe. His face was still obscured by shadow, but recognition flared nonetheless.

"Draílock?"

His arms extended outward, and he bowed as he responded, "The very same."

A dozen questions came to mind. *What are you doing here? How are you here? Why* . . . Kyllean decided to start with a little more formality. "It's . . . great to see you."

"Likewise, Kyllean Don-Votro."

Kyllean resumed pushing the cart up the slope and Draílock fell in beside him. Kyllean asked, "So, what exactly are you doing here? Weren't you supposed to be with Sindri down in Scritland looking for that missing boy?"

Draílock took a while to answer, but Kyllean recalled this trait from their weeks together onboard a small vessel between Brinkwell and Tung. He finally responded, "Suffice it to say there are a few things here that need doing."

"So did you and Sindri find the boy you were looking for? And what about . . . what was her name? Ari—something?"

"Arella remains with Sindri." He paused, then added, "I believe by now they should be close to finding the boy."

They had reached the northeast corner of the citadel where Kyllean was to turn right to spread the human waste while turning left would take them back to the barracks, the training grounds, and the main entrance to the citadel.

Draílock said, "Why don't you finish up here then meet me in the dining hall. There are a few others with whom I must speak." He held up a finger. "Oh, and bring your weapons."

"My swords?"

Draílock nodded. "Definitely." As if adding the word "definitely" was all the explanation that was needed. He started off in the opposite direction.

Kyllean was left feeling that something bad was about to happen, but he had no idea what. There was just something about Draílock that gave Kyllean the impression of . . . change. A disquieting calm surrounded his very essence. The whole thing about bringing his swords didn't do anything to diminish these thoughts. Kyllean felt the same foreboding one feels at the calming winds that precede a great storm. He did not like it one bit.

Draílock mumbled something under his breath.

"What's that?" asked Kyllean.

Draílock ignored the question. "This blade is quite curious and also . . . marvelous," said the wizard as he held the marbled weapon in his hands, inspecting it closely enough to convince Kyllean that he might have experience as a blacksmith. "They just gave this to you, mmm?"

"Well, it doesn't do anything, or at least nothing that anyone knows."

Draílock handed it back to him carefully. "Is that so? Hmm. I suppose we'll find out soon enough."

Kyllean chuckled. "Yeah—wait. What's that supposed to mean?"

Draílock took a seat across the table from Kyllean in the empty dining hall. "So you've really not been chosen by a Lumále yet?"

This ignoring of his questions was a trait that irritated Kyllean. Had Draílock been this annoying on the ship?

Kyllean sighed. "I already told you I haven't." When Draílock didn't reply, Kyllean added, "It's not like there are many untethered left to begin with."

Draílock just stared up at the sky with an expression of perplexity, which as far as Kyllean could recall was *not* normal for the man.

"This will certainly be . . . interesting," Draílock said, more to himself than Kyllean.

Several candles cast dim light within the dining hall. Kyllean strained as he tore a piece of bread from the cold, hard loaf he had taken from the kitchen. He didn't mind the stuff. He'd grown accustomed to eating his dinners cold ever since his appointment to the esteemed position of fortress fecal thrower.

Kyllean decided to try out a few more questions. Maybe Draílock would answer at least one of them. "So why again are you here? And how is it that you appear to know your way around?"

Draílock seemed to be somewhere else, but he managed a response. "Oh, I find riders to be a most intriguing lot. More important, I have a sense that something very interesting is going to be taking place here quite soon."

What kind of answer is that? Another non-answer.

Then something struck Kyllean, something that had itched at the back of his mind throughout the entire journey from Brinkwell. He'd had a sense that he had seen Draílock before. He hadn't been able to place him and had therefore dismissed the feeling after Draílock had brushed his question about it aside. But seeing Draílock's familiarity with the fortress renewed his sense of déjà vu, and with that a memory slammed into place. His parents had received a visitor to their home just a few weeks before Kyllean had been shipped off to Brinkwell. And this just days before Kyllean had been told that he would be attending Brinkwell, not the University of Scritler. Kyllean had arrived home just as the "visitor" was leaving. The man had held the door for him, Kyllean had thanked him, and he'd responded with just one word: "Indeed." An odd response, but if it had been Draílock . . . well, Draílock was odd. For some reason, Kyllean could not recall the man's face.

But what did this mean? Why would Draílock have been at *his* home? The peculiarity of it gave him further reason to doubt his suspicion.

Kyllean blurted, "Before I left for Brinkwell, you were at my parents' home. What were you doing there?"

Draílock's eyes finally seemed to focus on the here and now, and he slowly turned his gaze upon Kyllean. His expression was almost a glare, but with such little variation in any of his expressions, it was difficult to be certain. Draílock relaxed his shoulders and leaned back in his chair, one hand reaching up to stroke his lengthy beard. "So you remember that, do you?"

Now it was Kyllean's turn to glare.

Draílock chuckled. "Very well. Your father and I go back a ways. I happened to be visiting the fortress and I decided to pay him a special visit."

Friends with my father, huh? "Okay, just a special visit to my father, a friend of yours. And your visit had nothing to do with the sudden change in where I would attend university?"

Draílock brought his hands to rest upon the table, his long bony fingers interlocking as he did. "Tell me this, Kyllean. Would you be upset if it did? Or would you be upset if I told you that my visit had nothing to do with you whatsoever?"

Kyllean was growing more and more agitated by Draílock's flippant deflections. "I—I—I just want *something* to make sense. With the Lugienese invasion, my father being dead—Yeah, he's dead, by the way." Kyllean voice was beginning to crack. "But you already knew that, didn't you?" He continued without waiting for a response. "Dagmara, the fugitive princess, was chosen by a Lumále. She had absolutely no training, but that's all right, *completely* normal. And my best friend from Brinkwell is likely preparing to hang from a noose, and that's if the new acting King Kirous takes mercy on him. So yeah, I'd like for at least one thing, even if it's something small, to just . . . make . . . sense. Is that so much to ask?"

Draílock stared at him, seemingly unfazed by the agitation or accusation in his voice. He spoke irritatingly calmly. "You sound quite a bit like him, you know."

"Like who? Aynward?"

Draílock shook his head. "Your father."

That made no sense. His father had hardly ever raised his voice. The man was flustered by nothing, ever. Knowing that his father was no longer alive made the statement feel all the more wrong. "You don't know what you're talking about. And you still haven't answered a single question."

Draílock started to stand. "One of your statements is true. Perhaps sometime we'll get the chance to sit down for a while longer and I'll be able to tell you more. But right now, it sounds like there is a bit of a commotion outside." The old wizard waved a hand. "Come."

Kyllean didn't hear anything, but he followed Draílock out of the dining hall. As they entered the hallway, he did hear *something*; men and women shouting? Yes, it grew clearer. These weren't terrified pedestrians like Kyllean recalled from Brinkwell; this was the sound of battle, distant shouts of command. Draílock stopped before the door that would lead to the outside.

"What is going on?" Kyllean's mind initially went to the Lugienese, but that couldn't be. There was no way they could have marched an army here without being seen by the rider scouts. The only other possibility Kyllean could imagine was that it was a force from East End, but that also made no sense. The riders were protected by the covenant, or, rather, the Kingdom was protected by the riders via the covenant.

Draílock peeked out, then pulled his head back in and closed the door. "Klerósi priests."

Those words struck Kyllean like an anvil falling from the sky. "Klerósi? As in Lugienese? How is that possible?" His hands were already reaching for his swords, tingling with nervous anticipation. He drew upon the surrounding stone to enhance his speed and strength.

"Yes, you're going to need your strength for this." Draílock's expression remained that of stone. "They ride upon the backs of dordron. Come, we need to get to the citadel."

Kyllean heard what Draílock said, or at least he thought he did. "Wait—dordron? You mean to tell me—"

A thundering crash shook the ground just a few paces away, and Kyllean stumbled into Draílock. Debris littered the dining hall precisely where they had just been seated. A spear of dim light shone through the man-sized opening in the roof; a massive chunk of stone had splintered the very chair that Kyllean had been seated in just moments earlier.

"We need to be going," said Draílock firmly.

"That is the sanest thing you've said since arriving," remarked Kyllean dryly.

They stepped out into a rectangular practice arena that ran the length of the connected barracks and dining hall. Across from them, beyond the empty practice arena, stood the citadel.

With the fortress absent its main force of riders, they would have a limited means of defense against their flying adversaries. Kyllean had no idea how many there might be. He looked up and saw at least a dozen of the massive birds silhouetted in the air, circling the citadel as they dropped human-sized boulders upon its defenders. Meanwhile the priests atop the winged creatures hurled magical blasts of energy. The citadel turrets and towers were sprinkled with men and women shooting arrows at the dordron and their riders. They worked in pairs, one with a blade to absorb the magical attacks while the other shot arrows. The priests atop the dordron had no difficulty batting the shafts aside with their magic as they tormented the citadel. The air thrummed with the use of magic.

Just as Draílock and Kyllean prepared to dash across the open space to the closest entrance, two riders sprinted from the barracks thirty paces away. They looked up, saw no danger, and continued toward the massive double-door entrance across the way. Kyllean looked on in horror as a dordron swooped in unseen from behind. He shouted, "Behind you!"

One of the two turned just in time to meet a collection of sharp talons head on. He brought his sword to bear a moment too late. He was picked up and carried into the air before being released about twenty paces up. He crashed into the citadel wall as if he were made from wet clay, his body twisting and bending at wrong angles.

Kyllean recognized the second rider as Thompson, a middle-aged untethered rider. He had dodged to the side of the attack on the other dordron rider, but the creature had turned and was now flying to meet him head on. The priest atop the beast shot a blast of energy at

Thompson, but the energy melted harmlessly into Thompson's blade. This would do the man little good when the full force of the dordron crashed into him.

"We need to do something!" Kyllean cried.

Draílock shook his head. "We need to get to the citadel."

Kyllean sprinted toward Thompson.

Fueled by his magic, Kyllean was very fast, but within the first few steps he saw that he would not get there in time. But maybe he could distract the attackers. Still at least twenty-five paces away, he shouted at the top of his lungs. The dordron and its rider were unaffected by his efforts and Kyllean was too late to help.

Kyllean suddenly felt two simultaneous sensations. One was a powerful wind, the sort of gust consistent with a storm; *or* the flapping wings of a flying man-killing bird ridden by an evil priest. This flashed across his awareness in the same instant as a vast swath of magic.

Then the ground beside him ripped open, exploding stone and dirt shot into the sky and knocking Kyllean off his feet. His enhanced agility was useless against the disorientation he experienced spinning through the air amid the debris.

Kyllean landed hard on his shoulder and rolled to his stomach. He got to his knees, covering his face and eyes as dirt and stone continued to rain all about. He dared look up not a moment too soon. An unseated Klerósi priest was sprinting toward him. He shot a line of energy directly at Kyllean. *My swords!* He'd lost both in his tumble. Reacting on instinct, he flattened against the ground as a wave of hot, powerful air zipped just above him. Then Kyllean sprang to his feet just as the priest leaped toward him with a knife in each hand. The moment Kyllean's foot touched the ground he propelled himself to the left while his upper body ducked beneath the slash of the blade. Kyllean's rider training proved its effectiveness; he maintained his grip on his magic. Without it, he would have been too slow.

Instead, he managed to twist around to land a fist in the priest's ribs as the blade caught only air. Kyllean followed this up with his opposite knee, and a final shot to the face that sent the priest stumbling backward.

Kyllean spotted the marbled blade to his right and dove to retrieve it. His left hand caught the hilt and he rolled back to his feet, weapon in hand. This was just in time as another blast of magic hurtled toward him. *Please work!* he begged the sword. Before he could find out if it did, the energy blast was pushed aside by another wave of magic, from Draílock. However, the edges of the energy still struck, shooting right past the marbled blade to strike Kyllean on the outside of his arm. He yelled and looked over to see that his sleeve had been torn and the skin beneath it singed. The injury was otherwise insignificant.

The priest shouted what Kyllean imagined was a curse and focused his attention on Draílock. Before Kyllean could take advantage of the distraction, a shriek rang out to Kyllean's left and he spotted a monstrous creature barreling toward him. Just as its beak opened to bite, a blast of magical air careened into its chest and sent it tumbling to the side.

Draílock called out from behind Kyllean, "We need to go. Now!"

Kyllean spotted the priest before him creating some sort of shield, the air around him rippling. Then the ground beneath him softened and swallowed him whole. *I'm thinking that was not his own doing,* Kyllean had a moment to think before Draílock yelled out again. "Run!"

Kyllean snatched up his other weapon and darted to the citadel, praying that Draílock would be able to keep any other dangers at bay.

Two riders shut the door behind them then slammed the lock bars into place.

Kyllean put hands to his knees and bent over to catch his breath. He was not physically fatigued, but nearly dying had a way of sapping a person's mental energy.

"Why are they here? They must have somehow known that the Lumáles were gone."

Draílock nodded. "Indeed. That is precisely why they are here. And *that* is also part of why I have come."

Draílock gestured down the long hallway that led to the foray, the place where Aynward had been healed weeks earlier.

"If you hope to survive this, you need to do as exactly as I say," commanded Draílock. "Do you understand me?"

Kyllean nodded, his heart thumping hard in his chest. "Except we need to go get Dagmara."

Draílock smiled, an unsettling sight worn upon his face. "Where do you think we're going?"

CHAPTER 75

DAGMARA

THE CLASH OF STEEL, SHOUTS of battle, and shaking of the very walls created a chilling chorus as Dagmara waiting nervously in her room. Whatever was going on out there, it did not appear to be going well for the riders.

Dagmara was already wearing her rider's uniform, armor and all, which included a breastplate, visorless helm, and a few other pieces of minor protection. She also still had the sword she had brought with her from Salmune. It had no magical qualities like the true riders' blades, but it was sharp enough. She couldn't abide just huddling in her room while everyone else fought and died. Headmaster Forestone had told her to stay put until further instructions came. Well, he could discipline her later if they all survived. She wasn't helpless. She had one of the few Lumáles still here at the fortress and she intended to use her.

As she neared the door, footsteps pounded down the hall. She stepped away and lifted her weapon above her head, poised to strike the intruders. The door was thrown open and she let out a battle cry as she started to swing.

Kyllean dodged out of the way of her weapon, which lost its momentum as recognition took hold.

536

"Nice to see you, too!" he said in his ever-jovial manner. Another man filled the space of the door behind him. Dagmara experienced a feeling of wrongness at the sight of him. He was tall and thin, with sunken temples, dark eyes, and cheekbones that appeared too sharp, too extreme for the rest of his face. He carried himself with unsettling confidence, giving the impression of a man who had seen much and was frightened by little. The robe he wore was just as disturbing. It seemed to absorb the light without reflecting any. Like the gloom of night as it worked to suffocate the light of a candle.

Kyllean stepped to the side and gestured with a hand. "Princess Rider Dagmara, allow me to introduce—"

"Draílock," he interrupted, bowing slightly as he did. "It is a great pleasure to meet the princess who rides. It has been a very long time since we have had such a blessing within the Kingdom. If only the circumstances were less . . . perilous. I should love to learn more about how this came to be."

The name Draílock was familiar, though she was certain she had never met him. She tried to place the name. *Oh yes.* One of the wizards Aynward had spoken of. But what was he doing here?

He interrupted her thoughts. "Come along, much to do. Little time."

Dagmara shook her head. "I'm going to call my Lumále. That's where I belong."

Draílock had turned to leave but he whirled on her. "You will do no such thing. Not yet, anyhow. You need to keep your Lumále away from the fight for now. Trust me."

Dagmara was taken aback by the severity of the man's stare and the finality of his words, but she recovered quickly.

"I'm the one with the Lumále, not you. I have a duty—"

"No." Draílock's voice seemed to reverberate, both loud and somehow not. His voice washed out the din of battle that grew louder with every passing moment "You have a duty to survive, and if you go out there right now, I assure you, you *will* perish. If you have any intention of remaining alive, you will do as I say."

Kyllean nodded to her, then said in a soft tone, "Come on, Princess, I know this gangly wizard has poor facial hair hygiene, but he's already saved my life twice today. I think you should trust him."

Dagmara's inner rebellion deflated and she nodded.

Draílock ignored the gibe and spun on his heel, his robes following on a delayed schedule behind him. He led the way down a series of hallways as if he'd been living there for his entire life, which seemed strange since he most certainly had not. Then again, Klerósi priests were supposedly assailing the citadel from atop the backs of birds the size of Lumáles so perhaps confusion was just the order of the day.

The floor continued to shudder beneath their feet as they ran down dark halls lit only by the occasional torch. Dagmara couldn't imagine what was going on out there that could cause the walls and ground to shake; an entire army fit with trebuchets and ballistae?

Draílock stopped at a door, then knocked loudly. "It's me. Open up."

A moment later they heard the clinking of keys, followed by the creaking of hinges as the door slowly opened. The three passed into a vast circular chamber lit by several bright torches around the perimeter.

Dagmara recognized the citadel's Great Hall. She had read about it, even seen sketches in one of her books about the Lumáles. But to stand within it herself, even at dusk, took her breath away. The chamber was immense, with a high domed ceiling of stone further supported by eight marble pillars that formed a wide semicircle that faced outward toward a main double-door entrance large enough to easily accommodate several Lumáles at once. She wished she could see it during the full light of day. The domed ceiling contained dozens of thin strips of stained glass, visible only as lines of light gray as the darkness of night began to take hold.

In the center of the room stood Headmaster Forestone, Master Hilde, and over a dozen riders, dressed for battle, their light armor glittering as the torchlight played against the smooth surfaces of polished metal. They comprised not even a quarter of the riders from the fortress, but they formed a sizable force considering they were arguably the best swordsmen in the world, enhanced by magical speed and strength.

Draílock stopped in the center of the room and paused, closing his eyes.

Dagmara leaned into Kyllean. "What's he doing?"

Then she felt the magic radiating from the man. Kyllean glanced in his direction at that moment.

"I have no idea. He's not particularly normal."

Draílock opened his eyes and looked over to Headmaster Forestone. "This is it. Did you bring the artifact as instructed?"

Headmaster Forestone nodded hesitantly. "Yes."

"Good."

Dagmara looked to Kyllean once again, eyebrows raised. He shrugged.

Then a faint knock sounded from the recently locked door, directly behind the pair. They had paused after only a few steps into the hall and both jumped at the sound, then spun to look.

Kyllean said, "Uh, what should we do?"

Dagmara felt the tingle of magic then heard a click as the metal inside the lock moved. She tensed and reached to unsheathe her weapon. Footsteps shuffled behind her but her eyes were trained on the door.

It opened just a crack, and a soft, strongly accented voice floated into the room, somehow drowning out all other sounds. "It is only I."

The woman who had saved Aynward's life weeks earlier stepped through the door, then closed and locked it behind her.

Headmaster Forestone said, "Lady Lillith, I am very glad to see that you are safe. I grew worried when my men were unable to find you in your rooms earlier."

She waved a dismissive hand. "I can take care of myself."

Forestone nodded. "Yes, well, I suspect we'll find out for certain very soon."

Kyllean spoke. "So what's the plan here? We hide out here until . . . when? Are we hoping they don't find us and just leave? Seems a wee bit cowardice, if you ask me."

Draílock smiled. "Fighting out in the open benefits the Lugienese and their flying friends. We wait here so as to limit their key advantage."

"Huh."

Draílock remarked dryly, "I'm so very glad that you approve."

The monstrous door that separated them from their enemy boomed as something very large struck it with great force. "Soon," said Draílock. "Very soon."

Headmaster Forestone yelled, "Riders! Prepare to fight. They think to take advantage of us while the bulk of our tethered riders protect the Kingdom elsewhere. Show this scum just how much you're worth even without a Lumále to fly upon!"

The men and woman around the room let out a cheer just as the door splintered and cracked in the middle.

"What is that?" asked Dagmara, afraid.

Headmaster Forestone replied angrily, "The dordron are dropping large stones they have loosened from elsewhere around the fortress." His anger was not directed at her, but it was clear that the destruction of the fortress by the Lugienese was being taken personally. And Draílock was right, this fight was coming to them all very soon.

Dagmara was terrified.

She shuffled her feet, bracing for the battle to begin. Her hands were slick with sweat, nerves tightening every muscle in her body to the point of near immobility. Master Hilde came up behind her. "Dagmara, stand behind the rest of us for now. Those priests will be wielding magic against which your sword will be no help."

Dagmara felt wrong about cowering behind the others, but Master Hilde was right. If she stood toward the front, she would be killed the moment the first priest used their magic. She would be far more useful if she waited until the fighting grew more chaotic. She would step in to take down enemy priests as they focused their attention, and their magic, on those who could defend against it.

Another loud crack, then another, and another. Then the door exploded inward, two massive stone projectiles bringing with them shards and splinters of wood as they careened toward the riders.

Draílock stepped forward and lifted a hand. A wave of energy shot toward the maelstrom of objects and reversed their direction. Both sides of the door were then blown outward off their enormous hinges.

Dagmara watched in awe as at least three flying creatures that had appeared in the opening were thrown from the sky in the blast. She didn't know much about magic, but she did know that the amount of energy needed to do what Draílock had just done was tremendous, and it felt to her as though she had been plunged into Lake Salmune in the dead of winter.

A chilly silence filled the room, and what she could see of the darkening sky was empty. For a moment Dagmara wondered if Draílock's effort had convinced the rest of the Lugienese to flee.

Kyllean broke the silence. "Master Hilde, you might consider having Draílock teach us how to do stuff like that with our magic. Seems like a useful thing, you know?"

A single shriek sounded and a moment later a dordron came into view, flying directly toward the opening to the citadel chambers. A chill washed over Dagmara as the creature's screech was echoed by a chorus of similar angry cries. Within a few heartbeats, the sky filled with them, and they were all flying toward Dagmara and the other riders.

Headmaster Forestone yelled, "Ready your weapons!"

Dagmara raised her own blade, but then she felt the enemy's magic and understood. Several blasts of magic shot out from the priests astride the dordron, but the riders were prepared and their weapons turned the magic into puffs of nothingness. As the first few dordron flew into the large space, Dagmara spotted movement beside her. A shape in her peripheral vision shifted and she ducked and turned to face . . . a Lumále crawling out from the shadowy depths of the room.

She knew it wasn't her own Lumále, as she could sense her a safe distance away and sent the message for her to remain so. This monstrous creature before her continued to move slowly out of hiding before suddenly launching itself into the air. To Dagmara's shock, it was not the only one; five Lumáles took to the air from hiding. None bore their riders, but they all attacked the oncoming enemy, who, in the limited space of the room had nowhere else to go.

For a moment Dagmara believed that this would be enough and the dordron would be turned away, but more continued to flood into the large space. Three of the Lumáles took their prey down to the ground then used their tails to assault both the priest and the dordron, but this was not enough.

Several dordron landed just beyond the entrance, their riders dismounting in order to approach on foot. After a few diffuse blasts of magic, they drew swords of their own and continued to advance.

Two Lumáles battled with dordron in the space between the entrance and where Dagmara and the riders stood in wait. Dagmara watched in wonder as the Lumále used its barbed tail to hack away at the violent beak and razor-sharp talons of the dordron. One of the Lugienese mounts released a gurgling shriek as its throat was cut open. Dagmara cheered under her breath, but saw another set of dordron, these unencumbered by riders, half running, half flying to attack the Lumále that had slain their brother.

The approaching priests gave this central area a wide birth as they continued forward to meet the much smaller contingent of riders, Dagmara included. The reality of their situation settled on her like a heavy cloak; she might die this day. Seeing the approaching invaders was a sobering sight, as if everything else had been theoretical. The potential for death was now fewer than a dozen paces away, and it wore the crimson color of blood.

CHAPTER 76

KYLLEAN

KYLLEAN BALANCED ON THE BALLS of his feet, ready for battle. He raised both swords, prepared to defend against magic should any of these priests decide to try their luck again before clashing steel. He sent his magic into both weapons, though he recognized that only the black one functioned to absorb enemy magic. The action still caused the steel of the marbled blade to grow lighter so Kyllean counted it worth the effort.

A priest who appeared not more than a few years older than himself let out a bellow and suddenly sprinted forward, and others following suit.

It's on.

As the man raised his scimitar, his other hand shot a thin line of deadly magic. Kyllean absorbed the blow with his black weapon and felt a strange coldness as the magic diffused into his sword. The sensation fled a heartbeat later and his marbled blade intercepted the priest's sword attack.

Kyllean allowed his own magic to flow throughout his body and felt the ease of movement as the priest before him seemed to slow. As they exchanged blows, Kyllean had to admit that he was impressed with the priest's skill. He recalled the Lugienese fighters from Brinkwell and thought with his newfound skill and speed, he would be cutting the Lugienese to pieces like a scythe to wheat, but it appeared these priests would not be so easily dispatched.

Even so, with his enhanced speed and strength, Kyllean never once felt legitimately threatened by their swordsmanship. However, the priest continued to sprinkle magical blades of power into the fight, and this kept Kyllean on his toes. He dodged some of the attacks, while others he absorbed with his weapon. It took him a few rallies to adjust to this added complexity, but he finally managed a counterattack and his black blade cut clean through the man's leg, shortening him on one side. The priest cried out and Kyllean finished him with the marbled blade. As the marbled blade met flesh, heat rushed up Kyllean's arm. The man cried out as he died, and his eyes met Kyllean's, an expression of shocked betrayal locked eternally upon his face. Kyllean was so surprised by the sensation that he dropped the marbled weapon.

Dagmara's voice behind him dragged him out of his temporary stupor. "Kyllean!"

He spun and raised his black blade, but it was too late. Or would have been had Dagmara's own weapon not stopped the attack. This snapped him back into the flow of battle, joining the fray once again, though he was forced to turn his attention to an oncoming priestess, who while smaller seemed more adept than the last priest he had fought. He didn't have time to reach down to collect the marbled blade so he fought on with just his black rider's blade. Once he deciphered her fighting pattern, the effectiveness of her skills diminished and he set up for a killing blow. Just before he cut past her defense, she caught him in the thigh with a thin spear of magic and he lost his balance.

As he fell, a pair of massive talons materialized, missing him by a hand's breadth. He felt the air as the winged monster swooped by and then he hit the ground.

Where did that thing come from?

He used his time on the ground to snatch his marbled blade, then shuffled back and inspected his leg. It wasn't as bad as he initially thought, and he was able to stand once again. He noted that several dordron had taken flight to join in the mayhem without their riders. That was not good. The riders were outnumbered as it were. And while each rider was arguably worth two or three Klerósi priests, the larger number of dordron would surely balance out the odds, and perhaps tip them against the Tal-Don riders.

The five Lumáles in the chambers were not enough to combat the dozens of dordron that had entered this space. They would soon be overwhelmed by the sheer numbers against them.

The priestess attempted another shot of magic, but Kyllean was ready for this one.

No more games.

Kyllean determined that his black blade would need to be relegated to the task of absorbing magical attacks while his marbled blade would be used for all the dirty work. Pushing more magic into his body, he no longer felt the pain of the wound in his leg. Another robed priest attempted to engage Kyllean as he stalked the priestess, but he batted the attack aside, and launched a quick and lethal counterattack, his black blade sinking deep into the chest of the overzealous priest who thought he would catch Kyllean unawares.

Then Kyllean launched a series of offensive attacks against the priestess. He was a single swing away from landing the killing blow when he was forced to duck beneath another set of dangerous talons. The priestess scored a minor cut on Kyllean's already injured leg as he did so. He responded with a minor slash to her other arm, this one with his marbled blade. Again, he felt heat flow through him before it disappeared. The priestess pulled back, eyes wide in horror. Kyllean looked for a secondary attacker, for the cut he had made barely scratched the surface, but he saw none.

She stood straight and continued to back away, her eyes accusatory as she did. And then as he readied to dodge away from an oncoming dordron, the creature swooped down and caught the priestess's arm in its beak and lifted her from the ground before tossing her into a pillar a dozen paces away.

Kyllean stared in shock as the dordron then flew out of the space altogether.

I don't think that the dordron was supposed to do that, he thought. He was allowed no further time to reflect as another priest stepped forward to replace the priestess.

Just before Kyllean engaged the man, a spray of stone from the ground between them shot up and then forward to strike the priest. Draílock's voice interrupted Kyllean's surprise. "We need to go."

"Go? We're sort of in the middle of something aren't we?" asked Kyllean, incredulous.

"Everyone. Behind me—now!" Draílock's voice cut through the battle din as if by some magic. It probably was, Kyllean supposed. He did as Draílock said, keeping his black blade at the ready in case any of the Klerósi priests decided to shoot more of their stupid magic at him.

"Lillith! Contingency. Now!" yelled Draílock.

The healer nodded and stepped forward, lifting her hands. Nothing happened, at least nothing Kyllean could see, but he felt a sudden surge of magic. A few riders fought on against their opponents, unable to separate from them as directed by Draílock. Kyllean didn't understand what Lillith had actually done until one of the priestesses strode toward him before falling on her face for no reason Kyllean could discern. She stood up and swung her sword in frustration, which stopped in the exact same place mid-swing. A moment later a dordron flew toward them at full speed. Kyllean prepared to dive out of the way, but the dordron suddenly struck this same invisible barrier as the priestess. Blood from the impact gave visual substance to the otherwise unseen barrier erected by Lillith. The sound was just as disturbing to Kyllean as the streak of blood still suspended in the air.

"We need to leave right now. This will not hold for long," said Lillith.

Master Forestone yelled, "To the lower hall."

Two riders had been caught on the wrong side of Lillith's wall and fought on in vain, while one female rider continued fighting an opponent on their side. Two other riders rushed over to help her finish the priest off. They managed to back the Lugienese man up against the invisible wall, where he was slain within another heartbeat. Kyllean and Dagmara turned and followed the rest out of the chambers, Lillith hurrying alongside them. Kyllean noted that not everyone would be following them. The two that remained on the wrong side of the barrier, plus an additional four lay amid the bodies of unmoving Lugienese.

As they ran down the hall, Lillith matched their pace. Kyllean said dryly, "I see you've found your running legs."

Lillith merely grunted in response.

They hurried down a dark hallway, and the sound of shouting and the sensation of magic became distant. They descended a narrow stone staircase following the light of a single torch ahead. Kyllean continued to look back, praying that Draílock would catch up with them soon.

Then a vibration shook the ground so strongly, Kyllean lost his footing and was forced to brace himself against the wall, which also shook. Dagmara fell into him, holding herself up by wrapping arms around his neck. Under different circumstances, it could have been almost intimate. But then they both began coughing as dust fell from the ceiling along with several smaller stones.

"What was that?" asked Dagmara loudly.

Master Hilde was not far away and she responded, "I believe Draílock has collapsed the chambers of the citadel. Come, we must continue."

Kyllean's head shot up. "He did what?" First Dwapek, now Draílock? Kyllean was growing a little tired of people sacrificing themselves around him.

Lillith clarified, "He will meet us at the rendezvous. He is not one to draft plans lightly, nor to easily perish."

That satisfied Kyllean for the time being. *He'd better still be alive! He has an ever-growing list of things to explain.*

Dagmara let go of Kyllean and they continued following others until they had reached another large, dark room. Master Forestone turned to face the group: Lillith, Dagmara, Kyllean, Master Hilde, and five other riders. "We should be safe to exit up above now. Keep moving."

They came up a few minutes later, opening a door to a hallway that led outside. Kyllean still didn't know the layout of the citadel particularly well and with it being dark, less so. It wasn't until they stepped out into the open that he recognized where they were. They were just west of the citadel's main chambers, which were nothing more than a heap of rubble now. The domed ceiling had collapsed, crushing everything and everyone beneath it—except Draílock, Kyllean prayed.

"What now?" asked Kyllean of Master Forestone.

He brought his sword to bear and smiled. "We fight."

Two Lumáles landed just a few paces away, and both Master Hilde and Headmaster Forestone started toward them. Master Hilde turned and grinned, her teeth shining bright under the light of the dual moons, which had begun their rise into the otherwise darkening sky. "It's time to show these Lugienese what more than two centuries of riding experience really looks like."

In spite of the toll Draílock's trick had taken on the Klerósi priests, there were still dozens of dordron flying about, and riders continued to battle them from a few strongholds throughout the fortress.

Movement from the collapsed citadel chambers caught Kyllean's attention. The rubble was moving in three places. *Oh no.* Kyllean held his breath until he saw someone who looked an awful lot like Draílock climb out of a depression within the rubble. Kyllean recognized the two Lumáles as more stones were shifted from where they had landed! One of the creatures took to the sky, apparently still in fighting shape. It flew directly toward them, and Kyllean saw Gerald step forward and climb up, but the Lumále did not immediately take flight. Gerald was looking at the northern fortress wall. Kyllean followed his gaze, where it remained for a time as he attempted to understand what was happening. The crenelated wall was filling up with a row of dordron, and their Klerósi riders.

A horn sounded and the remaining dordron flocked to the area, though a select few landed on the ground below the wall about twenty paces from where Kyllean and the surviving riders from the citadel stood in anticipation. Draílock continued toward them and several other riders joined their ranks.

"Soooo, are we all just regrouping before round two begins?" asked Kyllean.

Glancing around at the number of riders who remained, his confidence grew. They appeared to outnumber their enemy, though not by much. "I have an idea," said Kyllean loudly. "Whoever has more survivors is declared the winner. The other side has to apologize and return home and make sad faces the entire time."

Dagmara looked over at him. "We are home right now."

Kyllean smiled. "I know. That's part of what makes this plan so great!"

More Lugienese continued to gather, and Kyllean noticed a number of them were entering on foot through the east gate. Kyllean quickly realized that they were still outnumbered.

A priestess stepped forward and spoke, her accented words amplified by magic. "We have come of here to find the Stone. If you relinquish of this item, we will not harm of any more of you today. Refuse and all of you will perish."

Kyllean looked around to see if anyone knew what this woman was talking about. *The Stone?* Perhaps this portion of what she said had been lost in translation. There appeared to be plenty of stone about. Or . . . was this the thing Draílock had mentioned earlier? The artifact?

Headmaster Forestone turned his Lumále sideways and spoke from atop the majestic creature of power. "We will bequeath no such thing to you. The Stone has been hidden such that you might raise every pebble here without coming any closer to possessing it. And I think you'll find the task of killing *all* of us a great deal more difficult than you believe." He gestured toward the collapsed citadel. The riders behind him chuckled at that.

Then, as if on cue, the rubble began to shift. Stones and dust fell away to reveal a number of priests and dordron that were very much *not* dead.

Kyllean spoke loud enough for only Dagmara to hear. "I think now might be a good time to summon your Lumále so you can leave. And hey, if you have any extra room, I'd be happy to join you."

Headmaster Forestone was unmoved by the Lugienese threat. "You will only find death here, priests of the false god."

Kyllean saw the collective shift in their enemy at the insult to their god. As if they were dogs and he had just waltzed into their yard uninvited. All eyes were now trained on him, all salivating with the hunger to kill.

Dagmara responded to Kyllean, "I'm not abandoning this fight. But I agree, perhaps it's time to get my Lumále down here for the fun."

Kyllean shook his head. "I wish I could see Aynward one last time to let him know that his own courage has been overshadowed by that of his sister."

Dagmara's eyes moistened at the mention of Aynward, then narrowed as she turned to regard the enemy. Kyllean did the same. The priests all moved at once as if a horn had just announced the start of the battle. A spray of pebbles and dust struck the line of riders, Dagmara and Kyllean included. The Klerósi priests had used their magic to attack the ground between them. Kyllean closed his eyes and turned his head but maintained focus enough to keep his sword out to protect him.

By the sounds of the shouts from around him, not everyone else had managed to do the same. After this, the battle devolved into organized chaos.

CHAPTER 77

KYLLEAN

THE FEROCITY OF THE LUGIENESE attack was far greater now than it had been while inside the citadel, and a number of dordron continued to swoop in to attack the riders as they fought the priests on the ground.

Master Hilde yelled, "To the arena!"

They weren't far; it was only about twenty paces behind them. Kyllean understood immediately. The entrance on foot was narrow and the tall barrier would prevent the flying dordron from being able to swoop in and attack at full speed.

Knowing that Dagmara's sword would not protect her from magical attacks, Kyllean took it upon himself to remain in front of her as much as he could. The defensive formation of the riders regained some semblance of order as they reached the entrance to the arena. Kyllean and Dagmara were at the back, but it was soon discovered that there was no back. The dordron flew their riders over the wall, then landed them in the arena so Kyllean, Dagmara, and number of others turned to face these attackers.

Kyllean engaged the closest Klerósi priest and was annoyed to find the priest giving ground without allowing himself to be cut. "Just stay put and fight! Would you?"

Then a dordron lunged forward and snapped at Kyllean's head. He ducked and stabbed upward, but his blade sank into something and the shadow of the creature disappeared for the time being.

Kyllean rolled backward then came back up with both blades ready to reengage. "That was rather uncouth!"

The priest returned some words in kind, but Kyllean's command of the Lugienese tongue was about as strong as his control of the dordron that attacked at the moment.

The priest reengaged and this time Kyllean landed a deep cut to the shoulder of his enemy. As soon as that marbled blade made contact with flesh, the heat sensation rushed up his arm and into his body. The priest cried out and stumbled back. Then he extended a hand toward Kyllean, who raised his black blade in defense against the magical attack, but nothing happened. The priest stared down at his hand then back at Kyllean. Then he fell to his knees, tears filling his eyes.

"Oh, get up and let me kill you like a man!" Kyllean was beginning to believe that something more was happening when the marbled blade made contact with the flesh of those priests.

The man staggered back to his feet, then narrowed his eyes as they fixed once again upon Kyllean. "You steal of Klerós's power. I send of you to death!" The priest rushed forward, swinging without concern for his own safety, only intending to kill. The unpredictability of someone who no longer cared to live made this a different bout than before, but Kyllean managed to maneuver beyond the man's reckless swings and put him out of his misery.

Then he paused to stare down at the marbled blade in wonder. *You separate people from their magic, don't you?*

He grinned wider than anyone should in the midst of such death, but he couldn't help it. *Let's find out for certain.*

The knowledge that he merely needed to break the skin of a priest with the marbled blade changed Kyllean's strategy. He turned his attention to the priest who was currently trying very hard to stab holes in Dagmara. She was giving ground but holding her own admirably. Distracted as the priest was with his own fight, it didn't take much to slip in and score a minor cut, especially powered by his magic.

The man cried out and looked to the heavens as if the attack had come from there. Dagmara ran him through, and then had to dive out of the way as a dordron charged them. Instead of attacking Dagmara, Kyllean, or any of the other riders, the creature took the dying priest in its beak and swung its head from side to side like a dog that has caught a rabbit.

Another revelation sank in. The dordron were not willing participants in whatever compulsion bound them to their Klerósi riders. Kyllean doubled down on the task of freeing as many dordron as possible.

The clang of steel and the cries of pain and grunts of exertion melted together into a terrible ballad as Kyllean began his campaign of chaos. It had a numbing effect, as if having so much stimuli dulled the horrific reality. Their choice to fight beneath the tall wall of the arena minimized the dordron attacks upon them. But the priests riding their dordron began dropping chunks of stone upon the riders. They quickly abandoned this strategy as Draílock or the healer—one of the two who could wield more than just rider magic—redirected the projectiles toward the attacking priests on either side.

Kyllean felt another plume of magic and halted his approach toward his next target just in time to see the stone wall beneath which they fought begin to collapse. It would crush half of the riders who were using it as protection from the dordron. In that instant, Kyllean looked for Dagmara to try to make sure she had gotten to safety. Where had she gone?

Panic surfaced and he was out of time—the wall was coming down and he had no way of knowing whether Draílock would be able to protect them all. Then a tug on his wrist caught his attention.

"Get out of the way!" It was Dagmara, who had somehow ended up behind him. He responded to the pull, following her blindly into the ranks of Lugienese attackers. He felt the rumble as the base of the tall pillars collapsed. Fueled by his magic, Kyllean leaped further than any normal human could, holding his weapons out at the ready to intercept any assaults that came as he soared through the air.

He batted away a sword strike to his left and landed close enough to counterstrike successfully with the marbled blade. He spun, ducked, and sliced the leg of another priest, then returned his attention to the first. Then he heard a loud boom, and a cloud of dust and debris rose from where the riders had been packed in their two-sided defense against greater numbers.

Kyllean swallowed hard. Draílock had apparently been unable to keep the stone from crushing them. Motion out of the corner of his eye prevented him from further consideration; he blocked with his marbled blade and stepped back in retreat as two Lugienese attempted to cut him down.

He felt the momentum of the fight tilting against the riders. They were outnumbered and overwhelmed and the core of their numbers had just been swallowed by the collapse of the arena wall. Kyllean spotted Dagmara similarly pressed. This was the point in a battle where warriors could only try to kill as many of the enemy as they could before the inevitable end. Caution and defense were no longer the way. Kyllean let himself go, let the tension fade into the background. As he did, the sick feeling of loss disappeared along with the tightness that came with the fear of losing, the fear of death. His mind, which had been filled with too many questions to count, became focused on one thing: death to the enemy.

Kyllean had only ever tasted the kind of unencumbered freedom that came to him here. There had been moments during his sparring when the politics and concerns about pleasing his father, or satisfying his own goals to earn a Lumále, had become distant considerations. But none of those things mattered now. He knew he was going to die, knew Dagmara would die, everyone there would die. There was no aid coming for her, for him, for anyone. The only thing he could do was send a lasting message to the Lugienese that the people of the free lands would not go down easy. Before he breathed his last, the Lugienese would wonder if it was worth the loss in lives required to put these people down.

Time disappeared as Kyllean unleashed a flurry with his swords that he'd never known existed within him. He became numb as he danced in and about the tightening field of enemies, swords trailing blood as he did. The only sense he acknowledged was that of his hands and feet and only insomuch as they connected to his weapons and the ground that pressed against his boots.

It wasn't until a sharp pain bit into the base of his spine that Kyllean's blood lust relented. He felt his body go limp and a true numbness took hold as he fell face up upon the bloodstained ground. He tried to move, but his body would not respond. There was an initial sense of panic as he tried to reconcile the paralysis, but it was short-lived, replaced with acceptance. He had long imagined himself fighting at the end of this life in some battle, dragging a badly wounded leg behind him, holding a broken arm or some such injury, bleeding slowly to death in the midst of death and dying. That sounded horrible. A quick death was really the way to go. Granted, he preferred a stab to the heart or some such, preferably otherwise unharmed, but he supposed this would have to do.

He stared up at a Klerósi priestess towering over him triumphantly as she reversed the grip on her scimitar, raising it high above her head as she prepared to deliver a quick death. He saw her take in a deep breath of air, and her eyes fixed on him; cold, menacing eyes set on the task of extermination on behalf of her God. There was no satisfaction in her expression, just grim determination.

This is it. Shame. I didn't even keep count of how many I took with me before the end. Had to have been at least ten. No. Eleven. I think it was ten. Oh well. On to meet the gods. Please be quick.

A shadow suddenly darkened everything, his executioner turned toward the source just in time to be knocked to the side. She was struck hard enough that it seemed she had simply vanished into thin air. *Oh, come on! Maybe I don't deserve a quick death. But lying on the ground paralyzed as the life slowly drains out of me? This day could not get—*

In the priestess's place appeared a wall of gray, a massive, muscular Lumále. It released the deepest roar Kyllean had ever heard from one of the creatures, then its tail whipped out once again and the cry of its victim echoed across the arena. Another roar answered from nearby, a different Lumále. The roar of several others followed.

Someone leaped from atop the other creature and landed almost precisely where the priestess had moments ago prepared to give him the quick death he so now desired, but apparently did not deserve. Before him stood a woman dressed in full battle armor, bloodstains streaking various places along the steel and tunic of a rider. Hair obscured the face until she ran a hand through it to reveal . . .

Evra? He tried to say this out loud, but again managed only a soft grunt. She looked from side to side, then said, "I brought us some help." She gestured with her hands. "Yup. All the remaining Lumáles, including the one that just returned from only the gods know where. Looks like a vet to me. We're still outnumbered, but this should give you a chance to—"

Her expression changed as she inspected him more closely. "Kyllean? Kyllean!"

His inability to respond was torturous.

She knelt beside him, and started feeling around, or at least he assumed that was what she was doing. He couldn't feel anything from the neck down so he had no idea what she was actually doing, but he saw her shadowed expression darken still.

"Kyllean, can you hear me?" She brought her hand up, covered in blood, and her face paled. "Kyllean. Don't die on me."

He just stared back at her. *Just kill me. It's too late,* he wanted to say.

Then the large head of a Lumále interrupted their one-sided conversation. The creature brought its snout right down to his face, sniffing his body. Evra moved to the side and Kyllean spotted a familiar mark upon its chest, but . . . *No that can't be. I'm hallucinating.*

It craned its neck up and roared, then lashed out behind with its barbed tail before returning its attention to Kyllean.

Evra said, "I have to keep fighting. Just don't die."

Kyllean was growing dizzy with blood loss and closed his eyes, which appeared to be the only thing over which he still had control. He attempted to speak, but again was only able to produce a pathetic grunt. Then, in spite of the fact that he could feel nothing of his body, he did feel something within his mind, a presence. Or was that his imagination?

No. There it was again, stronger. And there was something familiar about it, though he could hardly discern it. Not in his current state. All he knew was that whatever this entity was, it wanted in, and his will to withstand it diminished with his will to remain conscious.

Moreover, something about this sensation tugged at a memory. Had one of his masters discussed something like this in his training? He knew they didn't do much training of the mind until after one was . . . *tethered.*

Oh, he thought. *Talk about bad timing.* If that was what was happening, the present circumstances painted a painful irony indeed.

CHAPTER 78

DAGMARA

SEVERAL LUMÁLES MATERIALIZED AND BEGAN tearing their way through the Lugienese with a ferocity that frightened even Dagmara. *Glad we're on the same side.*

They quickly formed a protective circle around the remaining riders and blade bearers, of which a sad few remained. This small contingent of Lumáles had followed the young rider named Evra. Dagmara didn't know her well, but they had sparred and the girl certainly knew her way around a blade. Her arrival with a small flock of flying monsters gave Dagmara a momentary sliver of hope that they may yet survive this battle. And if not, they would at least take several more Lugienese to the grave before the end.

Dagmara landed a solid kick to the stomach of the priest before her. The man stumbled back and Dagmara took that moment to survey her surroundings. The arrival of the Lumáles all around them had created a commotion. *Where's Kyllean?* He had been fighting by her side before this but she didn't see him now. Then she spotted the marbled blade to her left and beside that, lying motionless on the ground, was Kyllean. *Oh, no.*

Before she could attend him, her Lugienese opponent resumed his interest in killing her. She rolled away from his attack then came to her feet to begin her own attack. Fueled by anger over Kyllean's condition, she felt an inner savagery previously checked by her own fear. Perhaps it was seeing Kyllean in such a state, perhaps it was her own mental fatigue that had eroded her sense of self-preservation, but she launched into an attack and her training did the rest.

Dagmara made a deposit of steel to the Klerósi priest's midsection in short order. Her chest heaved after such exertion, then she rushed over to Kyllean.

She knelt down beside him. "Kyllean?" She patted his face, but he was unresponsive. "Kyllean!"

She glanced up to confirm that no one was going to stab her while she was distracted, then returned her attention to Kyllean. She would not have much time. The Lumáles, while apparently impervious to direct magical attacks, were not immune to attacks of steel, giant talons, or dordron mouths.

Kyllean's chest still moved up and down, barely. Sindri put her ear close to his mouth to listen for breathing and was relieved to hear something, but each breath was shallow and ragged. Then she noticed the patch of blood soaking the front of his tunic at his waist.

She swallowed hard. He was as good as dead.

Then Draílock's voice sounded from somewhere behind her. "Lillith! Your skills are needed here, now. It is time to leave." Dagmara turned to see him pointing to Kyllean.

The ghostly pale woman was covered in dust and grime like the rest of them. The powder from the collapsed structure stuck to her sweaty skin, while vertical streaks of light skin marked perspiration down the sides of her face and eyebrows. Dagmara saw the fatigue in her drawn expression, and yet she moved with grace. Dagmara moved aside to allow Lillith access to Kyllean.

The healer stepped over his immobile body then crouched beside him, placing a hand upon his midsection where blood stained his tunic.

Lillith placed a hand on Kyllean's head and held it there for a few heartbeats. "I will heal the boy." Then her hand went to the location of the wound.

Dagmara felt the shift in magical expenditure in the area and knew Lillith had immediately begun the healing. Moments later, the woman sagged and her upper half fell toward the bloodstained earth. Dagmara dropped to a knee and caught her behind the neck, helping her return to a seated position. Lillith's body had gone slack, but some of her strength seemed to return with Dagmara's support.

Dagmara recalled Lillith leaning heavily on Kyllean as he helped her return to her room after healing Aynward. That had been without a prologue of prolonged magical combat. She marveled that the woman could even sit. So far as Dagmara understood the magic, Lillith had to have already come dangerously close to turning her bones to mush.

Lillith whispered in a weak voice, "Thank you, dear."

Dagmara glanced over to Kyllean. He sat up slowly, felt his stomach, his back, and then reached down and touched his legs. He turned to regard Lillith. "I can feel my . . . everything! You . . . thank you." Then his head swiveled and looked out at the brutal fighting between the Lumáles and the Lugienese. His eyes closed, then opened wide. "I—I—I think . . . I think . . . I was tethered!"

Draílock turned away from shooting blades of magic at the enemy for a moment and offered a hand to both Kyllean and Dagmara, then helped Lilith to her feet. "Come. It's time to leave."

Kyllean looked around at the small cohort of blade bearers. "But . . ."

Draílock finished, "This fight is not yet finished, true, but this is not where you or I are meant to die. None of us here, none of us today." Looking flatly at Kyllean, he said, "Had I known you would take so long to be tethered, I would have made different arrangements." He looked over at the fighting. "But the time for that is past." He raised his voice for all to hear. "Each rider will carry one person besides themselves." He gestured with his hands. "Come, I have nearly reached my limits."

Dagmara felt the tingle of magic, then he said, "This shield will not hold for long."

One of the blade bearers spoke up then. "Uh, how are any of us to ride these Lumáles? Most are unteth—" The Lumáles had all suddenly turned to face the remaining blade bearers and riders. One Lumále's head drew close enough to him that his hair stood up with its intake of breath.

Dagmara knew what was about to happen before she felt the tingle of their magic.

Master Hilde stood beside Dagmara and whispered to herself, "Extraordinary. I've never seen something like this before."

Draílock allowed an unusual grin to crack his grim stoicism for the briefest moment. "Nor will you again."

Each of the remaining untethered Lumáles had chosen a master. They then lowered themselves to the ground, continuing to ignore the Lugienese threat just paces away.

A Klerósi priestess ran forward and Dagmara prepared to blurt out a warning. Just before the call escaped Dagmara's lips, the attacking priestess struck the invisible barrier and fell to the side, shouting a curse before returning to her feet, striking the threshold with magical blasts and steel alike.

Dagmara turned her attention to her own Lumále, whose silent, mental call she had been overlooking.

Draílock said, "We must leave." There were seven Lumáles, each capable of carrying their own rider and one more. "I ride with Kyllean. Lillith, you ride with Gerald."

Everyone was looking around and Dagmara knew they were making the same calculations. There were close to twenty remaining in their group.

Draílock continued, "I know this seems unfair. It is. And yet, this is our reality."

Master Hilde, and the remaining blade bearers, looked about, but no one moved. Not a single one of them was willing to value their lives above that of their brethren.

Draílock scooped up Lillith and nodded to Gerald. "You will need to carry her until her strength returns."

Gerald nodded, but Lillith shook her head.

"I am too far gone." Looking to Draílock, she said, "You of all people know how much of the future is not carved of stone. This was always one of the paths. I must remain here. I have one last task left in me."

Draílock's expression darkened, and he closed his eyes. Dagmara expected him to insist, but he opened his eyes and nodded. "Thank you for all you have done in the service of good."

Lillith closed her eyes in turn, and for a time even the floating dust in the air seemed to pause. Her words broke the stillness. "The Lugienese have found my people. They have taken the other stone. I believe you know where they plan to take it." She waved a weak hand to point a finger. "Do not let my people down, or I swear my spirit will take vengeance on you whenever your end does come. For even *you* cannot evade death forever."

Draílock narrowed his eyes slightly, then cracked a smile. "Your spirit will likely need to wait in line." The smile faded and he added, "But I will continue the course." He turned to Kyllean and said coldly, "Come, rider. It is time."

Kyllean moved slowly, confusedly.

No smart remark? He must not be fully healed. Dagmara clambered up to sit upon the back of her Lumále, clinging to its fur as she settled into the space at the base of its long neck. There was bickering among the remaining blade bearers about who would abandon the fight to escape alongside the riders. It was Master Hilde who spoke up.

"Tanner, Jannice, Thresh, Nilda, and Tarn, you will go with Draílock. This is my last order to you."

They all looked around, but no one moved.

"If you're looking for Headmaster Forestone, he has fallen. I am the highest-ranking master here."

Gerald spoke up from atop his Lumále. "With all due respect, as the highest-ranking master here, you should be among those who live on to fight another day. Your strength and expertise will be needed in the coming weeks."

She shook her head and said firmly, "My Lumále has fallen. I can feel the loss stealing the strength from me, more with every moment. I will remain to avenge this loss and then we will rejoin each other in the beyond."

Gerald didn't argue further and the rest took this as the cue to follow her orders while the others became reenergized for battle. Dagmara noted how young some of them appeared. She knew the Tal-Dons lived longer than ordinary humans, but they just seemed too young.

A blade bearer, Nilda, stole Dagmara's attention as she settled in behind her. Dagmara did not know Nilda, but she was at least two decades older than Dagmara. Dagmara felt all the more inadequate as one of the few to have been tethered. Looking out and seeing a contingent of blade bearers who had dedicated years in the service to their training, all of whom were far more competent warriors than she, all slated for death, she felt the weight of the world upon her. *Why me? I don't deserve this.* Drailock's words echoed in her mind: *I know this seems unfair. It is. And yet, this is our reality.*

With that, she urged her Lumále into the air.

She blinked away tears of guilt and shame as she watched a scene of unfolding carnage grow smaller below.

CHAPTER 79

KYLLEAN

KYLLEAN FELT CLUMSILY FOR THE connection between himself and the Lumále, his father's Lumále. That was easy enough, like reaching up to feel for a bump on his head.

How do I communicate ideas to it? He focused his attention on the connection, on the presence he felt within his mind. *Fly*, he thought.

Nothing happened for long enough to assume that he had done something wrong.

I don't have time for this. "Fly!" he yelled out loud. He assumed that they had ears. The creature craned its head around and looked right at him and he felt a little foolish—a lot foolish. This thing could fling him off and eat him in a few bites if it wished. He shrugged. "Fly, please?"

The Lumále snorted and turned away. Then it opened its wings and they were lifted into the air. *All right!*

Draílock spoke dryly from his position just behind Kyllean. "You're going to need to improve your communication with the Lumále."

"Really? I thought that went rather well."

Draílock did not reward his sarcasm with a response.

Kyllean looked down and saw the shrinking dark forms of blade bearers, the healer, and Master Hilde vastly outnumbered, yet eagerly charging into their last battle. Kyllean opened his mouth to ask Draílock why they would attack with such recklessness, but the question never left his lips. They did so in order to help protect everyone else's escape. *Songs need to be sung in their memory.*

Even as he realized this, he saw that it would not be enough. Several of the remaining dordron took to the air with Klerósi riders astride.

Why can't something ever just be simple for once?

Then he felt a burst of magic emanate from below. He looked back down and braced himself, but all he saw was a dordron spiraling helplessly to the ground. Several more blasts of magic followed and half of the eight remaining dordron that had taken to the sky in pursuit were on their way back to the ground at the speed of any other object. It was like the gods themselves had decided to punch them from the sky.

Lillith remained where they had left her and Kyllean saw her extend a shaky arm, slowly as if lifting something of enormous size. A burst of magic shot forth, and Kyllean followed it to the dordron. The energy struck its wing and the Lugienese chase was reduced to a mere three dordron.

When Kyllean glanced back at Lillith's shrinking form, she was no longer sitting. Her body was a heap of formless flesh. She had spent her last so that the rest of them might escape with their lives. Kyllean hoped that when his time came, he might have the courage to do the same. He said as much out loud to Draílock.

Draílock didn't respond for a time. Then he finally said, "She was a brave woman. Leaving this world in such a fashion is a worthy aspiration."

Kyllean looked back and saw that the dordron giving chase were closing in on them. Carrying two people each, and with most of the riders being new and without any sort of saddle, Kyllean knew they were far from free. But an idea materialized. It was risky, but what was the worst that could happen; he gave his life to save others? *A worthy aspiration, right?*

He assumed a standing position as the nearest dordron and rider closed in.

Draílock yelled, "What do you think you're doing?"

Kyllean knew he needed to act before his innate sense of self-preservation reminded him just how foolish this was. "I'm going to release this dordron."

Draílock drew back a hand and Kyllean knew what Draílock planned to do. Kyllean drew both of his weapons. The black blade captured Draílock's magic. Whatever its intended purpose, it was unsuccessful. Before Draílock could do anything more, Kyllean yelled to his Lumále. "Catch me!"

Kyllean was still clinging to the leftover power he had drawn in before taking flight and was glad for this because there was nothing from which to draw upon up here. He had enough to power his weapons, and hopefully a little more.

With that, he leaped.

The Klerósi priest didn't expect to see a human soaring unencumbered through the air toward him. His weapon was still sheathed so he reacted with magic. Kyllean snapped out his obsidian weapon and attacked from the air as he continued past the priest. Then he stabbed with the marbled weapon. He aimed for the priest's outstretched hand, but the man retracted it. Kyllean missed completely.

The priest and dordron continued on past, and Kyllean realized he had risked his life for nothing. *No.*

He contorted his body and redirected his marbled blade. It was an awkward, ugly maneuver, but he managed to extend the very tip of his weapon just far enough to nick the boot of the priest. He didn't know whether or not he broke the skin, but he had other problems now.

His high-speed leap through the open air became even more of a nightmare after the acrobatics he performed while in flight, and he spiraled out of control toward the earth below.

In spite of his panic, Kyllean managed to cross his arms to hold each of his weapons tight against his body. If he was rescued, he would not wish to impale himself or his rescuer, nor would he wish to misplace his weapons. He lost track of all sense of direction as he spun through the air toward his death. He closed his eyes and prayed. One way or another, it would be over soon.

Pain suddenly shot through his midsection, then he screamed.

CHAPTER 80

SINDRI

SINDRI SQUEEZED BETWEEN TWO THICK bushes, her face attacked by branches covered in tiny vines. She felt an adhesive texture pulling on the fabric of her robes, making each step into the forest a task far more difficult than it should otherwise have been.

There is nothing natural about this. Nothing at all.

"Ohh—" sounded Arella up ahead. *THUMP*. "Ow!"

"You okay?" asked Sindri.

A delayed response. "Yes. But I'm near to abandoning this foolishness about not using magic." Each word was accompanied by a grunt and occasional groan. "At this point, I think maybe you had it right. Better to just get the witch women's attention and have a quick death if that's to be our fate."

Arella had insisted they use no magic unless absolutely necessary. She wanted to be able to locate Kibure before their arrival was detected.

A few hundred heartbeats and scratches later, Sindri stepped out of the brambles into a less overtly restrictive forest. She saw Arella emerge a moment later to her left.

"Finally!" exclaimed Arella.

The forest canopy continued to choke out most of the sunlight, but Sindri could tell that Arella's face was covered in small cuts and scrapes. The burning on Sindri's own face told a similar story.

As she looked around, the way forward did not appear nearly as perilous. Sindri believed passage might be easier now that they had forged beyond the vicious barrier of bramble.

She took the lead, finding the forest remarkably beautiful. Unlike the wooded pine forest in the foothills of the Drisko Mountains she had traveled with Kibure, this forest allowed nothing to exist without some form of vegetation. There were no stone outcroppings, or pine-needle havens where nothing else grew. Even the passable area was filled with an array of multicolored flowers and hanging vines, and she began to enjoy the animal sounds she had been unable to appreciate while trouncing through the brush.

As they walked, Sindri noticed a particularly enchanting, purple flower nearly the size of her head and was drawn toward its shiny petals. The flower seemed to open further in greeting as she approached. *It's so beautiful*, thought Sindri. But then a strong hand caught her arm and pulled hard—right as the flower shot forward like a serpent. Its long, soft petals brushed Sindri's face, but the bulk of the attack missed. Sindri's heart leaped then pounded and her breathing came fast.

"Thank you," was all she could manage.

Arella replied, "In places like this, the prettier the object, the more dangerous."

Sindri gulped, and they continued on, eyeing every living object with suspicion. Arella stopped ahead and Sindri understood why as soon as she caught up. They faced another barrier of vegetation like the one they had traversed before. Arella turned left as soon as Sindri was within a few paces, and they walked along the barrier for another thousand heartbeats before Arella stopped and turned to face Sindri.

Frowning, she said, "I was hoping I was wrong."

Sindri was missing something. "Wrong about what?"

Arella reached into her pack and withdrew a waterskin and drank, then said, "Whoever created this barrier did so for the same reason someone might construct a wall, with intentions of keeping people out. I was hoping this was merely a small grove, but I've no doubt at this point. I think if we continue to try to circumvent it, we'll miss what we're looking for."

That made sense. Sindri asked, "So whatever semblance of civilization exists here must lie beyond this barrier?"

Arella nodded as she extended a hand to lean on a nearby tree. She dabbed her forehead with the sleeve of her robe, and then fell to one knee.

Sindri tried to rush over to help, but she couldn't move as fast as she wanted. Dread took hold as she felt at the cuts on her face. Barely had she started toward Arella before her foot caught against a fallen log and she plummeted to the forest floor.

The landing was at least soft. Despite her growing lethargy, she began climbing to her knees by using the log over which she had tripped. Her hand pressed into an unexpected texture. The bark held a soft warmth unlike any bark she had ever felt, and it was completely smooth. She should not have been surprised, as all the vegetation here was different from what she had seen in Angolia, but it was even more different than she'd thought. Looking closely, she noticed a dark-green pattern of geometric shapes that seemed oddly familiar. She had seen similar patterns as a girl, but on a much smaller scale. But this couldn't be. *Snakes don't grow this large, do they?* The fallen dark-green tree curved slightly, then disappeared behind a massive gray trunk decorated in brown vines that disappeared into the thick canopy above.

Slowly coming to her feet, she saw that Arella had resumed her own upright position. That's when she saw a circular object the size of a drogal fruit wink in and out of sight. She swallowed hard and opened her mouth, knowing she needed to say something. Then a much larger green shape came into focus and there was no more mistaking what she saw. It was the head of the largest serpent she had ever seen, and it was slowly creeping toward Arella.

In a trembling voice, Sindri said, "Do not panic, but you need to stop of your moving, right now."

Arella froze in place. "To your right is a . . . a *very* big . . . snake," Sindri said. "It has size enough to eat of a human."

The creature stopped moving and Sindri released a silent breath. With the risks of using magic outweighed by the risk of not, Sindri attempted to draw on her surroundings. She felt the energy around her, but as she fixed on a large tree trunk, she found that her mind slid clumsily over the energy. *I'm too nervous.* She tried again and again, the imaginary fingers of her mind slipping awkwardly over the energy as if it wasn't there. *Something is wrong.*

She saw Arella raise a hand slowly, then tilt her head in confusion. She turned slowly and her expression told Sindri that she'd just had the same realization about her magic.

Sindri's hands found their blades, and then she waited. Maybe this monstrosity would pass them by if they remained completely still. Arella had slowly pulled her scimitar free. Without magic, this did not seem like a fight they could hope to win, and as Sindri slowly attempted to position herself to fight, her physical fatigue grew worse. Her legs felt like they weighed twice what they should and even her arms felt like they were dragging thick iron shackles.

A vast tongue shot forth to taste the air, and then the head started to move away from the Arella. Sindri began to hope she had been right about remaining still. But as she looked at the angle of the neck, she realized that the serpent was not moving away, it was poising to strike.

Without another thought, Sindri located the body of the snake and drove both daggers down as hard as her weakened state would allow. The response was instantaneous. The body, as thick as Sindri's own, jerked forward and turned, throwing Sindri into a nearby tree trunk, and without one of her daggers, which remained rammed into the snake's flesh. Staggering back to her feet, she saw that she had successfully arrested the beast's attention from Arella, but that made her its primary target.

She gripped the dagger tight in her hand and prepared her feet to move when the attack came. She didn't have to wait long. The massive serpent slithered the short distance, its body flattening the foliage. It was positioned to strike for only an instant before its head shot forward. At full strength, perhaps Sindri could have reacted well enough to avoid the attack altogether, but in her current state, her reaction was far too slow. She dodged to one side—sort of—and her single dagger thrust missed, glancing off at an ineffective angle as it caught the corner of the wide-open maw. The snake's head connected with Sindri, and while not lethal, knocked her off of her feet.

She rolled as best she could to another position of defense, but her momentum was stopped by a root that had grown out of the ground at a strange angle. Instead, she lay on her back staring up at a deadly-looking set of eyes as the beast prepared to attack once more. She tried to shuffle backward, but the bramble wall prevented her from moving more than a single pace. She had nowhere to go.

Then movement to her left alerted her to Arella, who darted forth, sword in hand. The serpent noticed the movement as well and turned its head to meet the attack. Arella leaped into the air and swung. Sindri's hopes were dashed when the snake simply lifted its head so Arella's harrowing attack looked more like a solitary dance routine. The serpent waited for Arella to land and then snapped forward. Sindri threw her only remaining weapon and it sank into the snake's neck. The serpent continued forward toward Arella but altered course just enough that she was not swallowed whole. She was instead merely knocked hard from her feet, her scimitar sailing through the air to sink into the soft earth beneath their feet.

The serpent's attention fell again upon Sindri. In her weaponless state, she had no further option but to run. Yet her legs felt like stone. *What is happening?* The edges of her vision were beginning to blur. Whatever was preventing them from using their magic was also slowly sedating them. It was either death by poison or death by giant serpent. She faced the dark-green monster, and stood, shaking, but ready to die. She had no further defense.

Then something zipped by and just missed the snake, but it was enough to give it pause. Then she heard Arella's voice. "Hey! Greeny. Over here." A fist-sized stone struck the snake in the side of the head, bouncing harmlessly to the forest floor. This was enough to turn its attention back to Arella.

The reptile wasted no time, and Arella backed away. She had withdrawn a single dagger. Sindri knew this back and forth was unsustainable; one of them needed to inflict real harm or they would both find themselves being digested inside this monster. The hilt of Arella's scimitar stuck up from the ground like a beacon. Sindri ran, or tried to, but every step was like slogging against a fast-moving current. Sindri reached the blade and pulled it free of the earth.

The serpent was upon Arella. There was no more time.

Sindri took one awkward step toward the body of the snake, raised the blade as high as she could reach, then slammed it down with everything she had.

A loud hiss escaped the beast's wide-open mouth, which had stopped halfway along its journey to consume Arella. Sindri looked down to see that she had cut clean through the body, though this part of the snake was not as thick as the rest. She had only cut off the last few paces of length, but that portion was writhing like a worm while the rest of the thing disappeared into the gloom of the forest. Sindri didn't fully trust that the snake was gone. But she called over to Arella.

"You have health?"

Arella replied through heavy breathing, "Yes. Though for a moment there I thought I was snake food. How did you—?" Arella came a few steps closer.

Sindri hadn't moved, but her blade was still dripping red blood, and behind her the snake tail continued to move about.

"I see."

Sindri's legs felt impossibly weak and she sat backward. Arella took one more step closer and did likewise.

An exhausted Arella said, "Now that we're not being eaten by a giant snake, we should probably talk about why our magic appears to be inaccessible."

Sindri commented, "Or why it feels like someone is holding of my ankles when I try to move?"

Arella nodded. "Precisely . . ." She touched her face. "I suspect the thick brush we pushed through in the beginning was lined with some form of poison."

Sindri was not surprised to hear her suspicion confirmed. "What are we to do now?"

Arella scowled. "As I see it, we have three options, and none of them good. One: We go forward into the thickness of bramble to be poisoned further, but maybe discover whatever lies on the other side before we die. Two: We continue along the path of least resistance alongside this very unnatural barrier, which will assuredly lead us into a trap and probably more monster serpents. Last: We wait here and hope the poison wears off without killing us, then try to use magic to move through this brush up ahead, thereby notifying these magic users of our presence and location. Oh, and maybe still be eaten by another serpent as we wait."

Sindri looked at Arella and said, "You have correctness about one thing. None of those options are good."

CHAPTER 81

SINDRI

T HE PAIR AGREED THAT THE best course was to try to make it
through the next vegetation barrier. Unfortunately, the first batch
of poison had not yet reached its peak. Standing alone was almost an
insurmountable challenge, and a few laborious steps forward ended
with Sindri falling to her face when her foot simply refused to lift high
enough to step over a fallen limb in her path. Arella was worse off, unable
to fully stand. She fell twice before accepting defeat. They managed to
crawl over to a nearby tree to lean their backs against it. Arella remarked
through slurred speech, "At least the bark is smooth."

Sindri grunted. The rest of her attempt to respond was rendered
impossible due to her mouth's refusal to cooperate. Then her head
slumped to the side and she was unable to right it. Her mind too began
to slip.

Then the unnatural weight of the poison lifted, and she sat up
straight. Relief was quickly replaced by confusion. *How?* And then she
understood.

The sound of the forest was gone, and so too were the vibrant colors.
She had slid into the realm of dreams. *Gods, not now!* But perhaps this
wasn't such a bad thing. She felt none of the effects of the poison here.

She would be free to inspect the terrain so they'd know where to go once the poison wore off, if it wore off. She considered the fact that it might just slowly kill them. In any case, she had no idea how long she might have, so she jumped to her feet and rushed toward the brush that had stopped them where they were.

The brush and bramble that had been so restrictive in the waking world was hardly an obstacle within this reflected reality. She moved through it with ease, picking up speed until reaching a fast-paced jog. Then she spilled onto a stone-covered path.

She looked left, then right, but neither direction offered any insight into what lay beyond. She was fairly certain that turning right would lead her back toward the beach, so she decided to go left and ran along the path in that direction. Not long after, she was rewarded with a sudden end of the path . . . at the base of a cliff.

There was no town, no civilization, just a dead-end path, which meant either she had chosen the wrong direction or she was missing a hidden opening somewhere. She looked back at the forest, then turned to the seamless cliff wall where the path stopped. She walked up to it and inspected the area more closely. *Makes no sense to have a path that leads to nowhere.* Recalling the labyrinth of secret tunnel entrances beneath the city of Brinkwell, she decided this had to be the case here. The problem, among many, was that there was no color, which removed some of the subtleties that might give visual clues as to where to search. Placing her hands along the stone right where the path led, she pressed.

The response was immediate and unexpected; her hands sank right into the stone. She would have gasped if sound existed in this place. Instead, she silently watched as her hands disappeared all the way to the elbows before pressing against what could only be described as a "force." Her hands pressed against this "barrier." She willed them further but it was like pressing against the hind end of the world's strongest, stubbornest donkey. She redoubled her efforts but felt no change. She could go no further. She was just beginning to relieve her pressure against the wall when her entire body was thrown back. The force was mostly painless until she landed, regardless, it was powerful enough to send her catapulting through the air at least a dozen paces. The shock of the reaction was chilling. But when she came to her feet, she shook off her surprise and smiled. *I've found him.*

Now she just had to pray that she would wake up in the real world to find a body that was no longer under the effects of the poison of the forest, then figure out a way to get through to this place without falling prey to it once more. Perhaps not enough to celebrate, but she at least had reason to believe that she was in the right place.

She had started back the way she had come when she spotted movement further down the path and dove off it into dense foliage. She watched from the cover of a thick, twisted tree as a plainly dressed man walked confidently in her direction. As he drew closer, she recognized the same man she had seen within the dream world back on the road from Scritler. She had a better opportunity to watch him this time, and his hood was not drawn so she was able to see his face. The man's head was shaven, and he had a thick beard, but there were certain features that were too distinct to hide within without the giveaway of skin tone. *A Lugienese slave?* There was something else familiar about him. But she couldn't place it. Was it the race alone? The revelation that he was of the slave-breed was shocking enough unto itself. There was no way a Lugienese slave would be working with Magog, not like this. They were despised by the Kleról. This gave her hope that he might be able to help.

Not having to worry about producing sound, she easily followed him. Sindri stopped at the edge of the forest where the trail opened up at the base of the cliff. She watched as the man stood patiently staring at the wall. *He must be attempting to find a way in,* thought Sindri. *Perhaps I should go help. He must know something.* Just then a woman materialized from within the cliff wall where Sindri had just been repelled. She appeared to be young but was without a doubt one of the gray-cloaked women Sindri had pursued in Brinkwell. The woman handed something to the man, but Sindri didn't get a good look at what it was. *What is going on here?* The woman turned as if to return to the hidden doorway when another figure emerged and Sindri could not believe her eyes.

He wore a white robe as opposed to the gray cloak worn by the woman, but she had little doubt regarding his identity. It was Kibure. Sindri stepped out from hiding without another thought. She had to tell him she was here.

CHAPTER 82

KIBURE

KIBURE SAT UP AND DUSTED himself off after being catapulted through the air in an explosion of energy. He located the area where Arabelle had just been, but she was gone. *Well, looks like it worked . . .*

He readied his mind to leave the spiritual realm. *Except . . . no,* he thought. *She wouldn't have been able to escape without my help so it's just as much my right as it is hers. I deserve to see a bit of the world, and I'll be much safer doing so with someone like Arabelle.*

So he followed her out of the opening.

He pushed past the barest of resistance where the barrier had once been impenetrable. He squinted and raised hands to shield his eyes, but the blinding light of the sun never came. The spiritual realm did not only mute color, it appeared to also dim its intensity. Squinting was wholly unnecessary. His expression shifted then to one of confusion as he spotted Arabelle a few paces ahead, speaking with a hooded figure. She handed him a small object, wrapped in cloth, which quickly disappeared into the folds of the man's robes. Then he turned his head and met Kibure's eyes with a penetrating glare. Kibure stumbled back in surprise. *Jengal?* He shook his head to reassess, but the more he focused, the more certain he became. Yet how could he be? Jengal was surely

579

dead. And even if he had somehow survived his wounds wrought by the Kraken, the Lugienese would not have taught him to walk the spiritual realm? It made no sense.

Kibure sent a hesitant mental message to the man. *"Jengal? Is that you?"*

The eyes were nothing short of *wrong* as they stared back. *"I was once called by that name, but I have been given a new name, a new purpose."*

The man turned away and started down a path leading back into the forest.

"Wait! Jengal, I have many questions for you."

"I suspect that we shall see each other again soon enough, old friend."

Kibure started after Jengal, refusing to let him get away, but Arabelle turned to face him. *"I'm afraid I can't let you do that."*

"Do wh—" He stopped his mental speech as he saw another form emerge from the foliage, barring Jengal's way. *Impossible.* This had to be a dream, a dream that simply looked and felt like the spiritual realm. *Is that possible?*

Sindri stood just a dozen paces away. But unlike Jengal, Sindri appeared just as confused as Kibure to see him. Her expression quickly became one of excitement and she took a step forward. That is, until she was lifted into the air and thrown from the path in response to a few hand gestures from Jengal.

What—no!

Jengal continued down the path and out of sight. Meanwhile, Kibure froze, unsure whether to follow Jengal or see to Sindri. Arabelle had just handed Jengal something. What did that mean? *"Arabelle, what is going on here?"*

She appeared amused by the entire spectacle. "Well, it looks like we've both had a visitor. But your visitor got in the way of mine. I'm sure she's fine. And I would love to stick around and chat, but I have places to be." She spun and trotted back toward the barrier.

Kibure let her go. He needed to see Sindri.

CHAPTER 83

SINDRI

SINDRI REORIENTED HERSELF AFTER BEING suddenly thrown from the path by the slave-born man. The experience had been painful, but not to the same degree as if it had occurred in the "real" world. She started back toward the path in search of Kibure when something crashed hard into her. Her body responded without thought, capturing an arm and pulling as she twisted her body. This landed her atop the attacking shape, though she had no weapon in this place with which to inflict further damage. This thought came only after her body's instincts responded, however.

The point became moot when the offender blinked out of existence upon landing, leaving her straddling nothing but the foliage beneath her.

Then she heard his voice inside of her mind. No, not so much heard, but felt.

"*Sindri, what are you doing here?*"

Sindri tossed her head from side to side in search of the source of the "sound."

There! Kibure hovered above her like an apparition.

How are you doing that? she thought. Of course she had no means of communicating this to him, so she just shrugged and pointed at her mouth and shook her head in an attempt to communicate the fact that she had no means of speaking in this place.

"*I see. Are you here on the island in the flesh as well?*"

Sindri nodded.

He cringed ever so slightly and shook his head. "*You should not have come here. They will not allow you to enter, nor will they allow you to leave should you find a way inside.*"

Sindri was dimly pleased she had been right about him being held captive, and that he had received some sort of training, but shook her head against the thought. She hadn't come all this way for nothing. She was going to finish her mission: rescue Kibure, continue to expand her skills with ateré magic, and finally seek revenge against the Kleról.

But how could she communicate all of this to him while in this netherworld? She didn't even know how she might get inside in the first place.

He interrupted her. "*I need to follow Jengal. I need to know why he has come to this place.*"

Jengal? Why did that name sound familiar? She couldn't place it. He must be referring to the slave-breed she had seen, but his identity remained a mystery to her. Whoever he was, he had been given something by one of the gray-cloaked women. Something was *very* off about all of this.

"*Please, Sindri, leave before something bad happens to you.*"

He disappeared in a blink and Sindri felt her own existence in this place waver. She would be returning to her true body at any moment and still had no idea how she might rescue Kibure.

CHAPTER 84

KIBURE

KIBURE MATERIALIZED AT THE LAST place he had seen Jengal. Being able to transport himself at will within the spiritual realm was a useful skill, but there were limitations: he couldn't transport himself unless he could visualize the place he wished to go. He didn't know where exactly Jengal had gone so he was forced to go on foot. He raced down the path in the direction Jengal had gone. He paused at a fork in the path for half a breath then determined that he had no time to ponder; he just picked the path to the left and continued forward. The path emptied onto a beach, from where he spotted two ships anchored out in the water. A small boat alongside one of them was being pulled out of the water by a series of ropes. Inside was a hooded figure; that had to be Jengal.

Kibure materialized upon the deck of the ship just as Jengal stepped onto it. Four hooded figures stood around the hoisted boat and all took a step back as they spotted Kibure's sudden appearance. Then blades materialized in their hands. *Uh oh.*

Kibure held up weaponless hands to signify peace and no one moved. But Kibure noted that two of the hooded figures possessed the translucent hair of the Lugienese as it spilled out from beneath their cowls. He also spotted the sigil on their cloaks: two crescent moons surrounding a four-sided star. Klerósi priests.

A sword took shape in Kibure's right hand and he widened his stance.

Jengal spoke: "*You need to leave, now, before someone gets hurt.*"

Kibure held his ground. "*Why have you come? And why are you with Klerósi priests?*"

"*I do the will of our God, unlike you, servant of the Asaaven, servant of the Dark Lord.*"

Kibure felt as if Jengal had just plunged a sword into his chest. His excitement at seeing Jengal alive and well was wholly corrupted by his alignment with the Kleról. That and Jengal's belief that Kibure was associated with the Dark Lord. And that name again, Asaaven. It loosed a memory. The nightmare and the visitation from Magog. But instead of casting doubt, the thought enraged Kibure. Magog had bewitched his friend. And if Jengal was alive, did that mean Tenk was, too?

He had to find out. "*I am no agent of the Dark Lord. And I'm not going anywhere. Not until—*"

One of the robed figures lashed out with his weapon. Kibure blocked with his own. Then took a step back as another priest swung his weapon. Kibure was quickly overwhelmed. He blinked out of existence, then materialized a dozen paces above the deck. "*Why did you come here, Jengal?*"

Jengal looked up and shook his head. "*You had something that we needed. And now we have it. Goodbye, Kibure.*"

"*Wait!*" Kibure needed to know. "*Is Tenk . . . is Tenk still alive?*"

But Jengal only smiled. Several more figures had come on deck and Kibure knew he could not hope to stay and fight. He needed to tell Drymus about this. What was Jengal talking about? What had Arabelle given him?

A bolt of pain erupted in his side, then another, and another. He managed to gather enough focus to relocate his consciousness back to the entrance to Purgemon before any further harm could be done to him. When he reappeared, the pain had diminished only slightly and he winced. He looked down and saw dark rivulets of blood. It wasn't red, but he knew. He stumbled back through the barrier, then returned his mind to the physical realm.

He opened his eyes to color, and the sound of his own voice screaming. He was in the bed of his room and reached down to touch his side where the most grievous of wounds had been in the spiritual realm. To his utter horror, his hand came away with blood.

"Help! Someone help!" he yelled.

Vardya entered within a few heartbeats. "Kibure, what is it?"

Kibure extended his blood-soaked hand and her eyes widened. She rushed over to inspect the wound. Her expression gave nothing away, but she made several sounds of disapproval as she poked around. Finally, she said, "Nothing lethal, but you'll need a healer. I'll return shortly and then you'll explain how you acquired such injuries while lying in your own bed."

He nodded as she slipped out of the room. He had no choice. He needed to tell them about the Klerósi priests, about Jengal, that they had stolen something, or been given something. That Arabelle had helped. That *he* had helped. Even if he hadn't been aware of his role at the time, he had helped, though he still had no idea just what he helped with. Drymus had warned him that Arabelle was not to be trusted. The truth of this warning come to fruition hurt worse than his physical wounds. What would they do when they found out? Would he be returned to the cave? *Oh gods, no.*

What about Sindri? What would happen if she didn't heed his warning? His heart was racing. Too many problems.

Vardya returned with Drymus and a healer named Surin, who went to work right away as Drymus glared hard at him. "Explain yourself." She appeared to already suspect his involvement, and that aggravated him. He wanted so badly to prove her clear expectation for him wrong. Unfortunately, her glare was warranted. *Where to begin?*

His body tingled with healing magic as he provided a brief summary, including his role in boring a hole in the barrier within the spiritual realm. After he mentioned the stolen object, Drymus and Vardya exchanged a look that chilled Kibure's blood. Drymus nodded to Vardya. "The kosmí Go! And set someone to locating my granddaughter. She will answer for this."

"The kosmí? What would they possibly want with that? Aren't I the only one able to wield it?"

"Fool boy, no. Why do you think we've remained hidden for all these years?"

Kibure had no response for that. Then his mind backtracked to the other command. "Arabelle is your granddaughter?"

Drymus grunted.

Vardya rushed back in. "Lady Atticus has called for an assembling of the flock."

Kibure gave Drymus a look. "What does that mean?"

Drymus took him by the arm and said gruffly, "It means something bad. Let's go."

CHAPTER 85

KIBURE

THE ASSEMBLY WITHIN THE AMPHITHEATER contained perhaps every resident. Kibure guessed that there must have been five hundred in attendance. It had been only a few hours since he had helped Arabelle escape the barrier in the spiritual realm.

Drymus had him posted beside her right in the front row of the assembly so Kibure had to crane his neck to look about for Arabelle; she was nowhere to be seen. With her involvement in the disappearance of the kosmí, Kibure wondered if she might have been taken into custody. Would he be next or would his ignorance give him a free pass? The fact that Drymus had him in the front worried him. Would they pull him to the stage for a public flogging or questioning? His heart thumped painfully.

Lady Atticus extended a hand and the din of noise grew silent. "The kosmí has been taken from us."

Gasps rang out from the assembled. Kibure gulped.

Lady Atticus brought her hands up to quiet them once again. "The enemy was acting in concert with one of our own." Her eyes drifted over to Kibure for the briefest moment and he felt the blood drain from his face.

One of the women from the assembled yelled out, "Impossible! Who among us would do such a thing?"

Kibure's heart began pumping faster, louder.

Lady Atticus waited for the noise to die down before responding. "Our Lady Arabelle drugged Lady Ardent, then took possession of the kosmí. We believe that Arabelle then moved the kosmí into the spiritual realm before turning it over to the Lugienese and their allies. She then fled with the enemy before we realized what had taken place."

Kibure felt relieved at not being outwardly associated with Arabelle's treachery, but he could not shed the guilt he felt in knowing the role he played in her scheme. *I could have said no. I could have told Drymus about her plans to bore a hole in the barrier. She might have been able to puzzle out Arabelle's intentions. Instead, I've doomed this people's, my people's hopes of ever returning to their homeland.*

Kibure wasn't given the chance to dwell further as Lady Atticus continued.

"I have deployed one of our fastest vessels to follow the enemy at a distance. Our sisters will report their whereabouts to us from within the spiritual realm so that we don't lose the artifact. Additionally, word has reached us from Lady Lillith and our kinsmen in the north. The Dark Lord's minions have attacked them as well, and the outcome is as of yet unknown to us. Should the Dark Lord secure both . . ." She shook her head. "It would mark the beginning of the passage to dark, an end to our prophecies of redemption. We *must* retake the kosmí."

The open space grew eerily silent, except for Kibure who whispered to Drymus, "What is the passage to dark?"

Drymus leaned in. "The *other* prophecy. It speaks of the beginning of 'the darkness,' an age of the thousand-year rule and the restructuring of all humanity under the Dark Lord's supervision."

Kibure's head sagged. "Oh."

Lady Atticus waited to ensure every eye was upon her before she said, "I know this news paints a bleak picture, but all is not lost. We have the prophesied savior in our midst." She gestured toward Kibure, who shrank back. Lady Atticus continued, "However, without the kosmí, our prophesied savior cannot fulfill his destiny. And while the prophecies do not speak of such dark tidings within the passage to dawn, such challenges may yet be a part of Olem's plan. We must be vigilant; we must be strong. Victory is not ordained, it is earned! So for the first time in nearly five millennia, we will leave our place of hiding to follow the kosmí, wherever this takes us. We will do what must be done in Olem's name that we might be freed from the sins of our forebears, freed from the destruction our enemy will wreak against the fallen world. Go now and prepare. Our exodus begins at dawn."

Kibure's mind reeled. They were going to follow the Klerósi priests? Then what? Confront them and steal the kosmí back?

"Come," said Drymus firmly.

Kibure stood and his body obeyed, but his mind remained a jumble of questions. Chasing and fighting the Lugienese? Kinsmen to the north? Sindri? Here? What would become of her? He had told her to leave, but would she listen?

CHAPTER 86

SINDRI

SINDRI CAME AWAKE FEELING LIKE she had been roused far too early from a fitful sleep. That and her neck felt like it had been stuck in the most precarious pos—

The snake! Poison! Kibure! It all came back, primary among her memories that of having found Kibure.

Her body felt stiff as she attempted to stand. Fortunately, she no longer felt the lethargy caused by the poison. She reached over and squeezed Arella's wrist. Arella opened her eyes slowly, appearing to fight a similar haze. "So . . . we are not dead."

"Not dead," agreed Sindri.

Sindri proceeded to tell her about seeing Kibure, and the slave, Jengal, both of whom she had both seen from within that strange dream place. Before Sindri could voice her intentions, Arella said, "You plan to ignore Kibure's advice, no matter the danger."

Sindri considered how to respond for several heartbeats before finally nodding. "I must. You do not have to go with me. You have done your part to get me here."

Arella nodded and Sindri was glad that her decision would not affect the wizardess. But then Arella replied, "I will accompany you on your fool's mission. I was told by Draílock to keep you safe and I can't do that from the ship."

Sindri was prepared to argue with Arella but stopped herself short. They didn't have time for arguing, and it would likely do her no good anyhow. Arella was a woman grown, capable of making her own choices, even rash ones like Sindri's own.

Arella stood and brushed herself off. "So what is your plan for bypassing the poisonous boundary that stands between your friend and us?"

Sindri stared into the thick wall of vegetation that would work to immobilize them long before reaching their destination. She saw no other way to get through than to risk revealing themselves. She reasoned that the woman in the gray robes she had seen with Kibure had spotted her, anyway, so they would likely be pursued soon no matter their course. It was either go forward with force or abandon the plan as a whole. Sindri could not abide the latter.

Sindri answered by extending her mind into the jungle before her, feeling the life within, and taking hold. With the energy in her grasp, she took a deep breath, gritted her teeth, and drew in its power. The forest shriveled before her and she was filled with its vitality. She then used this power to send a blast of energy further down the line into the forest toward the stone wall that she believed was a hidden entrance to where Kibure was being held.

Arella scowled. "I see caution is no longer a consideration."

Sindri narrowed her eyes. "As I said, I was seen by one of them. The time to have of stealth has passed."

Arella muttered to herself, "Very well. Let's hope the old man was right about . . ." She trailed off then stepped onto the newly cleared path and repeated what Sindri had just done, continuing to clear a line in the forest to avoid being poisoned again.

Once more each and they reached the spot where Sindri had seen Kibure. The stone path, once located, led right to the stone cliff face then continued around a bend. Sindri would never have found the opening without having seen Kibure step out from within it. She walked up to it, studying the smooth, seamless surface. She saw no indication of any door whatsoever. She ran her hands along the smooth stone; nothing.

"The door is right here . . . somewhere."

Arella replied, "Slightly to the left actually."

Sindri looked back to see Arella standing a pace behind her, eyes closed, hand extended toward the wall. *Of course! She's sinking her mind into the stone itself.* That was likely going to be the only way to open the door, anyhow. *Why didn't I think of that?*

Sindri did the same. Mentally probing the stone, she began to see the contours in her mind's eye. More important, she could see the absence of stone that formed a tunnel leading down . . . beyond where she dared reach. This still left a thick door of stone between them and the tunnel.

"How do we move of this stone door?" asked Sindri.

Arella replied, "I'm not sure. We could try to drain it of substance to weaken it like we've done with the vegetation, but to dissolve it completely would be extremely taxing and I think we're going to want some magic left over to protect ourselves just in case the gray-cloaks greet us with the hospitality befitting unannounced visitors who intend to steal their prized guest."

Sindri didn't like the sound of that option, but it got her thinking. "Can we weaken of the perimeter, then move stone? This uses of less power, yes?"

Arella considered the idea. "Yes, that *might* work. It would certainly be a more economic course, though draining a specific line of stone in a rectangular ring will require a very precise pull of energy." Her talking slowed. "Except . . . oh."

"Oh?" responded Sindri.

"Aha."

"What is it?" asked Sindri.

Arella was working magic, Sindri could feel it. Not much was being used, but she could tell by Arella's expression that whatever she was doing required a fair amount of mental attention. Then she felt *something*. The faintest vibration. She probably wouldn't have noticed were she not standing completely still so close to the door. She stepped back, not sure if the effect was something Arella had created or if one of the gray-cloaked women was about to step out from the wall.

"Something is happening," she said as she backed away.

Arella nodded. "At my behest."

That was a relief. Arella took a step forward and Sindri watched in awe as her hand disappeared into the stone.

"How did you do that?"

Arella turned and smiled. "It's an illusion. I was able to unlatch the actual stone door and open that, but the illusion remains intact. It's quite the clever design."

Sindri nodded and gestured with a hand. "Shall we?"

Arella nodded and stepped back. "After you."

Sindri smiled, but her heart was pumping to the beat of battle, and her stomach turned over on itself as she realized she was about to walk into a completely unknown space filled with who knew how many skilled wielders. Perhaps they weren't all wielders. Perhaps they only had a few, and the rest were just regular people. It was wishful thinking, but Sindri needed some of that to convince herself to move forward with this suicide mission. She swallowed and stepped into the—

Arella grabbed her arm and pulled her back. "Wait!"

Her left leg had passed the threshold of the illusion and disappeared into the empty space, but Arella pulled her back just before her leg was struck by stone. Her momentum carried her and her limb out of danger as stone slammed into the space where she would have been standing. She would have been crushed.

"How did you know?"

Arella's expression was angry. "I continued probing the area and noticed a few oddities in the wall of the entrance, a few very thin lines of energy that seemed unattached to the rest. I'm surprised my arm didn't trigger one of them when I pushed through. A trap for unwanted visitors. Your leg triggered one of these strands of energy."

"So how do we get in?" asked Sindri wearily.

"I think I can disable them, now that I know what I'm looking at."

A few minutes later, Arella had moved the stone that had slid over to crush them, as well as rerouted the lines of energy that would trigger the stone to move again if they were broken. Arella wasn't certain how the defensive door had been powered to begin, but she believed it would not be able to do so again without being somehow reloaded with energy. To be safe, however, she waved her hand about the area in an attempt to catch any errant lines of energy she had missed.

"Would you like to do the honors?" she asked.

Sindri swallowed hard. "Not particularly. But this is my journey, so I must have of the courage." And with that, she stepped into the darkness of the tunnel.

CHAPTER 87

KIBURE

DRYMUS LED KIBURE TO THE small building that she called her home, then stopped a few paces away from the front door.

"Wait here."

She returned a few moments later, closing the door behind her, then tossed a bundle of fabric at him. His reaction was too slow to do anything but let it hit him. The silvery wad struck his shoulder and began to unfurl itself. The shimmering fabric soon lay draped across him like a Klerósi sash.

"What's this?" he asked, confused.

"Your new outfit."

He looked down at it, then back up at her still unsure.

Drymus rolled her eyes. "If you're ever going to be a real wizard, you need to start looking the part. Plus, I promised you'd get a robe once you earned it. And in spite of your foolish assistance to Arabelle, I believe you worthy of a wizard's robe. Now get dressed, we will be departing shortly."

Kibure did so as quickly as he could without time to investigate the new look. He certainly enjoyed the softness of the silky fabric. *No wonder they all wear these!*

He looked up and saw Drymus tilting her head in confusion. "What is it?" he asked. "Am I wearing it wrong?" He looked down at the finery. It was silver, but unlike the robes worn by the women, his had golden trim and a wrapping of golden fabric at the waist. He felt unworthy of wearing something of such opulence, but if he was going to do it, he should at least put the thing on right.

Drymus had a far-off look, like she was seeing something entirely different within her mind than that which was before her. She shook her head and returned to the present. "No, no, you appear precisely as you are meant to. You look like a real wizard."

Now I just have to become one, thought Kibure.

Drymus brought a hand to her chin and said, "We will be leaving this place in a matter of hours and I have a few things to take care of before we do. Why don't you go for a walk, or practice your forms?"

Kibure left Drymus to her business and headed down the main street past the amphitheater over toward the garden. He hadn't spent as much time as he would have liked admiring the gardens, especially in the physical realm.

The area was largely empty, as it was most of the time, however Kibure did notice that the adjacent orchards were buzzing with activity. Gathering food for the journey, he knew. He felt a stab of guilt. This was his fault, at least partially. These women had to leave the only place they'd ever called home, and all because he had been too foolish to see that he was being used by Arabelle. A touch of anger sparked at the thought of her conniving.

He wandered aimlessly throughout the garden, zigzagging between aisles and through a section of maze, where he paused at a flower that had bent over, sagging awkwardly into the center of the path. He cupped the large, red blossom in his hand, gently lifting it and its stalk to reposition it among the others. As soon as he let go, it sagged even further into the path. Kibure attempted to reposition it and brought his hand down the stalk to the roots to see if he could prop it up there, but realized the futility as he looked at the other flowers in the grouping. This one had grown too large for its slim stalk to support it. Kibure stared at the once beautiful flower that now sagged pathetically into the path, and without much further consideration, extended his mind into the stone at his feet, using that energy to strengthen the flower's base. He grew a shoot off the side, then another, and another, then tethered these to the neighboring flowers until this the flower was able to support itself. When he had finished, he admired his handiwork. "That's better," he said out loud to it.

Of course, this garden and everything within would die within a few weeks of the women's departure. All the plants in here served at the pleasure of the women. Without sunlight or someone to infuse them with energy from the stone, they would all shrivel up and die. It seemed a cruelty, but that, he supposed, was part of life. His own life would possibly find a similar end, and according to the prophecy, so too then would the rest of these women, even the world. It seemed unfair, unwise even, to place so much on the shoulders of a single individual, no matter who.

Kibure rose and started back toward his room. He spotted Rave flittering past. He hadn't noticed the raaven nearby, but that was the way with Rave. The creature somehow managed to maintain a semblance of total indifference while simultaneously being around whenever Kibure needed him most. His time here in Purgemon had been without much need, so Rave had been absent more often than not, though he seemed always near. Kibure looked out at the marvel that was this underground oasis and another wave of guilt passed through him. It was a true marvel, and it would be left to wither like a field left untended. He wondered how long the garden would survive with the women's magic.

Kibure stopped at the edge of the garden just before stepping onto the cobbled street leading back into the city. He felt an odd sensation, but he couldn't pinpoint precisely what it was. *Probably nerves*, he thought. He glanced over at Rave, who had landed atop the lamppost. Rave was facing the city, but his head was craning back toward the orchard. His head was also tilted to the side as if in curiosity or confusion. Then an undeniable sensation struck Kibure and he understood the feeling that had given him pause moments earlier: it was magic.

The sensation would not ordinarily give him pause, as the use of magic was commonplace in Purgemon, a near constant buzz of it, actually. However, it was nearly always used in small, controlled ways. What she had just felt was a bubble. He turned and faced the orchard and saw that the five women who had been busy harvesting had stopped. They all faced the same direction, the door to the outside. The same door Kibure had opened in the spiritual realm, right near where he had seen . . . Sindri.

By the time Kibure had made his way to the door, he was accompanied by the five women who had been working in the orchard. He presumed more would come as the evidence of magic continued to flare from the location of the door. Kibure stopped a few paces away, waiting for whoever, or whatever, emerged.

One of the She'yaren stepped in front of him. "You should go. Whoever is attempting to enter this place is not one of our own. Someone of your value cannot be risked."

Kibure might have listened. The intruder could be Klerósi priests, after all, but something in his gut told him otherwise. And if it was who he thought it was, he had to be here.

He felt another ripple of magic and the stone within the doorway slid soundlessly into the rest of the wall. Kibure braced himself for who or what would come through.

He knew that every single woman within the semicircle of She'yaren was drawing in power from the stone below. No matter the danger to himself or the women, Kibure prayed he would see a Klerósi priest step into view. His prayer was answered with defiance.

CHAPTER 88

KIBURE

AN OLIVE-SKINNED WOMAN WITH BLOND hair and a brown robe stepped into view and Kibure sighed in relief, then tilted his head in confusion. She was certainly no Lugienese. Then again, the Kleról appeared to be expanding their view of who should wear the robes. In any event, Kibure was simply glad not to see—

Sindri stepped into view right behind the other woman. Kibure's breath caught in his throat. *No. Oh no. Sindri, why did you not listen?*

One of the She'yaren before Kibure spoke using some dialect of Lugienese, probably in response to seeing Sindri, whose bronze skin and translucent hair left no room to question her heritage. The She'yaren woman said calmly but firmly, "You have entered the home of the She'yar without permission, agent of the darkness."

Sindri came to stand beside the other woman, who looked to Kibure to be an Isles native, though he wasn't certain, and didn't care enough to consider further. Sindri responded in even tones, "I speak of the common tongue for I have abandoned the ways of my people. I come only for Kibure. I do not wish for to fight of you."

Switching seamlessly to the common tongue, the same She'yaren woman replied tersely, "Kibure is a guest of ours. He will not be going anywhere, not with you. As for you, your people have stolen something precious of ours."

This was not going to end well, Kibure knew that much. He needed to do something. He stepped forward, or tried to. The She'yaren who had taken on the role of speaker put her hand out behind her to prevent Kibure from stepping up beside her. "Stay back," she hissed.

Kibure took a step back and said, "Sindri, please. You need to leave, now." He didn't need to add urgency to his voice. It was more a matter of finding bits of strength to balance it out.

Unless the woman Sindri had brought with her wielded the power of a god, this was not going to end well for either of them.

Sindri peered over at Kibure, her expression one of determination, and he knew she would not back down. She said calmly, "I have come a long way to find you, Kibure. Risked my life to help you escape the Empire, and more, to find you here. Do you now expect me to simply turn around and leave you in the custody of thieves?"

Kibure's heart was racing and he felt his mind was going to explode from the many directions it was being pulled. He knew this moment balanced on a head of a pin, that the slightest wrong move would begin a magical assault that would likely be the end of Sindri. He needed to convince her that he was being well taken care of, and that she needed to leave; that he *wanted* her to leave.

Kibure took a step backward to be free of the woman who was blocking him and extended both arms out from his sides, palms up like a priest speaking to his followers. "Sindri, I was given a choice to leave upon arrival. I have *chosen* to be here and am being well taken care of. These women have taught me to wield ateré magic as well as how to navigate the spiritual realm. I do not need to be rescued."

Sindri scowled and looked to her companion, who raised eyebrows and shrugged, both still appearing poised to strike just like the residents of Purgemon who faced them. Sindri opened her mouth and said, "I . . ." but trailed off, unsure how to respond.

"Sindri, please," said Kibure.

She lifted her left sandaled foot ever so slightly, her body still tense and prepared for battle. *Gods, no . . .*

CHAPTER 89

SINDRI

INDRI STOOD WITHIN THE LARGEST cavern she could have imagined might exist; an entire civilization housed inside; it was like an entire underground world. Several paces away grew a fruit-filled garden, but beyond that, a city of dazzling glowing orbs, stone structures, and probably hundreds of inhabitants. It took her breath away. But the majesty of the place bore down on her resolve. How could she challenge a people responsible for constructing such a place? There was a gentle thrum of power, a soft symphony of magical threads that seemed to blow about like a breeze within the stone enclosure.

No, I'm here for a purpose. I will not be seduced by this.

She had drawn in a dangerous amount of power, feeling the glorious potential within. And yet, each of the women before her had likely done the same and had been wielding this power for much longer than she. She shook her head. *You can't think about that.* She needed to clear her mind of everything but one fact: she *needed* this. Needed to rescue Kibure.

But what if he didn't need rescuing? Surely his words were coerced. But what if they weren't? Kibure was not dressed in a way that suggested that he was being held captive. He wore an elaborate silver robe with a golden, frilly pad on the left shoulder. Instead of a flat, simple flow of fabric as worn by the other women, his robe gathered at the waist with another band of golden fabric before continuing down to cover the rest of his legs. He looked like a wizard from the stories.

Would Sindri drag Arella to her death alongside her own folly, all because she was too stubborn to admit that Kibure didn't need her help in the first place? Had people died in the wake of her determination to accomplish . . . nothing? *No. This has to have been for something.* She lifted her foot and started forward for an attack, to free Kibure from their influence. A distant part of her mind, a hand of doubt, reached out and gripped her. With a shaky sigh that released much of the magical potential she had taken in, she slowly relaxed her position, lowering her arms to her sides.

She glanced at Arella and shook her head as she said to Kibure, "I will leave you. I—I'm glad that you are being well cared for, Kibure."

As if she needed further proof of the futility that would have been this fight, another gray-cloaked woman approached from within a maze of flowers to the left of the fruit.

Unlike the ageless appearance of the other gray-cloaked witches, the approaching woman appeared ancient. She said angrily, "What in the depths of suffering hell is going on here?"

One of the gray-cloaks turned and said, "Lady Drymus, we have before us a pair of intruders come to steal away with—"

Drymus cut her off. "I would hear it from the intruders themselves."

Sindri did not like the tone but attempted to answer with as little venom as possible. If she was not going to rescue Kibure, she would prefer to leave with her life, so she explained her original intentions in brief, followed by her decision to now leave without him.

Drymus said, "This is a wise decision you have made. It would not have gone well for you to attempt to steal away with such a most precious artifact as he."

Sindri nodded and bowed her head. She wasn't sure why, but this felt right. She then turned and nodded to Arella, who turned to follow her out.

The original gray-cloak who had questioned them spoke up. "We can't just let these two leave. For all we know, they're in league with those who stole the kosmí."

Sindri stopped mid-step at the words. The accusation was bitter, and wrong. She spoke without turning: "I have of nothing to do with the Lugienese."

The woman replied, "Your obvious heritage, and the timing of your arrival, would suggest otherwise. You'll at least need to stay long enough for the council to rule on the matter."

Sindri turned slowly. Drymus spoke up, but not to Sindri. "Rubbish. If the boy has confirmed her identity as an ally and she agrees to go, we let her go. We are leaving, anyhow. We have no care for her knowledge of this place."

The gray-cloak curled up her lip as she said, "Rumor has it that the last person our 'savior' deemed trustworthy turned out to be much the opposite. This matter will be brought to Lady Atticus and the council."

Sindri's nerves were beginning to tingle as the chance for a safe departure was removed from her control. She glanced at Arella, whose cool, composed face spoke of deep concentration. They met eyes and Sindri knew that Arella was preparing to fight. Sindri had better do the same. She drew in as much power from her surroundings as she could on short notice.

The gray-cloak intent on not allowing Sindri to leave, said to the others, "Seize them."

Four of the silver-robed sorceresses stepped forward to take Sindri and Arella, who sidled up beside each other to form a V shape of defense. Sindri suspected a spell of immobilization, a spell she wished she had been taught. In any event, she did know how to defend against an attack of magic, no matter the nature.

Draílock's training echoed as both women ducked while deflecting the initial magical attacks with shields of air. They both shot forth their own retorts. Sindri sent a blast of compact air, while Arella was more tactical. She shot a blade of energy into the ground at the feet of her attackers, spraying them with stone and dirt. She then rolled forward and engaged the surprised women with a mix of martial prowess and magic.

Sindri's attack was easily defended, so she rose from her crouch to engage in closer combat. Unfortunately, her first step sank unexpectedly into the earth before her, causing her to lose her balance. She was forced to use her next step to maintain her upright position. A moment later, a blast of energy sent her spiraling to the ground with a hard thud.

She expected the assault to continue, but when she looked up to her opponents, she saw only a man in silver and gold standing tall between her and the gray-cloaks. "Leave them be."

His words were commanding, unlike anything she had ever heard him say before, but there was no denying that this was Kibure. There was obvious hesitation in the voice of the gray-cloak in charge as she responded, "Stand aside. We can't place the entire tribe at risk simply because our 'savior' is too naïve to see the threat before him."

Kibure stood his ground. "I may be naïve, but I know Sindri and she is no ally of the Lugienese. Now leave—them—be."

None of the original five were willing to strike with Kibure standing in their way, but neither did they stand down. One of the women who had yet to speak sneered and said, "The prophecies have been wrong before. I begin to wonder if he isn't another failed interpretation."

Drymus moved to stand beside Kibure and said, "This is madness. Would you truly risk attacking the only person capable of returning us? Risking it all over two insignificant travelers? He has drawn upon the kosmí, I have seen it with my own eyes. *He* is our last hope." She gestured toward Sindri and Arella. "What care have we for these women?"

Sindri was taken aback. These women believed Kibure to be some sort of prophesied savior? She shouldn't have been surprised; it wasn't the first time such claims had been made regarding him. This would explain why they had captured and trained him in the first place.

The gray-cloak who had last spoken responded to Drymus. "We'll try not to hurt him, or you, but if you're fool enough to stand in our way . . ."

As if a telepathic message had been sent, all five gray-cloaks attacked in unison.

Sindri drew in more power and rolled to the side, narrowly avoiding a blast of heat that would have left her painfully charred. She realized these women had no intention of delivering their quarry to their council in good health, if at all. Surrender was no longer an option.

Sindri knew she was severely outmatched. Her skills of ateré magic were still rudimentary when compared to these gray-cloaks. *No. Don't think like that. You've been fighting with magic for over a decade. You were one of the best of the Kleról.* This was just like fighting with a blade, just a different shape. She could adapt. Needed to adapt.

That thought gave her an idea.

She reached down and removed one of her knives from hiding, then another. She leaped over a blast of power shot toward her knees, then used her magic to deflect a follow-up meant to take her airborne body by surprise.

Sindri was only a few paces away from the woman intent on ending her existence. She said a quick prayer, then attempted an old trick from years past. She had nothing to lose but her life.

She sent her first blade arcing high into the air toward the woman, followed by a magical blade of air sent toward the woman's feet. This was immediately followed by a flick of her other knife sent zipping straight toward the woman's chest. Sindri had taken a step forward to throw this last knife and followed through with the rest of her body. The sorceress before her deflected the magical attack while still dodging away from each of the thrown knives. She was, however, not prepared for Sindri to be close enough to strike with a closed fist. That was the thing with magic users, Sindri thought; they tended to overlook attacks of the mundane. Her knuckles slammed into the underside of the sorceress's jaw and her head snapped backward. Sindri had just enough time to grin to herself before pain erupted from her knee, which had been kicked by the adjacent witch. Sindri grunted, then struck the first sorceress with an elbow to the stomach for good measure before spinning to face her new opponent.

She was immediately engaged. Sindri had hoped that close quarters fighting with limited magic would give her an edge. It didn't. These women trained in the martial arts. While Sindri had been one of the better fighters within the Klerósi priesthood, she was unable to land a single blow as the woman flowed through smooth movements of deflection and reattack like rising water surrounding a stationary stone. An outstretched foot to the stomach sent Sindri stumbling backward and she managed to roll instead of falling flat on her back. She ended her backward roll in a crouch just in time to deflect an attack of summoned magic.

Her peripheral vision picked up continued fighting from the others, but she also spotted movement from other sides, more women had arrived, forming a ring. Of course the use of magic would have attracted the attention of others in this place. There was no getting out of it. And she suspected that even if she decided to go willingly before this "council," their ruling would not be in her and Arella's favor. She was fighting for her life. She could not surrender.

If she was going to go down, she'd go down fighting. She formed a shield of air, and filled it with her remaining summoned power, hoping it would give her long enough to figure out her next move. A cry to her left shifted her attention to Kibure, who had just landed a decisive blow against one of their opponents, who sank against the stone wall to Sindri's right. He turned and immediately engaged another. Sindri also spotted Arella, still up and fighting, though she was being backed against the wall by two of the gray-cloaks. Drymus seemed to merely act in defense, perhaps hoping her opponent would tire.

Sindri's eye was drawn back to Kibure, who fought with an awe-inspiring grace unbefitting someone so new to the act. He looked the part of a performer playing out a choreographed drama as the silver fabric of his robes flowed about his arms and legs like the trailing tassels of a baton. It was beautiful and she could hardly believe he was the same helpless boy whom she had rescued just a short time ago. He looked a true wizard through and through. But before Sindri had time to appreciate this thought, the woman with whom he was engaged caught one of his wrists in her hand, twisted her body away from him and pulled, her other arm flying up past his armpit as if to wave to those who were watching. This action sent Kibure sailing in a high arc over her, his wrist acting the part of an anchor. He landed on his back with a thud, following by a cloud of dust, and a groan of pain and surprise. "Some prodigy," snarled the woman as she struck him with a wave of magic. He didn't move, but his eyes remained open, growing wide in fear, then anger. *A spell of immobilization.*

Sindri felt something stir within her. A feral frustration built upon a foundation years in the making, beginning with the death of her brother. To unleash this anger would be to burn the bridge of negotiation once and for all. There would be no turning back. She didn't care. She extended her mind back into the hard earth beneath her feet. She met with unexpected resistance, finding the magic difficult to draw. For a moment she thought she was doing something wrong, but then she considered the amount of magic being used in such a small space. They were likely exhausting the residual levels of power within the stone. The ground itself would be holding tighter to what remained of its energy in order to keep its shape. This meant she would either have to draw harder and risk destabilizing the stone around her or extend her mind to draw energy from further away. In either case, the process would be less efficient and put even more strain on her bones as she channeled the energy. Looking over at Kibure, she decided it no longer mattered.

She closed her eyes and released the fury of a trapped and cornered animal as she swallowed that last semblance of restraint. She extended her mind deep into the bedrock beneath her and to either side. Her mind spidered out in every direction in search of whatever power it could sense. Then she gripped it with the mental strength of a steel-forging smith as he hoisted his great hammer.

She drew in and felt the euphoria of such vast a volume of power. She had never held so much at one time. A small part of her mind recoiled in fear of what might happen should she actually channel all of it. But that part of her mind was a whisper amid the torrent of anger she felt toward these gray-cloaks, toward a world that had brought her to this place, toward a god that had birthed an Empire that stole the lives of people like her brother. So much anger. So many things wrong. And she now held within her the ability to enact justice, at least in this small way.

She sensed an attack from behind; one of the newly arrived onlookers had decided to join the fight. Sindri instinctually pushed a portion of the drawn energy into her shield, a mere drip when compared to the ocean of power she held. The shield expanded to fully envelop her as she rose to her feet. A blast of energy came directly for her from behind, then another from the woman with whom she'd been engaged. Both fizzled away like a wisps of air striking stone. Two more joined the attack, two more failed to break her shield.

Sindri noted confusion then concern upon the faces of the gray-cloaks who had gathered around, drawn by the use of magic. A few began moving backward. *Is that fear I see? Good. You should all be afraid.*

Sindri narrowed her eyes and lifted her hands. She heard voices, but it was just noise, and justice had closed its ears to the rabble of the guilty. She squeezed her eyes shut and felt for the essence that made up Kibure, then that of Arella. She would spare them. No one else mattered.

She gritted her teeth and released the tempest of raw power within.

CHAPTER 90

KIBURE

KIBURE STARED UP WIDE-EYED, BUT unable to move due to the spell of immobilization. He cursed himself for leaving the opening to allow such a fate to befall him. And now he watched, helpless, as Sindri employed a protective shield strong enough to rebuff simultaneous attacks from several of the long-lived, magically adept She'yaren. He wouldn't have thought such a feat possible, not for someone so new to ateré magic. But her strength alone was not what frightened him; it was the look in her eyes, a look that foretold a menacing violence. That, in addition to the fact that she seemed to have summoned more power than she could manage to keep stored. He sensed tendrils of pure energy seeping out of her as if her reservoir was an old bucket filled too high with water.

Drymus had spoken of such folly with regards to novice wielders who became intoxicated with the euphoria of channeling the magic of the world. Each wielder had their own natural limits, which could be improved with practice, but only to a limited extent. Sindri could not have had much more practice than he, but perhaps her previous adeptness with priestly magic meant she could also hold more ateré.

Kibure didn't need to know how much energy she held in comparison to others. He feared if she channeled all she held, enough that she couldn't even contain it within herself, she would kill not only herself but everyone around her, himself included. He strained against the magical bonds of immobilization, but they were as firm as steel, unwilling to bend in the slightest to his will. He was completely at the mercy of Sindri's rage. They all were.

He noted that the other She'yaren seemed to have recognized the same thing and had begun backing away as they employed modes of their own magical protection. The conflict between Drymus and her combatant must have ended because Drymus was suddenly by Kibure's side. She shouted, "Release the boy, you fool!" The woman must have sensed the combination of fear and command in her tone for she did so immediately. Kibure sat up and yelled, "Sindri, don't—"

A wave of pure energy shot out from her in every direction. It was *nearly* indiscriminate, though it appeared to mostly miss him. Still, tiny spears of heated air struck him, smoke swirling as his new robe singed in places. The ground beneath him gave way and he tumbled through the air, disoriented. He heard the cries of dozens of women.

Kibure landed hard, at an odd angle and slid along shiny smooth stone. Everything was suddenly still. Kibure blinked several times, but the landscape didn't change as he thought it might. He had fallen into a vast crater, the ground uneven but smooth. It spanned dozens upon dozens of paces in every direction. Spears of light shot into the space from the outside world, for whatever Sindri had done had destroyed a large portion of the wall that enclosed Purgemon. The smooth mini craters and mounds within the crater sparkled in the light like moving seawater illuminated by an early-morning sun.

Kibure turned his gaze in search of Sindri. She remained where she had been in the center of this crater standing on a thin pillar of stone, chest heaving after the exertion. Kibure rose to his feet, noting the trembling in her legs. Warnings he had received from Draílock, and again from Drymus, about the damage to bone mass that would come from channeling too much power put Kibure's feet to moving. He wasn't certain she would survive even a fall to the earth were she standing on flat ground. But he was certain that she would not survive a fall into the crater, and that was exactly what was about to happen. He attempted to draw in power from his surroundings, but the stone at his feet clung to its mass and Kibure didn't have the focus right to wrench any free, not while also navigating the uneven terrain. He propelled his legs forward as Sindri swayed and finally lost her ability to stand completely. Her head sagged backward and her body followed, arms limp at her sides.

Kibure pumped tired legs, but the uneven ground made the task too difficult. He stumbled to a knee, then scrambled back to a half run before stumbling again. *Nooooo!* He wasn't going to make it. He ran nonetheless.

Sindri's limp form cascaded through the air and Kibure extended a hand, helpless as he lost his footing once again, too far. "Nooooo!" he shouted.

He closed his eyes and turned away at the last moment, unable to witness such a horrific death.

Just then a splinter of magic cracked the air, followed by complete and utter silence. Silence? The sound of Sindri's body crunching against the stone below did not come. Did that mean . . . ? Kibure turned his head slowly, still afraid he would see Sindri's body lying in a heap of shattered bones and flesh. Instead, her body hovered in the air. But how?

Kibure looked around, seeing no one else except—there. A tall, thin She'yaren with stark white hair stood at the edge of the crater, sun glittering on her silver robe and hair. Lady Atticus. Sindri's body floated up and over to land gently at Atticus's feet, just above the rim of the crater created by Sindri's incredible feat of power.

Kibure's joy at seeing Sindri rescued was suddenly replaced by dread. To what end had Lady Atticus just saved her? Sindri had entered Purgemon unbidden in an attempt to steal away with the person they had traveled across the world to find in the first place. On top of this, Sindri had just attacked a dozen She'yaren. Kibure climbed out of the crater and was grateful to see the upright forms of several She'yaren who had been struck by Sindri's wave of power, including the individual with whom Kibure had just been dueling. Lady Atticus's arrival had ended the hostilities, as none of the women tried to reengage. That is until Sindri's accomplice rose to her feet a dozen paces away. Other She'yaren formed up, poised to attack, but Lady Atticus ended this with a word: "Peace."

Looks of confusion followed, but she was obeyed.

Sindri's friend looked just as befuddled as everyone else, but with no attack forthcoming, the woman did not seem eager to begin the violence anew, especially not when Lady Atticus held Sindri's life within her grasp.

Lady Atticus addressed this woman directly. "I have called for healers to see to your friend, though I cannot guarantee her survival from such a reckless use of power. In any case, we will see to her rehabilitation insomuch as we are able. What is your name, Isleslander?"

"My name is Arella." Arella executed a quick bow of the head.

Lady Atticus offered no such deference, but she did wave Arella over with a gesture of her hand. "Lady Arella, I offer you parlay so long as you swear to uphold the peace. During such a time, you will have the connection to your power dimmed so as to limit the threat to my people as we travel. Do you agree to these terms?"

Arella glanced around, eventually meeting Kibure's eyes before nodding begrudgingly. "I do not appear to have much choice in the matter, do I?"

Atticus allowed the slightest shrug and shook her head. "You do not. At least no other choice in which you would be permitted to remain alive." Her voice took on a sharp edge and Kibure was reminded that Atticus was centuries old and had just had her people's most valuable possession stolen from her by the Lugienese while Arella and Sindri attempted to take the other.

Arella then asked, "Might I ask to where you travel?"

To Kibure's surprise, Atticus projected an expression of consideration, followed by an answer. "We seek to regain something very important to our people. We travel by sea to wherever this leads us."

"I see," was all Arella said in response.

Kibure approached the place where Sindri lay at Atticus's feet. Lady Atticus said nothing, which Kibure took as a good sign. He knelt beside Sindri and was thankful to hear her breathing, though her breaths were ragged and shallow.

Kibure looked up. "Lady Atticus, I am thankful that you have decided to spare Sindri's life. But I have to ask: why?"

Atticus answered matter-of-factly, her emotionless voice defeating any notion that this was a mere act of kindness. "Her use of magic, while foolish, was beyond that which any single person should be capable of besides perhaps you, though I doubt you have the capacity to draw so much power without the kosmí. This makes her the subject of my curiosity, for now."

Kibure didn't know what to make of that. He simply replied, "Thank you. She is a trusted friend, though I wish her attempt to rescue me had not come to violence as it did."

Atticus nodded. "That was indeed most unfortunate, though it appears everyone had a chance to protect themselves from the worst of your friend's surge. This Sindri, she is the Lugienese woman of whom you spoke when you first arrived? The one who helped you escape from the Lugienese Empire?"

Kibure nodded, surprised she had put that together. He shouldn't have been. She was centuries old. He needed to continue reminding himself of this.

"You care about this woman."

Kibure nodded again. "She is a friend."

"Good. Then her safekeeping will be enough collateral to guarantee no further violence between you and your sisters as we travel."

Kibure gulped but nodded.

Atticus looked to someone behind Kibure and said, "Ah, Lady Drymus. I am glad to see you are well."

Drymus responded with her typical sarcasm, "A generous lie."

Atticus ignored the invitation to banter. "Your accommodations have changed. You will now be traveling with myself, the boy, and our two new friends. We have much to discuss, you and I, especially your decision to raise arms against your own. You will walk with me now."

Then Atticus spoke loud enough for everyone in the general vicinity to hear: "The ships are prepared to set sail. We will depart as soon as everyone has boarded. Rosell and Gengriel, you will see Kibure and Lady Arella to the ship. Lady Arella is to be given tea straight away. If she resists in any way, you have my permission to use whatever force necessary, including deadly. Fandriel, you will wait here with the wounded intruder until our healers arrive to care for and transport her to my ship."

Atticus turned and started back toward the city of Purgemon, Drymus by her side.

Two She'yaren approached from the groups of departing women. "I am Lady Rosell. You heard Lady Atticus. You two will be coming with us." She indicated Lady Gendriel beside her. Kibure was thankful not to be placed in chains. Atticus was right about one thing; using Sindri's safety as collateral would keep Kibure compliant. Not that he had intended rebellion of any sort in the first place. The attempt on Sindri's life had given him little choice in the matter. Granted, none of that would have taken place had she simply listened to him. That was a conversation to be had at a later date, for now Kibure was simply praying she would wake up.

CHAPTER 91

KIBURE

KIBURE TRUDGED ALONGSIDE ARELLA AS they followed the She'yaren charged with escorting them to the ship. They had passed through the waterfall that Kibure recalled from his initial arrival, but from there the women took them down a different path, this one following the river. Kibure enjoyed the sounds of the forest, the chirping of birds, the hum of life. Even the natural light of the sun, while initially painful to his eyes, worked to rejuvenate him with its warm touch.

Rave flew around excitedly now that he was in a space without a stone ceiling. This also lifted Kibure's spirits, if only slightly. The raaven suddenly flitted up and over the tops of the trees, disappearing from sight. Kibure watched him go and missed the opening of the forest and the path emptying out into a clearing.

Kibure gasped when he finally returned his gaze to what lay before him. The path opened to a vast lake, fed by the river they had accompanied on their walk. Four ships floated on the lake, each as breathtaking as the next.

Kibure didn't know much about ships, but he did know that these looked nothing like any he had ever seen. He considered the ship he had taken from the Palpanese Union to Brinkwell and then the one from Brinkwell to this place. Compared with them, all four of the ships before him were altogether majestic. The wood of the hull was dark amber, but it glistened like marble. The front of each boasted a carving of a leafless tree that sprouted outward toward the sun like a hand, becoming a statue jutting off the prow. It looked like a tree was growing out of the side of a cliff, only it belonged to a ship, as if the roots of the tree were the ship itself. Kibure became more enamored with the image as he drew closer. Could the ship have been grown from a single tree? Considering his most recent training and knowledge of growing plants, he realized that might very well be the case, though he could only imagine the volume of magic and skill necessary to build an entire ship in this fashion.

He marveled at it as he climbed the plank leading him onto the deck, Rave landing upon his shoulder as he did. There were no seams, nails, or notches—anywhere. This ship, in all its intricacies, was a single unit of wood, though "grown" would be a more suitable word. The realization brought with it the recurring question of how these women could possibly need *him* to grow something they did not collectively have the power to grow. It still seemed like a bad case of mistaken identity, but he was in too deep to turn around, especially knowing that his perceived significance was likely the only reason Sindri had been kept alive. What would happen when they discovered he was not who they needed him to be?

"Thank you for defending my friend and me," said Kibure to Drymus. He had found her standing alone at the bow of the ship, her face in its ordinary scowl. He wasn't certain if it was the brighter light or recent events, but she appeared even more aged than he remembered, her skin deathly pale, wisps of hair blowing carelessly in the breeze that pushed the sails.

Drymus grumbled, "I was protecting you, though for what reason I'm still not sure. Should you be so foolish as to raise arms against my sisters again, I may be inclined to let them do as they must."

"Your 'sisters' left me few other options."

Drymus nodded. "True," she sighed. "We are living in very strange times, and as such, I suspect we'll find many people acting outside the realm of normal reason." Looking up, Drymus added, "Speaking of . . ."

Kibure followed her line of sight to the approaching figure of Lady Atticus. "Kibure. Lady Drymus."

Kibure's heart tightened. He was awaiting news of Sindri's health, as she had remained unconscious and it was unknown whether or not she would live. Lady Atticus's expression gave nothing away, of course.

"Your friend lives."

Kibure felt a sudden release of tension.

Atticus continued, her tone darkening, "However, she has not woken and may remain in such a state indefinitely."

Kibure gave her a pleading look and she continued explaining.

"Our healers stabilized her breathing and have worked to protect her body from collapsing in upon itself, but with the amount of magic she channeled, it's difficult to say if any permanent damage was done."

Kibure spoke over the lump that formed in his throat. "Can't your healers do something to restore her bones?"

Atticus shook her head. "I'm afraid her bones must repair themselves, and in their own time. But if the cavity that houses the mind collapsed at any point, it could have caused irreparable damage to the mind. Her past training as a priestess is likely the only reason she remains alive at all. Any novice wielder's bones would have turned to dust after channeling just a quarter of what she did, at least without some sort of jewelry or a tool like the kosmí."

Kibure felt anxiety building. "When will we know? You know, if she is okay?"

"If all goes well, her bones should be fully restored in at least one week, possibly two."

Kibure exhaled in relief, though even one week would be an agonizing length of time. "And what happens to her if she does wake up?"

Atticus responded coolly, "She will remain in our care, under guard, until either she breaks the peace and is sent to the bottom of the sea, or you fulfill your agreed-upon role for us and we release you and your friends from our care."

That was probably the best set of options Kibure could have hoped for and he nodded his thanks.

Atticus added, "Kibure, you should know, the healers are not optimistic. They say that if everything were truly okay with her she should have woken by now."

"I . . . see," was all Kibure dared say as his voice failed him.

Atticus nodded. "I know she was your friend, Kibure, but I must remind you that we are headed to face Klerósi priests and perhaps other monsters of the Dark Lord's making. No matter your friend's outcome, you must continue to grow as a wielder if we are to survive." Nodding to Drymus, she said, "See that his instruction continues, and that no further 'incidents' take place."

Atticus drifted away like a fog, leaving Kibure and Drymus alone.

Drymus grumbled, "The fool girl. It's no wonder the two of you are friends."

Kibure scowled. "Can we at least wait to see if she lives before we start in on the insults?"

Drymus rolled her eyes. "Would that change the reality of who she is, her choices that lead me to call her a fool?"

Kibure didn't respond.

Drymus huffed. "So sensitive. Never mind that, fool or no fool, we have training to do."

Kibure was in no mood to train, but he was also in no mood to fight Drymus on the subject. "Okay."

Drymus sighed. "Let's see. Where to begin? Ah yes, how to not get killed when you're less powerful, less skilled, and less mentally prepared than your enemy. How about we begin with your magical defenses, then finish with more work on your ability to shape plants. Much room for improvement in both areas."

Kibure stared down at Sindri's sleeping form, though he wasn't certain he could rightly call it sleeping after being in such a state unchanged for multiple days.

"When will she wake?" Kibure asked the healer as she gently removed the damp rag from Sindri's forehead.

The healer shrugged as she took up a bowl of broth to feed her. "There is little more we can do but wait and see. Her body has recovered remarkably well, but whether or not the mind wakes is beyond our ability to know or control. I must tell you, however, that with every passing day, the likelihood of a sudden return to consciousness becomes less and less likely."

Kibure remained even after the feeding had concluded. He sat beside the bed which hung suspended from the ceiling by a series of vines. The bed swayed gently back and forth in response to the ship's movement. The frame was made from the same smooth, dark wood as the rest of the vessel, but the bedding consisted of a thick growth of tiny ivy leaves which had begun to absorb Sindri's immobile body into itself. Kibure had used his magic twice already to push this growth back, but it continued its attempt to wrap her within its hungry webbing. A message from the universe, perhaps.

Kibure watched as Sindri's chest rose and fell, slowly, ever slowly. *Is it my imagination, or does her breathing grow fainter with every passing day?* "Sindri," he whispered, then glanced around to be certain he was alone. "I . . . don't know if you can hear me, don't know if your mind is still with us at all, but if you are, please, please wake up. We follow the Lugienese who stole an object of great power. These women plan to confront the Lugienese and I am not ready. I don't know if I ever will be but having you there to fight alongside me would be . . . it would be good. Plus, if we survive this, I think these women may have some of the answers to the questions you've been seeking all this time. But you *have* to wake up, *and* maybe try not to fight them while you're at it. I . . ." He trailed off. *This is stupid. Pointless.*

He slunk out of the cabin, up the ladder, and around the deck to the stern of the ship, hoping to avoid being seen by—

"Ah, Kibure, there you are!"

Kibure winced at the sound of Drymus's voice. His combat training had grown increasingly rigorous since their departure, taking place exclusively in the physical realm, which meant the bumps and bruises were all quite real. His most recent injuries flared to life as he considered another bout. Drymus had taken to selecting a different woman from the ship to visit for each session, so he never had a chance to grow used to one person's particular style. Not that there was much discernible difference among the women. The result was nearly always the same no matter who inflicted the beating.

Kibure dragged himself to his feet after another session, this one with a She'yaren named Jesmiere.

"It is slow, but you show improvement," remarked Drymus dryly.

"Doesn't feel like it," replied Kibure. He longed for his sessions with Arabelle. Knowing that she had been using him for her own gain the entire time, that none of their friendship had been real, made little difference; he still missed the time they'd spent together. The realization made him angry, and his anger, he knew, would cause his focus to wane during the lecture portions of his training when Drymus went over the theoretical aspects of floranity—plant shaping.

He might earn nearly as many welts from Drymus during such training as he would from the combat itself. He chided himself for having such thoughts of Arabelle, such frivolous complaints about his training. Drymus was right about one thing: whatever pain he experienced now would pale in comparison to what he might endure should the Dark Lord gain the power held by the kosmí. Nevertheless, he needed to be ready in the event that they were able to obtain the kosmí, so they ended each session with a task of growing one thing or another to whatever specifications Drymus presented to him.

After they had finished, Kibure stalked away on shaky legs before Drymus had a chance to expand upon the session. He headed away from the belowdecks dining area upon glimpsing Atticus, but she spotted him.

"Kibure, come. We must speak."

Reluctantly he followed her down into the cramped dining space and sat across from her on the smooth wooden bench at a large table, empty but for himself, Lady Atticus, and Rave, who had flown down to curl around Kibure's neck before he descended the first ladder.

"Kibure. We have done all that we can for your friend, but as we draw near the enemy, we will be faced with a reality that you will find difficult. That is, keeping Sindri alive in such a state will be an added drain upon our resources that we cannot afford to maintain. We will need all of our healers, and beds, when this time comes."

Kibure had a bad feeling about where she was going with this conversation. He asked, "What does this mean for Sindri, then?"

Atticus spoke low and calm. "There is also the possibility that things do not go as we would wish. Consider what the enemy might do with one of their own should they recover her in such a state."

Kibure recalled his experience in Brinkwell when Grobennar and whatever that thing had been invaded his mind. He had been a most unholy violation. The knot in his stomach tightened.

"How much longer?" he asked, afraid to hear the answer.

"One day."

Kibure nearly fell from the bench. He had thought they would give her at least another week. "One day?" Rave responded to the change in Kibure's tension by cooing his angry coo, the one that typically signified danger.

Atticus ignored the raaven, giving Kibure a sympathetic smile, if it could even be called that. Her lips hadn't moved, but her cold eyes did seem to soften as she explained, "I have spoken with the healers. They are not optimistic that she will ever wake. It is likely her mind has already fled, and we currently hold her body captive while her soul waits at the gates of the afterlife to be let free. It will be a mercy."

Kibure could not believe what he was hearing. "But you don't know for certain! How can you order the death of someone simply because there's a chance they might not live?"

Atticus's expression hardened. "When you have lived as long as I, you come to understand that life is filled with difficult choices. Painful alternatives. Each weighed against the other. I have sought the opinions of the healers and used this information to make the best choice for my people, and for your friend. Whether you see it the same way is irrelevant. I know that I make this choice with the health and safety of my people as priority. It will not be the first time I have borne the burden of someone's life, of a choice between bad and worse. That is leadership at its core, Kibure. And that is the best answer I can give. I am sorry about your friend. I too very much wish to see her wake."

This was a knife to the stomach that Kibure had not expected. He didn't know what he had expected should Sindri not wake, but it wasn't this. Lady Atticus spoke of murder.

Rave curled around Kibure's neck as he ventured down to see Sindri for the last time. He hadn't slept that night, thinking about what was to come. He revisited his time with Sindri and imagined her journey to find him, only to wind up here, waiting to die. He could hardly reconcile the notion. Everything about it felt wrong.

He approached the bed where she lay, still motionless but for her slow, shallow breathing. He had no idea what to say so he said nothing at all. He reached down and took her hand between both of his and gave a slight squeeze. His eyes filled with tears but he fought hard against the weeping his emotions called for. He knew it would come, but he wished to wait until he was completely alone before it did. Yet his lips quivered and he felt an unbearable weight upon his chest, as if he were being smothered by an eager mob seeking food handouts from the city watch.

"Why couldn't you have just listened," he whispered through the trembling. "Why couldn't you have just left and gone back to . . ."

There was nowhere for her to go. That didn't matter, not anymore. She had learned something of magic in his absence. She could have gone anywhere. But instead she had come here and refused to leave in spite of Kibure's warning. It was infuriating. What's more, looking at the shell of a person that lay before him, he could hardly maintain the frustration that he wished to feel toward her. Those feelings would get him through what was to come. But even they betrayed him, overpowered by his sorrow.

Rave hopped from Kibure's shoulder onto Sindri's chest and walked nimbly toward her head and nestled in as if he was going to simply take a nap with her. Vexing. Kibure had never seen Rave do this with anyone else. Perhaps the raaven knew what was to come. He did seem to have an unusual understanding of what went on. Kibure could no longer be surprised by the odd creature. Rave made a few soft cooing sounds. They seemed like notes of sadness and Kibure could only agree.

Still holding her hand in his, he gave it one last squeeze, and said, "Goodbye, Sindri. And thank you for—everything."

Kibure felt another wave of sadness and wished to be alone when the floodgates broke. He raced out, Rave zipping to catch up. He passed Lady Atticus. "Kibure, it is time to—"

"I know. Do as you must. I've said my goodbyes."

He hurried back to his tiny cabin. Rave flew past him and away, voicing concern through his cooing and cawing, but Kibure was in no mood for Rave's games. He slammed his door behind him then leaned with his back to the door and slid down to the floor in the blackness of the unlit room. If Kibure was certain of one thing, it was that he did not wish to be present when the She'yaren did whatever it was they intended to do to Sindri. He knew that if he was there, he'd never be able to remove the connection between those people and Sindri's untimely death. He had said his good-byes and that would have to be good enough. This was the way it needed to be, lest his sorrow be replaced by resentment and anger.

At this point, sorrow was better for him. And so he cried. He cried until his abdominal muscles grew fatigued and his chest ached. He was winding down when the sound of nails on the door caught his attention, accompanied by a faint whining. He held his breath to listen and heard it again. *Rave?* This was not his mischievous cooing; this was a warning of danger.

Had the Lugienese somehow circled back to attack them? His emotions shifted in an instant, driven by fear, then anger. If he wished to take his frustrations out on anyone, let it be the Lugienese.

Kibure scrambled to his feet and opened the door. Rave hobbled through on his hind legs. Kibure absently lit the sconce by his bed with an orb of gentle light then closed the door behind Rave. In an odd gesture, Rave extended one of his little hands toward Kibure. Kibure slowly protracted his own hand, palm up and Rave deposited *something* onto it. A leaf? It was dried and shriveled so he couldn't identify it based on the shape.

"Rave, I'm not in the mood to play." *What am I supposed to do with this?* He brought it up to his nose, sniffed, then withdrew it quickly as the pungent smell struck him. He recognized the scent instantly. This was the tea leaf that would send him to the spiritual realm.

"What's this about? I don't need tea to travel to the spiritual realm anymore." Rave flew up and snatched the leaf out of Kibure's hand, and then landed on his shoulder and used one of his hands to hold the leaf just below the nose. Kibure used his left hand to gently lower the leaf.

"Rave, what is this about?" he asked, annoyed but also intrigued. Rave did not behave in such a way without reason; Kibure just often failed to initially recognize the reasons for Rave's behavior. "Do you wish me to enter the spiritual realm?"

Rave cooed his affirmation. *This had better be good.* He was in no mood for games, but he was not fool enough to ignore the mysterious creature.

Kibure sighed heavily. "Very well."

Lying down, he calmed his mind as best he could, then he descended into the spiritual realm. He opened his eyes to an empty grayscale replica of his room, his nerves tingling with anticipation. He had the distinct fear that danger would befall him at any moment, that a group of Klerósi priests was converging on the ship to somehow attack from within this other plane of reality. Would he see Jengal again? What would he do if he did?

Movement to his right caught his eye and he turned and relaxed, though only slightly. There was something unsettling about seeing Rave's reflection in this place. The small black creature had a different sort of presence about him when he glowed all white and stood just as tall as Kibure. Kibure half-expected the gleaming entity to speak to him, but he merely gestured with one of his not-so-small hands for Kibure to follow.

Rave led him quickly up to the cabin where Sindri was lying. Kibure couldn't hear it, but he felt the pressure of his heart thumping hard as they neared. He didn't know what he expected to see, but he was fairly confident that Rave would not lead him to an empty room.

Kibure slowly pressed against the door, which swung soundlessly open. He stepped into the cabin nervously, his eyes drawn immediately to the bed where Sindri lay in the physical realm.

His hope drained away. The bed was empty. Kibure's emotions were so splintered, the slightest shift in circumstances could swing him from joy to rage in an instant. In this case, it was a shift from nervous anticipation to anger. Why had Rave dragged him into this realm then led him into an empty room? As mysterious as the creature often was, he didn't take direct action such as this without good cause. So, then, what was Rave attempting to communicate by bringing him into the spiritual realm? It had something to do with Sindri, since Rave had led him to her room.

Perhaps Rave thought she might be in the spiritual realm? Clearly she wasn't, or if she was, she had not remained in this cabin. Perhaps she was searching the vessel for help right now. In fact, Kibure worried what would happen if she did come upon one of the She'yaren. They traveled from vessel to vessel from within the spiritual realm in order to communicate as they tracked the enemy's ships. Kibure doubted that Sindri's presence in the spiritual realm would be well received. They'd likely think her a Lugienese spy. He needed to find her.

Kibure turned toward the door, but Rave suddenly appeared in the doorway, blocking his way. *"What are you doing?"*

At this point, Kibure would hardly have been surprised to hear Rave respond as a voice within his mind, but of course he did not. The hulking form of the glowing white raaven was off-putting, to say the least. His eyes were black and unblinking, and his expression was as emotionless as the most stoic She'yaren. Kibure turned back to regard the place where Sindri's body lay within the physical realm, then back to Rave. *"Why am I here?"*

Rave finally moved, his dainty arm lifted and he pointed at his head, then over to Sindri, then back to his head.

Kibure took a step to the side and turned so he could observe both Sindri and Rave at the same time. Then he raised his arms in an exaggerated shrug. *"I don't know what you want me to do. Her mind is gone. They're going to . . ."* He noticed the rippling of air, and the faint glow he knew to be the souls of others. The She'yaren had entered the physical realm. Sindri's time was up.

In spite of the fact that Kibure knew the cause was lost, he felt a panicked need to help. Was there a way to contact her mind from within the spiritual realm? Not one in which she was aware, however. Magog had entered one of his dreams. There! That was it—maybe. He had no idea how to do so. And according to Drymus, this practice was considered so dangerous that even the She'yaren no longer used it.

No time. If Sindri's mind remained intact, perhaps he could locate it this way. He had to try. He ignored the fact that the rippling figures appeared to be moving Sindri's body. No time. He looked at Rave one last time and the creature seemed to understand his thoughts, for he nodded.

Then Kibure's mind shot back into the place between places, the consciousness between realms that existed only within the mind. He slowed at the slight pull he knew represented the realm of dreams. Drymus referred to it as a place of danger and chaos. And Kibure knew that just like the spiritual realm, he could perish here.

He steeled his nerves, then shot forth toward it.

CHAPTER 92

KIBURE

KIBURE PICKED UP SPEED ALONG the mental corridor that he hoped would take him into the realm of dreams. His sense of movement suddenly ended and he looked about, sort of. Unlike within the spiritual realm, he had no sense of body, no sense of form. He "looked" around him, but with no head or neck the act was difficult to control. Everything around him blurred for a moment, then when he stopped, that which had been in front of him was simply different.

He blinked, except, no he couldn't blink. He just stopped seeing for a moment and then his sight returned the instant he willed it. Though what exactly he saw was yet another mystery altogether. The space was dark, very dark. If he had eyes in this place, he would have been squinting to try to make out his surroundings. As he looked about in confusion, he began to recognize nuances within the darkness. There were subtle variations within the shadows and there was one brighter orb, like the dimness of the sun hidden behind clouds on an overcast day. He thought through where he had been within the physical realm and managed to sort out that he was in this exact same place within the dream realm. It was simply another reflection of the physical realm, if dimmer and darker than the reflection represented by the spiritual realm. And he did not appear to have a corporeal form while within this place. That should make moving around easier, so long as he knew where he wished to go. The weight of Sindri's situation pressed firmly against him. *I don't have time to experiment. If she is somewhere in this place, I need to find her.* He had been hoping that Rave would be here to help in some way but that did not appear to be the case. He was on his own.

Praying that the principles of travel here were similar to those of the spiritual realm, he willed himself into the room where Sindri was being held. He experienced no sense of vertigo or movement, but his surrounding did appear to shift. He was able to make out the rough outline of Sindri's bed, hanging as it was from the ceiling by weblike lines of black, and two orbs of light were visible on either side of the bed, their glow barely touching the rest of the room.

But no sign of Sindri, or anyone else, for that matter. No ripples in the air or glowing orbs. Panic began to set in. He didn't have time to learns the ins and out of this place. He needed to find Sindri and . . . he didn't even know that part yet. Wouldn't matter if he couldn't find her.

He thought back to what little Drymus had said about visiting people's dreams. That it was possible to visit someone's dream as long as you had come into contact with them within the spiritual realm or knew precisely where they were located. He thought he knew where her body was in the physical realm, but she was not here. Unless—

He visualized the deck and willed himself there. His world brightened considerably, though it was still far darker than the spiritual realm's version would have been. The bright blaze of the sun was but a hazy ring in the sky here. But Kibure's attention was arrested by the awareness of other vague lights moving about the deck. One in particular shone brighter than the rest, and it swirled with color. As soon as Kibure caught sight of it, he felt himself drawn toward it. His instincts warned him against anything that pulled so strongly, but he knew that this was Sindri, that her true body was being carried to the edge of the vessel to be thrown overboard. He needed to find a way to wake her, if such a thing could be done.

So he allowed himself to be pulled toward the force that was this sphere of color. As soon as he stopped resisting, his awareness shot out toward it like a bird diving into water after a fish.

Kibure's vision shifted before his eyes and when it had finished, he found himself standing in the middle of a noisy dirt street he did not recognize. The buildings closest to him were single-story, shabby-looking structures, but he spotted the taller markings of a vast city etched into the horizon, a bright sun beating down to warm them from above. He saw color and heard sound and had a body as real as that which waited for him back in the physical realm.

Kibure scanned his surroundings, looking for Sindri, but she was nowhere to be seen. Yet his eyes were drawn to the door to a nearby dwelling. He couldn't explain it, but something about it tugged at him. With nothing else to go by, he approached the door. He pushed and the door swung easily open. He stepped in and closed the door behind.

He had entered a small, one-room home. The floor was dirt, like the street, but it appeared well-kept insofar as his limited understanding of such things was concerned. Everything was neatly put in its place, while the flames of a small cook fire licked a small pot. The smell of soup materialized the moment he noticed the pot was there.

Then a whimper sent his attention to the corner of the room beside a small table. There, huddled in the corner, was a woman cradling a young boy in her arms. "It's okay. Don't worry, everything will be all right. Shh, shh." The woman rubbed the boy's back as she continued to whisper words of comfort.

Her face was partially hidden, but Kibure knew her.

"Sindri?"

She looked up, eyes filled with terror in spite of what she had just said to the boy. "Kibure. You should not be here. They're coming for him, for me!"

"Who?"

The door exploded inward from behind him and he felt spikes in his back through his clothes, which he realized for the first time consisted of the brown tunic and trousers of a common Lugienese citizen. It was the sort of outfit Kibure recalled most of the overseers wearing at Zagreb's estate.

The shock of the pain alongside the intrusion wore off and Kibure turned to meet the source. Four Klerósi priests had entered the small space. Kibure looked from face to face in confusion, noticing that they all appeared to be the exact same person.

The closest one pointed to where Sindri remained, though she had stood, the boy cowering helplessly behind her. The priest shouted, "You there, hand over the boy."

Sindri's face was filled with fear, but her eyes narrowed, fingers grasping at the air. "You can't have him. He's my brother."

Kibure had to remind himself that this was a dream. Yet, this was her dream. And that meant that he could be harmed here. He could die here. He needed Sindri to wake up. The vivid nature of this dream was evidence that her mind still existed, that it was somewhere inside of her. But he needed to somehow get her to depart from the realm of dreams before her true body was thrown into the sea. He had no idea if time worked the same here as in the physical realm, but he had no reason to believe otherwise, which meant they had very little time indeed.

"Sindri, you need to—"

His words were cut short as he dodged to the side, a blast of energy shooting past where he had just been to strike the pot of cooking soup. The fire sizzled as the pot tipped, steam filling the air around it. Kibure sent his mind into his surroundings and found nothing. *Not good.* A second attack was coming any moment and he had no magic. *This isn't the physical realm. This is Sindri's dream. Maybe—*

Just as the second blast of energy came zipping toward his abdomen, Kibure willed a defensive barrier to exist before him, and though he still attempted to dodge to the side, it didn't matter because the barrier held. He sent a counterattack at the nearest priest, which took him square in the chest. The priest stumbled back, then straightened and smiled.

"What the—"

Another attack came and his barrier crumbled. Another blast shot forth, striking Kibure's shoulder. Pain exploded. In spite of this, Kibure managed to put up another defensive barrier of compressed air, but he knew it would not be enough. Not here.

This makes no sense. But of course it didn't need to; this was a dream. The entire sequence of events was a construct of Sindri's mind. Those priests could be as powerful as she imagined them to be. However, Kibure was an external component with a direct connection to the physical realm; if he perished here, he would perish in the physical realm, while Sindri could die again and again, moving from nightmare to nightmare without recourse.

Kibure was able to manipulate this place by force of will, but only to an extent. Sindri's will, however, seemed to hold the upper hand while within her own dream. Or perhaps her will was simply stronger in and of itself. In any case, the only way he was going to survive this exchange was to convince Sindri to return to the physical realm, to convince her that none of this was real. More importantly, this was the only way Sindri's physical body was going to survive being thrown into the sea. She needed to wake up!

Kibure growled, and with as much mental will as he could muster, he gripped the table to his left within his mind and sent it barreling toward the group of priests. It knocked two of them over, and Kibure used the distraction to execute a forward roll toward Sindri and the boy. He came up beside the pair.

"Sindri, you have to wake up. Your true body is in serious danger."

She looked at him, her expression glazed over with fear. "They're coming for him. I can't stop them. You have to help. Please help."

"Sindri!" Kibure shouted. "This is a dream! None of this is real. Your body is dying in the real world as we speak! Please."

There was no indication she heard him. "I can't protect him."

Kibure erected another shield of air as the priests fanned out before them. "Sindri, your brother is already dead. He died over five years ago. You, on the other hand, are not dead. Not yet. And neither am I."

Sindri's eye narrowed, and she stood, leaving her huddled brother shaking in the corner as she regarded Kibure, eyes ablaze with anger.

"My brother is right here." She pointed. The room grew darker and she appeared to gather power, or her mind's idea of power.

"They've turned you against me, too, haven't they?" She sent a wave of power toward him and he flew across the room, right past the Klerósi priests, who had paused their efforts for the time being.

Kibure used his own will to buffet his collision with the wall. He still crashed into the hard adobe lined with clay bowls and plates, shattering most.

Kibure rose to his feet, deathly afraid yet determined to do what he had come here to do. He had no other recourse. He felt himself being pressed backward, into the wall, and realized he had not the strength to do otherwise. She wielded too much power in this place. He couldn't match wills with her within her own dream. This was what Drymus had warned him about. This was why this place was so dangerous for people to visit. Only someone like Magog could dare enter someone else's mind and hope to return unharmed. "You came to Purgemon. You faced the She'yaren and nearly killed yourself—"

Kibure remained immobile, pressed so hard against the wall that he knew he had very little time left to live. He felt the weight of Sindri's mind pressing into him like a boulder. Thinking back to Magog's visit, he remembered that Magog had started out as Tenkoran. So did that mean one could change their appearance while here? If so, it might be the only way to reach her.

Kibure looked to the cowering child behind Sindri, then closed his eyes. He needed to become that boy. He focused his attention on that idea. Focused his mind not just on what the boy looked like, but what the boy felt like. The helpless fear of being a tazamine. Kibure clung to that feeling and became the boy.

When he opened his eyes, he felt the weight of Sindri's attack falter. She looked behind her in confusion then back to Kibure in shock; the boy was gone. No. Not gone. *He* was now the boy. He had become her vision of Lyson. But he didn't know how long he could maintain it.

Sindri turned back to face him, confused. But dreams often did strange things without the dreamer realizing how strange or nonsensical such changes often were. "Sindri. You need to wake up. This is a dream.

Your physical body is in trouble. Sindri. I'm dead. I'm not real. None of this is real. I love you. Please. Please, wake up!"

Sindri looked from side to side. "I have to protect—"

"I'm dead. I'm already dead! You can't save me. But you can save yourself. You can avenge my death by not dying yourself. And Kibure needs your help. You need to wake up!"

She was beginning to shake. "I—no. You can't be dead. I have to . . ."

The pressure keeping him against the wall was gone and the Lugienese in the room were also gone. It was just him and her. "Sindri. You've done all you can for me. You have to save yourself. You're needed in the real world."

"I—I don't know how to get there."

Kibure allowed himself to revert back to himself as Kibure. "I will help you. But we have to go now. It may already be too late."

This time, Sindri nodded, tears streaking her eyes.

CHAPTER 93

SINDRI

S INDRI'S TEARS REMAINED THROUGHOUT THE journey between
realms. When she finally opened her eyes to the physical realm,
her vision was a painful blur of murky blueness. Her body had become
weightless, and a sudden coldness crashed into her from every direction.
She breathed in and choked.

At this point she registered her predicament: she had been submerged
in water.. Drowning had always been on her list of ways to *not* die. She
panicked and kicked her legs, but they had been tied together, as had
her wrists, plus, she had no idea which direction was up. Her lungs
burned as she continued to choke on seawater. She turned her head to
the left, then the right and lastly spotted lighter waters. She attempted
to coordinate her body movements but it was useless. She opened her
mouth, knowing she needed air but found none. It was too late.

She flailed her limbs as she willed herself to the surface, toward air,
toward life, but mere strength of will would not be enough, not in the
physical realm. She strained her muscles, wide-open eyes dragging her
toward the surface, but it was too far and her body failed. Finally, a
calm came over her and she stopped moving. She felt a sense of peace,
the pain of her lungs departed, and she knew she was dying, but it was

okay. Everything was going to be okay. There was relief in knowing that her fight was over. She wasn't sure how long the feeling would last, how long it would take for her consciousness to fade, but she cherished this moment of euphoria before she passed into whatever came next.

Then she felt *something,* a faint touching sensation that wrapped itself beneath her right armpit and across to her neck. *That's strange,* she thought. Maybe this was the God above come to take her soul for judgment. That thought made her nervous, but the sense of serenity about her was so powerful that she couldn't help but feel the tranquility of knowing that everything was as it should be.

She drifted into the darkness, into her final slumber.

CHAPTER 94

SINDRI

PAIN AND UNCONTROLLABLE COUGHING. WATER spewed from her mouth, and yet more water shot forth. When the coughing finally came to an end, Sindri lay on her side, temple resting on the ground feeling that her skull weighed the same as a barrel of ale. She rolled to her back, her entire body tingling, and not just from her sense of magic that had just been thrust upon her.

Sindri stared up at the faces of a dozen women in shimmering silver robes, two others were completely nude, black hair slick and dripping as they worked to dress themselves in similar silver robes as the rest.

Coughing to her right caused her to look over. There beside her lay a male, his silver and gold robes dark and wet, clinging to him like the roots of a shrub grown into the side of a cliff. His chest heaved as if he was a messenger who had just arrived from across a large city with an urgent message. As Sindri's mind continued to recover, she realized that this man was Kibure.

Another woman entered the room, her robes more elaborate, including a golden cape. The others parted to make way. She looked about the room, a look of disgust upon her face. No one spoke, no one moved. The woman appeared older than the stone upon which Sindri lay. Except, Sindri ran her fingers along the surface and confirmed that she didn't lie upon stone. She was on wood. The gentle swaying of a ship upon the sea corroborated this, though she had no idea how she had come to such a place. *That explains the drowning.*

The newest arrival finally broke the silence that hung in the air like thick fog. "It appears our decision to dispose of the intruder was made in haste. She is to be returned to the infirmary to be examined and nursed back to health. She will have no visitors until after I have spoken with her." The woman paused, seeming to a bore a hole into Kibure with her stare. "Is that understood?"

Kibure sat up but gave no response. He looked down at Sindri with a tired, expressionless face, and said, "It's good to see you with your eyes open, Sindri. I'll visit you as soon as I can." Fatigue was evident in his every gesture, as if gravity itself had turned against him and was pulling harder on his every movement than all else around him.

Then he stood, turned, and shouldered past the women who still crowded around Sindri. One of them crouched down beside her and helped her sit up. "There, there. Slowly now. Your body and mind have been through much trauma." She took Sindri's wet, weak arm and draped it over her own shoulder and around her neck, then three others joined and lifted Sindri into the air. "My name is Jezrael, I am a healer." Her voice was gentle, unlike the tone of the other woman. They began moving her out of the room.

A stern voice from behind said, "Jezrael, see that she is given the tea immediately. I do not wish for any errant magical outbursts before we have spoken."

"Yes, of course, Lady Atticus," responded the healer. The mention of magic shook loose a flood of memories in Sindri that had remained hidden behind the fog of pain and confusion. Of what she had done before her body failed her. What little strength she had vacated her body and she nearly fell to the deck. Jezrael managed to stabilize her. "Whoa, easy, now." Another woman came up from behind and took Sindri's other arm.

The pair helped Sindri down belowdecks, which under normal circumstances would have been a wonder to explore and admire, but at this moment was nothing more than an obstacle to her ability to rest. She finally lay back upon a bed suspended in the air by vines of green and brown, the room illuminated by orbs of soft yellow light.

She might have resisted the tea, but her mind remained clouded with confusion over where she was, what she had done, and oh how much she simply wished to sleep again. The healer used some sort of magic to drain away the pain from her lungs and even managed to restore some of her body's energy.

"Where am I?" she finally asked.

Jezrael continued with her work, moving tea leaves and jars along the wall where they were secured by various vines, which seemed to move at the behest of Jezrael's will. The healer answered without turning. "You are in the infirmary."

"The infirmary of where? We are at sea, yes?"

The woman nodded, the back of her black hair shimmering like her silver robes. "Our ship, the *Masa*, travels west along what is now called the Sotaric Sea."

Sindri still had little idea how they had gone from an underground city to a ship sailing along the sea. She hardly knew what questions to even ask. "Where do we go and why?"

The woman turned and smiled. "I think it best that any further questions be directed to Lady Atticus. She should be along shortly."

True to Jezrael's word, Lady Atticus entered within minutes. Without a word, Jezrael bowed and started toward the door. "Please let me know if you need anything."

Lady Atticus nodded and said, "She has taken her tea?"

"Of course," responded Jezrael as she closed the door behind her.

Sindri recognized the woman who had entered as the same who had ordered that Sindri be brought here. She also recognized the woman's robe as different from the rest. The silver of the ankle-length fabric appeared similar, but her shoulders bore fabric of gold, which flowed behind her, a cape. This Lady Atticus was clearly the leader, or at the very least a woman of prominence within this society. She stood silently in observation for an uncomfortable period before gliding over toward Sindri's bed, golden cape billowing as she did. Then, with a wave of her hand and a sprinkle of magic, vines grew from the ceiling and floor to form a chair upon which the woman sat gracefully.

Once seated, Atticus said dryly, "You have invaded my home. You have attacked my people." These were not questions but statements of fact, yet Sindri decided to argue the point. But first she worked tired muscles to bring herself to a seated position, her back leaning against the wall of vines that held the bed suspended in the air. Once upright, Sindri responded. "You speak half of truth."

The woman eyed her curiously but said nothing, so Sindri continued, "I entered of your city without invitation, truth, but I attempted to leave of it without fight. *Your* people attacked of *me*. I did not wish to fight of them."

Atticus's expression did not change. "Mmm, perhaps. But you did not expect a people who had worked so hard to remain hidden for thousands of years to allow you to enter uninvited then simply walk away. Especially after arriving alongside Klerósi priests who stole away an object of great value to us. Do you enter the den of a bear then act surprised when it claws and bites?"

The woman had a point and Sindri was too tired to argue further. "So why then does this bear keep of me alive now?"

"Ah. That is the question indeed, is it not?"

Sindri waited silently for Atticus to continue. *Is she looking for me to respond?* She finally said, "I . . . Yes, I suppose it is."

"Indeed," affirmed Atticus. "The truth, Sindri, is that were it not for Kibure, you and your very tight-lipped companion would be fertilizing the soil we left behind in Purgemon."

Sindri gulped.

"However, Kibure seems to believe that he owes you his life. And Kibure, you see, has a very important role to play in the future of my people. Because of this, he and I have entered into a bargain for your life and that of your companion."

Sindri did not have the patience for games. "So you have come to tell of me that I am now a prisoner and that if I attempt to disrupt your plans for Kibure, you will kill of me, bargain or not. Very good. I will be good prisoner until your business with him is finished. I have understanding."

Atticus smiled, and Sindri did not like the way it looked. "This is true, in a sense. But there is more."

Sindri stared at her confused, but eager with anticipation.

"What you did back there against my people was foolish beyond measure, and it nearly killed you—you should have perished in the process. It was *the* largest volume of raw magic I have ever seen wielded by any one person at once, and I have lived a *very* long life. People have died wielding far less."

Sindri had no idea what to say so she remained silent, awaiting the explanation of how this fit into the woman's "more." Atticus continued, "Your skills are elementary, this much is obvious by the fact that none of my sisters were fatally wounded by your outburst. But the power you wielded . . . during times such as these, my people need to expand our circle of trust if we hope to survive. Allies of allies must become friends and I would be remiss to ignore such a potential ally. To this end, I would ask that you and your companion not only remain under close watch but join us in our quest to retrieve this stolen object of power, an object that threatens the stability of the world as we know it. If we're able to retrieve 'the stone,' and Kibure is able to do his part in fulfilling our prophecies, then our business will be concluded and you, your companion, and Kibure will all be free to do as you wish."

Sindri felt a weight lift, and her mind returned to her promise of revenge against the Lugienese. Now it was her turn to smile. "This object was stolen by Klerósi priests, yes?"

Atticus nodded.

Sindri's smile widened. "If helping you retrieve this thing means I will be able to kill of Klerósi priests, then yes, I agree to do of this thing."

Her excitement at a life prolonged shifted to that of the pragmatic. These women were old, perhaps ancient, and might well possess some of the very answers she had been seeking since her brother's death years ago. She needed to press her advantage while she had it. "But if I do this thing, you will teach of me more of the magic, and answer of me any questions I ask of you with full truth."

Atticus sat in silence as she weighed the question, but her eyes twinkled with . . . was that triumph? "It just so happens that I have questions of my own for you. Perhaps we might exchange such truths. And so long as you understand that until your side of the agreement has been fulfilled, you are under my complete authority, we have an agreement."

Sindri swallowed hard, her sense of relief slipping from her grasp to be replaced with the weight of obligations and bargains. Not that she had other options. But her sense of victory was deflated by a sense that some aspect of this bargain weighed heavier in favor of the woman sitting beside her.

Sindri shook her head, resigned to her new fate. "We have of an agreement." At least she had earned *something* in the bargain; she just couldn't help but feel like she had been swindled by the stoic woman before her.

Lady Atticus rose to her feet. "You will begin further instruction in magic as soon as the tea wears off. I will inform Kibure that you are now accepting guests. And your other companion will be presented with a similar set of options. Should she agree, I will release her to visit you as well. If not, she will remain under lock and key, though unharmed, until such a time as your side of the bargain has been fulfilled."

Lady Atticus left the room, her golden cape trailing behind her like a procession of Klerósi priests during a Blood Moon parade.

Kibure's arrival seemed to take an eternity, but this gave Sindri more time to digest exactly what she had done back in Purgemon, as well as the bargain she had just made with these women. Her thoughts meandered to the trials she had undergone to find Purgemon in the first place. Then a sickening guilt formed over the fate of the merchant, Galdred, who had died at her expense. And his son had been caught up in it, too. What would Keldred's fate be? Had they simply killed him and tossed him overboard? Considering what had been done to Tenk's brother Jengal, she thought the quick death would be a mercy. It seemed like everything she touched turned to rubble. No, not rubble. Fire. Everything and everyone she touched caught fire.

This brought Sindri's mind back to Kibure. Kibure, the mere slave boy who had somehow managed to become a major target of the Kleról, of Magog himself, was seen as some sort of "savior" to this ancient tribe of extremely skilled wielder-women. Kibure, who was accompanied by some sort of magical raaven whose exact powers and purpose remained undefined. One of these things would have been reason to believe he was something more than ordinary, but all of them? There was no way to rationalize such a coincidence beyond saying that it was no coincidence at all. Accepting this, she must also accept the fact that she would either be far safer, or far more in danger, by remaining tethered to his future. At this point, it was looking more like the latter. However, considering her previous vow to take vengeance on the Lugienese for what they had done to her brother, she was pleased to discover that her current predicament would at least be in agreement with that. And if she perished in the process, she would at least do so in pursuit of something worthwhile. Then again, Kibure seemed to be doing well enough under the tutelage of these women. Perhaps he was better off without Sindri around to turn things to flame.

The sound of feet padding their way toward her door brought her eyes up to meet Kibure's own as he stepped into sight, his silver and gold robe now dry and gleaming as if possessing a source of illumination.

His raaven stared at her from its perch upon his shoulder. To Sindri's surprise, the creature flew over to land on her lap, cooed, then curled up and snuggled in. The effect on her mood was immediate; like the bright rays of the sun in early spring, bringing welcome warmth along with their light. She felt suddenly more at ease than she had in a *very* long time.

Kibure walked over and sat in the seat left behind by Lady Atticus. He placed a hand upon her shoulder. "Thank you."

She considered playing the humble fool, but she was too mentally exhausted. She nodded and said, "You're welcome. And thank you, too."

He smiled. "Who would have thought that you, the woman hired to remove me from my magic, would someday be readying to use this very magic to fight alongside me?"

She just shook her head. "It's been quite the journey for both of us."

Kibure squeezed her shoulder then removed his hand.

Sindri said, "I'd be lying if I said it has been pleasant, but I'd be lying too if I said I regretted any of it."

Kibure stood and gave her a weak smile. "Rest up. I suspect the next leg of our journey is going to be the most dangerous yet."

Sindri could hardly believe this was the same boy she'd met less than a year earlier. She nodded. "I'm glad I was able to find you, Kibure. And if I'm to die, I'll be glad to die fighting the Lugienese alongside you."

"Me too," he said as he strode out of the room. Rave took to the air to follow him and Sindri just shook her head in amazement.

She swung her feet toward the floor and attempted to stand. She nearly toppled forward as the boat swayed, but the room was small enough that she was able to quickly find a wall to brace herself then closed her eyes and said out loud, "To the next adventure." She opened her eyes and stared up at the ceiling, toward the sky and the heaven above. "May my vengeance against the Lugienese be pleasing to you, whoever you are."

CHAPTER 95

DAGMARA

AGMARA SAT UPON A LOG beside the cook fire, emotions completely drained along with her physical and mental energy. It had been a dreadful thing to witness death, and worse yet to take a life at the palace in Quinson. But those experiences had been mild compared with what she had just taken part in. The sacrifice of so many warriors, all fighting against an evil beyond the scope of her understanding that meant to scourge the world. Yet those men and women sacrificed themselves without any concern for their own safety. It was both beautiful and terrible. She knew many of them. Not for long, but long enough to respect and care for them. There had been a kinship in training alongside them, and now most of them were dead. Why did she deserve to live? Because some creature had selected her at random?

Her emotions were numb.

Draílock stooped beside her, attending a makeshift spit cooking deer meat that the Lumáles had fetched for them before taking their own rest.

Kyllean groaned as he attempted to reposition himself beside her. "Say, Draí, you've got to have some tricks for healing, right?"

Draílock nodded. "I have some minor skills, yes."

Kyllean gave him a look, but Draílock did not make eye contact. Kyllean persisted, wincing as he breathed in. "So, how about lending me a little help, then? I'm certain I have at least a cracked rib. Several, actually."

Draílock reached up and turned the meat, then returned to his perch upon the log. "I find that pain is one of the best educators."

"Uh—yeah. Listen, Draílock." Kyllean emphasized the name as he said it, tasting the sound of the word in his mouth, then continued, "Draílock, while your name may be derived from the word draconian, please be reminded that in spite of my unorthodox methods, the remaining dordron ended their pursuit after one of their own suddenly turned on its rider then attacked the others, thereby ending their pursuit of us indefinitely."

Draílock nodded. "This is true. However, I had my own plan to remove their interest; a plan that didn't involve you falling to within a stride of your own death. You're fortunate that your Lumále managed to catch you at all. Therefore, your method, your consequence."

Kyllean scoffed, "Well, maybe if you were a little more transparent with your plans, the rest of us wouldn't be forced to improvise. Even now. Where exactly are we headed? You've an idea, I'm sure, but does anyone else know?"

Dagmara leaned in with interest in spite of the fact that she sat between the pair and could hear just fine.

Draílock said flatly, "We're going to be off-script for a while."

Kyllean threw up his hands, then yelped. "Yeow!" His hand went to his ribs and he coughed, wincing each time. In more of a whisper, he said, "But see?" He took a moment to control his breathing, then continued, "Off-script? What does that even mean?"

Draílock stood and reached over with cloth-wrapped hands to remove the meat from the fire, then set it off to the side to cool.

Dagmara joined the conversation. "Kyllean has a point. We deserve to know where we are headed, and these riddles of yours are less than helpful."

The old wizard sighed. "Very well. I was thinking that we might go rescue your brother from your brother, or possibly from the Lugienese. It's difficult to say based on our timing. But if you two are going to continue bombarding me with questions, we'll run out of time for either and have to just skip that part."

Dagmara knew that her mouth was hanging open. She didn't care. She readied to speak but silenced the question. *Rescue her brother? Lugienese?*

Darkness descended upon her mood and she did nothing to mask this as she half growled, "Surely *this* requires further explanation?"

Draílock raised a calming hand. "Yes, I suppose it would." He sighed. "I'll tell you what I know, and then you and Kyllean will leave me be to plan and think. Understood?"

"Yes, yes," harrumphed an impatient Dagmara.

Draílock responded in his ever calm, ever more agonizingly slow manner of speaking. "It is my belief that the Lugienese are presently in the midst of attacking Quinson. This is much sooner than what the city had expected or was prepared to defend against. Scritlandian troops are on their way to provide aid, but I do not believe that they will arrive in time."

That was a gut punch. Dagmara asked, "Will Kingdom forces be able to push the Lugienese back once reinforcements arrive?"

Draílock shook his head. "Perhaps under normal circumstances, but betrayal from within is afoot. I doubt very much that the Kingdom will be capable of holding the city."

Kyllean spoke up. "Forgive me, but how could you know all of this? I mean, I know you're a wizard, and you're older than . . ." He looked around then finally scooped up a handful of soil, ". . . you know. But by golly, you're giving me the creeps with all of the mysterious *knowing* of stuff."

Draílock nodded appreciatively. "When you've lived as long as I, you simply gather a sense for such things. There are patterns that to the young and unobservant go completely unnoticed, but for one who has seen a certain breeze come and go a thousand times, the path becomes more . . . predictable."

Kyllean rolled his eyes. "So then, what does the breeze have to say about how exactly we're going to rescue Aynward?"

Draílock smiled. "I do not ordinarily prefer chaos, but in this instance, I believe it will serve our needs well, providing the perfect opportunity from which to swoop in and extract your friend."

Kyllean appeared unimpressed. "Well, that's awfully . . . light on detail. And what about that artifact you've taken from the Tal-Dons?"

Dagmara had missed that. *Artifact?*

Draílock reached into his cloak and pulled out a yellow sphere the size of a fist. It was semi-transparent, and as it sat in his hand, the fire dimmed, as if it was somehow drawing on the flames' energy. Meanwhile the sphere radiated a faint glow of its own. Bright enough to suggest that it was glowing, but not bright enough to be certain at first glance. Draílock massaged the stone with his thumb as it rested in the palm of his hand.

He said, "This is why the Lugienese came to the fortress."

Dagmara stared, confused. "A stone? All that death, for one mildly pretty stone?"

Draílock didn't look up as he said, "It is one of only seven such stones in existence. Each with the capacity to do terrible things if allowed to fall into the hands of the wrong wielder. The Lugienese are in the process of reassembling their own stone, which was dismantled long ago. And I have reason to believe that they recently obtained another such artifact from the sisters of the gray. The world will be fatally imperiled if we allow the Lugienese to wield even these two together. So I think after rescuing Aynward, I will be heading south for a bit. There's a little place called Nineveh. I've heard it's quite nice this time of year. I also believe that it is where this other stone is soon to be. I would like to help take it back."

No one spoke for a time, and then Kyllean finally said, "So you're hoping that by helping us rescue Aynward, we'll be indebted to you and will in turn help you to steal back this other stone?"

Dagmara understood Kyllean's train of thought now. Surely the wizard did not need Aynward for his plans. But he did need their Lumáles. What better way to indebt those who controlled the Lumáles than to help them save someone they cared about?

Draílock provided no visual reaction to the question. But he responded, "I rather like Aynward. It would pain me to know that any harm befell him, especially if I knew I could help prevent such. Any debt owed me for my part in this would be an unrelated matter." Then his eyebrow rose slightly. "Although it does now occur to me that you may feel inclined to reciprocate. I also believe you may come to appreciate the severity of the threat the Lugienese pose to the world, regardless of Aynward's fate. And I assure you that these stones are of more importance to them than any single battle, or the control of any dozen cities."

Kyllean narrowed his eyes. "So you're going to risk your life rescuing Aynward on the off chance that this might help convince us to help you save the world, as you see it?"

Draílock stood and retrieved deer meat, then used a bit of magic to strip it from the bone. He handed Dagmara and Kyllean each a hunk. "It is as you say."

Kyllean shook his head. "So smug."

A gruff and unfamiliar voice answered from somewhere in the nearby darkness, "Your instructions for finding this place were quite unsagely, but were right about one thing, Quinson will fall."

Startled by intrusion, Dagmara lost her balance on the log. She fell backward and Kyllean extended an arm to try to catch her. He yelped in pain and both landed unceremoniously upon their backs, further disturbing the trampled grass and weeds.

Kyllean cursed.

Dagmara whispered, "Sorry" as she stood, then offered a hand to Kyllean. Hand still outstretched, she turned her head to scan the darkness from which the intruder's voice had come.

Kyllean caught her hand and spoke loudly, voice straining as she helped him back to his feet. "You know, I had this counselor back in Brinkwell. He was the most grouchy, temperamental, irritating, and—"

He was cut short by the same voice from before. "This coming from the fool with bruised ribs, and a best friend who's drawn to prison like a mutt to vomit?"

Dagmara finally located the source of the voice as a small form stepped into the light cast by the flickering fire. She would be wrong to call the man child sized, but he was certainly child height. Bearded and burly, his scowl matched the tone right up until he smiled wide. "Good to see you alive, Kyllean, though I'd hoped you had wizened a bit more by now." He turned to face Draílock. "My, my, Draílock, you look . . . about as old and sagelike as always." Lastly, he regarded Dagmara. "Who's the lass? Wait, don't tell me. She's the master of fools' sister, isn't she? Looks about as Kingdom-born as you big'ns come."

Draílock nodded. "Dwapek, please make the acquaintance of Princess Dagmara Dowe, though I'm not sure that she retains that title now that she is a fugitive-turned-rider."

Dwapek's eyebrows lifted. "A rider? Tethered and all?"

Dwapek returned his gaze to Dagmara and bowed his head slightly. She suddenly felt very self-conscious. "Like a flower taking to root in a salty sea. Well done, lass."

Aynward had mentioned the half-man, as he called him, though she was pretty sure that Aynward believed him to be dead at the hands of the Lugienese. In any event, now that she saw and heard him, she understood Aynward's mixed feelings about him. He certainly lacked all manner of decorum, but there was something avuncular about him. In any case, there were far more important matters to worry over at the moment. Like the city of Quinson.

Dagmara replied, "Thank you."

"Kyllean has also been tethered," added Draílock

Dwapek's eyebrows rose once again. "Has he now? Well, well, the boy becomes less useless by the day."

Kyllean grinned. "It's high praise such as this that makes it all worth it."

Dagmara interrupted, "How is it that you know Quinson will fall?"

Dwapek replied in as matter of fact a tone as one might expect from a farmer discussing the butchering of a cow. "Because the Kingdom doesn't have the numbers or the mages to withstand the Lugienese and their turncoat allies. And by the time the Scritlandians arrive, the Lugienese will have dug into Quinson like a viper to its hole."

"I . . . see," was all Dagmara could manage to say in response. Even if they somehow managed to rescue Aynward, her home had been captured and now the rest of the Kingdom. It was difficult to feel anything but sad at the news. Exile or not, this was her home.

Draílock interrupted Dagmara's introspection. "Dwapek, how went your venture to the jungles of the east?"

"Not well," he grumbled.

"Hmm. Seems you'll need to journey north after all."

Dwapek's mood soured even further at that. "Yes, yes, you had the right of it. Don't have to be so smug about it. They're as likely to kill me, as they are to recognize my claim. Traveling there in search of the Etzem Tzaraath will be risky enough business as it is."

Draílock was unmoved. "I have great confidence that you will succeed."

Dwapek huffed. "Pray the same for you. Your dealings to the south are just as likely to doom us, aye?"

Draílock shrugged. "There are many possibilities, many variables, but failure is close at hand in nearly every scenario I can fathom. Which brings me to one of the reasons I had you meet us here." He held up the glowing artifact. "Considering where I'm headed, it is best that you take this with you for safekeeping. Not that there is much hope, should we fail, but placing this tool into the lion's mouth would be a great way to expedite the process."

Dwapek took the sphere in his miniature hands, turning it over. "I would have thought these things would be . . . prettier."

Draílock rose to his full height. "Let's you and I take a walk. We have much to discuss, and I would like to hear more about your adventure into the northlands, failure or not." Draílock had taken a few steps away from the fire but stopped and turned to regard Kyllean and Dagmara. "Please excuse us while you consider your plans for after we rescue Aynward."

Dwapek gave a curt nod before turning. "Pleasure to meet this much prettier version of Aynward." He paused, then made eye contact with Kyllean and simply added, "Kyllean." He then turned and followed Draílock into the gloom.

Dagmara felt Kyllean's gaze upon her. Keeping his voice down, he said, "What a strange man."

"Which one?"

Kyllean chuckled. "A fair question. Say, did you recognize that name, Etzem Tzar—something?

Dagmara shook her head, "No. Why?"

Kyllean's forehead scrunched in thought. "Sounded familiar but I can't place it. Sounds like we'll either find out soon, or we'll all be dead and it won't matter."

Images of the carnage from which they had just fled spilled into Dagmara's mind. She saw droves of Kingdom soldiers being obliterated by Klerósi priests. Then she thought of Aynward, a prisoner in a city on the brink of collapse.

Kyllean drew her away from the butchery, lifting his hands and looking around as he said, "So, what do you think about all of this?"

Dagmara responded without much thought at all. "If Aynward is truly alive, I will go with Draílock to rescue him."

"Of course you will, and so will I. But I mean beyond that?"

She sighed heavily and weighed her words. "I'm not sure. My gut tells me to run as far away from here as possible, but my heart tells me if I can do something that may help stop the Lugienese, then . . ."

Kyllean shook his head and cursed under his breath. "Duty. Responsibility. I'm beginning to think those might be the worse communicable diseases known to man, or woman."

Dagmara nodded. "Well, I was born with this *disease*. It's always uncomfortable, but you sort of learn to get used to it. To be honest, I'm certain I'd rather be here than stuffed in some tower for my own protection alongside the Kingdom's treasury. At least this disease *feels* like a choice."

Kyllean snorted. "Yes, it does at least offer the *illusion* of choice. At the very least, I like our odds a lot better if the half-man sticks around to help. He's like those gross little insects that are so hard to kill . . . what are they called?"

"Do you mean roaches?"

"Yes! Roaches! He's like one of them, except he's on our side, I think."

Dagmara rolled her eyes. "That's awfully reassuring."

The eastern sky was beginning to glow with the light of dawn. Dagmara took out the cloak Draílock had packed for her and wrapped as much of her arms and legs as the wool would allow, then lay down beside the fire. She hoped the shade of the forest would keep the brightest of the sun's rays out of her eyes long enough for her to catch at least a few hours of sleep before they had to begin anew. Draílock had said they would resume their travels at midday and should arrive at Quinson by nightfall. Her stomach twisted at the thought of what they would find there.

"Good night, Kyllean."

"Good night, my duty-stricken princess."

Dagmara suddenly regretted using herself to continue Kyllean's analogy, but exhaustion prevented her from lamenting for long.

CHAPTER 96

GROBENNAR

THE TWO LUGIENESE FUGITIVES SAT side by side on the ground staring into the remnants of their campfire at the northwestern edge of the Luguinden desert. Grobennar glanced over as Paranja shook her head. He knew her well enough to understand that she was making up her mind about something. She reached over and gently touched Grobennar's shoulder. "We need to talk."

"Very well."

She exhaled slowly, then said, "We will be arriving within the next few days. It's time I give you the explanation you deserve."

Grobennar nodded for her to go on, though he cared little at this point. He had been harboring a growing sense of emptiness, a pit, a lack of purpose. Sure, he was alive, but what did his life matter? He was nothing. The prophecies he had once believed applied to him were the fancies of a self-important fraud. He was nothing more than a disgraced heretic.

Paranja began, "My mother was a Luguinden prophetess, one of the most powerful seers born to our people in centuries."

Jaween commented, *"Never trust a person who believes themselves acting out prophecy."*

654

Grobennar nearly interrupted Paranja to respond to Jaween's nonsensical statement. After all, he had been doing just that for most of his life. But he remained silent as she continued.

"She followed this 'sight' decades into the future, all the way to the Lugienese Empire where she was to marry the Lugienese man shown to her in these visions. It was foretold that the fruit of this union would one day return with the one destined to reunite the stone of power, and with this, the five tribes of old would once again rally beneath a single banner as they had in the days of old. Since birth, she taught me everything I needed to know, at least insofar as my small role would be in guiding such events into being."

Before Grobennar opened his mouth to ask exactly what she meant by that, she clarified, "Such foretellings are never without potential wrinkles. They are closer to maps with directions to a particular destination rather than a story with a definitive end. In the foretelling I have been attempting to see to fruition, the one who discovered the shards is the one to reunite them. When Rajuban informed me what he wished for me to do to you, I knew I had reached another fork."

Grobennar attempted to process what she said, but it was too ridiculous. A seer? Another prophecy? None of that mattered; there was already a wrinkle in her little story. "We don't have all of the shards. Rajuban wears one of them embedded within his . . ." He trailed off as she smiled and extended her hand, fingernails still caked in dried blood. Between forefinger and thumb was a red, circular shard. She had not been aiming to slice Rajuban's throat at all. She had struck precisely where she intended, cutting free his shard. Grobennar had been so busy attempting to survive that he had missed this detail.

Still in a haze of disbelief, he asked, "So what happens now?"

Paranja smiled. "Only a few steps remain until we reach the limits of how far my mother was able to see."

Jaween concluded, "*She's mad, but she did save your life.*"

Grobennar responded, "Well? What are they?"

Paranja's eyes and attention shifted to focus upon something behind Grobennar. She grinned wider still. "One such approaches as we speak."

Grobennar turned to see the growing silhouette of a figure in a tattered brown cloak. As this visitor neared, the hood fell away and Grobennar saw the face of a woman, dark skin too weathered by age to quickly determine race. Shoulder-length hair of gray and white was matted by the sweat and grime of travel.

She bowed and said, "Greetings, I am called Ruka. I was told that you are in need of a lapidary."

CHAPTER 97

RAJUBAN

THE CONNECTION WITH HIS SPIRIT felt stronger since transferring it into the ordinary gemstone, though it was subtle enough to overlook. And yet, as he carried the pouch containing all of the others, he felt a collective draw that he had not felt when they were all still within the shards.

"Shards almighty!" he said the word as a curse. *Paranja was more cunning than she portrayed herself to be.*

Rajuban was not the sort to be deceived. The fact that Paranja had betrayed him, and on behalf of Grobennar of all people, made it all the more infuriating. Rajuban had been confident that he had manipulated her toward his own ends; he had allowed her into his inner circle, and all the while her allegiance to Grobennar had remained unbroken. *Hubris can bring down even the greatest of towers.* He had been on his way toward the door but held up his index finger and stopped. "I should record that token of wisdom." He moved back to retrieve the notebook dedicated to such proverbs, a treatise in the making titled, "Fatu Mazi's Infallible Refrains." He had to pick through several items upon his small, cluttered desk to find it. "This cabin is much too cramped. Dry land cannot come soon enough."

His thoughts darkened as he finished scribbling his latest tidbit, the meaning of which returned him to thoughts of the shortcoming. *I will uncover and eradicate the both of them once and for all.* Neither one served any use to him or the Empire, not anymore. He just had to pray that they didn't do something insipid like hide the shards, or, worse yet, hand them over to the enemies of the Empire.

The spirit in the gemstone said, "You mustn't dwell on the past. Trust me, the longer you live, the larger and more perilous a playground it becomes. One could get lost in there if they are not careful."

"Sage advice, almost notebook-worthy. But it is not the past that causes me trepidation. It is our future sans the stones. Thus far, we have recently absconded with one, failed to secure another, and our own has yet to be reassembled from the shards. We must now rely on Grobennar's propensity for power and the hope that Paranja believes him to be the foretold Uniter of the Tribes."

"Did you not uncover that her mother is the Luguinden seer?"

"Indeed," confirmed Rajuban.

"Then surely this is why she follows him still." He felt the warmth of satisfaction flow through the connection to the orange sapphire that now housed the spirit. "Oh, you needn't worry over his destination. He will not be able to ignore the promise of glory. And the bloodshed will be all the more glorious when it comes."

"Perchance." *That snare had been set regardless of Grobennar's involvement. I simply have to make certain to allow no means of escape this time.* Another axiom revealed itself and he jotted it down with relish. "One who does not account for failure is destined to meet it."

THANK YOU FOR READING

WORD-OF-MOUTH IS CRUCIAL FOR ANY author to succeed. If you enjoyed *The Other Way,* please pay it forward by posting an honest review to Goodreads, Amazon, Bookbub, or wherever you post reviews.

ABOUT THE AUTHOR

DERRICK SMYTHE HAS BEEN FASCINATED with all things elvish, dwarvish, and magical since his days of running through the woods with sharpened sticks in defense of whatever fortification he and his brothers had built that summer. After consuming nearly every fantasy book he could find, he was driven to begin work on one of his own. When he isn't dreaming up new stories, he can be spotted hiking the Adirondack Mountains or traveling the world. He currently resides near his hometown in upstate New York with his enchanting wife, ethereal daughters, and his faithful-if-neurotic Australian Shepherd, Magnus.

Derricks Smythe's debut novel, *The Other Magic*, is the award-winning first installment of his passage to dawn series, an epic fantasy set in the World of Doréa.

To learn more about Derrick and his work visit:
Website: derricksmythe.com
Facebook: derricksmythe.author
Email: author@derricksmythe.com

Printed in Great Britain
by Amazon